WARRIORS

WARRIORS

EDITED BY

GEORGE R. R. MARTIN

AND

GARDNER DOZOIS

TOR®

A TOM DOHERTY ASSOCIATES BOOK

NEW YORK

This is a work of fiction. All of the characters, organizations, and events portrayed in these stories are either products of the authors' imaginations or are used fictitiously.

WARRIORS

A Tor Book
Published by Tom Doherty Associates, LLC
175 Fifth Avenue
New York, NY 10010

www.tor-forge.com

Tor® is a registered trademark of Tom Doherty Associates, LLC.

Library of Congress Cataloging-in-Publication Data

Warriors / edited by George R. R. Martin and Gardner Dozois. —1st ed.
    p. cm.
  "A Tom Doherty Associates book."
  ISBN 978-0-7653-2048-3
  1. War stories, American.   2. Soldiers—Fiction.   I. Martin, George R. R.   II.
Dozois, Gardner R.
  PS648.W34W37 2010
  813'.010806—dc22

                                                                    2009041233

First Edition: March 2010

Printed in the United States of America

0 9 8 7 6 5 4 3 2 1

Copyright Acknowledgments

To Lauren and Jeff,
to Tyler and Isabella,
to Sean and Dean,

may you be strangers to war

Contents

Introduction

Stories from the Spinner Rack
by George R. R. Martin

There were no bookstores in Bayonne, New Jersey, when I was a kid.

Which is not to say there was no place to buy a book. There were plenty of places to buy books, so long as what you wanted was a paperback. (If you wanted a hardcover, you could take the bus into New York City.) Most of those places were what we called "candy stores" back then, but Hershey bars and Milky Ways and penny candy were the least of what they sold. Every candy store was a little different from every other. Some carried groceries and some didn't, some had soda fountains and some didn't, some offered fresh baked goods in the morning and would make you a deli sandwich all day long, some sold squirt guns and hula hoops and those pink rubber balls we used for our stickball games . . . but all of them sold newspapers, magazines, comic books, and paperbacks.

When I was growing up in Bayonne's projects, my local candy store was a little place on the corner of First Street and Kelly Parkway, across the street from the waters of the Kill Van Kull. The "book section" was a wire spinner rack, taller than I was, that stood right next to the comics . . . perfect placement for me, once my reading had expanded beyond funny books. My allowance was a dollar a week, and figuring out how I was going to split that up between ten-cent comic books (when the price went up to twelve cents, it really blew the hell out of my budget), thirty-five-cent paperbacks, a candy bar or two, the infrequent quarter malt or ice cream soda, and an occasional game of Skee-Ball at Uncle Milty's down the block was always one of the more agonizing decisions of the week, and honed my math skills to the utmost.

The comic book racks and the paperback spinner had more in common than mere proximity. Neither one recognized the existence of genre. In those days, the superheroes had not yet reached the same level of dominance in comics that they presently enjoy. Oh, we had Superman and Batman and the JLA, of course, and later on Spider-Man and the Fantastic Four came along to join them, but there were all sorts of other comic books as well—war comics, crime comics, western comics, romance comics for the girls, movie and television tie-ins, strange hybrids like *Turok, Son of Stone* (Indians meet dinosaurs, and call them "honkers"). You had Archie and Betty and Veronica and *Cosmo the Merry Martian* for laughs, you had Casper the Friendly Ghost and Baby Huey for littler kids (I was much too sophisticated for those), you had Carl Barks drawing Donald Duck and Uncle Scrooge. You had hot rod comics, you had comics about models complete with cut-out clothes, and, of course, you had *Classics Illustrated*, whose literary adaptations served as my first introduction to everyone from Robert Louis Stevenson to Herman Melville. *And all these different comics were mixed together.*

The same was true of the paperbacks in the adjacent spinner rack. There was only the one spinner, and it had only so many pockets, so there were never more than one or two copies of any particular title. I had been a science fiction fan since a friend of my mother's had given me a copy of Robert A. Heinlein's *Have Space Suit—Will Travel* one year for Christmas (for the better part of the decade, it was the only hardcover I owned), so I was always looking for more Heinlein, and more SF, but with the way all the books were mixed together, the only way to be sure of finding them was to flip through every book in every pocket, even if it meant getting down on your knees to check the titles in the back of the bottom level. Paperbacks were thinner then, so each pocket might hold four or five books, and every one was different. You'd find an Ace Double SF title cheek-by-jowl with a mass market reprint of *The Brothers Karamazov*, sandwiched in between a nurse novel and the latest Mike Hammer yarn from Mickey Spillane. Dorothy Parker and Dorothy Sayers shared rack space with Ralph Ellison and J. D. Salinger. Max Brand rubbed up against Barbara Cartland. (Barbara would have been mortified.) A. E. van Vogt, P. G. Wodehouse, and H. P. Lovecraft were crammed in together with F. Scott Fitzgerald. Mysteries, westerns, gothics, ghost stories, classics of English literature, the latest contemporary "literary" novels, and, of course, SF and fantasy and horror—you could find it all on that spinner rack in the little candy store at First Street and Kelly Parkway.

Looking back now, almost half a century later, I can see that that wire spinner rack had a profound impact on my later development as a writer.

All writers are readers first, and all of us write the sort of books we want to read. I started out loving science fiction and I still love science fiction . . . but inevitably, digging through those paperbacks, I found myself intrigued by other sorts of books as well. I started reading horror when a book with Boris Karloff on the cover caught my attention. Robert E. Howard and L. Sprague de Camp hooked me on fantasy, just in the time for J. R. R. Tolkien and *The Lord of the Rings*. The historical epics of Dumas and Thomas B. Costain featured sword fights too, so I soon started reading those as well, and that led me to other epochs of history and other authors. When I came upon Charles Dickens and Mark Twain and Rudyard Kipling on the spinner rack, I grabbed them up too, to read the original versions of some of my favorite stories, and to see how they differed from the *Classics Illustrated* versions. Some of the mysteries I found on the rack had cover art so salacious that I had to smuggle them into the apartment and read them when my mother wasn't watching, but I sampled those as well, and have been reading mysteries ever since. Ian Fleming and James Bond led me into the world of thrillers and espionage novels, and Jack Schaefer's *Shane* into westerns. (Okay, I confess, I never did get into romances or nurse novels.) Sure, I knew the differences between a space opera and a hard-boiled detective story and a historical novel . . . but I never *cared* about such differences. It seemed to me, then as now, that there were good stories and bad stories, and that was the only distinction that truly mattered.

My views on that have not changed much in the half century since, but the world of publishing and bookselling certainly has. I don't doubt that there are still some old spinner racks out there, with all the books jumbled up together, but these days most people buy their reading material in chain superstores, where genre is king. SF and fantasy over here, mystery over there, romance back of that, bestsellers up front. No mixing and no mingling, please, keep to your own kind. "Literature" has its own section, now that the so-called "literary novel" has become a genre itself. Children's books and YAs are segregated.

It's good for selling books, I guess. It's convenient. Easy to find the sort of books you like. No one has to get down on their knees in hopes of finding Jack Vance's *Big Planet* behind that copy of *How to Win Friends and Influence People*.

But it's not good for readers, I suspect, and it's definitely not good for writers. Books should broaden us, take us to places we have never been and show us things we've never seen, expand our horizons and our way of looking at the world. Limiting your reading to a single genre defeats that. It limits us, makes us smaller.

Yet genre walls are hardening. During my own career, I have written science fiction, fantasy, and horror, and occasionally a few hybrids that were part this and part that, sometimes with elements of the murder mystery and the literary novel blended in. But younger writers starting out today are actively discouraged from doing the same by their editors and publishers. New fantasists are told that they had best adopt a pseudonym if they want to do a science fiction novel . . . and god help them if they want to try a mystery.

It's all in the name of selling more books, and I suppose it does.

But I say it's spinach, and I say to hell with it.

Bayonne may not have had any bookstores when I was growing up, but it did have a lot of pizza parlors, and a bar pie from Bayonne is among the best pizza anywhere. Small wonder that pizza is my favorite food. That doesn't mean I want to eat it every day, and to the exclusion of every other food in the world.

Which brings me to the book you hold in your hands.

These days I am best known as a fantasy writer, but *Warriors* is not a fantasy anthology . . . though it does have some good fantasy in it. My co-editor, Gardner Dozois, edited a science fiction magazine for a couple of decades, but *Warriors* is not a science fiction anthology either . . . though it does feature some SF stories as good as anything you'll find in *Analog* or *Asimov's*. It also features a western, and some mystery stories, a lot of fine historical fiction, some mainstream, and a couple of pieces that I won't even begin to try to label. *Warriors* is our own spinner rack.

People have been telling stories about warriors for as long as they have been telling stories. Since Homer first sang the wrath of Achilles and the ancient Sumerians set down their tales of Gilgamesh, warriors, soldiers, and fighters have fascinated us; they are a part of every culture, every literary tradition, every genre. *All Quiet on the Western Front, From Here to Eternity,* and *The Red Badge of Courage* have become part of our literary canons, taught in classrooms all around the country and the world. Fantasy has given us such memorable warriors as Conan the Barbarian, Elric of Melnibone, and Aragorn son of Arathorn. Science fiction offers us glimpses of the wars and warriors of the future, in books like Robert A. Heinlein's *Star-*

ship Troopers, Joe W. Haldeman's *Forever War,* and the space operas of David Weber, Lois McMaster Bujold, and Walter Jon Williams. The gunslinger of the classic western is a warrior. The mystery genre has made an archetype of the urban warrior, be he a cop, a hit man, a wiseguy, or one of those private eyes who walks the mean streets of Chandler and Hammett. Women warriors, child soldiers, warriors of the gridiron and the cricket pitch, the Greek hoplite and Roman legionary, Viking, musketeer, crusader, and doughboy, the GI of World War II and the grunt of Vietnam . . . all of them are warriors, and you'll find many in these pages.

Our contributors make up an all-star lineup of award-winning and bestselling writers, representing a dozen different publishers and as many genres. We asked each of them for the same thing—a story about a warrior. Some chose to write in the genre for which they're best known. Some decided to try something different. You will find warriors of every shape, size, and color in these pages, warriors from every epoch of human history, from yesterday and today and tomorrow, and worlds that never were. Some of the stories will make you sad, some will make you laugh, many will keep you on the edge of your seat.

But you won't know which until you've read them, for Gardner and I, in the tradition of that old wire spinner rack, have mixed them all up. There's no science fiction section here, no shelves reserved just for historical novels, no romance rack, no walls or labels of any sort. Just stories. Some are by your favorite writers, we hope; others, by writers you may never have heard of (yet). It's our hope that by the time you finish this book, a few of the latter may have become the former.

So spin the rack and turn the page. We have some stories to tell you.

WARRIORS

Cecelia Holland

Cecelia Holland is one of the world's most highly acclaimed and respected historical novelists, ranked by many alongside other giants in that field, such as Mary Renault and Larry McMurtry. Over the span of her thirty-year career, she's written almost thirty historical novels, including *The Firedrake, Rakóssy, Two Ravens, Ghost on the Steppe, The Death of Attila, The King's Road, Pillar of the Sky, The Lords of Vaumartin, Pacific Street, The Sea Beggars, The Earl, The Kings in Winter, The Belt of Gold,* and more than a dozen others. She also wrote the well-known science fiction novel *Floating Worlds,* which was nominated for a Locus Award in 1975, and of late has been working on a series of fantasy novels, including *The Soul Thief, Witches' Kitchen, The Serpent Dreamer,* and *Varanger,* the most recent volume in the Soul Thief series. *The High City,* a historical novel set in the Byzantine Empire, was published in 2009.

In the violent and bloody story that follows, she takes us back to the days of the Vikings and sweeps us along with a swift-moving raiding party (hope you know how to row!) who find the stakes for that particular raid set a little higher than they had bargained for. . . .

The King of Norway

I

Conn Corbansson had fought for Sweyn Tjugas when Sweyn was just an outlaw rebelling against his father, King Harald Bluetooth, and the prince had promised him a war with England when he became King of Denmark. Now that Sweyn actually wore the crown, he had let the English king buy his peace with a ship full of silver. Conn took this very ill.

"England is the greatest prize. You swore this to me."

Sweyn pulled furiously at his long forked mustaches. His eyes glittered. "I have not forgotten. And the time will come. Meanwhile, there is Hakon the Jarl, up in Norway. I cannot turn my back on him."

"So you called in the Jomsvikings instead of fighting him yourself," Conn said. "I see being King has made you womanish as well as pursefond."

He turned on his heel, before Sweyn could speak, and walked off down the boardwalk toward the King's great hall. His cousin Raef, who went everywhere with him, followed at his side. Sweyn bellowed after them, but neither of them paid heed.

Conn said, "How can I believe anything he says ever again?"

Raef said, "Who would you rather fight for?"

"I don't know," Conn said. "But I will find out."

That night in his great hall at Helsingor, Sweyn had a feasting, and there came many of his own hirdmen, including Conn and Raef, but also the chiefs of the Jomsvikings, Sigvaldi Haraldsson and Bui the Stout. Raef sat down at the low table, since with Conn he was now on the King's sour side.

Conn sat beside him, his black curly hair and beard a wild mane around his head. His gaze went continually to the Jomsvikings at the table across the way. Raef knew his curiosity; they had heard much of the great company of the Jomsvikings, of their fortress in the east, and their skill at war, which they gave to whoever would pay them enough. They weren't actually supposed to have chiefs, but to hold all in common as free men, and Raef wondered if Sigvaldi here and the barrel-shaped Bui were messengers more than chiefs. They wore no fancy clothes, such as Sweyn's red coats of silk and fur, and their beards and hair hung shaggy and long. Sigvaldi was a big man, square shouldered, with curling yellow hair that flowed into his beard.

Beside him, Conn said, "I like their looks. They are hard men, and proud."

Raef said nothing, being slower to judgment. Across the way, Sigvaldi had seen Conn watching, indeed, and lifted a cup to him, and Conn drank with him. It was the strong beer, thick as bear piss, and the slaves were carrying around ewers of it to refill any cup that went even half-empty. Raef reached out and turned his empty cup upside down.

When they were finished with the meat and settling in to drink, Sweyn stood up and lifted his cup, and called on Thor and Odin and gave honor to them. The men all shouted and drank, but Sweyn was not finished.

"In their honor also, it's our Danish custom to offer vows, which are most sacred now—" He held out his cup to be filled again. "And here in the names of those most high, I swear one day to make myself King of England!"

The men all through the hall gave up a roar of excitement; across the field of waving arms and cheering faces, Raef saw Sweyn turn and glare at Conn. "Who else offers such a vow as this?"

The uproar faded a moment, and Sigvaldi lurched to his feet. "When the war for England comes, let it be, but we are here for the sake of Hakon the Jarl, in Norway, who is an oathbreaker and a turncoat."

Voices rose, calling Hakon the Jarl every sort of evil thing, traitor and thief and liar. And the slaves went around and filled the cups. Steeped in drink, red-faced Sigvaldi held his cup high so that all would look. When the hall was hushed, he shouted, "Therefore I vow here before the high gods to lead the Jomsvikings against Hakon, wherever he hides! And I will not give up until he is beaten."

There was a great yell from all there, and they drank. The hall was crowded with men now, those sitting at the tables, many of them Jomsvikings, and many others standing behind them who were Sweyn's housecarls and crews.

"A mighty vow," Sweyn called. "An honor to the gods Hakon has betrayed. The rest of you—will you follow your chief in this?" His eyes shot an oblique glance at Conn, down at the lower table. "Which of you will join the Jomsvikings?"

At this, Dane and Jomsviking alike began shouting out oaths and vows against Hakon, while the slaves with the jugs plied their work.

Then Conn rose.

Raef held his breath, alarmed at this, and around the hall, the other men hushed.

Conn held out his cup.

"I swear I will sail with you, Sigvaldi, and call out Hakon face-to-face, and not come back until I am the King of Norway." He raised his cup toward Sweyn and tilted it to his mouth.

There was a brief hush at this, as everybody saw it was an insult, or a challenge, but then they erupted again in another great roaring and stamping all through the hall, and more outpourings of vows. Raef, who had touched nothing since the first cup, marked that up there at the high seat, Sweyn's glinting eyes were fixed on Conn and his mouth wound tight with rage. Raef thought they had all probably gotten more than they wished for in this oath-taking at Helsingor.

The next morning Conn woke, sprawled on his bench in the hall, and went out into the yard to piss. His head pounded and his mouth tasted evil. He could not remember much of the night before. When he turned away from the fence, Sigvaldi the Jomsviking chief was walking up to him, beaming all across his face.

"Well," he boomed out, "maybe we promised some mighty doings, last night, with those vows, hah? But I'm glad you're with us, boy. We'll see if you'll make a Jomsviking." He put out his hand to Conn, who shook it, having nothing else to do. Sigvaldi went on, "Meet at the Limsfjord at the full moon, and we'll go raiding in Norway, and draw Hakon to us. Then we'll find out how well you fight."

He tramped away across the yard, where more of the Jomsvikings were coming out into the sun. Raef stood by the door into the hall.

Conn went over by him.

"What did I swear to?"

His cousin's long homely face was expressionless. "You said you would sail with them and challenge Hakon the Jarl face-to-face, and not return to Denmark until you were King of Norway."

Conn gave a yelp, amazed, and said, "What a fool I am in beer! That's something great to do, though, isn't it."

Raef said, "I'd say that."

"Well, then," Conn said, "let's get started."

II

So they sailed north to raid in Norway, around the Vik, where the riches were. Sometimes the whole fleet raided a village together, and sometimes they went out in parties and attacked farmsteads along the fjord, driving the people out and then ransacking their holdings. Whatever anybody found of gold went into a great chest, which Bui the Stout guarded like a dragon. All else they ate or drank, or packed off to the Jomsberg. Several ships went heavy-laden to the Jomsberg, but there was no sign of Hakon the Jarl.

They turned north, following the passageways between the islands and the coast, raiding as they went. Every day the sun stayed longer in the sky, and the nights barely darkened enough to let a man sleep an hour. Around them, above thin green seaside meadows, the land rose in curtains of rock, snow-cloaked. They stood far out to sea to weather the cloud-shrouded wind-blasted cape at Stad, and then rowed on, still north but now easterly, attacking whatever they found in the fjords. They were within a few good days' rowing now of the long waterway that led to the Trondelag, and still Hakon offered them no opposition.

III

Conn's muscles hurt; all day he had been rowing against the fierce north wind, and he stood on the beach and stretched the ache out of his arms. The sun was a great fat orange blob floating just above the western horizon. The sky burned with its fiery glow, the few low streaks of cloud gilt-edged. The dark sea rolled up against the pebble shore, broke, and withdrew in a long seething growl. Out past the ships, sixty of them, drawn up onto the beach like resting monsters, he caught a glimpse of a shark.

The coppery light of the long sundown made the campfires that covered the beach almost invisible. Over every pit a haunch turned, strips of meat and fish hung dripping on tripods and spits, their fats exploding in the coals below, and a man stood by in the hot glow with a cup, putting out burns with a douse of beer. Conn saw Sigvaldi Haraldsson up on the beach and went to him.

The chief of the Jomsvikings sat on a big log, his feet out in front of him, watching some lesser men turn his spit. Bui the Stout sat next to him, the Jomsvikings' treasure chest at his feet. As Conn came up, they raised their faces toward him. They were passing a cup between them, and Sigvaldi with a bellowed greeting held it out to him.

Conn drank. The beer tasted muddy. "Hakon has to come after us soon."

Sigvaldi gave a harsh crackle of a laugh, clapping his hands on his knees. "I told you, lad, he won't willingly fight us. We will have to go all the way up to the Trondelag to drag him out of his hole."

Bui laughed. "By then we will have beggared him anyway." He kicked the chest at his feet.

"Yes," Sigvaldi said, and reached out and slapped Conn's arm companionably. "We've taken great boot, and we'll feast again tonight as we do every night. This is the life of a Jomsviking, boy."

Conn blurted, "I came to throw down Hakon the Jarl, not to stick a few burghers for their gold chains."

Bui threw his head back at that. "There's a bit of Hakon in every link."

Sigvaldi gave another laugh at that. "Conn, heed me. You need to match this green eagerness with a cold wit. Before we can get to any real fighting, we have to run Hakon to ground like the rabbit he is. Meanwhile, we can feast on these villages."

Bui was still staring at Conn, unfriendly. "You know, your ship isn't bringing me much gold." He pushed at the treasure chest. "Maybe you ought to think about that more."

Conn said, "I'm not a Jomsviking," and turned and walked away. He did not say, I am not Sweyn Tujgas's hirdman anymore either.

He went back down the shore, past the ships, going toward his own fire. His crew had camped at the end of the beach, where the sandy bank cut the wind. The sundown cast a pink veil over the sea, which the waves broke in lines of light and dark. The wind sang among the ships, as if the dragons spoke to one another in their secret voices. Beyond, to the east, against the red-and-purple sky, the gaunt mountains of the coast seemed like sheer walls of rock, capped with the rosy glisten of a glacier.

He went in among his crew, clustered around the fire, cooking cow parts and drinking beer; they greeted him in a chorus. His cousin Raef was off by the foot of the sandy slope, sitting beside the wounded man, who lay stretched out flat on the ground.

Conn squatted down on his heels by the fire. He took the beer horn out of the hand of the man next to him, who was Finn, the youngest of them. "Go ask Aslak to come drink with me."

Finn got up and trotted off, a short, thin boy who had been pushing a plow two summers before. Conn drank what was left in the horn, which was better beer than Sigvaldi's. Since he had found out that after every raid any gold or silver they took went into Bui's chest, he shifted his interest to looting the best food and drink.

Opposite him, pop-eyed Gorm grinned at him over a half-burnt chunk of meat.

"Any word?"

Conn said, "Nothing." He looked around again at Raef, off in the gloom with the dying man, but then Aslak came up.

Conn got to his feet; Aslak was a captain, like him, and although he was a Jomsviking, he and Conn got on well. Also, he was from the Trondelag. They shook hands and sat, and Conn waited until Aslak had taken a long pull of the drinking horn.

Aslak smacked his lips. "That's the best of the sacred stuff I've tasted since the oath-taking at Helsingor."

Conn growled. He did not like being reminded of that. He said, "You're from here, aren't you? What's this coast?"

"Same as we've been sailing," Aslak said. "All inlets and bays and islands. Lots of wind. Lots of rock. And poor, these people, poor as an old field. Bui won't be happy here."

Conn laughed. "Bui isn't happy with me anyway."

Aslak saluted him with the horn. "You steal the wrong kind of gold, Conn."

Conn gave him back the salute and drank. "Sigvaldi thinks Hakon is too afraid to come after us, no matter how we harry his people."

Aslak grunted. The other men by the fire were watching them both intently. "That's wrong. Sigvaldi's making a bad mistake if he really believes that. Hakon's a devil of a fighter." Aslak wiped foam off his beard with one hand. "Hakon's kindred goes back to the Frost Giants, to gods older than Odin. That's why he didn't come south when we sacked Tonsberg, or come out to meet us below Stad. His power is in the North. And so now we are going North, and I doubt we'll be too much longer waiting."

"Let it happen," Conn said, and spat between his fingers. He nodded toward the fire. "Drink another horn, Aslak. Gorm, save me some of that meat." He got up and went in toward the bank, to where Raef sat beside the dying man.

This was Ketil, one of their rowers, no older than Conn himself. Their whole crew were boys who had joined off their farms when they first took their ship *Seabird*. After two years' sailing with Conn and Raef, none of them was green anymore, whatever Sigvaldi thought.

That day they had stormed a village on an inlet; some of the people had fought back, for a few moments, and one had bashed in the side of Ketil's head with a stick. He was still alive, and they had brought him here to keep him safe while he died. Raef was sitting there beside him, his back to the sandbank and his long legs drawn up to his chest. Conn sank down on his heels.

"Is he—?"

Raef shook his head. His pale hair hung lank to his shoulders. "Less and less."

Conn sat there thinking about the fight in the village, and he said, "These are Hakon's people. Why does he not defend them?" He put out one hand toward Ketil, but he did not touch him.

Raef shrugged. "Because we want him to."

"Then what will he do?"

"What we don't want," Raef said. "Here comes Bui."

The keg-shaped Jomsviking had sauntered up the beach toward the *Seabird*'s fire, and now seeing them apart from it, veered toward them.

"Hail, King of Norway!" he called, and snickered.

Conn stood up. "Let the Fates hear you. What is it?"

"Sigvaldi commands you. Just you. Right now. For a council."

Conn turned and glanced at Raef. "Are you coming?"

"Sigvaldi says you only," Bui said with a sniff.

"I'm staying here with Ketil," Raef said, and Conn went off without him.

IV

When he first sailed with the Jomsvikings, Conn had expected their council to be a great shouting and arguing and talking of everybody, but now he knew better; there was plenty of food and beer, but in the end, Sigvaldi stood in front of them and said what would happen, and they nodded. They were supposed to be free men, but they did as they were told. There was much about the Jomsvikings he liked better in the idea than in the actual practice.

Sigvaldi said, "We have word now that Hakon is just inside the bay, over there. Where that big island is."

A roar went up from the gathered captains. Bui stood.

"How many ships?"

"Not many," Sigvaldi said. "Six. Eight. He's waiting for his fleet to gather, that's clear. But we're going to catch him before they come." He swept his gaze around them all. "We'll leave before dawn. I'll take the left, with Bui. Aslak, you take the right, with Sigurd Cape, and Havard." His teeth shone. Conn felt a sudden shiver of excitement. Sigvaldi turned and fixed his gaze on him.

"And since you're so wild to get him, Conn Corbansson, you go first, in the middle."

In the short, bright night, they buried Ketil. The rest of *Seabird*'s crew laid him on his back at the foot of the sand bank, with his sword beside him and a little meat and beer for the last journey. Then each brought a stone from the beach.

Finn said, "Better to die like this than behind a plow, like an ox." He put his stone by Ketil's feet.

"Better still, in the battle tomorrow," Gorm said, at Ketil's head. He turned his wide eyes on Conn; he always looked a little pop-eyed. "How many ships does Hakon have?"

Conn said, "Sigvaldi says only a few. But I don't trust Sigvaldi anymore."

"Tomorrow," said Grim, "when we catch Hakon—"

Somebody else laughed; Rugr said, "If we catch him—"

"That will be a deed that will ring around the world."

Conn stooped and laid his stone down by Ketil's shoulder, moving other stones to fit. "Whatever we do tomorrow, we do it together."

"We take Ketil with us." Raef bent and put his stone by Ketil's hip.

"If we beat Hakon—" Odd laid his stone by Ketil's knee. Now the shape of stones was closed around the dead man, a ship to carry him on. "They will tell the story until the end of the world."

"The end of the world."

They stood then a moment silent, their eyes on Ketil, and then they brought the sand bank down to cover him. They all turned and looked at one another. They clasped each other's hands and laughed, sharp and uneasy and wild, their eyes shining. "Together," they said. "All together."

Then they went off to get ready, to see to their weapons, to sleep, if they could, so they could sail before dawn. Conn and Raef fetched extra water and food and stowed it on the ship, where she lay on the beach.

The others were lying down by the fire. Conn sat down beside his cousin on the sand beside the round breast of their ship. He thought he would never sleep. In his mind he thought about every fight and battle he had ever been in, but everything seemed like a blur suddenly.

It would all be different, anyway; it always was.

After a while, he said to Raef, "Are you ready?"

"I guess so," Raef said. His voice was tight as a plucked wire. "No. This feels bad to me. He put us first, out in front of everybody?"

"Yes," Conn said. "We have the chance to take Hakon ourselves, alone."

"Or be taken ourselves. He's trying to kill us," Raef said.

Conn nudged him with his elbow. "You think too much. When it starts, you won't have time to think." He yawned, leaning against the ship's side, suddenly exhausted. "Just follow me," he said, and shut his eyes finally, and slept.

Conn dreamt.

He was in a great battle, around him the clash of axes and shields, the horns blaring, a boat rocking under him, arms and hair and twisted faces packed around him. He could not tell his enemies from his friends. The heaving and screaming and struggle around him were like something trying to devour him, and in a frenzy he hacked around him with his sword to make himself room to stand. The blood sprayed over him, so he tasted it on his lips.

Then the clash of blades on shields became thunder rolling, and lightning flashed so bright, he was blinded. When he could see again, he was alone, fighting alone, a tiny man against a towering storm, not even on a ship anymore. The clouds rose hundreds of feet above him, billowing black and gray, and the lightning shot forth its arrows at him, the rain itself felt like showers of stones, and the fists of the thunder battered him.

The wind streamed out the cloud's long hair; in the billows he saw eyes, a mouth with teeth like boulders, a monstrous woman's shape of fog and mist. High above him, she stretched out her arm toward him, and from each fingertip the lightning blazed. He could not move, bound where he was, and the lightning bolts came straight at him and blasted him into pieces, so that where he had been, there was nothing.

He woke up on the ground beside the ship. The dream gripped him; he was surprised to find himself whole. He got to his feet and walked down the shore, toward the sunrise.

On the far edge of the purple sky, a hot red glow was spreading, and the air glimmered. He stood on the pebble beach, and the dream went on in his head, stronger than the day around him.

In a moment, Raef came up beside him. Conn told him the dream and, even in the dim light, saw his cousin turn pale.

"Is it true, do you think?" Conn asked.

"All dreams are true, somehow."

The crew was gathering by *Seabird*, and the sun was about to rise. "Fate takes us," Conn said, "and all there is for us to do is meet it well. Simple enough. Come on, let's get going."

V

They rowed out into the swelling sunlight, rounding the top end of the island and turning southeast toward the opening of the bay. The sea was high and rolling. *Seabird* flew over the water like a hunting hawk; without Ketil, Conn was rowing his oar, the first bench on the steerboard side. As he leaned into each stroke, he saw the rest of the fleet swinging out to row after them, ship after ship, stalking along on their oars, their bare masts and tall curled prows dark against the pale sky, the sea breaking white along their bows.

Something swelled in him, some irresistible joy. He glanced forward over his shoulder. They were passing the tip of the island, set to weather the low cape on the mainland, with the bay opening before them between the gaunt gouged hillsides. Behind hung the white curtain of the mountains. The sun was rising, spilling a sheet of light out over the water. The sky was white. He was glad they were turning south now, so he would fight with the glare of the sun on his side instead of in his eyes. He felt the sea smooth out as they came into the shelter of the hills; he called an order, and the crew gave a single shout in answer, flattened their oars so the blades bit the top of the sea and the ship seemed to lift into the air, skimming over the low chop. He felt a giddy pride in this, his crew, the best rowers in the fleet.

The bay opened its arms. In the middle of the channel, a ragged island humped up dark under a cloak of trees. Raef, at the helm, set them to pass to the west of it. The ship flew by a cluster of low rocks that barely broke up through the trough of the waves. Looking past the seven rowers in front of him, Conn saw Raef with his white hair streaming, staring up ahead and all around the bay, Raef with his long sight.

A pale spit ran like a tongue down into the water from the southern tip of the island. Beyond, the bay widened out, glistening with fresh light. Near the shore on either side, the waves broke white on barren skerries. Then Raef shouted, "Ship! Ship!" and pointed straight ahead of them.

Conn crossed his oar and leapt up, climbing onto the gunwale, one hand on the stempost. At first, all he saw was the broad glittering expanse of the water, another tree-covered island, farther south. Then, halfway to that island, the fresh new sun glinted on something gold.

Conn remembered that golden-headed dragon, which he had seen once before, in Denmark. He gave a yell. "That's him! That's Hakon's ship!"

Behind him, Raef shouted an answer. On one of the ships coming after them, a warhorn sounded its deep hollow note. *Seabird* shot out past the island onto the open bay, the rowers pulling strong and long. Conn twisted to look quickly back.

Behind them, the narrow waters between the island and the west shore were packed with the ships of the Jomsvikings, the masts like a moving forest. More horns sounded, and a roar of voices went up. They had seen the golden ship too.

He wheeled around. Up there, half a mile into the bay, the golden gleam turned and ran off into the south. His crew bellowed, and *Seabird* surged forward. The long warhorns were braying behind him. Conn slid down quickly to his oar again. On his left, Sigvaldi in his big dragon was striding after him, and on the right, Aslak's ship with its fanged and horned head was only a few lengths behind.

Conn screamed, "Go! Go!" and leaned into his stroke, and the rest of the crew smoothly picked up the rhythm with him. The fleet behind him was spreading out, as they rowed into the open water past the first island, and all were racing to be first. A screech of urgent voices rose. Conn saw Sigvaldi in the bow of his big dragon, bellowing orders. On the other side, Aslak was waving his men on with milling arms.

Smallest of them, still *Seabird* flew ahead of them all. Behind her was the great pack of the Jomsvikings, but ahead of her was only the dragon with the golden head, running away.

Then Raef shouted, "Ships! Ships—"

Conn crossed his oar again and leapt up onto the gunwale by the bow. His eyes swept the end of the bay, through the confusion of the ragged shore and the islands and the low skerries. Down there, the golden dragon was turning, was facing them, not running anymore. He climbed higher on the prow, teetering on the gunwale, and now he saw, first, the low hulls sliding through the water after Hakon, and then, on either side, other ships stroking hard into the bay from inlets, from behind capes.

"How many?" Raef bellowed.

"I don't know! Half row!" Conn sprang down from the bow, and as the ship slowed a little, he went back through his ship, from man to man. "Get ready," he said. "Get your swords, get your helmets on." Their eyes were already wild, and Finn's face was white as an egg, Gorm was swearing under his breath, Skeggi was swallowing over and over as if he were about to be sick. Conn reached the stern, where Raef had climbed up on the gunwale to see.

"A lot of ships," Raef said. "More than us. Hakon laid a trap for us, and we walked right into it."

"Sigvaldi did," Conn said. He reached into the stern counter and got his helmet out and pulled it on over his hair. "Just get us to Hakon." He shouted, "Full row! One! Two!" and ran back up to his oar in the forecastle.

Seabird surged forward. While they had slowed, the rest of the fleet had all but caught up to them, on every ship shouting and horns. Conn could see Aslak on his right, the big bald Jomsviking standing by his third oarsmen. He wore no helmet; he was bawling to the crew. Conn swung forward again, his heart hammering, and rowed. His ship hurtled across the flat water. Ahead, now, faint, he heard other horns and more shouting.

Raef shouted, "They're throwing something! Duck!"

Conn doubled over, hunching his shoulders; the bow would shield him well enough. A rattle of spears clattered down around *Seabird*, mostly just sharpened sticks, which hit nothing. Raef shouted, "Get ready!"

Conn crossed his oar again. "Gorm! Arn—Sigurd—" He leapt up; he had almost called Ketil's name. He drew his sword and, with his free hand, grabbed up a sharpened stick that had fallen into the ship. When he whirled around, the round head of a dragon was looming toward him, closing rapidly.

Not golden. A big black beast, a round weather-beaten curve of a prow. Behind him, Raef shouted: "Up oars!"

With the hand holding the sharp stick, Conn grabbed the gunwale, and *Seabird* plowed in past the black dragon, snapping off a few of her oars before the other crew managed to get them out of the way. Conn stepped up onto the gunwale and jumped across the narrowing water between the two ships.

Three men met him with their axes swinging. For a moment, balancing on the gunwale with his back to the sea, all he could do was weave and parry, jabbing with the stick with his left hand and his sword in his right. Then somebody else from *Seabird* landed next to him and one of the axemen staggered and Conn stuck him through and then lunging sideways and all the way onto the ship hacked down another Tronder axeman.

It was pop-eyed Gorm beside him. His whole forecastle crew was piling onto the enemy ship after him. The ship was pitching hard, as if it tried to throw them off. He ducked down under an axe blade swinging by him and thrust toward the body behind it. He fought for space on the tilting floor, his feet planted wide, stabbing and jabbing with his sword at the man before him. The Tronder reeled, cut across the chest. Lunging to hack him down, Conn smacked his knee on a bench and almost collapsed.

Suddenly the Tronders were turning, were leaping off the ship, and beyond them, he saw Aslak's bald head climbing over the black ship's stern.

He wheeled toward *Seabird*; the little dragon was drifting away. From the far side, more Tronders swarmed over her, battling the rest of his crew. Raef. He bellowed and charged back to his ship.

When they first closed with the black ship, half the crew had jumped off, and now the rest were leaning out to watch, their oars idle. *Seabird* was tipped hard to that direction. Raef held the steerboard out, to keep the ship close on the black dragon. Then another Tronder ship was veering straight at him.

He bellowed to the sterncastle crew, who were all backwards to this, and swung the steerboard up out of the way.

The crew wheeled around to meet the Tronders' charge. The bigger ship ground into *Seabird*'s bow and spilled men in a tide, roaring and waving their one-bladed axes. Tronders charged down the middle of the ship; Raef reached down at his feet for his sword, and before he stood up, a shaggy-bearded man was leaping toward him, his red mouth round and howling.

His axe swung, and, still sitting, Raef shrank away. The brow of the axe missed him by a finger's breadth and struck the gunwale just beyond him. A chunk of wood flew into the air. Awkward, stooping, Raef flailed his sword at the shaggy man, and the flat of the blade hit the Tronder's wrist with a crack like a stone splitting. The Tronder staggered. Raef lunged up and caught him in the gut with his shoulder and heaved him over the side of the ship.

The Tronder ship had backed off, was fighting somebody else. All around him, Raef saw ships jammed against ships, and men fighting up and down them; ahead of him, a big dragon wallowed awash to the tops of its benches, and men swam and bodies floated in the choppy water.

On *Seabird*, the remaining Tronders had taken over the forecastle, but the stern half of the crew had pushed them back and was holding them at the mast. Raef charged up to help them. As he got there, Finn went down hard right in front of him. A big man in a leather tunic reared over him, his single-bladed axe high; he never saw Raef coming and Raef never stopped. Still running, he drove his sword straight through the leather chest.

The Tronder fell backwards. Finn was trying to crawl out of the way, blocked by a sea chest and a misshipped oar, and Raef stepped over him to the mast. There Skeggi and Odd were clubbing away at two axemen in front of them; more beyond in the narrow waist of the ship were struggling to close enough to strike. Then suddenly the ship yawed. Up by the bow, Conn was climbing out of the bay, pulling himself over the gunwale behind the Tronders, his hair streaming in his face, and they wheeled, saw him and the men climbing in after him, and leapt off.

Raef turned around to Finn, who was clinging to the gunwale and trying to stand. His leg looked broken, maybe both legs. Raef hauled him back into the stern and sat him on the bench by the tiller. "Can you steer?"

"I—" The boy threw back his long brown hair. "Yes, I can." He reached out one hand to hold the side of the ship, but the other reached for the tiller. Raef swung the steerboard down and gave him the tiller bar.

"Stay off the rocks. And get us to that golden dragon." He ran back toward Conn, in the forecastle.

The sun was only halfway up the sky and the day already crackled with heat. Raef peeled off his shirt; his hair dripped. Hakon's golden ship seemed always just out of reach. They went side to side with a big snake-headed dragon, fighting across the gunwales. Twice Conn led the whole crew to charge the other ship, and twice the Tronders held them off. Then abruptly the Tronder was veering away, all her oars coming out, fleeing.

For a moment, *Seabird* was in a lull, ships all around them, but nobody fighting them. Raef leaned against the mast, breathing hard, looking around. There were fewer of them than before. Gorm lay flat on his back on the floor, his pop eyes open. But his arm was gone, and he was dead. Beyond him, Egil leaned on the gunwale and then slowly slumped down on his knees between two benches. Skeggi and Grim had simply disappeared. The others looked battered, but whole. They were sitting down, reaching for water or food, talking. He even heard Arn's girly laugh. Raef lifted his gaze toward the fighting.

The battle line stretched across the whole end of the bay in a long crescent moon curve, with Sigvaldi on the left arm of the curve. Raef could see them fighting hard there, every ship engaged. *Seabird* was near the center; on the other arm, the Jomsvikings shoved Hakon's men toward the beach, and here in the middle there were several idle ships—Hakon seemed to be falling back—he could not see the golden dragon. Then, at the end of the line where Sigvaldi fought, another stream of ships was rowing up into sight, past the big island.

"Hiyahh! What's that?"

Conn reared up beside him. Raef pointed to the leader of the line of ships now attacking Sigvaldi. The ship was bigger than most, with a broader bow, and her whole stem below the slender curve of her dragon neck was covered in bands of iron set with iron claws.

Conn said, "I don't know, but if he turns the end of Sigvaldi's line, we're surrounded. Come on."

He shouted, and the men jumped to their oars. Gorm still lay on the floor, and Egil was dead on his own bench, but Finn sat by the steerboard and nodded at Raef when he looked. Raef went up forward and took the oar opposite Conn.

Seabird flew across the choppy water, past clumps of ships fighting. Overhead, ravens and seagulls glided in circles. They passed a dragon sinking, bodies floating around her, loose oars. Raef pointed beyond. "Bui is there."

Conn lifted his head; to his right, he saw Bui the Stout in the bow of his long dragon charging toward the iron ship, and he spun around toward his crew and shouted, "Go—go—go—!"

Smoothly, they quickened their pace, their shoulders sunburnt, slick with sweat. On the backswing, he turned again to look ahead of them.

The great iron dragon was at the center of a wedge-line of ships, pushing slightly ahead of the rest. The armor on her sea swan's breast was set with massive hooks. Conn guessed the barbs stuck out below the waterline too. He thought also she would be slow to steer. He crossed his oar and stood.

Seabird swooped in on the iron ship from one side and Bui from the other. The big ship stayed steady on her course, and Conn yelled, "Half row!" trying to judge the distance so that *Seabird* and Bui's ship got to the Tronder at the same time. He drew his sword. A hail of spears and stones met them, but the iron ship did not veer. Then *Seabird* was sheering in along one bow, and Bui on the other.

The Tronders, caught in the middle, stood up and fought in place. Conn traded blows with the man opposite him, parrying and hitting; Conn flinched back and, when the man lunged after him, chopped his sword through the Tronder's shoulder and then hacked him in the back as he went down. He bounded into the open space this left on the iron ship and stood toe to toe with another man with an axe. Raef was coming behind him. Conn pushed in—so close, he felt the Tronder's hot breath on his face. The axe haft struck him a glancing blow on the elbow and his arm went dead and the sword clattered to the floor. He stooped and with his left hand gripped it and struck upward, and the odd angle caught the Tronder off balance and Conn's sword bit his side and he slumped.

Bui was climbing on over the iron ship's other gunwale. He saw Conn and shouted, "Ho, the King of Norway! Come help me!"

Raef stood at Conn's left shoulder; they fought their way along one line of benches, and Bui fought his way down the other. The Tronders gave way only by dying. Conn's right arm started to tingle alive again, and he switched his sword into that hand. Now he got to using his sword well again, and he and Raef reached the mast a step ahead of Bui. The burly Jomsviking was red in the face, his bare chest slick with blood streaming from a cut on his neck.

"Eirik," he shouted, his voice hoarse. "We've got you!"

In the stern stood a man who, in spite of the heat, wore a dark shirt and a long cloak. His helmet had a gold rim and he was yelling orders. He bellowed, "Somebody has somebody, Bui. Reverse! Reverse!"

Conn wheeled. "They'll take us in with them!" The iron ship was already sliding backwards on her sterncastle oars, rowing back in among the other Tronder ships. By the bow, *Seabird*, with six men at the oars, was staying near as she could, but she dared not go into the midst of the Tronders. Conn shouted and pushed Raef ahead of him, and Raef shoved the other men on up to the bow of the iron ship.

The first four men leapt easily enough into *Seabird*, and then Raef clambered up the gunwale and jumped across the widening water, but Conn threw off his helmet, and dived into the bay.

The iron ship was stroking steadily backwards, into the thick of Hakon's ships. A stretch of clear water opened between the Tronder fleet and the Jomsvikings. Conn swam hard through it toward his ship, her oars coming out, hanging in the air, ready to row. A spear sliced through the water just past his head. He reached the ship and Raef leaned down to haul him up. He went facefirst into the space between the front two benches, into several inches of water.

He rolled over and straightened, on his knees, looking back toward the iron ship. Raef pushed up beside him.

"We're full of water."

"Bail!" Conn yelled, and got his feet under him, to his ankles in water. *Seabird* was rowing rearward, sluggish; she was always stiff going stern first, but this was more sluggish than usual. All around the ship, the crew bent to slinging the water out.

The fighting everywhere had stopped. Between them and the Tronders now was a broad stretch of the bay. Hakon was pulling his whole fleet back toward shore. The water between was scummed with blood, filthy with broken gear, bits of ships and oars, bodies like unsteady islands bobbing in the little waves. Down past his own stempost, he could see an arm floating a few feet below the surface.

The water in his ship did not seem to be going down. He reached into the forecastle and found a bucket and began to throw water over the side. Raef vaulted over the gunwale into the bay, and went hand over hand around the outside of the ship.

"King of Norway!"

Conn straightened, looking around. Aslak's big dragon was gliding up just off his bow. The big bald Jomsviking stood by the mast.

"You don't look so good!" Aslak shouted. "Eirik's claws ripped you."

Conn pointed toward Hakon's fleet. "Is he giving up?" He bent to bail; the water was coming in as fast as he and his crew threw it out again.

"No—he's just gone for help," Aslak bellowed.

Raef's head appeared above the gunwale, near Conn's knee; he boosted himself smoothly up onto the ship. His left side was all bruised, Conn saw, and he was bleeding from a cut on his arm, but he looked hale enough.

Raef said, "The ship is sinking. I think that damned toothed thing tore one of the strakes loose."

Aslak bawled, "Come over here! Come on—half my crew's gone any-way." He turned and gave orders, and his ship began to scull sideways toward Conn's.

Conn shouted, "*Seabird*—everybody—go over!" He waved his arm. They were already scrambling over so fast, the ship rocked, even wallow-ing half-full of water. Conn went back into the stern and got Finn.

The boy was only half-conscious. His leg had swollen fat enough to split his legging, the flesh black underneath. Conn lifted him up and he whined. Raef came and helped him carry Finn onto Aslak's ship. They set him down in the hollow of the sterncastle, behind the steering bench. Raef went off immediately. Conn found some beer, but Finn choked on it. His eyes opened, wide and dark with pain. Conn left the beer by him and stood up.

Amidships he saw Raef standing also, his arms at his sides, watching *Seabird* go down. Conn went up beside him. For a while, their dragonship seemed to float, still, even awash, but then suddenly it went down out of sight into the dark green deep. The last thing he saw was her little fierce-eyed dragon head. Raef said nothing, only stood there. Conn felt the heart in him crack like a rock in the fire.

He looked around, and found Aslak up by the bow. He went there, looking toward Hakon's fleet against the far shore. Where they were, in the center of the bay, the Jomsvikings were drinking and eating and bailing their ships out. Conn could see three other ships sinking in a single glance.

He said, "What kind of help is Hakon looking for?"

Aslak had a little skin of beer, and he took a pull on it. He nodded with his head toward the island in the middle of the bay.

"You see that island? It's called the Blessed Place. There are altars there half as old as the Ash Tree. Hakon may have a problem. He switched sides once too often. I've heard his patron goddesses are still angry for when he turned Christian."

He slung an arm around Conn's shoulders. "I'm glad to have you on board, boy—you're a damned good fighter."

Conn flushed; to hide this pleasure he turned and glanced around at his crew. That took the glow away. He had not realized how many were gone. He was losing everything—his ship, the crew that made her fly. He had to win now.

He turned back to Aslak. "This Christian thing seems common enough. Even Sweyn's been primesigned." He took the skin and drank, and leaned out to pass the skin to Raef.

Aslak was sitting on the front bench, his knees wide and his arms bent across them. "Hakon didn't stay a Christer very long—just until he got away from Bluetooth."

"So he's betrayed everybody," Conn said.

"Oh, yes. At least once. And beaten everybody. German, Swede, Dane, and Norse. At least once." With a grimace, Aslak stretched one leg out and rubbed his calf. Blood squished from the top of his shoe.

Conn said, "But we are winning this one."

Aslak said, "Yes, I think so. So far."

VI

In the blazing sun past noon, Hakon's ships gathered again, and the golden dragon was in the center. They came forward again across the bay, and the Jomsvikings swung into lines to meet them.

Even as they rowed up, a cold wind began to blast. Conn, pulling an oar in the front of Aslak's ship, felt the harsh slash of the air on his cheek and looked west and saw a cloud boiling up over the horizon, black and swelling like a bruise on the sky. His skin went all to gooseflesh, and his dream came back to him. The line of the Jomsviking ships swept toward Hakon, and the stormcloud climbed up over half the sky, heavy and dark, the wind ripping streamers away like hair. Under it, the air flickered, thick and green.

Conn bent to his oar. Up the center of Aslak's ship came four men with spears, which they cast, but the wind flung them off like splinters. A roll of thunder boomed across the sky. Inside the towering cloud, lightning glowed. The first drops fell, and then all at once, sheets of rain hammered down.

Aslak was screaming the oar-chant, because of the mixed crew. Conn threw all his strength into each stroke. The rain battered on his head, his bare shoulders, streamed cold down his chest. Hakon's ships in their line loomed over them; he shipped the oar and, drawing his sword, wheeled toward the bow.

As he rose, the wind met him so hard, he had to stiffen himself against it, and then suddenly, as if the sky broke into tiny pieces and fell on him, it began to hail.

He stooped, half-blinded in the white deluge, feeling the ship under him rub another ship, and saw through the haze of flying ice the shape before him of a man with an axe. He struck. Raef was beside him, hip to hip. The axe came at him and he slashed again, blind, into the white whirling storm. Somebody screamed, somewhere. There was hail all in his beard, his hair, his eyebrows. Abruptly the booming fall stopped. The rain pattered away, and the sun broke through, glaring.

He staggered back a step. The ship was full of hailstones and water; Raef, beside him, slumped down on the bench, gasping for breath. Blood streamed down his face, his shoulders. Conn wheeled to look past the bow, toward Hakon's men.

The Tronder fleet had backed off again, but they were not fleeing; they were letting Sigvaldi flee.

Conn let out a howl of rage. Off toward the west, at the end of the Jomsviking line, Sigvaldi's big dragon suddenly had broken out of line, was stroking fast away up the bay, and behind it, the other Jomsviking ships were peeling out of their formation and following.

Conn leapt up onto the gunwale of Aslak's ship, his hand on the dragon's neck, and shouted, "Run! Run, Sigvaldi, you coward! Remember your vow? The Jomsviking way, is it—I'll not run—not if I'm the last man here and he sends all the gods against me, I'll not run!"

From behind him came a howl from Aslak's ship and the ships beyond. Conn pivoted his head to see them—back there all the other men shouted and shook their fists toward Sigvaldi and waved their swords at Hakon. Bui in their midst bellowed like a bull, red-faced. There were ten ships, he thought. Ten left, from sixty.

Aslak stood before him and put his hand on Conn's shoulder and met his eyes.

"If it's my doom here, I'll meet it like a man. Let's show them how true Jomsvikings fight!"

Conn gripped his hand. "To the last man!"

"It will be that," Raef said, behind him.

Bui shouted from the next dragon, "Aslak! Aslak! King of Norway! Lash the ships together!"

Aslak's head pivoted, looking toward Hakon. "He's coming."

"Hurry," Conn said.

They drew all the ships together, gunwale to gunwale, and lashed them with the rigging through the oar holes; so all the men were free to fight, and the ships formed a sort of fighting floor. The Tronder fleet was spreading out to encircle them. Conn went back into the stern of Aslak's dragon, where Finn lay, his eyes closed, still breathing, and pulled a shield across him. Then he went back up beside Raef.

VII

Horns blew in the Tronder fleet, the sound rolling around the bay, and then the ships all at once closed on the Jomsvikings on their floating ship-island. The air darkened; the cold wind blasted. The rain began to fall, and like icy rocks the hail descended on them again. Conn could barely stand against the wind and the pelting hailstones. Through the driving white, he saw a man with an axe heave up over the gunwale, another just behind, and he slashed out, and on the hailstrewn floor, he slipped and fell on his back. Raef strode across him. Raef slashed wildly side to side with his sword, battling two men at once, until Conn staggered up again and cut the first axeman across the knees and dropped him.

The hail stopped. In the rain, they battered at a wall of axeblades trying to hack their way over the gunwale. Horns blew. The Tronders were falling back again. Conn stepped back, breathing hard, his hair in his eyes; his knee was swelling and hurt as if somebody were driving a knife into it. The sun came out again, blazing bright.

On the next ship, Bui swayed back and forth, covered with blood. Both hands were gone. His face was hacked to the bone. He stooped, and looped his stumped arms through the handles of his chest of gold.

"All Bui's men overboard!" he shouted, and leapt into the bay, the gold in his arms. He sank at once into the deep.

The sunlight slanted in under a roof of cloud. The long sundown had begun. Beneath the clouds, the air was already turning dark. Hakon's horns blew their long booming notes, pulling his fleet off.

Aslak sank down on a bench. The side of his face was mashed so that one eye was almost invisible. Raef sat next to him, slack with fatigue. Conn went down the ship, whose whole side had taken the Tronder attack. He was afraid if he sat down, his knee would stiffen entirely. What he saw clenched his belly to a knot.

Arn lay dead on the floor, his head split to the red mush of his brain. The two men next to him, bleeding but alive, were Jomsvikings, not his. Beyond them, Rugr slumped, and Conn stooped beside him and tried to rouse him, but he fell over, lifeless. Two other dead men lay on the floor of the ship, and he had to climb across a bench to get around them. He went up to the stern, where Finn lay, still breathing, in the dark.

Conn laid one hand on him, as if he could hold the life in him. He looked back along the ship, at the living and wounded, and saw no other face that had rowed on *Seabird* with him save Raef's. Along the length of Aslak's ship, he met Raef's eyes and knew his cousin was thinking this too.

The ship-fortress was sinking. All over the cluster of lashed hulls, men were dipping and rising, bailing out the water and ice. Several other men came walking across the wooden island, stepping from gunwale to gunwale. They were gathering down by Aslak, and Conn went back that way, wading through a soup of hail and rainwater that got deeper toward the bow. He sat down next to Raef, with the other men, slumped wearily around Aslak.

All save him and Raef were Jomsvikings. Havard had a skin of beer and held it out to Conn as he sat. Beside him, another captain was looking around them. "How many of us are left?"

Aslak shrugged. "Maybe fifty. Half wounded. Some really bad wounded." His voice was a little thick from the mess of his face.

Conn took a deep pull on the skin of beer. The drink hit his stomach like a fist. But a moment later, warmth spread through him. He handed the skin on to Raef, just behind him.

The Jomsviking across from Conn said, "Hakon will sit out the night on the shore, in comfort. Then they'll finish us off tomorrow, unless we all just drown tonight."

Conn said, "We have to swim for it." He had a vague idea of reaching shore and walking around and surprising Hakon from behind.

Havard leaned forward, his bloody hands in front of him. "That's a good idea. We could probably make that side, there." He pointed the other way from Hakon.

"That's far," Raef said. "Some of these men can't swim two strokes."

Aslak said, "We could lash some spars together. Make a raft."

Havard leaned closer to Conn, his voice sinking. "Look. The ones who can make it, should. Leave the rest behind—they're dying anyway."

Conn thought of Finn, and red rage drove him to his feet. He hit Havard in the face as hard as he could. The Jomsviking pitched backwards head over heels into the half foot of water on the floor. Conn wheeled toward the others.

"We take everybody. All or none."

Aslak was grinning at him. The other men shifted a little, glaring down at Havard, who sat up.

"Look. I was just—"

"Shut up," Aslak said. "Let's get moving. This ship is sinking."

In the slow-gathering dark, they tied spars together into a square and bound sails over it. The rain held off. On the raft, they laid the ten wounded men who could not move by themselves, and the other men swam behind the raft to push it.

The icy water gripped them. They left the sinking ships behind them. At first, they moved steadily along, but after a while, men started to lag behind, to drag on the raft. Havard cried, "Keep up!" Across the way, someone tried to climb onto the spars, and the men beside him pulled him back.

Next to Conn, Aslak said, "We'll never make it." He was gasping; he laid his head down on the spar a moment. Conn knew it was true. He was exhausted; he could barely kick his legs. Aslak lost his grip, and Conn reached out and grabbed hold of him until the Jomsviking could get his hands back to the spar.

Raef said, breathless, "There's a skerry—"

"Go," Conn said.

The skerry was only a bare rock rising just above the surface of the bay. They hauled and kicked and dragged the raft into the low waves lapping it. The rock was slippery, and it took all Conn's strength to haul Finn up off the raft. Raef dragged Aslak after them, and above the waterline they lay down on the rock, and instantly Conn was asleep.

Hail fell again in the night. Conn woke and crawled over to Finn to protect him from the worst of it. After the brief crash abruptly stopped, he realized that the body under him was as cold as the rock.

He thought of the other dead—of pop-eyed Gorm; and Odd, whose sister he had loved once; and Skeggi and Orm; Sigurd and Rugr—he remembered how only the night before, they were all alive, speaking of the battle to come, how its fame and theirs would ring around the world until the end of time—now who would even remember their names, when all those who knew them were dead with them? The battle might be a long-told story, but the men were already forgotten.

He would remember. But he would be dead soon himself. Hakon had beaten him. He put his face against the cold stone and shut his eyes.

In the morning, Raef woke up, battered and stiff, starving and thirsty. All around him on the rock, the other men lay slumped asleep, or dead. Between him and Conn, Finn was dead. Raef crawled up higher on the skerry and found a hollow where some hail had fallen and mostly melted. He plunged his face into the ice-studded water and drank. When he lifted his head, he saw, on the bay, the dragons coming for them.

He slid back to Conn, yelling, the men stirring awake, all but the dead, but then the dragons reached them, and Hakon's men swarmed over them.

VIII

Raef had never heard exactly how the Jomsvikings had offended Thorkel Leira, but clearly the wergild was going to be very high. The big Tronder had killed three men already, all nearly dead anyway, and he was lining up the rest of the prisoners for the same. Now another wounded man stumbled exhausted between two slaves, who made him kneel down, and twisted a stick in his hair.

Raef had already counted; there were nine men in the line between him and Conn. The Tronders had tied their hands behind their backs and strung them along the beach, here, and bound their feet together, like trussed lambs. Down the shore, on the pebbles between them and the beached dragons, stood several men, passing a drinking horn and watching Thorkel Leira at his work. One was the man in the gold-rimmed helmet, captain of the iron ship, who was Eirik the Jarl; another was his father, Hakon the Jarl himself.

Thorkel Leira took a long pull on a drinking horn and gave it to one of the slaves. As he took hold of his sword again, Hakon said, "You, there, what do you think about dying?"

The Jomsviking, kneeling there, his hands bound, his head stretched out for the killing stroke, said, "I don't care. My father did it. Tonight I'll drink Odin's ale, Thorkel, but you will be despised for this forever. Slash away."

Thorkel raised the sword and struck off his head. The slave took the head by the hair and carried it off to the heap by the shore.

Conn said, "You know, I don't like how this is going."

Raef thought the Jomsvikings were too ready for dying. He was not; he rubbed his bound wrists frantically back and forth, and up and down, trying to get some play in the rope. The sun was hot on his shoulders. Another man went up before Thorkel Leira.

"I don't mind dying, but I will do it the way I have lived, facing everything. So I ask you to kill me straight ahead, and not bent over, and not from behind."

"So be it," said Thorkel, and stepping forward raised his sword over his shoulder and struck the man straight down the face, cleaving through the top of his skull. The Jomsviking never flinched, his eyes open until his body slumped.

Thorkel was getting tired, Raef thought; the big Tronder had trouble getting his sword out of the body. He called for the drinking horn again and drained it. Now another was kneeling down in front of Hakon and Eirik and the others, and Thorkel again asked him if he was afraid to die.

"I'm a Jomsviking," the kneeling man said. "I don't care one way or the other. But we have often spoken among us about whether a man remains conscious at all after his head is cut off, and here is a chance to prove it. Cut off my head, and if I am still conscious, I will raise my hand."

Beside Raef, Conn gave a choked incredulous laugh. Thorkel stepped forward and slashed off the head; it took him two strokes to get it entirely off. The two jarls and their men crowded around the body and looked. Then they stepped back, and solemnly Eirik the Jarl turned to the Jomsvikings and announced, "His hand did not move."

Conn said, "That was pretty stupid. In a few minutes, we'll all know for ourselves." Along the rope line, the Jomsvikings laughed as if they were at table hearing jokes.

Thorkel turned and glared at him, and then the next man knelt before him, and when he turned to this one, he missed the first stroke. He hit the back of the man's head, knocking him down, and then his shoulders, and didn't cut off his head until the third try.

"I hope you have better aim with your prick, Thorkel!" Conn shouted.

The Jomsvikings let up a yell of derision, and even Eirik the Jarl smiled, his hands on his hips. Someone called, "That's why his wife's always so glad to see me coming, I guess!"

Half a dozen men shouted, "You mean Ingebjorg? Is that why, do you think?"

Thorkel's face twisted. He wheeled around and pointed at Conn.

"Bring him. Bring him next!"

The guard came and untied Conn's feet. Raef suddenly saw some chance here; he licked his lips, afraid of croaking, a weakling voice, and called out, "Wait."

The Jomsvikings were yelling taunts at Thorkel, who stood there with his mouth snarling, his long sword tilted down, but Eirik heard Raef and looked toward him. "What do you want?"

"Kill me first," Raef said. "I love my brother too much, I don't want to see him die. If you kill me first, I won't have to."

Eirik scowled at him, and Hakon made a snort. "Why should we do what you want?" But Thorkel strode forward, the sword in both hands, shouting.

"Bring him! Bring him! I'll kill them both at once!"

The slave untied Raef's feet and pulled him up. Conn was already standing, and his feet were already untied. Raef gave him a swift look, walking past, and went down before the jarls on the shore.

His ribs hurt where he had taken blows in the battle, he was walking a little crooked, and he was tired and hungry, but he summoned himself together. Thorkel's slaves came up beside him and pushed him on the shoulder to make him kneel down; one had the stick to twist in his hair.

He stepped back from the hands on him. "I am a free man. No slave shall put his dirty hands in my hair."

The Norse all laughed, except Eirik the Jarl, who snapped, "He's just stalling. He's afraid to die. Somebody hold his hair for him, and we'll see how he does it."

One of his hirdmen stepped forward. "My privilege." He came up before Raef. "Kneel by yourself, then, if you're free."

Raef knelt down, and the Tronder took hold of his long pale hair and stepped back again, and so stretched Raef's head forward like a chicken on the block. Raef's heart was hammering in his chest, and he was sick to his stomach. His neck felt ten feet long and thin as a whisker; he watched Thorkel approaching in the corner of his eye.

He said, "Try to do this right, will you?" Up on the beach there was a chorus of jeers.

Thorkel snarled. He swung up his sword, the long sun glinting off the blade, and brought it down hard.

With all his strength, Raef lunged back and out from under that falling blade, yanking after him the man holding his hair, so that the Tronder's hands passed under the falling sword and Thorkel slashed them both off at the wrist. The Tronder howled, his arms spurting blood. Still on his knees, Raef staggered his chest up straight. The Tronder's hands had clenched in his hair, and he had to toss his head to get them out.

Thorkel wheeled around, hauling the sword back for a fresh blow. His hands still tied behind his back, Raef rolled sideways against the big man's ankles and brought him crashing down, so that the sword flew out of his hands.

Raef struggled to get to his feet. Thorkel sprawled on the ground. Even the jarls were laughing at him. But Conn had leapt forward even as the sword fell. He knelt astride it, ran his bound hands down the edge, and leapt up again, freed, the sword in his fists.

Thorkel staggered up. Conn took a long stride toward him, the sword swinging around level, and sliced Thorkel's head off while the big man was still rising.

A roar went up from the Jomsvikings. Conn wheeled toward Hakon.

"Hakon, I challenge you, face-to-face!"

Eirik the Jarl had drawn his sword, was shouting, waving his arms, calling his hirdmen to him. Raef lurched to his feet, close to Conn. Conn's hands were dripping blood; in his fury to get free, he had cut himself all over. Quickly he turned and sliced through Raef's bonds. Eirik and his men were closing in on them.

Then Hakon called out again. "Hold. Hold your hands. Who are you, there, Jomsviking? I've seen you two before."

The Tronders stood where they were. Conn lowered the sword. "I'm not a Jomsviking. I'm Conn Corbansson."

"I thought so," Hakon said. "These are the sons of that Irish wizard who helped Sweyn Tjugas overcome Bluetooth. I told you Sweyn was behind this."

Eric said, "So." He lowered the long sword in his hand. "Still, we've won. Good enough. That just now was cleverly done, and to go on is a waste of men. Thorkel's dead, he needs no more revenge. Let me have these two."

Hakon said, "Well, I remember the wizard, who once gave me good advice. I will not say his name. Do what you like with them all."

Eirik said, "You, Corbanssons, if I let you live, will you come into my service?"

Conn said, "You are a generous man, Jarl Eirik. But you should know I swore at Helsingor never to go back to Denmark until I was King of Norway, which I don't think will sit well with either Sweyn or you Tronders. But those men—" He swung his arm at the hillside, at the twenty men still roped together on the grass. "Those men will serve you, better than any other. Those are the true Jomsvikings!"

At that, there was a yell that went on for a while. Raef saw that Eirik started to smile, his hands on his hips, and Hakon shrugged and walked away toward the ships. Eirik gave a word, and the Jomsvikings were set free.

Then Hakon the Jarl came up to Conn. He was as Raef remembered him—not tall, with a crisp black beard, and the coldest eyes he had ever seen.

He said, "King of Norway, was it? I think anyone you do choose to serve will find you more trouble than help. But tell me what you will do now that you are free again."

Conn glanced at Raef beside him. "We won't go back to Sweyn, that's certain. We promise to go somewhere else and not bother you."

Aslak came up to them and shook their hands and clapped them both on the back. Even Havard grinned at them, over Hakon's shoulder.

Hakon said, "Then go. But if I catch you again in Norway you're done."

"Agreed," Conn said, and went on down the beach, Raef beside him. After a while, he said, "I think we hammered that vow."

"We, it is now," Raef said. "Don't get so drunk next time. We should both be dead. Like everybody else."

"But we're not," Conn said. He had lost his sword, his ship, his crew, but he felt light, fresh, as if he had just come new alive again. "I don't know what to make of that, but I will make something. I swear it. Let's go."

Joe Haldeman

Here's a fascinating look at the high-tech future of warfare—which, in its essentials, and particularly in its *costs*, turns out to be not all that different from the way that war has always been. . . .

Born in Oklahoma City, Oklahoma, Joe Haldeman took a B.S. degree in physics and astronomy from the University of Maryland, and did postgraduate work in mathematics and computer science. But his plans for a career in science were cut short by the U.S. Army, which sent him to Vietnam in 1968 as a combat engineer. Seriously wounded in action, Haldeman returned home in 1969 and began to write. He sold his first story to *Galaxy* in 1969, and by 1976 had garnered both the Nebula Award and the Hugo Award for his famous novel *The Forever War*, one of the landmark books of the '70s. He took another Hugo Award in 1977 for his story "Tricentennial," won the Rhysling Award in 1983 for the best science fiction poem of the year (although usually thought of primarily as a "hard-science" writer, Haldeman is, in fact, also an accomplished poet and has sold poetry to most of the major professional markets in the genre), and won both the Nebula and the Hugo Award in 1991 for the novella version of "The Hemingway Hoax." His story "None So Blind" won the Hugo Award in 1995. His other books include a mainstream novel, *War Year*, the SF novels *Mindbridge*, *All My Sins Remembered*, *There Is No Darkness* (written with his brother, SF writer Jack C. Haldeman II), *Worlds*, *Worlds Apart*, *Worlds Enough and Time*, *Buying Time*, *The Hemingway Hoax*, *Tools of the Trade*, *The Coming*, the mainstream novel *1968*, *Camouflage*, which won the prestigious James Tiptree, Jr. Award, and *Old Twentieth*. His short work has been gathered in the collections *Infinite Dreams*, *Dealing in Futures*, *Vietnam and Other Alien Worlds*, *None So Blind*, *A Separate War and Other Stories*, and an omnibus of fiction and nonfiction, *War Stories*. As editor, he has produced the anthologies *Study War No More*, *Cosmic Laughter*, *Nebula Award Stories 17*, and, with

Martin H. Greenberg, *Future Weapons of War*. His most recent books are two new science fiction novels, *The Accidental Time Machine* and *Marsbound*. Haldeman lives part of the year in Boston, where he teaches writing at the Massachusetts Institute of Technology, and the rest of the year in Florida, where he and his wife, Gay, make their home.

Forever Bound

I'd thought that being a graduate student in physics would keep me from being drafted. But I was sitting safely boxed in my library carrel, reading a journal article, when the screen went blank and then blinked PAPER DOCUMENT INCOMING, which had never happened before—who would bother to track you down at the library?—and I had a premonition that was instantly confirmed.

One sheet of paper slid out with the sigil of the National Service Commission. I turned it right side up and pressed my thumb onto the the thumbprint circle, and the words appeared: "You have been chosen to represent your country as a member of the Ninth Infantry Division, Twelfth Remote Combat Infantry Brigade," Soldierboys. "You will report to Fort Leonard Wood, Missouri, to begin RCIU training at 1200, 3 September 2054."

Just before class registration, how considerate. I wouldn't be pulled out of school. I even had two weeks to pack and say my good-byes.

Various options came to mind as I sat staring at the page. I could run to Sweden or Finland, where I'd also face national service, but it wouldn't have to be military. I could take the Commission itself to court, pleading pacifism, asking to be reassigned to Road Service or Forestry. But I didn't belong to any pacifist groups and couldn't claim any religion.

I could do like Bruce Cramer last year. Stoke up on painkillers and vodka and shoot off a toe. But his draft notice had been for the regular infantry, pretty dangerous.

People who ran soldierboys never got shot at directly—they sat in an underground bunker hundreds of miles from the battlefield and operated remote robots that were invincible and armed to the teeth. Sort of like a sim, but the people you kill actually are people, and they actually do die.

Most soldierboys didn't do that, I knew. There were about twenty thousand of them dispersed throughout Ngumi territory, and most of them just stood guard, huge and impregnable, unkillable, symbols of Alliance might. Which is to say, American might, though about 12 percent came from elsewhere.

My adviser, Blaze Harding, was in her office a couple of buildings away, and said to bring the document over.

She studied the letter for much longer than it would take to read it. "Let me explain to you . . . in how many dimensions you are fucked.

"You could run. Finland, Sweden, Formosa. Forget Canada. It's a combat assignment, and you'd be extradited. In any case, you'd lose your grant, and it would be the end of your academic career. Likewise with going to jail.

"If you obey the law and go in, you'll be like Sira Tolliver over in Mac Roman's office. You have to report 'only' ten days a month. But she seems to spend half her time recovering from those ten days."

"Just sitting in a little room?"

"A cage, she calls it. Evidently it's a little more strenuous than sitting."

"The plus side is that the department wouldn't dare drop you. If you just show up for work, your position with the Jupiter Project is as safe as tenure. As long as the grant holds out, which should be approximately forever." The Jupiter Project was building a huge supercollider in orbit around Jupiter, millions of electromagnetic doughnuts circling out by the orbit of Io.

"Once they turn it on," I said, "our worries will be over anyhow. Instantly sucked into a huge black hole."

"No, I favor the 'explode and be scattered to the edge of the universe' theory. I always wanted to travel." We shared a laugh. The Project would simulate conditions 10^{-35} seconds after the Big Bang, and the tabloids loved it.

"Well, at least I'll lose a few pounds in basic training. I've been putting on two or three pounds a year since I graduated and left the soccer team."

"Some of us like them a little plump," she said, pinching the skin on my forearm. It was a funny situation. We'd been attracted to each other since the day we met, three years ago, but it had never gone beyond banter. She was fifteen years older than me, and white. Which was not a problem on campus, but outside, Texas is Texas.

"I goo-wikied something you ought to see. Running a soldierboy isn't really just sitting around." She turned her clipboard around so I could read the screen.

DISABILITY AND DEATH

BY

MILITARY OCCUPATIONAL SPECIALTY

PER 100,000 ANNUALLY

	COMBAT INJURY/DEATH	NONCOMBAT INJURY/DEATH
INFANTRY	949.2/207.4	630.8/123.5
RCI	248.9/201.7	223.9/125.6

"Not really so safe, then."

"And the injuries in the RCI, combat or not, would all be brain injuries. You'd be out of a job here."

"You're just saying that to cheer me up."

"No, but I'm thinking you ought to try switching to the infantry, as crazy as that sounds. With your education and age, they'd put you behind a desk, for sure."

"Well, I've got two weeks to nose around. See how much latitude I'll have. But what about my job here?"

She waved a hand in dismissal. "You can do it in twenty days a month. Actually, I was going to take you off the physics lab babysitting anyhow; just grade papers for 60 and help me with the 299 special projects." She looked at her calendar. "I guess Basic Training will be full-time."

"I don't know. Sounds like it, from what I've heard."

"Find out for me. If I have to kidnap somebody for October and November, I'd better start looking around." She reached across the desk and patted my hand. "It's an inconvenience, Julian, but not a disaster. You'll come out on top."

Blaze hadn't brought up the largest danger and the biggest attraction of being a "mechanic," as the soldiers who operated the soldierboys were called. They all had to be jacked, a hole drilled into the back of the skull and an elecronic interface inserted, so you shared the thoughts and observations, feelings, of the rest of your platoon. There were five men and five women in a platoon, so you become like a mythical beast, with ten brains, twenty arms, and five cocks and five cunts. A lot of people tried to join up for that experience. That was not quite what the army was looking for.

Almost all mechanics were drafted, because the army needed a peculiar mix of attitudes and eptitudes. Empathy is obvious, being able to stay sane with nine other people sharing your deepest feelings and memories. But they also needed people who were comfortable with killing, for the so-called "hunter-killer" platoons. They were the ones who got all the attention, the bonuses, even fan clubs. I could assume I wasn't going to be one of them. I didn't even like to go fishing, because of the blood and guts and hurting the fish.

The installation of the jack was also risky. The rate of failure was classified, but various sources put it between 5 and 15 percent. Most of the failures didn't die, but I wondered how many of them went back to intellectual pursuits.

I found out that Basic Training was indeed full-time, for eight weeks. The first four weeks were intensely physical, old-fashioned boot camp—not obviously useful for people who would spend their military career sitting in a cage, thinking. After four weeks, they installed the jack, and you started training in tandem with your other nine.

I did apply to be reassigned, to infantry or medical or quartermaster. (They crossed that off; you can't join a noncombat arm in time of war.) I was rejected the day I applied.

So I increased my jogging from one mile a day to three, and worked out on the gym machines every other day. Basic training had a bad reputation, and I wanted to be ready for the physical side of it.

I also spent more social time with Blaze than I ever had before. She had no teaching load during the summer. I had legitimate reasons to drop by the Jupiter Project, though I could do most of my work from any computer console anywhere in the world. I tended to show up around lunchtime or when the office nominally closed at five.

You couldn't call it dating, given the difference in our ages, but it wasn't just coworkers having lunch, either. It could have evolved into something if there'd been more than two weeks, perhaps.

But on September 2, she took me to the airport and gave me a tight hug and a kiss that was a little more interesting than a coworker saying "goodbye for now."

———

When I got off the plane in St. Louis, there was a woman in uniform holding a card with my name and two others on it. She was bigger than me, and white, and looked pretty mean. I stifled the impulse to walk right by her and get a ticket to Finland.

When the other two, a woman and a man, showed up, she walked us to an emergency exit that apparently had been disabled, then down onto the tarmac in the 105-degree heat. We walked a fast quarter mile to where a couple of dozen people stood in ranks, sweating beside a military bus.

"*No* talking. Get your sorry ass in line." A big black man who didn't need a megaphone. "Put your bags on the cart. You'll get them back in eight weeks."

"My medicine—," a woman said.

"*Did I say no talking?*" He glared at her. "If you filled out your medical forms correctly, your pills will be waiting for you. If not, you'll just have to die."

A couple of people chuckled. "Shut up. I'm not kidding." He stepped up to the biggest man and spoke quietly, his face inches away. "I'm not kidding. In the next eight weeks, some of you may die. Usually from not following orders."

When the fiftieth person came, he loaded us all into the bus, a wheeled oven. My god, I thought, Fort Leonard Wood must be over a hundred miles away. The windows didn't open.

I sat down next to a pretty white woman. She glanced at me and then looked straight ahead. "Are you going to mechanics' school?"

"Go where they send me," she said with a South Texas drawl, not looking at me. Later that day, I would learn that mechanics train with the regular infantry, "shoes," for the first month, and it's not wise to reveal that you were going to spend all your subsequent career sitting down in the air-conditioning.

We drove only a couple of miles, though, to the military airport adjacent to the civil one, and piled into a flying-wing troop transport, where we were stuffed onto benches without seat belts. It was a fast and bumpy twenty-minute flight, the big sergeant standing in front of us, hanging on to a strap, glaring. "Anybody pukes, he has to clean it up while everybody else waits." Nobody did.

We landed on a seriously bumpy runway and were separated by gender and marched off in two different directions. The men, or "dicks," were led into a hot metal building, where we took off all our clothes and put them in plastic bags marked with our names. If they were going to ferment for eight weeks, the army could keep them.

They said we would get clothes when we needed them, and had us shuffle through a line, where we contributed blood and urine and got two shots in each arm and one in the butt, the old-fashioned way, painful. Then we walked through a welcome shower into a room with piles of towels and clothing, fatigues sorted more or less by size. Then we actually got to sit down while three dour men with robot assistants measured our feet and brought us boots.

There was a rotating holo of a handsome guy showing us what we were supposed to look like—the trouser legs "bloused" into boots, shirt seam perfectly aligned with belt buckle and fly, shirtsleeves neatly rolled to mid-forearm. His fatigues were new and tailored, though; ours were used and approximate. He wasn't sweating.

I thought I'd second-guessed the army by having my hair cut down to a half-inch burr. They shaved me down to the skin, in retribution.

The sun was low, and it had cooled down to about ninety, so they took us for a little run. That didn't bother me except for being overdressed. We went around a quarter-mile cinder track, in formation. After four laps, the women joined us, and together we did eight more.

Then they piled all of us, hot and dripping, into a freezing mess hall. We waited in a long line for cold greasy fried chicken, cold mashed potatoes, and warm wilted salad.

The woman who sat down across from me watched me strip the sodden fried batter from the chicken. "On a diet?"

"Yeah. No disgusting food."

"I think you goin' to lose a lot of weight." We shook hands across the table. Carolyn from Georgia, a pretty black woman a little younger than me. "What, you graduated and got nailed?"

"Yeah. Ph.D. in physics."

She laughed. "I know where *you're* goin'."

"You, too?"

"Yeah, but I don't know why. BFA in Creative Viewing."

"So what's your favorite show?"

"Hate 'em all. Unlike most folks, I *know* why I hate 'em. Now tell me you'd die if you didn't get your *Kill Squad* fix every week."

"Don't have a cube, or time to watch it. When I was a kid, my parents let me watch only ten hours a week."

"Wow . . . would you marry me? Or you got somethin' goin' already."

"I'm gay, except for sheep."

"Ewe." We both laughed a little too hard at that.

Shoe training was about half PT and half learning how to use weapons we'd never see again, as mechanics. Even the shoes would probably never use a bayonet or knife or bare hands—how often would you not have a gun, and face an enemy who didn't have one either?

(I knew the rationale was more subtle, training us to be aggressive. I wasn't sure that was a good idea for mechanics, though—your soldierboy might wipe out a village because you lost your temper.)

Carolyn's last name was Collins, and we were next to each other in the alphabet. We spent a lot of time talking, sometimes sotto voce when we were standing in formation, which got us into trouble a couple of times. ("One of you lovebirds runs around the track while the other finishes painting this wall.")

I was really smitten with her—I mean the kind of brain-chemistry-level addiction that you ought to be able to control by the time you're eighteen. I thought of her all the time, and lived to see her face when we mustered in the mornings. Her expressions and gestures made me think she felt the same way about me, though we carefully wouldn't use the word *love*.

After two weeks of constant training, they unexpectedly gave us half a Sunday off. A bus took us into St. Robert, a small town that existed to separate soldiers from their money. We had to be back by 6:00 sharp, or we'd be AWOL.

On the way to the bus station in St. Robert, we passed several hotels and motels that advertised HOURLY RATES / CLEAN SHEETS. When we got off the bus, I faltered, trying to frame a proposition, and she grabbed me by the arm and pulled me through the closest place's door.

We'd never even kissed before. So we did some of that while trying to get each other's fatigues off without popping any buttons.

Speaking of popping, I was not exactly the long-lasting partner-oriented lover I would've liked to have been. But I had a certain amount of hydrostatic as well as psychological pressure built up; the barracks offered no privacy for masturbation.

She laughed that off, though, and we just played around for a while, until I was ready for a more patient and slow coupling. It was better than my dreams.

We had an hour before we had to be on the bus. There was a bar next door, but Carolyn didn't feel like being stared at by our fellow draftees. So we sat on the damp and rumpled sheets and shared a glass of metallic-tasting water.

"Did you try to get out of it?" she asked.

"Well, yeah. My adviser pointed out that if I joined the infantry, at my age and with my education, I'd just have a desk job for a couple of years."

"Yeah, right. You believe that now?"

I laughed. "They'd put me in a bayonets-only platoon. Get out there and stab for your country."

"God and country. Don't forget God."

"If it weren't for God, we wouldn't get half of Sunday off."

"Praise the Lord." She took my penis between two fingers and wiggled it. "Don't suppose there's any juice left in this little guy."

"Not for a while. We could do it on the bus."

"Okay. Hold you to it." She yawned and stretched so hard, a couple of joints popped. "Maybe we should go get a beer. Show those lonely cunts who got her man."

"Let's." Though I doubted there was much loneliness in town.

She dressed me carefully, smoothing the uniform down with long slow strokes. Then she stroked my face and my hands, eyes closed, as if she were memorizing.

She held me close then, and took a long deep breath. "Thank you, Julian," she whispered. "It's been some while."

So I tried to dress her, but got the buttons wrong. All very romantic. It's also easier to take panties off of someone than to put them back on.

The nonsmoking part of the bar still had a whiff of tobacco and light weed. Ice-cold beer but no place to sit. So we stayed at the bar, loud with music and laughing, and nodded hello to some of our fellow trainees.

"You didn't grow up in the South," she said. "You talk funny, you don't mind my sayin'."

"Actually, I was born in Georgia, but my parents moved north before I started school, Delaware. Then four years at Harvard will screw up your accent forever."

"You majored in science."

"Physics, then astrophysics for the master's. Moved into particle physics for the doctorate. Post-doc, too, assuming basic doesn't kill me."

"I don't know shit about any of that."

"Never expect anyone to." I put my hand on hers. "Like I know anything about film."

"Joo-lian." She slid her hand away. "Never condescend to someone who can kill you with a single blow. Six different ways."

"Sorry. Takes you four years to get a degree at Harvard, and then forty to get over it."

"Well, I ain't waitin' forty. You best get your shit together." But she smiled and put her hand back.

A short private from the permanent party walked through the door with a megaphone. "Aw-right, you listen up. Trainees Charlie Company, you bus is heah. You not in that bus in five minutes, you AWOL. We come back heah and put you ass in chains."

There was a moment of silence when he went through the door, and then a low murmur.

"How could they put just your ass in chains, and not the rest of you?"

"Think big stapler," she said, and finished off her beer. "Chariot awaits."

The next two weeks didn't have any Sundays. Now that they were pretty sure no one was going to have a heart attack doing laps, they pushed us to the wall. The morning after our afternoon-long furlough, they woke us up at 2:30, striding through the barracks, beating on metal pans. Five minutes to dress, then a ten-mile run with full pack and rifle. When people stopped to puke, we had to run in place, shouting "Pussy, pussy!"

They continued with the early-morning runs about every third day, increasing them by a mile each time. The drill instructors acted like it was malicious torture, but it was obviously well planned. We had to get the running in, but if we did it during those hundred-degree-plus days, people would get heatstroke and die.

The instructors also made sure everybody knew that the intensity of training was our own fault. "Only got four weeks to turn these CGI pussies into soldiers" was the refrain.

Carolyn and I did have one more opportunity, a thirty-minute lunch break in thick woods. I got poison ivy on my butt, and she on her feet. We had the same medic look at us, and he advised us to next time take along something like a shelter half or at least a newspaper. But there never was a next time, not in Basic Training.

The first day of CGI training, they took the fifty of us in a bus with blacked-out windows to someplace that might have been a half hour away, or a mile, going in circles. It was in deep woods, though, and underground.

A camouflaged door slid open to reveal dimly lit stairs going down. The entrance was guarded by two huge soldierboys, whose camouflage perfectly mimicked the woods behind them. If you stood still, you couldn't see them; walking by them, they looked like a heat shimmer roughly the shape of a nine-foot-tall man.

The underground complex was large. We stood in formation in a foyer, and a private read our names off a clipboard and gave us platoon designations and room numbers. Carolyn and I were both Alpha Platoon and went to room A.

There were ten hard chairs in the room and, incongruously, a table with party snacks and a tub full of iced drinks. An older man in a jumpsuit with no insignia watched us file in.

He didn't speak until the last of us sat down. "I'm going to leave you here alone for one hour and thirty minutes. Your job is to get to know one another.

"In a couple of days, you're all going to be jacked, and none of you will have any secrets from the others. That's all I'm going to say.

"When I leave the room, please take off all your clothes. Get a drink and a snack and . . . tell each other your secrets, your problems. It will be easier for you to deal with one another if you have some preparation.

"When the bell rings, you should get dressed, and I'll come back to talk with you. Yes, private?"

"Sir," she said, "I . . . I've never been naked in front of a man. I—"

"You're about to be. You didn't have brothers?"

"No, sir."

"In a couple of days, you'll have five of them. And 'naked' does not begin to describe how exposed you'll be. But you will all be gentlemen?"

"Yes, sir," we all said. She was a pretty little blonde, and I was half looking forward to seeing the rest of her and half sympathetic with her anxiety.

He smiled, face crinkling. "Just look each other in the eyes and you'll be all right." He left the room.

I talked with Lou Mangiani while we undressed, both of us studiously not looking at the women (but *seeing* them with some intensity). Lou's in his late twenties, working as a baker in New York City for his father's Italian restaurant. That's about as much as I knew about anybody except Carolyn. For the past four weeks, we had trained till we dropped and got up hours before our bodies wanted to; not much time for chat.

Carolyn and Candi joined us. We'd wondered in shoe training what Candi was doing here. She was a gentle—you'd have to say "delicate"—woman, whose civilian job was grief counseling. I suppose you have to be pretty tough to do that, actually.

She was also a natural leader for this sort of thing. She clapped once. "Let's get these chairs in a circle," she said to everyone. "Get sorted out boy-girl, boy-girl."

Richard Lasalle was beet-red, with a large prominent erection. I was myself trying to think about anything else, running through prime numbers and tables of integrals.

None of the women were eager to sit next to him. Carolyn gave my hand a little tug and strode over to him, and stuck her hand out. "You're Richard, aren't you?" He nodded—"Dick" would not be a good choice—and she introduced herself and sat down. I took the other seat next to her and the pretty little blonde, Arlie, quickly perched on the other side of me, probably figuring I was "taken" and therefore safe. She crossed her perfect legs and hid her breasts behind folded arms.

Candi was the opposite, totally casual, leaning back, legs akimbo. Samantha and Sara, who had been in modest crouches, looked at Candi and unfolded.

"So let's go around the circle and everybody come up with something important that you normally keep secret. After tomorrow, we won't have any secrets." Slow nods. "I should start it." She paused for some time, rubbing her chin and the side of her face. "My clients, my patients, don't know this. Why I became a grief counselor. I was once so devastated I, I killed myself.

"I jumped off a bridge. In Cape Cod in January. I was dead for ten or twelve minutes, but the water was so cold, they were able to bring me back."

"What was it like?" Akeem said. "Being dead."

"Nothing; I just went unconscious. I think the impact knocked me out." She ran a finger between her breasts. "I woke up when they shocked my heart, in the ambulance."

"You had a reason," I said.

She nodded. "Watched my father die. We were on the interstate and the steering and the fail-safes cut out at the same time. We flipped and crashed into traffic. The air bags inflated, but the accident kept happening; another truck smashed into us and knocked us off an overpass. When we finally came to rest . . . my mother's head was crushed and my father was drowning in his own blood. I wasn't in too bad shape, but was pinned in place. I had to just hang there upside down and watch my father die. About two feet away.

"I couldn't get his image out of my head. So I jumped off the bridge. And somehow wound up here. Lou?"

He shrugged. "God, I never had anything like that." He shook his head a couple of times, looking down. "I was maybe thirteen. There was a gang my parents forbade me to hang around with, so of course I did. They thought I was out doing church stuff, but they never went, so I could fake it, I thought.

"These were junior goombahs, apprentice Mafia. I was the lookout while they did nickel-and-dime stuff. Robbing machines, shoplifting. Stealing cars for joyrides when people were careless enough to leave them unlocked.

"We got word that this old Jew who ran a news shop and candy store in the Bronx sold guns under the table. The back door looked like it would be easy enough to break in. So at one in the morning, I snuck down the fire escape and ran down a bunch of side streets to meet them.

"They knew for sure the old guy locked up and went home about ten. It was easy to crack the back door with a crowbar.

"This was the first thing we'd done where I wasn't 'the kid.' A younger boy stood lookout, and I went in first, because I was still a juvenile. If something went wrong, I wouldn't get hard time.

"I went in with a flashlight and started opening drawers, looking for guns. Well, I found one, but it was in the fist of the old Jew. He hadn't gone home that night.

"I heard him cock the gun and swung around, and I guess dazzled him with the light. 'Turn that off, boy,' he said. But the guy with the crowbar had come up behind him and bashed his head with a two-handed swing. He went down like a log, but the guy kept hitting him. Then he picked the gun up off the floor and thanked me for thinking fast.

"We ransacked the place, wearing rubber gloves, but there were no other guns, nor anything else of much value. We couldn't open or even move the cash box. We took a bunch of candy and cigarettes.

"The next day the newspaper reported the murder-robbery. I didn't say anything to anybody. I could have called in anonymously and identified the murderer, but I was afraid."

"He ever get caught?" Mel asked.

"Not that I know of. He went down for drug dealing and I went off to college. Now I'm here."

Everybody looked at Arlie. "I got caught having sex. With the wrong person." She looked at the floor. "By my husband. In our bedroom. I promised not to see this person again . . . not to see *her* again." She looked up with a trembling smile. "Details tomorrow."

My turn. "I got caught jerking off?" Some nervous laughter. "I guess the worst thing . . . it might seem even more trivial, to some. But it drove me crazy with guilt at the time, and it still bothers me, more than ten years later.

"I was, what, fifteen, walking down an alley, and I saw a turtle, which was rare. A pretty big box turtle. It pulled in its head and legs. I poked it with a stick and it just sat there, of course.

"On impulse, I picked up a brick and threw it down with all my might. The shell cracked open and the turtle squirmed around, all pale and bloody. I ran away as fast as I could go."

After a pause, Candi said, "Yeah, I can see that. Even though my family used to fish for turtles and cut them up for soup. I grew up thinking of them as food." She looked at Carolyn and raised her eyebrows.

She shook her head. "Guess I've led a sheltered life. Nothing sexy or violent. I did get caught masturbating, but my mother just laughed and told me to do it in my own room.

"There was a test, a chemistry final, when I was a junior in high school. A girl who worked in the office found a copy of it and sold it to me for ten bucks.

"That was bad enough; I mean, I'd never done anything like that before. But what was worse was that I already knew most of the answers—would've gotten a B, anyhow. And now this girl had proof that I was a cheat, and could tell anybody anytime.

"So I killed her." She looked up and grinned. "Only in my dreams, actually."

Richard had enlivened a grown-ups' party by putting a laxative in the punch, but he used a bit too much, and put several people in the hospital. (Including himself, to deflect attention.)

Samantha stole money from her mother's purse for years, whenever she came home drunk.

Mel played vicious tricks on his retarded brother.

Sara helped her father die.

Akeem struggled, and finally confessed that he had never believed in Allah, not even as a child, but had lacked the courage to admit it and leave the faith.

It was an exhausting and awkward two hours, but obviously necessary.

When we got the bell to get dressed, I was a little surprised to find that I wasn't looking at the women sexually anymore. But there were a couple that perhaps I could love.

We never went back to Fort Leonard Wood. The blacked-out bus took us to the St. Louis airport, where they gave us back the personal effects we'd surrendered a month before, laundered, and put us aboard a flight to Portobello.

The plane went over a lot of water, staying carefully away from Nicaraguan and Costa Rican airspace. Ngumi nations don't have air forces; our flyboys would just disintegrate them. But they could still throw missiles at us.

It was nighttime when we landed, the air thick and greasy. The base was an unremarkable collection of low buildings, with the solid gleaming presence of the occasional soldierboy. They stood guard around the perimeter of the base, which they said had never been successfully attacked. I had to wonder how much damage an "unsuccessful" attack could do.

But that's good. We would be spending a third of our lives here, somewhere underground, only dozens of miles from enemy territory. Nice to be safe behind a phalanx of invulnerable telepathic robots. Feel safe, anyhow.

Not really robots, and not completely invulnerable. Each was really an oversized, heavily armed suit of armor that was the telepresent avatar of one man or woman, who operated in instant concert with nine others. Each ten-person platoon was a telepathic family that, with training, would work as one powerful entity.

The enemy could destroy an individual soldierboy, but its operator, the mechanic, could instantly be switched to a reserve machine and be back in the field in minutes—or even seconds, if the backup was stored nearby. And whoever had destroyed the first one, they well knew, would get special attention from its replacement.

I suspected that was just propaganda, part of the mystique that personified the machines, to make them more effective psychological weapons. Any emotion that makes a human being dangerous, they had. But they couldn't die, or even be hurt.

(The "hurt" part was not completely true, which was a closely guarded secret and perennial rumor. If a soldierboy was disabled and captured, the Ngumi would elaborately torture it in front of cameras, before destroying it.)

Americans laughed that off, saying that it might work with voodoo dolls, but not machines. You turn a machine off, it's just a bag of bolts.

But you have to turn it off in time.

Our quarters in Portobello were neat but perfunctory, and barely large enough to turn around in. But we wouldn't be spending much time in them. Mechanics worked and slept, ate and drank and eliminated, without being unplugged, which took a certain amount of intrusive plumbing. But they didn't open you up for that surgery until they knew whether you could be jacked.

The first day in Portobello, we were wheeled off one at a time for the most dramatic "routine" surgery known to medicine—the installation of cybernetic cranial implants, or jacks, as they were always called. It seems more dangerous than it is. They've done it a hundred thousand times, and it's worked for about ninety thousand.

Of the one in ten for whom it doesn't work, most simply go back to regular life, without the ambiguous gift of being able to share another's mind and body totally. Some few for whom it doesn't work become mentally or emotionally handicapped. Some few die.

The numbers are not published.

Being a physicist, I can figure out some numbers by myself. If something—jacking successfully—has a 90 percent chance of success, and if ten people do it, the probability of one of them *failing* is one minus 0.9 to the tenth power, which equals 0.65. So 65 percent of the time, more than half, at least one of the ten is going to fail.

So logic would say "do eleven." But what if all eleven made it? You'd have to pull one out, and that would be like a casualty, they say. It's easier to add to a family than to subtract.

All ten of us made it, and spent the next two days in bed rest. The third day, we started exploring the gift.

The man who first led us through it, Kerry, was apparently a civilian, a therapist in his seventies.

"Your first time shouldn't be with a beginner," he said. We were back in a place like Room A, government-green walls, the hard chairs and tub of drinks, but with an addition: two couches waiting with a black box between them. Two cables snaked out of the black box.

"You're all going to jack with me for a few minutes first. That will take about an hour for ten people. I don't foresee any trouble, but if there is, best to have someone like me in the circuit."

"Like you, sir?" Candi said.

"You'll see why." He looked at a clipboard. "Azuzi first." Akeem stood and followed him to the couches.

"Close your eyes. Lie down." He took a cable and planted the jack in the base of Akeem's skull with a soft click. Then he sat on the edge of the other couch and did the same to himself.

He closed his eyes and rocked gently for a couple of minutes. Then he unplugged himself and Akeem.

Akeem shook his head and sat up with a shiver. "Oh. That was . . . extreme," he whispered.

Kerry nodded. Neither of them elaborated. "Julian Class?"

I went over and lay down and faced the wall away from him. There was a little click when the jack touched the metal implant, and then I was sort of seeing double with my whole body.

It's hard to describe accurately. I still saw the wall, two feet away, but almost as clearly, I saw what Kerry was looking at, the group of mechanics staring back at him and me.

And all at once, I *knew* him, almost the way I knew myself. I could feel the body in his clothes as well as the clothes on his body; the somatic shifting of soft organs inside, and the complex array of muscle and bone—things that we feel all the time, but which become invisible with familiarity—small twinges and itches and deep pain in the right shoulder I'd have to, he'd have to, stop ignoring. . . .

I remembered everything he routinely remembered about himself, bad and good and neutral. Comfortable childhood cut short by divorce, college a magnificent escape; a rewarding doctorate in developmental psychology. Sex with two women and dozens of men. Somehow that didn't seem even odd. Four years as a mechanic in Africa, driving trucks that got blown up regularly.

Like a memory of a memory, I could feel the union he'd felt with the other mechanics in his transportation platoon, and his longing for the sensation.

It was over with a click. I looked at him. "That's why you're doing this?"

He smiled. "Though it's not the same. Like singing in the shower when you used to be in a choir."

Carolyn was next, and when she sat back down next to me, she softly nudged me with her hip, and you didn't need telepathy to know we were thinking the same thing.

One by one, the others had their sample.

"Okay," Kerry said, "That was the first stage of your warm-up. Now we go to the next level." We followed him into an adjacent room.

Ten of the so-called cages were lined up along the far wall. They were like recliners with lots of plumbing and electronics attached.

We wouldn't have to do the plumbing until the end of Basic, since we wouldn't be plugged in for more than a few hours at a time. When it became ten days, our usual monthly stint, we'd have to be fed and emptied automatically, which they said wasn't bad once you got used to it.

The soldierboys we were going to be plugged into were in a vacant lot somewhere outside. For the first couple of days, we did "raise your right foot, raise your left foot" exercises; then walking and going up stairs. By the third day, we were jogging in formation, having crossed a major threshold: knowing you had to stop thinking about what you were doing, and just do it. Trust the machine. The machine is you.

Meanwhile, we started hooking up to each other in the evenings, without the soldierboys, one on one and then in larger groups.

Being with Carolyn was thrilling and a little scary—if anything, she felt even more strongly about me than I did about her. And we were so totally different—her intuitive intelligence versus my analytical nature, her streetwise emotionally jarring youth played out against the support and love I'd gotten from my family. Our bodies were different, not just in female/male matters; she was small and fast and I was neither. We enjoyed experimenting with each other's bodies; she said every girl should have a dick of her own for a while. I enjoyed the strangeness of being her, and then the familiarity, though the first time I menstruated, it was like a shocking wound, even though I was ready for it. She was sympathetic but amused—"you big pussy"—and I eventually got over it, though I never got to the point, like her, of looking forward to it, as a kind of affirmation of "my" womanhood.

(None of the other women had that attitude, I came to find out. Sara and Arlie had suppressed ovulation for an indefinite length of time, and the other two didn't especially like it, but didn't like the anti-fertility drugs either.)

Being linked to the others, male and female, was less intense than with Carolyn, though it was pretty sexual with Sara, Candi, and Mel. That was odd enough—Mel wasn't like Kerry; he'd never had or desired sex with a man. When he was linked with me or one of the other guys, though, it was pretty obvious that he'd been suppressing a natural attraction to his own sex, and that's something you couldn't hide from another mechanic even if you wanted to. After some initial embarrassment, he didn't want to hide it.

When we were just doing one-on-one, the other eight people's life stories were pretty far away, like a novel you'd intensely studied in school. When we started doing threesomes and more, it was a lot more complicated. At first, you'd lose track of who—or where—the "I" was. With two, you could be in a state where both lives merged in a kind of selfless integration. I could do that with about half of them.

With three in the circuit, that couldn't happen. At first, there was a kind of existential battle for possession, for "turf," but with experience, it became obvious that each person had to hold on to his or her own sense of "I," or the asymmetries would drive everybody crazy. It was hard for me and Carolyn, and a few other pairs, like Samantha and Arlie, to let go of one another and let a third person in, but if you didn't, the triad would never work together. One person always on the outside, looking in on a love feast.

We spent a lot of time, about four days, switching around among triads. That made the foursomes and larger groups pretty simple, having mastered the basic trick: Each of us was an "I" identified by the life story we had when we weren't jacked, but you had a number of partners, between two and nine of them, each with the same degree of autonomy as you, who intimately shared their pasts and presence.

We could be jacked for a maximum of only two hours running, followed by at least thirty minutes unplugged, which was frustrating. It would be years before we understood why: if you stayed jacked for too long, the feeling of empathy with others became so strong that any human became a part of you; killing anybody would be as impossible as suicide. Which could be a real handicap for a soldier.

We did learn about soldiering at visceral secondhand, by jacking into crystals other people had recorded during battle. It was confusing at first, because you were intimate with ten strangers, and you had no physical control over the soldierboy you inhabited. But the combat was real enough, more real than it could ever be, secondhand, merely human.

Candi was deeply depressed by the experience, and I think only Mel was eager to repeat it. But we all saw how necessary it was. A dress rehearsal for Hell.

I was surprised when they made me platoon leader. I was the oldest, but not by much, and the most educated, but particle physics wasn't exactly relevant to leadership. The unflattering truth became obvious early on. They didn't want a "natural leader," like Lou or Candi, in charge, because he or she would take over the platoon too completely—instead of ten people working in concert, you'd have one guy making all the decisions, with nine people reviewing them after the fact. That would mirror old-fashioned hierarchic military organization, with the alpha male calling the shots and the lesser doggies falling into line. But if that happened, you'd just wasted a lot of time and money, and risked ten brains in surgery, for no advantage. A soldierboy platoon was like one huge machine that could take over acres of battlefield, making instant decisions with a kind of gestalt intelligence. It was eerie to watch, but became less and less strange to be part of.

We had the minor surgery that took care of nutrition, hydration, and excretion, recovered for a couple of days, and then went out on our first "field exercise"—in the middle of enemy territory.

The ten of us, of course, were safe underground, in a bombproof bunker in Portobello. But our soldierboys walked out ten miles beyond the perimeter, where any pedro could risk his life and attack. But there was an experienced hunter-killer platoon in a protective circle around our machines. Safer than sitting at home, watching it on the cube. You could get struck by lightning there.

We had two more walkabouts like that, never confronting an enemy, and then Basic was over, and we could go home for twenty days. None of us went straight home, though. We had to try the jack joints that ringed the base at Portobello.

At a jack joint, you could pay to plug into other people's experiences. A lot of them were records of soldierboy battle encounters, which we didn't have to pay for, thank you. The flyboy crystals did look appealing, "being" an aircraft capable of banks and dives and accelerations that no human pilot could execute.

But apart from the military ones, there were adventure crystals, of people doing dangerous things in odd places, and "appetite" ones, where you could experience food and drink you could never afford. There were even suicide crystals, for the most extreme experience possible, though you had to sign a waiver before they'd let you enjoy it, in case you empathized enough to die yourself. It was the ultimate in something, like that Japanese sushi with natural neurotoxins, that will kill you if the chef makes a mistake.

And of course, there was sex. Sex with beautiful people who in real life would never even say hello to you, sex in places where you would be arrested if they caught you, daredevil sex, weird sex, sweet and sour and salty sex.

Sex with Carolyn.

During training they only jacked you through cages, to get used to it, so you couldn't physically touch anyone you were jacked with. Most of the jack joints outside the base offered only solitary experiences, but in a few expensive ones, two people could jack together in real time, in private. Sort of like the motels in Rock City, though they advertised *environmentos sanitos* rather than clean sheets, and charged by the minute rather than by the hour.

We asked around and went to Cielito Lindo, a place that did look clean. The women who hovered around the entrance, so-called jills, didn't molest us, but stared deeply at me, and some at Carolyn: if you think it's good with an amateur, come back and try it again with a pro.

The *mamacita* in charge was fat and jolly, and told us the rules: Timer starts the second you close the door, and stops when you come back to the desk and pick up your credit card. Lie there and murmur sweet nothings; they cost the same as sweet somethings.

I asked her whether people ever burst out of the room stark naked and sprint for the credit card. "I have them arrested for indecent exposure," she said, "unless I'm extremely entertained." I decided not to press my luck.

The room was small and clean and smelled heavily of jasmine. There was nothing in it but a large bed with a pile of pillows. The sheet felt like freshly starched cotton, but was dispensed by a practical and unromantic roller.

We'd had sex a couple of hours earlier, so it wouldn't be over immediately, but we were both more than ready when we shucked our clothes and jacked and fell into bed. I kissed and tasted her all over, feeling our mutual tongue on the skin we shared. When we tasted me inside her, I shared her orgasm, but kept just enough "I" not to ejaculate.

She straddled me and slid back and forth once, and I snapped into her with the springy force of a horny teenager. She held my hips still, telling me wordlessly not to thrust, and for a few moments we merged completely, as I flowed into her and she into me, until neither of us could stand it, and we bucked so hard, we rolled off the bed and lay there gasping.

"Nice carpet," she said while we felt our skin against the rough pile. One of us had bruised a hip in the fall. When we unjacked, I realized it was hers.

"Sorry," I said. "Clumsy." She stroked my retreating dick.

"That musta been at least ten seconds," she said huskily. "Why don't you put on some pants and go get your card."

We went to the Cielito Lindo three more times, and once tried *Falling In Love,* where you made love, or had sex, during an endless fall from an airplane, and floated gently to earth afterwards. But then we did have to literally get back down to earth, Carolyn to her studies and me to my measurements and equations.

Parting was like losing a limb, or part of your mind, but knowing you'd be whole again in three weeks.

I tried to explain it to Blaze, the first day I was back. We were having coffee in a quiet corner of the Student Center.

"You know what it sounds like," she said, "and I'm just being an old mother hen here . . . but it's like you had an intense summer romance, rendered even more intense by the pressure of the military environment, and then the jacking squared it, and then making love while you were jacked cubed it. But you can square x and cube x, and it's still x."

"Still just an infatuation."

She nodded. "You really think it will last forever, though."

"As much of forever as we get."

She sipped her coffee, still nodding. "The Siamese twin aspect. That's a little creepy."

I laughed. "It is. It's really impossible to explain in words."

She stared at me in a funny way. "Wish I could try it. I'm just jealous." Maybe I blushed. "Not of *Carolyn,* silly. Of you both, of the whole experience."

Blaze would lose her grant and her job if she got jacked. Most contracts for intellectual jobs had no-jacking clauses, for obvious reasons; I was protected because my military jack wasn't voluntary. The operation for jacking wasn't even legal in the States for civilians, though hundreds crossed the border every day to have it done.

I had tremendous respect for Blaze, and wanted so much for her to understand. But I suppose it was like a deeply religious person trying to explain her ecstasy to someone like me, before. Samantha was like that, and I understood her instantly, below the level of words, the moment we jacked together. As she understood me, and forgave my unbelief.

Blaze did have legitimate professional concerns, because I was far from being an ideal coworker. I couldn't concentrate well. At some level, I was never not thinking about Carolyn, and at another level it had to show. I couldn't look at a calendar without counting the days until I gave up my freedom again.

"Why don't you take the weekend off and go to Georgia?" Blaze said on Thursday morning. "Can't you soldierboys fly for free?"

I was a mechanic, and the machine was a soldierboy, but it was a mistake often made. "I was planning to work over the weekend, catch up."

She laughed. "Why don't you catch up with Carolyn instead? The Jupiter Project will lurch along somehow without you."

I wasn't happy about being so transparent, but couldn't pass it up. I called Carolyn, and she was ecstatic. Her roommate agreed to get lost for a few days, and I got booked on a transport headed for Macon Friday afternoon.

It turned out strange. Of course, there was no place to jack in Macon, and we were back to basics. We had the unspoken assumption that that would be enough, but in fact, it wasn't. I wasn't impotent, exactly, and she wasn't unreceptive, exactly. But early Saturday morning we took a bus to Atlanta and got a cheap room a couple of blocks from the jack joints outside Fort McPherson.

The Stars and Stripes Forever was the cheapest place, no frills, which was fine with both of us. Sunday morning, though, we counted our pennies and splurged on Private Space, which gave the illusion of zero gravity, surrounded by whirling galaxies, and that was extraordinary.

We did talk a little bit about it. It was unsettling, but we agreed it was in large measure the fact that jacking was still new to us. We parted very much in love, but a little shaken by the contrast between the normal and enhanced states.

Making love in her apartment, we'd both been fantasizing like mad about the previous week.

In a couple of weeks, we were on our first independent combat mission.

Bravo Platoon was H&I, a Harassment and Interdiction unit. So our main job was to go in there and screw things up for the enemy. Confusion rather than killing.

In this case, our assignment was a little focused chaos. The Ngumi had put together a command center in a remote valley in Costa Rica, laboriously carrying in equipment and munitions by night, by hand. No heat signature visible from above the tree canopy. They didn't know yet that we had seeded the entire countryside with microscopic olfactory devices whose simple job was to ping their location when a sweating human walked by. So we knew exactly where the enemy was and what trails they had taken.

We stayed off those trails. If you're careful and slow, you can move the heavy soldierboy through pretty thick brush without a sound. I guided the ten of us up both sides of the main trail, averaging about one mile per hour. Twice, their patrols tiptoed right through our platoon without noticing us, our suits set on camo in the dark.

Arlie got to their perimeter first. She stood quietly a few yards away from a dozing sentry while the rest of us encircled the camp. I was poised to start the attack instantly if one of us was detected, but we all got into place without a hitch.

I was nominally in charge, but all ten of us were essentially wired in parallel. At my thought, we all attacked at once.

No weapons at first but light and sound: ten lights much brighter than the sun; ten deafening speakers shrieking a dissonant chord. Then a billow of gas from ten directions.

They were out of their tents firing wildly, but almost all took one breath of KO gas and fell unconscious. Two had been able to don gas masks. Mel took one and I took the other. Knocked away his rifle and tapped him on the chest, which flung him to the ground. I pulled off his gas mask and tossed it away, and moved with the others to the central objective, a tetrahedral mini-fort of some bulletproof plastic. They'd evidently brought it up piecemeal and glued it together.

Our forces had encountered them in the African desert (invisible to radar and tough on flyboys), but this was the first one we knew of in Costa Rica. They fired 155 mm explosive armor-piercing shells, which could disable a soldierboy, but the barrel was external. It spun around fast, but we could anticipate it and duck. They were firing dumb shells, fortunately.

We could just keep ducking and dodging until he ran out of ammunition, but he was firing all over the place, and liable to kill some of his own people, or civilian mules. So Carolyn and I fried two corners of the thing with lasers, reaiming several times a second as we evaded its fire, which finally heated up the inside and filled it with burning-plastic fumes. A door popped open and two people spilled out, coughing. We KO'ed them, too, and then gathered up all the sleeping bodies and stacked them. Then we lasered a clearing out of the forest to use as a landing zone and called for a chopper to come get them.

From turning on the lights to loading the "captives" aboard the chopper, it was about twelve minutes. No casualties.

Mel was not able to hide his resentment at that. *Thanks . . . we're still virgins*. He apologized, but it hung in the air.

I would have called it a textbook-perfect operation, but while we were waiting for pickup, we got the word from the officers' review board, which had been hooked up with us for evaluation. Three out of the seven thought we should have destroyed the mini-fort and its two occupants immediately, before they could harm a soldierboy or bystanders.

Okay, I thought, *you* come down and kill them. While the soldierboys were on the chopper back, and we were unjacked in the relative privacy of the situation room, we chewed that over. Seven of the platoon agreed with me, predictably; all but Mel and Sara. The disagreement was mild, though; they said they would have done it differently, but it was my call. They didn't think much of the long-distance quarterbacking.

Of course, the officers had really been no further from the action than we were.

They gave us Sunday afternoon off, and I managed to get an advance in pay (borrowing against it, actually; paying the government 10 percent interest) so we could go downtown and jack.

It was called the *Hotel de Dream*. An uninhabited desert island this time, and I paid ahead for thirty minutes, so after we made love in the low morning sun, we swam in the warm water for a few minutes, and then sat and held each other while the gentle surf rolled over us. It was jarring when the time ran out suddenly and we were in that hard plain bed, hardly even touching.

No money for a hotel room. We had hot dogs for dinner and a couple of beers, and then walked back to the base and our separate beds.

Blaze was amused but shook her head. "You're in for four years, ten days at a time?"

"Yeah. I see what you mean." We were alone at the coffee place, mid-morning.

"By the time you get out, you'll owe the army a million dollars. At ten percent interest."

I could just shrug, and I guess smile sheepishly.

"You know it's like addictive behavior. If the army had gotten you hooked on DDs, we'd be down there with a brace of lawyers, getting you pulled from service and into detox. But they've got you hooked on *love!*"

"Come on . . ."

"Try to be objective about it. I know Carolyn's a nice girl and so forth—"

"Watch out, Blaze."

"Listen to me for just one minute, okay?" She took out her notebook and clicked a couple of times. "Do you know what your brain chemistry looks like when you go down to that *Motel de Dream?*"

"Hotel. Pretty strange, I suppose."

"Not strange at all. It's a seething stew of oxytocin, serotonin, and endogenous opioids. Your vasopressin receptors are wide open. You would be totally juiced even if Carolyn was a gerbil!"

I could feel myself almost grinning. "Nice job of objectifying it. But if you haven't been there, you just don't know. It really *is* love."

"Okay. So do me a favor. Do it with one of the other women. Watch yourself fall in love with *her.*"

"No." Just the thought was disgusting. "Blaze, that's awful. It's like I was a lovesick teenager, and Dad gives me a wad of money to go to a whorehouse and get it out of my system."

"Nothing like that. I just want you to engage your critical side, your objectivity."

"Yeah. That always works with love."

We didn't talk about that any more that month—or much else. I went to the airport alone.

Carolyn and I had one embrace, and then off to the cages.

It was a routine show of force. The governor-general of Panama, our well-loved puppet, was giving a speech in Panama City, and we were there to stand at attention and look ominous. Which we did, I had to admit, nine of the soldierboys set to "camouflage" in the bright sun. That didn't hide them; it made them glittering, shifting statues you couldn't quite focus on. Scary. My own soldierboy, platoon leader, was shiny black.

Our presence wasn't really needed, except for the press. The crowd was hand-selected, and applauded and cheered on cue, no doubt eager to have it over with and get back into the air-conditioning. It was in the high nineties and steamy still.

Do you feel warm? Carolyn asked without words. I thought back that it was psychosomatic, sympathy for those poor proles outside, and she agreed.

Then the speech was over, and we got together in a line for our dramatic exit. It was a routine extraction, but it was a good demonstration of our inhuman strength: we stood shoulder to shoulder with our left hands raised, and a cargo helicopter with a retrieval bar came swooping in, churning along below treetop-level at more than a hundred miles per hour, and snatched us away. It would have torn off a human's arm, but we hardly felt it.

Carolyn's output suddenly went black, apparently unplugged by the mechanical shock. "Carolyn?" I said over the emergency vocal circuit.

When she didn't respond, I asked permission to disengage. There was no reason for us to stay in the soldierboys, other than the convenience of walking them to storage after we landed. My request wasn't answered by Command. They were probably off fighting a war someplace, I figured.

So we landed by the service bay and walked our machines in. Carolyn's wasn't under her control, obviously; the soldierboy normally mimicked her natural physical grace. This time it staggered like a cartoon robot, some tech moving it with a joystick.

I popped our cages and we were suddenly in the real world, naked and sweaty, joints popping as we stretched.

Carolyn's cage was open, but she wasn't there.

One person in the room was dressed, a medical officer. She walked over. "Private Collins had a massive cerebrovascular failure, just prior to extraction. She's in surgery now."

I felt the blood chase away from my face and arms. "She'll be all right?"

"No, Sergeant. They're trying, but I'm afraid she's . . . well, she's clinically dead."

I sat down on the edge of the cage base, hard concrete, my head spinning. "How is that different from plain dead?"

"She has no higher brain function. We are contacting her next of kin. I'm sorry."

"But . . . I—I was *in* her brain just minutes ago."

She looked at her clipboard. "Time of death was 13:47. Twenty-five minutes."

"That's not enough time. They bring people back."

"They're trying, Sergeant. Mechanics are too valuable to throw away. That's all I can tell you." She turned to go.

"Wait! Can I see her?"

"I don't know where she is, Sergeant. Sorry."

The others had gathered around me. I was surprised I wasn't crying, or even trying not to cry. I felt gut-punched, helpless.

"She's gotta be at the base hospital," Mel said. "Let's go find her."

"And do what?" Candi said. "Get in the way?" She sat down next to me and put an arm around my shoulders. "We should go into the lounge and wait."

We did, me walking like a zombie. Like a soldierboy without a mechanic. Lou got a credit card from his locker and bought us all beers from the machine. We dressed and drank in awkward silence.

Akeem didn't drink. "Sometimes one wishes one could pray." Samantha looked up from her meditation and nodded. The rest of us just drank and watched the door.

I got up to buy a round, and the medical officer came back. I took one look at her eyes and collapsed.

I woke up suddenly in a hospital bed, like a noiseless splash of ice water. A nurse stepped away with a hypodermic, and behind her was Blaze.

"What time is it?"

"Five in the morning," she said. "Wednesday. I came as soon as I heard, and they said they were about to wake you up anyway." She picked up a plastic cup and held the straw toward me. "Water?"

I shook my head. "What, I just passed out? Twelve hours ago?"

"And they gave you something, to help you sleep. It's what they do, when someone has a loss like yours."

It all came back and hit me like a car. "Carolyn." She took my hand in both of hers, and I jerked it away. Then I sat partway up and took her hand back.

I closed my eyes and I was floating, falling. Maybe the drug. I swallowed, and couldn't find my voice.

"They said you're on compassionate leave for the rest of the month. Come home with me."

"What about my people? My platoon?"

"Most of them are waiting in the hall. They let me come in first."

I sat up and held her, she held me, until I was ready to see my mates. They came in as a group, and Blaze waited outside in the hall while we made a wheel, each right arm a spoke. Mel and Candi and Samantha whispered a few words, but it was more the silent communion than any specific sentiment, that gave me a place to be. A place where I could breathe for a while.

Blaze took me home with her, and after some long time, I was her lover rather than the friend who needed a strong arm, a soft breast. Later on, we laughed because neither of us could remember the exact night, or afternoon or morning, when it became sex. But I think I know when it became love.

The army counselor I'd been going to said I should see my loss as a wound, which had to be protected by stitches, which is to say a set of responses that could protect me while it healed. Stitches that would fall away when they were no longer needed.

But Blaze, a doctor of physics rather than of medicine, said he didn't understand. There are wounds too large to close with stitches. You have to leave them open, and protect them, while keloid tissue grows over them. Keloid tissue doesn't have normal nerve endings. It keeps you alive, but numb.

That's where I am, years later. For ten days each month, I lock myself into the cage that gives me superhuman power. The rest of the time, I have her calm and sweet acceptance of the loss that will always be my center.

The soft cage of arms and legs that protects me, and gives me a measure of amnesia.

Robin Hobb

New York Times bestseller Robin Hobb is one of the most popular writers in fantasy today, having sold more than one million copies of her work in paperback. She's perhaps best known for her epic fantasy Farseer series, including *Assassin's Apprentice, Royal Assassin,* and *Assassin's Quest,* as well as the two fantasy series related to it, the Liveship Traders series, consisting of *Ship of Magic, The Mad Ship,* and *Ship of Destiny,* and the Tawny Man series, made up of *Fool's Errand, Golden Fool,* and *Fool's Fate.* Recently, she's started a new fantasy series, the Soldier Son series, composed of *Shaman's Crossing, Forest Mage,* and her most recently published novel, *Renegade's Magic.* Her early novels, published under the name Megan Lindholm, include the fantasy novels *Wizard of the Pigeons, Harpy's Flight, The Windsingers, The Limbreth Gate, Luck of the Wheels, The Reindeer People, Wolf's Brother,* and *Cloven Hooves,* the science fiction novel *Alien Earth,* and, with Steven Brust, the collaborative novel *The Gypsy.*

Here she takes us to the edge of human endurance and considerably beyond, for a harrowing study of the ultimate meaning of loyalty, when everything else has been lost.

The Triumph

The evening winds swept across the plains to the city and pushed on the iron-barred cage hung in the arch of the gate. The man in the cage braced himself against the bite of the inward-facing spikes and stared into the westering sun. He had small choice in that. Before they'd hoisted his cage into position, they'd cut away his eyelids and lashed his wrists to the bars, so that he could not turn away from the fiery gaze of the Carthaginian sun.

The dust-laden wind was drying his bared eyes, and his vision was dwindling. Tears, the tears of his body rather than the tears of his heart, ran unchecked down his cheeks. The severed muscles that had once worked his eyelids twitched in helpless reflex; they could not moisten his eyeballs and renew his vision. Just as well; there was little out there he wished to see.

Earlier in the day, there had been a crowd below him. They'd lined the street to watch the laughing, mocking soldiers roll him along inside the spiked barrel of his cage. Despite the earlier torture he had endured, he'd still had a bit of defiance in him then. He'd seized the bars of the cage and braced himself, fighting the momentum of the bumping, bouncing cage as they tumbled him along. He hadn't been completely successful. The spikes inside the cage were too long for that. They'd scored his body in a dozen places. Still, he'd avoided any immediately mortal wounds. He now doubted the wisdom of that.

At the bottom of the hill, beneath the arch of the city gates, the crowd had roared with avid approval when his guards dragged him out and sliced the eyelids from his face. "Face the sunset, Regulus! It's the last one you'll see, dog of a Roman! You'll die with the sun today!" Then they'd forced him back into his spiked prison, lashing his wrists to the bars before they hoisted him up high so that all might have a good view of the Roman consul's slow death.

His torment had drawn a sizable crowd. The Carthaginians hated him, and with good reason. Very good reason. They'd never forgive him for the many defeats he'd dealt them, or forget the impossible treaty terms he'd offered them after the battle at Adys. He bared what remained of his broken teeth in a grin. He still had that to be proud of. His gallery had pelted his cage with rocks and rotten vegetables and offal. Some of the missiles had ricocheted off the iron bars that confined him, a shield wall that flung their insults back into their upturned faces. Others had found their mark. Well, that was to be expected. No defense was completely impenetrable. Even the Carthaginians could hit a target sometimes. He had tucked his chin to his chest to offer his eyes what shelter he could from the dazzling African sun and looked down at the crowd. They'd been both exultant and furious. They had him caged, Marcus Atillius Regulus, and their torturers had wreaked on him all that for so long they had desired to do, but feared. His final defiance of them had pressured them to do their worst. And now they would watch him die in a cage hung from the city gates of Carthage.

His cracked lips pulled wide in a smile as he looked down at the hazy crowd. A film obscured his vision, but it seemed to him that there were not so many of them as there had been. Watching a man die painfully offered an hour or two of amusement to vary their tepid lives, but Regulus had prolonged their voyeurism too long, and they had wearied of it. Most had returned to the routine tasks of their ordinary lives. He gripped the bars firmly, and with all his will he bade his fingers to hold fast and his trembling legs braced him upright. It would be his last victory, to deny them any spectacle at his passing. He willed himself to take another breath.

Flavius looked up at the man in the cage. He swallowed. Marcus appeared to be looking straight at him. He resisted the temptation to look aside and tried to meet his old friend's gaze. Either Marcus could not see Flavius or knew that if he recognized him and reacted to him in any way, his old friend would pay with his life. Or perhaps more than four years of slavery in Carthage had changed Flavius so much that even his childhood friend could not recognize him. He had never been a fleshy man, and the hardships of slavery had leaned even his soldier's muscles from his frame. He was a bone man now, skeletal and ravaged by the harsh African sun. He was ragged and he stank, not just his unwashed body but also the dirty sodden bandage that wrapped the still-oozing injury on his left thigh.

He'd "escaped" from his master a scant month ago; it had not required much subterfuge. The overseer was a sot, more intent on drinking each day than on wringing work out of slaves that were no longer capable of real labor. One night, as the slaves made their weary way in from the grain fields, Flavius had lagged behind. He had limped more and more slowly and finally, while the overseer was haranguing another slave, he had dropped down amongst the rustling stalks and lain still. The grain was tall enough to conceal his supine body; they would not locate him without a search, and even so, in the failing light, they might miss him. But the old sot had not seemed to notice even that he was one slave short. When the moonless night had deepened, Flavius had crawled to the far edge of the field and then tottered to his feet and limped away. The old injury to his leg had already been suppurating. He had known then that the broken dragon tooth inside it had begun to move again. The pain had awakened memories of how he'd taken the injury, and made him think of Marcus and wonder about his friend's fate.

How long had it been since he'd last seen him? Time slipped around when a man was a slave. Days seemed longer when someone else owned every minute of your time. A summer of forced labor in Carthage could seem a lifetime with the sun beating down on a man's head and back. He counted the harvests he could recall and then decided that it had been over four years since he'd seen Marcus. Over four years since that disastrous battle where everything went wrong. On the plains of the Bagradas, not far from the cursed river of the same name, Consul Marcus Atillius Regulus had gone down in defeat. Flavius had been one of the five hundred soldiers taken prisoner. Some of those who had survived had pointed out that being captured alive was one step above being one of the twelve thousand Roman dead who littered the bloody battlefield. On the longest days of his slavery, Flavius had doubted that.

His eyes were drawn again to his friend and commander. The spikes had pierced him in a dozen places, but blood no longer trickled from the injuries. The dust-laden summer wind had crusted them over. His chest and belly looked like a map of a river system where the red trickles had dried to brown. Stripped of armor and garments, naked as a slave, Marcus' body still showed the musculature and bearing of a Roman soldier. They had tortured him and hung him up to die, but they still hadn't managed to break him. The Carthaginians never would.

After all, it had not been the Carthaginians who managed to defeat Consul Regulus, but a hired general, one Xanthippus, a Spartan, a man who led his troops not out of love for his country but for cold coin. The Carthaginians had hired him when their own Hamilcar had been unable to deliver the victories they needed. If Marcus had been fully cognizant of what that change in command would mean, perhaps he would not have pressed his men so hard toward their last encounter. That fateful day, the sun had beat down on them as fiercely as if it were a Carthaginian ally. Dust and heat had tormented the troops as Marcus had marched his forces round a lake. Toward evening, the weary soldiers approached the river Bagradas. On the other side, their enemy awaited them. Everyone had expected that their leader would order them to strike a camp, to fortify it with a wall and a ditch. They'd counted on a meal and a night of rest before they engaged in battle. But Marcus had promptly ordered his forces to cross the river and confront the waiting army, thinking to confound the Carthaginian force with his bravado.

Had Hamilcar been the Carthaginian general, the tactic might have worked. Everyone knew that Carthaginians avoided fighting in the open, for they dared not stand against the organized might of a Roman army. But Xanthippus was a Spartan and not to be taken in by show. Nor did he allow his men to fight like Carthaginians. Marcus had drawn his force confidently into their standard formation, infantry in the middle and their cavalry flanking them on both sides, and moved boldly forward. But Xanthippus had not drawn back. Instead, he sent his elephants crashing squarely into the middle of the infantry formation. Even so, the beleaguered square of infantry had held. Flavius had been there. They had fought like Romans, and the lines had held. But then Xanthippus had split his cavalry, a tactic that Flavius had never seen in such a situation. When the horses thundered down on them from both sides, their own outnumbered cavalry had gone down, and then the flanks of the infantry formation had caved in and given way. It had been chaos and bloody slaughter the like of which he'd never seen. Some men, he had heard, had escaped, to flee to Aspis and be rescued later by the Roman fleet. Those soldiers had gone home. Flavius and close to five hundred others had not.

Consul Marcus Atillius Regulus had been a prized captive and a valuable hostage and was treated as such. But Flavius had been only a soldier, and not even one from a wealthy family. His body and the work he could do had been his only worth to the victors. As a spoil of war, he'd been sold for labor. He'd taken a blow to the head in the course of the defeat; he'd never know if it had been from a horse's hoof or a random slingstone. But for a time, he'd seen rings around torches at night and staggered to the left whenever he tried to walk. He'd been sold cheap, and his new master put him to work in his grain fields. And there he had toiled for the last four years. Some seasons he plowed and some he planted, and in the heat of the summer as the grain began to ripen, he'd moved through the field, shouting and flapping his arms to keep the greedy birds at bay. Rome and his soldiering days, his wife and his children, and even Marcus, the boyhood friend who had gotten him into this situation, all had begun to fade from his thoughts. Sometimes he'd felt that he had been a slave always.

And then one night he'd awakened to a familiar pain, and known that the dragon's tooth was once more moving inside his flesh. And within a handful of days, he'd limped away from his overseer.

Had the shifting tooth in the old wound been an omen, a warning from the gods of what was to come? Flavius had given small thought to such things in recent years. The gods of his youth had forsaken him; why should he care any longer to give them honor or even regard? Yet it seemed to him now that the tooth's stirring on the final leg of its journey through his flesh might have come close to the time when Marcus was making his final appearance before the Chief Magistrates of Rome. In the days that followed, the old wound had swollen, turned scarlet, and then began to crust and ooze. And on those same days, he heard the gossip that even Carthaginian slaves would repeat. "The war will soon be over. They paroled the Consul to Rome, to present their treaty terms for them. Consul Regulus is to meet with the Roman magistrates and convince them that it's useless to defy us. He gave his word that if Rome did not accept the terms, he'd return to Carthage."

Flavius had shaken his head and turned wordlessly away from their rumors. Marcus had gone home without him? Marcus had gone home, abandoning the five hundred men who had once served him? Marcus would present Carthaginian terms of surrender to Rome and urge them to accept them? That did not seem like Marcus. For three days, he had mulled it over as he limped through a grain field, flapping his arms at black birds. Then he had decided that the moving tooth inside his flesh was a message. That very day, he had made his escape and begun his slow journey back toward the city of Carthage.

It was a long and weary way for a man half-crippled, without a coin or a purse to put it in. He'd traveled by night, stealing what he could from fields and outlying farmsteads. He avoided speaking to anyone, for although he had learned Punic during his servitude, his Roman accent was strong and would betray him. As the miles between him and his former owner had increased, he'd become a bit more bold. He'd stolen worn garments from a ragpicker's cart that were much more serviceable than the twist of cloth his owner had given him. He'd begged, too, sitting at a village gate and showing his oozing wound and bony body, and a few fools had taken pity on him. And so he had made his slow way, step by step, toward Carthage.

Two nights ago, he had camped in sight of the city walls. As evening fell, he'd found a place to sleep in the dubious shelter of a leafless grove of trees. In the night, he'd wakened to the fever of his wound. In the feeble light of a full moon, he had mustered his courage, set his teeth, and bore down on the swollen tissue. He'd gripped his thigh's hot flesh in both hands and squeezed, pushing up and away from the bone. The dragon's tooth had emerged slickly, jabbing its way out of his body just as bloodily as it had gone in. It had passed through his entire leg, from back to front. He'd pulled it from his flesh, his wet fingers slipping on the gleaming white tooth's smooth surface. When he'd finally tugged it from its hiding place, a gush of foul liquid and pus had followed it. And for the first time in over six years, he finally felt alone in his body, freed of the dragon's tooth and its presence in his life. For a short time, he had held the tooth in his hands, sick with marvel at how long he had carried it. It was sharper than any arrow, and longer than his forefinger. The snapped-off stump where it had broken from the monster's jaw was still sharp-edged. He clutched it in his hand and slept well that night, despite hunger and a bed that was no more than dirt and tree roots.

The next morning, he had risen, bound his old injury afresh, and limped off in search of Marcus. Midway through his first day of walking, he found a likely stick along the roadside and made it his staff. At dusk that day, he came to a sluggish flow of water in a sunken stream. He'd followed it upstream, into a farmer's field, and found a quiet place to bathe his wound and wash out his scant clothing and his bandaging. He'd stolen handfuls of underripe grain from the field, filling his belly with the milky, chewy kernels. When he lay down that night to sleep, he'd dreamed of home, but not of his wife and his sons. No. He'd dreamed of a time before them.

His father's small acreage had been adjacent to that of Marcus' family.

Neither parent was a wealthy man, but while Flavius' father was a farmer who had been to war, Marcus' father had risen to the rank of Consul and never forgotten it. His family holding had been twelve acres, while Marcus' father could claim only a scanty seven, yet when Marcus was recounting his father's heroism, Flavius had always felt he was the poorer of the two boys. He smiled bitterly to himself. When Marcus' father had died, Marcus had been devastated, not just by the man's death but also by the thought that his days as a warrior were finished. Marcus had gone to the Roman Senate and reluctantly requested to be freed from his military duty, so that he might return home to till his seven acres and support his wife and children and mother, for with his father gone, there was no one else to shoulder that task. Yet even in that early flush of his career, the Senate had recognized his military worth. They'd taken from taxes the funds to hire a man to till the lands of Marcus Atillius Regulus and sent him forth yet again to serve Rome where he functioned best, at the bloody forefront of the war.

Marcus had gone joyfully. Flavius had shaken his head over it then even as he did now. War and its glory were all Marcus had ever wanted. When they were boys, in the green of their youth, they had both dreamed of escaping their chores for the adventure of soldiering. They'd counted down the musterings until they reached an age when they, too, could stand with the other eligible men in the town square and await a chance to be chosen to serve. They'd both been seventeen years tall and of a like height at that first dilectus, and it had been Marcus who had contrived that they must find a way to stand four men apart. "For we shall be called forward four at a time, for the tribunes to have the pick of us. If we go up together, one will choose me and another you, and then we shall certainly be separated. So, see that you come up after me, for if I can at all, I shall whisper to the tribune that chooses me that although you may not have the muscle I show, there is no one like to you for an arrow well shot or a spear flung straight. I'll see that so long as we march to war, we always march together. That I promise you."

"And what of our marching home? Do you promise we shall always be together then?"

Marcus had stared at him, affronted. "Of course we shall! In triumph!"

Small matter to Marcus that, if Flavius had had his way after his first stint of soldiering, he might have stayed at home, well away from the gore and boredom of a soldier's life. But of course, he had no choice; no son of a Roman citizen did. And so at that first muster he stood, knees slightly bent to blend in with three shorter youths, and watched Marcus being chosen. He saw his frantic whispering and pointing, and he saw the stony-faced tribune who waved an angry hand at him to silence him. But when the time came for the tribune to choose from the four men offered him, he had chosen Flavius. And thus the two boyhood friends had marched off together for their first foray into a soldier's life.

Marcus thrived on a military life. As Marcus' talent for strategy had blossomed, he had risen in rank. Although Marcus was his commander on the battlefield each year, when they returned home, they resumed being friends and neighbors. As the years had passed, and especially after the dragon had damn near taken his leg off, Flavius had answered the muster more reluctantly each year. He had begun to hope that the tribunes would see that the injury to his leg had made him an old man before his time. But every year when he presented himself for the dilectus, Marcus contrived that Flavius was chosen to serve in his legion. And at the end of each campaign, when they returned home together, always they slipped comfortably back into their old friendship.

Had Marcus ever wanted to be anything but a soldier? Even now, as Flavius looked up at him in his cage, he doubted it. When they were boys, after their chores, Marcus had always wanted to be fighting with staves or staging ambushes on the neighbor's goats. Flavius had preferred the hunt to a battle, and on the evenings when he persuaded Marcus to follow him on his quests, his friend had been unstinting in his amazement and praise of Flavius' skills. He excelled at stealth and marksmanship. Flavius well remembered the sweetness of the long evenings of late summer, when the two boys had lounged by a small fire, savoring the smell of plundered apples baking by the embers and a small game bird sizzling over the last of the flames. Flavius' thoughts would wander to whether he might persuade his father to let him range farther in search of larger game, but for Marcus, the dream was always the same.

"I know my destiny," he had confided to Flavius, more than once. "I've seen it in my dreams. I shall rise through the ranks, to be a praetor or a consul, just as my father did before me. And then I shall lead my troops forth into war."

"To kill a thousand of the enemy?" Flavius would ask, grinning.

"A thousand? No! Five thousand, ten thousand will fall to my strategy. And I shall be summoned back to Rome and awarded a Triumph. I shall be paraded through the streets, with wagons full of my plunder, and my captives walking barefoot behind me. My army will follow me, of course, and you, Flavius, you I promise will be in the first rank. My wife and my grown sons will be honored with me. And I, I shall be stained as red as this apple, and my toga whiter than snow. At Jupiter's temple, I will sacrifice six white bulls to him. All of Rome will line the streets to cheer me. This I know, Flavius. I've seen it."

He'd smiled at his friend's posturing. "Don't forget the best part of it, Marcus. There will be a slave in the chariot with you, standing just back of your shoulder and leaning forward to whisper into your ear the words that remind you that every hero is mortal. And thus you will be kept humble." He grinned. "Perhaps, instead of a slave, they will let me do that!"

"Mortal? The body perhaps is mortal, Flavius. But once a man has had a Triumph, once he is an imperator, then his legend is immortal and will be passed on through all the generations of soldiers that will ever spill blood on the earth."

One of the stolen apples had popped on the fire, spitting out a tiny missile of pulp and then draining a sweet stream of hot juice into the embers. Flavius had speared it with the small stick he was using to tend their meal and drawn it back from the fire's edge. He held it up gravely on its skewer. "Memento mori!" he had toasted it gravely, and then blown on it before scalding his mouth with an incautious bite of it.

Regulus tried to decide if the evening was as chill as it seemed. The day had been hot enough to bake him. But now, as the sunlight that jabbed through his hazed vision turned the world to a bloody red, he felt chilled.

His eyeballs were too dried to see clearly, but he could still perceive that the light was fading. So the cooler evening was finally coming. Or death. Blindness would make the light fade, and blood loss could make a man cold. He well knew that. He'd lost count of the times when he'd lent his cloak to wrap a dying man. Flavius, he suddenly thought. He'd knelt by Flavius and tucked his cloak around him as he shivered. But Flavius hadn't died, had he? Had he? No, not then. Not then, but now? Was Flavius alive now? Or had he left him dead on that last battlefield?

Men always complained of the cold when they were dying, if they had breath left to speak. The cold and the enveloping darkness troubled them, or they expressed regrets in a muttered word or a sigh as he knelt beside the fallen man. As if the cold or the dark were what a man should worry about when his entrails were spilled in the dust next to him, or half his body's blood was congealing in a pool beneath him. Still, it was a small comfort to offer, the lending of a cloak for the usually brief time it took a man to bleed out from a battle wound. A small comfort he would have welcomed just now. The touch of one friendly hand, one word from a friend to send him on his way. But he was alone.

No one would come to wrap him in a cloak, or to take his hand, or even to speak his name. No one would crouch down beside him and say, "Regulus, you died well. You were a fine consul, a loyal centurion, and a good citzen. Rome will remember you. You died a hero's death." No. His parched tongue tried to wet his cracked lips. Another stupid reflex of the body. Tongue, lips, teeth. Silly, useless words now. None of them applied to him. As stupid as his mind, going on thinking, thinking, thinking while his body spiraled down into death.

Something landed on the top of his suspended cage. A bird, it would have to be a bird up here. Not a serpent, not a dragon. It was not heavy, he didn't think, but it was enough to make the cage rock a tiny bit.

And enough to make the spikes bite just that much deeper. He held his breath and waited. Soon, they'd reach something vital, and he would die. But not just yet. No. Not just yet. He tightened his grip on the bars of his cage, or tried to. They'd shackled his hands higher than his heart, and they were numb now. It made no sense to cling to life when his body was already ruined. They'd broken so many parts of him that he could no longer catalog them. He did remember the moment when he suddenly knew that they weren't going to stop. He'd known that before they began, of course. They'd promised him that. The Carthaginians had sent him forth, bound doubly by his word and their promise. They'd made him promise to return. In turn, the Carthaginians had promised that if he did not convince the Roman magistrates to accept the terms of the treaty, they would kill him on his return.

He recalled standing among slaves as the Carthaginian envoys presented their terms. He had not shouted out that he was a Roman citizen, had not announced that he was Consul Marcus Attillius Regulus. No. He was ashamed to return to Rome in such a way and he had no intention of being a tool for the Carthaginians. They had had to bring him forward and announce him to the Magistrates themselves. And then he had done the only thing he could do. He denounced the treaty and its harsh terms, and advised the Magistrates to refuse it.

And they had.

And then he had kept his honor by keeping his word to his captors. He returned to Carthage with them.

So, he'd known all along that the Carthaginians would kill him. Known with his mind. But that was different from knowing with his body. His body hadn't known. His body had believed that somehow, he'd be able to go on living. If his body hadn't believed that, his torturers would not have been able to wring scream after scream from him.

He'd tried not to scream, of course. All men tried, at first, not to scream under torture. But sooner or later, they all did. And sooner or later, they all stopped even pretending to try not to scream. He could command one hundred men and they'd obeyed him in his days as a centurion, and as a general and as a consul he could command thousands. When he had told the Magistrates that they should refuse the terms of the treaty, they had listened. But when he had commanded his own body not to scream, it hadn't listened to him. It had screamed and screamed, as if somehow that would mitigate the pain. It didn't. And then, at some crucial point, when they had broken so many parts of him that he could no longer keep count, when really, no part of him was left whole, even his body had known that he was going to die. And then it had stopped screaming.

A very long time after that, or perhaps only a short time that seemed like a long time, they'd stopped actively torturing him. Was it hours or days ago that they'd rolled him down to the city gates inside his spiked cage? Did it matter?

He listened to the sounds of the city below him. Earlier, there had been crowd noises. Exclamations, shouts of disgust and ridicule, mocking laughter and the stupid shouts of triumph from men who had never fought, never even tortured, but somehow thought they could claim his death as their victory. *By virtue of what?* he'd wanted to ask them. *That you were whelped on a piece of dirt somewhere near the place where my torturer was born? Does that make seeing me dangle in a cage over your city gate a victory for you? You have no victory here. I told the Magistrates to refuse the treaty. Rome will not go down on its knees before you. I saw to that. If I could not give my country the victory it deserved, at least I have preserved it from accepting a defeat.*

He hadn't said any such words to his gallery, of course. His mouth, tongue, and teeth were no longer useful for talking. He'd almost wished, at one point, that his torturers were pretending to wring information from him. If that had been their pretense, they'd have left him a mouth to babble with when they'd hurt him badly enough. But they'd been freed from any need to pretend they were doing anything other than hurting him as much as they could without killing him. And so they had done their worst, or perhaps they thought of it as their best. Torturers, he knew from employing them, were not interested in information or confessions. They weren't even interested in reforming the wicked or making them sorry for their misdeeds. Torturers were interested in hurting people. That was all. He'd seen how it aroused them, how their eyes glittered and their mouths grew wet. It was in how lovingly they handled their tools and the great thought they gave to how they applied them. Torture, he thought, was sex for the sexless. Not a one of them ever worked for anything except his own joy in hurting. They were not warriors, not soldiers; perhaps they were not men at all. They were torturers. Consumers of pain, and they'd fed off his screams, just as the carrion birds waited to consume his flesh. The torturers were tools, servants of the ones who commanded them. And in his case, the men who had commanded the torturers were simply keeping a promise to him.

His thoughts were jumping around like fleas evacuating the carcass of a dead animal. The mental image pleased him for a moment, and then it vanished from his mind. He cast his thoughts wider, tried to find an image or an idea to cling to, anything that would distract him from the slow pain of dying. There was his wife to think of, Julia. She would mourn and miss him. How many soldiers could say that of women left behind and know that it was true? And his sons, Marcus and Gaius. They would hear of their father's death, and it would stiffen their resolution to defend Rome. They'd realize more clearly just what evil dogs these Carthaginians were. They would not feel shamed that he had been defeated and captured. They would take pride in how he had not scrabbled for a chance at life by betraying his country. No. He'd defied Carthage. If he could not leave his boys a Triumph to remember him by, at least he would leave them his honorable death as a loyal Roman.

They'd hear how he died. He had no doubt of that. The Senate would noise it about. It would put some fire in their bellies, to think of Marcus Atillius Regulus, once a proud consul of the Roman legions, tormented and hung up to die like fresh meat hung to bleed in a butcher's stall. The Senate would make certain that everyone heard of how he died.

It would be the last use they'd make of him. He knew that and didn't resent it. But gods, gods, how much longer must it take him to die?

Flavius realized that he had been standing and staring too long. The stream of people moving into the city had parted to go around him. Earlier, he was sure, there had been a standing audience for Marcus' last moments. But the stubborn soldier had defeated those gawkers. He'd refused to die for them.

Flavius crossed the street to a merchant hawking slabs of flat bread. It smelled wonderful. He had a few coins from a purse he'd cut last week. At one time, he would have been shamed to resort to common thievery, but he had learned to justify it to himself. Even if he no longer wore the armor of a Roman soldier, soldier he was, and every Carthaginian remained his enemy. Stealing from them, even killing one if the opportunity were offered, was no different from hunting any other sort of prey. It had been a good pouch he'd cut, a leather one with woven throngs, and inside it was half a dozen coins, a small knife, a man's ring, and a slab of wax. He took out his smallest coin and held it up for the bread merchant to see, scowling darkly all the while. The merchant shook his head disdainfully. Flavius let his scowl darken as he brought another small coin from the twisted rag at his hip and offered it as well. The merchant muttered, "You will beggar me!" but picked up one of his smaller loaves and offered it. Flavius handed over the two bits of metal and took the bread without thanks. Today he would take no chance of his accent betraying him.

He broke the bread into small pieces and ate it dry, casting furtive glances up at Marcus as he did so. It felt traitorous to eat while his friend was dying, but he was hungry, and the activity gave him an excuse to loiter where he was. Marcus held steady. He gripped the bars of his cage and stared down at the passing folk. Some still looked up at him as they passed, but others scarcely noticed the dying man in the cage. Perhaps it was because he did not look as if he were dying. Yet Flavius looked up at him and knew. His boyhood friend was past saving. Even if a Roman legion had miraculously appeared to rescue him, Marcus would still die. There was a dusky color to his hands and feet that spoke of blood settling. The attentions of the torturers had left streaks of blood that had dried as brown stripes on his face and his chest and thighs. Yet Marcus stood and waited and Flavius stood and watched and waited, even though he could not say why.

It seemed only fitting. After all, Marcus had once kept a death watch for him.

It had been years ago. Six years? Seven? And it had not been that far from this dusty, evil city. They had been trying to cross the Bagradas River at a place where it ran through thick brush and verdant reeds that grew higher than a man's head. The Bagradas Valley was a rich and fertile swath of ground that received the waters from the Tells on either side of it. On the flanks of the Tells, cork and oak and pine forests grew. The banks of the wide river were thick with both vegetation and stinging insects. Marcus had been a general then, but not yet risen to the rank of consul. That title he would earn by cutting a swath of destruction across Carthage. It had been a summer of conquest for him. That day, Marcus pushed infantry, horse, and archers to move swiftly as he sought for the best place to ford the Bagradas. He had chosen a prime spot for his evening camp, on a rise that overlooked a river. The troops settled in to create the standard fortification, a ditch and a wall made from the upflung dirt. Marcus had sent his scouts ahead to survey the fording place. They had returned too soon, to report unusual activity by the water's edge.

"We saw a snake, sir. A huge snake. By the river."

Flavius had been in earshot of that first report. Sometimes of an evening, after the boundaries were set for the night, he'd go by Marcus' tent. If the general was not too busy, he'd find time for some talk with his old friend. But that evening, as he approached, he was blocked by a huddle of men clustered around the tent. Marcus stood scowling, while the two velites reporting to him looked at the ground and shifted sheepishly. Flavius had seen Marcus' consternation that they had even dared to return to report such a thing. "Amazing," he had responded, his voice dripping sarcasm. "That we should encounter a snake on an African riverbank. Is that why you fled back here before determining if we can ford there tomorrow?"

The velites had exchanged glances. They were among the poorest of the soldiers that were recruited, often without enough money to equip themselves well and accorded little status by their fellows. In battle, they were skirmishers and javelin throwers, not recognized as formally belonging to any group. They had been sent to scout precisely because they were expendable. They knew it and did not like it. Flavius could scarcely blame them for retreating from whatever they had seen. They had to watch out for their own backs. One of the men was wet to the waist. The other man spoke. "We couldn't see all of it, sir. But what we saw was, well, immense. We saw a piece of its side moving past us through the tall river grass. It was the diameter of a hogshead, sir, and that was close to the end of it. We aren't cowards. We went toward it, for a better look. And then, close to a hundred feet away, this head reared up from the reeds."

"Glowing eyes!" broke in the other scout. "On my word, sir, big glowing eyes. And it hissed at us, but the hiss was more like whistling. I had to cover my ears. It kept to the water, and the reeds hid most of it from us, but what we could see was immense. From the size of its eyes and head, it had to be—"

"That's twice now that you've admitted coming back to report to me on something that you haven't completely seen," Marcus had observed coldly. "It is the function of a scout, is it not, to see things and then come back to report? Rather than to come back to report what he has *not* seen?"

The first man scowled and looked at his feet. The second scout flushed a deep red. He didn't meet Marcus's gaze, but there was no shame in his voice as he said, "Some things are so strange that even a glimpse of one should be reported. That is no ordinary snake, sir. And I'm not just speaking of its size, though it dwarfs any other snake I've ever seen. Its eyes glowed when it looked at us. And it more whistled than hissed. It didn't flee at the sight of us, as most snakes would. No. It challenged us. And so we came back to report it to you."

"River dragon," someone said into the silence that followed the scout's words.

Marcus' eyes snapped to the men clustered at the edge of the firelight's reach. Perhaps he knew who had spoken, but Flavius didn't. In any event, he didn't single out anyone. "Ridiculous," he said scathingly.

"You didn't see it," the first scout said abruptly, but before he could continue, Marcus cut in with, "And neither did you! You saw something. Probably a glimpse of a hippo, and then a glimpse of a snake, and in the reeds and the evening light, you thought they were one and the same." He pointed a finger at the one scout and demanded, "How did you get wet?"

The man drew himself up. "If I could finish my report, sir. That head came up out of the reeds. It lifted its head higher than I'm tall, and it looked down on us. Then it whistled. Startled us both, and I shouted back at it. Big as it was, I still thought it would turn aside and go its way. Instead, it came at us. It darted its head at me, mouth open, and all I could see was row after row of teeth, in a maw the size of a cart. Carus shouted at him and threw his javelin. It stuck in him, made him angry. He roared again and went for me. I jumped to one side and ran. I thought it was solid riverbank, but it wasn't and I went right over the edge and into the water. Lucky for me, because it lost sight of me."

The other man took up the tale. "That's when it turned on me and came after me, but I was already moving by then. It stopped to rub my javelin off. I heard the shaft snap, like it was nothing. I'd run up the bank and I think it was reluctant to come out of the reeds and cattails. I thought Tullus was dead. When he came out of the reeds and joined me, we decided we'd best come back to report this."

Marcus had crossed his arms on his chest. "And the light is almost gone. And no doubt by the time we reach the river tomorrow, your giant snake will be gone as well. Go about your duties, both of you. Glowing eyes!"

And with that sharp remark, he dismissed not only the two scouts but all of the men as well. Just before he turned away, his eyes met Flavius' and he gave a small toss of his head. He knew that he was summoned, but privately. In the dark and almost quiet hours of the restive camp, he went to Marcus' tent.

"I need to know what they saw. Can you go out, before dawn, and then come back to me? If anyone can read the ground and let me know what is out there, you can. I need to get our troops across the river, Flavius. I'd like to cross here, at first light. But if there are hippos and crocodiles, then I need to know before we enter the water, not when we're halfway across."

"Or giant snakes?" Flavius asked him.

Marcus gave a dismissive laugh. "They're young and poorly armed. I don't blame them for running back here, but they have to learn that what I need is information, not rumors. I'll have them here to hear your report in the morning. And that's when they'll face their discipline as well."

Flavius had nodded, and gone off to take what sleep he could.

A Roman camp stirs early, but he was the first to arise that morning. He took with him not the arms of a warrior but the tools of a hunter. It did not take a lot of modification to turn a pike into a pole sling. It had greater range and could launch a heavier weapon than his small sling. If there were an irritable hippo or basking crocodiles, he wished to turn them away before they got too close to him. The gladius at his side was for closer occasions. The short blade was good for both stabbing and slashing. Flavius hoped it came to neither.

The banks of the Bagradas River teemed with life. Brush edged it and deep reed beds lined it. He followed the same well-trodden game trail that the scouts had investigated the day before. Animals knew the best places to water and the safest places to cross. That this path was so well trodden made him suspect he'd find a safe fording for the troops. Closer to the river, the brush to either side grew thicker and the reeds and cattails before him loomed taller. He was reassured by the plentiful birdsong and the darting of the busy feathered creatures. Off to one side, he heard some larger creature startle out of its wallow and then crash off into deep brush. It was a four-legged beast, he was sure of that. It increased his wariness, and he went more slowly. The ground began to become bog. He reached the edge of the reed bed and looked down a clear channel, almost a tunnel of a path that led out into the open moving waters of the river. On the far side, a similar muddy track led up the opposite bank. So. A place to cross. He decided to wade out and check the strength of the current and the footing. He was knee-deep in the water when suddenly all the bird noises stopped.

Flavius halted and stood still, listening. His eyes sought not color or shape but motion. He heard only the lapping rush of the water, saw only the normal movement of the reeds in harmony with the water's flow.

Then, a sling's shot away from him, the tops of the cattails moved *against* the current. He remained as he was, breathing slowly. A bank of the cattails bowed in unison, and then, a distance from that motion, a group of reeds bowed in the opposite direction. The next motion of the reeds was closer to him, and suddenly he realized that he was hearing a sound, one that had blended with the water noises when it was distant. But now it was closer. Something scraped through the reeds. The tall standing grasses rubbed against a creature's hide in a long, smooth chorus. Flavius parted his lips, took a silent breath. He'd find out what it was now, before it came any closer. His pole sling was loaded. In a motion so practiced and natural that he gave it no thought, he tipped the pole and snapped it forward.

The missile was one of his own devising, heavier than he would have launched from a hand sling and with one end pointed. Sometimes it tumbled and struck blunt end first. Other times, the sharpened end bit. He cared little what happened this time; his intent was to startle whatever it was into betraying itself. His missile flew silently but when it struck, all silence ended.

The creature's whistle was like a shriek of wind. Much closer than he had expected, a head reared up from the reeds. It turned its outraged gaze from its own body to see what had dared to attack it. Flavius was already backing up before it turned its boxy head and fixed its eyes on him. Even in the clear morning light, they burned orange. It took in breath with a sound like cold water hitting hot stone, its slit nostrils flaring as it did so. Then it opened wide its mouth and he saw, just as the scout had reported, a maw the size of a cart, lined with rows of inward-leaning teeth. He stumbled backwards, then spun and fled. The massive head struck the ground a pike's length behind him. The shock of the impact traveled through the wet soil; he felt the weight of the creature's head through the soles of his feet, and abruptly he was running as he had never run before. He risked one glance back when he gained the top of the bank. He saw nothing.

Then, just as he dared to take a breath, the immense head on its thick neck rose again from the reeds and rushes. It stared at him, and a long forked tongue emerged from its blunt snout, flickering and tasting the air. It regarded him with nothing of fear, only malevolence, with lidless orange eyes. It opened its maw and again that whistling shriek shattered the air around him. Then it came on, moving much faster than any legless creature had a right to. Flavius turned and fled. He ran and heard the gruesome sounds of an immense footless creature coming after him. His terror put the spring of a boy in his man's legs and his heart thundered in his ears. When he finally mustered the courage to glance back, the snake was gone, but still he ran, unable to stop, almost to the outskirts of the camp.

He hurried through a camp that had begun to stir, pausing to speak to no one. He would start no rumors until Marcus had heard his news and decided how to deal with it. His mouth was dry; his heart still shaking when he stood before Regulus to make his report. It was to his commander, not to his old friend that he said, "They told you true, sir. It's an immense snake, the likes of which no one has ever seen. I'd estimate it at one hundred feet long. And it's aggressive. I hit it with a sling stone, and it came after me."

He watched his friend absorb the news. He peered at him and perhaps a smile threatened as he challenged him quietly, "One hundred feet long, Flavius? A snake one hundred feet long?"

He swallowed in a dry throat. "My best estimate, sir. From the size of the head and how high he lifted it, and from how far away the reeds were stirred by his tail." He cleared his throat. "I'm serious."

He watched Marcus rethink his words, his face growing still, and then his jaw setting. He saw his commander announce his decision. "Regardless of its size, it's still just a snake. A wolf or a bear may stand and face one man, or even half a dozen, but no creature will take a stand against a legion. We'll form up and march down there. Doubtless the noise and activity will scare it off. What did you think of the river? Are the baggage train carts going to have any problems crossing there?"

Before Flavius could reply, they heard wild yells, and then a sound that stood all the hair up on Flavius' back. A shrill whistle split the air. It was followed by shouts of "Dragon! Dragon!" The whistling shriek of the creature was repeated, more loudly. It was followed by screams, very human screams that abruptly stopped. More shouting, panicky, wordless yells.

Marcus had been half-dressed when Flavius arrived. Now he hastily buckled his breastplate and snatched up his helm. "Let's go," he said, and though a dozen men fell in at his heels, Flavius felt the words had been meant for him. They went at a dogtrot through the camp and toward the river. Flavius drew his shortsword as he ran, hoping he'd never be near enough to use it. All around him, other men in various stages of dress joined the hurrying throng. "Archers to me!" Marcus shouted, and within a score of strides, he was flanked by bowmen. Flavius doggedly held his place just behind Marcus' left shoulder.

They did not reach the edge of camp before a tide of shouting men met them. They carried one man, and though he was still roaring with pain, Flavius knew him for a dead man. His left leg had been shorn away at the hip.

"It's a dragon!"

"Snake got two of them right way. They just went to fetch water."

"Eyes the size of cartwheels!"

"Knocked down six men and crushed them. Just crushed them!"

"It ate them. Gods help us, it ate them!"

"It's a demon, a Carthaginian demon!"

"They've set a dragon on us!"

"It's coming! It's coming!"

Behind the fleeing men, Flavius saw the great head rise. Up it went and up, higher and higher. It looked down on all of them, eyes gleaming, forked tongue long as a bullwhip flickering in and out of its mouth. Flavius felt cold, as if evil had looked directly at him. The creature, dragon or snake, whistled then, a high powerful gust of sound. Some men cried out and others clapped their hands to their ears.

"Archers!" shouted Regulus, and a score of flights took wing, their hiss lost in the snake's long whistle. Some arrows missed; others skipped over the creature's scaled back. Some struck, stuck briefly, and then fell as the snake shook itself. Perhaps six hit and sank into the creature. If it felt any pain, it did not show it. Instead, it struck, the immense head, mouth open wide, darting down to seize two soldiers. The men shrieked as it lifted them into the air. It threw back its head and gulped, and their comrades were suddenly visible lumps moving down the snake's throat. Flavius felt cold. The snake had seized them so quickly, they could not be dead. They had been swallowed alive.

Flavius had not heard the command given to fire again, but another phalanx of arrows was arching toward the beast. It had come closer and they struck more true. Of those that hit, most stuck well. This time, the snake gave a whistle of fury. It flung itself flat and wallowed, trying to dislodge the arrows. Its whipping tail cleared brush from the riverside.

"Fall back!" Regulus shouted, and in a matter of moments they were in full retreat from the creature. It was not the most orderly withdrawal that Flavius had ever participated in, but it achieved its goal. The ranks of men reformed defensively as they put distance between themselves and the Carthaginian monster. Flavius' knees felt rubbery and his mind still reeled from that one revealing glimpse of the full extent of the creature. It was more than a hundred feet long; of that, he was sure. How much longer, he had no desire to know.

"It's not following!" someone shouted.

"Keep moving!" Regulus ordered. "Back to the camp and man the fortifications." Then he cast a sideways look at Flavius. "Go see," he said quietly. Heart in his throat, Flavius turned and began to walk back through the crowd of oncoming men. When he had passed the last stragglers, he pushed on, ears strained and his sling at the ready. He knew it would not do much, but it was his oldest and most familiar weapon. And, he thought to himself, it had a lot more range than a gladius. He grinned, surprising himself, and walked on.

When he could see the bodies of the fallen, he stopped. He scanned the surrounding brush and saw no sign of the immense creature. It had wallowed out a section of brush and grasses where it rolled to dislodge the arrows. He stood a time longer, surveying the scene. When first one carrion bird and then another swept in and landed near the bodies, he judged that the serpent was truly gone. Still, his advance was cautious.

All the downed men were dead. One breathed a little still, air rasping in and out of his slack mouth, but his torso was crushed and there was no light in his eyes. Sometimes the body took a little time to know it was dead. He stood from appraising the man and forced himself to walk on. The serpent had cut a large swath through the brush in its retreat. He found no blood or any sign that they had dealt it significant injuries. He followed it until he could see the river and the crushed reeds where the creature had returned to the water. Down there, it could conceal itself. He would go no farther. There was no need of it.

When he reported back to Marcus, he realized how shaken his friend was. He listened gravely to what Flavius told him, then shook his head. "We are here to fight Carthaginians, not deal with a giant snake. The idea that it is some kind of demon or dragon set on us by the Carthaginians has shaken them. I don't intend to challenge it again. I'll send a burial detail for the fallen, but I've decided to move downriver. I've already sent the scouts ahead, looking for a place to cross. We can't linger here. We'll move on."

Flavius had felt relief but also surprise that Marcus would follow so sensible a course. He had expected his friend to dig in and do battle with it. Marcus' next words cleared away the mystery. "It's big, but it's only a snake. It's not worth our time."

Flavius nodded to that and withdrew. Marcus had always been about being a soldier. The stalking that a hunter did and the necessity of trying to think like his prey in order to hunt it had never appealed to him. War he saw as a challenge between men, demanding an understanding of strategy. He had never seen animals as complex and unpredictable, as Flavius did. He had never seen animals as worthy opponents, never understood Flavius' fascination with hunting.

Now, as Flavius looked up at his friend in his cage, he saw too clearly the animal that Marcus had always lived inside. The man's mind was slowly giving way to the beast that enclosed him. Pain wracked him and demanded his attention. He saw the tremors that had begun to run over Marcus' body.

His knees shook, and a trickle of blood-tinged urine ran down his leg and dripped onto the street and the passersby below him. A shout of outrage greeted this, and the market crowd that had almost forgotten the dying man above them once more turned their eyes upward.

The woman who had been spattered tore her scarf from her shoulders and threw it to the ground. She looked up at Marcus and shook her fist and shouted obscenities at him. A wave of mocking laughter followed her words, along with pointing gestures and other mocking shouts. A few onlookers stooped to pick up stones.

The pain, for a time, had come in waves that threatened to sweep his consciousness away. Through each engulfing surge, he had held tight to the bars of his cage as a drowning sailor might cling to a bit of floating wreckage. He knew it offered him no safety, but he would not release his grip. He'd die standing, and not just because a fall would mean being impaled on one of the coarse spikes sticking up from the bottom of his cage. He'd die upright, a Roman citizen, a consul, a soldier, not curled like a speared dog.

The pain had not abated, but it had turned into something else. Just as the crash of storm waves can eventually lull a man to sleep, so it was with the pain now. It was there, and so constant that his thoughts floated on top of it, only disconnecting when an especially sharp jab penetrated his mind. The pain seemed to provoke his memories, waking the sharpest and most potent of them. His triumph at Aspis; he had seized the whole city with scarcely a blow. That had been a summer! Hamilcar had avoided him, and his army had virtually had the run of Carthage. The plunder had been rich, and he'd lost count of how many captured Roman soldiers he had regained. Oh, he had been the Senate's darling then. Then, the prospect of being granted a Triumph and paraded through Rome had loomed large and fresh before him, as keenly imagined as when he had been a boy. It would be his. He would be acknowledged as a hero by cheering, adoring crowds.

But then Manlius, his fellow consul, had decided to sail back to Rome, taking the best of their plunder home. And Hamilcar, general for the Carthaginians, had perhaps decided that gave him some sort of advantage. He had brought his army to an encampment on high wooded ground on the far side of the Bagradas River. Regulus had not been daunted. He'd set out to meet and challenge him, taking infantry, cavalry, and a good force of ballistae.

But then they had come to the river. And that damn African snake. Some of his men had believed it a Carthaginian demon, sent by Hamilcar to attack them. When he had seen it for himself, he hadn't been able to comprehend the creature. Flavius had tried to tell him; that was the first and last time he'd ever doubted his friend's evaluation of an animal. He'd lost thirteen men in his first encounter with the creature, too big a loss against such an adversary. He'd been intent on Hamilcar and fearful of losing his element of surprise. And so, he'd withdrawn his men, surrendering the riverbank to the immense snake, as he never would have conceded it to any human opponent. He'd marched his men downriver, looking for a good place to ford, while his baggage train and the heavier wheeled artillery had followed on the higher, firmer ground.

A few hours of marching and he'd found a good fording place. He'd congratulated himself on losing so little time. Mounted on his horse, he'd led his men to the river and halted there on the bank to watch the crossing of his troops. He'd posted archers on what little higher ground there was, a standard precaution he took whenever he committed that many troops to a river crossing. The Bagradas was wide, shallow at the edges and mucky, with muddy banks forested with reeds and cattails taller than a man on horseback. The front ranks of his soldiers pushed their way forward through them. He watched them go, the leading men disappearing into the green ranks of river plants, pushing a narrow path that those who followed would soon trample into a wide swath.

He hoped the bottom would be more gravel than muck as they got closer to the middle of the river. He wanted to get across quickly and out onto the other side, and then up onto firmer ground. Fording a river was always a vulnerable time for any military force. A man chest-deep in moving water presents a good target without being capable of defending himself. Anxiously, he scanned the far side of the river through the fence of reeds and grasses. He saw no sign of the enemy. He would not relax until his first ranks were on the other side of the river and posting more archers there to guard the crossing place.

But he was not looking in the right place, or for the right opponent.

Flavius had been standing near his horse. He heard his friend gasp and turned his head. For a moment, his eyes could make no sense of what he saw. And then he realized that he was staring at a wall of snakeskin, a pattern of animal hide that was sliding through the tall bank of reeds, headed directly for his vulnerable troops.

Who could ever have imagined that a snake of that size could move so swiftly, let alone so quietly? Who could ever have imagined that any animal would have anticipated that they would move downriver and attempt another crossing? It might have been a coincidence. It might have been that the creature was hungry and had followed the noise of the troops on the march.

Or it might truly be a Carthaginian demon, some ancient evil summoned by them to put an end to his domination of their lands. The creature slid near soundlessly through the water and the bowing reeds. For a moment, he was stunned again at the size of it. It seemed impossible that such a long movement of grasses could be caused by a single creature. He saw it raise its blunt-nosed head, saw its jaws gape wide.

"Ware serpent!" he shouted, the first to give the warning, and then a hundred voices took up his cry. "Serpent!" Now there was an inadequate word to describe the nightmare that attacked them! A serpent was a creature that a man might tread underfoot. At its worst, here in Africa one might encounter a boa crushing a goat in its coils. *Serpent* was not a word that could apply to a creature the length of a city wall and almost the height of one.

It moved like a wish, like a sigh, like a gleaming scythe, newly sharpened, mowing down grain. He glimpsed it as a moving wall seen between the vertical spikes of the upright reeds. Scales glittered when the sun touched them and gleamed in the gentle shade of the reeds. It moved in a relentless, remorseless way that seemed more like a wave or a landslide than like a living creature as it sliced through the ranked men in the water. Some it caught up in its jaws. It swallowed them whole, the great muscles on the sides of its throat working as it crushed the men down its throat. Others were pushed down into the water, if not by the creature's own body, then by the wave that its undulating motion created. It moved swiftly through the formation, and then, with a lash of its gigantic tail, it slashed again at the struggling men who either swam or tried to regain their footing in the current.

"Archers!" Regulus had shouted, but their arrows were already bouncing off the snake's smooth hide or sticking like wobbly pins, barely penetrating its armor. The missiles did no good and much harm, for the snake doubled back on itself. A rank reptilian stench suddenly filled the air as the creature lashed like a massive whip through the struggling men in the water. It caught some of them in its jaws, crushed them, and flung the bodies aside in a fury. One man in the water, brave or foolish, most likely both, tried to plunge his pike into the creature. The sharp point skittered along the snake's scales to no effect. An instant later, the snake bent its head and engulfed the man in its mouth. A shake sent his pike flying. A convulsive swallow, and its enemy was gone. Whistling scream after scream split the air. The few bodies it snapped up and swallowed seemed afterthoughts to its wrath.

Regulus fought his mount. Battle-trained, nonetheless, she reared, screaming in terror, and when he tightened his reins, she backed and fought for her head. Was that struggle what turned the snake's attention to him? Perhaps it was only that a man mounted on a horse was a larger creature than the frantic men drowning in the river. Whatever it was, the snake's gleaming gaze fell on him, and suddenly it came straight for him. The lashing tail that drove it whipped the river to brown froth. The snake turned its immense head sideways, jaws gaping wide, plainly intending to seize both man and horse in its jaws.

Useless to flee. He'd never escape the snake's speed. Might as well stand his ground and die a hero, as flee and be remembered as a coward. Strange. Even now, he recalled clearly that he had not been afraid. Surprised, a bit, that he would die in battle against a snake rather than against the Carthaginians. He recalled thinking clearly that men would remember his death. His sword was already in his hand, though he could not recall drawing it. Foolish weapon for an encounter such as this, and yet he would draw blood if he could. The snake whistled as it came, a sky-splitting sound that made thought impossible. He felt stunned by the impact against his ears, his skin.

Around him, he was dimly aware of his men scattering. The mare reared and he held her in with sheer strength. The snake's gaping mouth came at him; the stench was overpowering. Then, as the creature's jaws were all around him, he felt a sudden slam of a body against his. "Marcus!" the man might have shouted, but that smaller sound was lost in the snake's whistle.

He didn't recognize Flavius when he tackled him from the horse. He only knew him as he hit the muddy bank of the river, and looked up, to see the snake lifting both horse and Flavius from the ground. The creature's jaws had closed on the horse's chest. Flavius' flying dive to drive Marcus from the horse meant that one of his legs had been caught in the snake's jaws as it gripped his unfortunate mare. Flavius dangled, head down, roaring with terror and pain as the mare struggled wildly in the snake's mouth.

Marcus had rolled as he struck the ground. He came instinctively back to his feet and then leaped upward and caught his friend round the chest. His added weight literally tore Flavius from the serpent's jaws. Lightened of Flavius' weight, the snake was content to continue its battle to engulf the wildly kicking horse. He scarcely noticed the men who fell back to the ground. That time, Marcus had landed heavily with Flavius' weight on top of him. Gasping for air, he rolled out from under his friend, then seized him under the arms and dragged him back, away from the open riverbank and into the protective brush.

They both stank of serpent, and Flavius was bleeding profusely. His thigh was scored deeply in several long gashes where the serpent's teeth had gripped him. He fought Marcus as Marcus tried to bind his leg firmly to stop the bleeding. Only as he tied the last knot did he realize that his friend was not fighting him, but was convulsing. The snake's bite was toxic. Flavius was going to die. He'd taken Marcus' death as his own.

A shiver shook Marcus and he came a little back to himself. He still gripped the bars of his cage. The sun and wind had dried his eyes to uselessness. He could sense there still was light; that was all. How many days had he stood here, he wondered, and how many more must he endure until death took him? His cracked lips parted, snarl or smile, he did not know. His mind shaped words his mouth could no longer form. *Flavius, you took my hero's death from me. And left me to find this one. It was no favor, my friend. No favor at all to me.*

Flavius saw him shudder. So did the rest of the crowd. Like jackals attracted to an injured beast, they fixed their eyes on him. Flavius glanced from face to face. Flared nostrils, parted lips, shining eyes. They wagged their head knowingly to one another and readied their dirty little missiles. They would see that Marcus' last moments were full of torment and mockery. With flung stones and vile words, they would claim his dog's death as a bizarre victory for themselves.

Anger swept through him, and he longed for a sword. He had no weapon, only the pole sling he'd manufactured from the stolen purse and his walking staff. Last night, he'd used it to kill a bird perched in a tree. It had been a small meal, but he'd been pleased to discover that he hadn't lost his skill. But it was a hunter's or a marksman's weapon, not something to turn against a mob.

He could turn his walking staff against them, perhaps, but there would not be the satisfaction of teaching them anything. Even if he'd had a gladius, he could not kill them all, but he could teach them the difference between tormenting a man in a cage and dying in a battle against a bared blade. Not that it would save Marcus. There would still be the rattle of stones against the iron bars of his prison and the small batterings of the ones that reached him. He would still hear their insults and mockery hurled along with the stones. His friend had stood strong all day, but now he would go down ignominiously. Flavius looked around him, sick with knowledge. He could not save Marcus.

He could not save Marcus from death. But, perhaps, he could save him from this particular death. He stooped for a stone, picked up a likely one, and retreated to the edge of the street. He'd have to work quickly. The crowd was already winging stones at Marcus. Most of them fell short, and even the missiles that struck had little power. He was satisfied to see that they fell back into the gathering crowd, striking some of the gawkers' upturned faces.

In the shelter of a doorway, he considered the stone he'd chosen. Then he groped in the knotted rag at his waist, and found the wad of wax from the stolen purse. He jabbed himself on the serpent's tooth as he took it out. The damnable thing was still sharp as ever, despite all the time it had festered inside his body.

He remembered too well the day he'd acquired it. He'd leaped, intending only to knock Marcus out of the way. He could still recall, in ghastly detail, how the serpent's jaws had closed on his leg. He'd dangled, upside down, the pain from the stabbing teeth as sharp as the toxin from the creature's mouth. Instantly, he'd felt the hot acid kiss of it and known he was poisoned. He'd been saved by the horse's harness. The serpent's teeth had passed completely through his leg; they grated on something, perhaps a buckle or bronze plate. He'd felt the snake's fury as it clenched its teeth all the tighter. And then, as teeth ground against metal, he'd felt one break.

The snake had briefly loosened its grip just as Marcus leaped for him and seized him. He'd literally been torn from the jaws of death by his friend. "Leave me!" he'd gasped, knowing that he was dying, and he'd sunk into blackness.

When next he'd found light, all had changed. His leg was tightly bandaged, his swollen flesh rippling next to the wrapping, and fever burned him. Marcus had been crouched beside him. He looked up at the leaves of an oak tree against the evening sky and smelled pine needles. So Marcus had withdrawn from the snake. Had he given up his river crossing, then? He'd blinked dully, knowing that, for him, the fight was done. Whatever became of him now was in the hands of his friend and commander. Marcus had grinned at him, a wolf's smile. "You're awake then? Good. I want you to see, my friend. If you should die this night, I want you to know that I did not suffer your enemy to outlive you."

"Sit him up," Marcus commanded someone, and, with a fine disregard for Flavius' wishes, two men did just that. He realized dizzily that he was on a slight rise scarcely worthy to be called a foothill, looking down on the river valley. They were not, then, that far away from the snake's territory. He felt queasy, and not just from the poison. Fear could do that to a man.

"What?" he managed, and with the word, felt that it was not just his leg, but his entire body that swelled with the venom.

"Give him water," Marcus directed one of the men, but he didn't even look toward Flavius. He was watching the river. Watching and waiting. "There," he breathed. "There you are. We see you now." He turned and shouted to someone behind them, "Do you mark him now? You can't miss him. He's as big as a city wall, and so shall we treat him. Take your best aim and let fly."

One of the men held water in a cup to his mouth. Flavius tried to drink. His lips, his tongue, all parts of his mouth were stupid and swollen. He wet his tongue, choked, gasped in air, gulped water, and then managed to pull his face away from the offered cup. Someone, somewhere was beating a drum, a slow thwacking noise. It made no sense. As he pulled his face away from the cup, he heard the familiar thud and then deep vibration as a ballista launched a shot. Four others followed in succession. He knew them now, knew the deep *thock-thock-thock* as the bowstring was racheted back, and then the release, followed by the deep hum of vibrating leather. They were using shot, not bolts, and the men on the rise were shouting and leaping in excitement as each missile was launched. "That's a hit!" someone shouted, and "Look at him thrash! Look at him thrash!" another replied.

Flavius forced his eyes wider and managed to focus them on the scene. Marcus had chosen to attack the snake with ballistae. The men on the weapons were working frantically, loading and cranking and adjusting each launch to target the writhing snake. Below, each heavy shot of stone either sent up a plume of brown water as it missed, or thudded harshly against the scaled back of the snake before splashing into the river. The snake was in the deep reeds, but from his vantage, Marcus could look down on him. He had glimpses of the broad scaled back and his lashing tail, but even when no part of the snake was visible, they could track him by the way he parted the reeds and sent brown tendrils of mud unfurling into the tan waters of the river.

"Can't kill him," Flavius said, but it came out as a muted mumble and no one paid him any heed. He caught only glimpses of the battle, for the men in front of him shouted and leaped and pounded one another with each successful hit on the snake. But Flavius knew snakes. He'd held them in his hands when he was a boy and knew how supple they were, how flexible their ribs. "Head," he suggested, and then, from swollen lips, he shouted at Marcus, "Head. Skull!"

Had he heard him, or had he figured it out for himself? "Aim for his head. All of you. Focus your missiles on his head! Quickly, before he finds better cover or goes back deep into the river."

His men complied, ratcheting and loading and raining a hail of rocks down on the snake below. Battered and confused, the creature turned first one way and then another, trying to elude its mysterious enemy. Its tail, Flavius saw, did not thrash so wildly as it had; perhaps one of the missiles had done some damage to its spine after all. Another hit, this one closer to the snake's wedge-shaped head, and suddenly its movements slowed and became more labored. It more twisted than thrashed now; Flavius caught a glimpse of pale belly scales as the creature rolled in agony.

And then, the hit. Flavius knew the death blow when he saw it. The rock struck the snake's head and stuck there, wedged into the animal's skull. The twitches became ever slower; undeterred, the men on the ballistae continued to rain stone after stone down on the creature. Even after it was still, they assaulted it, pelting its yielding body over and over.

"Enough!" Marcus shouted at last, long after Flavius knew the snake was dead. He turned to someone, spoke over Flavius' head. "Send two men down to be sure of it. And when they are sure it's dead, I want them to measure it."

"It's a hundred foot if it's one," someone observed.

"Closer to a hundred and twenty," someone else opined.

"No one's going to believe us," someone else laughed sourly.

Flavius saw Marcus stiffen. The poison was working in him, and his vision wavered before him. He had a glimpse of Marcus' set jaw and grim eyes. Then, as he gave in and closed his own eyes, he heard Marcus say, "They'll believe us. This is no wild tale from Africa, no braggart's boast. They'll believe because we'll send them the hide. And the head. We'll skin it out and send it back to Rome. They'll believe."

And they had. Flavius had ridden in the oxcart alongside the salted and stinking hide. The severed head, missing a number of souvenir teeth, had been at the end of the wagon. The sight and the smell of it baking under the hot African sun had sickened him almost as much as the poison and infection coursing through his body. He had leaned against the side of the wagon, his bandaged leg propped up before him and stared at it blearily. He could see the broken tooth in the snake's jaw, and knew where the rest of it was. Up against the bone in his thigh, snugged in tight. The healer had judged it safest to leave it where it was. "You'll heal up around it, never know it's there," the man had lied to Flavius. And Flavius, too sick and weary to consider the idea of letting him dig in the wound for it, had nodded and accepted the lie.

Marcus had come to bid him farewell. "You know I'd keep you by my side if I could, but it's for the best that you go home. You can tell my tale better than anyone else. And no one will doubt you when you've got both skull and hide to back you up. I'm sorry to send you home like this. But I promise that at the next muster, you'll join me again. I hope you don't think I'm breaking my promise."

They both knew to what he referred. Flavius had sighed. Even if he had told Marcus that he never wanted to go soldiering again, his friend would not have believed it. So he summoned a smile and said, "As I recall, you only promised that you'd never go to war without me. And I don't recall that I ever said I wouldn't go home without you!"

"That's true, old friend. The promise was mine, not yours. Well, travel well. And send me word of my family, and tell my boys of our deeds. I'll be home again soon enough. And next time we form up, be sure that you will march with me again."

And he *was* home again soon. That time. Flavius squeezed his eyes shut for a moment, wishing he could shut out the sounds of the crowd as well. The catcalls were getting louder. Marcus had never grasped that for Flavius, war was a duty, not a call to glory. So the next time there had been a muster, as Flavius limped forward on the leg that had never fully healed, Marcus kept his word. Flavius was once more chosen to march with him.

And he'd ended up here. An escaped slave in Carthage.

He looked at what he had fashioned from the serpent's tooth. He balanced it in his hand, considering. A pole sling worked best with a rounded stone. This missile might well tumble. The bars of the cage might deflect it. It was a stupid plan, a hopeless gesture. He looked up at his friend, and what he saw decided him.

Some flung object had struck Marcus' brow. Bright blood trickled from the split. But more than that, the setting sun cast a red light on him. His bared skin looked scarlet in the dying light. Red painted him, just as if he were riding in a chariot through Rome, riding to have his Triumph recognized. He stood upright, trembling with the effort of remaining so. His ruined eyes stared to the west.

Flavius stepped out into the street, walked determinedly to the best vantage point. He'd have one chance, and the pole sling demanded space. Marcus was visibly failing as petty stones and flung insults filled the air and his ears. Flavius considered well. Then he took a deep breath.

"Ware serpent!" he shouted.

Marcus did not turn toward him. Perhaps, his grip on the bars tightened. Perhaps not. He might never know that his friend was there to witness him die, might never know what Flavius risked in raising his voice. A few people had turned to stare at him, hearing his foreign words. He busied himself, settling his missile in his sling, testing the swing of it. He fixed his eyes and his heart on his friend. He nodded a farewell Marcus could not see. Then he launched the tooth. It flew true. He saw it strike Marcus' chest, saw it sink into his heart. Marcus jerked with the impact.

"Memento mori!" he shouted, and at those words, his friend did, for the last time, turn toward him. Then he sank, dead but never relinquishing his grip on the bars, onto the spikes that had so long awaited him. The crowd roared in triumph, but he was past hearing them. Consul Marcus Attilius

Regulus was dead, slain by a serpent. It no longer mattered that fools continued to hurl stones and offal at him. He was gone.

Flavius stood but a moment longer. A few people had marked what he had done, but they marked also that he gripped his staff tightly, and that he did not avoid their stares. They turned away from him and continued to pick up stones and hurl them at Marcus' body. Like soldiers hurling rocks at a dead serpent. Better to taunt a dead lion than a live jackal, Flavius thought to himself.

Then he turned and walked away. Home was a long way from here, but he knew he would make it. He had never promised Marcus that he wouldn't go home without him. He would. He spoke a new promise to the gathering evening. "I'll never go to war again, Marcus. Not without you."

Lawrence Block

New York Times bestseller Lawrence Block, one of the kings of the modern mystery genre, is a Grand Master of Mystery Writers of America, winner of four Edgar Awards and six Shamus Awards, and has also been the recipient of the Nero Wolfe Award, the Philip Marlowe Award, a Lifetime Achievement Award from the Private Eye Writers of America, and a Cartier Diamond Dagger for Life Achievement from the Crime Writers' Association. He's written more than fifty books and numerous short stories. Block is perhaps best known for his long-running series about alcoholic ex-cop Private Investigator Matthew Scudder, protagonist of novels such as *The Sins of the Fathers, In the Midst of Death, A Stab in the Dark,* and thirteen others, but he's also the author of the bestselling four-book series about the assassin Keller, including *Hit Man, Hit List,* and *Hit Parade,* the eight-book series about globe-trotting insomniac Evan Tanner, including *The Thief Who Couldn't Sleep* and *The Canceled Czech,* and the eleven-book series about burglar and antiquarian book dealer Bernie Rhodenbarr, including *Burglars Can't Be Choosers, The Burglar in the Closet,* and *The Burglar Who Liked to Quote Kipling.* He's also written stand-alone novels such as *Small Town, Death Pulls a Double Cross,* and sixteen others, as well as writing novels under the names Chip Harrison, Jill Emerson, and Paul Kavanagh. His many short stories have been collected in *Sometimes They Bite, Like a Lamb to Slaughter, Some Days You Get the Bear, By the Dawn's Early Light, One Night Stands, The Collected Mystery Stories, Death Wish and Other Stories,* and *Enough Rope: Collected Stories.* He's also edited twelve mystery anthologies, including *Murder on the Run, Blood on Their Hands,* and, with Otto Penzler, *The Best American Mystery Stories 2001,* and produced seven books of writing advice and nonfiction, including *Telling Lies for Fun & Profit.* His most recent books are *Hit and Run,* the new Keller novel, *One Night Stands and*

Lost Weekends, a new collection, and, as editor, the anthology *Speaking of Wrath.* He lives in New York City.

In the terse and hard-edged story that follows, he shows us that obsession can take us down some curious paths indeed . . . and lead us to some very dark destinations.

Clean Slate

There was a Starbucks just across the street from the building where he had his office, and she settled in at a window table a little before five. She thought she might be in for a long wait. In New York, young associates at law firms typically worked until midnight and took lunch and dinner at their desks. Was it the same in Toledo?

Well, the cappuccino was the same. She sipped hers, making it last, and was about to go to the counter for another when she saw him.

But was it him? He was tall and slender, wearing a dark suit and a tie, clutching a briefcase, walking with purpose. His hair when she'd known him was long and shaggy, a match for the jeans and tee shirt that were his usual costume, and now it was cut to match the suit and the briefcase. And he wore glasses now, and they gave him a serious, studious look. He hadn't worn them then, and he'd certainly never looked studious.

But it was Douglas. No question, it was him.

She rose from her chair, hit the door, quickened her pace to catch up with him at the corner. She said, "Doug? Douglas Pratter?"

He turned, and she caught the puzzlement in his eyes. She helped him out. "It's Kit," she said. "Katherine Tolliver." She smiled softly. "A voice from the past. Well, a whole person from the past, actually."

"My God," he said. "It's really you."

"I was having a cup of coffee," she said, "and looking out the window and wishing I knew somebody in this town, and when I saw you I thought you were a mirage. Or that you were just somebody who looked the way Doug Pratter might look eight years later."

"Is that how long it's been?"

"Just about. I was fifteen and I'm twenty-three now. You were two years older."

"Still am. That much hasn't changed."

"And your family picked up and moved right in the middle of your junior year of high school."

"My dad got a job he couldn't say no to. He was going to send for us at the end of the term, but my mother wouldn't hear of it. We'd all be too lonely is what she said. It took me years before I realized she just didn't trust him on his own."

"Was he not to be trusted?"

"I don't know about that, but the marriage failed two years later anyway. He went a little nuts and wound up in California. He got it in his head that he wanted to be a surfer."

"Seriously? Well, good for him, I guess."

"Not all that good for him. He drowned."

"I'm sorry."

"Who knows? Maybe that's what he wanted, whether he knew it or not. Mom's still alive and well."

"In Toledo?"

"Bowling Green."

"*That's* it. I knew you'd moved to Ohio, and I couldn't remember the city, and I didn't think it was Toledo. Bowling Green."

"I've always thought of it as a color. Lime green, forest green, and bowling green."

"Same old Doug."

"You think? I wear a suit and go to an office. Christ, I wear glasses."

"And a wedding ring." And, before he could tell her about his wife and kiddies and adorable suburban house, she said, "But you've got to get home, and I've got plans of my own. I want to catch up, though. Have you got any time tomorrow?"

It's Kit. Katherine Tolliver.

Just saying her name had taken her back in time. She hadn't been Kit or Katherine or Tolliver in years. Names were like clothes; she'd put them on and wear them for a while and then let them go. The analogy went only so far, because you could wash clothes when you'd soiled them, but there was no dry cleaner for a name that had outlived its usefulness.

Katherine "Kit" Tolliver. That wasn't the name on the ID she was carrying, or the one she'd signed on the motel register. Once she'd identified herself to Doug Pratter, she'd become the person she'd proclaimed herself to be. She was Kit again—and, at the same time, she wasn't.

Interesting, the whole business.

Back in her motel room, she surfed her way around the TV channels, then switched off the set and took a shower. Afterwards she spent a few minutes studying her nude body and wondering how it would look to him. She was a little fuller in the breasts than she'd been eight years before, a little rounder in the butt, a little closer to ripeness overall. She had always been confident of her attractiveness, but she couldn't help wondering what she might look like to those eyes that had seen her years ago.

Of course, he hadn't needed glasses back in the day.

She had read somewhere that a man who has once had a particular woman somehow assumes he can have her again. She didn't know how true this might be, but it seemed to her that something similar applied to women. A woman who had once been with a particular man was ordained to doubt her ability to attract him a second time. And so she felt a little of that uncertainty, but willed herself to dismiss it.

He was married, and might well be in love with his wife. He was busy establishing himself in his profession, and settling into an orderly exis-tence. Why would he want a meaningless fling with an old girlfriend, who'd had to say her name before he could even place her?

She smiled. *Lunch*, he'd said. *We'll have lunch tomorrow.*

Funny how it started.

She was at a table with six or seven others, a mix of men and women in their twenties. And one of the men mentioned a woman she didn't know, though she seemed to be known to most if not all of the others. And one of the women said, "That slut."

And the next thing she knew, the putative slut was forgotten while the whole table turned to the question of just what constituted sluttiness. Was it a matter of attitude? Of specific behavior? Was one born to slutdom, or was the status acquired?

Was it solely a female province? Could you have male sluts?

That got nipped in the bud. "A man can take sex too casually," one of the men asserted, "and he can consequently be an asshole, and deserving of a certain measure of contempt. But as far as I'm concerned, the word *slut* is gender-linked. Nobody with a Y chromosome can qualify as a genuine slut."

And, finally, was there a numerical cutoff? Could an equation be drawn up? Did a certain number of partners within a certain number of years make one a slut?

"Suppose," one woman suggested, "suppose once a month you go out after work and have a couple—"

"A couple of men?"

"A couple of drinks, you idiot, and you start flirting, and one thing leads to another, and you drag somebody home with you."

"Once a month?"

"It could happen."

"So that's twelve men in a year."

"When you put it that way," the woman allowed, "it seems like a lot."

"It's also a hundred and twenty partners in ten years."

"Except you wouldn't keep it up for that long, because sooner or later one of those hookups would take."

"And you'd get married and live happily ever after?"

"Or at least live together more or less monogamously for a year or two, which would cut down on the frequency of hookups, wouldn't it?"

Throughout all of this, she barely said a word. Why bother? The conversation buzzed along quite well without her, and she was free to sit back and listen, and to wonder just what place she occupied in what someone had already labeled "the saint–slut continuum."

"With cats," one of the men said, "it's nice and clear-cut."

"Cats can be sluts?"

He shook his head. "With women and cats. A woman has one cat, or even two or three cats, she's an animal lover. Four or more cats, and she's a demented cat lady."

"That's how it works?"

"That's exactly how it works. With sluts, it looks to be more complicated."

Another thing that complicated it, someone said, was if the woman in question had a significant other, whether husband or boyfriend. If she didn't, and she hooked up half a dozen times a year, well, she certainly wasn't a slut.

If she was married and still fit in that many hookups on the side, well, that changed things, didn't it?

"Let's get personal," one of the men said to one of the women. "How many partners have you had?"

"Me?"

"Well?"

"You mean in the past year?"

"Or lifetime. You decide."

"If I'm going to answer a question like that," she said, "I think we definitely need another round of drinks."

The drinks came, and the conversation slid into a game of truth, though it seemed to Jennifer—these people knew her as Jennifer, which had lately become her default name—it seemed to her that the actual veracity of the responses was moot.

And then it was her turn.

"Well, Jen? How many?"

Would she ever see any of these people again? Probably not. So it scarcely mattered what she said.

And what she said was, "Well, it depends. How do you decide what counts?"

"What do you mean? Like blow jobs don't count?"

"That's what Clinton said, remember?"

"As far as I'm concerned, blow jobs count."

"And hand jobs?"

"They don't count," one man said, and there seemed to be general agreement on that point. "Not that there's anything wrong with them," he added.

"So what's your criterion here, exactly? Something has to be inside of something?"

"As far as the nature of the act," one man said, "I think it has to be subjective. It counts if you think it counts. So, Jen? What's your count?"

"Suppose you passed out, and you know something happened, but you don't remember any of it?"

"Same answer. It counts if you think it counts."

The conversation kept going, but she was detached from it now, thinking, remembering, working it out in her mind. How many men, if gathered around a table or a campfire, could compare notes and tell each other about her? That, she thought, was the real criterion, not what part of her anatomy had been in contact with what portion of his. Who could tell stories? Who could bear witness?

And, when the table quieted down again, she said, "Five."

"Five? That's all? Just five?"

"Five."

She had arranged to meet Douglas Pratter at noon in the lobby of a downtown hotel not far from his office. She arrived early and sat where she could watch the entrance. He was five minutes early himself, and she saw him stop to remove his glasses, polishing their lenses with a breast-pocket handkerchief. Then he put them on again and stood there, his eyes scanning the room.

She got to her feet, and now he caught sight of her, and she saw him smile. He'd always had a winning smile, optimistic and confident. Years ago, it had been one of the things she liked most about him.

She walked to meet him. Yesterday she'd been wearing a dark gray pantsuit; today she'd paired the jacket with a matching skirt. The effect was still business attire, but softer, more feminine. More accessible.

"I hope you don't mind a ride," he told her. "There are places we could walk to, but they're crowded and noisy and no place to have a conversation. Plus they rush you, and I don't want to be in a hurry. Unless you've got an early afternoon appointment?"

She shook her head. "I had a full morning," she said, "and there's a cocktail party this evening that I'm supposed to go to, but until then I'm free as the breeze."

"Then we can take our time. We've probably got a lot to talk about."

As they crossed the lobby, she took his arm.

The fellow's name was Lucas. She'd taken note of him early on, and his eyes had shown a certain degree of interest in her, but his interest mounted when she told the group how many sexual partners she'd had. It was he who'd said, "Five? That's all? Just five?" When she'd confirmed her count, his eyes grabbed hers and held on.

And now he'd taken her to another bar, a nice quiet place where they could really get to know each other. Just the two of them.

The lighting was soft, the décor soothing. A pianist played show tunes unobtrusively, and a waitress with an indeterminate accent took their order and brought their drinks. They touched glasses, sipped, and he said, "Five."

"That really did it for you," she said. "What, is it your lucky number?"

"Actually," he said, "my lucky number is six."

"I see."

"You were never married."

"No."

"Never lived with anybody."

"Only my parents."

"You don't still live with them?"

"No."

"You live alone?"

"I have a roommate."

"A woman, you mean."

"Right."

"Uh, the two of you aren't . . ."

"We have separate beds," she said, "in separate rooms, and we live separate lives."

"Right. Were you ever, uh, in a convent or anything?"

She gave him a look.

"Because you're remarkably attractive, you walk into a room and you light it up, and I can imagine the number of guys who must hit on you on a daily basis. And you're how old? Twenty-one, twenty-two?"

"Twenty-three."

"And you've only been with five guys? What, were you a late bloomer?"

"I wouldn't say so."

"I'm sorry, I'm pressing and I shouldn't. It's just that, well, I can't help being fascinated. But the last thing I want is to make you uncomfortable."

The conversation wasn't making her uncomfortable. It was merely boring her. Was there any reason to prolong it? Was there any reason not to cut to the chase?

She'd already slipped one foot out of its shoe, and now she raised it and rested it on his lap, massaging his groin with the ball of her foot. The expression on his face was worth the price of admission all by itself.

"My turn to ask questions," she said. "Do you live with your parents?"

"You're kidding, right? Of course not."

"Do you have a roommate?"

"Not since college, and that was a while ago."

"So," she said. "What are we waiting for?"

The restaurant Doug had chosen was on Detroit Avenue, just north of I-75. Walking across the parking lot, she noted a motel two doors down and another across the street.

Inside, it was dark and quiet, and the décor reminded her of the cocktail lounge where Lucas had taken her. She had a sudden memory of her foot in his lap, and the expression on his face. Further memories followed, but she let them glide on by. The present moment was a nice one, and she wanted to live in it while it was at hand.

She asked for a dry Rob Roy, and Doug hesitated, then ordered the same for himself. The cuisine on offer was Italian, and he started to order the scampi, then caught himself and selected a small steak instead. Scampi, she thought, was full of garlic, and he wanted to make sure he didn't have it on his breath.

The conversation started in the present, but she quickly steered it back to the past, where it properly belonged. "You always wanted to be a lawyer," she remembered.

"Right, I was going to be a criminal lawyer, a courtroom whiz. The defender of the innocent. So here I am doing corporate work, and if I ever see the inside of a courtroom, that means I've done something wrong."

"I guess it's hard to make a living with a criminal practice."

"You can do okay," he said, "but you spend your life with the scum of the earth, and you do everything you can to keep them from getting what they damn well deserve. Of course I didn't know any of that when I was seventeen and starry-eyed over *To Kill a Mockingbird.*"

"You were my first boyfriend."

"You were my first real girlfriend."

She thought, Oh? And how many unreal ones were there? And what made her real by comparison? Because she'd slept with him?

Had he been a virgin the first time they had sex? She hadn't given the matter much thought at the time, and had been too intent upon her own role in the proceedings to be aware of his experience or lack thereof. It hadn't really mattered then, and she couldn't see that it mattered now.

And, she'd just told him, he'd been her first boyfriend. No need to qualify that; he'd truly been her first boyfriend, real or otherwise.

But she hadn't been a virgin. She'd crossed that barrier two years earlier, a month or so after her thirteenth birthday, and had had sex in one form or another perhaps a hundred times before she hooked up with Doug.

Not with a boyfriend, however. I mean, your father couldn't be your boyfriend, could he?

Lucas lived alone in a large L-shaped studio apartment on the top floor of a new building. "I'm the first tenant the place has ever had," he told her. "I've never lived in something brand-spanking-new before. It's like I've taken the apartment's virginity."

"Now you can take mine."

"Not quite. But this is better. Remember, I told you my lucky number."

"Six."

"There you go."

And just when, she wondered, had six become his lucky number? When she'd acknowledged five partners? Probably, but never mind. It was a good-enough line, and one he was no doubt feeling proud of right about now, because it had worked, hadn't it?

As if he'd had any chance of failing . . .

He made drinks, and they kissed, and she was pleased but not surprised to note that the requisite chemistry was there. And, keeping it company, there was that delicious surge of anticipatory excitement that was always present on such occasions. It was at once sexual and nonsexual, and she felt it even when the chemistry was not present, even when the sexual act was destined to be perfunctory at best, and at worst distasteful. Even then she'd feel that rush, that urgent excitement, but it was greatly increased when she knew the sex was going to be good.

He excused himself and went to the bathroom, and she opened her purse and found the little unlabeled vial she kept in the change compartment. She looked at it and at the drink he'd left on the table, but in the end she left the vial in her purse, left his drink untouched.

As it turned out, it wouldn't have mattered. When he emerged from the bathroom he reached not for his drink but for her instead, and it was as good as she'd known it would be, inventive and eager and passionate, and finally they fell away from each other, spent and sated.

"Wow," he said.

"That's the right word for it."

"You think? It's the best I can come up with, and yet it somehow seems inadequate. You're—"

"What?"

"Amazing. I have to say this, I can't help it. It's almost impossible to believe you've had so little experience."

"Because I'm clearly jaded?"

"No, just because you're so good at it. And in a way that's the complete opposite of jaded. I swear to God this is the last time I'll ask you, but were you telling the truth? Have you really only been with five men?"

She nodded.

"Well," he said, "now it's six, isn't it?"

"Your lucky number, right?"

"Luckier than ever," he said.

"Lucky for me, too."

She was glad she hadn't put anything in his drink, because after a brief rest they made love again, and that wouldn't have happened otherwise.

"Still six," he told her afterwards, "unless you figure I ought to get extra credit."

She said something, her voice soft and soothing, and he said something, and that went on until he stopped responding. She lay beside him, in that familiar but ever-new combination of afterglow and anticipation, and then finally she slipped out of bed, and a little while later she let herself out of his apartment.

All by herself in the descending elevator, she said out loud, "Five."

A second round of Rob Roys arrived before their entrées. Then the waiter brought her fish and his steak, along with a glass of red wine for him and white for her. She'd had only half of her second Rob Roy, and she barely touched her wine.

"So you're in New York," he said. "You went there straight from college?"

She brought him up to date, keeping the responses vague for fear of contradicting herself. The story she told was all fabrication; she'd never even been to college, and her job résumé was a spotty mélange of waitressing and office temp work. She didn't have a career, and she worked only when she had to.

If she needed money—and she didn't need much, she didn't live high— well, there were other ways to get it beside work.

But today she was Connie Corporate, with a job history to match her clothes, and yes, she'd gone to Penn State and then tacked on a Wharton MBA, and ever since she'd been in New York, and she couldn't really talk about what had brought her to Toledo, or even on whose behalf she was traveling, because it was all hush–hush for the time being, and she was sworn to secrecy.

"Not that there's a really big deal to be secretive about," she said, "but, you know, I try to do what they tell me."

"Like a good little soldier."

"Exactly," she said, and beamed across the table at him.

"You're my little soldier," her father had told her. "A trooper, a little warrior."

In the accounts she sometimes found herself reading, the father (or the stepfather, or the uncle, or the mother's boyfriend, or even the next-door neighbor) was a drunk and a brute, a bloody-minded savage, forcing himself upon the child who was his helpless and unwilling partner. She would get angry, reading those case histories. She would hate the male responsible for the incest, would sympathize with the young female victim, and her blood would surge in her veins with the desire to even the score, to exact a cruel but just vengeance. Her mind supplied scenarios—castration, mutilation, disembowelment—all of them brutal and heartless, all richly deserved.

But her own experience was quite unlike what she read.

Some of her earliest memories were of sitting on her father's lap, his hands touching her, patting her, petting her. Sometimes he was with her at bath time, making sure she soaped and rinsed herself thoroughly. Sometimes he tucked her in at night, and sat by the side of the bed stroking her hair until she fell asleep.

Was his touch ever inappropriate? Looking back, she thought that it probably was, but she'd never been aware of it at the time. She knew that she loved her daddy and he loved her, and that there was a bond between them that excluded her mother. But it never consciously occurred to her that there was anything wrong about it.

Then, when she was thirteen, when her body had begun to change, there was a night when he came to her bed and slipped beneath the covers. And he held her and touched her and kissed her.

The holding and touching and kissing were different that night, and she recognized it as such immediately, and somehow knew that it would be a secret, that she could never tell anybody. And yet no enormous barriers were crossed that night. He was very gentle with her, always gentle, and his seduction of her was infinitely gradual. She had since read how the Plains Indians took wild horses and domesticated them, not by breaking their spirit but by slowly, slowly, winning them over, and the description resonated with her immediately, because that was precisely how her father had turned her from a child who sat so innocently on his lap into an eager and spirited sexual partner.

He never broke her spirit. What he did was awaken it.

He came to her every night for months, and by the time he took her virginity she had long since lost her innocence, because he had schooled her quite thoroughly in the sexual arts. There was no pain on the night he led her across the last divide. She had been well prepared, and was entirely ready.

Away from her bed, they were the same as they'd always been.

"Nothing can show," he'd explained. "No one would understand the way you and I love each other. So we must not let them know. If your mother knew—"

He hadn't needed to finish that sentence.

"Someday," he'd told her, "you and I will get in the car, and we'll drive to some city where no one knows us. We'll both be older then, and the difference in our ages won't be that remarkable, especially when we've tacked on a few years to you and shaved them off of me. And we'll live together, and we'll get married, and no one will be the wiser."

She tried to imagine that. Sometimes it seemed like something that could actually happen, something that would indeed come about in the course of time. And other times it seemed like a story an adult might tell a child, right up there with Santa Claus and the Tooth Fairy.

"But for now," he'd said more than once, "for now we have to be warriors. You're my little soldier, aren't you? Aren't you?"

"I get to New York now and then," Doug Pratter said.

"I suppose you and your wife fly in," she said. "Stay at a nice hotel, see a couple of shows."

"She doesn't like to fly."

"Well, who does? What they make you go through these days, all in the name of security. And it just keeps getting worse, doesn't it? First they started giving you plastic utensils with your in-flight meal, because there's nothing as dangerous as a terrorist with a metal fork. Then they stopped giving you a meal altogether, so you couldn't complain about the plastic utensils."

"It's pretty bad, isn't it? But it's a short flight. I don't mind it that much. I just open up a book, and the next thing I know I'm in New York."

"By yourself."

"On business," he said. "Not that frequently, but every once in a while. Actually, I could get there more often, if I had a reason to go."

"Oh?"

"But lately I've been turning down chances," he said, his eyes avoiding hers now. "Because, see, when my business is done for the day I don't know what to do with myself. It would be different if I knew anybody there, but I don't."

"You know me," she said.

"That's right," he agreed, his eyes finding hers again. "That's right. I do, don't I?"

Over the years, she'd read a lot about incest. She didn't think her interest was compulsive, or morbidly obsessive, and in fact it seemed to her as if it would be more pathological if she were not interested in reading about it.

One case imprinted itself strongly upon her. A man had three daughters, and he had sexual relations with two of them. He was not the artful Daughter Whisperer that her own father had been, but a good deal closer to the Drunken Brute end of the spectrum. A widower, he told the two older daughters that it was their duty to take their mother's place. They felt it was wrong, but they also felt it was something they had to do, and so they did it.

And, predictably enough, they were both psychologically scarred by the experience. Almost every incest victim seemed to be, one way or the other.

But it was their younger sister who wound up being the most damaged of the three. Because Daddy never touched her, she figured there was something wrong with her. Was she ugly? Was she insufficiently feminine? Was there something disgusting about her?

Jeepers, what was the matter with her, anyway? Why didn't he want her?

After the dishes were cleared, Doug suggested a brandy. "I don't think so," she said. "I don't usually drink this much early in the day."

"Actually, neither do I. I guess there's something about the occasion that feels like a celebration."

"I know what you mean."

"Some coffee? Because I'm in no hurry for this to end."

She agreed that coffee sounded like a good idea. And it was pretty good coffee, and a fitting conclusion to a pretty good meal. Better than a person might expect to find on the outskirts of Toledo.

How did he know the place? Did he come here with his wife? She somehow doubted it. Had he brought other women here? She doubted that as well. Maybe it was something he'd picked up at the office water cooler. *"So I took her to this Eye-tie place on Detroit Avenue, and then we just popped into the Comfort Inn down the block, and I mean to tell you that girl was good to go."*

Something like that.

"I don't want to go back to the office," he was saying. "All these years, and then you walk back into my life, and I'm not ready for you to walk out of it again."

You were the one who walked, she thought. Clear to Bowling Green.

But what she said was, "We could go to my hotel room, but a downtown hotel right in the middle of the city—"

"Actually," he said, "there's a nice place right across the street."

"Oh?"

"A Holiday Inn, actually."

"Do you think they'd have a room at this hour?"

He managed to look embarrassed and pleased with himself, all at the same time. "As a matter of fact," he said, "I have a reservation."

She was four months shy of her eighteenth birthday when everything changed.

What she came to realize, although she hadn't been consciously aware of it at the time, was that things had already been changing for some time. Her father came a little less frequently to her bed, sometimes telling her he was tired from a hard day's work, sometimes explaining that he had to stay up late with work he'd brought home, sometimes not bothering with an explanation of any sort.

Then one afternoon he invited her to go for a ride. Sometimes rides in the family car would end at a motel, and she thought that was what he planned on this occasion. In anticipation, no sooner had he backed the car out of the driveway than she'd dropped her hand into his lap, stroking him, awaiting his response.

He pushed her hand away.

She wondered why, but didn't say anything, and he didn't say anything either, not for ten minutes of suburban streets. Then abruptly he pulled into a strip mall, parked opposite a shuttered bowling alley, and said, "You're my little soldier, aren't you?"

She nodded.

"And that's what you'll always be. But we have to stop. You're a grown woman, you have to be able to lead your own life, I can't go on like this. . . ."

She scarcely listened. The words washed over her like a stream, a babbling stream, and what came through to her was not so much the words he spoke but what seemed to underlie those words: *I don't want you anymore.*

After he'd stopped talking, and after she'd waited long enough to know he wasn't going to say anything else, and because she knew he was awaiting her response, she said, "Okay."

"I love you, you know."

"I know."

"You've never said anything to anyone, have you?"

"No."

"Of course you haven't. You're a warrior, and I've always known I could count on you."

On the way back, he asked her if she'd like to stop for ice cream. She just shook her head, and he drove the rest of the way home.

She got out of the car and went up to her room. She sprawled on her bed, turning the pages of a book without registering their contents. After a few minutes she stopped trying to read and sat up, her eyes focused on a spot on one wall where the wallpaper was misaligned.

She found herself thinking of Doug, her first real boyfriend. She'd never told her father about Doug; of course he knew that they were spending time together, but she'd kept their intimacy a secret. And of course she'd never said a word about what she and her father had been doing, not to Doug or to anybody else.

The two relationships were worlds apart in her mind. But now they had something in common, because they had both ended. Doug's family had moved to Ohio, and their exchange of letters had trickled out. And her father didn't want to have sex with her anymore.

Something really bad was going to happen. She just knew it.

A few days later, she went to her friend Rosemary's house after school. Rosemary, who lived just a few blocks away on Covington, had three brothers and two sisters, and anybody who was still there at dinnertime was always invited to stay.

She accepted gratefully. She could have gone home, but she just didn't want to, and she still didn't want to a few hours later. "I wish I could just stay here overnight," she told Rosemary. "My parents are acting weird."

"Hang on, I'll ask my mom."

She had to call home and get permission. "No one's answering," she said. "Maybe they went out. If you want, I'll go home."

"You'll stay right here," Rosemary's mother said. "You'll call right before bedtime, and if there's still no answer, well, if they're not home, they won't miss you, will they?"

Rosemary had twin beds, and fell asleep instantly in her own. Kit, a few feet away, had this thought that Rosemary's father would let himself into the room, and into her bed, but of course this didn't happen, and the next thing she knew she was asleep.

In the morning she went home, and the first thing she did was call Rosemary's house, hysterical. Rosemary's mother calmed her down, and then she was able to call 911 to report the deaths of her parents. Rosemary's mother came over to be with her, and shortly after that the police came, and it became pretty clear what had happened. Her father had killed her mother and then turned the gun on himself.

"You sensed that something was wrong," Rosemary's mother said. "That's why it was so easy to get you to stay for dinner, and why you wanted to sleep over."

"They were fighting," she said, "and there was something different about it. Not just a normal argument. God, it's my fault, isn't it? I should have been able to do something. The least I could have done was to say something."

Everybody told her that was nonsense.

After she'd left Lucas's brand-new high-floor apartment, she returned to her own older less-imposing sublet, where she brewed a pot of coffee and sat up at the kitchen table with a pad and paper. She wrote down the numbers one through five in descending order, and after each she wrote a name, or as much of the name as she knew. Sometimes she added an identifying phrase or two. The list began with 5, and the first entry read as follows:

Said his name was Sid. Pasty complexion, gap between top incisors. Met in Philadelphia at bar on Race Street (?), went to his hotel, don't remember name of it. Gone when I woke up.

Hmmm. Sid might be hard to find. How would she even know where to start looking for him?

At the bottom of the list, her entry was simpler and more specific. *Douglas Pratter. Last known address Bowling Green. Lawyer? Google him?*

She booted up her laptop.

Their room in the Detroit Avenue Holiday Inn was on the third floor in the rear. With the drapes drawn and the door locked, with their clothes hastily discarded and the bedclothes as hastily tossed aside, it seemed to her for at least a few minutes that she was fifteen years old again, and in bed with her first boyfriend. She tasted a familiar sweetness in his kisses, a familiar raw urgency in his ardor.

But the illusion didn't last. And then it was just lovemaking, at which each of them had a commendable proficiency. He went down on her this time, which was something he'd never done when they were teenage sweethearts, and the first thought that came to her was that he had turned into her father, because her father had done that all the time.

Afterwards, after a fairly long shared silence, he said, "I can't tell you how many times I've wondered."

"What it would be like to be together again?"

"Well, sure, but more than that. What life would have been like if I'd never moved away in the first place. What would have become of the two of us, if we'd had the chance to let things find their way."

"Probably the same as most high school lovers. We'd have stayed together for a while, and then we'd have broken up and gone separate ways."

"Maybe."

"Or I'd have gotten pregnant, and you'd have married me, and we'd be divorced by now."

"Maybe."

"Or we'd still be together, and bored to death with each other, and you'd be in a motel fucking somebody new."

"God, how'd you get so cynical?"

"You're right, I got off on the wrong foot there. How about this? If your father hadn't moved you all to Bowling Green, you and I would have stayed together, and our feeling for each other would have grown from teenage hormonal infatuation to the profound mature love it was always destined to be. You'd have gone off to college, and as soon as I finished high school I'd have enrolled there myself, and when you finished law school I'd have my undergraduate degree, and I'd be your secretary and office manager when you set up your own law practice. By then we'd have gotten married, and by now we'd have one child with a second on the way, and we would remain unwavering in our love for one another, and as passionate as ever." She gazed wide-eyed at him. "Better?"

His expression was hard to read, and he appeared to be on the point of saying something, but she turned toward him and ran a hand over his flank, and the prospect of a further adventure in adultery trumped whatever he might have wanted to say. Whatever it was, she thought, it would keep.

"I'd better get going," he said, and rose from the bed, and rummaged through the clothes he'd tossed on the chair.

She said, "Doug? Don't you think you might want to take a shower first?"

"Oh, Jesus. Yeah, I guess I better, huh?"

He'd known where to take her to lunch, knew to make a room reservation ahead of time, but he evidently didn't know enough to shower away her spoor before returning to home and hearth. So perhaps this sort of adventure was not the usual thing for him. Oh, she was fairly certain he tried to get lucky on business trips—those oh-so-lonely New York visits he'd mentioned, for instance—but you didn't have to shower after that sort of interlude, because you were going back to your own hotel room, not to your unsuspecting wife.

She started to get dressed. There was no one waiting for her, and her own shower could wait until she was back at her own motel. But she changed her mind about dressing, and was still naked when he emerged from the shower, a towel wrapped around his middle.

"Here," she said, handing him a glass of water. "Drink this."

"What is it?"

"Water."

"I'm not thirsty."

"Just drink it, will you?"

He shrugged, drank it. He went and picked up his undershorts, and kept losing his balance when he tried stepping into them. She took his arm and led him over to the bed, and he sat down and told her he didn't feel so good. She took the undershorts away from him and got him to lie down on the bed, and she watched him struggling to keep a grip on consciousness.

She put a pillow over his face, and she sat on it. She felt him trying to move beneath her, and she watched his hands make feeble clawing motions at the bedsheet, and observed the muscles working in his lower legs. Then he was still, and she stayed where she was for a few minutes, and an involuntary tremor, a very subtle one, went through her hindquarters.

And what was that, pray tell? Could have been her coming, could have been him going. Hard to tell, and did it really matter?

When she got up, well, duh, he was dead. No surprise there. She put her clothes on, cleaned up all traces of her presence, and transferred all the cash from his wallet to her purse. A few hundred dollars in tens and twenties, plus an emergency hundred-dollar bill tucked away behind his driver's license. She might have missed it, but she'd learned years ago that you had to give a man's wallet a thorough search.

Not that the money was ever the point. But they couldn't take it with them and it had to go somewhere—so it might as well go to her. Right?

How it happened: That final morning, shortly after she left for school, her father and mother had argued, and her father had gone for the handgun he kept in a locked desk drawer and shot her mother dead. He left the house and went to his office, saying nothing to anyone, although a coworker did say that he'd seemed troubled. And sometime during the afternoon he returned home, where his wife's body remained undiscovered. The gun was still there (unless he'd been carrying it around with him during the intervening hours) and he put the barrel in his mouth and blew his brains out.

Except that wasn't really how it happened; it was how the police figured it out. What did in fact happen, of course, is that she shot her mother before she left for school, and called her father on his cell as soon as she got home from school, summoning him on account of an unspecified emergency. He came right home, and by then she would have liked to change her mind, but how could she with her mother dead in the next room? So she shot him and arranged the evidence appropriately, and then she went over to Rosemary's.

Di dah di dah di dah.

You could see Doug's car from the motel room window. He'd parked in the back and they'd come up the back stairs, never going anywhere near the front desk. So no one had seen her, and no one saw her now as she went to his car, unlocked it with his key, and drove it downtown.

She'd have preferred to leave it there, but her own rental was parked near the Crowne Plaza, so she had to get downtown to reclaim it. You couldn't stand on the corner and hail a cab, not in Toledo, and she didn't want to call one. So she drove to within a few blocks of the lot where she'd stowed her Honda, parked his Volvo at an expired meter, and used the hankie with which he'd cleaned his glasses to wipe away any fingerprints she might have left behind.

She redeemed her car and headed for her own motel. Halfway there, she realized she had no real need to go there. She'd packed that morning and left no traces of herself in her room. She hadn't checked out, electing to keep her options open, so she could go there now with no problem, but for what? Just to take a shower?

She sniffed herself. She could use a shower, no question, but she wasn't so rank that people would draw away from her. And she kind of liked the faint trace of his smell coming off her flesh.

And the sooner she got to the airport, the sooner she'd be out of Toledo.

She managed to catch a 4:18 flight that was scheduled to stop in Cincinnati on its way to Denver. She'd stay in Denver for a while, until she decided where she wanted to go next.

She hadn't had a reservation, or even a set destination, and she took the flight because it was there to be taken. The leg from Toledo to Cincinnati was more than half-empty, and she had a row of seats to herself, but she was stuck in a middle seat from Cincinnati to Denver, wedged between a fat lady who looked to be scared stiff of something, possibly the flight itself, and a man who tapped away at his laptop and invaded her space with his elbows.

Not the most pleasant travel experience she'd ever had, but nothing she couldn't live through. She closed her eyes, let her thoughts turn inward.

After her parents were buried and the estate settled, after she'd finished the high school year and collected her diploma, after a Realtor had listed her house and, after commission and closing costs, netted her a few thousand over and above the outstanding first and second mortgages, she'd stuffed what she could into one of her father's suitcases and boarded a bus.

She'd never gone back. And, until her brief but gratifying reunion with Douglas Pratter, Esq., she'd never been Katherine Tolliver again.

On the tram to Baggage Claim, a businessman from Wichita told her how much simpler it had been getting in and out of Denver before they built Denver International Airport. "Not that Stapleton was all that wonderful," he said, "but it was a quick, cheap cab ride from the Brown Palace. It wasn't stuck out in the middle of a few thousand square miles of prairie."

It was funny he should mention the Brown, she said, because that's where she was staying. So of course he suggested she share his cab, and when they reached the hotel and she offered to pay half, well, he wouldn't hear of it. "My company pays," he said, "and if you really want to thank me, why don't you let the old firm buy you dinner?"

Tempting, but she begged off, said she'd eaten a big lunch, said all she wanted to do was get to sleep. "If you change your mind," he said, "just ring my room. If I'm not there, you'll find me in the bar."

She didn't have a reservation, but they had a room for her, and she sank into an armchair with a glass of water from the tap. The Brown Palace had its own artesian well, and took great pride in its water, so how could she turn it down?

"Just drink it," she'd told Doug, and he'd done what she told him. It was funny, people usually did.

"Five," she'd told Lucas, who'd been so eager to be number six. But he'd managed it for only a matter of minutes, because the list was composed of men who could sit around that mythical table and tell each other how they'd had her, and you had to be alive to do that. So Lucas had dropped off the list when she'd chosen a knife from his kitchen and slipped it right between his ribs and into his heart. He fell off her list without even opening his eyes.

After her parents died, she didn't sleep with anyone until she'd graduated and left home for good. Then she got a waitress job, and the manager took her out drinking after work one night, got her drunk, and performed something that might have been date rape; she didn't remember it that clearly, so it was hard to say.

When she saw him at work the next night he gave her a wink and a pat on the behind, and something came into her mind, and that night she got him to take her for a ride and park on the golf course, where she took him by surprise and beat his brains out with a tire iron.

There, she'd thought, Now it was as if the rape—if that's what it was, and did it really matter what it was? Whatever it was, it was as if it had never happened.

A week or so later, in another city, she quite deliberately picked up a man in a bar, went home with him, had sex with him, killed him, robbed him, and left him there. And that set the pattern.

Four times the pattern had been broken, and those four men had joined Doug Pratter on her list. Two of them, Sid from Philadelphia and Peter from Wall Street, had escaped because she drank too much. Sid was gone when she woke up. Peter was there, and in the mood for morning sex, after which she'd laced his bottle of vodka with the little crystals she'd meant to put in his drink the night before. She'd gone away from there wondering who'd drink the vodka. Peter? The next girl he managed to drag home? Both of them?

She thought she'd read about it in the papers, sooner or later, but if there'd been a story it escaped her attention, so she didn't really know whether Peter deserved a place on her list.

It wouldn't be hard to find out, and if he was still on the list, well, she could deal with it. It would be a lot harder to find Sid, because all she knew about him was his first name, and that might well have been improvised for the occasion. And she'd met him in Philadelphia, but he was already registered at a hotel, so that meant he was probably from someplace other than Philadelphia, and that meant the only place she knew to look was the one place where she could be fairly certain he didn't live.

She knew the first and last names of the two other men on her list. Graham Weider was a Chicagoan she'd met in New York; he'd taken her to lunch and to bed, then jumped up and hurried her out of there, claiming an urgent appointment and arranging to meet her later. But he'd never turned up, and the desk at his hotel told her he'd checked out.

So he was lucky, and Alan Reckson was lucky in another way. He was an infantry corporal on leave before they shipped him off to Iraq, and if she'd realized that she wouldn't have picked him up in the first place, and she wasn't sure what kept her from doing to him as she did to the other men who entered her life. Pity? Patriotism? Both seemed unlikely, and when she thought about it later she decided it was simply because he was a soldier. That gave them something in common, because weren't they both warriors? Wasn't she her father's little soldier?

Maybe he'd been killed over there. She supposed she could find out. And then she could decide what she wanted to do about it.

Graham Weider, though, couldn't claim combatant status, unless you considered him a corporate warrior. And while his name might not be unique, neither was it by any means common. And it was almost certainly his real name, too, because they'd known it at the front desk. Graham Weider, from Chicago. It would be easy enough to find him, when she got around to it.

Of them all, Sid would be the real challenge. She sat there going over what little she knew about him and how she might go about playing detective. Then she treated herself to another half glass of Brown Palace water and flavored it with a miniature of Johnnie Walker from the minibar. She sat down with the drink and shook her head, amused by her own behavior. She was dawdling, postponing her shower, as if she couldn't bear to wash away the traces of Doug's lovemaking.

But she was tired, and she certainly didn't want to wake up the next morning with his smell still on her. She undressed and stood for a long time in the shower, and when she got out of it, she stood for a moment alongside the tub and watched the water go down the drain.

Four, she thought. Why, before you knew it, she'd be a virgin all over again.

Tad Williams

Tad Williams became an international bestseller with his very first novel, *Tailchaser's Song,* and the high quality of his output and the devotion of his readers have kept him on the top of the charts ever since as a *New York Times* and *London Sunday Times* bestseller. His other novels include *The Dragonbone Chair, Stone of Farewell, To Green Angel Tower, City of Golden Shadow, River of Blue Fire, Mountain of Black Glass, Sea of Silver Light, Caliban's Hour, Child of an Ancient City* (with Nina Kiriki Hoffman), *Tad Williams' Mirrorworld: An Illustrated Novel, The War of the Flowers, Shadowmarch,* and a collection of two novellas, one by Williams and one by Raymond E. Feist, *The Wood Boy/The Burning Man.* As editor, he has produced the big retrospective anthology *A Treasury of Fantasy.* His most recent book is a collection, *Rite: Short Work.* In addition to his novels, Williams writes comic books and film and television scripts, and is cofounder of an interactive television company. He lives with his family in Woodsie, California.

And Ministers of Grace

The seed whispers, sings, offers, instructs.

A wise man of the homeworld once said, "Human beings can alter their lives by altering their attitudes of mind." Everything is possible for a committed man or woman. The universe is in our reach.

Visit the Orgasmium—now open 24 hours. We take Senior Credits. The Orgasmium—where YOU *come first!*

Your body temperature is normal. Your stress levels are normal, tending toward higher than normal. If this trend continues, you are recommended to see a physician.

I'm almost alive! And I'm your perfect companion—I'm entirely portable. I want to love you. Come try me. Trade my personality with friends. Join the fun!

Comb properties now available. Consult your local environment node. Brand new multifamily and single-family dwellings, low down payment with government entry loans! . . .

Commodity prices are up slightly on the Sackler Index at this hour, despite a morning of sluggish trading. The Prime Minister will detail her plans to reinvigorate the economy in her speech to Parliament. . . .

A wise woman of the homeworld once said, "Keep your face to the sunshine and you cannot see the shadow."

His name is Lamentation Kane and he is a Guardian of Covenant—a holy assassin. His masters have placed a seed of blasphemy in his head. It itches like unredeemed sin and fills his skull with foul pagan noise.

The faces of his fellow travelers on the landing shuttle are bored and vacuous. How can these infidels live with this constant murmur in their heads? How can they survive and stay sane with the constant pinpoint flashing of attention signals at the edge of vision, the raw, sharp pulse of a world bristling and burbling with information?

It is like being stuck in a hive of insects, Kane thinks—insects doing their best to imitate human existence without understanding it. He longs for the sweet, singular voice of Spirit, soothing as cool water on inflamed skin. Always before, no matter the terrors of his mission, that voice has been with him, soothing him, reminding him of his holy purpose. All his life, Spirit has been with him. All his life until now.

Humble yourselves therefore under the strong hand of God, so that He may raise you up in due time.

Sweet and gentle like spring rain. Unlike this unending drizzle of filth, each word Spirit has ever spoken has been precious, bright like silver.

Cast all your burdens on Him, for He cares for you. Be in control of yourself and alert. Your enemy, the devil, prowls around like a roaring lion, looking for someone to devour.

Those were the last words Spirit spoke to him before the military scientists silenced the Word of God and replaced it with the endless, godless prattle of the infidel world, Archimedes.

For the good of all mankind, they assured him: Lamentation Kane must sin again so that one day all men would be free to worship God. Besides, the elders pointed out, what was there for him to fear? If he succeeds and escapes Archimedes, the pagan seed will be removed and Spirit will speak in his thoughts again. If he does not escape—well, Kane will hear the true voice of God at the foot of His mighty throne. *Well done, my good and faithful servant. . . .*

Beginning descent. Please return to pods, the pagan voices chirp in his head, prickling like nettles. *Thank you for traveling with us. Put all food and packaging in the receptacle and close it. This is your last chance to purchase duty-free drugs and alcohol. Cabin temperature is twenty degrees centigrade. Pull the harness snug. Beginning descent. Cabin pressure stable. Lander will detach in twenty seconds. Ten seconds. Nine seconds. Eight seconds . . .*

It never ends, and each godless word burns, prickles, itches.

Who needs to know so much about nothing?

A child of one of the Christian cooperative farms on Covenant's flat and empty plains, he was brought to New Jerusalem as a candidate for the elite

Guardian unit. When he saw for the first time the white towers and golden domes of his planet's greatest city, Kane had been certain that Heaven would look just that way. Now, as Hellas City rises up to meet him, capital of great Archimedes and stronghold of his people's enemies, it is bigger than even his grandest, most exaggerated memories of New Jerusalem—an immense sprawl with no visible ending, a lumpy white and gray and green patchwork of complex structures and orderly parks and lacy polyceramic web skyscrapers that bend gently in the cloudy upper skies like an oceanic kelp forest. The scale is astounding. For the first time ever in his life, Lamentation Kane has a moment of doubt—not in the rightness of his cause, but in the certainty of its victory.

But he reminds himself of what the Lord told Joshua: *Behold I have given into thy hands Jericho, and the king thereof, and all the valiant men. . . .*

Have you had a Creemy Crunch today? It blares through his thoughts like a Klaxon. *You want it! You need it! Available at any food outlet. Creemy Crunch makes cream crunchy! Don't be a bitch, Mom! Snag me a CC—or three!*

The devil owns the Kingdom of Earth. A favorite saying of one of his favorite teachers. *But even from his high throne, he cannot see the City of Heaven.*

Now with a subdermal glow-tattoo in every package! Just squeeze it in under the skin—and start shining!

Lord Jesus, protect me in this dark place and give me strength to do your work once more, Kane prays. *I serve You. I serve Covenant.*

It never stops, and only gets more strident after the lander touches down and they are ushered through the locks into the port complex. *Remember the wise words, air quality is in the low thirties on the Teng Fuo scale today, first-time visitors to Archimedes go here, returning go there*, where to stand, what to say, what to have ready. Restaurants, news feeds, information for transportation services, overnight accommodations, immigration law, emergency services, yammer yammer yammer until Kane wants to scream. He stares at the smug citizens of Archimedes around him and loathes every one of them. How can they walk and smile and talk to each other with this Babel in their heads, without God in their hearts?

Left. Follow the green tiles. Left. Follow the green tiles. They aren't even people, they can't be—just crude imitations. And the variety of voices with which the seed bedevils him! High-pitched, low-pitched, fast and persuasive, moderately slow and persuasive, adult voices, children's voices, accents of a dozen sorts, most of which he can't even identify and can barely understand. His blessed Spirit is one voice and one voice only, and he longs for her desperately. He always thinks of Spirit as "her," although it could just as easily be the calm, sweet voice of a male child. It doesn't matter. Nothing so crass as earthly sexual distinctions matter, any more than with God's holy angels. Spirit has been his constant companion since childhood, his advisor, his inseparable friend. But now he has a pagan seed in his brain and he may never hear her blessed voice again.

I will never leave thee, or forsake thee. That's what Spirit told him the night he was baptized, the night she first spoke to him. Six years old. *I will never leave thee, or forsake thee.*

He cannot think of that. He will not think of anything that might undermine his courage for the mission, of course, but there is a greater danger: some types of thoughts, if strong enough, can trigger the port's security E-Grams, which can perceive certain telltale patterns, especially if they are repeated.

A wise man of the homeworld once said, "Man is the measure of all things. . . ." The foreign seed doesn't want him thinking of anything else, anyway.

Have you considered living in Holyoake Harbor? another voice asks, cutting through the first. *Only a twenty-minute commute to the business district, but a different world of ease and comfort.*

. . . And of things which are not, that they are not, the first voice finishes, swimming back to the top. *Another wise fellow made the case more directly: "The world holds two classes of men—intelligent men without religion, and religious men without intelligence."*

Kane almost shivers despite the climate controls. *Blur your thoughts*, he reminds himself. He does his best to let the chatter of voices and the swirl of passing faces numb and stupefy him, making himself a beast instead of a man, the better to hide from God's enemies.

He passes the various mechanical sentries and the first two human guard posts as easily as he hoped he would—his military brethren have prepared his disguise well. He is in line at the final human checkpoint when he catches a glimpse of her, or at least he thinks it must be her—a small brown-skinned woman sagging between two heavily armored port security guards who clutch her elbows in a parody of assistance. For a moment their eyes meet and her dark stare is frank before she hangs her head again in a convincing imitation of shame. The words from the briefing wash up in his head through the fog of Archimedean voices—*Martyrdom Sister*—but he does his best to blur them again just as quickly. He can't imagine any word that will set off the E-Grams so quickly as *martyrdom*.

The final guard post is more difficult, as it is meant to be. The sentry, almost faceless behind an array of enhanced light scanners and lenses, does not like to see Arjuna on Kane's itinerary, his last port of call before Archimedes. Arjuna is not a treaty world for either Archimedes or Covenant, although both hope to make it so, and is not officially policed by either side.

The official runs one of his scanners over Kane's itinerary again. "Can you tell me why you stopped on Arjuna, Citizen McNally?"

Kane repeats the story of staying there with his cousin who works in the mining industry. Arjuna is rich with platinum and other minerals, another reason both sides want it. At the moment, though, neither the Rationalists of Archimedes nor the Abramites of Covenant can get any traction there: the majority of Arjuna's settlers, colonists originally from the homeworld's Indian subcontinent, are comfortable with both sides—a fact that makes both Archimedes and Covenant quite uncomfortable indeed.

The guard post official doesn't seem entirely happy with Lamentation Kane's explanation and is beginning to investigate the false personality a little more closely. Kane wonders how much longer until the window of distraction is opened. He turns casually, looking up and down the transparent U-glass cells along the far wall until he locates the one in which the brown-skinned woman is being questioned. Is she a Muslim? A Copt? Or perhaps something entirely different—there are Australian Aboriginal Jews on Covenant, remnants of the Lost Tribes movement back on the homeworld. But whoever or whatever she is doesn't matter, he reminds himself: she is a sister in God and she has volunteered to sacrifice herself for the sake of the mission—*his* mission.

She turns for a moment, and their eyes meet again through the warping glass. She has acne scars on her cheeks but she's pretty, surprisingly young to be given such a task. He wonders what her name is. When he returns—if he returns—he will go to the Great Tabernacle in New Jerusalem and light a candle for her.

Brown eyes. She seems sad as she looks at him before turning back to the guards. Could that be true? The Martyrs are the most privileged of all during their time in the training center. And she must know she will be looking on the face of God Himself very soon. How can she not be joyful? Does she fear the pain of giving up her earthly body?

As the sentry in front of him seems to stare out at nothing, reading the information that marches across his vision, Lamentation Kane opens his mouth to say something—to make small talk the way a real returning citizen of Archimedes would after a long time abroad, a citizen guilty of nothing worse than maybe having watched a few religious broadcasts on Arjuna—when he sees movement out of the corner of his eye. Inside the U-glass holding cell, the young brown-skinned woman lifts her arms. One of the armored guards lurches back from the table, half-falling; the other reaches out his gloved hand as though to restrain her, but his face has the hopeless slack expression of a man who sees his own death. A moment later, bluish flames run up her arms, blackening the sleeves of her loose dress, and then she vanishes in a flare of magnesium white light.

People are shrieking and diving away from the glass wall, which is now spiderwebbed with cracks. The light burns and flickers, and the insides of the walls blacken with a crust of what Kane guesses must be human fat turning to ash.

A human explosion—nanobiotic thermal flare—that partially failed. That will be their conclusion. But of course, the architects of Kane's mission didn't want an actual explosion. They want a distraction.

The sentry in the guardpost polarizes the windows and locks up his booth. Before hurrying off to help the emergency personnel fight the blaze that is already leaking clouds of black smoke into the concourse, he thrusts Kane's itinerary into his hand and waves him through, then locks off the transit point.

Lamentation Kane would be happy to move on, even if he were the innocent traveler he pretends to be. The smoke is terrible, with the disturbing, sweet smell of cooked meat.

What had her last expression been like? It is hard to remember anything except those endlessly deep, dark eyes. Had that been a little smile or is he trying to convince himself? And if it had been fear, why should that be surprising? Even the saints must have feared to burn to death.

Yea, though I walk through the valley of the shadow of death, I will fear no evil. . . .

Welcome back to Hellas, Citizen McNally! a voice in his head proclaims, and then the other voices swim up beneath it, a crowd, a buzz, an itch.

He does his best not to stare as the cab hurtles across the metroscape, but he cannot help being impressed by the sheer size of Archimedes' first city. It is one thing to be told how many millions live there and to try to understand that it is several times the size of New Jerusalem, but another entirely to see the hordes of people crowding the sidewalks and skyways. Covenant's population is mostly dispersed on pastoral settlements like the one on which Kane was raised, agrarian cooperatives that, as his teachers explained to him, keep God's children close to the earth that nurtures them. Sometimes it is hard to realize that the deep, reddish soil he had spent his childhood digging and turning and nurturing was not the same soil as the Bible described. Once he even asked a teacher why if God made Earth, the People of the Book had left it behind.

"God made all the worlds to be earth for His children," the woman explained. "Just as he made all the lands of the old Earth, then gave them to different folk to have for their homes. But he always kept the sweetest lands, the lands of milk and honey, for the children of Abraham, and that's why when we left earth, he gave us Covenant."

As he thinks about it now, Kane feels a surge of warmth and loneliness commingled. It's true that the hardest thing to do for love is to give up the beloved. At this moment he misses Covenant so badly, it is all he can do not to cry out. It is astounding in one as experienced as himself. *God's warriors don't sigh*, he tells himself sternly. *They make others sigh instead. They bring lamentation to God's enemies. Lamentation.*

He exits the cab some distance from the safe house and walks the rest of the way, floating in smells both familiar and exotic. He rounds the neighborhood twice to make sure he is not followed, then enters the flatblock, takes the slow but quiet elevator up to the eighteenth floor, and lets himself in with the key code. It looks like any other Covenant safe house on any of the other colony worlds, cupboards well stocked with nourishment and medical supplies, little in the way of furniture but a bed and a single chair and a small table. These are not places of rest and relaxation; these are way stations on the road to Jericho.

It is time for him to change.

Kane fills the bathtub with water. He finds the chemical ice, activates a dozen packs and tosses them in. Then he goes to the kitchen and locates the necessary mineral and chemical supplements. He pours enough water into the mixture to make himself a thick, bitter milk shake and drinks it down while he waits for the water in the tub to cool. When the temperature has dropped far enough, he strips naked and climbs in.

"You see, Kane," one of the military scientists had explained, "we've reached a point where we can't smuggle even a small hand-weapon onto Archimedes, let alone something useful, and they regulate their own citizens' possession of weapons so thoroughly that we cannot chance trying to obtain one there. So we have gone another direction. We have created Guardians—human weapons. That is what you are, praise the Lord. It started in your childhood. That's why you've always been different from your peers—faster, stronger, smarter. But we've come to the limit of what we can do with genetics and training. We need to give you what you need to make yourself into the true instrument of God's justice. May He bless this and all our endeavors in His name. Amen."

"Amen," the Spirit in his head told him. "You are now going to fall asleep."

"Amen," said Lamentation Kane.

And then they gave him the first injection.

When he woke up that first time he was sore, but nowhere near so sore as he was the first time he activated the nanobiotes or "notes" as the scientists liked to call them. When the notes went to work, it was like a terrible sunburn on the outside and the inside both, and like being pounded with a roundball bat for at least an hour, and like lying in the road while a good-sized squadron of full-dress Holy Warriors marched over him.

In other words, it hurt.

Now, in the safe house, he closes his eyes, turns down the babble of the Archimedes seed as far as it will let him, and begins to work.

It is easier now than it used to be, certainly easier than that terrible first time when he was so clumsy that he almost tore his own muscles loose from tendon and bone.

He doesn't just *flex*, he thinks about where the muscles are that would flex if he wanted to flex them, then how he would just begin to move them if he were going to move them extremely slowly, and with that first thought comes the little tug of the cells unraveling their connections and reknitting in different, more useful configurations, slow as a plant reaching toward the sun. Even with all this delicacy his temperature rises and his muscles spasm and cramp, but not like the first time. That was like being born—no, like being judged and found wanting, as though the very meat of his earthly body were trying to tear itself free, as though devils pierced his joints with hot iron pitchforks. Agony.

Had the sister felt something like this at the end? Was there any way to open the door to God's house without terrible, holy pain? She had brown eyes. He thinks they were sad. Had she been frightened? Why would Jesus let her be frightened, when even He had cried out on the cross?

I praise You, Lord, Lamentation Kane tells the pain. *This is Your way of reminding me to pay attention. I am Your servant, and I am proud to put on Your holy armor.*

It takes him at least two hours to finish changing at the best of times. Tonight, with the fatigue of his journey and long entry process and the curiously troubling effect of the woman's martyrdom tugging at his thoughts, it takes him over three.

Kane gets out of the tub shivering, most of the heat dispersed and his skin almost blue-white with cold. Before wrapping the towel around himself he looks at the results of all his work. It's hard to see any differences except for a certain broadness to his chest that was not there before, but he runs his fingers along the hard shell of his stomach and the sheath of gristle that now protects his windpipe and is satisfied. The thickening beneath the skin will not stop high-speed projectiles from close up, but they should help shed the energy of any more distant shot and will allow him to take a bullet or two from nearer and still manage to do his job. Trellises of springy cartilage strengthen his ankles and wrists. His muscles are augmented, his lungs and circulation improved mightily. He is a Guardian, and with every movement he can feel the holy modifications that have been given to him. Beneath the appearance of normality he is strong as Goliath, scaly and supple as a serpent.

He is starving, of course. The cupboards are full of powdered nutritional supplement drinks. He adds water and ice from the kitchen unit, mixes the first one up and downs it in a long swallow. He drinks five before he begins to feel full.

Kane props himself up on the bed—things are still sliding and grinding a little inside him, the last work of change just finishing—and turns the wall on. The images jump into life and the seed in his head speaks for them. He wills his way past sports and fashion and drama, all the unimportant gibberish with which these creatures fill their empty hours, until he finds a stream of current events. Because it is Archimedes, hive of Rationalist pagans, even the news is corrupted with filth, gossip and whoremongering, but he manages to squint his way through the offending material to find a report on what the New Hellas authorities are calling a failed terrorist explosion at the port. A picture of the Martyrdom Sister flashes onto the screen—taken from her travel documents, obviously, anything personal in her face well hidden by her training—but seeing her again gives him a strange jolt, as though the notes that tune his body have suddenly begun one last forgotten operation.

Nefise Erim, they call her. Not her real name, that's almost certain, any more than Keenan McNally is his. *Outcast*, that's her true name. *Scorned*—that could be her name too, as it could be his. Scorned by the unbelievers, scorned by the smug, faithless creatures who like Christ's ancient tormentors fear the Word of God so much, they try to ban Him from their lives, from their entire planet! But God can't be banned, not so long as one human heart remains alive to His voice. As long as the Covenant system survives, Kane knows, God will wield his mighty sword and the unbelievers will learn real fear.

Oh, please, Lord, grant that I may serve you well. Give us victory over our enemies. Help us to punish those who would deny You.

And just as he lifts this silent prayer, he sees *her* face on the screen. Not his sister in martyrdom, with her wide, deep eyes and dark skin. No, it is her—the devil's mistress, Keeta Januari, Prime Minister of Archimedes.

His target.

Januari is herself rather dark skinned, he cannot help noticing. It is disconcerting. He has seen her before, of course, her image replayed before him dozens upon dozens of times, but this is the first time he has noticed a shade to her skin that is darker than any mere suntan, a hint of something else in her background beside the pale Scandinavian forebears so obvious in her bone structure. It is as if the martyred sister Nefise has somehow suffused everything, even his target. Or is it that the dead woman has somehow crept into his thoughts so deeply that he is witnessing her everywhere?

If you can see it, you can eat it! He has mostly learned to ignore the horrifying chatter in his head, but sometimes it still reaches up and slaps his thoughts away. *Barnstorm Buffet! We don't care if they have to roll you out the door afterwards—you'll get your money's worth!*

It doesn't matter what he sees in the Prime Minister, or thinks he sees. A shade lighter or darker means nothing. If the devil's work out here among the stars has a face, it is the handsome, narrow-chinned visage of Keeta Januari, leader of the Rationalists. And if God ever wanted someone dead, she is that person.

She won't be his first: Kane has sent eighteen souls to judgment already. Eleven of them were pagan spies or dangerous rabble-rousers on Covenant. One of those was the leader of a cryptorationalist cult in the Crescent—the death was a favor to the Islamic partners in Covenant's ruling coalition, Kane found out later. Politics. He doesn't know how he feels about that, although he knows the late Dr. Hamoud was a doubter and a liar and had been corrupting good Muslims. Still . . . politics.

Five were infiltrators among the Holy Warriors of Covenant, his people's army. Most of these had half-expected to be discovered, and several of them had resisted desperately.

The last two were a politician and his wife on the unaffiliated world of Arjuna, important Rationalist sympathizers. At his masters' bidding, Kane made it look like a robbery gone wrong instead of an assassination: this was not the time to make the Lord's hand obvious in Arjuna's affairs. Still, there were rumors and accusations across Arjuna's public networks. The gossipers and speculators had even given the unknown murderer a nickname—the Angel of Death.

Dr. Prishrahan and his wife had fought him. Neither of them had wanted to die. Kane had let them resist even though he could have killed them both in a moment. It gave credence to the robbery scenario. But he hadn't enjoyed it. Neither had the Prishrahans, of course.

He will avenge the blood of His servants, and will render vengeance to His adversaries, Spirit reminded him when he had finished with the doctor and his wife, and he understood. Kane's duty is not to judge. He is not one of the flock, but closer to the wolves he destroys. Lamentation Kane is God's executioner.

———

He is now cold enough from his long submersion that he puts on clothes. He is still tender in his joints as well. He goes out onto the balcony, high in the canyons of flatblocks pinpricked with illuminated windows, thousands upon thousands of squares of light. The immensity of the place still unnerves him a little. It's strange to think that what is happening behind one little lighted window in this expanse of sparkling urban night is going to rock this massive world to its foundations.

It is hard to remember the prayers as he should. Ordinarily Spirit is there with the words before he has a moment to feel lonely. *"I will not leave you comfortless: I will come to you."*

But he does not feel comforted at this moment. He is alone.

"Looking for love?" The voice in his head whispers this time, throaty and exciting. A bright twinkle of coordinates flicker at the edge of his vision. *"I'm looking for you . . . and you can have me for almost nothing. . . ."*

He closes his eyes tight against the immensity of the pagan city.

Fear thou not; for I am with thee: be not dismayed; for I am thy God.

He walks to the auditorium just to see the place where the Prime Minister will speak. He does not approach very closely. It looms against the grid of light, a vast rectangle like an axe head smashed into the central plaza of Hellas City. He does not linger.

As he slides through the crowds, it is hard not to look at the people around him as though he has already accomplished his task. What would they think if they knew who he was? Would they shrink back from the terror of the Lord God's wrath? Or would a deed of such power and piety speak to them even through their fears?

I am ablaze with the light of the Lord, he wants to tell them. *I have let God make me His instrument—I am full of glory!* But he says nothing, of course, only walks amid the multitudes with his heart grown silent and turned inward.

Kane eats in a restaurant. The food is so overspiced as to be tasteless, and he yearns for the simple meals of the farm on which he was raised. Even military manna is better than this! The customers twitter and laugh just like the Archimedes seed in their heads, as if it is that babbling obscenity that has programmed them instead of the other way around. How these people surrounded themselves with distraction and glare and noise to obscure the emptiness of their souls!

He goes to a place where women dance. It is strange to watch them, because they smile and smile and they are all as beautiful and naked as a dark dream, but they seem to him like damned souls, doomed to act out this empty farce of love and attraction throughout eternity. He cannot get the thought of martyred Nefise Erim out of his head. At last he chooses one of the women—she does not look much like the martyred one, but she is darker than the others—and lets her lead him to her room behind the place where they dance. She feels the hardened tissues beneath his skin and tells him he is very muscular. He empties himself inside her and then, afterwards, she asks him why he is crying. He tells her she is mistaken. When she asks again, he slaps her. Although he holds back his strength, he still knocks her off the bed. The room adds a small surcharge to his bill.

He lets her go back to her work. She is an innocent, of sorts: she has been listening to the godless voices in her head all her life and knows nothing else. No wonder she dances like a damned thing.

Kane is soiled now as he walks the streets again, but his great deed will wipe the taint from him as it always does. He is a Guardian of Covenant, and soon he will be annealed by holy fire.

His masters want the deed done while the crowd is gathered to see the Prime Minister, and so the question seems simple: Before or after? He thinks at first that he will do it when she arrives, as she steps from the car and is hurried into the corridor leading to the great hall. That seems safest. After she has spoken it will be much more difficult, with her security fully deployed and the hall's own security acting with them. Still, the more he thinks about it, the more he feels sure that it must be inside the hall. Only a few thousand would be gathered there to see her speak, but millions more will be watching on the screens surrounding the massive building. If he strikes quickly his deed will be witnessed by this whole world—and other worlds, too.

Surely God wants it that way. Surely He wants the unbeliever destroyed in full view of the public waiting to be instructed.

Kane does not have time or resources to counterfeit permission to be in the building—the politicians and hall security will be checked and rechecked, and will be in place long before Prime Minister Januari arrives. Which means that the only people allowed to enter without going through careful screening will be the Prime Minister's own party. That is a possibility, but he will need help with it.

Making contact with local assets is usually a bad sign—it means something has gone wrong with the original plan—but Kane knows that with a task this important he cannot afford to be superstitious. He leaves a signal in the established place. The local assets come to the safe house after sunset. When he opens the door, he finds two men, one young and one old, both disconcertingly ordinary-looking, the kind of men who might come to tow your car or fumigate your flat. The middle-aged one introduces himself as Heinrich Sartorius, his companion just as Carl. Sartorius motions Kane not to speak while Carl sweeps the room with a small object about the size of a toothbrush.

"Clear," the youth announces. He is bony and homely, but he moves with a certain grace, especially while using his hands.

"Praise the Lord," Sartorius says. "And blessings on you, brother. What can we do to help you with Christ's work?"

"Are you really the one from Arjuna?" young Carl askes suddenly.

"Quiet, boy. This is serious." Sartorius turns back to Kane with an expectant look on his face. "He's a good lad. It's just—that meant a lot to the community, what happened there on Arjuna."

Kane ignores this. He is wary of the Death Angel nonsense. "I need to know what the Prime Minister's security detail wears. Details. And I want the layout of the auditorium, with a focus on air and water ducts."

The older man frowns. "They'll have that all checked out, won't they?"

"I'm sure. Can you get it for me without attracting attention?"

"Course." Sartorius nods. "Carl'll find it for you right now. He's a whiz. Ain't that right, boy?" The man turns back to Kane. "We're not backward, you know. The unbelievers always say it's because we're backward, but Carl here was up near the top of his class in mathematics. We just kept Jesus in our hearts when the rest of these people gave Him up, that's the difference."

"Praise Him," says Carl, already working the safe house wall, images flooding past so quickly that even with his augmented vision Kane can barely make out a tenth of them.

"Yes, *praise* Him," Sartorius agrees, nodding his head as though there has been a long and occasionally heated discussion about how best to deal with Jesus.

Kane is beginning to feel the ache in his joints again, which usually means he needs more protein. He heads for the small kitchen to fix himself another nutrition drink. "Can I get you two anything?" he asks.

"We're good," says the older man. "Just happy doing the Lord's work."

They make too much noise, he decides. Not that most people would have heard them, but Kane isn't most people.

I am the sword of the Lord, he tells himself silently. He can scarcely hear himself think it over the murmur of the Archimedes seed, which although turned down low is still spouting meteorological information, news, tags of philosophy and other trivia like a madman on a street corner. Below the spot where Kane hangs, the three men of the go-suited security detail communicate among themselves with hand signs as they investigate the place he has entered the building. He has altered the evidence of his incursion to look like someone has tried and failed to get into the auditorium through the intake duct.

The guards seem to draw the desired conclusion: after another flurry of hand signals, and presumably after relaying the all clear to the other half of the security squad, who are doubtless inspecting the outside of the same intake duct, the three turn and begin to walk back up the steep conduit, the flow of air making their movements unstable, headlamps splashing unpredictably over the walls. But Kane is waiting above them like a spider, in the shadows of a high place where the massive conduit bends around one of the building's pillars, his hardened fingertips dug into the concrete, his augmented muscles tensed and locked. He waits until all three pass below him then drops down silently behind them and crushes the throat of the last man so he can't alert the others. He then snaps the guard's neck and tosses the body over his shoulder, then scrambles back up the walls into the place he has prepared, a hammock of canvas much the same color as the inside of the duct. In a matter of seconds he strips the body, praying fervently that the other two will not have noticed that their comrade is missing. He pulls on the man's go-suit, which is still warm, then leaves the guard's body in the hammock and springs down to the ground just as the second guard realizes there is no one behind him.

As the man turns toward him, Kane sees his lips moving behind the face shield and knows the guard must be talking to him by seed. The imposture is broken, or will be in a moment. Can he pretend his own communications machinery is malfunctioning? Not if these guards are any good. If they work for the Prime Minister of Archimedes, they probably are. He has a moment before the news is broadcast to all the other security people in the building.

Kane strides forward, making nonsensical hand signs. The other guard's eyes widen: he does not recognize either the signs or the face behind the polymer shield. Kane shatters the man's neck with a two-handed strike even as the guard struggles to pull his sidearm. Then Kane leaps at the last guard just as he turns.

Except it isn't a he. It's a woman and she's fast. She actually has her gun out of the holster before he kills her.

He has only moments, he knows: the guards will have a regular check-in to their squad leader. He sprints for the side shaft that should take him to the area above the ceiling of the main hall.

Women as leaders. Women as soldiers. Women dancing naked in public before strangers. Is there anything these Archimedeans will not do to debase the daughters of Eve? Force them all into whoredom, as the Babylonians did?

The massive space above the ceiling is full of riggers and technicians and heavily armed guards. A dozen of those, at least. Most of them are sharpshooters keeping an eye on the crowd through the scopes on their high-powered guns, which is lucky. Some of them might not even see him until he's on his way down.

Two of the heavily armored troopers turn as he steps out into the open. He is being queried for identification, but even if they think he is one of their own, they will not let him get more than a few yards across the floor. He throws his hands in the air and takes a few casual steps toward them, shaking his head and pointing at his helmet. Then he leaps forward, praying they do not understand how quickly he can move.

He covers the twenty yards or so in just a little more than a second. To confound their surprise, he does not attack but dives past the two who have already seen him and the third just turning to find out what the conversation is about. He reaches the edge and launches himself out into space, tucked and spinning to make himself a more difficult target. Still, he feels a high-speed projectile hit his leg and penetrate a little way, slowed by the guard's go-suit and stopped by his own hardened flesh.

He lands so hard that the stolen guard helmet pops off his head and bounces away. The first screams and shouts of surprise are beginning to rise from the crowd of parliamentarians but Kane can hardly hear them. The shock of his fifty-foot fall swirls through the enhanced cartilage of his knees and ankles and wrists, painful but manageable. His heart is beating so fast it almost buzzes, and he is so accelerated that the noise of the audience seemed like the sound of something completely inhuman, the deep scrape of a gla-cier, the tectonic rumbling of a mountain's roots. Two more bullets snap into the floor beside him, chips of concrete and fragments of carpet spinning slowly in the air, hovering like ashes in a fiery updraft. The woman at the lectern turns toward him in molasses-time, and it is indeed her, Keeta Januari, the Whore of Babylon. As he reaches toward her he can see the in-dividual muscles of her face react—eyebrows pulled up, forehead wrinkling, surprised . . . but not frightened.

How can that be?

He is already leaping toward her, curving the fingers of each hand into hardened claws for the killing strike. A fraction of a second to cross the space between them as bullets snap by from above and either side, the noise scything past a long instant later, *wow, wow, wow.* Time hanging, disconnected from history. God's hand. He *is* God's hand, and this is what it must feel like to be in the presence of God Himself, this shimmering, endless, bright NOW. . . .

And then pain explodes through him and sets his nerves on fire and everything goes suddenly and irrevocably

black.

Lamentation Kane wakes in a white room, the light from everywhere and nowhere. He is being watched, of course. Soon the torture will begin.

"Beloved, think it not strange concerning the fiery trial which is to try you, as though some strange thing happened unto you. . . ." Those were the holy words Spirit whispered to him when he lay badly wounded in the hospital after capturing the last of the Holy Warrior infiltrators, another augmented soldier

like himself, a bigger, stronger man who almost killed him before Kane managed to put a stiffened finger through his eyeball into his brain. Spirit recited the words to him again and again during his recuperation: "*But rejoice, inasmuch as ye are partakers of Christ's sufferings; that, when his glory . . . when his glory . . .*"

To his horror, he cannot remember the rest of the passage from Peter.

He cannot help thinking of the martyred young woman who gave her life so that he could fail so utterly. He will see her soon. Will he be able to meet her eye? Is there shame in Heaven?

I will be strong, Kane promises her shade, *no matter what they do to me.*

One of the cell's walls turns from white to transparent. The room beyond is full of people, most of them in military uniforms or white medical smocks. Only two wear civilian clothing, a pale man and . . . her. Keeta Januari.

"You may throw yourself against the glass if you want." Her voice seems to come out of the air on all sides. "It is very, very thick and very, very strong."

He only stares. He will not make himself a beast, struggling to escape while they laugh. These people are the ones who think themselves related to animals. Animals! Kane knows that the Lord God has given his people dominion.

"Over all the beasts and fowls of the earth," he says out loud.

"So," says Prime Minister Januari. "So, this is the Angel of Death."

"That is not my name."

"We know your name, Kane. We have been watching you since you reached Archimedes."

A lie, surely. They would never have let him get so close.

She narrows her eyes. "I would have expected an angel to look more . . . angelic."

"I'm no angel, as you almost found out."

"Ah, if you're not, then you must be one of the ministers of grace." She sees the look on his face. "How sad. I forgot that Shakespeare was banned by your mullahs. 'Angels and ministers of grace defend us!' From *Macbeth.* It precedes a murder."

"We Christians do not have mullahs," he says as evenly as he can. He does not care about the rest of the nonsense she speaks. "Those are the people of the Crescent, our brothers of the Book."

She laughed. "I thought you would be smarter than the rest of your sort, Kane, but you parrot the same nonsense. Do you know that only a few generations back your 'brothers' as you call them set off a thermonuclear device, trying to kill your grandparents and the rest of the Christian and Zionist 'brothers'?"

"In the early days, before the Covenant, there was confusion." Everyone knew the story. Did she think to shame him with old history, ancient quotations, banned playwrights from the wicked old days of Earth? If so, then both of them had underestimated each other as adversaries.

Of course, at the moment she did hold a somewhat better position.

"So, then, not an angel but a minister. But you don't pray to be protected from death, but to be able to cause it."

"I do the Lord's will."

"Bullshit, to use a venerable old term. You are a murderer many times over, Kane. You tried to murder me." But Januari does not look at him as though at an enemy. Nor is there kindness in her gaze, either. She looks at him as though he is a poisonous insect in a jar—an object to be careful with, yes, but mostly a thing to be studied. "What shall we do with you?"

"Kill me. If you have any of the humanity you claim, you will release me and send me to Heaven. But I know you will torture me."

She raises an eyebrow. "Why would we do that?"

"For information. Our nations are at war, even though the politicians have not yet admitted it to their peoples. You know it, woman. I know it. Everyone in this room knows it."

Keeta Januari smiles. "You will get no argument from me or anyone here about the state of affairs between Archimedes and the Covenant system. But why would we torture you for information we already have? We are not barbarians. We are not primitives—like some others. We do not force our citizens to worship savage old myths—"

"You force them to be silent! You punish those who would worship the God of their fathers. You have persecuted the People of the Book wherever you have found them!"

"We have kept our planet free from the mania of religious warfare and extremism. We have never interfered in the choices of Covenant."

"You have tried to keep us from gaining converts."

The Prime Minister shakes her head. "Gaining converts? Trying to hijack entire cultures, you mean. Stealing the right of colonies to be free of

Earth's old tribal ghosts. We are the same people that let your predecessors worship the way they wished to—we fought to protect their freedom, and were repaid when they tried to force their beliefs on us at gunpoint." Her laugh is harsh. "'Christian tolerance'—two words that do not belong together no matter how often they've been coupled. And we all know what your Islamist and Zionist brothers are like. Even if you destroy all of the Archimedean alliance and every single one of us unbelievers, you'll only find yourself fighting your allies instead. The madness won't stop until the last living psychopath winds up all alone on a hill of ashes, shouting praise to his god."

Kane feels his anger rising and closes his mouth. He suffuses his blood with calming chemicals. It confuses him, arguing with her. She is a woman and she should give comfort, but she is speaking only lies—cruel, dangerous lies. This is what happens when the natural order of things is upset. "You are a devil. I will speak to you no more. Do whatever it is you're going to do."

"Here's another bit of Shakespeare," she says. "If your masters hadn't banned him, you could have quoted it at me. '*But man, proud man,/dressed in a little brief authority,/most ignorant of what he's most assured*'—that's nicely put, isn't it?—'*His glassy essence, like an angry ape,/plays such fantastic tricks before high heaven/as make the angels weep.*'" She puts her hands together in a gesture disturbingly reminiscent of prayer. He cannot turn away from her gaze. "So—what *are* we going to do with you? We could execute you quietly, of course. A polite fiction—died from injuries sustained in the arrest—and no one would make too much fuss."

The man behind her clears his throat. "Madame Prime Minster, I respectfully suggest we take this conversation elsewhere. The doctors are waiting to see the prisoner—"

"Shut up, Healy." She turns to look at Kane again, really look, her blue eyes sharp as scalpels. She is older than the Martyrdom Sister by a good twenty years, and despite the dark tint, her skin is much paler, but somehow, for a dizzying second, they are the same.

Why do you allow me to become confused, Lord, between the murderer and the martyr?

"Kane comma Lamentation," she says. "Quite a name. Is that your enemies lamenting, or is it you, crying out helplessly before the power of your

God?" She holds up her hand. "Don't bother to answer. In parts of the Covenant system you're a hero, you know—a sort of superhero. Were you aware of that? Or have you been traveling too much?"

He does his best to ignore her. He knows he will be lied to, manipulated, that the psychological torments will be more subtle and more important than the physical torture. The only thing he does not understand is this: Why her—why the prime minister herself? Surely he isn't so important. The fact that she stands in front of him at this moment instead of in front of God is, after all, a demonstration that he is a failure.

As if in answer to this thought, a voice murmurs in the back of his skull, *"Arjuna's Angel of Death captured in attempt on PM Januari."* Another inquires, *"Have you smelled yourself lately? Even members of Parliament can lose freshness—just ask one!"* Even here, in the heart of the beast, the voices in his head will not be silenced.

"We need to study you," the Prime Minister says at last. "We haven't caught a Guardian-class agent before—not one of the new ones, like you. We didn't know if we could do it—the scrambler field was only recently developed." She smiles again, a quick icy flash like a first glimpse of snow in high mountains. "It wouldn't have meant anything if you'd succeeded, you know. There are at least a dozen more in my party who can take my place and keep this system safe against you and your masters. But I made good bait—and you leaped into the trap. Now we're going to find out what makes you such a nasty instrument, little Death Angel."

He hopes now that the charade is over they will at least shut off the seed in his head. Instead, they leave it in place but disable his controls so that he can't affect it at all. Children's voices sing to him about the value of starting each day with a healthy breakfast, and he grinds his teeth. The mad chorus yammers and sings to him nonstop. The pagan seed shows him pictures he does not want to see, gives him information about which he does not care, and always, always, it denies that Kane's God exists.

The Archimedeans claim they have no death penalty. Is this what they do instead? Drive their prisoners to suicide?

If so, he will not do their work for them. He has internal resources they cannot disable without killing him, and he was prepared to survive torture of a more obvious sort—why not this? He dilutes the waves of despair that wash through him at night when the lights go out and he is alone with the idiot babble of their idiot planet.

No, Kane will not do their job for him. He will not murder himself. But it gives him an idea.

If he had done it in his cell, they might have been more suspicious, but when his heart stops in the course of a rather invasive procedure to learn how the note biotech has grown into his nervous system, they are caught by surprise.

"It must be a fail-safe!" one of the doctors cries. Kane hears him as though from a great distance—already his higher systems are shutting down. "Some kind of autodestruct!"

"Maybe it's just cardiac arrest . . . ," says another, but it's only a whisper, and he is falling down a long tunnel. He almost thinks he can hear Spirit calling after him. . . .

And God shall wipe away all tears from their eyes; and there shall be no more death, neither sorrow, nor crying, neither shall there be any more pain: for the former things are passed away.

His heart starts pumping again twenty minutes later. The doctors, unaware of the sophistication of his autonomic control, are trying to shock his system back to life. Kane hoped he would be down longer and that they would give him up for dead, but that was overly optimistic: instead he has to roll off the table, naked but for trailing wires and tubes, and kill the startled guards before they can draw their weapons. He must also break the neck of one of the doctors who has been trying to save him but now makes the mistake of attacking him. Even after he leaves the rest of the terrified medical staff cowering on the emergency room floor and escapes the surgical wing, he is still in a prison.

"Tired of the same old atmosphere? Holyoake Harbor, the little village under the bubble—we make our own air and it's guaranteed fresh!"

His internal modifications are healing the surgical damage as quickly as possible, but he is staggering, starved of nutrients and burning energy at brushfire speed. God has given him this chance and he must not fail, but if he does not replenish his reserves, he *will* fail.

Kane drops down from an overhead air duct into a hallway and kills a two-man patrol team. He tears the uniform off one of them and then, with stiffened, clawlike fingers, pulls gobbets of meat off the man's bones and swallows them. The blood is salty and hot. His stomach convulses at what he is doing—the old, terrible sin—but he forces himself to chew and swallow. He has no choice.

Addiction a problem? Not with a NeoBlood transfusion! We also feature the finest life-tested and artificial organs. . . .

He can tell by the sputtering messages on the guards' communicators that the security personnel are spreading out from the main guardroom. They seem to have an idea of where he has been and where he now is. When he has finished his terrible meal he leaves the residue on the floor of the closet and then makes his way toward the central security office, leaving red footprints behind him. He looks, he feels sure, like a demon from the deepest floors of Hell.

The guards make the mistake of coming out of their hardened room, thinking numbers and weaponry are on their side. Kane takes several bullet wounds, but they have nothing as terrible as the scrambling device that captured him in the first place; he moves through his enemies like a whirlwind, snapping out blows of such strength that one guard's head is knocked from his shoulders and tumbles down the hall.

Once he has waded through the bodies into the main communication room, he throws open as many of the prison cells as he can and turns on the escape and fire alarms, which howl like the damned. He waits until the chaos is ripe, then pulls on a guard's uniform and heads for the exercise yard. He hurries through the shrieking, bloody confusion of the yard, then climbs over the three sets of razor-wire fencing. Several bullets smack into his hardened flesh, burning like hot rivets. A beam weapon scythes across the last fence with a hiss and pop of snapping wire, but Kane has already dropped to the ground outside.

He can run about fifty miles an hour under most circumstances, but fueled with adrenaline he can go almost half again that fast for short bursts. The only problem is that he is traveling over open, wild ground and has to watch for obstacles—even he can badly injure an ankle at this speed because he cannot armor his joints too much without losing flexibility. Also, he is so exhausted and empty even after consuming the guard's flesh that black spots caper in front of his eyes: he will not be able to keep up this pace very long.

Here are some wise words from an ancient statesman to consider: "You can do what you have to do, and sometimes you can do it even better than you think you can."

Kids, all parents can make mistakes. How about yours? Report religious paraphernalia or overly superstitious behavior on your local Freedom Council tip node. . . .

Your body temperature is far above normal. Your stress levels are far above normal. We recommend you see a physician immediately.

Yes, Kane thinks. *I believe I'll do just that.*

He finds an empty house within five miles of the prison and breaks in. He eats everything he can find, including several pounds of frozen meat, which helps him compensate for a little of the heat he is generating. He then rummages through the upstairs bedrooms until he finds some new clothes to wear, scrubs offs the blood that marks him out, and leaves.

He finds another place some miles away to hide for the night. The residents are home—he even hears them listening to news of his escape, although it is a grossly inaccurate version that concentrates breathlessly on his cannibalism and his terrifying nickname. He lays curled in a box in their attic like a mummy, nearly comatose. When they leave in the morning, so does Kane, reshaping the bones of his face and withdrawing color from his hair. The pagan seed still chirps in his head. Every few minutes, it reminds him to keep an eye open for himself, but not to approach himself, because he is undoubtedly very, very dangerous.

"Didn't know anything about it." Sartorius looks worriedly up and down the road to make sure they are alone, as if Kane hadn't already done that better, faster, and more carefully long before the two locals had arrived at the rendezvous. "What can I say? We didn't have any idea they had that scrambler thing. Of course, we would have let you know if we'd heard."

"I need a doctor—somebody you'd trust with your life, because I'll be trusting him with mine."

"Cannibal Christian," says young Carl in an awed voice. "That's what they're calling you now."

"That's crap." He is not ashamed, because he was doing God's will, but he does not want to be reminded, either.

"Or the Angel of Death, they still like that one, too. Either way, they're sure talking about you."

The doctor is a woman too, a decade or so past her child-bearing years. They wake her up in her small cottage on the edge of a blighted park that looks like it was manufacturing space before a halfway attempt to redeem it. She has alcohol on her breath and her hands shake, but her eyes, although a little bloodshot, are intelligent and alert.

"Don't bore me with your story and I won't bore you with mine," she says when Carl begins to introduce them. A moment later, her pupils dilate. "Hang on—I already know yours. You're the Angel everyone's talking about."

"Some people call him the Cannibal Christian," says young Carl helpfully.

"Are you a believer?" Kane asks her.

"I'm too flawed to be anything else. Who else but Jesus would keep forgiving me?"

She lays him out on a bedsheet on her kitchen table. He waves away both the anesthetic inhaler and the bottle of liquor.

"They won't work on me unless I let them, and I can't afford to let them work. I have to stay alert. Now please, cut that godless thing out of my head. Do you have a Spirit you can put in?"

"Beg pardon?" She straightens up, the scalpel already bloody from the incision he is doing his best to ignore.

"What do you call it here? My kind of seed, a seed of Covenant. So I can hear the voice of Spirit again—"

As if to protest its own pending removal, the Archimedes seed abruptly fills his skull with a crackle of interference.

A bad sign, Kane thinks. He must be overworking his internal systems. When he finishes here he'll need several days' rest before he decides what to do next.

"Sorry," he tells the doctor. "I didn't hear you. What did you say?"

She shrugs. "I said I'd have to see what I have. One of your people died on this very table a few years ago, I'm sad to say, despite everything I did to save him. I think I kept his communication seed." She waves her hand a little, as though such things happen or fail to happen every day. "Who knows? I'll have a look."

He cannot let himself hope too much. Even if she has it, what are the odds that it will work, and even more unlikely, that it will work here on Archimedes? There are booster stations on all the other colony worlds, like Arjuna, where the Word is allowed to compete freely with the lies of the Godless.

The latest crackle in his head resolves into a calm, sweetly reasonable voice. . . . *No less a philosopher than Aristotle himself said, "Men create gods after their own image, not only with regard to their form, but with regard to their mode of life."*

Kane forces himself to open his eyes. The room is blurry, the doctor a faint shadowy shape bending over him. Something sharp probes in his neck.

"There it is," she says. "It's going to hurt a bit coming out. What's your name? Your real name?"

"Lamentation."

"Ah." She doesn't smile, at least he doesn't think she does—it's hard for him to make out her features—but she sounds amused. "'She weepeth sore in the night, and her tears are on her cheeks: among all her lovers she hath none to comfort her: all her friends have dealt treacherously with her, they are become her enemies.' That's Jerusalem they're talking about," the doctor adds. "The original one."

"Book of Lamentations," he says quietly. The pain is so fierce that it's all he can do not to reach up and grab the hand that holds the probing, insupportable instrument. At times like this, when he most needs to restrain himself, he can most clearly feel his strength. If he were to lose control and loose that unfettered power, he feels that he could blaze like one of the stellar torches in heaven's great vault, that he could destroy an entire world.

"Hey," says a voice in the darkness beyond the pool of light on the kitchen table—young Carl "Hey. Something's going on."

"What are you talking about?" demands Sartorius. A moment later, the window explodes in a shower of sparkling glass and the room fills with smoke.

Not smoke, gas. Kane springs off the table, accidentally knocking the doctor back against the wall. He gulps in enough breath to last him a quarter of an hour and flares the tissues of his pharynx to seal his air passages. If it's a nerve gas, there is nothing much he can do, though—too much skin exposed.

In the corner, the doctor struggles to her feet, emerging from the billows of gas on the floor with her mouth wide and working but nothing coming out. It isn't just her. Carl and Sartorius are holding their breath as they shove furniture against the door as a makeshift barricade. The bigger, older man already has a gun in his hand. Why is it so quiet outside? What are they doing out there?

The answer comes with a stuttering roar. Small arms fire suddenly fills the kitchen wall with holes. The doctor throws up her hands and begins a terrible jig, as though she is being stitched by an invisible sewing machine. When she falls to the ground, it is in pieces.

Young Carl stretches motionless on the floor in a pool of his own spreading blood and brains. Sartorius is still standing unsteadily, but red bubbles seep through his clothing in several places.

Kane is on the ground—he has dropped without realizing it. He does not stop to consider the near-certainty of failure, but instead springs to the ceiling and digs his fingers in long enough to smash his way through with the other hand, then hunkers in the crawlspace until the first team of troopers comes in to check the damage, flashlights darting through the fog of gas fumes. How did they find him so quickly? More important, what have they brought to use against him?

Speed is his best weapon. He climbs out through the vent. He has to widen it, and the splintering brings a fusillade from below. When he reaches the roof dozens of shots crack past him and two actually hit him, one in the arm and one in the back, these from the parked security vehicles where the rest of the invasion team are waiting for the first wave to signal them inside. The shock waves travel through him so that he shakes like a wet dog. A moment later, as he suspected, they deploy the scrambler. This time, though, he is ready: he saturates his neurons with calcium to deaden the electromagnetic surge, and although his own brain activity ceases for a moment and he drops bonelessly across the roof crest, there is no damage. A few seconds later, he is up again. Their best weapon spent, the soldiers have three seconds to shoot at a dark figure scrambling with incredible speed along the roofline; then Lamentation Kane jumps down into the hot tracery of their fire, sprints forward and leaps off the hood of their own vehicle and over them before they can change firing positions.

He can't make it to full speed this time—not enough rest and not enough refueling—but he can go fast enough that he has vanished into the Hellas City sewers by time the strike team can remobilize.

The Archimedes seed, which has been telling his enemies exactly where he is, lies behind him now, wrapped in bloody gauze somewhere in the ruins of the doctor's kitchen. Keeta Januari and her Rationalists will learn much about the ability of the Covenant scientists to manufacture imitations of Archimedes technology, but they will not learn anything more about Kane. Not from the seed. He is free of it now.

He emerges almost a full day later from a pumping station on the outskirts of one of Hellas City's suburbs, but now he is a different Kane entirely, a Kane never before seen. Although the doctor removed the Archimedes seed, she had no time to locate, let alone implant, a Spirit device in its place: for the first time in as long as he can remember his thoughts are entirely his own, his head empty of any other voices.

The solitude is terrifying.

He makes his way up into the hills west of the great city, hiding in the daytime, moving cautiously by night because so many of the rural residents have elaborate security systems or animals who can smell Kane even before he can smell them. At last he finds an untended property. He could break in easily, but instead extrudes one of his fingernails and hardens it to pick the lock. He wants to minimize his presence whenever possible—he needs time to think, to plan. The ceiling has been lifted off his world and he is confused.

For safety's sake, he spends the first two days exploring his new hiding place only at night, with the lights out and his pupils dilated so far that even the sudden appearance of a white piece of paper in front of him is painful. From what he can tell, the small modern house belongs to a man traveling for a month on the eastern side of the continent. The owner has been gone only a week, which gives Kane ample time to rest and think about what he is going to do next.

The first thing he has to get used to is the silence in his head. All his life since he was a tiny unknowing child, Spirit has spoken to him. Now he cannot hear her calm, inspiring voice. The godless prattle of Archimedes is silenced too. There is nothing and no one to share Kane's thoughts.

He cries that first night as he cried in the whore's room, like a lost child. He is a ghost. He is no longer human. He has lost his inner guide, he has botched his mission, he has failed his God and his people. He has eaten the flesh of his own kind, and for nothing.

Lamentation Kane is alone with his great sin.

He moves on before the owner of the house returns. He knows he could kill the man and stay for many more months, but it seems time to do things differently, although Kane can't say precisely why. He can't even say for certain what things he is going to do. He still owes God the death of Prime Minister Januari, but something seems to have changed inside him, and he is in no hurry to fulfill that promise. The silence in his head, at first so frightening, has begun to seem something more. Holy, perhaps, but certainly different from anything he has experienced before, as though every moment is a waking dream.

No, it is more like waking up from a dream. But what kind of dream has he escaped, a good one or a bad one? And what will replace it?

Even without Spirit's prompting, he remembers Christ's words: *You shall know the truth, and the truth shall set you free.* In his new inner silence, the ancient promise seem to have many meanings. Does Kane really want the truth? Could he stand to be truly free?

Before he leaves the house, he takes the owner's second-best camping equipment, the things the man left behind. Kane will live in the wild areas in the highest parts of the hills for as long as seems right. He will think. It is possible that he will leave Lamentation Kane there behind him when he comes out again. He may leave the Angel of Death behind as well.

What will remain? And whom will such a new sort of creature serve? The angels, the devils . . . or just itself?

Kane will be interested to find out.

Joe R. Lansdale

Prolific Texas writer Joe R. Lansdale has won the Edgar Award, the British Fantasy Award, the American Horror Award, the American Mystery Award, the International Crime Writer's Award, and seven Bram Stoker Awards. Although perhaps best known for horror/thrillers such as *The Nightrunners, Bubba Ho-Tep, The Bottoms, The God of the Razor,* and *The Drive-In,* he also writes the popular Hap Collins and Leonard Pine mystery series—*Savage Season, Mucho Mojo, The Two-Bear Mambo, Bad Chili, Rumble Tumble, Captains Outrageous*—as well as western novels such as *A Fine Dark Line* and *Blood Dance,* and totally unclassifiable cross-genre novels such as *Zeppelins West, Magic Wagon,* and *Flaming London.* His other novels include *Dead in the West, The Big Blow, Sunset and Sawdust, Act of Love, Freezer Burn, Waltz of Shadows,* and *The Drive-In 2: Not Just One of Them Sequels.* He has also contributed novels to series such as Batman and Tarzan. His many short stories have been collected in *By Bizarre Hands, Tight Little Stitches in a Dead Man's Back; The Shadows, Kith and Kin; The Long Ones; Stories by Mama Lansdale's Youngest Boy; Bestsellers Guaranteed; On the Far Side of the Cadillac Desert with Dead Folks; Electric Gumbo; Writer of the Purple Rage; A Fist Full of Stories (and Articles); Steppin' Out, Summer '68; Bumper Crop; The Good, the Bad, and the Indifferent; For a Few Stories More; Mad Dog Summer and Other Stories; The King and Other Stories;* and *High Cotton: Selected Stories of Joe R. Lansdale.* As editor, he has produced the anthologies *The Best of the West, Retro-Pulp Tales, Razored Saddles* (with Pat LoBrutto), *Dark at Heart* (with wife Karen Lansdale), and the Robert E. Howard tribute anthology, *Cross Plains Universe* (with Scott A. Cupp). An anthology in tribute to Lansdale's work is *Lords of the Razor.* His most recent books are *Leather Maiden* and a novel written with John Lansdale, *Hell's Bounty.* The newest anthology, *Son of Retro Pulp*

Tales, was published in 2009. He lives with his family in Nacogdoches, Texas.

Here's a funny and sizzlingly fast-paced look at two men who do what Huck and Tom only dream about doing and actually do "light out for the territories"—and run into a lot more trouble there than they bargained for.

Soldierin'

They said if you went out West and joined up with the colored soldiers, they'd pay you in real Yankee dollars, thirteen of them a month, feed and clothe you, and it seemed like a right smart idea since I was wanted for a lynchin'. It wasn't that I was invited to hold the rope or sing a little spiritual. I was the guest of honor on this one. They was plannin' to stretch my neck like a goozle-wrung chicken at Sunday dinner.

Thing I'd done was nothin' on purpose, but in a moment of eyeballin' while walkin' along the road on my way to cut some firewood for a nickel and a jar of jam, a white girl who was hangin' out wash bent over and pressed some serious butt up against her gingham, and a white fella, her brother, seen me take a look, and that just crawled all up in his ass and died, and he couldn't stand the stink.

Next thing I know, I'm wanted for being bold with a white girl, like maybe I'd broke into her yard and jammed my arm up her ass, but I hadn't done nothin' but what's natural, which is glance at a nice butt when it was available to me.

Now, in the livin' of my life, I've killed men and animals and made love to three Chinese women on the same night in the same bed and one of them with only one leg, and part of it wood, and I even ate some of a dead fella once when I was crossin' the mountains, though I want to rush in here and make it clear I didn't know him all that well, and we damn sure wasn't kinfolks. Another thing I did was I won me a shootin' contest up Colorady way against some pretty damn famous shooters, all white boys, but them's different stories and not even akin to the one I want to tell, and I'd like to add, just like them other events, this time I'm talking about is as true as the sunset.

Pardon me. Now that I've gotten older, sometimes I find I start out to tell one story and end up tellin' another. But to get back to the one I was talkin' about . . . So, havin' been invited to a lynchin', I took my daddy's horse and big ole loaded six-gun he kept wrapped up in an oilcloth from under the floorboards of our shack, and took off like someone had set my ass on fire. I rode that poor old horse till he was slap worn out. I had to stop over in a little place just outside of Nacogdoches and steal another one, not on account of I was a thief, but on account of I didn't want to get caught by the posse and hung and maybe have my pecker cut off and stuck in my mouth. Oh. I also took a chicken. He's no longer with me, of course, as I ate him out there on the trail.

Anyway, I left my horse for the fella I took the fresh horse and the chicken from, and I left him a busted pocket watch on top of the railing post, and then I rode out to West Texas. It took a long time for me to get there, and I had to stop and steal food and drink from creeks and make sure the horse got fed with corn I stole. After a few days, I figured I'd lost them that was after me, and I changed my name as I rode along. It had been Wiliford P. Thomas, the *P* not standing for a thing other than *P*. I chose the name Nat Wiliford for myself, and practiced on saying it while I rode along. When I said it, I wanted it to come out of my mouth like it wasn't a lie.

Before I got to where I was goin', I run up against this colored fella taking a dump in the bushes, wiping his ass on leaves. If I had been a desperado, I could have shot him out from over his pile and taken his horse, 'cause he was deeply involved in the event—so much, in fact, that I could see his eyes were crossed from where I rode up on a hill, and that was some distance.

I was glad I was downwind, and hated to interrupt, so I sat on my stolen horse until he was leaf wiping, and then I called out. "Hello, the shitter."

He looked up and grinned at me, touched his rifle lying on the ground beside him, said, "You ain't plannin' on shootin' me, are you?"

"No. I thought about stealin' your horse, but it's sway back and so ugly in the face it hurts my feelings."

"Yeah, and it's blind in one eye and has a knot on its back comes right through the saddle. When I left the plantation, I took that horse. Wasn't much then, and it's a lot less now."

He stood up and fastened his pants and I seen then that he was a pretty big fellow, all decked out in fresh-looking overalls and a big black hat with a feather in it. He came walkin' up the hill toward me, his wipin' hand stuck out for a shake, but I politely passed, because I thought his fingers looked a little brown.

Anyway, we struck it up pretty good, and by nightfall we found a creek, and he washed his hands in the water with some soap from his saddlebag, which made me feel a mite better. We sat and had coffee and some of his biscuits. All I could offer was some conversation, and he had plenty to give back. His name was Cullen, but he kept referrin' to himself as The Former House Nigger, as if it were a rank akin to general. He told a long story about how he got the feather for his hat, but it mostly just came down to he snuck up on a hawk sittin' on a low limb and jerked it out of its tail.

"When my master went to war against them Yankees," he said, "I went with him. I fought with him and wore me a butternut coat and pants, and I shot me at least a half dozen of them Yankees."

"Are you leaking brains out of your gourd?" I said. "Them rebels was holdin' us down."

"I was a house nigger, and I grew up with Mr. Gerald, and I didn't mind going to war with him. Me and him was friends. There was lots of us like that."

"Y'all must have got dropped on your head when you was young'ns."

"The Master and the older Master was all right."

"'Cept they owned you," I said.

"Maybe I was born to be owned. They always quoted somethin' like that out of the Bible."

"That ought to have been your clue, fella. My daddy always said that book has caused more misery than chains, an ill-tempered woman, and a nervous dog."

"I loved Young Master like a brother, truth be known. He got shot in the war, right 'tween the eyes by a musket ball, killed him deader than a goddamn tree stump. I sopped up his blood in a piece of his shirt I cut off, mailed it back home with a note on what happened. When the war was over, I stayed around the plantation for a while, but everything come apart then, the old man and the old lady died, and I buried them out back of the place a good distance from the privy and uphill, I might add. That just left me and the Old Gentleman's dog.

"The dog was as old as death and couldn't eat so good, so I shot it, and went on out into what Young Master called The Big Wide World. Then, like you, I heard the guv'ment was signing up coloreds for its man's army. I ain't no good on my own. I figured the army was for me."

"I don't like being told nothin' by nobody," I said, "but I surely love to get paid." I didn't mention I also didn't want to get killed by angry crackers and the army seemed like a good place to hide.

About three days later, we rode up on the place we was looking for. Fort McKavett, between the Colorady and the Pecos rivers. It was a sight, that fort. It was big and it didn't look like nothin' I'd ever seen before. Out front was colored fellas in army blue drilling on horseback, looking sharp in the sunlight, which there was plenty of. It was hot where I come from, sticky even, but you could find a tree to get under. Out here, all you could get under was your hat, or maybe some dark cloud sailing across the face of the sun, and that might last only as long as it takes a bird to fly over.

But there I was. Fort McKavett. Full of dreams and crotch itch from long riding, me and my new friend sat on our horses, lookin' the fort over, watchin' them horse soldiers drill, and it was prideful thing to see. We rode on down in that direction.

In the Commanding Officer's quarters, me and The Former House Nigger stood before a big desk with a white man behind it, name of Colonel Hatch. He had a caterpillar mustache and big sweat circles like wet moons under his arms. His eyes were aimed on a fly sitting on some papers on his desk. Way he was watchin' it, you'd have thought he was beading down on a hostile. He said, "So you boys want to sign up for the colored army. I figured that, you both being colored."

He was a sharp one, this Hatch.

I said, "I've come to sign up and be a horse rider in the Ninth Cavalry."

Hatch studied me for a moment, said, "Well, we got plenty of ridin' niggers. What we need is walkin' niggers for the goddamn infantry, and I can get you set in the right direction to hitch up with them."

I figured anything that was referred to with *goddamn* in front of it wasn't the place for me.

"I reckon ain't a man here can ride better'n me," I said, "and that would be even you, Colonel, and I'm sure you are one ridin' sonofabitch, and I mean that in as fine a way as I can say it."

Hatch raised an eyebrow. "That so?"

"Yes, sir. No brag, just fact. I can ride on a horse's back, under his belly, make him lay down and make him jump, and at the end of the day, I take a likin' to him, I can diddle that horse in the ass and make him enjoy it enough to brew my coffee and bring my slippers, provided I had any. That last part about the diddlin' is just talkin', but the first part is serious."

"I figured as much," Hatch said.

"I ain't diddlin' no horses," The Former House Nigger said. "I can cook and lay out silverware. Mostly, as a Former House Nigger, I drove the buggy."

At that moment, Hatch come down on that fly with his hand, and he got him too. He peeled it off his palm and flicked it on the floor. There was this colored soldier standing nearby, very stiff and alert, and he bent over, picked the fly up by a bent wing, threw it out the door and came back. Hatch wiped his palm on his pants leg. "Well," he said, "let's see how much of what you got is fact, and how much is wind."

They had a corral nearby, and inside it, seeming to fill it up, was a big black horse that looked like he ate men and shitted out saddlebags made of their skin and bones. He put his eye right on me when I came out to the corral, and when I walked around on the other side, he spun around to keep a gander on me. Oh, he knew what I was about, all right.

Hatch took hold of one corner of his mustache and played with it, turned and looked at me. "You ride that horse well as you say you can, I'll take both of you into the cavalry, and The Former House Nigger can be our cook."

"I said I could cook," The Former House Nigger said. "Didn't say I was any good."

"Well," Hatch said, "what we got now ain't even cookin'. There's just a couple fellas that boil water and put stuff in it. Mostly turnips."

I climbed up on the railing, and by this time, four colored cavalry men had caught up the horse for me. That old black beast had knocked them left and right, and it took them a full twenty minutes to get a bridle and a saddle on him, and when they come off the field, so to speak, two was limpin' like they had one foot in a ditch. One was holding his head where he had been kicked, and the other looked amazed he was alive. They had tied the mount next to the railin', and he was hoppin' up and down like a little girl with a jump rope, only a mite more vigorous.

"Go ahead and get on," Hatch said.

Having bragged myself into a hole, I had no choice.

I wasn't lyin' when I said I was a horse rider. I was. I could buck them and make them go down on their bellies and roll on their sides, make them strut and do whatever, but this horse was as mean as homemade sin, and I could tell he had it in for me.

Soon as I was on him, he jerked his head and them reins snapped off the railing and I was clutchin' at what was left of it. The sky came down on my head as that horse leaped. Ain't no horse could leap like that, and soon me and him was trying to climb the clouds. I couldn't tell earth from heaven, 'cause we bucked all over that goddamn lot, and ever time that horse come down, it jarred my bones from butt to skull. I come out of the saddle a few times, nearly went off the back of him, but I hung in there, tight as a tick on a dog's nuts. Finally he jumped himself out and started to roll. He went down on one side, mashing my leg in the dirt, and rolled on over. Had that dirt in the corral not been tamped down and soft, giving with me, there wouldn't been nothing left of me but a sack of blood and broken bones.

Finally the horse humped a couple of sad bucks and gave out, started to trot and snort. I leaned over close to his ear and said, "You call that buckin'?" He seemed to take offense at that, and run me straight to the corral and hit the rails there with his chest. I went sailin' off his back and landed on top of some soldiers, scatterin' them like quail.

Hatch come over and looked down on me, said, "Well, you ain't smarter than the horse, but you can ride well enough. You and The Former House Nigger are in with the rest of the ridin' niggers. Trainin' starts in the morning."

We drilled with the rest of the recruits up and down that lot, and finally outside and around the fort until we was looking pretty smart. The horse they give me was that black devil I had ridden. I named him Satan. He really wasn't as bad as I first thought. He was worse, and you had to be at your best every time you got on him, 'cause deep down in his bones, he was always thinking about killing you, and if you didn't watch it, he'd kind of act casual, like he was watching a cloud or somethin', and quickly turn his head and take a nip out of your leg, if he could bend far enough to get to it.

Anyway, the months passed, and we drilled, and my buddy cooked, and though what he cooked wasn't any good, it was better than nothin'. It was a good life as compared to being hung, and there was some real freedom to it and some respect. I wore my uniform proud, set my horse like I thought I was somethin' special with a stick up its ass.

We mostly did a little patrollin', and wasn't much to it except ridin' around lookin' for wild Indians we never did see, collectin' our thirteen dollars at the end of the month, which was just so much paper 'cause there wasn't no place to spend it. And then, one mornin', things changed, and wasn't none of it for the better, except The Former House Nigger managed to cook a pretty good breakfast with perfect fat biscuits and eggs with the yolks not broke and some bacon that wasn't burned and nobody got sick this time.

On that day, Hatch mostly rode around with us, 'cause at the bottom of it all, I reckon the government figured we was just a bunch of ignorant niggers who might at any moment have a watermelon relapse and take to gettin' drunk and shootin' each other and maybe trying to sing a spiritual while we diddled the horses, though I had sort of been responsible for spreadin' the last part of that rumor on my first day at the fort. We was all itchin' to show we had somethin' to us that didn't have nothin' to do with no white fella ridin' around in front of us, though I'll say right up front, Hatch was a good soldier who led and didn't follow, and he was polite too. I had seen him leave the circle of the fire to walk off in the dark to fart. You can't say that about just anyone. Manners out on the frontier was rare.

You'll hear from the army how we was all a crack team, but this wasn't so, at least not when they was first sayin' it. Most of the army at any time, bein' they the ridin' kind or the walkin' kind, ain't all that crack. Some of them fellas didn't know a horse's ass end from the front end, and this was pretty certain when you seen how they mounted, swinging into the stirrups, finding themselves looking at the horse's tail instead of his ears. But in time everyone got better, though I'd like to toss in, without too much immodesty, that I was the best rider of the whole damn lot. Since he'd had a good bit of experience, The Former House Nigger was the second. Hell, he'd done been in war and all, so in ways, he had more experience than any of us, and he cut a fine figure on a horse, being tall and always alert, like he might have to bring somebody a plate of something or hold a coat.

Only action we'd seen was when one of the men, named Rutherford, got into it with Prickly Pear—I didn't name him, that come from his mother—and they fought over a biscuit. While they was fightin', Colonel Hatch come over and ate it, so it was a wasted bout.

But this time I'm tellin' you about, we rode out lookin' for Indians to scare, and not seein' any, we quit lookin' for what we couldn't find, and come to a little place down by a creek where it was wooded and there was a shade from a whole bunch of trees that in that part of the country was thought of as being big, and in my part of the country would have been considered scrubby. I was glad when we stopped to water the horses and take a little time to just wait. Colonel Hatch, I think truth be told, was glad to get out of that sun much as the rest of us. I don't know how he felt, being a white man and having to command a bunch of colored, but he didn't seem bothered by it a'tall, and seemed proud of us and himself, which, of course, made us all feel mighty good.

So we waited out there on the creek, and Hatch, he come over to where me and The Former House Nigger were sitting by the water, and we jumped to attention, and he said, "There's a patch of scrub oaks off the creek, scatter-ing out there across the grass, and they ain't growin' worth a damn. Them's gonna be your concern. I'm gonna take the rest of the troop out across the ground there, see if we can pick up some deer trails. I figure ain't no one gonna mind if we pot a few and bring them back to camp. And besides, I'm bored. But we could use some firewood, and I was wantin' you fellas to get them scrubs cut down and sawed up and ready to take back to the fort. Stack them in here amongst the trees, and I'll send out some men with a wagon when we get back, and have that wood hauled back before it's good and dark. I thought we could use some oak to smoke the meat I'm plannin' on gettin'. That's why I'm the goddamn colonel. Always thinkin'."

"What if you don't get no meat?" one of the men with us said.

"Then you did some work for nothin', and I went huntin' for nothin'. But, hell, I seen them deer with my binoculars no less than five minutes ago. Big fat deer, about a half dozen of them running along. They went over the hill. I'm gonna take the rest of the troops with me in case I run into hostiles, and because I don't like to do no skinnin' of dead deer myself."

"I like to hunt," I said.

"That's some disappointin' shit for you," Colonel Hatch said. "I need you here. In fact, I put you in charge. You get bit by a snake and die, then, you, The Former House Nigger, take over. I'm also gonna put Rutherford, Bill, and Rice in your charge . . . some others. I'll take the rest of them. You get that wood cut up, you start on back to the fort and we'll send out a wagon."

"What about Indians?" Rutherford, who was nearby, said.

"You seen any Indians since you been here?" Hatch said.

"No, sir."

"Then there ain't no Indians."

"You ever see any?" Rutherford asked Hatch.

"Oh, hell yeah. Been attacked by them, and I've attacked them. There's every kind of Indian you can imagine out here from time to time. Kiowa. Apache. Comanche. And there ain't nothin' they'd like better than to have your prickly black scalps on their belts, 'cause they find your hair funny. They think it's like the buffalo. They call you buffalo soldiers on account of it."

"I thought it was because they thought we was brave like the buffalo," I said.

"That figures," Hatch said. "You ain't seen no action for nobody to have no opinion of you. But, we ain't seen an Indian in ages, and ain't seen no sign of them today. I'm startin' to think they've done run out of this area. But, I've thought that before. And Indian, especially a Comanche or an Apache, they're hard to get a handle on. They'll get after somethin' or someone like it matters more than anything in the world, and then they'll wander off if a bird flies over and they make an omen of it."

Leaving us with them mixed thoughts on Indians and buffalo, Hatch and the rest of the men rode off, left us standing in the shade, which wasn't no bad place to be. First thing we did when they was out of sight was throw off our boots and get in the water. I finally just took all my clothes off and cleaned up pretty good with a bar of lye soap and got dressed. Then leaving the horses tied up in the trees near the creek, we took the mule and the equipment strapped on his back, carried our rifles, and went out to where them scrubs was. On the way, we cut down a couple of saplings and trimmed some limbs, and made us a kind of pull that we could fasten on to the mule. We figured we'd fill it up with wood and get the mule to drag it back to the creek, pile it and have it ready for the wagon.

Rigged up, we went to work, taking turns with the saw, two other men working hacking off limbs, one man axing the trimmed wood up so it fit good enough to load. We talked while we worked, and Rutherford said, "Them Indians, some of them is as mean as snakes. They do all kind of things to folks. Cut their eyelids off, cook them over fires, cut off their nut sacks and such. They're just awful."

"Sounds like some Southerners I know," I said.

"My master and his family was darn good to me," The Former House Nigger said.

"They might have been good to you," Rice said, pausing at the saw, "but that still don't make you no horse, no piece of property. You a man been treated like a horse, and you too dumb to know it."

The Former House Nigger bowed up like he was about to fight. I said, "Now, don't do it. He's just talkin'. I'm in charge here, and you two get into it, I'll get it from Hatch, and I don't want that, and won't have it."

Rice tilted his hat back. His face looked dark as coffee. "I'm gonna tell you true. When I was sixteen, I cut my master's throat and raped his wife and run off to the North."

"My God," The Former House Nigger said. "That's awful."

"And I made the dog suck my dick," Rice said.

"What?" The Former House Nigger said.

"He's funnin' you," I said.

"That part about the master's throat," Rice said, "and runnin' off to the North. I really did that. I would have raped his wife, but there wasn't any time. His dog didn't excite me none."

"You are disgustin'," The Former House Nigger said, pausing from his job of trimming limbs with a hatchet.

"Agreed," I said.

Rice chuckled, and went back to sawin' with Rutherford. He had his shirt off, and the muscles in his back bunched up like prairie dogs tunnelin', and over them mounds was long, thick scars. I knew them scars. I had a few. They had been made with a whip.

Bill, who was stackin' wood, said, "Them Indians. Ain't no use hatin' them. Hatin' them for bein' what they is, is like hatin' a bush 'cause it's got thorns on it. Hatin' a snake 'cause it'll bite you. They is what they is just like we is what we is."

"And what is we?" The Former House Nigger said.

"Ain't none of us human beings no 'count. The world is just one big mess of no 'counts, so there ain't no use pickin' one brand of man or woman over the other. Ain't none of them worth a whistlin' fart."

"Ain't had it so good, have you, Bill?" I asked.

"I was a slave."

"We all was," I said.

"Yeah, but I didn't take it so good. Better'n Rutherford, but not so good. I was in the northern army, right there at the end when they started lettin' colored in, and I killed and seen men killed. Ain't none of my life experience give me much of a glow about folks of any kind. I even killed buffalo just for the tongues rich folks wanted to have. We left hides and meat in the fields to rot. That was to punish the Indians. Damned ole buffalo. Ain't nothin' dumber, and I shot them for dollars and their tongues. What kind of human beings does that?"

We worked for about another hour, and then, Dog Den—again, I didn't name him—one of the other men Hatch left with us, said, "I think we got a problem."

On the other side of the creek, there was a split in the trees, and you could see through them out into the plains, and you could see the hill Hatch had gone over some hours ago, and comin' down it at a run was a white man. He was a good distance away, but it didn't take no eagle eye to see that he was naked as a skinned rabbit, and runnin' full out, and behind him, whoopin' and having a good time, were Indians. Apache, to be right on the money, nearly as naked as the runnin' man. Four of them was on horseback, and there was six of them I could see on foot runnin' after him. My guess was they had done been at him and had set him loose to chase him like a deer for fun. I guess livin' out on the plains like they did, with nothin' but mesquite berries and what food they could kill, you had to have your fun where you could find it.

"They're funnin' him," Rutherford said, figurin' same as me.

We stood there lookin' for a moment; then I remembered we was soldiers. I got my rifle and was about to bead down, when Rutherford said, "Hell, you can't hit them from here, and neither can they shoot you. We're out of range, and Indians ain't no shots to count for."

One of the runnin' Apaches had spotted us, and he dropped to one knee and pointed his rifle at us, and when he did, Rutherford spread his arms wide, and said, "Go on, shoot, you heathen."

The Apache fired.

Rutherford was wrong. He got it right on the top of the nose and fell over with his arms still spread. When he hit the ground, The Former House Nigger said, "I reckon they been practicin'."

We was up on a hill, so we left the mule and run down to the creek where the horses was, and waded across the little water and laid out between the trees and took aim. We opened up and it sounded like a bunch of mule skinners crackin' their whips. The air filled with smoke and there was some shots fired back at us. I looked up and seen the runnin' man was makin' right smart time, his hair and johnson flappin' as he run. But then one of the horseback Apaches rode up on him, and with this heavy knotted-looking stick he was carrying, swung and clipped the white fella along the top of the head. I seen blood jump up and the man go down and I could hear the sound of the blow so well, I winced. The Apache let out a whoop and rode on past, right toward us. He stopped to beat his chest with his free hand, and when he did, I took a shot at him. I aimed for his chest, but I hit the horse square in the head and brought him down. At least I had the heathen on foot.

Now, you can say what you want about an Apache, but he is about the bravest thing there is short of a badger. This'n come runnin' right at us, all of us firin' away, and I figure he thought he had him some big magic, 'cause not a one of our shots hit him. It was like he come haint-like right through a wall of bullets. As he got closer, I could see he had some kind of mud paint on his chest and face, and he was whoopin' and carryin' on somethin' horrible. And then he stepped in a hole and went down. Though he was still a goodly distance from us, I could hear his ankle snap like a yanked suspender. Without meaning to, we all went, "Ooooooh." It hurt us, it was so nasty soundin'.

That fall must have caused his magic to fly out of his ass, 'cause we all started firing at him, and this time he collected all our bullets, and was deader than a guv'ment promise before the smoke cleared.

This gave the rest of them Apache pause, and I'm sure, brave warriors or not, a few assholes puckered out there.

Them ridin' Apaches stopped their horses and rode back until they was up on the hill, and the runnin' Indians dropped to the ground and lay there. We popped off a few more shots, but didn't hit nothin', and then I remembered I was in charge. I said, "Hold your fire. Don't waste your bullets."

The Former House Nigger crawled over by me, said, "We showed them."

"They ain't showed yet," I said. "Them's Apache warriors. They ain't known as slackers."

"Maybe Colonel Hatch heard all the shootin'," he said.

"They've had time to get a good distance away. They figured on us cuttin' the wood and leavin' it and goin' back to the fort. So maybe they ain't missin' us yet and didn't hear a thing."

"Dang it," The Former House Nigger said.

I thought we might just mount up and try to ride off. We had more horses than they did, but three of them ridin' after us could still turn out bad. We had a pretty good place as we was, amongst the trees with water to drink. I decided best thing we could do was hold our position. Then that white man who had been clubbed in the head started moaning. That wasn't enough, a couple of the braves come up out of the grass and ran at his spot. We fired at them, but them Spencer single shots didn't reload as fast as them Indians could run. They come down in the tall grass where the white man had gone down, and we seen one of his legs jump up like a snake, and go back down, and the next moment came the screaming.

It went on and on. Rice crawled over to me and said, "I can't stand it. I'm gonna go out there and get him."

"No, you're not," I said. "I'll do it."

"Why you?" Rice said.

" 'Cause I'm in charge."

"I'm goin' with you," The Former House Nigger said.

"Naw, you ain't," I said. "I get rubbed out, you're the one in charge. That's what Colonel Hatch said. I get out there a ways, you open up on them other Apache, keep 'em busier than a bear with a hive of bees."

"Hell, we can't even see them, and the riders done gone on the other side of the hill."

"Shoot where you think they ought to be, just don't send a blue whistler up my ass."

I laid my rifle on the ground, made sure my pistol was loaded, put it back in the holster, pulled my knife, stuck it in my teeth, and crawled to my left along the side of that creek till I come to tall grass, then I worked my way in. I tried to go slow as to make the grass seem to be moved by the wind, which had picked up considerable and was helpin' my sneaky approach.

As I got closer to where the white man had gone down and the Apaches had gone after him, his yells grew somethin' terrible. I was maybe two or three feet from him. I parted the grass to take a look, seen he was lying on his side, and his throat was cut, and he was dead as he was gonna get.

Just a little beyond him, the two Apache was lying in the grass, and one of them was yellin' like he was the white man bein' tortured, and I thought, Well, if that don't beat all. I was right impressed.

Then the Apache saw me. They jumped up and come for me. I rose up quick, pulling the knife from my teeth. One of them hit me like a cannon ball, and away we went rollin'.

A shot popped off and the other Apache did a kind of dance, about four steps, and went down holdin' his throat. Blood was flying out of him like it was a fresh-tapped spring. Me and the other buck rolled in the grass and he tried to shoot me with a pistol he was totin', but only managed to singe my hair and give me a headache and make my left ear ring.

We rolled around like a couple of doodle bugs, and then I came up on top and stabbed at him. He caught my hand. I was holding his gun hand to the ground with my left, and he had hold of my knife hand.

"Jackass," I said, like this might so wound him to the quick, he'd let go. He didn't. We rolled over in the grass some more, and he got the pistol loose and put it to my head, but the cap and ball misfired, and all I got was burned some. I really called him names then. I jerked my legs up and wrapped them around his neck, yanked him down on his back, got on top of him and stabbed him in the groin and the belly, and still he wasn't finished.

I put the knife in his throat, and he gave me a look of disappointment, like he's just realized he'd left somethin' cookin' on the fire and ought to go get it; then he fell back.

I crawled over, rolled the white man on his back. They had cut his balls off and cut his stomach open and sliced his throat. He wasn't gonna come around.

———

I made it back to the creek bank and was shot at only a few times by the Apache. My return trip was a mite brisker than the earlier one. I only got a little bit of burn from a bullet that grazed the butt of my trousers.

When I was back at the creek bank, I said, "Who made that shot on the Apache?"

"That would be me," The Former House Nigger said.

"Listen here, I don't want you callin' yourself The Former House Nigger no more. I don't want no one else callin' you that. You're a buffalo soldier, and a good'n. Rest of you men hear that?"

The men was strung out along the creek, but they heard me, and grunted at me.

"This here is Cullen. He ain't nothing but Cullen or Private Cullen, or whatever his last name is. That's what we call him. You hear that, Cullen? You're a soldier, and a top soldier at that."

"That's good," Cullen said, not so moved about the event as I was. "But, thing worryin' me is the sun is goin' down."

"There's another thing," Bill said, crawlin' over close to us. "There's smoke over that hill. My guess is it ain't no cookout."

I figured the source of that smoke would be where our white fella had come from, and it would be what was left of whoever he was with or the remains of a wagon or some such. The horse-ridin' Apache had gone back there either to finish them off and torture them with fire or to burn a wagon down. The Apache was regular little fire starters, and since they hadn't been able to get to all of us, they was takin' their misery out on what was within reach.

As that sun went down, I began to fret. I moved along the short line of our men and decided not to space them too much, but not bunch them up either. I put us about six feet apart and put a few at the rear as lookouts. Considerin' there weren't many of us, it was a short line, and them two in the back was an even shorter line. Hell, they wasn't no line at all. They was a couple of dots.

The night crawled on. A big frog began to bleat near me. Crickets was sawin' away. Upstairs, the black-as-sin heavens was lit up with stars and the half moon was way too bright.

Couple hours crawled on, and I went over to Cullen and told him to watch tight, 'cause I was goin' down the line and check the rear, make sure no one was sleepin' or pullin' their johnsons. I left my rifle and unsnapped my revolver holster flap, and went to check.

Bill was fine, but when I come to Rice, he was facedown in the dirt. I grabbed him by the back of his collar and hoisted him up, and his head fell near off. His throat had been cut. I wheeled , snappin' my revolver into my hand. Wasn't nothin' there.

A horrible feelin' come over me. I went down the row. All them boys was dead. The Apache had been pickin' em off one at a time, and doin' it so careful like, the horses hadn't even noticed.

I went to the rear and found that the two back there was fine. I said, "You fellas best come with me."

We moved swiftly back to Cullen and Rice, and we hadn't no more than gone a few paces, when a burst of fire cut the night. I saw an Apache shape grasp at his chest and fall back. Runnin' over, we found Cullen holding his revolver, and Bill was up waving his rifle around. "Where are they? Where the hell are they?"

"They're all around. They've done killed the rest of the men." I said.

"Ghosts," Bill said. "They're ghosts."

"What they are is sneaky," I said. "It's what them fellas do for a livin'."

By now, I had what you might call some real goddamn misgivin's, figured I had reckoned right on things. I thought we'd have been safer here, but them Apache had plumb snuck up on us, wiped out three men without so much as leavin' a fart in the air. I said, "I think we better get on our horses and make a run for it."

But when we went over to get the horses, Satan, soon as I untied him, bolted and took off through the wood and disappeared. "Now, that's the shits," I said.

"We'll ride double," Cullen said.

The boys was gettin' their horses loose, and there was a whoop, and an Apache leap-frogged over the back of one of them horses and came down on his feet with one of our own hatchets in his hand. He stuck the blade of it deep in the head of a trooper, a fella whose name I don't remember, be-ing now in my advanced years, and not really havin' known the fella that good in the first place. There was a scramble, like startled quail. There wasn't no military drill about it. It was every sonofabitch for himself. Me and Cullen and Bill tore up the hill, 'cause that was the way we was facin'.

We was out of the wooded area now, and the half moon was bright, and when I looked back, I could see an Apache coming up after us with a knife in his teeth. He was climbin' that hill so fast, he was damn near runnin' on all fours.

I dropped to one knee and aimed and made a good shot that sent him tumbling back down the rise. Horrible thing was, we could hear the other men in the woods down there gettin' hacked and shot to pieces, screamin' and a pleadin', but we knew wasn't no use in tryin' to go back down there. We was outsmarted and outmanned and outfought.

Thing worked in our favor, was the poor old mule was still there wearing that makeshift harness and carry-along we had put him in, with the wood stacked on it. He had wandered a bit, but hadn't left the area.

Bill cut the log rig loose, and cut the packing off the mule's back; then he swung up on the beast and pulled Cullen up behind him, which showed a certain lack of respect for my leadership, which, frankly, was somethin' I could agree with.

I took hold of the mule's tail, and off we went, them ridin', and me runnin' behind holdin' to my rifle with one hand, holdin' on to the mule's tail with the other, hopin' he didn't fart or shit or pause to kick. This was an old Indian trick, one we had learned in the cavalry. You can also run along-side, you got somethin' to hang on to. Now, if the horse, or mule, decided to run full out, well, you was gonna end up with a mouth full of sod, but a rider and a horse and a fella hangin', sort of lettin' himself be pulled along at a solid speed, doin' big strides, can make surprisin' time and manage not to wear too bad if his legs are strong.

When I finally chanced a look over my shoulder, I seen the Apache were comin', and not in any Sunday picnic stroll sort of way either. They was all on horseback. They had our horses to go with theirs. Except Satan. That bastard hadn't let me ride, but he hadn't let no one else ride either, so I gained a kind of respect for him.

A shot cut through the night air, and didn't nothin' happen right off, but then Bill eased off the mule like a candle meltin'. The shot had gone over Cullen's shoulder and hit Bill in the back of the head. We didn't stop to check his wounds. Cullen slid forward, takin' the reins, slowed the mule a bit and stuck out his hand. I took it, and he helped me swing up behind him. There's folks don't know a mule can run right swift, it takes a mind to, but it can. They got a gait that shakes your guts, but they're pretty good runners. And they got wind and they're about three times smarter than a horse.

What they don't got is spare legs for when they step in a chuck hole, and that's what happened. It was quite a fall, and I had an idea then how that Apache had felt when his horse had gone out from under him. The fall chunked me and Cullen way off and out into the dirt, and it damn sure didn't do the mule any good.

On the ground, the poor old mule kept tryin' to get up, but couldn't. He had fallen so that his back was to the Apache, and we was tossed out in the dirt, squirmin'. We crawled around so we was between his legs, and I shot him in the head with my pistol and we made a fort of him. On came them Apache. I took my rifle and laid it over the mule's side and took me a careful bead, and down went one of them. I fired again, and another hit the dirt. Cullen scuttled out from behind the mule and got hold of his rifle where it had fallen, and crawled back. He fired off a couple of shots, but wasn't as lucky as me. The Apache backed off, and at a distance they squatted down beside their horses and took pot shots at us.

The mule was still warm and he stunk. Bullets were splatterin' into his body. None of them was comin' through, but they was lettin' out a lot of gas. Way I had it figured, them Indians would eventually surround us and we'd end up with our hair hangin' on their wickiups by mornin'. Thinkin' on this, I made an offer to shoot Cullen if it looked like we was gonna be overrun.

"Well, I'd rather shoot you then shoot myself," he said.

"I guess that's a deal, then," I said.

It was a bright night and they could see us good, but we could see them good too. The land was flat there, and there wasn't a whole lot of creepin' up they could do without us noticin', but they could still outflank us because they outnumbered us. There was more Apache now than we had seen in the daytime. They had reinforcements. It was like a gatherin' of ants.

The Apache had run their horses all out, and now they was no water for them, so they cut the horse's throats and lit a fire. After a while we could smell horse meat sizzlin'. The horses had been killed so that they made a ring of flesh they could hide behind, and the soft insides was a nice late supper.

"They ain't got no respect for guv'ment property," Cullen said.

I got out my knife and cut the mule's throat, and he was still fresh enough blood flowed, and we put our mouths on the cut and sucked out all we could. It tasted better than I would have figured, and it made us feel a mite better too, but with there just bein' the two of us, we didn't bother to start a fire and cook our fort.

We could hear them over there laughin' and a cuttin' up, and I figure they had them some mescal, 'cause after a bit, they was actually singin' a white man song, "Row, row, row you boat," and we had to listen to that for a couple of hours.

"Goddamn missionaries," I said.

After a bit, one of them climbed over a dead horse and took his breech-cloth down and turned his ass to us and it winked dead-white in the moon-light, white as any Irishman's ass. I got my rifle on him, but for some reason I couldn't let the hammer down. It just didn't seem right to shoot some drunk showin' me his ass. He turned around and peed, kind of pushin' his loins out, like he was doin' a squaw, and laughed, and that was enough. I shot that sonofabitch. I was aimin' for his pecker, but I think I got him in the belly. He fell over and a couple of Apache come out to get him. Cullen shot one of them, and the one was left jumped over the dead horses and disappeared behind them.

"Bad enough they're gonna kill us," Cullen said, "but they got to act nasty too."

We laid there for a while. Cullen said, "Maybe we ought to pray for deliverance."

"Pray in one hand, shit in the other, and see which one fills up first."

"I guess I won't pray," he said. "Or shit. Least not at the moment. You remember, that's how we met. I was—"

"I remember," I said.

Well, we was waitin' for them to surround us, but like Colonel Hatch said, you can never figure an Apache. We laid there all night, and nothin' happen. I'm ashamed to say, I nodded off, and when I awoke it was good and daylight and hadn't nobody cut our throats or taken our hair.

Cullen was sittin' with his legs crossed, lookin' in the direction of the Apache. I said, "Damn, Cullen. I'm sorry. I fell out."

"I let you. They're done gone."

I sat up and looked. There was the horses, buzzards lightin' on them, and there were a few of them big ole birds on the ground eyeballin' our mule, and us. I shooed them, said, "I'll be damn. They just packed up like a circus and left."

"Yep. Ain't no rhyme to it. They had us where they wanted us. Guess they figured they'd lost enough men over a couple of buffalo soldiers, or maybe they saw a bird like Colonel Hatch was talkin' about, and he told them to take themselves home."

"What I figure is they just too drunk to carry on, and woke up with hangovers and went somewhere cool and shaded to sleep it off."

"Reckon so," Cullen said. Then: "Hey, you mean what you said about me bein' a top soldier and all?"

"You know it."

"You ain't a colonel or nothin', but I appreciate it. Course, I don't feel all that top right now."

"We done all we could do. It was Hatch screwed the duck. He ought not have separated us from the troop like that."

"Don't reckon he'll see it that way," Cullen said.

"I figure not," I said.

We cut off chunks of meat from the mule and made a little fire and filled our bellies, then we started walkin'. It was blazin' hot, and still we walked. When nightfall come, I got nervous, thinkin' them Apache might be comin' back, and that in the long run they had just been funnin' us. But they didn't show, and we took turns sleepin' on the hard plains.

Next mornin' it was hot, and we started walkin'. My back hurt and my ass was draggin' and my feet felt like someone had cut them off. I wished we had brought some of that mule meat with us. I was so hungry, I could see cornbread walkin' on the ground. Just when I was startin' to imagine pools of water and troops of soldiers dancin' with each other, I seen somethin' that was a little more substantial.

Satan.

I said to Cullen, "Do you see a big black horse?"

"You mean, Satan?"

"Yep."

"I see him."

"Did you see some dancin' soldiers?"

"Nope."

"Do you still see the horse?"

"Yep, and he looks strong and rested. I figure he found a water hole and some grass, the sonofabitch."

Satan was trottin' along, not lookin' any worse for wear. He stopped when he seen us, and I tried to whistle to him, but my mouth was so dry, I might as well have been trying to whistle him up with my asshole.

I put my rifle down and started walkin' toward him, holdin' out my hand like I had a treat. I don't think he fell for that, but he dropped his head and let me walk up on him. He wasn't saddled, as we had taken all that off when we went to cut wood, but he still had his bridle and reins. I took hold of the bridle. I swung onto his back, and then he bucked. I went up and landed hard on the ground. My head was spinnin', and the next thing I know, that evil bastard was nuzzlin' me with his nose.

I got up and took the reins and led him over to where Cullen was leanin' on his rifle. "Down deep," he said, "I think he likes you."

We rode Satan double back to the fort, and when we got there, a cheer went up. Colonel Hatch come out and shook our hands and even hugged us. "We found what was left of you boys this mornin', and it wasn't a pretty picture. They're all missin' eyes and balls sacks and such. We figured you two had gone under with the rest of them. Was staked out on the plains some-where with ants in your eyes. We got vengeful and started trailin' them Apache, and damn if we didn't meet them comin' back toward us, and there was a runnin' fight took us in the direction of the Pecos. We killed one, but the rest of them got away. We just come ridin' in a few minutes ahead of you."

"You'd have come straight on," Cullen said, "you'd have seen us. And we killed a lot more than one."

"That's good," Hatch said, "and we want to hear your story and Nate's soon as you get somethin' to eat and drink. We might even let you have a swallow of whiskey. Course, Former House Nigger here will have to do the cookin', ain't none of us any good."

"That there's fine," I said, "but, my compadre here, he ain't The Former House Nigger. He's Private Cullen."

Colonel Hatch eyeballed me. "You don't say?"

"Yes sir, I do, even if it hair lips the United States Army."

"Hell," Hatch said. "That alone is reason to say it."

There ain't much to tell now. We said how things was, and they did some investigatin', and damn if we wasn't put in for medals. We didn't never get them, 'cause they was slow about given coloreds awards, and frankly, I didn't think we deserved them, not with us breakin' and runnin' the way we did, like a bunch of little girls tryin' to get in out of the rain, leavin' them men behind. But we didn't stress that part when we was tellin' our story. It would have fouled it some, and I don't think we had much choice other than what we did. We was as brave as men could be without gettin' ourselves foolishly killed.

Still, we was put in for medals, and that was somethin'. In time, Cullen made the rank of Top Soldier. It wasn't just me tellin' him no more. It come true. He become a sergeant, and would have made a good one too, but he got roarin' drunk and set fire to a dead pig and got his stripes taken and spent some time in the stockade. But that's another story.

I liked the cavalry right smart myself, and stayed on there until my time run out and I was supposed to sign up again, and would have too, had it not been for them Chinese women I told you about at the first. But again, that ain't this story. This is the one happened to me in the year of 1870, out there on them hot West Texas plains. I will add a side note. The army let me keep Satan when I was mustered out, and I grew to like him, and he was the best horse I ever had, and me and him became friends of a sort, until 1872, when I had to shoot him and feed him to a dog and a woman I liked better.

Peter S. Beagle

Peter S. Beagle was born in New York City in 1939. Although not prolific by genre standards, he has published a number of well-received fantasy novels, at least two of which, *A Fine and Private Place* and *The Last Unicorn*, were widely influential and are now considered to be classics of the genre. In fact, Beagle may be the most successful writer of lyrical and evocative modern fantasy since Bradbury, and is the winner of two Mythopoeic Fantasy Awards and the Locus Award, as well as having often been a finalist for the World Fantasy Award. Beagle's other books include the novels *The Folk of the Air*, *The Innkeeper's Song*, and *Tamsin*. His short fiction has appeared in places as varied as *The Magazine of Fantasy & Science Fiction*, *The Atlantic Monthly*, *Seventeen*, and *Ladies' Home Journal*, and has been collected in *The Rhinoceros Who Quoted Nietzsche and Other Odd Acquaintances*, *Giant Bones*, *The Line Between*, and *We Never Talk About My Brother*. He won the Hugo Award in 2006 and the Nebula Award in 2007 for his story "Two Hearts." He has written screenplays for several movies, including the animated adaptations of *The Lord of the Rings* and *The Last Unicorn;* the libretto of an opera, *The Midnight Angel;* the fan-favorite *Star Trek: The Next Generation* episode "Sarek"; and a popular autobiographical travel book, *I See By My Outfit*. His most recent book is the new collection *Mirror Kingdoms: The Best of Peter S. Beagle*, and 2010 will see the publication of two long-awaited new novels, *Summerlong* and *I'm Afraid You've Got Dragons*.

You may find the opening pages of this story a bit confusing, but stick with it, and we promise you that you'll be rewarded with a compelling study of the price of compassion—and introduced to perhaps the strangest and most unlikely warrior in this whole anthology.

Dirae

Red.

    Wet red.

    My feet in the red.

    Look. Bending in the red. Shiny in his hand—other hand tears, shakes at something in the red.

    Moves.

    In the red, it moves.

    Doesn't want it to move. Kicks at it, lifts shiny again.

    Doesn't see me.

    In the red, it makes a sound.

    Sound hurts me.

    Doesn't want sound, either. Makes a sound, brings shiny down.

    Stop him.

    Why?

    Don't know.

    In my hand, his hand. Eyes wide. Pulls free, swings shiny at me.

    Take it away.

    Swing shiny across his face. Opens up, flower. Red teeth. Swing shiny again, other way.

    Red. Red.

    Another sound—high, hurting. Far away, but coming closer. Eyes white in red, red face. He turns, feet slipping in red. Could catch him.

    Sound closer. At my feet, moves in red. Hurts me. Hurts me.

    Sound too close.

    Go away.

    Darkness.

    Darkness.

DARK.

I . . .

What? Which? Who?

Who *I*? Think.

What is *think*?

Loud. Hurting. Loud.

A fence. Boys. *Loud.* Hurts me.

One boy, curled on ground.

Other boys.

Feet. So many *feet*.

Hurts.

I walk to them. *I.*

A boy in each hand. I throw them away. *I.*

More boys, more feet. Pick them up, bang together. Throw away.

Like this. *I like this.*

Boys gone.

Curled-up boy. Clothes torn, face streaked red. This is blood. *I* know. How do *I* know?

Boy stands up. Falls.

Face wet, not the blood. Water from his eyes. What?

Stands again. Speaks to me, words. Walks away. Almost falls, but not. Wipes face, walks on.

Turn, faces looking at me. *I* look back, they turn away. Alone here.

Here. Where?

Doors. Windows. Noise. People. In one dark window, a figure.

I move, it moves. *I* go close to see—it comes toward, reaching out.

Me?

Darkness. **Darkness. DARK** . . .

the one with the knife, just out of reach. Drops back, comes close, darts away again. Waiting, waiting, in the corner of my left eye. Old woman screams and screams. The one riding my back, forearm across my throat, laughing, grunting. I snap my head back, feel the nose go, kick between his legs as he falls away. Knife man moves in then, and I catch his wrist and break it, *yes.* Third one, with the gun, frightened, fires, *whong*, garbage can rolls on its edge, falls over. He drops the gun, runs, and I lose him in the alley.

The one I kicked, wriggling on his side toward the gun when I turn back. Stops when he sees me. The old woman gone at last, the knife man huddling against the warehouse wall. "Bitch, you broke my fucking wrist!" *Bitch,* over and over. Other words. I pick up knife and gun and walk away, find a place to drop them. The sky is brightening toward the river, pretty.

Dark...

and I am rolling on the ground, trying to take an automatic rifle away from a crying man. Hits out, bites, kicks, tries to club me with the gun. People crowding in everywhere—legs, shoes, too close, shopping bags, too close, someone steps on my hand. Bodies on the ground, some moving, most not. In my arms, he struggles and wails, wife who left him, job he lost, children taken from him, *voices, voices.* Gives up suddenly—eyes roll back, gone away, harmless. I fight off a raging man, little girl limp in his arms, wants the gun, *Give me that gun!* I am on my feet, standing over the gunman, surrounded, protecting *him* now. Police.

Revolving lights, red and blue and white, ringing us all in together, they yank the man to his feet and run him away, barely letting him touch the ground. Still weeping, head thrown back as though his neck were broken. Bodies lying everywhere, most of them dead. I know dead.

One policeman comes to me, thanks me for preventing more deaths. I give him the rifle, he takes out a little notebook. Wants my story—what happened, what I saw, what I did. Kind face, happy eyes. I begin to tell him.

... then the darkness.

Where do I go?

When the dark takes me—just after I am snatched up out of one war and whirled off into another—where am I? No time between, no memories except blurred battles, no name, no needs, no desires, no relation to anything but my reflection in a shop window or a puddle of rain ... where do I live? Who am I when I am there?

Do I live?

No, I am not a *who,* cannot be. I am a *what.* A walking weapon, a tool, a force, employed by someone or something unknown to me, for reasons I don't understand.

But—

If I was made to be a weapon, consciously manufactured for one purpose alone, then why do I question? That poor madman's rifle had no such interest in its own identity, nor its master's, nor where it hung between uses. No, I am something more than a rifle: I must be something that . . .

wonders. Wonders even while I am taking a gas can away from a giggling young couple who are bending over the ragged woman blinking drowsily on the sidewalk, the man holding his cigarette lighter open, thumb on its wheel. I hit them with the can until they fall down and stay there; then pour the gasoline over them and throw the lighter into a sewer. The ragged woman sniffs, offended by the smell, gets up and mumbles away. She gives me a small nod as she passes by.

And for just an instant, before the darkness takes me, I stand in the empty street, staring after her: a weapon momentarily in no one's hands, aimed at no one, a weapon trying to imagine itself. Only that moment . . .

then dark again, *think about the darkness* . . .

and it is daylight this time, late afternoon. I can see her ahead of me, too far ahead, the calm, well-dressed woman placidly dropping the second child into the river that wanders back and forth through this city. I can see the head of the first one, already swept almost out of sight. The third is struggling now, crying in her arms as she picks it up and raises it over the rail. Other people are running, but I am weaving through, I am past them, I am *there*, hitting her as hard as I can, so that she is actually lifted off the ground, slamming into a sign I cannot read. But the child is already in the air, falling . . .

. . . and so am I, hitting the water only seconds behind her. That one is easy—I have her almost immediately, a little one, a girl, gasping and choking, but unharmed. I set her on the narrow bank—there are stairs ahead, someone will come down and get her—and head after the others, kicking my shoes off as I swim. *As I swim* . . .

How do I know how to swim? Is that part of being a weapon? I am cutting through the water effortlessly, moving faster than the people running along the roadway—how did I learn to use my legs and arms just so? The current is with me, but it is sweeping the children along in the same way. Ahead, one small face turned to the sky, still afloat, but not for long. I swim faster.

A boy, this one, older than the first. I tread water to scoop him up and hold him over my shoulder, while he spews what seems like half the river down my back. But he is trying to point ahead, downstream, even while he vomits, after the third child, the one I can't see anywhere. People are calling from above, but there's no time, no time. I tuck him into the crook of my left arm and set off again, paddling with the right, using my legs and back like one thing, keeping my head out of the water to stare ahead. Nothing. No sign.

Sensible boy, he wriggles around to hold onto my shoulders as I swim, so that the left arm is free again. But I can't find the other one—*I can't* . . .

. . . and then I can. Floating face down, drifting lifelessly, turning and turning. A second girl. I have her in another moment, but the river is fighting me for the two of them now, and getting them to the bank against the current is hard. But we manage it. We manage.

Hands and faces, taking the children from me. The boy and the little one will be all right—the older girl . . . I don't know. The police are here, and two of them are kneeling over her, while the other two are being wrapped in blankets. There is a blanket around my shoulders too, I had not noticed. People pressing close, praising me, their voices very far away. I need to see about the girl.

The police have the mother, a man on either side of her, holding her arms tightly, though she moves with them willingly. Her face is utterly tranquil, all expression smoothed away; she looks at the children with no sign of recognition. The boy looks back at her . . . I will not think about that look. If I am a weapon, I don't have to. I start toward the motionless girl.

One of the policemen trying to start her breath again looks up—then recognizes me, as I know him. He was the one who was asking me questions about the weeping man with the rifle, and who actually saw me go with the darkness. I back away, letting the blanket fall, ready to leap back into the river, soaked through and weary as I am. He points at me, begins to stand up . . .

. . . the darkness comes for me, and for once I am grateful. Except . . . except . . .

Except that now I will never know about that girl, whether she lived or died. I will never know what happened to the mother . . .

Once I would not—*could* not—have thought such thoughts. I would have had neither the words nor the place in me where the words should go. I would not have known to separate myself from the darkness—to remain *me,* even in the dark, waiting. Can a weapon do that? Can a weapon remember that small boy's face above the water, and the way he tried to help me save his sister?

Then that is not all I am, even as I wish it. *Who am I?*

If I am a person, I must have a name. Persons have names. What is my name?

What is my name?

Where do I live?

Could I be mad? Like that poor man with the gun?

I wake. That must mean that I sleep. Doesn't it? Then where do I . . . no, no distractions. What is sure is that I come suddenly awake—on the street, every time, somewhere in the city. Wide awake, instantly . . . dressed—neatly, practically, and entirely unremarkably—and on my feet, *moving,* either already in the midst of trouble, or heading straight for it. And I will know what to do when I find it, because . . . because I will *know,* that's all. I always know.

No name, then . . . no home . . . nowhere to be, except when I am hurrying toward it. And even in daylight, darkness always near . . . silent, void, always lost before, but now this new place in the dark when I can feel that there *is* a *now,* and that *now* is different from *after-now.* If that's so, then I ought to be able to stand still in *after-now* and look back . . .

standing beneath a flickering street light, watching two young black girls walking together, arm in arm. They look no more than fifteen—thirteen, more likely—and they have just come from seeing a movie. *How do I know what a movie is?* This must have been a funny one, because they are giggling, quoting lines, acting out scenes for each other. But they walk rapidly, almost hurrying, and there is a strained pitch to their laughter that makes me think they know it is dangerous for them to be here. I parallel their progress on the other side of the street.

The five white boys materialize silently out of the shadows—three in front of the girls, two behind them, cutting off any chance of flight. The moment is perfectly soundless: everybody knows what everybody else is there for. The black girls look desperately around them; then back slowly against the wall of a building, holding hands like the children they are. One of the boys is already unbuckling his belt.

I am the first one to speak. I walk forward slowly, crossing the empty street, saying, "No. This is not to happen."

I speak strangely, I know that, though I can never hear what it is that I do wrong. The boys turn to look at me, giving the two girls an instant when they might well have made a successful dash for safety. But they are too frightened; neither of them could move a finger at this moment. I keep coming. I say, "I think everyone should go home."

The big one begins to smile. *The leader. Good.* He says loudly to the others, "Right, I'll take this one. Dark meat's bad for my diet." The rest of them laugh, turning back toward the black girls.

I walk straight up to him, never hesitating. The smile stays on his broad blond face, but there is puzzlement in the eyes now, because I am not supposed to be doing this. I say, "You should have listened," and kick straight up at his crotch.

But this one saw that coming, and simply turns his thigh to block me. Huge, grinning—small teeth, kernels of white corn—he hurls himself at me, and we grapple on our feet for a moment before we fall together. His hand covers my entire face; he could smother me like that, easily, but I know better than to bite the heel and anchor myself to the consequences. Instead, I grab his free hand and start breaking fingers. He roars and pulls the hand away from my face, closing it into a fist that will snap my neck if it lands. It doesn't. I twist. Then my own hand, rigid fingers joined and extended, catches him under the heart—again, around the side, kidneys, once, twice—and he gasps and sags. I roll him off me fast and stand up.

The boys haven't noticed the fate of their leader; they are entirely occupied with the black girls, who are screaming now, crying to me for help. I take a throat in each hand and bang two heads together—really hard, there is blood. I drop them, grab another by the shirt, slam him against a parked car, hit him until he sits down in the street. When I turn from him, the last one is halfway down the block, looking back constantly as he runs. He is fat and slow, easily caught—but I had better see to the girls.

"This is not a good place," I say. "Come, I will walk you home."

They are paralyzed at first, almost unable to believe that they have not been raped and beaten, perhaps murdered. Then they are all questions, hysterical with questions I cannot answer. Who am I? What is my name? Where did I come from—do I live around here? How did I happen to be right there when they needed help?

I just saw, that's all, I tell them. Lucky.

"Where you ever learn all that martial arts shit?"

No martial arts, I tell them, no exotic fighting technique, I was just irritated—which makes them laugh shakily, and breaks the tension. Beyond that, I talk to them as little as I can, my voice still something unpracticed, oddly wrong. They do most of the talking, anyway, so glad merely to be alive.

I do walk them all the way to their apartment house—they are cousins, living with their grandmother—and they both hug me with all their strength when we say good-bye. The older girl says earnestly, "I'm going to pray for you every night," and I thank her. They both wave back to me as they run into the building.

I am glad the darkness did not snatch me away while I was with them: my vanishing before their eyes would surely have terrified them, and they have been frightened enough for one night. And I am glad to have at least a moment to be a *who*, fumbling and confused, before I must once again be an invincible *what*, taken down from the wall and aimed at some new target.

This time, when the darkness takes me . . . this time my memory remains whole, clear, unhazy. Everything is still there: nothing tattered or smudged, gone. The two black girls stay with me. I *remember* them, even things they said to each other about the movie they had just seen, and their telling me that their grandmother worked in a school cafeteria. And from there I remember more, though I have no sure way of measuring when any of it happened. *The drunken old man stumbling in front of a bus . . . the two toddlers playing on a rusty, sagging fire escape on a hot night . . . the children driving so slowly down a wide trash-strewn street, training a pistol through the passenger window on another child who has just come out of a liquor store . . . the woman looking behind her into a stir of shadows, walking a little faster . . .*

And each time—me. Rescuer. Savior. Wrath of God . . . somehow fortunately there at just the right moment; there, where I am necessary. But where is *there*?

I am beginning to know. It is a city—how big a city I cannot guess—

and there is a river I almost remember swimming . . . yes, the children. (*What happened to the third one?*) There is a street or two that I have come to recognize. A handful of buildings that give me some kind of bearing as I hurry past on this or that night's mission. One particular row of crowded, crumbling houses has become almost familiar, as have a few shops, a few street corners, a few markets—even a face, now and then . . .

This city, then, is where I live.

No. This is where I *am*.

They live, but I am only *real*. There is a difference I cannot name . . .

outside an apartment door with bright brass numerals on it—4 and 2 and 9; for the first time they are more than shapes to me—my leg in mid-snap, heel of my foot slamming once, just under the lock, breaking cheap wood away from dead bolt and mortise to give me entry. And there they are, the pair of them, sitting together on a couch, his eyes all pupil, the skin of her arms covered with deep scratches. I have seen that before.

This time I could not care less about it. I am here for the baby.

Hallway, door on the right. Closed, but I can hear the whimpering, even though the man is on his feet, making outraged noises, and the woman— pretty, once—is telling him to call nine-one-one. I pay no heed to either of them, not yet. No time, no time.

I can smell the urine even before I have opened the door. He's soaked, and the mattress is soaked, and the blanket, but that's not what stops my breath. It's the little cry he gives when I pick him up: a cry that ought to be a scream, with those bruises, and the way his left arm is hanging—but he hasn't even got the strength to scream. I cannot even tell when I'm hurting him. I lift him, and look into his eyes. What I see there I have never seen before.

And I go completely insane.

Somewhere far away, the woman is tugging at me, shrieking something at me. The man is on the floor, not moving, his face bloody. Not bloody enough. I can fix that. I start toward him, but she keeps getting in my way, she keeps making that sound. What has she got to make noise about? Her arm's not broken, her body isn't one big bruise—she doesn't have those marks that had better not be cigarette burns. Pulling on the arm holding the baby, she will make me drop him. No, now she has stopped, now she is down there, quiet, like the man. Both in the red. Wet red. Good.

Still noise, so much noise. People shouting—the apartment is full of people, when did that happen? Police, lots of police—and one of them *that* one. He stares at me. Says, under all the racket, "What are you doing here? Who *are* you?"

"I am no one," I say. I hand the baby to him. He looks down at it, and his young face goes a terrible color. Before he can raise his head again, the darkness . . .

. . . but no. Different this time. I am back almost immediately, ordinary night, and I am on the street, outside an apartment house I have never seen, where two police cars stand blinking redly at the curb. It is a warm night, but I'm shaking, and cannot stop. Something on my face, I brush at it, impatient. I have been . . . crying.

No purpose here: I know this. I walk away down the street. Keep walking, maybe that will help. For the moment, no place I should be, no helpless, desperate appeal closing on me. No one to save, only escape, evasion. A little time to wonder . . . to ask myself questions—did I kill those two? I was trying, I really wanted to kill them.

Blood crusting on the knuckles of both hands—my blood as well as theirs. My back pains me where the man hit me with some sort of kitchen object before I threw him through the door. I never have time to notice or remember pain; this is new. Yet nothing tonight hurt me as much as the look in the eyes of that urine-soaked child with his little arm dangling so . . . that was when I started crying and trying to kill, not merely protect. I can cry, then; there's something else I know.

Perhaps learning to think was not a good idea. My head is crowded now, heaving and churning with faces, voices, moments . . . *the old man hammering an older one with a heavy paint can, swinging it by the handle . . . the wild-eyed homeless man ringed by jeering boys, who finally catches hold of the one constantly darting in to steal his possessions out of his shopping cart, and has him down, hands around his throat, as the others swarm over him . . . the man with the tire iron, and the bleeding, half-naked woman who attacked me so furiously when I was taking it away from him . . .*

But even so, even so, I can feel it coming closer, a fleeting space *between* strangers, between rescues, when *something* becomes almost clear, like the instant before dawn: the rush of paling sky, the first lights going on in windows, the earliest sounds of birds waking on rooftops. While in it I sense that there is a source of me, a *point* to me; a place, and a memory—and a name—and even my own dawn, where I belong . . .

wake not on the street but in a strange room, where I can see the sky—soft with early morning light, incomplete, the world heavy still with sleep—through tall narrow windows.

There are eight beds in this room, with bodies rounding the blankets in three of them, but no sound, except for the soft buzz and wheeze of machinery. A hospital. The woman in the nearest bed lies on her back, but twisted toward the right; if the tube plugged into a hole in her throat and a monitor beyond were not preventing it, she would be curled up on her side. Her breath is short and soundless, and too fast, and she smells like mildew. She is a big woman, but lying so makes her look shrunken, and older than she probably is. The chart at the foot of the bed is labeled JANE DOE. I sit down in a chair close to her.

She is very ugly. Her arms are thick, heavy, with tiny hands, the fingers all more or less the same size; you can hardly tell the thumb from the rest. Her black hair is lank and tangled, and her face is so pale that the blotches and faded pockmarks stand out like whip scars. Something once broke her nose and the bones of her face, badly. They are not right and clearly never will be. But her expression is utterly peaceful, serenely empty.

I know her.

The red. In the red, moving. Wants it not to move. Sound hurts me.

I say it out loud: "I know you." *You moved in the red. He kicked you. Shiny. I took it away.*

Why am I here?

Jane Doe does not answer me. I never expected that she would. But the young nurse does, a moment later, when she comes storming into the room, demanding to know who I am. I could tell her that I am constantly asking myself the same question, but instead I say that I am Jane Doe's friend. She promptly reaches for the telephone, saying that "Jane Doe" is the name they use for people whose real name no one knows—as I obviously do not. I could tear the phone out of her hand, out of the wall, but instead I sit and wait. She turns away to speak into the phone for a few moments, looking more and more puzzled and annoyed; then hangs it up and turns back to glare at me.

"How the hell did you get in here? Security says no one looking like you has been through at all." She is black, tall and slender, with a small, delicate head, a naturally somber face. Quite pretty, but the confusion is making her really angry.

I say, "There was no one at the door. I just walked in."

"Somebody dies for this," she mumbles. She looks at her watch, makes a note on a pad of paper. "Oh, heads will *roll*, I swear." Calming herself: "Go away, please, or I'll have to have Security up. You don't belong here."

I look back at Jane Doe. "What is the matter with her?"

The nurse shakes her head. "I don't think that's any of your business."

I stand up. I say, "Tell me."

The nurse looks at me for a long moment. I wonder what she sees. "I do that, you'll leave without making any trouble?"

"Yes."

"She was mugged. Ten, eleven months ago. Attacked on the street and beaten really badly—she almost died. They never caught the guy who did it. When she fell, she must have hit her head against something, a building. There was brain damage, bleeding. She's been in a vegetative state ever since." She gestures around her at the other silent beds. "Like the others here."

"And you don't know who she is."

"Nobody does. Do you? Is there something you're not telling me?"

Oh yes. Yes.

"Will she always be like this?"

The nurse—the name on her blue and white breast pin says FELICIA—frowns and backs slowly toward the door. "On second thought, maybe you better stay right there. I'm going to go get someone who can answer your questions."

She will come back with guards.

I sit down. I stare down into the big, blind, ugly face from my very first memory, trying to understand why the darkness brought me here. I watch the blinking monitors and wonder about so many things I do not even have *thoughts* for, let alone words. But it is more than I can grasp, and I have understood nothing when once more I lose the world.

Her name! Her name is . . .

another strange, dim street, and I am carrying a weeping, forlornly struggling girl out of a storefront that advertises ASIAN MAS AGE in its grimy window. She appears to be thirteen or fourteen years old. I cannot understand what she is saying to me.

But she is looking past me, over my shoulder; and when I turn, I see the group massing behind me. A hardfaced middle-aged couple, two younger men—squat, but burly in a top-heavy way—and a boy likely not very much older than the girl in my arms. He is the one holding the broken bottle.

I set the girl down on her feet, still holding her by the shoulders. She has a round, sweet face, but her eyes are mad with terror. I point at the sidewalk and say loudly, "*Stay here!*" several times, until it seems to get through, and she nods meekly. I cannot begin to guess how many times she must have made just that same gesture of bewildered submission in the face of power. I try to pat her shoulder, but she cringes away from me. I let her go, and turn back to face my new batch of enemies.

They are all shouting furious threats at me, but the boy seems to be the only one who speaks English. He eases toward me, waving the half bottle as menacingly as he can, saying, "You give her, get away. My sister."

"She is no more your sister than I am," I answer him. "She is a child, and I am taking her out of here." Neighbors, fellow entrepreneurs, and curious nightwalkers are already gathering around the scene, silent, unfriendly. I say, "Tell the rest of them if they get in my way, that bottle goes up your nose, for a start, and I will beat those two fat boys to death with you. Tell them I am in a very bad mood."

In truth, I am anxious for the police to show up before things get worse than they are. My mood is actually a kind of detached anger, nothing like the madness that took me over so completely when I saw that baby's broken arm. Something changed then, surely. Even if it is what I am for—all I am for—I have no desire to fight anyone just at the moment. I want to go somewhere by myself and think. I want to go back to the hospital, and sit by Jane Doe's bed, and look at her, and think.

But the two burly men are moving slowly out to left and right, trying to flank me, and that stupid boy is getting closer, in little dancy jump-steps. The girl is standing where I left her, wide-eyed, a finger in her mouth. There is a woman just behind her, middle-aged, with a heavy face and kind eyes. I ask her with my own eyes to keep the girl safe while I deal with her former employers, and she nods slightly.

The boy, seeing my attention apparently distracted, chooses this moment to lunge, his arm fully extended, his notion of a war cry carrying and echoing off the low storefronts. I spin, trip him up—the half bottle crashes in the gutter—and hurl him by his shirtfront into the path of the bravo on my left. They go down together, and I turn on the other one, catching him under the nose with the heel of my right hand, between belly and breath with the balled left. He clutches hard at me as he falls, but he does fall.

There are women spilling out of the massage parlor now, all very young, all wearing cut-off shorts and T-shirts that show their flat, childish stomachs. Most simply stare; a few run back into the storefront; two or three slip away down a half-hidden alley. The boy struggles to his feet and here he comes again, jabbing the air with a single jagged splinter of the broken bottle, cutting his own hand where he holds it. I am trying not to hurt him more than necessary, but he is not making it easy. I kick the glass shard out of his grasp, so he won't fall on it when I side-kick his feet out from under him on my way toward the older couple. They back away fast—maybe from me, more likely from the lights and sirens coming up the street. I back off myself, and sigh with relief.

The girl is still where I left her, with the older woman's hand resting lightly on her trembling shoulder. I catch the woman's eye, nod my thanks, gesture toward the patrol car, and start to drift slowly away from there, eyes lowered.

One of the two policemen, Asian himself, is interrogating the massage parlor owners in their own language. But the other, much younger, sees me . . . looks past me . . . then looks again and heads straight for me. Through the shouting and the street noise, I hear his voice. "You! You hold it right there!"

I could still follow the escaping girls down the alley, but I stand where I am. He plants himself a foot in front of me, forefinger aimed at my chest. Surprisingly, he is smiling, but it is a tense, determined smile, not at all pleasant. He says, "We're going to stop meeting like this, right now. Who the hell *are* you?"

"I don't know."

"Yeah, right. And I'll bet you aren't carrying any ID, either." He is too agitated to wait for me to answer. He charges on: "Goddammit, first I see you at that mall shooting, but you just *disappear* on me, I don't know how. Then it was that crazy woman dropping her kids into the river—you dived in, went after them like some TV superhero—"

I interrupt him to ask, "The girl, the older one. Is she . . . will she be all right?"

His face changes; he stops pointing at me. He says nothing for a while, and his voice is lower when he speaks again. "We tried everything. If you'd bothered to stick around, you'd have known. But no—it's another disappearing act, like a damn special effect. Then that couple with the baby, those two meth-heads." It is a different smile this time. "Okay, they had it coming, but *you're* coming downtown with us on that one, and lucky it's not a murder charge. Both of them still in the hospital, you know that?"

I wonder whether they are in the same hospital as Jane Doe. I wonder where the baby is, and I am about to ask him, when he continues, "Now *this*. What, you think you're Batman, the Lone Ranger, rousting massage parlors, beating the crap out of rapists? You're really starting to leave a trail, lady, and we need to have a conversation. You can't *do* this shit."

He reaches for the handcuffs at his belt. My hands raise automatically and he steps back, reaching for his holstered gun instead. I begin to explain why I cannot let him arrest me . . .

but then it is bright afternoon, and I am standing on a street across from a schoolyard in time to see a boy push a smaller boy down hard and run off, laughing. The little one is whimpering dazedly over ripped new blue jeans or a scraped knee, and doesn't see the car coming. Other children and passersby do, but they're too far away, and their warning screams are drowned by the shriek of brakes. No one can possibly reach him in time.

But of course I am there. It is what I do, being there.

Not even a spare second to scoop him up—I crash into him from the side, and the two of us roll away into the gutter as the car slews by, skidding in a half circle, so that it comes to rest on the far side of the street, facing us. The boy ends up in my arms, his eyes wide and frantic, but not crying at all now, because he cannot get his breath. Children are running toward us, adults are coming out of the school; the driver is already down on his knees beside us, easily as hysterical as the boy. But it's all right. It is over. I was there.

My left shoulder hurts where I hit the asphalt, and I have banged my head on something, maybe the curb. Like Jane Doe. I stand up carefully and, as always, ease myself slowly away from the rejoicing and the praise. The boy has started to cry fully now, which is a relief to me.

Jane Doe doesn't cry. She hasn't cried for a very long time.

It is confusing to be suddenly thinking about her. She is somehow there with me, an intrusion, surplus from the darkness, only being felt now because there is no one I must save. Why? I am a ghost myself, always vanishing. How can I be haunted?

Her name is . . .

Oh. I—

I know her name.

I walk until I come to a bridge over that milky river which divides and defines this city. I sit on the stone guardrail to wait for the darkness. I feel a weariness in me more frightening than any boy with a broken bottle. I am real enough to break a jaw or a rib defending a child prostitute; not real enough ever to understand that child's life, her terror, her pain. I can go as mad with rage as any human over a beaten, half-dead infant, and do my very best to murder its abusers—and feel dreadfully *satisfied* to have done so—but now I think . . . now I think it is not my outrage and terrible pity I am satisfying; it is all, all of it, happening in that hospital room, behind those closed eyes whose color I do not know.

I gaze down from the bridge, watching a couple of barges sliding silently by, just below me. *If I were to leap down to them, right now, would I be killed? Can a dream commit suicide?*

Darkness . . .

that policeman is actively looking for me. We have not met again, but I have seen him from a distance once or twice, during one rescue—one *being there*—or another.

My ever-faithful darkness keeps returning for me, carrying me off to do battle with other exploiters, other abusers, other muggers, rapists, molesters, gang thugs, drive-by assassins. See me: lithe, swift, fearless, always barehanded, always alone, always conquering . . . and never in control, not of anything, not of the smallest choice I make. She is. I am certain of that now.

My missions—*her* missions—have always favored children, but lately they seem to feature them constantly, exclusively. More and more I wake to other massage parlors—endless, those—and trucks crammed full of ten-year-old immigrant laborers packed into shipping crates. Garment sweatshops in basement factories. Kitchens in alley diners. Lettuce fields outside the city. At the airport I intercept two girls arriving for hand-delivery to an old man from their home village. In a basement I break a man's arm and leg, then free his pregnant daughter and pregnant granddaughters from the two rooms he has kept them locked in for years. I have grown sharper, more peremptorily violent. I rarely speak now. There is no time. We have work to do, Jane Doe and I, and it is growing so late.

The blind force in the darkness grows fiercer, angrier, more *hurried.* Sometimes I am not even finished when I am snatched up once again—by the back of my neck, really, like a kitten—and plopped straight into another crisis, another horror, another rescue. And I do what I do, what I am for, what Jane Doe birthed me to be: guardian, defender, invincible fighter for the weak and the injured. But it is all wearing thin; so thin that often I can see the next mission through the fabric of this one, the dawn through an increasingly transparent darkness. *Wearing thin . . .*

it happens while I am occupied in rescuing a convenience-store manager and his wife from three large men in ski masks. They are all drunk, they are all armed, and the manager has just made the mistake of hauling out the shotgun from behind the counter. All very noisy and lively; but so far no one is dead, and I have the old couple stashed safely out of the way. But the sirens are coming.

The bandits hear the sirens too, and the two who can still walk actually push past me to get out of the store. I hardly notice them, because I am starting to feel a vague, sickly unease—a psychic nausea surging up and over me in a wave of dislocation and abandonment. Outside, I double over against a wall, gasping, struggling for breath, unable to stand straight, with the patrol cars sounding in the next street over. Somehow I stumble to safety, out of sight behind a couple of huge garbage trucks, and lean there until the spasm passes. No—until it eases a bit. Whatever it is, it is not passing.

The sun is just clear of the horizon. I can feel the dark clutching blindly and feebly at me, but it hasn't the strength to carry me away. I am on my own. I look around to get my bearings; then push myself away from the garbage trucks and start wobbling off.

A car horn close beside me, almost in my ear. I sense who it is before I turn my head and see the blue-and-white police car. He is alone, glaring at me as he pulls to the curb. "Get in, superhero," he calls. "Don't make me chase you."

I am too weak, too weary for flight. I open the front passenger door and sit down beside him. He raises his eyebrows. "Usually we keep the escape artists in the back, with no door handles. What the hell." He does not start up again, but eyes me curiously, fingertips lightly drumming on the steering wheel. He says, "You look terrible. You look really sick." I do not answer. "You going to throw up in my car?"

I mumble, "No. I don't know. I don't think so."

"Because we've had nothing but pukers for the last week—I mean, *nothing* but pukers. So I'd really appreciate it, you know . . ." He does not finish the sentence, but keeps eyeing me warily. "Boy, you look bad. You think you ate a bad clam or something?" Abruptly he makes up his mind. "Look, before we go anywhere, I'm taking you to the hospital. Put your seat belt on."

I leave the belt catch not quite clicked, but as he pulls away into traffic an alarm goes off. He reaches over, snaps the catch into place. I am too slow to prevent him. The alarm stops. With a quick glance my way he says, "You don't *look* crazy or anything—you look like a nice, normal girl. How'd you get into the hero business?"

I am actually dizzy and sweating, as though I *were* going to throw up. I say again, "I don't know. I try to help, that is all."

"Uh-huh. Real commendable. I mean, pulling whole families out of the river and all, the mayor gives you medals for that stuff. Rescuing abused children, taking down mall shooters—that's *our* job, you're kind of making us look bad." He slaps the steering wheel, trying to look sterner than his nature. "But beating up the bad guys, *that's* a no-no. Doesn't matter how bad they are, you get into some really deep shit doing that. They sue. And somebody like me has to go and arrest you . . . not to mention explaining about sixteen million times to my boss, and *his* boss, why I didn't do it already, you being right there on the scene and all. All the damn time."

My head is swimming so badly I have trouble making sense of his words. Something very bad is happening; whether to me or to Jane Doe I cannot tell. *Could this hospital he is taking me to be her hospital?* The policeman is speaking again, his face and voice serious, even anxious. He says, far away, "That vanishing act of yours, now that worries me. Because if you're not crazy, then either you really *are* some kind of superhero, or *I'm* crazy. And I just don't want to be crazy, you know?"

In the midst of my faintness, I feel strangely sorry for him. I manage to reply, "Perhaps there is another choice . . . another possibility . . ." *Even if it is the right hospital, if the darkness does not come again, I will never reach Jane Doe's silent room—not in handcuffs, which are surely coming, and with his hand tight on my shoulder. What must I do?*

"Another possibility?" His eyebrows shoot up again. "Well, now you've got me trying to figure what the hell that could be."

I do not answer him.

He parks the patrol car in front of a squat gray-white building. I can see other cars coming and going: people on crutches, people being pushed in wheelchairs—an ambulance out front, another in the parking lot. He cuts the engine, turns to look straight at me. "Look, doesn't matter whether I *want* to bust you on a filing cabinet full of assault charges or not. I *got* to do that. But what I'd way rather do is just talk to you, first, because that other possibility . . . that other possibility is I've got reality wrong, flat wrong. All of it. And I don't think I'm ready to know that, you understand?"

It *is* Jane Doe's hospital. I can feel her there. This close, the pull of the darkness is still erratic but convulsively stronger. I know she is reaching for me.

With one hand I reach for the door handle, very slowly, holding his glance. With the other I start to unbuckle the seat belt.

"Don't—"

I start to say, "I never had your choice." But I don't finish, any more than I get a chance to throw the door open and bolt into the hospital. Between one word and the next the darkness takes hold of me, neck and heels, and I am gone . . .

once again in Jane Doe's room, standing at the foot of her bed.

And Felicia has seen me appear.

Her silence is part of the silence of the room; her breath comes as roughly as her patients' through the tubes in their throats; the speechless fear in her wide dark eyes renders me just as mute. All I can do for her is to move aside, leaving a clear path to the door. I croak her name as she stumbles through, but the only response is the soft click as she closes the door and locks it from outside. I think I hear her crying, but I could be wrong.

There is a little bathroom, just to the right of the door, with a toilet and sink for visitors. I walk in and wash my face—still dirty and bruised from my convenience store battle—for the first time. Then I take a moment to study the mask that Jane Doe made for me. The woman in the mirror has black hair, like hers, but longer—almost to the shoulders—and fuller. The eyes looking back at me are dark gray. The skin around them is a smooth light-olive. It is blankly calm, this face, the features regular yet somehow uninteresting: easily ignored, passed over, missed in a crowd. And why not, since that so clearly suited Jane Doe's purpose? Whatever terrified instinct first clothed me in flesh chose well.

It is a good face. A *useful* face. I wonder if I will ever see it again.

I walk back to Jane Doe's bed. The strange near-nausea has not left me—if anything, it seems to rise and fall with Jane Doe's breathing, which is labored now. She moves jerkily beneath the cover of her sheets, eyes still closed, her face sweaty and white. Some of the noises coming from the machines attached to her are strong and regular, but others chirp with staccato alarm: whether she is conscious or not, the machines say her body is in pain. And in the same way I know so many things now, I know why. The gift unleashed by the damage she suffered—the talent to give me life from nothingness, to sense danger, fear, cruelty from afar and send her own unlikely angel flying to help—has become too great for the form containing it.

I sit down by her, taking her heavy, limp hand between my own, and the darkness touches me.

There are too many.

My lips feel too cold to move, so I do not even try to speak. All I can do is look.

There are too many, and she cannot do enough.

Images comes to me, falling through my mind like leaves.

Red.

Wet red.

My feet in the red.

She made me up to save her, but I was too late. So we saved others, she and I. We saved so many others.

I look at the door. With every small sound I expect clamor and warning—gunshots, even, or barking dogs. I wonder whether Felicia will be back with the nice young policeman. I wish I could have explained to him.

There is warmth in the darkness. I feel it in my head, I feel it on my skin. It is pain . . . but something beyond pain, too.

On the wall next to the telephone there is a white board with words written on it, and a capped marker. Writing is new to me—I have never had to do it before—so it does not go as quickly or as well as I would like, but I manage. In a child's block letters I write down the name I found in the darkness, and three more words: WE THANK YOU.

Then I go back to her bed.

Voices in the hall now—Felicia, and another woman, and two or three men. I cannot tell whether the young policeman is one of them. No sound yet of Felicia's key in the lock; are they afraid of a woman who comes and goes by magic arts?

I think I would have liked to have a name of my own, but no matter. I lean forward and remove the cables, then the tubes. So many of them. Some of the machines go silent, but others howl.

Fumbling at the lock . . . now the sound of the key. It is so easy to close my hands around her throat, and I feel her breath between my fingers.

Diana Gabaldon

International bestseller Diana Gabaldon is the winner of a Quill Award (for science fiction/fantasy/horror), a RITA Award (for best book of the year, genre unspecified), given by the Romance Writers of America, and the Corine International Prize for Fiction—all for the same series of books. Her hugely popular Outlander series includes *Outlander, Dragonfly in Amber, Voyager, Drums of Autumn, The Fiery Cross, A Breath of Snow and Ashes,* and *An Echo in the Bone.* The bestselling Lord John stories are a subset of the main Outlander series, historical mysteries featuring Lord John Grey, an important minor character from the main novels. Lord John's adventures include *Lord John and the Private Matter, Lord John and the Brotherhood of the Blade,* and *Lord John and the Hand of Devils* (a collection of shorter pieces that includes "Lord John and the Hell-fire Club," "Lord John and the Succubus," and "Lord John and the Haunted Soldier"). A graphic novel, *The Exile* (based on *Outlander,* with artwork by Hoang Nguyen), is due to be released in September 2010. She has also written *The Outlandish Companion,* a nonfiction reference/guide/addendum that covers the first four volumes of the series (the second volume of the *Companion* is due out in a year or so), and is working on a contemporary mystery (working title: *Red Ant's Head*).

Here she takes her swashbuckling military adventurer, Lord John Grey, on a journey to the New World, where at the Siege of Quebec, he faces dangers much more subtle than the usual shot, shell, and steel.

The Custom of the Army

All things considered, it was probably the fault of the electric eel. John Grey could—and for a time, did—blame the Honorable Caroline Woodford as well. And the surgeon. And certainly that blasted poet. Still . . . no, it was the eel's fault.

The party had been at Lucinda Joffrey's house. Sir Richard was absent; a diplomat of his stature could not have countenanced something so frivolous. Electric eel parties were a mania in London just now, but owing to the scarcity of the creatures, a private party was a rare occasion. Most such parties were held at public theaters, with the fortunate few selected for encounter with the eel summoned onstage, there to be shocked and sent reeling like nine-pins for the entertainment of the audience.

"The record is forty-two at once!" Caroline had told him, her eyes wide and shining as she looked up from the creature in its tank.

"Really?" It was one of the most peculiar things he'd seen, though not very striking. Nearly three feet long, it had a heavy squarish body with a blunt head that looked to have been inexpertly molded out of sculptor's clay, and tiny eyes like dull glass beads. It had little in common with the lashing, lithesome eels of the fish-market—and certainly did not seem capable of felling forty-two people at once.

The thing had no grace at all, save for a small thin ruffle of a fin that ran the length of its lower body, undulating as a gauze curtain does in the wind. Lord John expressed this observation to the Honorable Caroline, and was accused in consequence of being poetic.

"Poetic?" said an amused voice behind him. "Is there no end to our gallant major's talents?"

Lord John turned, with an inward grimace and an outward smile, and bowed to Edwin Nicholls.

"I should not think of trespassing upon your province, Mr. Nicholls," he said politely. Nicholls wrote execrable verse, mostly upon the subject of love, and was much admired by young women of a certain turn of mind. The Honorable Caroline wasn't one of them; she'd written a very clever parody of his style, though Grey thought Nicholls had not heard about it. He hoped not.

"Oh, don't you?" Nicholls raised one honey-colored brow at him and glanced briefly but meaningfully at Miss Woodford. His tone was jocular, but his look was not, and Grey wondered just how much Mr. Nicholls had had to drink. Nicholls was flushed of cheek and glittering of eye, but that might be only the heat of the room, which was considerable, and the excitement of the party.

"Do you think of composing an ode to our friend?" Grey asked, ignoring Nicholls's allusion and gesturing toward the large tank that contained the eel.

Nicholls laughed, too loudly—yes, quite a bit the worse for drink—and waved a dismissive hand.

"No, no, Major. How could I think of expending my energies upon such a gross and insignificant creature, when there are angels of delight such as this to inspire me?" He leered—Grey did not wish to impugn the fellow, but he undeniably leered—at Miss Woodford, who smiled—with compressed lips—and tapped him rebukingly with her fan.

Where was Caroline's uncle? Grey wondered. Simon Woodford shared his niece's interest in natural history, and would certainly have escorted her. . . . Oh, there. Simon Woodford was deep in discussion with Mr. Hunter, the famous surgeon—what had possessed Lucinda to invite *him*? Then he caught sight of Lucinda, viewing Mr. Hunter over her fan with narrowed eyes, and realized that she *hadn't* invited him.

John Hunter was a famous surgeon—and an infamous anatomist. Rumor had it that he would stop at nothing to bag a particularly desirable body—whether human or not. He did move in society, but not in the Joffreys' circles.

Lucinda Joffrey had the most expressive eyes. Her one claim to beauty, they were almond-shaped, amber in color, and capable of sending remarkably minatory messages across a crowded room.

Come here! they said. Grey smiled and lifted his glass in salute to her, but made no move to obey. The eyes narrowed further, gleaming dangerously, then cut abruptly toward the surgeon, who was edging toward the tank, his face alight with curiosity and acquisitiveness.

The eyes whipped back to Grey.

Get rid of him! they said.

Grey glanced at Miss Woodford. Mr. Nicholls had seized her hand in his and appeared to be declaiming something; she looked as though she wanted it back. Grey looked back at Lucinda and shrugged, with a small gesture toward Mr. Nicholls's ochre-velvet back, expressing regret that social responsibility prevented his carrying out her order.

"Not only the face of an angel," Nicholls was saying, squeezing Caroline's fingers so hard that she squeaked, "but the skin as well." He stroked her hand, the leer intensifying. "What do angels smell like in the morning, I wonder?"

Grey measured him up thoughtfully. One more remark of that sort, and he might be obliged to invite Mr. Nicholls to step outside. Nicholls was tall and heavily built, outweighed Grey by a couple of stone, and had a reputation for bellicosity. *Best try to break his nose first*, Grey thought, shifting his weight, *then run him headfirst into a hedge. He won't come back in if I make a mess of him.*

"What are you looking at?" Nicholls inquired unpleasantly, catching Grey's gaze upon him.

Grey was saved from reply by a loud clapping of hands—the eel's proprietor calling the party to order. Miss Woodford took advantage of the distraction to snatch her hand away, cheeks flaming with mortification. Grey moved at once to her side, and put a hand beneath her elbow, fixing Nicholls with an icy stare.

"Come with me, Miss Woodford," he said. "Let us find a good place from which to watch the proceedings."

"Watch?" said a voice beside him. "Why, surely you don't mean to *watch*, do you, sir? Are you not curious to try the phenomenon yourself?"

It was Hunter himself, bushy hair tied carelessly back, though decently dressed in a damson-red suit, and grinning up at Grey; the surgeon was broad-shouldered and muscular, but quite short—barely five foot two, to Grey's five-six. Evidently he had noted Grey's wordless exchange with Lucinda.

"Oh, I think—," Grey began, but Hunter had his arm and was tugging him toward the crowd gathering round the tank. Caroline, with an alarmed glance at the glowering Nicholls, hastily followed him.

"I shall be most interested to hear your account of the sensation," Hunter was saying chattily. "Some people report a remarkable euphoria, a momentary disorientation . . . shortness of breath, or dizziness—sometimes pain in the chest. You have not a weak heart, I hope, Major? Or you, Miss Woodford?"

"Me?" Caroline looked surprised.

Hunter bowed to her.

"I should be particularly interested to see your own response, ma'am," he said respectfully. "So few women have the courage to undertake such an adventure."

"She doesn't want to," Grey said hurriedly.

"Well, perhaps I *do*," she said, and gave him a little frown before glancing at the tank and the long gray form inside it. She gave a little shiver—but Grey recognized it, from long acquaintance with the lady, as a shiver of anticipation, rather than of revulsion.

Mr. Hunter recognized it, too. He grinned more broadly and bowed again, extending his arm to Miss Woodford.

"Allow me to secure you a place, ma'am."

Grey and Nicholls both moved purposefully to prevent him, collided, and were left scowling at each other as Mr. Hunter escorted Caroline to the tank and introduced her to the eel's owner, a dark-looking little creature named Horace Suddfield.

Grey nudged Nicholls aside and plunged into the crowd, elbowing his way ruthlessly to the front.

Hunter spotted him and beamed.

"Have you any metal remaining in your chest, Major?"

"Have I—what?"

"Metal," Hunter repeated. "Arthur Longstreet described to me the operation in which he removed thirty-seven pieces of metal from your chest—most impressive. If any bits remain, though, I must advise you against trying the eel. Metal conducts electricity, you see, and the chance of burns—"

Nicholls had made his way through the throng as well, and gave an unpleasant laugh, hearing this.

"A good excuse, Major," he said, a noticeable jeer in his voice.

He was very drunk indeed, Grey thought. Still—

"No, I haven't," he said abruptly.

"Excellent," Suddfield said politely. "A soldier, I understand you are, sir? A bold gentleman, I perceive—who better to take first place?"

And before Grey could protest, he found himself next to the tank, Caroline Woodford's hand clutching his, her other held by Nicholls, who was glaring malevolently.

"Are we all arranged, ladies and gentlemen?" Suddfield cried. "How many, Dobbs?"

"Forty-five!" came a call from his assistant from the next room, through which the line of participants snaked, joined hand to hand and twitching with excitement, the rest of the party standing well back, agog.

"All touching, all touching?" Suddfield cried. "Take a firm grip of your friends, please, a very firm grip!" He turned to Grey, his small face alight. "Go ahead, sir! Grip it tightly, please—just there, just there before the tail!"

Disregarding his better judgement and the consequences to his lace cuff, Grey set his jaw and plunged his hand into the water.

In the split second when he grasped the slimy thing, he expected something like the snap one got from touching a Leiden jar and making it spark. Then he was flung violently backwards, every muscle in his body contorted, and he found himself on the floor, thrashing like a landed fish, gasping in a vain attempt to recall how to breathe.

The surgeon, Mr. Hunter, squatted next to him, observing him with bright-eyed interest.

"How do you feel?" he inquired. "Dizzy, at all?"

Grey shook his head, mouth opening and closing like a goldfish's, and with some effort, thumped his chest.

Thus invited, Mr. Hunter leaned down at once, unbuttoned Grey's waistcoat and pressed an ear to his shirtfront. Whatever he heard—or didn't—seemed to alarm him, for he jerked up, clenched both fists together and brought them down on Grey's chest with a thud that reverberated to his backbone.

This blow had the salutary effect of forcing breath out of his lungs; they filled again by reflex, and suddenly, he remembered how to breathe. His heart also seemed to have been recalled to a sense of its duty, and began beating again. He sat up, fending off another blow from Mr. Hunter, and sat blinking at the carnage round him.

The floor was filled with bodies. Some still writhing, some lying still, limbs outflung in abandonment, some already recovered and being helped to their feet by friends. Excited exclamations filled the air, and Suddfield stood by his eel, beaming with pride and accepting congratulations. The eel itself seemed annoyed; it was swimming round in circles, angrily switching its heavy body.

Edwin Nicholls was on hands and knees, Grey saw, rising slowly to his feet. He reached down to grasp Caroline Woodford's arms and help her to rise. This she did, but so awkwardly that she lost her balance and fell face-first into Mr. Nicholls. He in turn lost his own balance and sat down hard, the Honorable Caroline atop him. Whether from shock, excitement, drink, or simple boorishness, he seized the moment—and Caroline—and planted a hearty kiss upon her astonished lips.

Matters thereafter were somewhat confused. He had a vague impression that he *had* broken Nicholls's nose—and there was a set of burst and swollen knuckles on his right hand to give weight to the supposition. There was a lot of noise, though, and he had the disconcerting feeling of not being altogether firmly confined within his own body. Parts of him seemed to be constantly drifting off, escaping the outlines of his flesh.

What *was* still inside was distinctly jangled. His hearing—still somewhat impaired from the cannon explosion a few months before—had given up entirely under the strain of electric shock. That is, he could still hear, but what he heard made no sense. Random words reached him through a fog of buzzing and ringing, but he could not connect them sensibly to the moving mouths around him. He wasn't at all sure that his own voice was saying what he meant it to, for that matter.

He was surrounded by voices, faces—a sea of feverish sound and movement. People touched him, pulled him, pushed him. He flung out an arm, trying as much to discover where it was as to strike anyone, but felt the impact of flesh. More noise. Here and there a face he recognized: Lucinda, shocked and furious; Caroline, distraught, her red hair disheveled and coming down, all its powder lost.

The net result of everything was that he was not positive whether he had called Nicholls out, or the reverse. Surely Nicholls must have challenged him? He had a vivid recollection of Nicholls, gore-soaked handkerchief held to his nose and a homicidal light in his narrowed eyes. But then he'd found himself outside, in his shirtsleeves, standing in the little park that fronted the Joffreys' house, with a pistol in his hand. He wouldn't have chosen to fight with a strange pistol, would he?

Maybe Nicholls had insulted him, and he had called Nicholls out without quite realizing it?

It had rained earlier, was chilly now; wind was whipping his shirt round his body. His sense of smell was remarkably acute; it seemed to be the only thing working properly. He smelled smoke from the chimneys, the damp green of the plants, and his own sweat, oddly metallic. And something faintly foul—something redolent of mud and slime. By reflex, he rubbed the hand that had touched the eel against his breeches.

Someone was saying something to him. With difficulty, he fixed his attention on Dr. Hunter, standing by his side, still with that look of penetrating interest. *Well, of course. They'd need a surgeon,* he thought dimly. *Have to have a surgeon at a duel.*

"Yes," he said, seeing Hunter's eyebrows raised in inquiry of some sort. Then, seized by a belated fear that he had just promised his body to the surgeon were he killed, seized Hunter's coat with his free hand.

"You . . . don't . . . touch me," he said. "No . . . knives. Ghoul," he added for good measure, finally locating the word.

Hunter nodded, seeming unoffended.

The sky was overcast, the only light that shed by the distant torches at the house's entrance. Nicholls was a whitish blur, coming closer.

Suddenly someone grabbed Grey, turned him forcibly about, and he found himself back to back with Nicholls, the bigger man's heat startling, so near.

Shit, he thought suddenly. *Is he any kind of a shot?*

Someone spoke and he began to walk—he thought he was walking—until an outthrust arm stopped him, and he turned in answer to someone pointing urgently behind him.

Oh, hell, he thought wearily, seeing Nicholls's arm come down. *I don't care.*

He blinked at the muzzle-flash—the report was lost in the shocked gasp from the crowd—and stood for a moment, wondering whether he'd been hit. Nothing seemed amiss, though, and someone nearby was urging him to fire.

Frigging poet, he thought. *I'll delope and have done. I want to go home.* He raised his arm, aiming straight up into the air, but his arm lost contact with his brain for an instant, and his wrist sagged. He jerked, correcting it, and his hand tensed on the trigger. He had barely time to jerk the barrel aside, firing wildly.

To his surprise, Nicholls staggered a bit, then sat down on the grass. He sat propped on one hand, the other clutched dramatically to his shoulder, head thrown back.

It was raining quite hard by now. Grey blinked water off his lashes and shook his head. The air tasted sharp, like cut metal, and for an instant, he had the impression that it smelled . . . purple.

"That can't be right," he said aloud, and found that his ability to speak seemed to have come back. He turned to speak to Hunter, but the surgeon had, of course, darted across to Nicholls, was peering down the neck of the poet's shirt. There was blood on it, Grey saw, but Nicholls was refusing to lie down, gesturing vigorously with his free hand. Blood was running down his face from his nose; perhaps that was it.

"Come away, sir," said a quiet voice at his side. "It'll be bad for Lady Joffrey, else."

"What?" He looked, surprised, to find Richard Tarleton, who had been his ensign in Germany, now in the uniform of a lieutenant in the Lancers. "Oh. Yes, it will." Dueling was illegal in London; for the police to arrest Lucinda's guests before her house would be a scandal—not something that would please her husband, Sir Richard, at all.

The crowd had already melted away, as though the rain had rendered them soluble. The torches by the door had been extinguished. Nicholls was being helped off by Hunter and someone else, lurching away through the increasing rain. Grey shivered. God knew where his coat or cloak was.

"Let's go, then," he said.

Grey opened his eyes.

"Did you say something, Tom?"

Tom Byrd, his valet, had produced a cough like a chimney sweep's, at a distance of approximately one foot from Grey's ear. Seeing that he had obtained his employer's attention, he presented the chamber pot at port arms.

"His Grace is downstairs, me lord. With Her Ladyship."

Grey blinked at the window behind Tom, where the open drapes showed a dim square of rainy light.

"Her Ladyship? What, the duchess?" What could have happened? It couldn't be past nine o'clock. His sister-in-law never paid calls before afternoon, and he had never known her to go anywhere with his brother during the day.

"No, me lord. The little 'un."

"The little—oh. My goddaughter?" He sat up, feeling well but strange, and took the utensil from Tom.

"Yes, me lord. His Grace said as he wants to speak to you about 'the events of last night.'" Tom had crossed to the window and was looking censoriously at the remnants of Grey's shirt and breeches, these stained with grass, mud, blood, and powder, and flung carelessly over the back of the chair. He turned a reproachful eye on Grey, who closed his own, trying to recall exactly what the events of last night had been.

He felt somewhat odd. Not drunk, he hadn't been drunk; he had no headache, no uneasiness of digestion. . . .

"Last night," he repeated, uncertain. Last night had been confused, but he did remember it. The eel party. Lucinda Joffrey, Caroline . . . why on earth ought Hal to be concerned with . . . what, the duel? Why should his brother care about such a silly affair—and even if he did, why appear at Grey's door at the crack of dawn with his six-month-old daughter?

It was more the time of day than the child's presence that was unusual; his brother often did take his daughter out, with the feeble excuse that the child needed air. His wife accused him of wanting to show the baby off—she was beautiful—but Grey thought the cause somewhat more straightforward. His ferocious, autocratic, dictatorial brother, Colonel of his own regiment, terror of both his own troops and his enemies—had fallen in love with his daughter. The regiment would leave for its new posting within a month's time. Hal simply couldn't bear to have her out of his sight.

Thus, he found the Duke of Pardloe seated in the morning room, Lady Dorothea Jacqueline Benedicta Grey cradled in his arm, gnawing on a rusk her father held for her. Her wet silk bonnet, her tiny rabbit-fur bunting, and several letters, some already opened, lay upon the table at the Duke's elbow.

Hal glanced up at him.

"I've ordered your breakfast. Say hallo to Uncle John, Dottie." He turned the baby gently round. She didn't remove her attention from the rusk, but made a small chirping noise.

"Hallo, sweetheart." John leaned over and kissed the top of her head, covered with a soft blond down and slightly damp. "Having a nice outing with Daddy in the pouring rain?"

"We brought you something." Hal picked up the opened letter and, raising an eyebrow at his brother, handed it to him.

Grey raised an eyebrow back and began to read.

"What!" He looked up from the sheet, mouth open.

"Yes, that's what I said," Hal agreed cordially, "when it was delivered to my door, just before dawn." He reached for the sealed letter, carefully balancing the baby. "Here, this one's yours. It came just after dawn."

Grey dropped the first letter as though it were on fire, and seized the second, ripping it open.

"*Oh, John,*" it read without preamble, "*forgive me, I couldn't stop him, I really couldn't, I'm so sorry. I told him, but he wouldn't listen. I'd run away, but I don't know where to go. Please, please do something!*" It wasn't signed, but didn't need to be. He'd recognized the Honorable Caroline Woodford's writing, scribbled and frantic as it was. The paper was blotched and puckered—with tearstains?

He shook his head violently, as though to clear it, then picked up the first letter again. It was just as he'd read it the first time—a formal demand from Alfred, Lord Enderby, to His Grace the Duke of Pardloe, for satisfaction regarding the injury to the honor of his sister, the Honorable Caroline Woodford, by the agency of His Grace's brother, Lord John Grey.

Grey glanced from one document to the other, several times, then looked at his brother.

"What the devil?"

"I gather you had an eventful evening," Hal said, grunting slightly as he bent to retrieve the rusk Dottie had dropped on the carpet. "No, darling, you don't want that anymore."

Dottie disagreed violently with this assertion, and was distracted only by Uncle John picking her up and blowing in her ear.

"Eventful," he repeated. "Yes, it was, rather. But I didn't do anything to Caroline Woodford save hold her hand whilst being shocked by an electric eel, I swear it. Gleeglgleeglgleegl-ppppppsssssshhhhh," he added to Dottie, who shrieked and giggled in response. He glanced up to find Hal staring at him.

"Lucinda Joffrey's party," he amplified. "Surely you and Minnie were invited?"

Hal grunted. "Oh. Yes, we were, but I had a prior engagement. Minnie didn't mention the eel. What's this I hear about you fighting a duel over the girl, though?"

"What? It wasn't—" He stopped, trying to think. "Well, perhaps it was, come to think. Nicholls—you know, that swine who wrote the ode to Minnie's feet?—he kissed Miss Woodford, and she didn't want him to, so I punched him. Who told you about the duel?"

"Richard Tarleton. He came into White's card-room late last night, and said he'd just seen you home."

"Well, then, you likely know as much about it as I do. Oh, you want Daddy back now, do you?" He handed Dottie back to his brother and brushed at a damp patch of saliva on the shoulder of his coat.

"I suppose that's what Enderby's getting at." Hal nodded at the Earl's letter. "That you made the poor girl publicly conspicuous and compromised her virtue by fighting a scandalous duel over her. I suppose he's got a point."

Dottie was now gumming her father's knuckle, making little growling noises. Hal dug in his pocket and came out with a silver teething ring, which he offered her in lieu of his finger, meanwhile giving Grey a sidelong look.

"You don't want to marry Caroline Woodford, do you? That's what Enderby's demand amounts to."

"God, no." Caroline was a good friend—bright, pretty, and given to mad escapades, but marriage? Him?

Hal nodded.

"Lovely girl, but you'd end in Newgate or Bedlam within a month."

"Or dead," Grey said, gingerly picking at the bandage Tom had insisted on wrapping round his knuckles. "How's Nicholls this morning, do you know?"

"Ah." Hal rocked back a little, drawing a deep breath. "Well . . . dead, actually. I had rather a nasty letter from his father, accusing you of murder. That one came over breakfast; didn't think to bring it. Did you mean to kill him?"

Grey sat down quite suddenly, all the blood having left his head.

"No," he whispered. His lips felt stiff and his hands had gone numb. "Oh, Jesus. No."

Hal swiftly pulled his snuffbox from his pocket, one-handed, dumped out the vial of smelling-salts he kept in it and handed it to his brother. Grey was grateful; he hadn't been going to faint, but the assault of ammoniac fumes gave him an excuse for watering eyes and congested breathing.

"Jesus," he repeated, and sneezed explosively several times in a row. "I didn't aim to kill—I swear it, Hal. I deloped. Or tried to," he added honestly.

Lord Enderby's letter suddenly made more sense, as did Hal's presence. What had been a silly affair that should have disappeared with the morning dew had become—or would, directly the gossip had time to spread—not merely a scandal, but quite possibly something worse. It was not unthinkable that he *might* be arrested for murder. Quite without warning, the figured carpet yawned at his feet, an abyss into which his life might vanish.

Hal nodded, and gave him his own handkerchief.

"I know," he said quietly. "Things . . . happen sometimes. That you don't intend—that you'd give your life to have back."

Grey wiped his face, glancing at his brother under cover of the gesture. Hal looked suddenly older than his years, his face drawn by more than worry over Grey.

"Nathaniel Twelvetrees, you mean?" Normally, he wouldn't have mentioned that matter, but both men's guards were down.

Hal gave him a sharp look, then looked away.

"No, not Twelvetrees. I hadn't any choice about that. And I did mean to kill him. I meant . . . what led to that duel." He grimaced. "Marry in haste, repent at leisure." He looked at the note on the table and shook his head. His hand passed gently over Dottie's head. "I won't have you repeat my mistakes, John," he said quietly.

Grey nodded, wordless. Hal's first wife had been seduced by Nathaniel Twelvetrees. Hal's mistakes notwithstanding, Grey had never intended marriage with anyone, and didn't now.

Hal frowned, tapping the folded letter on the table in thought. He darted a glance at John and sighed, then set the letter down, reached into his coat and withdrew two further documents, one clearly official, from its seal.

"Your new commission," he said, handing it over. "For Krefeld," he said, raising an eyebrow at his brother's look of blank incomprehension. "You were brevetted lieutenant-colonel. You didn't remember?"

"I—well . . . not exactly." He had a vague feeling that someone—probably Hal—had told him about it, soon after Krefeld, but he'd been badly wounded then, and in no frame of mind to think about the army, let alone to care about battlefield promotion. Later—

"Wasn't there some confusion over it?" Grey took the commission and opened it, frowning. "I thought they'd changed their minds."

"Oh, you do remember, then," Hal said, eyebrow still cocked. "General Wiedman gave it you after the battle. The confirmation was held up, though, because of the inquiry into the cannon explosion, and then the . . . ah . . . kerfuffle over Adams."

"Oh." Grey was still shaken by the news of Nicholls's death, but mention of Adams started his brain functioning again. "Adams. Oh. You mean Twelvetrees held up the commission?" Colonel Reginald Twelvetrees, of the Royal Artillery—brother to Nathaniel, and cousin to Bernard Adams, the traitor awaiting trial in the Tower, as a result of Grey's efforts the preceding autumn.

"Yes. Bastard," Hal added dispassionately. "I'll have him for breakfast, one of these days."

"Not on my account, I hope," Grey said dryly.

"Oh, no," Hal assured him, jiggling his daughter gently to prevent her fussing. "It will be a purely personal pleasure."

Grey smiled at that, despite his disquiet, and put down the commission. "Right," he said, with a glance at the fourth document, which still lay folded on the table. It was an official-looking letter, and had been opened; the seal was broken. "A proposal of marriage, a denunciation for murder, and a new commission—what the devil's that one? A bill from my tailor?"

"Ah, that. I didn't mean to show it to you," Hal said, leaning carefully to hand it over without dropping Dottie. "But under the circumstances . . ."

He waited, noncommittal, as Grey opened the letter and read it. It was a request—or an order, depending how you looked at it—for the attendance of Major Lord John Grey at the court-martial of one Captain Charles Carruthers, to serve as witness of character for the same. In . . .

"In Canada?" John's exclamation startled Dottie, who crumpled up her face and threatened to cry.

"Hush, sweetheart." Hal jiggled faster, hastily patting her back. "It's all right; only Uncle John being an ass."

Grey ignored this, waving the letter at his brother.

"What the devil is Charlie Carruthers being court-martialed for? And why on earth am I being summoned as a character witness?"

"Failure to suppress a mutiny," Hal said. "As to why you—he asked for you, apparently. An officer under charges is allowed to call his own witnesses, for whatever purpose. Didn't you know that?"

Grey supposed that he had, in an academic sort of way. But he had never attended a court-martial himself; it wasn't a common proceeding, and he had no real idea of the shape of the proceedings.

He glanced sideways at Hal.

"You say you didn't mean to show it to me?"

Hal shrugged, and blew softly over the top of his daughter's head, making the short blond hairs furrow and rise like wheat in the wind.

"No point. I meant to write back and say that as your commanding officer, I required you here; why should you be dragged off to the wilds of Canada? But given your talent for awkward situations . . . what did it feel like?" he inquired curiously.

"What did—oh, the eel." Grey was accustomed to his brother's lightning shifts of conversation, and made the adjustment easily. "Well, it was rather a shock."

He laughed—if tremulously—at Hal's glower, and Dottie squirmed round in her father's arms, reaching out her own plump little arms appealingly to her uncle.

"Flirt," he told her, taking her from Hal. "No, really, it was remarkable. You know how it feels when you break a bone? That sort of jolt before you feel the pain, that goes right through you, and you go blind for a moment and feel like someone's driven a nail through your belly? It was like that, only much stronger, and it went on for longer. Stopped my breath," he admitted. "Quite literally. And my heart, too, I think. Dr. Hunter—you know, the anatomist?—was there, and pounded on my chest to get it started again."

Hal was listening with close attention, and asked several questions, which Grey answered automatically, his mind occupied with this latest surprising communiqué.

Charlie Carruthers. They'd been young officers together, though from different regiments. Fought beside one another in Scotland, gone round London together for a bit on their next leave. They'd had—well, you couldn't call it an affair. Three or four brief encounters—sweating, breathless quarters of an hour in dark corners that could be conveniently forgotten in daylight, or shrugged off as the result of drunkennness, not spoken of by either party.

That had been in the Bad Time, as he thought of it; those years after

Hector's death, when he'd sought oblivion wherever he could find it—and found it often—before slowly recovering himself.

Likely he wouldn't have recalled Carruthers at all, save for the one thing.

Carruthers had been born with an interesting deformity—he had a double hand. While Carruthers's right hand was normal in appearance and worked quite as usual, there was another, dwarf hand that sprang from his wrist and nestled neatly against its larger partner. Dr. Hunter would probably pay hundreds for that hand, Grey thought with a mild lurch of the stomach.

The dwarf hand had only two short fingers and a stubby thumb—but Carruthers could open and close it, though not without also opening and closing the larger one. The shock when Carruthers had closed both of them simultaneously on Grey's prick had been nearly as extraordinary as had the electric eel's.

"Nicholls hasn't been buried yet, has he?" he asked abruptly, the thought of the eel party and Dr. Hunter causing him to interrupt some remark of Hal's.

Hal looked surprised.

"Surely not. Why?" He narrowed his eyes at Grey. "You don't mean to attend the funeral, surely?"

"No, no," Grey said hastily. "I was only thinking of Dr. Hunter. He, um, has a certain reputation . . . and Nicholls did go off with him. After the duel."

"A reputation as what, for God's sake?" Hal demanded impatiently.

"As a body-snatcher," Grey blurted.

There was a sudden silence, awareness dawning in Hal's face. He'd gone pale.

"You don't think—no! How could he?"

"A . . . um . . . hundredweight or so of stones being substituted just prior to the coffin's being nailed shut is the usual method—or so I've heard," Grey said, as well as he could with Dottie's fist being poked up his nose.

Hal swallowed. Grey could see the hairs rise on his wrist.

"I'll ask Harry," Hal said, after a short silence. "The funeral can't have been arranged yet, and if . . ."

Both brothers shuddered reflexively, imagining all too exactly the scene as an agitated family member insisted upon raising the coffin lid, to find . . .

"Maybe better not," Grey said, swallowing. Dottie had left off trying to remove his nose and was patting her tiny hand over his lips as he talked. The feel of it on his skin . . .

He peeled her gently off and gave her back to Hal.

"I don't know what use Charles Carruthers thinks I might be to him—but all right, I'll go." He glanced at Lord Enderby's note, Caroline's crumpled missive. "After all, I suppose there are worse things than being scalped by Red Indians."

Hal nodded, sober.

"I've arranged your sailing. You leave tomorrow." He stood and lifted Dottie. "Here, sweetheart. Kiss your uncle John good-bye."

A month later, Grey found himself, Tom Byrd at his side, climbing off the *Harwood* and into one of the small boats that would land them and the battalion of Louisbourg grenadiers with whom they had been traveling on a large island near the mouth of the St. Lawrence River.

He had never seen anything like it. The river itself was larger than any he had ever seen, nearly half a mile across, running wide and deep, a dark blue-black under the sun. Great cliffs and undulating hills rose on either side of the river, so thickly forested that the underlying stone was nearly invisible. It was hot, and the sky arched brilliant overhead, much brighter and much wider than any sky he had seen before. A loud hum echoed from the lush growth—insects, he supposed, birds, and the rush of the water, though it felt as though the wilderness were singing to itself, in a voice heard only in his blood. Beside him, Tom was fairly vibrating with excitement, his eyes out on stalks, not to miss anything.

"Cor, is that a Red Indian?" he whispered, leaning close to Grey in the boat.

"I don't suppose he can be anything else," Grey replied, as the gentleman loitering by the landing was naked save for a breech-clout, a striped blanket slung over one shoulder, and a coating of what—from the shimmer of his limbs—appeared to be grease of some kind.

"I thought they'd be redder," Tom said, echoing Grey's own thought. The Indian's skin was considerably darker than Grey's own, to be sure, but a rather pleasant soft brown in color, something like dried oak leaves. The Indian appeared to find them nearly as interesting as they had found him; he was eyeing Grey in particular with intent consideration.

"It's your hair, me lord," Tom hissed in Grey's ear. "I told you you ought to have worn a wig."

"Nonsense, Tom." At the same time, Grey experienced an odd frisson up the back of the neck, constricting his scalp. Vain of his hair, which was blond and thick, he didn't commonly wear a wig, choosing instead to bind and powder his own for formal occasions. The present occasion wasn't formal in the least. With the advent of fresh water aboard, Tom had insisted upon washing his hair that morning, and it was still spread loose upon his shoulders, though it had long since dried.

The boat crunched on the shingle, and the Indian flung aside his blanket and came to help the men run it up the shore. Grey found himself next the man, close enough to smell him. He smelled quite unlike anyone Grey had ever encountered; gamy, certainly—he wondered, with a small thrill, whether the grease the man wore might be bear-fat—but with the tang of herbs and a sweat like fresh-sheared copper.

Straightening up from the gunwale, the Indian caught Grey's eye and smiled.

"You be careful, Englishman," he said, in a voice with a noticeable French accent, and reaching out, ran his fingers quite casually through Grey's loose hair. "Your scalp would look good on a Huron's belt."

This made the soldiers from the boat all laugh, and the Indian, still smiling, turned to them.

"They are not so particular, the Abenaki who work for the French. A scalp is a scalp—and the French pay well for one, no matter what color." He nodded genially to the grenadiers, who had stopped laughing. "You come with me."

There was a small camp on the island already; a detachment of infantry under a Captain Woodford—whose name gave Grey a slight wariness, but who turned out to be no relation, thank God, to Lord Enderby's family.

"We're fairly safe on this side of the island," he told Grey, offering him a flask of brandy outside his own tent after supper. "But the Indians raid the other side regularly—I lost four men last week, three killed and one carried off."

"You have your own scouts, though?" Grey asked, slapping at the mosquitoes that had begun to swarm in the dusk. He had not seen the Indian who had brought them to the camp again, but there were several more in camp, mostly clustered together around their own fire, but one or two squatting among the Louisbourg grenadiers who had crossed with Grey on the *Harwood*, bright-eyed and watchful.

"Yes, and trustworthy for the most part," Woodford said, answering Grey's unasked question. He laughed, though not with any humor. "At least we hope so."

Woodford gave him supper, and they had a hand of cards, Grey exchanging news of home for gossip of the current campaign.

General Wolfe had spent no little time at Montmorency, below the town of Quebec, but had nothing but disappointment from his attempts there, and so had abandoned that post, regathering the main body of his troops some miles upstream from the Citadel of Quebec. A so-far impregnable fortress, perched on sheer cliffs above the river, commanding both the river and the plains to the west with her cannon, obliging English warships to steal past under cover of night—and not always successfully.

"Wolfe'll be champing at the bit, now his grenadiers are come," Woodford predicted. "He puts great store by those fellows, fought with 'em at Louisbourg. Here, Colonel, you're being eaten alive—try a bit of this on your hands and face." He dug about in his campaign chest and came up with a tin of strong-smelling grease, which he pushed across the table.

"Bear-grease and mint," he explained. "The Indians use it—that, or cover themselves with mud."

Grey helped himself liberally; the scent wasn't quite the same as what he had smelled earlier on the scout, but it was very similar, and he felt an odd sense of disturbance in its application. Though it did discourage the biting insects.

He had made no secret of the reason for his presence, and now asked openly about Carruthers.

"Where is he held, do you know?"

Woodford frowned and poured more brandy.

"He's not. He's paroled; has a billet in the town at Gareon, where Wolfe's headquarters are."

"Ah?" Grey was mildly surprised—but then, Carruthers was not charged with mutiny, but rather with failure to suppress one—a rare charge. "Do you know the particulars of the case?"

Woodford opened his mouth, as though to speak, but then drew a deep breath, shook his head, and drank brandy. From which Grey deduced that probably everyone knew the particulars, but that there was something fishy about the affair. Well, time enough. He'd hear about the matter directly from Carruthers.

Conversation became general, and after a time, Grey said good-night. The grenadiers had been busy; a new little city of canvas tents had sprung up at the edge of the existing camp, and the appetizing smells of fresh meat roasting and brewing tea were rising on the air.

Tom had doubtless managed to raise his own tent, somewhere in the mass. He was in no hurry to find it, though; he was enjoying the novel sensations of firm footing and solitude, after weeks of crowded shipboard life. He cut outside the orderly rows of new tents, walking just beyond the glow of the firelight, feeling pleasantly invisible, though still close enough for safety—or at least he hoped so. The forest stood only a few yards beyond, the outlines of trees and bushes still just visible, the dark not quite complete.

A drifting spark of green drew his eye, and he felt delight well up in him. There was another . . . another . . . ten, a dozen, and the air was suddenly full of fireflies, soft green sparks that winked on and off, glowing like tiny distant candles among the dark foliage. He'd seen fireflies once or twice before, in Germany, but never in such abundance. They were simple magic, pure as moonlight.

He could not have said how long he watched them, wandering slowly along the edge of the encampment, but at last he sighed and turned toward the center, full-fed, pleasantly tired, and with no immediate responsibility to do anything. He had no troops under his command, no reports to write . . . nothing, really, to do until he reached Gareon and Charlie Carruthers.

With a sigh of peace, he closed the flap of his tent and shucked his outer clothing.

He was roused abruptly from the edge of sleep by screams and shouts, and sat bolt upright. Tom, who had been asleep on his bedsack at Grey's feet, sprang up like a frog onto hands and knees, scrabbling madly for pistol and shot in the chest.

Not waiting, Grey seized the dagger he had hung on the tent-peg before retiring, and flinging back the flap, peered out. Men were rushing to and fro, colliding with tents, shouting orders, yelling for help. There was a glow in the sky, a reddening of the low-hanging clouds.

"Fire-ships!" someone shouted. Grey shoved his feet into his shoes and joined the throng of men now rushing toward the water.

Out in the center of the broad dark river stood the bulk of the *Harwood*, at anchor. And coming slowly down upon her were one, two, and then three blazing vessels—a raft, stacked with flammable waste, doused with oil and set afire. A small boat, its mast and sail flaming bright against the night. Something else—an Indian canoe, with a heap of burning grass and leaves? Too far to see, but it was coming closer.

He glanced at the ship and saw movement on deck—too far to make out individual men, but things were happening. The ship couldn't raise anchor and sail away, not in time—but she was lowering her boats, sailors setting out to try to deflect the fire-ships, keep them away from the *Harwood*.

Absorbed in the sight, he had not noticed the shrieks and shouts still coming from the other side of the camp. But now, as the men on the shore fell silent, watching the fire-ships, they began to stir, realizing belatedly that something else was afoot.

"Indians," the man beside Grey said suddenly as a particularly high, ululating screech split the air. "Indians!"

This cry became general, and everyone began to rush in the other direction.

"Stop! Halt!" Grey flung out an arm, catching a man across the throat and knocking him flat. He raised his voice in the vain hope of stopping the rush. "You! You and you—seize your neighbor, come with me!" The man he had knocked down bounced up again, white-eyed in the starlight.

"It may be a trap!" Grey shouted. "Stay here! Stand to your arms!"

"Stand! Stand!" A short gentleman in his nightshirt took up the cry in a cast-iron bellow, adding to its effect by seizing a dead branch from the ground and laying about himself, turning back those trying to get past him to the encampment.

Another spark grew upstream, and another beyond it: more fire-ships. The boats were in the water now, mere dots in the darkness. If they could fend off the fire-ships, the *Harwood* might be saved from immediate destruction; Grey's fear was that whatever was going on in the rear of the encampment was a ruse designed to pull men away from the shore, leaving the ship protected only by her marines, should the French then send down a barge loaded with explosives, or a boarding craft, hoping to elude detection whilst everyone was dazzled or occupied by the blazing fire-ships and the raid.

The first of the fire-ships had drifted harmlessly onto the far shore, and was burning itself out on the sand, brilliant and beautiful against the night. The short gentleman with the remarkable voice—clearly he was a sergeant, Grey thought—had succeeded in rallying a small group of soldiers, whom he now presented to Grey with a brisk salute.

"Will they go and fetch their muskets, all orderly, sir?"

"They will," Grey said. "And hurry. Go with them, Sergeant—it is sergeant?"

"Sergeant Aloysius Cutter, sir," the short gentleman replied with a nod, "and pleased to know an officer what has a brain in his head."

"Thank you, Sergeant. And fetch back as many more men as fall conveniently to hand, if you please. With arms. A rifleman or two, if you can find one."

Matters thus momentarily attended to, he turned his attention once more to the river, where two of the *Harwood*'s small boats were herding one of the fire-ships away from the transport, circling it and pushing water with their oars; he caught the splash of their efforts, and the shouts of the sailors.

"Me lord?"

The voice at his elbow nearly made him swallow his tongue. He turned with an attempt at calmness, ready to reproach Tom for venturing out into the chaos, but before he could summon words, his young valet stooped at his feet, holding something.

"I've brought your breeches, me lord," Tom said, voice trembling. "Thought you might need 'em, if there was fighting."

"Very thoughtful of you, Tom," he assured his valet, fighting an urge to laugh. He stepped into the breeches and pulled them up, tucking in his shirt. "What's been happening in the camp, do you know?"

He could hear Tom swallow hard.

"Indians, me lord," Tom said. "They came screaming through the tents, set one or two afire. They killed one man I saw, and . . . and scalped him." His voice was thick, as though he might be about to vomit. "It was nasty."

"I daresay." The night was warm, but Grey felt the hairs rise on arms and neck. The chilling screams had stopped, and while he could still hear considerable hubbub in the camp, it was of a different tone now; no random shouting, just the calls of officers, sergeants, and corporals ordering the men, beginning the process of assembly, of counting noses and reckoning damage.

Tom, bless him, had brought Grey's pistol, shot-bag, and powder, as well as his coat and stockings. Aware of the dark forest and the long, narrow trail between the shore and the camp, Grey didn't send Tom back, but merely told him to keep out of the way as Sergeant Cutter—who with good military instinct, had also taken time to put his breeches on—came up with his armed recruits.

"All present, sir," Cutter said, saluting. "'Oom 'ave I the honor of h'addressing, sir?"

"I am Lieutenant-Colonel Grey. Set your men to watch the ship, please, Sergeant, with particular attention to dark craft coming downstream, and then come back to report what you know of matters in camp."

Cutter saluted and promptly vanished with a shout of "Come on, you shower o' shit! Look lively, look lively!"

Tom gave a brief strangled scream, and Grey whirled, drawing his dagger by reflex, to find a dark shape directly behind him.

"Don't kill me, Englishman," said the Indian who had led them to the camp earlier. He sounded mildly amused. "*Le capitaine* sent me to find you."

"Why?" Grey asked shortly. His heart was still pounding from the shock. He disliked being taken at a disadvantage, and disliked even more the thought that the man could easily have killed him before Grey knew he was there.

"The Abenaki set your tent on fire; he supposed they might have dragged you and your servant into the forest."

Tom uttered an extremely coarse expletive and made as though to dive directly into the trees, but Grey stopped him with a hand on his arm.

"Stay, Tom. It doesn't matter."

"The bloody hell you say," Tom replied heatedly, agitation depriving him of his normal manners. "I daresay I can find you more smallclothes, not as that will be easy, but what about your cousin's painting of her and the little 'un she sent for Captain Stubbs? What about your good hat with the gold lace!"

Grey had a brief moment of alarm—his young cousin Olivia had sent a miniature of herself and her newborn son, charging him to deliver this to her husband, Captain Malcolm Stubbs, presently with Wolfe's troops. He clapped a hand to his side, though, and felt with relief the oval shape of the miniature in its wrappings, safe in his pocket.

"That's all right, Tom; I've got it. As to the hat . . . we'll worry about that later, I think. Here—what is your name, sir?" he inquired of the Indian, unwilling to address him simply as *you*.

"Manoke," said the Indian, still sounding amused.

"Quite. Will you take my servant back to the camp?" He saw the small determined figure of Sergeant Cutter appear at the mouth of the trail, and firmly overriding Tom's protests, shooed him off in care of the Indian.

In the event, all five fire-ships either drifted or were steered away from the *Harwood*. Something that might—or might not—have been a boarding craft did appear upstream, but was frightened off by Grey's impromptu troops on the shore, firing volleys—though the range was woefully short; there was no possibility of hitting anything.

Still, the *Harwood* was secure, and the camp had settled into a state of uneasy watchfulness. Grey had seen Woodford briefly upon his return, near dawn, and learned that the raid had resulted in the deaths of two men and the capture of three more, dragged off into the forest. Three of the Indian raiders had been killed, another wounded—Woodford intended to interview this man before he died, but doubted that any useful information would result.

"They never talk," he'd said, rubbing at his smoke-reddened eyes. His face was pouchy and gray with fatigue. "They just close their eyes and start singing their damned deathsongs. Not a blind bit of difference what you do to 'em—they just keep singing."

Grey had heard it, or thought he had, as he crawled wearily into his borrowed shelter toward daybreak. A faint high-pitched chant that rose and fell like the rush of the wind in the trees overhead. It kept up for a bit, then stopped abruptly, only to resume again, faint and interrupted, as he teetered on the edge of sleep.

What was the man saying? he wondered. Did it matter that none of the men hearing him knew what he said? Perhaps the scout—Manoke, that was his name—was there; perhaps he would know.

Tom had found Grey a small tent at the end of a row. Probably he had ejected some subaltern, but Grey wasn't inclined to object. It was barely big enough for the canvas bedsack that lay on the ground and a box that served as table, on which stood an empty candlestick, but it was shelter. It had begun to rain lightly as he walked up the trail to camp, and the rain was now pattering busily on the canvas overhead, raising a sweet musty scent. If the deathsong continued, it was no longer audible over the sound of the rain.

Grey turned over once, the grass stuffing of the bedsack rustling softly beneath him, and fell at once into sleep.

He woke abruptly, face-to-face with an Indian. His reflexive flurry of movement was met with a low chuckle and a slight withdrawal, rather than a knife across the throat, though, and he broke through the fog of sleep in time to avoid doing serious damage to the scout Manoke.

"What?" he muttered, and rubbed the heel of his hand across his eyes. "What is it?" *And why the devil are you lying on my bed?*

In answer to this, the Indian put a hand behind his head, drew him close, and kissed him. The man's tongue ran lightly across his lower lip, darted like a lizard's into his mouth, and then was gone.

So was the Indian.

He rolled over onto his back, blinking. A dream. It was still raining, harder now. He breathed in deeply; he could smell bear-grease, of course, on his own skin, and mint—was there any hint of metal? The light was stronger—it must be day; he heard the drummer passing through the aisles of tents to rouse the men, the rattle of his sticks blending with the rattle of the rain, the shouts of corporals and sergeants—but still faint and gray. He could not have been asleep for more than half an hour, he thought.

"Christ," he muttered, and turning himself stiffly over, pulled his coat over his head and sought sleep once again.

The *Harwood* tacked slowly upriver, with a sharp eye out for French marauders. There were a few alarms, including another raid by hostile Indians while camped on shore. This one ended more happily, with four marauders killed, and only one cook wounded, not seriously. They were obliged to loiter for a time, waiting for a cloudy night, in order to steal past the fortress of Quebec, menacing on its cliffs. They were spotted, in fact, and one or two cannon fired in their direction, but to no effect. And at last came into port at Gareon, the site of General Wolfe's headquarters.

The town itself had been nearly engulfed by the growing military encampment that surrounded it, acres of tents spreading upward from the settlement on the riverbank, the whole presided over by a small French Catholic mission, whose tiny cross was just visible at the top of the hill that lay behind the town. The French inhabitants, with the political indifference of merchants everywhere, had given a Gallic shrug and set about happily overcharging the occupying forces.

The General himself was elsewhere, Grey was informed, fighting inland, but would doubtless return within the month. A lieutenant-colonel without brief or regimental affiliation was simply a nuisance; he was provided with suitable quarters and politely shooed away. With no immediate duties to fulfill, he gave a shrug of his own and set out to discover the whereabouts of Captain Carruthers.

It wasn't difficult to find him. The *patron* of the first tavern Grey visited directed him at once to the habitat of *le Capitaine*, a room in the house of a widow named Lambert, near the mission church. Grey wondered whether he would have received the information as readily from any other tavern-keeper in the village. Charlie had liked to drink when Grey knew him, and evidently still did, judging from the genial attitude of the *patron* when Carruthers's name was mentioned. Not that Grey could blame him, under the circumstances.

The widow—young, chestnut-haired and quite attractive—viewed the English officer at her door with a deep suspicion, but when he followed his request for Captain Carruthers by mentioning that he was an old friend of the Captain's, her face relaxed.

"*Bon,*" she said, swinging the door open abruptly. "He needs friends."

He ascended two flights of narrow stairs to Carruthers's attic, feeling the air about him grow warmer. It was pleasant at this time of day, but must grow stifling by midafternoon. He knocked, and felt a small shock of pleased recognition at hearing Carruthers's voice bid him enter.

Carruthers was seated at a rickety table in shirt and breeches, writing, an inkwell made from a gourd at one elbow, a pot of beer at the other. He looked at Grey blankly for an instant; then joy washed across his features, and he rose, nearly upsetting both.

"John!"

Before Grey could offer his hand, he found himself embraced—and returned the embrace wholeheartedly, a wash of memory flooding through him as he smelled Carruthers's hair, felt the scrape of his unshaven cheek against Grey's own. Even in the midst of this sensation, though, he felt the slightness of Carruthers's body, the bones that pressed through his clothes.

"I never thought you'd come," Carruthers was repeating, for perhaps the fourth time. He let go and stepped back, smiling as he dashed the back of his hand across his eyes, which were unabashedly wet.

"Well, you have an electric eel to thank for my presence," Grey told him, smiling himself.

"A what?" Carruthers stared at him blankly.

"Long story—tell you later. For the moment, though—what the devil have you been doing, Charlie?"

The happiness faded somewhat from Carruthers's lean face, but didn't disappear altogether. "Ah. Well. That's a long story, too. Let me send Martine for more beer." He waved Grey toward the room's only stool, and went out before Grey could protest. He sat gingerly, lest the stool collapse, but it held his weight. Besides the stool and table, the attic was very plainly furnished; a narrow cot, a chamber pot, and an ancient washstand with an earthenware basin and ewer completed the ensemble. It was very clean, but there was a faint smell of something in the air—something sweet and sickly, which he traced at once to a corked bottle standing at the back of the washstand.

Not that he had needed the smell of laudanum; one look at Carruthers's gaunt face told him enough. Returning to the stool, he glanced at the papers Carruthers had been working on. They appeared to be notes in preparation for the court-martial; the one on top was an account of an expedition undertaken by troops under Carruthers's command, on the orders of a Major Gerald Siverly.

> "Our orders instructed us to march to a village called Beaulieu, some ten miles to the east of Montmorency, there to ransack and fire the houses, driving off such animals as we encountered. This we did. Some men of the village offered us resistance, armed with scythes and other implements. Two of these were shot, the others fled. We re-

turned with two waggons filled with flour, cheeses, and small house-hold goods, three cows, and two good mules."

Grey got no further before the door opened.

Carruthers came in and sat on the bed, nodding toward the papers.

"I thought I'd best write everything down. Just in case I don't live long enough for the court-martial." He spoke matter-of-factly, and seeing the look on Grey's face, smiled faintly. "Don't be troubled, John. I've always known I'd not make old bones. This—" He turned his right hand upward, letting the drooping cuff of his shirt fall back. "—isn't all of it."

He tapped his chest gently with his left hand.

"More than one doctor's told me I have some gross defect of the heart. Don't know, quite, if I have two of those, too—" He grinned at Grey, the sudden charming smile he remembered so well. "—or only half of one, or what. Used to be, I just went faint now and then, but it's getting worse. Sometimes I feel it stop beating and just flutter in my chest, and every-thing begins to go all black and breathless. So far, it's always started beat-ing again—but one of these days, it isn't going to."

Grey's eyes were fixed on Charlie's hand, the small dwarf hand curled against its larger fellow, looking as though Charlie held a strange flower cupped in his palm. As he watched, both hands opened slowly, the fingers moving in strangely beautiful synchrony.

"All right," he said quietly. "Tell me."

Failure to suppress a mutiny was a rare charge; difficult to prove, and thus unlikely to be brought, unless other factors were involved. Which in the present instance, they undoubtedly were.

"Know Siverly, do you?" Carruthers asked, taking the papers onto his knee.

"Not at all. I gather he's a bastard." Grey gestured at the papers. "What kind of bastard, though?"

"A corrupt one." Carruthers tapped the pages square, carefully evening the edges, eyes fixed on them. "That—what you read—it wasn't Siverly. It's General Wolfe's directive. I'm not sure whether the point is to deprive the fortress of provisions, in hopes of starving them out eventually, or to put pressure on Montcalm to send out troops to defend the countryside, where Wolfe could get at them—possibly both. But he means deliberately to ter-rorize the settlements on both sides of the river. No, we did this under the

General's orders." His face twisted a little, and he looked up suddenly at Grey. "You remember the Highlands, John?"

"You know that I do." No one involved in Cumberland's cleansing of the Highlands would ever forget. He had seen many Scottish villages like Beaulieu.

Carruthers took a deep breath.

"Yes. Well. The trouble was that Siverly took to appropriating the plunder we took from the countryside—under the pretext of selling it in order to make an equitable distribution among the troops."

"What?" This was contrary to the normal custom of the army, whereby any soldier was entitled to what plunder he took. "Who does he think he is, an admiral?" The navy did divide shares of prize money among the crew, according to formula—but the navy was the navy; crews acted much more as single entities than did army companies, and there were Admiralty courts set up to deal with the sale of captured prize-ships.

Carruthers laughed at the question.

"His brother's a commodore. Perhaps that's where he got the notion. At any rate," he added, sobering, "he never did distribute the funds. Worse— he began withholding the soldiers' pay. Paying later and later, stopping pay for petty offenses, claiming that the paychest hadn't been delivered—when several men had seen it unloaded from the coach with their own eyes.

"Bad enough—but the soldiers were still being fed and clothed adequately. But then he went too far."

Siverly began to steal from the commissary, diverting quantities of supplies and selling them privately.

"I had my suspicions," Carruthers explained, "but no proof. I'd begun to watch him, though—and he knew I was watching him, so he trod carefully for a bit. But he couldn't resist the rifles."

A shipment of a dozen new rifles, vastly superior to the ordinary Brown Bess musket, and very rare in the army.

"I think it must have been a clerical oversight that sent them to us in the first place. We hadn't any riflemen, and there was no real need for them. That's probably what made Siverly think he could get away with it."

But he hadn't. Two private soldiers had unloaded the box, and, curious at the weight, had opened it. Excited word had spread—and excitement had turned to disgruntled surprise when, instead of new rifles, muskets showing considerable wear were later distributed. The talk—already angry—had escalated.

"Egged on by a hogshead of rum we confiscated from a tavern in Levi," Carruthers said with a sigh. "They drank all night—it was January, the nights are damned long in January here—and made up their minds to go and find the rifles. Which they did—under the floor in Siverly's quarters."

"And where was Siverly?"

"In his quarters. He was rather badly used, I'm afraid." A muscle by Carruthers's mouth twitched. "Escaped through a window, though, and made his way through the snow to the next garrison. It was twenty miles. Lost a couple of toes to frostbite, but survived."

"Too bad."

"Yes, it was." The muscle twitched again.

"What happened to the mutineers?"

Carruthers blew out his cheeks, shaking his head.

"Deserted, most of them. Two were caught and hanged pretty promptly; three more rounded up later; they're in prison here."

"And you—"

"And I." Carruthers nodded. "I was Siverly's second-in-command. I didn't know about the mutiny—one of the ensigns ran to fetch me when the men started to move toward Siverly's quarters—but I did arrive before they'd finished."

"Not a great deal you could do under those circumstances, was there?"

"I didn't try," Carruthers said bluntly.

"I see," Grey said.

"Do you?" Carruthers gave him a crooked smile.

"Certainly. I take it Siverly is still in the army, and still holds a command? Yes, of course. He might have been furious enough to prefer the original charge against you, but you know as well as I do that under normal circumstances, the matter would likely have been dropped as soon as the general facts were known. You insisted on a court-martial, didn't you? So that you can make what you know public." Given Carruthers's state of health, the knowledge that he risked a long imprisonment if convicted apparently didn't trouble him.

The smile straightened, and became genuine.

"I knew I chose the right man," Carruthers said.

"I am exceeding flattered," Grey said dryly. "Why me, though?"

Carruthers had laid aside his papers, and now rocked back a little on the cot, hands linked around one knee.

"Why you, John?" The smile had vanished, and Carruthers's gray eyes were level on his. "You know what we do. Our business is chaos, death, destruction. But you know why we do it, too."

"Oh? Perhaps you'd have the goodness to tell me, then. I've always wondered."

Humor lighted Charlie's eyes, but he spoke seriously.

"Someone has to keep order, John. Soldiers fight for all kinds of reasons, most of them ignoble. You and your brother, though . . ." He broke off, shaking his head.

Grey saw that his hair was streaked with gray, though he knew Carruthers was no older than himself.

"The world is chaos and death and destruction. But people like you—you don't stand for that. If there is any order in the world, any peace—it's because of you, John, and those very few like you."

Grey felt he should say something, but was at a loss as to what that might be. Carruthers rose and came to Grey, putting a hand—the left—on his shoulder, the other gently against his face.

"What is it the Bible says?" Carruthers said quietly. "Blessed are they that hunger and thirst for justice, for they shall be satisfied? I hunger, John," he whispered. "And you thirst. You won't fail me." The fingers of Charlie's secret moved on his skin, a plea, a caress.

> *"The custom of the army is that a court-martial be presided over by a senior officer and such a number of other officers as he shall think fit to serve as council, these being generally four in number, but can be more but not generally less than three. The person accused shall have the right to call witnesses in his support, and the council shall question these, as well as any other persons whom they may wish, and shall thus determine the circumstances, and if conviction ensue, the sentence to be imposed."*

That rather vague statement was evidently all that existed in terms of written definition and directive regarding the operations of courts-martial—or was all that Hal had turned up for him in the brief period prior to his departure. There were no formal laws governing such courts, nor did the law of the land apply to them. In short, the army was—as always, Grey thought—a law unto itself.

That being so, he might have considerable leeway in accomplishing what Charlie Carruthers wanted—or not, depending upon the personalities and professional alliances of the officers who composed the court. It would behoove him to discover these men as soon as possible.

In the meantime, he had another small duty to discharge.

"Tom," he called, rummaging in his trunk, "have you discovered Captain Stubbs's billet?"

"Yes, me lord. And if you'll give over ruining your shirts, there, I'll tell you." With a censorious look at his master, Tom nudged him deftly aside. "What you a-looking for in there, anyway?"

"The miniature of my cousin and her child." Grey stood back, permitting Tom to bend over the open chest, tenderly patting the abused shirts back into their tidy folds. The chest itself was rather scorched, but the soldiers had succeeded in rescuing it—and Grey's wardrobe, to Tom's relief.

"Here, me lord." Tom withdrew the little packet and handed it gently to Grey. "Give me best to Captain Stubbs. Reckon he'll be glad to get that. The little 'un's got quite the look of him, don't he?"

It took some little time, even with Tom's direction, to discover Malcolm Stubbs's billet. The address—insofar as it could be called one—lay in the poorer section of the town, somewhere down a muddy lane that ended abruptly at the river. Grey was surprised at this; Stubbs was a most sociable sort, and a conscientious officer. Why was he not billeted in an inn, or a good private house, near his troops?

By the time he found the lane, he had an uneasy feeling; this grew markedly as he poked his way through the ramshackle sheds and the knots of filthy polyglot children that broke from their play, brightening at the novel sight, and followed him, hissing unintelligible speculations to each other, but who stared blankly at him, mouths open, when he asked after Captain Stubbs, pointing at his own uniform by way of illustration, with a questioning wave at their surroundings.

He had made his way down the lane, and his boots were caked with mud, dung, and a thick plastering of the leaves that sifted in a constant rain from the giant trees, before he discovered someone willing to answer him. This was an ancient Indian, sitting peacefully on a rock at the river's edge, wrapped in a striped British trade blanket, fishing. The man spoke a mixture of three or four languages, only two of which Grey understood, but this basis of understanding was adequate.

"*Un, deux, trois,* in back," the ancient told him, pointing a thumb up the lane, then jerking this appendage sideways. Something in an aboriginal tongue followed, in which Grey thought he detected a reference to a woman—doubtless the owner of the house where Stubbs was billeted. A concluding reference to *"le bon Capitaine"* seemed to reinforce this impression, and thanking the gentleman in both French and English, Grey retraced his steps to the third house up the lane, still trailing a line of curious urchins like the ragged tail of a kite.

No one answered his knock, but he went round the house—followed by the children—and discovered a small hut behind it, smoke coming from its gray stone chimney.

The day was beautiful, with a sky the color of sapphires, and the air was suffused with the tang of early autumn. The door of the hut was ajar, to admit the crisp, fresh air, but he did not push it open. Instead, he drew his dagger from his belt and knocked with the hilt—to admiring gasps from his audience at the appearance of the knife. He repressed the urge to turn round and bow to them.

He heard no footsteps from within, but the door opened suddenly, revealing a young Indian woman whose face blazed with sudden joy at beholding him.

He blinked, startled, and in that blink of an eye, the joy disappeared and the young woman clutched at the door-jamb for support, her other hand fisted into her chest.

"*Batinse!*" she gasped, clearly terrified. "*Qu'est-ce qui s'passe?*"

"*Rien,*" he replied, equally startled. "*Ne t'inquiete pas, madame. Est-ce que Capitaine Stubbs habite ici?*" Don't perturb yourself, madam. Does Captain Stubbs live here?

Her eyes, already huge, rolled back in her head, and he seized her arm, fearing lest she faint at his feet. The largest of the urchins following him rushed forward and pushed the door open, and he put an arm round the woman's waist and half dragged, half carried her into the house.

Taking this as invitation, the rest of the children crowded in behind him, murmuring in what appeared to be sympathy, as he lugged the young woman to the bed and deposited her thereon. A small girl, wearing little more than a pair of drawers snugged round her insubstantial waist with a piece of string, pressed in beside him and said something to the young woman. Not receiving an answer, the girl behaved as though she had, turning and racing out of the door.

Grey hesitated, not sure what to do. The woman was breathing, though pale, and her eyelids fluttered.

"Voulez-vous un peu de l'eau?" he inquired, turning about in search of water. He spotted a bucket of water near the hearth, but his attention was distracted from this by an object propped beside it. A cradle-board, with a swaddled infant bound to it, blinking large, curious eyes in his direction.

He knew already, of course, but knelt down before the infant and waggled a tentative forefinger at it. The baby's eyes were big and dark, like its mother's, and the skin a paler shade of her own. The hair, though, was not straight, thick and black. It was the color of cinnamon, and exploded from the child's skull in a nimbus of the same curls that Malcolm Stubbs kept rigorously clipped to his scalp and hidden beneath his wig.

"Wha' happen with *le Capitaine?*" a peremptory voice demanded behind him. He turned on his heels, and, finding a rather large woman looming over him, rose to his feet and bowed.

"Nothing whatever, madam," he assured her. *Not yet, it hasn't.* "I was merely seeking Captain Stubbs, to give him a message."

"Oh." The woman—French, but plainly the younger woman's mother or aunt—left off glowering at him and seemed to deflate somewhat, settling back into a less threatening shape. "Well, then. *D'un urgence,* this message?" She eyed him; clearly other British officers were not in the habit of visiting Stubbs at home. Most likely Stubbs had an official billet elsewhere, where he conducted his regimental business. No wonder they thought he'd come to say that Stubbs was dead or injured. *Not yet,* he added grimly to himself.

"No," he said, feeling the weight of the miniature in his pocket. "Important, but not urgent." He left then. None of the children followed him.

Normally, it was not difficult to discover the whereabouts of a particular soldier, but Malcolm Stubbs seemed to have disappeared into thin air. Over the course of the next week, Grey combed headquarters, the military encampment, and the village, but no trace of his disgraceful cousin-by-marriage could be found. Still odder, no one appeared to have missed the Captain. The men of Stubbs's immediate company merely shrugged in confusion, and his superior officer had evidently gone off upriver to inspect the state of various postings. Frustrated, Grey retired to the riverbank to think.

Two logical possibilities presented themselves—no, three. One, that Stubbs had heard about Grey's arrival, supposed that Grey would discover exactly what he *had* discovered and had in consequence panicked and deserted. Two, he'd fallen foul of someone in a tavern or back alley, been killed, and was presently decomposing quietly under a layer of leaves in the woods. Or three—he'd been sent somewhere to do something, quietly.

Grey doubted the first exceedingly; Stubbs wasn't prone to panic, and if he had heard of Grey's arrival, Malcolm's first act would have been to come and find him, thus preventing his poking about in the village and finding what he'd found. He dismissed that possibility accordingly.

He dismissed the second still more promptly. Had Stubbs been killed, either deliberately or by accident, the alarm would have been raised. The army did generally know where its soldiers were, and if they weren't where they were meant to be, steps were taken. The same held true for desertion.

Right, then. If Stubbs was gone and no one was looking for him, it naturally followed that the army had sent him to wherever he'd gone. Since no one seemed to know where that was, his mission was presumably secret. And given Wolfe's current position and present obsession, that almost certainly meant that Malcolm Stubbs had gone downriver, searching for some way to attack Quebec. Grey sighed, satisfied with his deductions. Which in turn meant that—barring his being caught by the French, scalped or abducted by hostile Indians or eaten by a bear—Stubbs would be back, eventually. There was nothing to do but wait.

He leaned against a tree, watching a couple of fishing canoes make their way slowly downstream, hugging the bank. The sky was overcast and the air light on his skin, a pleasant change from the summer heat. Cloudy skies were good for fishing; his father's game-keeper had told him that. He wondered why—were the fish dazzled by sun, and thus sought murky hiding places in the depths, but rose toward the surface in dimmer light?

He thought suddenly of the electric eel, which Suddfield had told him lived in the silt-choked waters of the Amazon. The thing did have remarkably small eyes, and its proprietor had opined that it was able to use

its remarkable electrical abilities in some way to discern, as well as to elec-
trocute, its prey.

He couldn't have said what made him raise his head at that precise moment, but he looked up to find one of the canoes hovering in the shallow
water a few feet from him. The Indian paddling the canoe gave him a brilliant smile.

"Englishman!" he called. "You want to fish with me?"

A small jolt of electricity ran through him and he straightened up.
Manoke's eyes were fixed on his, and he felt in memory the touch of lips
and tongue, and the scent of fresh-sheared copper. His heart was racing—
go off in company with an Indian he barely knew? It might easily be a
trap. He could end up scalped or worse. But electric eels were not the only
ones to discern things by means of a sixth sense, he thought.

"Yes!" he called. "Meet you at the landing!"

Two weeks later, he stepped out of Manoke's canoe onto the landing, thin,
sunburnt, cheerful, and still in possession of his hair. Tom Byrd would be
beside himself, he reflected; he'd left word as to what he was doing, but
naturally had been able to give no estimate of his return. Doubtless poor
Tom would be thinking he'd been captured and dragged off into slavery or
scalped, his hair sold to the French.

In fact, they had drifted slowly downriver, pausing to fish wherever the
mood took them, camping on sandbars and small islands, grilling their catch
and eating their supper in smoke-scented peace, beneath the leaves of oak
and alder. They had seen other craft now and then—not only canoes, but also
many French packet boats and brigs, as well as two English warships, tacking
slowly up the river, sails bellying, the distant shouts of the sailors foreign to
him just then as the tongues of the Iroquois.

And in the late summer dusk of the first day, Manoke had wiped his fingers after eating, stood up, casually untied his breech-clout and let it fall.
Then waited, grinning, while Grey fought his way out of shirt and breeches.

They'd swum in the river to refresh themselves before eating; the Indian
was clean, his skin no longer greasy. And yet he seemed to taste of wild
game, the rich, uneasy tang of venison. Grey had wondered whether it was
the man's race that was responsible, or only his diet?

"What do I taste like?" he'd asked, out of curiosity.

Manoke, absorbed in his business, had said something that might have been, "Cock," but might equally have been some expression of mild disgust, so Grey thought better of pursuing this line of inquiry. Besides, if he *did* taste of beef and biscuit or Yorkshire pudding, would the Indian recognize that? For that matter, did he really want to know, if he did? He did not, he decided, and they enjoyed the rest of the evening without benefit of conversation.

He scratched the small of his back where his breeches rubbed, uncomfortable with mosquito bites and the peel of fading sunburn. He'd tried the native style of dress, seeing its convenience, but had scorched his bum by lying too long in the sun one afternoon, and thereafter resorted to breeches, not wishing to hear any further jocular remarks regarding the whiteness of his arse.

Thinking such pleasant but disjointed thoughts, he'd made his way halfway through the town before noticing that there were many more soldiers in evidence than there had been before. Drums were pattering up and down the sloping, muddy streets, calling men from their billets, the rhythm of the military day making itself felt. His own steps fell naturally into the beat of the drums, he straightened, and felt the army reach out suddenly, seizing him, shaking him out of his sunburnt bliss.

He glanced involuntarily up the hill and saw the flags fluttering above the large inn that served as field headquarters. Wolfe had returned.

Grey found his own quarters, reassured Tom as to his well-being, submitted to having his hair forcibly untangled, combed, perfumed, and tightly bound up in a formal queue, and with his clean uniform chafing his sunburnt skin, went to present himself to the general, as courtesy demanded. He knew James Wolfe by sight; Wolfe was his own age, had fought at Culloden, been a junior officer under Cumberland during the Highland campaign—but did not know him personally. He'd heard a great deal about him, though.

"Grey, is it? Pardloe's brother, are you?" Wolfe lifted his long nose in Grey's direction, as though sniffing at him, in the manner of one dog inspecting another's backside.

Grey trusted he would not be required to reciprocate, and instead bowed politely.

"My brother's compliments, sir."

Actually, what his brother had had to say had been far from complimentary.

"Melodramatic ass," was what Hal had said, hastily briefing him before his departure. "Showy, bad judgment, terrible strategist. Has the Devil's own luck, though, I'll give him that. *Don't* follow him into anything stupid."

Wolfe nodded amiably enough.

"And you've come as a witness for, who is it—Captain Carruthers?"

"Yes, sir. Has a date been set for the court-martial?"

"Dunno. Has it?" Wolfe asked his adjutant, a tall, spindly creature with a beady eye.

"No, sir. Now that His Lordship is here, though, we can proceed. I'll tell Brigadier Lethbridge-Stewart; he's to chair the proceeding."

Wolfe waved a hand.

"No, wait a bit. The Brigadier will have other things on his mind. 'Til after . . ."

The adjutant nodded and made a note.

"Yes, sir."

Wolfe was eyeing Grey, in the manner of a small boy bursting to share some secret.

"D'you understand Highlanders, Colonel?"

Grey blinked, surprised.

"Insofar as such a thing is possible, sir," he replied politely, and Wolfe brayed with laughter.

"Good man." The General turned his head to one side and eyed Grey some more, appraising him. "I've got a hundred or so of the creatures; been thinking what use they might be. I think I've found one—a small adventure."

The adjutant smiled, despite himself, then quickly erased the smile.

"Indeed, sir?" Grey said cautiously.

"Somewhat dangerous," Wolfe went on carelessly. "But then, it's the Highlanders . . . no great mischief should they fall. Would you care to join us?"

Don't follow him into anything stupid. Right, Hal, he thought. Any suggestions on how to decline an offer like that from one's titular commander?

"I should be pleased, sir," he said, feeling a brief ripple of unease down his spine. "When?"

"In two weeks—at the dark of the moon." Wolfe was all but wagging his tail in enthusiasm.

"Am I permitted to know the nature of the . . . er . . . expedition?"

Wolfe exchanged a look of anticipation with his adjutant, then turned eyes shiny with excitement on Grey.

"We're going to take Quebec, Colonel."

So Wolfe thought he had found his point *d'appui*. Or rather, his trusted scout, Malcolm Stubbs, had found it for him. Grey returned briefly to his quarters, put the miniature of Olivia and little Cromwell in his pocket, and went to find Stubbs.

He didn't bother thinking what to say to Malcolm. It was as well, he thought, that he hadn't found Stubbs immediately after his discovery of the Indian mistress and her child; he might simply have knocked Stubbs down, without the bother of explanation. But time had elapsed, and his blood was cooler now. He was detached.

Or so he thought, until he entered a prosperous tavern—Malcolm had elevated tastes in wine—and found his cousin-by-marriage at a table, relaxed and jovial among his friends. Stubbs was aptly named, being approximately five foot four in both dimensions, a fair-haired fellow with an inclination to become red in the face when deeply entertained or deep in drink.

At the moment, he appeared to be experiencing both conditions, laughing at something one of his companions had said, waving his empty glass in the barmaid's direction. He turned back, spotted Grey coming across the floor, and lit up like a beacon. He'd been spending a good deal of time out of doors, Grey saw; he was nearly as sunburnt as Grey himself.

"Grey!" he cried. "Why, here's a sight for sore eyes! What the devil brings you to the wilderness?" Then he noticed Grey's expression, and his joviality faded slightly, a puzzled frown growing between his thick brows.

It hadn't time to grow far. Grey lunged across the table, scattering glasses, and seized Stubbs by the shirtfront.

"You come with me, you bloody swine," he whispered, face shoved up against the younger man's, "or I'll kill you right here, I swear it."

He let go then, and stood, blood hammering in his temples.

Stubbs rubbed at his chest, affronted, startled—and afraid. Grey could see it in the wide blue eyes. Slowly, Stubbs got up, motioning to his companions to stay.

"No bother, chaps," he said, making a good attempt at casualness. "My cousin—family emergency, what?"

Grey saw two of the men exchange knowing glances, then look at Grey, wary. They knew, all right.

Stiffly, he gestured for Stubbs to precede him, and they passed out of the door in a pretense of dignity. Once outside, though, he grabbed Stubbs by the arm and dragged him round the corner into a small alleyway. He pushed Stubbs hard, so that he lost his balance and fell against the wall; Grey kicked his legs out from under him, then knelt on his thigh, digging his knee viciously into the thick muscle. Stubbs uttered a strangled noise, not quite a scream.

Grey dug in his pocket, hand trembling with fury, and brought out the miniature, which he showed briefly to Stubbs before grinding it into the man's cheek. Stubbs yelped, grabbed at it, and Grey let him have it, rising unsteadily off the man.

"How dare you?" he said, low-voiced and vicious. "How dare you dishonor your wife, your son?"

Malcolm was breathing hard, one hand clutching his abused thigh, but was regaining his composure.

"It's nothing," he said. "Nothing to do with Olivia at all." He swallowed, wiped a hand across his mouth, and took a cautious glance at the miniature in his hand. "That the sprat, is it? Good . . . good-looking lad. Looks like me, don't he?"

Grey kicked him brutally in the stomach.

"Yes, and so does your *other* son," he hissed. "How could you do such a thing?"

Malcolm's mouth opened, but nothing came out. He struggled for breath like a landed fish. Grey watched without pity. He'd have the man split and grilled over charcoal before he was done. He bent and took the miniature from Stubb's unresisting hand, tucking it back in his pocket.

After a long moment, Stubbs achieved a whining gasp, and the color of his face, which had gone puce, subsided back toward its normal brick color. Saliva had collected at the corners of his mouth; he licked his lips, spat, then sat back, breathing heavily, and looked up at Grey.

"Going to hit me again?"

"Not just yet."

"Good." He stretched out a hand, and Grey took it, grunting as he helped Stubbs to his feet. Malcolm leaned against the wall, still panting, and eyed him.

"So, who made you God, Grey? Who are you, to sit in judgment of me, eh?"

Grey nearly hit him again, but desisted.

"Who am *I*?" he echoed. "Olivia's fucking cousin, that's who! The nearest male relative she's got on this continent! And you, need I remind you—and evidently I do—are her fucking husband. Judgment? What the devil d'you mean by that, you filthy lecher?"

Malcolm coughed, and spat again.

"Yes. Well. I said, it's nothing to do with Olivia—and so it's nothing to do with you." He spoke with apparent calmness, but Grey could see the pulse hammering in his throat, the nervous shiftiness of his eyes. "It's nothing out of the ordinary—it's the bloody custom, for God's sake. Everybody—"

He kneed Stubbs in the balls.

"Try again," he advised Stubbs, who had fallen down and was curled into a fetal position, moaning. "Take your time; I'm not busy."

Aware of eyes upon him, he turned to see several soldiers gathered at the mouth of the alley, hesitating. He was still wearing his dress uniform, though—somewhat the worse for wear, but still clearly displaying his rank—and when he gave them an evil look, they hastily dispersed.

"I should kill you here and now, you know," he said to Stubbs after a few moments. The rage that had propelled him was draining away, though, as he watched the man retch and heave at his feet, and he spoke wearily. "Better for Olivia to have a dead husband—and whatever property you leave—than a live scoundrel, who will betray her with her friends—likely with her own maid."

Stubbs muttered something indistinguishable, and Grey bent, grasping him by the hair, and pulled his head up.

"What was that?"

"Wasn't . . . like that." Groaning and clutching himself, Malcolm maneuvered himself gingerly into a sitting position, knees drawn up. He gasped for a bit, head on his knees, before being able to go on.

"You don't know, do you?" He spoke low-voiced, not raising his head. "You haven't seen the things I've seen. Not . . . done what I've had to do."

"What do you mean?"

"The . . . the killing. Not . . . battle. Not an honorable thing. Farmers. Women . . ." He saw Stubbs's heavy throat move, swallowing. "I—we—for months now. Looting the countryside, burning farms, villages." He sighed, broad shoulders slumping. "The men, they don't mind. Half of them are brutes to begin with." He breathed. "Think . . . nothing of shooting a man on his doorstep and taking his wife next to his body." He swallowed. "'Tisn't only Montcalm who pay for scalps," he said in a low voice. Grey couldn't avoid hearing the rawness in his voice; a pain that wasn't physical.

"Every soldier's seen such things, Malcolm," he said after a short silence, almost gently. "You're an officer. It's your job to keep them in check." *And you know damn well it isn't always possible*, he thought.

"I know," Malcolm said, and began to cry. "I couldn't."

Grey waited while he sobbed, feeling increasingly foolish and uncomfortable. At last, the broad shoulders heaved and subsided.

After a moment, Malcolm said, in a voice that quivered only a little.

"Everybody finds a way, don't they? And there're not that many ways. Drink, cards, or women." He raised his head and shifted a little, grimacing as he eased into a more comfortable position. "But you don't go in much for women, do you?" he added, looking up.

Grey felt the bottom of his stomach drop, but realized in time that Malcolm had spoken matter-of-factly, with no tone of accusation.

"No," he said, and drew a deep breath. "Drink, mostly."

Malcolm nodded, wiping his nose on his sleeve.

"Drink doesn't help me," he said. "I fall asleep, but I don't forget. I just dream about . . . things. And whores—I—well, I didn't want to get poxed and maybe . . . well, Olivia," he muttered, looking down. "No good at cards," he said, clearing his throat. "But sleeping in a woman's arms—I can sleep, then."

Grey leaned against the wall, feeling nearly as battered as Malcolm Stubbs. Bright leaves drifted through the air, whirling round them, settling in the mud.

"All right," he said eventually. "What do you mean to do?"

"Dunno," Stubbs said in a tone of flat resignation. "Think of something, I suppose."

Grey bent and offered a hand; Stubbs got carefully to his feet and, nodding to Grey, shuffled toward the alley's mouth, bent over and holding himself as though his insides might fall out. Halfway there, though, he stopped and looked back over his shoulder.

There was an anxious look on his face, half-embarrassed.

"Can I—the miniature? They are still mine, Olivia and the . . . my son."

Grey heaved a sigh that went to the marrow of his bones; he felt a thousand years old.

"Yes, they are," he said, and digging the miniature out of his pocket, tucked it carefully into Stubbs's coat. "Remember it, will you?"

Two days later, a convoy of troop ships arrived, under the command of Admiral Holmes. The town was flooded afresh with men hungry for unsalted meat, fresh-baked bread, liquor and women. And a messenger arrived at Grey's quarters, bearing a parcel for him from his brother, with the Admiral's compliments.

It was small, but packaged with care, wrapped in oilcloth and tied about with twine, the knot sealed with his brother's crest. That was unlike Hal, whose usual communiqués consisted of hastily dashed-off notes, generally employing slightly fewer than the minimum number of words necessary to convey his message. They were seldom signed, let alone sealed.

Tom Byrd appeared to think the package slightly ominous, too; he had set it by itself, apart from the other mail, and weighted it down with a large bottle of brandy, apparently to prevent it escaping. That, or he suspected Grey might require the brandy to sustain him in the arduous effort of reading a letter consisting of more than one page.

"Very thoughtful of you, Tom," he murmured, smiling to himself and reaching for his pen-knife.

In fact, the letter within occupied less than a page, bore neither salutation nor signature, and was completely Hal-like.

> *Minnie wishes to know whether you are starving, though I don't know what she proposes to do about it, should the answer be yes. The boys wish to know whether you have taken any scalps—they are confident that no Red Indian would succeed in taking yours; I share this opinion. You had better bring three tommyhawks when you come home.*
>
> *Here is your paperweight; the jeweler was most impressed by the*

quality of the stone. The other thing is a copy of Adams's confession.
They hanged him yesterday.

The other contents of the parcel consisted of a small wash-leather pouch and an official-looking document on several sheets of good parchment, this folded and sealed—this time with the seal of George II. Grey left it lying on the table, fetched one of the pewter cups from his campaign chest and filled it to the brim with brandy, wondering anew at his valet's perspicacity.

Thus fortified, he sat down and took up the little pouch, from which he decanted a small, heavy gold paperweight, made in the shape of a half moon set among ocean waves, into his hand. It was set with a faceted—and very large—sapphire, which glowed like the evening star in its setting. Where had James Fraser acquired such a thing? he wondered.

He turned it in his hand, admiring the workmanship, but then set it aside. He sipped his brandy for a bit, watching the official document as though it might explode. He was reasonably sure it would.

He weighed the document in his hand and felt the breeze from his window lift it a little, like the flap of a sail just before it fills and bellies with a snap.

Waiting wouldn't help. And Hal plainly knew what it said, anyway; he'd tell Grey eventually, whether he wanted to know or not. Sighing, he put by his brandy and broke the seal.

I, Bernard Donald Adams, do make this confession of my own free
will. . . .

Was it? he wondered. He did not know Adams's handwriting, could not tell whether the document had been written or dictated—no, wait. He flipped over the sheets and examined the signature. Same hand. All right, he had written it himself.

He squinted at the writing. It seemed firm. Probably not extracted under torture, then. Perhaps it was the truth.

"Idiot," he said under his breath. "Read the god-damned thing and have done with it!"

He drank the rest of his brandy at a gulp, flattened the pages upon the stone of the parapet and read, at last, the story of his father's death.

The Duke had suspected the existence of a Jacobite ring for some time, and had identified three men whom he thought involved in it. Still, he made no move to expose them, until the warrant was issued for his own arrest, upon the charge of treason. Hearing of this, he had sent at once to Adams, summoning him to the Duke's country home at Earlingden.

Adams did not know how much the Duke knew of his own involvement, but did not dare to stay away, lest the Duke, under arrest, denounce him. So he armed himself with a pistol, and rode by night to Earlingden, arriving just before dawn.

He had come to the conservatory's outside doors and been admitted by the Duke. Whereupon "some conversation" had ensued.

> *I had learned that day of the issuance of a warrant for arrest upon the charge of treason, to be served upon the body of the Duke of Pardloe. I was uneasy at this, for the Duke had questioned both myself and some colleagues previously, in a manner that suggested to me that he suspected the existence of a secret movement to restore the Stuart throne.*
>
> *I argued against the Duke's arrest, as I did not know the extent of his knowledge or suspicions, and feared that if placed in exigent danger himself, he might be able to point a finger at myself or my principal colleagues, these being Joseph Arbuthnot, Lord Creemore, and Sir Edwin Bellman. Sir Edwin was urgent upon the point, though, saying that it would do no harm; any accusations made by Pardloe could be dismissed as simple attempts to save himself, with no grounding in fact—while the fact of his arrest would naturally cause a widespread assumption of guilt, and would distract any attentions that might at present be directed toward us.*
>
> *The Duke, hearing of the warrant, sent to my lodgings that evening, and summoned me to call upon him at his country home, immediately. I dared not spurn this summons, not knowing what evidence he might possess, and therefore rode by night to his estate, arriving soon before dawn.*

Adams had met the Duke there, in the conservatory. Whatever the form of this conversation, its result had been drastic.

*I had brought with me a pistol, which I had loaded outside the house.
I meant this only for protection, as I did not know what the Duke's
demeanor might be.*

Dangerous, evidently. Gerard Grey, Duke of Pardloe, had also come
armed to the meeting. According to Adams, the Duke had withdrawn his
own pistol from the recesses of his jacket—whether to attack or merely
threaten was not clear—whereupon Adams had drawn his own pistol in
panic. Both men fired; Adams thought the Duke's pistol had misfired,
since the Duke could not have missed, at the distance.

Adams's shot did not misfire, nor did it miss its target, and seeing
the blood upon the Duke's bosom, Adams had panicked and run. Looking
back, he had seen the Duke, mortally stricken but still upright, seize the
branch of the peach tree beside him for support, whereupon the Duke had
used the last of his strength to hurl his own useless weapon at Adams before collapsing.

John Grey sat still, slowly rubbing the parchment sheets between his
fingers. He wasn't seeing the neat strokes in which Adams had set down
his bloodless account. He saw the blood. A dark red, beautiful as a jewel
where the sun through the glass of the roof struck it suddenly. His father's
hair, tousled as it might be after hunting. And the peach, fallen to those
same tiles, its perfection spoilt and ruined.

He set the papers down on the table; the wind stirred them, and by reflex, he reached for his new paperweight to hold them down.

What was it Carruthers had called him? *Someone who keeps order. You
and your brother,* he'd said. *You don't stand for it. If the world has peace and order, it's because of men like you.*

Perhaps. He wondered if Carruthers knew the cost of peace and order—
but then recalled Charlie's haggard face, its youthful beauty gone, nothing
left in it now save the bones and the dogged determination that kept him
breathing.

Yes, he knew.

Just after full dark, they boarded the ships. The convoy included Admiral
Holmes's flagship, the *Lowestoff*; three men of war, the *Squirrel, Sea Horse,*
and *Hunter*; a number of armed sloops, others loaded with ordnance, powder

and ammunition, and a number of transports for the troops—1,800 men in all. The *Sutherland* had been left below, anchored just out of firing range of the fortress, to keep an eye on the enemy's motions; the river there was littered with floating batteries and prowling small French craft.

He traveled with Wolfe and the Highlanders aboard *Sea Horse*, and spent the journey on deck, too keyed up to bear being below.

His brother's warning kept recurring in the back of his mind—*Don't follow him into anything stupid*—but it was much too late to think of that, and to block it out, he challenged one of the other officers to a whistling contest—each party to whistle the entirety of "The Roast Beef of Old England," the loser the man who laughed first. He lost, but did not think of his brother again.

Just after midnight, the big ships quietly furled their sails, dropped anchor and lay like slumbering gulls on the dark river. L'Anse au Foulon, the landing spot that Malcolm Stubbs and his scouts had recommended to General Wolfe, lay seven miles downriver, at the foot of sheer and crumbling slate cliffs that led upward to the Heights of Abraham.

"Is it named for the biblical Abraham, do you think?" Grey had asked curiously, hearing the name, but had been informed that, in fact, the clifftop comprised a farmstead belonging to an ex-pilot named Abraham Martin.

On the whole, he thought this prosaic origin just as well. There was likely to be drama enough enacted on that ground, without thought of ancient prophets, conversations with God, or any calculation of how many just men might be contained within the fortress of Quebec.

With a minimum of fuss, the Highlanders and their officers, Wolfe and his chosen troops—Grey among them—debarked into the small *bateaux* that would carry them silently down to the landing point.

The sounds of oars were mostly drowned by the river's rushing, and there was little conversation in the boats. Wolfe sat in the prow of the lead boat, facing his troops, looking now and then over his shoulder at the shore. Quite without warning, he began to speak. He didn't raise his voice, but the night was so still that those in the boat had little trouble in hearing him. To Grey's astonishment, he was reciting "Elegy Written in a Country Churchyard."

Melodramatic ass, Grey thought—and yet could not deny that the recitation was oddly moving. Wolfe made no show of it. It was as though he were simply talking to himself, and a shiver went over Grey as he reached the last verse.

" 'The boast of heraldry, the pomp of pow'r,
And all that beauty, all that wealth e'er gave,
Awaits alike the inexorable hour.

The paths of glory lead but to the grave,' " Wolfe ended, so low-voiced that only the three or four men closest heard him. Grey was close enough to hear him clear his throat with a small *hem* noise, and saw his shoulders lift.

"Gentlemen," Wolfe said, lifting his voice as well, "I should rather have written those lines than have taken Quebec."

There was a faint stir, and a breath of laughter among the men.

So would I, Grey thought. *The poet who wrote them is likely sitting by his cozy fire in Cambridge eating buttered crumpets, not preparing to fall from a great height or get his arse shot off.*

He didn't know whether this was simply more of Wolfe's characteristic drama. Possibly—possibly not, he thought. He'd met Colonel Walsing by the latrines that morning, and Walsing had mentioned that Wolfe had given him a pendant the night before, with instructions to deliver it to Miss Landringham, to whom Wolfe was engaged.

But then, it was nothing out of the ordinary for men to put their personal valuables into the care of a friend before a hot battle. Were you killed or badly injured, your body might be looted before your comrades managed to retrieve you, and not everyone had a trustworthy servant with whom to leave such items. He himself had often carried snuff-boxes, pocket-watches, or rings into battle for friends—he'd had a reputation for luck, prior to Krefeld. No one had asked him to carry anything tonight.

He shifted his weight by instinct, feeling the current change, and Simon Fraser, next him, swayed in the opposite direction, bumping him.

"Pardon," Fraser murmured. Wolfe had made them all recite poetry in French round the dinner table the night before, and it was agreed that Fraser had the most authentic accent, he having fought with the French in Holland some years prior. Should they be hailed by a sentry, it would be his job to reply. Doubtless, Grey thought, Fraser was now thinking frantically in French, trying to saturate his mind with the language, lest any stray bit of English escape in panic.

"De rien," Grey murmured back, and Fraser chuckled, deep in his throat.

It was cloudy, the sky streaked with the shredded remnants of retreating rain clouds. That was good; the surface of the river was broken, patched with faint light, fractured by stones and drifting tree branches. Though even so, a decent sentry could scarcely fail to spot a train of boats.

Cold numbed his face, but his palms were sweating. He touched the dagger at his belt again; he was aware that he touched it every few minutes, as if needing to verify its presence, but couldn't help it, and didn't worry about it. He was straining his eyes, looking for anything—the glow of a careless fire, the shifting of a rock that was not a rock . . . nothing.

How far? he wondered. Two miles, three? He'd not yet seen the cliffs himself, was not sure how far below Gareon they lay.

The rush of water and the easy movement of the boat began to make him sleepy, tension notwithstanding, and he shook his head, yawning exaggeratedly to throw it off.

"Quel est c'est bateau?" What boat is that? The shout from the shore seemed anticlimax when it came, barely more remarkable than a night bird's call. But the next instant, Simon Fraser's hand crushed his, grinding the bones together as Fraser gulped air and shouted, *"Celui de la Reine!"*

Grey clenched his teeth, not to let any blasphemous response escape. If the sentry demanded a password, he'd likely be crippled for life, he thought. An instant later, though, the sentry shouted, *"Passez!"* and Fraser's death-grip relaxed. Simon was breathing like a bellows, but nudged him and whispered *"Pardon,"* again.

"De fucking *rien,"* he muttered, rubbing his hand and tenderly flexing the fingers.

They were getting close. Men were shifting to and fro in anticipation, more than Grey, checking their weapons, straightening coats, coughing, spitting over the side, readying themselves. Still, it was a nerve-wracking quarter hour more before they began to swing toward shore—and another sentry called from the dark.

Grey's heart squeezed like a fist, and he nearly gasped with the twinge of pain from his old wounds.

"Qui etes-vous? Que sont ces bateaux?" a French voice demanded suspiciously. *Who are you? What boats are those?*

This time, he was ready, and seized Fraser's hand himself. Simon held on, and leaning out toward the shore, called hoarsely, *"Des bateaux de provisions! Tasiez-vous—les anglais sont proches!" Provision boats! Be quiet—the British are nearby!* Grey felt an insane urge to laugh, but didn't. In fact, the *Sutherland* was nearby, lurking out of cannon shot downstream, and doubtless the frogs knew it. In any case, the guard called, more quietly, "*Passez!*" and the train of boats slid smoothly past and round the final bend.

The bottom of the boat grated on sand, and half the men were over at once, tugging it farther up. Wolfe half leapt, half fell over the side in eagerness, all trace of somberness gone. They'd come aground on a small sandbar, just offshore, and the other boats were beaching now, a swarm of black figures gathering like ants.

Twenty-four of the Highlanders were meant to try the ascent first, finding—and insofar as possible, clearing, for the cliff was defended not only by its steepness but also by abatis, nests of sharpened logs—a trail for the rest. Simon's bulky form faded into the dark, his French accent changing at once into the sibilant Gaelic as he hissed the men into position. Grey rather missed his presence.

He was not sure whether Wolfe had chosen the Highlanders for their skill at climbing, or because he preferred to risk them rather than his other troops. The latter, he thought. Like most English officers, Wolfe regarded the Highlanders with distrust and a certain contempt. Those officers, at least, who'd never fought with them—or against them.

From his spot at the foot of the cliff, he couldn't see them, but he could hear them; the scuffle of feet, now and then a wild scrabble and a clatter of falling small stones, loud grunts of effort and what he recognized as Gaelic invocations of God, His mother and assorted saints. One man near him pulled a string of beads from the neck of his shirt and kissed the tiny cross attached to it, then tucked it back and, seizing a small sapling that grew out of the rock-face, leapt upward, kilt swinging, broadsword swaying from his belt in brief silhouette, before the darkness took him. Grey touched his dagger's hilt again, his own talisman against evil.

It was a long wait in the darkness; to some extent, he envied the Highlanders, who, whatever else they might be encountering—and the scrabbling noises and half-strangled whoops as a foot slipped and a comrade grabbed a hand or arm suggested that the climb was just as impossible as it seemed—were not dealing with boredom.

A sudden rumble and crashing came from above, and the shore-party scattered in panic as several sharpened logs plunged out of the dark above, dislodged from an abatis. One of them had struck point down no more than six feet from Grey, and stood quivering in the sand. With no discussion, the shore-party retreated to the sandbar.

The scrabblings and gruntings grew fainter, and suddenly ceased. Wolfe, who had been sitting on a boulder, stood up, straining his eyes upward.

"They've made it," he whispered, and his fists curled in an excitement that Grey shared. "God, they've made it!"

Well enough, and the men at the foot of the cliff held their breaths; there was a guard post at the top of the cliff. Silence, bar the everlasting noise of tree and river. And then a shot.

Just one. The men below shifted, touching their weapons, ready, not knowing for what.

Were there sounds above? He could not tell, and out of sheer nervousness, turned aside to urinate against the side of the cliff. He was fastening his flies when he heard Simon Fraser's voice above.

"Got 'em, by God!" he said. "Come on, lads—the night's not long enough!"

The next few hours passed in a blur of the most arduous endeavor Grey had seen since he'd crossed the Scottish Highlands with his brother's regiment, bringing cannon to General Cope. No, actually, he thought, as he stood in darkness, one leg wedged between a tree and the rock-face, thirty feet of invisible space below him, and rope burning through his palms with an unseen deadweight of two hundred pounds or so on the end, this was worse.

The Highlanders had surprised the guard, shot their fleeing captain in the heel, and made all of them prisoner. That was the easy part. The next thing was for the rest of the landing party to ascend to the clifftop, now that the trail—if there was such a thing—had been cleared, where they would make preparations to raise not only the rest of the troops now coming down the river aboard the transports, but also seventeen battering cannon, twelve howitzers, three mortars and all of the necessary encumbrances in terms of shell, powder, planks and limbers necessary to make this artillery effective. At least, Grey reflected, by the time they were done, the vertical trail up the cliffside would likely have been trampled into a simple cowpath.

As the sky lightened, Grey looked up for a moment from his spot at the top of the cliff, where he was now overseeing the last of the artillery as it was heaved over the edge, and saw the *bateaux* coming down again like a flock of swallows, they having crossed the river to collect an additional 1,200 troops that Wolfe had directed to march to Levi on the opposite shore, there to lie hidden in the woods until the Highlanders' expedient should have been proved.

A head, cursing freely, surged up over the edge of the cliff. Its attendant body lunged into view, tripped, and sprawled at Grey's feet.

"Sergeant Cutter!" Grey said, grinning as he bent to yank the little sergeant to his feet. "Come to join the party, have you?"

"Jesus fuck," replied the sergeant, belligerently brushing dirt from his coat. "We'd best win, that's all I can say." And without waiting for reply, turned round to bellow down the cliff, "Come *on*, you bloody rascals! 'Ave you all eaten lead for breakfast, then? Shit it out and step lively! *Climb*, God damn your eyes!"

The net result of this monstrous effort being that as dawn spread its golden glow across the Plains of Abraham, the French sentries on the walls of the Citadel of Quebec gaped in disbelief at the sight of more than four thousand British troops, drawn up in battle array before them.

Through his telescope, Grey could see the sentries. The distance was too great to make out their facial expressions, but their attitudes of alarm and consternation were easy to read, and he grinned, seeing one French officer clutch his head briefly, then wave his arms like one dispelling a flock of chickens, sending his subordinates rushing off in all directions.

Wolfe was standing on a small hillock, long nose lifted as though to sniff the morning air. Grey thought he probably considered his pose noble and commanding; he reminded Grey of a dachshund scenting a badger; the air of alert eagerness was the same.

Wolfe wasn't the only one. Despite the ardors of the night, skinned hands, battered shins, twisted knees and ankles, and a lack of food and sleep, a gleeful excitement ran through the troops like wine. Grey thought they were all giddy with fatigue.

The sound of drums came faintly to him on the wind: the French, beating hastily to quarters. Within minutes, he saw horsemen streaking away from the fortress, and smiled grimly. They were going to rally whatever troops Montcalm had within summoning distance, and he felt a tightening of the belly at the sight.

The matter hadn't really been in doubt; it was September, and winter was coming on. The town and fortress had been unable to provision themselves for a long siege, owing to Wolfe's scorched-earth policies. The French were there, the English before them—and the simple fact, apparent to both sides, was that the French would starve long before the English did. Montcalm would fight; he had no choice.

Many of the men had brought canteens of water, some a little food. They were allowed to relax sufficiently to eat, to ease their muscles—though none of them ever took their attention from the gathering French, massing before the fortress. Employing his telescope further, Grey could see that while the mass of milling men was growing, they were by no means all trained troops; Montcalm had called his militias from the countryside— farmers, fishermen, and *coureurs du bois*, by the look of them—and his Indians. Grey eyed the painted faces and oiled topknots warily, but his acquaintance with Manoke had deprived the Indians of much of their terrifying aspect—and they would not be nearly so effective on open ground, against cannon, as they were sneaking through the forest.

It took surprisingly little time for Montcalm to ready his troops, impromptu as they might be. The sun was no more than halfway up the sky when the French lines began their advance.

"*Hold* your fucking fire, you villains! Fire before you're ordered, and I'll give your fuckin' heads to the artillery to use for cannonballs!" He heard the unmistakable voice of Sergeant Aloysius Cutter, some distance back but clearly audible. The same order was being echoed, if less picturesquely, through the British lines, and if every officer on the field had one eye firmly on the French, the other was fixed on General Wolfe, standing on his hillock, aflame with anticipation.

Grey felt his blood twitch, and moved restlessly from foot to foot, trying to ease a cramp in one leg. The advancing French line stopped, knelt, and fired a volley. Another from the line standing behind them. Too far, much too far to have any effect. A deep rumble came from the British troops— something visceral and hungry.

Grey's hand had been on his dagger for so long that the wire-wrapped hilt had left its imprint on his fingers. His other hand was clenched upon a saber. He had no command here, but the urge to raise his sword, gather the eyes of his men, hold them, focus them, was overwhelming. He shook his shoulders to loosen them and glanced at Wolfe.

Another volley, close enough this time that several British soldiers in the front lines fell, knocked down by musket fire.

"Hold, hold!" The order rattled down the lines like gunfire. The brimstone smell of slow match was thick, pungent above the scent of powder-smoke; the artillerymen held their fire as well.

French cannon fired, and balls bounced murderously across the field, but they seemed puny, ineffectual despite the damage they did. How many French? he wondered. Perhaps twice as many, but it didn't matter. It wouldn't matter.

Sweat ran down his face, and he rubbed a sleeve across to clear his eyes. "Hold!"

Closer, closer. Many of the Indians were on horseback; he could see them in a knot on the left, milling. Those would bear watching. . . .

"Hold!"

Wolfe's arm rose slowly, sword in hand, and the army breathed deep. His beloved grenadiers were next him, solid in their companies, wrapped in sulfurous smoke from the matchtubes at their belts.

"Come on, you buggers," the man next to Grey was muttering. "Come on, come on!"

Smoke was drifting over the field, low white clouds. Forty paces. Effective range.

"Don't fire, don't fire, don't fire . . ." Someone was chanting to himself, struggling against panic.

Through the British lines, sun glinted on the rising swords, the officers echoing Wolfe's order.

"Hold . . . hold . . ."

The swords fell as one.

"Fire!" And the ground shook.

A shout rose in his throat, part of the roar of the army, and he was charging with the men near him, swinging his saber with all his might, finding flesh.

The volley had been devastating; bodies littered the ground. He leaped over a fallen Frenchman, brought his saber down upon another caught halfway in the act of loading, took him in the cleft between neck and shoulder, yanked his saber free of the falling man and went on.

The British artillery was firing as fast as the guns could be served. Each boom shook his flesh. He gritted his teeth, squirmed aside from the point of a half-seen bayonet, and found himself panting, eyes watering from the smoke, standing alone.

Chest heaving, he turned round in a circle, disoriented. There was so much smoke around him that he could not for a moment tell where he was. It didn't matter.

An enormous blur of something passed him, shrieking, and he dodged by instinct and fell to the ground as the horse's feet churned past, hearing as an echo the Indian's grunt, the rush of the tomahawk blow that had missed his head.

"Shit," he muttered, and scrambled to his feet.

The grenadiers were hard at work nearby; he heard their officers' shouts, the bang and pop of their explosions as they worked their way stolidly through the French like the small mobile batteries they were.

A grenade struck the ground a few feet away, and he felt a sharp pain in his thigh; a metal fragment had sliced through his breeches, drawing blood.

"Christ," he said, belatedly becoming aware that being in the vicinity of a company of grenadiers was not a good idea. He shook his head to clear it and made his way away from them.

He heard a familiar sound, which made him recoil for an instant from the force of memory—wild Highland screams, filled with rage and berserk glee. The Highlanders were hard at work with their broadswords—he saw two of them appear from the smoke, bare legs churning beneath their kilts, pursuing a pack of fleeing Frenchmen, and felt laughter bubble up through his heaving chest.

He didn't see the man in the smoke. His foot struck something heavy and he fell, sprawling across the body. The man screamed, and Grey scrambled hastily off him.

"Sorry. Are you—Christ, Malcolm!"

He was on his knees, bending low to avoid the smoke. Stubbs was gasping, grasping desperately at his coat.

"Jesus." Malcolm's right leg was gone below the knee, flesh shredded and the white bone splintered, butcher-stained with spurting blood. Or . . . no. It wasn't gone. It—the foot, at least—was lying a little way away, still clad in shoe and tattered stocking.

Grey turned his head and threw up.

Bile stinging the back of his nose, he choked and spat, turned back, and grappled with his belt, wrenching it free.

"Don't . . ." Stubbs gasped, putting out a hand as Grey began wrapping the belt round his thigh. His face was whiter than the bone of his leg. "Don't. Better . . . Better if I die."

"The devil you will," Grey replied briefly.

His hands were shaking, slippery with blood. It took three tries to get the end of the belt through the buckle, but it went, at last, and he jerked it tight, eliciting a yell from Stubbs.

"Here," said an unfamiliar voice by his ear. "Let's get him off. I'll— shit!" He looked up, startled, to see a tall British officer lunge upward, blocking the musket butt that would have brained Grey. Without thinking, he drew his dagger and stabbed the Frenchman in the leg. The man screamed, his leg buckling, and the strange officer pushed him over, kicked him in the face and stamped on his throat, crushing it.

"I'll help," the man said calmly, bending to take hold of Malcolm's arm, pulling him up. "Take the other side; we'll get him to the back." They got Malcolm up, his arms round their shoulders, and dragged him, paying no heed to the Frenchman thrashing and gurgling on the ground behind them.

Malcolm lived, long enough to make it to the rear of the lines, where the army surgeons were already at work. By the time Grey and the other officer had turned him over to the surgeons, it was over.

Grey turned to see the French scattered and demoralized, fleeing toward the fortress. British troops were flooding across the trampled field, cheering, overrunning the abandoned French cannon.

The entire battle had lasted less than a quarter of an hour.

He found himself sitting on the ground, his mind quite blank, with no notion how long he had been there, though he supposed it couldn't have been much time at all.

He noticed an officer standing near him, and thought vaguely that the man seemed familiar. Who . . . Oh, yes. Wolfe's adjutant. He'd never learned the man's name.

He stood up slowly, stiff as a nine-day pudding.

The adjutant was simply standing there. His eyes were turned in the direction of the fortress and the fleeing French, but Grey could tell that he wasn't really seeing either. Grey glanced over his shoulder, toward the hillock where Wolfe had stood earlier, but the General was nowhere in sight.

"General Wolfe—?" he said.

"The General . . . ," the adjutant said, and swallowed thickly. "He was struck."

Of course he was, silly ass, Grey thought uncharitably. *Standing up there like a bloody target, what could he expect?* But then he saw the tears standing in the adjutant's eyes, and understood.

"Dead, then?" he asked, stupidly, and the adjutant—why had he never thought to ask the man's name?—nodded, rubbing a smoke-stained sleeve across a smoke-stained countenance.

"He . . . in the wrist, first. Then in the body. He fell, and crawled—then he fell again. I turned him over . . . told him the battle was won; the French were scattered."

"He understood?"

The adjutant nodded and took a deep breath that rattled in his throat. "He said—" He stopped and coughed, then went on, more firmly. "He said that in knowing he had conquered, he was content to die."

"Did he?" Grey said blankly. He'd seen men die, often, and imagined it much more likely that if James Wolfe had managed anything beyond an inarticulate groan, his final word had likely been either "Shit," or "Oh, God," depending upon the general's religious leanings, of which Grey had no notion.

"Yes, good," he said meaninglessly, and turned toward the fortress himself. Ant-trails of men were streaming toward it, and in the midst of one such stream, he saw Montcalm's colors, fluttering in the wind. Below the colors, small in the distance, a man in general's uniform rode his horse, hatless, hunched and swaying in the saddle, his officers bunched close on either side, anxious lest he fall.

The British lines were reorganizing, though it was clear no further fighting would be required. Not today. Nearby, he saw the tall officer who had saved his life and helped him to drag Malcolm Stubbs to safety, limping back toward his troops.

"The major over there," he said, nudging the adjutant and nodding. "Do you know his name?"

The adjutant blinked, then firmed his shoulders.

"Yes, of course. That's Major Siverly."

"Oh. Well, it would be, wouldn't it?"

Admiral Holmes, third in command after Wolfe, accepted the surrender of Quebec three days later, Wolfe and his second, Brigadier Monckton, having perished in battle. Montcalm was dead, too; had died the morning following the battle. There was no way out for the French save surrender; winter was coming on, and the fortress and its city would starve long before its besiegers.

Two weeks after the battle, John Grey returned to Gareon, and found that smallpox had swept through the village like an autumn wind. The mother of Malcolm Stubbs's son was dead; her mother offered to sell him the child. He asked her politely to wait.

Charlie Carruthers had perished, too, the smallpox not waiting for the weakness of his body to overcome him. Grey had the body burned, not wishing Carruthers's hand to be stolen, for both the Indians and the local habitants regarded such things superstitiously. He took a canoe by himself, and on a deserted island in the St. Lawrence, scattered his friend's ashes to the wind.

He returned from this expedition to discover a letter, forwarded by Hal, from Mr. John Hunter, surgeon. He checked the level of brandy in the decanter, and opened it with a sigh.

> *My dear Lord John,*
>
> *I have heard some recent conversation regarding the unfortunate death of Mr. Nicholls last spring, including comments indicating a public perception that you were responsible for his death. In case you shared this perception, I thought it might ease your mind to know that in fact you were not.*

Grey sank slowly onto a stool, eyes glued to the sheet.

> *It is true that your ball did strike Mr. Nicholls, but this accident contributed little or nothing to his demise. I saw you fire upward into the air—I said as much, to those present at the time, though most of them did not appear to take much notice. The ball apparently went up at a slight angle, and then fell upon Mr. Nicholls from above. At this point, its power was quite spent, and the missile itself being negligible in size and weight, it barely penetrated the skin above his collarbone, where it lodged against the bone, doing no further damage.*
>
> *The true cause of his collapse and death was an aortic aneurysm, a weakness in the wall of one of the great vessels emergent from the*

*heart; such weaknesses are often congenital. The stress of the electric
shock and the emotion of the duello that followed apparently caused
this aneurysm to rupture. Such an occurrence is untreatable, and invariably fatal, I am afraid. There is nothing that could have saved
him.*

*Your Servant,
John Hunter, Surgeon*

Grey was conscious of a most extraordinary array of sensations. Relief,
yes, there was a sense of profound relief, as of one waking from a nightmare. There was also a sense of injustice, colored by the beginnings of indignation; by God, he had nearly been married! He might, of course, also
have been maimed or killed as a result of the imbroglio, but that seemed
relatively inconsequent; he was a soldier, after all—such things happened.

His hand trembled slightly as he set the note down. Beneath relief, grat-
itude and indignation was a growing sense of horror.

I thought it might ease your mind. . . . He could see Hunter's face, saying
this; sympathetic, intelligent, and cheerful. It was a straightforward remark, but one fully cognizant of its own irony.

Yes, he was pleased to know he had not caused Edwin Nicholls's death.
But the means of that knowledge . . . gooseflesh rose on his arms and he
shuddered involuntarily, imagining . . .

"Oh, God," he said. He'd been once to Hunter's house—to a poetry reading, held under the auspices of Mrs. Hunter, whose salons were famous. Dr.
Hunter did not attend these, but sometimes would come down from his part
of the house to greet guests. On this occasion, he had done so, and falling
into conversation with Grey and a couple of other scientifically minded gentlemen, had invited them up to see some of the more interesting items of his
famous collection: the rooster with a transplanted human tooth growing in
its comb, the child with two heads, the fetus with a foot protruding from its
stomach.

Hunter had made no mention of the walls of jars, these filled with eyeballs, fingers, sections of livers . . . or of the two or three complete human
skeletons that hung from the ceiling, fully articulated and fixed by a bolt
through the tops of their skulls. It had not occurred to Grey at the time to
wonder where—or how—Hunter had acquired these.

Nicholls had had an eyetooth missing, the front tooth beside the empty space badly chipped. If he ever visited Hunter's house again, might he come face-to-face with a skull with a missing tooth?

He seized the brandy decanter, uncorked it, and drank directly from it, swallowing slowly and repeatedly, until the vision disappeared.

His small table was littered with papers. Among them, under his sapphire paperweight, was the tidy packet that the widow Lambert had handed him, her face blotched with weeping. He put a hand on it, feeling Charlie's doubled touch, gentle on his face, soft around his heart.

You won't fail me.

"No," he said softly. "No, Charlie, I won't."

With Manoke's help as translator, he bought the child, after prolonged negotiation, for two golden guineas, a brightly colored blanket, a pound of sugar, and a small keg of rum. The grandmother's face was sunken, not with grief, he thought, but with dissatisfaction and weariness. With her daughter dead of the smallpox, her life would be harder. The English, she conveyed to Grey through Manoke, were cheap bastards; the French were much more generous. He resisted the impulse to give her another guinea.

It was full autumn now, and the leaves had all fallen. The bare branches of the trees spread black ironwork flat against a pale blue sky as he made his way upward through the town to the small French mission. There were several small buildings surrounding the tiny church, with children playing outside; some of them paused to look at him, but most of them ignored him—British soldiers were nothing new.

Father LeCarré took the bundle gently from him, turning back the blanket to look at the child's face. The boy was awake; he pawed at the air, and the priest put out a finger for him to grasp.

"Ah," he said, seeing the clear signs of mixed blood, and Grey knew the priest thought the child was his. He started to explain, but after all, what did it matter?

"We will baptize him as a Catholic, of course," Father LeCarré said, looking up at him. The priest was a young man, rather plump, dark and clean-shaven, but with a gentle face. "You do not mind that?"

"No." Grey drew out a purse. "Here—for his maintenance. I will send an additional five pounds each year, if you will advise me once a year of his continued welfare. Here—the address to which to write." A sudden inspiration struck him—not that he did not trust the good father, he assured himself—only . . . "Send me a lock of his hair," he said. "Every year."

He was turning to go when the priest called him back, smiling.

"Has the infant a name, sir?"

"A—" He stopped dead. His mother had surely called him something, but Malcolm Stubbs hadn't thought to tell him what it was before being shipped back to England. What should he call the child? Malcolm, for the father who had abandoned him? Hardly.

Charles, maybe, in memory of Carruthers . . .

. . . one of these days, it isn't going to.

"His name is John," he said abruptly, and cleared his throat. "John Cinnamon."

"Mais oui," the priest said, nodding. *"Bon voyage, monsieur—et voyez avec le Bon Dieu."*

"Thank you," he said politely, and went away, not looking back, down to the riverbank where Manoke waited to bid him farewell.

Naomi Novik

Born in New York City, where she still lives with her mystery-editor husband and six computers, Naomi Novik is a first-generation American who was raised on Polish fairy tales, Baba Yaga, and Tolkien. After doing graduate work in computer science at Columbia University, she participated in the development of the computer game *Neverwinter Nights: Shadows of Undrentide,* and then decided to try her hand at novels. A good decision! The resultant Temeraire series—consisting of *His Majesty's Dragon, Black Powder War, Throne of Jade,* and *Empire of Ivory*—describing an alternative version of the Napoleonic Wars where dragons are used as living weapons, has been phenomenally popular and successful. Her most recent book is a new Temeraire novel, *Victory of Eagles.*

Here she takes us on an evocative visit to a distant planet of intricate and interlocking biological mysteries for a harrowing demonstration that it's unwise to strike at an enemy before you're sure they can't strike *back.* . . .

Seven Years from Home

Preface

Seven days passed for me on my little raft of a ship as I fled Melida; seven years for the rest of the unaccelerated universe. I hoped to be forgotten, a dusty footnote left at the bottom of a page. Instead I came off to trumpets and medals and legal charges, equal doses of acclaim and venom, and I stumbled bewildered through the brassy noise, led first by one and then by another, while my last opportunity to enter any protest against myself escaped.

Now I desire only to correct the worst of the factual inaccuracies bandied about, so far as my imperfect memory will allow, and to make an offering of my own understanding to that smaller and more sophisticated audience who prefer to shape the world's opinion rather than be shaped by it.

I engage not to tire you with a recitation of dates and events and quotations. I do not recall them with any precision myself. But I must warn you that neither have I succumbed to that pathetic and otiose impulse to sanitize the events of the war, or to excuse sins either my own or belonging to others. To do so would be a lie, and on Melida, to tell a lie was an insult more profound than murder.

I will not see my sisters again, whom I loved. Here we say that one who takes the long midnight voyage has leaped ahead in time, but to me it seems it is they who have traveled on ahead. I can no longer hear their voices when I am awake. I hope this will silence them in the night.

Ruth Patrona
Reivaldt, Janvier 32, 4765

The First Adjustment

I disembarked at the port of Landfall in the fifth month of 4753. There is such a port on every world where the Confederacy has set its foot but not yet its flag: crowded and dirty and charmless. It was on the Esperigan continent, as the Melidans would not tolerate the construction of a spaceport in their own territory.

Ambassador Kostas, my superior, was a man of great authority and presence, two meters tall and solidly built, with a jovial handshake, high intelligence, and very little patience for fools; that I was likely to be relegated to this category was evident on our first meeting. He disliked my assignment to begin with. He thought well of the Esperigans; he moved in their society as easily as he did in our own, and would have called one or two of their senior ministers his personal friends, if only such a gesture were not highly unprofessional. He recognized his duty, and on an abstract intellectual level the potential value of the Melidans, but they revolted him, and he would have been glad to find me of like mind, ready to draw a line through their name and give them up as a bad cause.

A few moments' conversation was sufficient to disabuse him of this hope. I wish to attest that he did not allow the disappointment to in any way alter the performance of his duty, and he could not have objected with more vigor to my project of proceeding at once to the Melidan continent, to his mind a suicidal act.

In the end he chose not to stop me. I am sorry if he later regretted that, as seems likely. I took full advantage of the weight of my arrival. Five years had gone by on my homeworld of Terce since I had embarked, and there is a certain moral force to having sacrificed a former life for the one unknown. I had observed it often with new arrivals on Terce: their first requests were rarely refused even when foolish, as they often were. I was of course quite sure my own were eminently sensible.

"We will find you a guide," he said finally, yielding, and all the machinery of the Confederacy began to turn to my desire, a heady sensation.

Badea arrived at the embassy not two hours later. She wore a plain gray wrap around her shoulders, draped to the ground, and another wrap around her head. The alterations visible were only small ones: a smattering of green freckles across the bridge of her nose and cheeks, a greenish tinge to her lips and nails. Her wings were folded and hidden under the wrap, adding the bulk roughly of an overnight hiker's backpack. She smelled a little like the sourdough used on Terce to make roundbread, noticeable but not unpleasant. She might have walked through a spaceport without exciting comment.

She was brought to me in the shambles of my new office, where I had barely begun to lay out my things. I was wearing a conservative black suit, my best, tailored because you could not buy trousers for women ready-made on Terce, and, thankfully, comfortable shoes, because elegant ones on Terce were not meant to be walked in. I remember my clothing particularly because I was in it for the next week without opportunity to change.

"Are you ready to go?" she asked me as soon as we were introduced and the receptionist had left.

I was quite visibly *not* ready to go, but this was not a misunderstanding: she did not want to take me. She thought the request stupid, and feared my safety would be a burden on her. If Ambassador Kostas would not mind my failure to return, she could not know that, and to be just, he would certainly have reacted unpleasantly in any case, figuring it as his duty.

But when asked for a favor she does not want to grant, a Melidan will sometimes offer it anyway, only in an unacceptable or awkward way. Another Melidan will recognize this as a refusal, and withdraw the request. Badea did not expect this courtesy from me; she only expected that I would say I could not leave at once. This she could count to her satisfaction as a refusal, and she would not come back to offer again.

I was, however, informed enough to be dangerous, and I did recognize the custom. I said, "It is inconvenient, but I am prepared to leave immediately." She turned at once and walked out of my office, and I followed her. It is understood that a favor accepted despite the difficulty and constraints laid down by the giver must be necessary to the recipient, as indeed this was to me; but in such a case, the conditions must then be endured, even if artificial.

I did not risk a pause at all even to tell anyone I was going; we walked out past the embassy secretary and the guards, who did not do more than give us a cursory glance—we were going the wrong way, and my citizen's button would likely have saved us interruption in any case. Kostas would not know I had gone until my absence was noticed and the security logs examined.

The Second Adjustment

I was not unhappy as I followed Badea through the city. A little discomfort was nothing to me next to the intense satisfaction of, as I felt, having passed a first test: I had gotten past all resistance offered me, both by Kostas and Badea, and soon I would be in the heart of a people I already felt I knew. Though I would be an outsider among them, I had lived all my life to the present day in the self-same state, and I did not fear it, or for the moment anything else.

Badea walked quickly and with a freer stride than I was used to, loose-limbed. I was taller, but had to stretch to match her. Esperigans looked at her as she went by, and then looked at me, and the pressure of their gaze was suddenly hostile. "We might take a taxi," I offered. Many were passing by empty. "I can pay."

"No," she said, with a look of distaste at one of those conveyances, so we continued on foot.

After Melida, during my black-sea journey, my doctoral dissertation on the Canaan movement was published under the escrow clause, against my will. I have never used the funds, which continue to accumulate steadily. I do not like to inflict them on any cause I admire sufficiently to support, so they will go to my family when I have gone; my nephews will be glad of it, and of the passing of an embarrassment, and that is as much good as it can be expected to provide.

There is a great deal within that book that is wrong, and more that is wrongheaded, in particular any expression of opinion or analysis I interjected atop the scant collection of accurate facts I was able to accumulate in six years of overenthusiastic graduate work. This little is true: The Canaan movement was an offshoot of conservation philosophy. Where the traditionalists of that movement sought to restrict humanity to dead worlds and closed enclaves on others, the Canaan splinter group wished instead to alter themselves while they altered their new worlds, meeting them halfway.

The philosophy had the benefit of a certain practicality, as genetic engineering and body modification were and remain considerably cheaper than terraforming, but we are a squeamish and a violent species, and nothing invites pogrom more surely than the neighbor who is different from us, yet still too close. In consequence, the Melidans were by our present day the last surviving Canaan society.

They had come to Melida and settled the larger of the two continents some eight hundred years before. The Esperigans came two hundred years later, refugees from the plagues on New Victoire, and took the smaller continent. The two had little contact for the first half millennium; we of the Confederacy are given to think in worlds and solar systems, and to imagine that only a space voyage is long, but a hostile continent is vast enough to occupy a small and struggling band. But both prospered, each according to their lights, and by the time I landed, half the planet glittered in the night from space, and half was yet pristine.

In my dissertation, I described the ensuing conflict as natural, which is fair if slaughter and pillage are granted to be natural to our kind. The Esperigans had exhausted the limited raw resources of their share of the planet, and a short flight away was the untouched expanse of the larger continent, not a tenth as populated as their own. The Melidans controlled their birthrate, used only sustainable quantities, and built nothing that could not be eaten by the wilderness a year after they had abandoned it. Many Esperigan philosophes and politicians trumpeted their admiration of Melidan society, but this was only a sort of pleasant spiritual refreshment, as one admires a saint or a martyr without ever wishing to be one.

The invasion began informally, with adventurers and entrepreneurs, with the desperate, the poor, the violent. They began to land on the shores of the Melidan territory, to survey, to take away samples, to plant their own foreign roots. They soon had a village, then more than one. The Melidans told them to leave, which worked as well as it ever has in the annals of colonialism, and then attacked them. Most of the settlers were killed; enough survived and straggled back across the ocean to make a dramatic story of murder and cruelty out of it.

I expressed the conviction to the Ministry of State, in my preassignment report, that the details had been exaggerated, and that the attacks had been provoked more extensively. I was wrong, of course. But at the time I did not know it.

Badea took me to the low quarter of Landfall, so called because it faced on the side of the ocean downcurrent from the spaceport. Iridescent oil and a floating mat of discards glazed the edge of the surf. The houses were mean and crowded tightly upon one another, broken up mostly by liquor stores and bars. Docks stretched out into the ocean, extended long to reach out past the pollution, and just past the end of one of these floated a small boat, little more than a simple coracle: a hull of brown bark, a narrow brown mast, a gray-green sail slack and trembling in the wind.

We began walking out toward it, and those watching—there were some men loitering about the docks, fishing idly, or working on repairs to equipment or nets—began to realize then that I meant to go with her.

The Esperigans had already learned the lesson we like to teach as often as we can, that the Confederacy is a bad enemy and a good friend, and while no one is ever made to join us by force, we cannot be opposed directly. We had given them the spaceport already, an open door to the rest of the settled worlds, and they wanted more, the moth yearning. I relied on this for protection, and did not consider that however much they wanted from our outstretched hand, they still more wished to deny its gifts to their enemy.

Four men rose as we walked the length of the dock, and made a line across it. "You don't want to go with that one, ma'am," one of them said to me, a parody of respect. Badea said nothing. She moved a little aside, to see how I would answer them.

"I am on assignment for my government," I said, neatly offering a red flag to a bull, and moved toward them. It was not an attempt at bluffing: on Terce, even though I was immodestly unveiled, men would have at once moved out of the way to avoid any chance of the insult of physical contact. It was an act so automatic as to be invisible: precisely what we are taught to watch for in ourselves, but that proves infinitely easier in the instruction than in the practice. I did not *think* they would move; I knew they would.

Perhaps that certainty transmitted itself: the men did move a little, enough to satisfy my unconscious that they were cooperating with my expectations, so that it took me wholly by surprise and horror when one reached out and put his hand on my arm to stop me.

I screamed, in full voice, and struck him. His face is lost to my memory, but I still can see clearly the man behind him, his expression as full of appalled violation as my own. The four of them flinched from my scream, and then drew in around me, protesting and reaching out in turn.

I reacted with more violence. I had confidently considered myself a citizen of no world and of many, trained out of assumptions and unaffected by the parochial attitudes of the one where chance had seen me born, but in that moment I could with actual pleasure have killed all of them. That wish was unlikely to be gratified. I was taller, and the gravity of Terce is slightly higher than of Melida, so I was stronger than they expected me to be, but they were laborers and seamen, built generously and rough-hewn, and the male advantage in muscle mass tells quickly in a hand-to-hand fight.

They tried to immobilize me, which only panicked me further. The mind curls in on itself in such a moment; I remember palpably only the sensation of sweating copiously, and the way this caused the seam of my blouse to rub unpleasantly against my neck as I struggled.

Badea told me later that, at first, she had meant to let them hold me. She could then leave, with the added satisfaction of knowing the Esperigan fishermen and not she had provoked an incident with the Confederacy. It was not sympathy that moved her to action, precisely. The extremity of my distress was as alien to her as to them, but where they thought me mad, she read it in the context of my having accepted her original conditions and somewhat unwillingly decided that I truly did need to go with her, even if she did not know precisely why and saw no use in it herself.

I cannot tell you precisely how the subsequent moments unfolded. I remember the green gauze of her wings overhead perforated by the sun, like a linen curtain, and the blood spattering my face as she neatly lopped off the hands upon me. She used for the purpose a blade I later saw in use for many tasks, among them harvesting fruit off plants where the leaves or the bark may be poisonous. It is shaped like a sickle and strung upon a thick elastic cord, which a skilled wielder can cause to become rigid or to collapse.

I stood myself back on my feet panting, and she landed. The men were on their knees screaming, and others were running toward us down the docks. Badea swept the severed hands into the water with the side of her foot and said calmly, "We must go."

The little boat had drawn up directly beside us over the course of our encounter, drawn by some signal I had not seen her transmit. I stepped into it behind her. The coracle leapt forward like a springing bird, and left the shouting and the blood behind.

We did not speak over the course of that strange journey. What I had thought a sail did not catch the wind, but opened itself wide and stretched out over our heads, like an awning, and angled itself toward the sun. There were many small filaments upon the surface wriggling when I examined it more closely, and also upon the exterior of the hull. Badea stretched herself out upon the floor of the craft, lying under the low deck, and I joined her in the small space: it was not uncomfortable or rigid, but had the queer unsettled cushioning of a waterbed.

The ocean crossing took only the rest of the day. How our speed was generated I cannot tell you; we did not seem to sit deeply in the water and our craft threw up no spray. The world blurred as a window running with rain. I asked Badea for water, once, and she put her hands on the floor of the craft and pressed down: in the depression she made, a small clear pool gathered for me to cup out, with a taste like slices of cucumber with the skin still upon them.

This was how I came to Melida.

The Third Adjustment

Badea was vaguely embarrassed to have inflicted me on her fellows, and having deposited me in the center of her village made a point of leaving me there by leaping aloft into the canopy where I could not follow, as a way of saying she was done with me, and anything I did henceforth could not be laid at her door.

I was by now hungry and nearly sick with exhaustion. Those who have not flown between worlds like to imagine the journey a glamorous one, but at least for minor bureaucrats, it is no more pleasant than any form of transport, only elongated. I had spent a week a virtual prisoner in my berth, the bed folding up to give me room to walk four strides back and forth, or to unfold my writing-desk, not both at once, with a shared toilet the size of an ungenerous closet down the hall. Landfall had not arrested my forward motion, as that mean port had never been my destination. Now, however, I was arrived, and the dregs of adrenaline were consumed in anticlimax.

Others before me have stood in a Melidan village center and described it for an audience—Esperigans mostly, anthropologists and students of biology and a class of tourists either adventurous or stupid. There is usually a lyrical description of the natives coasting overhead among some sort of vines or tree branches knitted overhead for shelter, the particulars and adjectives determined by the village latitude, and the obligatory explanation of the typical plan of huts, organized as a spoked wheel around the central plaza.

If I had been less tired, perhaps I, too, would have looked with so analytical an air, and might now satisfy my readers with a similar report. But to me the village only presented all the confusion of a wholly strange place, and I saw nothing that seemed to me deliberate. To call it a village gives a false air of comforting provinciality. Melidans, at least those with wings, move freely among a wide constellation of small settlements, so that all of these, in the public sphere, partake of the hectic pace of the city. I stood alone, and strangers moved past me with assurance, the confidence of their stride saying, "I care nothing for you or your fate. It is of no concern to me. How might you expect it to be otherwise?" In the end, I lay down on one side of the plaza and went to sleep.

I met Kitia the next morning. She woke me by prodding me with a twig, experimentally, having been selected for this task out of her group of schoolmates by some complicated interworking of personality and chance. They giggled from a few safe paces back as I opened my eyes and sat up.

"Why are you sleeping in the square?" Kitia asked me, to a burst of fresh giggles.

"Where should I sleep?" I asked her.

"In a house!" she said.

When I had explained to them, not without some art, that I had no house here, they offered the censorious suggestion that I should go back to wherever I did have a house. I made a good show of looking analytically up at the sky overhead and asking them what our latitude was, and then I pointed at a random location and said, "My house is five years that way."

Scorn, puzzlement, and at last delight. I was from the stars! None of their friends had ever met anyone from so far away. One girl who previously had held a point of pride for having once visited the smaller continent, with an Esperigan toy doll to prove it, was instantly dethroned. Kitia possessively took my arm and informed me that as my house was too far away, she would take me to another.

Children of virtually any society are an excellent resource for the diplomatic servant or the anthropologist, if contact with them can be made without giving offense. They enjoy the unfamiliar experience of answering real questions, particularly the stupidly obvious ones that allow them to feel a sense of superiority over the inquiring adult, and they are easily impressed with the unusual. Kitia was a treasure. She led me, at the head of a small pied-piper procession, to an empty house on a convenient lane. It had been lately abandoned, and was already being reclaimed: the walls and floor were swarming with tiny insects with glossy dark blue carapaces, munching so industriously the sound of their jaws hummed like a summer afternoon.

I with difficulty avoided recoiling. Kitia did not hesitate: she walked into the swarm, crushing beetles by the dozens underfoot, and went to a small spigot in the far wall. When she turned this on, a clear viscous liquid issued forth, and the beetles scattered from it. "Here, like this," she said, showing me how to cup my hands under the liquid and spread it upon the walls and the floor. The disgruntled beetles withdrew, and the brownish surfaces began to bloom back to pale green, repairing the holes.

Over the course of that next week, she also fed me, corrected my manners and my grammar, and eventually brought me a set of clothing, a tunic and leggings, which she proudly informed me she had made herself in class. I thanked her with real sincerity and asked where I might wash my old clothing. She looked very puzzled, and when she had looked more closely at my clothing and touched it, she said, "Your clothing is dead! I thought it was only ugly."

Her gift was not made of fabric but a thin tough mesh of plant filaments with the feathered surface of a moth's wings. It gripped my skin eagerly as soon as I had put it on, and I thought myself at first allergic, because it itched and tingled, but this was only the bacteria bred to live in the mesh assiduously eating away the sweat and dirt and dead epidermal cells built up on my skin. It took me several more days to overcome all my instinct and learn to trust the living cloth with the more voluntary eliminations of my body also. (Previously I had been going out back to defecate in the woods, having been unable to find anything resembling a toilet, and meeting too much confusion when I tried to approach the question to dare pursue it further, for fear of encountering a taboo.)

And this was the handiwork of a child, not thirteen years of age! She could not explain to me how she had done it in any way that made sense to me. Imagine if you had to explain how to perform a reference search to someone who had not only never seen a library, but did not understand electricity, and who perhaps knew there was such a thing as written text, but did not himself read more than the alphabet. She took me once to her classroom after hours and showed me her workstation, a large wooden tray full of grayish moss, with a double row of small jars along the back each holding liquids or powders that I could distinguish only by their differing colors. Her only tools were an assortment of syringes and eyedroppers and scoops and brushes.

I went back to my house and in the growing report I would not have a chance to send for another month I wrote, *These are a priceless people. We must have them.*

The Fourth Adjustment

All these first weeks, I made no contact with any other adult. I saw them go by occasionally, and the houses around mine were occupied, but they never spoke to me or even looked at me directly. None of them objected to my squatting, but that was less implicit endorsement and more an unwillingness even to acknowledge my existence. I talked to Kitia and the other children, and tried to be patient. I hoped an opportunity would offer itself eventually for me to be of some visible use.

In the event, it was rather my lack of use that led to the break in the wall. A commotion arose in the early morning, while Kitia was showing me the plan of her wings, which she was at that age beginning to design. She would grow the parasite over the subsequent year, and was presently practicing with miniature versions, which rose from her worktable surface gossamer-thin and fluttering with an involuntary muscle-twitching. I was trying to conceal my revulsion.

Kitia looked up when the noise erupted. She casually tossed her example out of the window, to be pounced upon with a hasty scramble by several nearby birds, and went out the door. I followed her to the square: the children were gathered at the fringes, silent for once and watching. There were five women laid out on the ground, all bloody, one dead. Two of the others looked mortally wounded. They were all winged.

There were several working already on the injured, packing small brownish-white spongy masses into the open wounds and sewing them up. I would have liked to be of use, less from natural instinct than from the colder thought, which inflicted itself upon my mind, that any crisis opens social barriers. I am sorry to say I did not refrain from any noble self-censorship, but from the practical conviction that it was at once apparent my limited field-medical training could not in any valuable way be applied to the present circumstances.

I drew away, rather, to avoid being in the way as I could not turn the situation to my advantage, and in doing so ran up against Badea, who stood at the very edge of the square, observing.

She stood alone; there were no other adults nearby, and there was blood on her hands. "Are you hurt also?" I asked her.

"No," she returned shortly.

I ventured on concern for her friends, and asked her if they had been hurt in fighting. "We have heard rumors," I added, "that the Esperigans have been encroaching on your territory." It was the first opportunity I had been given of hinting at even this much of our official sympathy, as the children only shrugged when I asked them if there were fighting going on.

She shrugged, too, with one shoulder, and the folded wing rose and fell with it. But then she said, "They leave their weapons in the forest for us, even where they cannot have gone."

The Esperigans had several kinds of land mine technologies, including a clever mobile one that could be programmed with a target either as specific as an individual's genetic record or as general as a broadly defined body type—humanoid and winged, for instance—and set loose to wander until it found a match, then do the maximum damage it could. Only one side could carry explosive, as the other was devoted to the electronics. "The shrapnel, does it come only in one direction?" I asked, and made a fanned-out shape with my hands to illustrate. Badea looked at me sharply and nodded.

I explained the mine to her and described their manufacture. "Some scanning devices can detect them," I added, meaning to continue into an offer, but I had not finished the litany of materials before she was striding away from the square, without another word.

I was not dissatisfied with the reaction, in which I correctly read intention to put my information to immediate use, and two days later my patience was rewarded. Badea came to my house in the midmorning and said, "We have found one of them. Can you show us how to disarm them?"

"I am not sure," I told her honestly. "The safest option would be to trigger it deliberately, from afar."

"The plastics they use poison the ground."

"Can you take me to its location?" I asked. She considered the question with enough seriousness that I realized there was either taboo or danger involved.

"Yes," she said finally, and took me with her to a house near the center of the village. It had steps up to the roof, and from there we could climb to that of the neighboring house, and so on until we were high enough to reach a large basket, woven not of ropes but of a kind of vine, sitting in a crook of a tree. We climbed into this, and she kicked us off from the tree.

The movement was not smooth. The nearest I can describe is the sensation of being on a child's swing, except at that highest point of weightlessness you do not go backwards, but instead go falling into another arc, but at tremendous speed, and with a pungent smell like rotten pineapple all around from the shattering of the leaves of the trees through which we were propelled. I was violently sick after some five minutes. To the comfort of my pride if not my stomach, Badea was also sick, though more efficiently and over the side, before our journey ended.

There were two other women waiting for us in the tree where we came to rest, both of them also winged: Renata and Paudi. "It's gone another three hundred meters, toward Ighlan," Renata told us—another nearby Melidan village, as they explained to me.

"If it comes near enough to pick up traces of organized habitation, it will not trigger until it is inside the settlement, among as many people as possible," I said. "It may also have a burrowing mode, if it is the more expensive kind."

They took me down through the canopy, carefully, and walked before and behind me when we came to the ground. Their wings were spread wide enough to brush against the hanging vines to either side, and they regularly leapt aloft for a brief survey. Several times they moved me with friendly hands into a slightly different path, although my untrained eyes could make no difference among the choices.

A narrow trail of large ants—the reader will forgive me for calling them ants, they were nearly indistinguishable from those efficient creatures—paced us over the forest floor, which I did not recognize as significant until we came near the mine, and I saw it covered with the ants, who did not impede its movement but milled around and over it with intense interest.

"We have adjusted them so they smell the plastic," Badea said, when I asked. "We can make them eat it," she added, "but we worried it would set off the device."

The word *adjusted* scratches at the back of my mind again as I write this, that unpleasant tinny sensation of a term that does not allow of real translation and which has been inadequately replaced. I cannot improve upon the work of the official Confederacy translators, however; to encompass the true concept would require three dry, dusty chapters more suited to a textbook on the subject of biological engineering, which I am ill-qualified to produce. I do hope that I have successfully captured the wholly casual way she spoke of this feat. Our own scientists might replicate this act of genetic sculpting in any of two dozen excellent laboratories across the Confederacy—given several years, and a suitably impressive grant. They had done it in less than two days, as a matter of course.

I did not at the time indulge in admiration. The mine was ignoring the inquisitive ants and scuttling along at a good pace, the head with its glassy eye occasionally rotating upon its spindly spider-legs, and we had half a day in which to divert it from the village ahead.

Renata followed the mine as it continued on, while I sketched what I knew of the internals in the dirt for Badea and Paudi. Any sensible mine-maker will design the device to simply explode at any interference with its working other than the disable code, so our options were not particularly satisfying. "The most likely choice," I suggested, "would be the transmitter. If it becomes unable to receive the disable code, there may be a failsafe, which would deactivate it on a subsequent malfunction."

Paudi had on her back a case that, unfolded, looked very like a more elegant and compact version of little Kitia's worktable. She sat crosslegged with it on her lap and worked on it for some two hours' time, occasionally reaching down to pick up a handful of ants, which dropped into the green matrix of her table mostly curled up and died, save for a few survivors, which she herded carefully into an empty jar before taking up another sample.

I sat on the forest floor beside her, or walked with Badea, who was pacing a small circle out around us, watchfully. Occasionally she would un-sling her scythe-blade, and then put it away again, and once she brought down a mottie, a small lemurlike creature. I say lemur because there is nothing closer in my experience, but it had none of the charm of an Earthnative mammal; I rather felt an instinctive disgust looking at it, even before she showed me the tiny sucker-mouths full of hooked teeth with which it latched upon a victim.

She had grown a little more loquacious, and asked me about my own homeworld. I told her about Terce, and about the seclusion of women, which she found extremely funny, as we can only laugh at the follies of those far from us which threaten us not at all. The Melidans by design maintain a five-to-one ratio of women to men, as adequate to maintain a healthy gene pool while minimizing the overall resource consumption of their population. "They cannot take the wings, so it is more difficult for them to travel," she added, with one sentence dismissing the lingering mystery that had perplexed earlier visitors, of the relative rarity of seeing their men.

She had two children, which she described to me proudly, living presently with their father and half siblings in a village half a day's travel away, and she was considering a third. She had trained as a forest ranger, another inadequately translated term, which was at the time beginning to take on a military significance among them under the pressure of the Esperigan incursions.

"I'm done," Paudi said, and we went to catch up Renata and find a nearby ant-nest, which looked like a mound of white cotton batting rising several inches off the forest floor. Paudi introduced her small group of infected survivors into this colony, and after a little confusion and milling about, they accepted their transplantation and marched inside. The flow of departures slowed a little momentarily, then resumed, and a file split off from the main channel of workers to march in the direction of the mine.

These joined the lingering crowd still upon the mine, but the new arrivals did not stop at inspection and promptly began to struggle to insinuate themselves into the casing. We withdrew to a safe distance, watching. The mine continued on without any slackening in its pace for ten minutes, as more ants began to squeeze themselves inside, and then it hesitated, one spindly metal leg held aloft uncertainly. It went a few more slightly drunken paces, and then abruptly the legs all retracted and left it a smooth round lump on the forest floor.

The Fifth Adjustment

They showed me how to use their communications technology and grew me an interface to my own small handheld, so my report was at last able to go. Kostas began angry, of course, having been forced to defend the manner of my departure to the Esperigans without the benefit of any understanding of the circumstances, but I sent the report an hour before I messaged, and by the time we spoke, he had read enough to be in reluctant agreement with my conclusions if not my methods.

I was of course full of self-satisfaction. Freed at long last from the academy and the walled gardens of Terce, armed with false confidence in my research and my training, I had so far achieved all that my design had stretched to encompass. The Esperigan blood had washed easily from my hands, and though I answered Kostas meekly when he upbraided me, privately I felt only impatience, and even he did not linger long on the topic: I had been too successful, and he had more important news.

The Esperigans had launched a small army two days before, under the more pleasant-sounding name of expeditionary defensive force. Its purpose was to establish a permanent settlement on the Melidan shore, some nine hundred miles from my present location, and begin the standard process of terraforming. The native life would be eradicated in spheres of a hundred miles across at a time: first the broad strokes of clear-cutting and the electrified nets, then the irradiation of the soil and the air, and after that the seeding of Earth-native microbes and plants. So had a thousand worlds been made over anew, and though the Esperigans had fully conquered their own continent five centuries before, they still knew the way.

He asked doubtfully if I thought some immediate resistance could be offered. Disabling a few mines scattered into the jungle seemed to him a small task. Confronting a large and organized military force was on a different order of magnitude. "I think we can do something," I said, maintaining a veneer of caution for his benefit, and took the catalog of equipment to Badea as soon as we had disengaged.

She was occupied in organizing the retrieval of the deactivated mines, which the ants were now leaving scattered in the forests and jungles. A bird-of-paradise variant had been *adjusted* to make a meal out of the ants and take the glittery mines back to their treetop nests, where an observer might easily see them from above. She and the other collectors had so far found nearly a thousand of them. The mines made a neat pyramid, as of the harvested skulls of small cyclopean creatures with their dull eyes staring out lifelessly.

The Esperigans needed a week to cross the ocean in their numbers, and I spent it with the Melidans, developing our response. There was a heady delight in this collaboration. The work was easy and pleasant in their wide-open laboratories full of plants, roofed only with the fluttering sailcloth eating sunlight to give us energy, and the best of them coming from many miles distant to participate in the effort. The Confederacy spy-satellites had gone into orbit perhaps a year after our first contact: I likely knew more about the actual force than the senior administrators of Melida. I was in much demand, consulted not only for my information but also for my opinion.

In the ferment of our labors, I withheld nothing. This was not yet deliberate, but neither was it innocent. I had been sent to further a war, and if in the political calculus that had arrived at this solution the lives of soldiers were only variables, yet there was still a balance I was expected to preserve. It was not my duty to give the Melidans an easy victory, any more than it had been Kostas's to give one to the Esperigans.

A short and victorious war, opening a new and tantalizing frontier for restless spirits, would at once drive up that inconvenient nationalism which is the Confederacy's worst obstacle, and render less compelling the temptations we could offer to lure them into fully joining galactic society. On the other hand, to descend into squalor, a more equal kind of civil war has often proved extremely useful, and the more lingering and bitter the better. I was sent to the Melidans in hope that, given some guidance and what material assistance we could quietly provide without taking any official position, they might be an adequate opponent for the Esperigans to produce this situation.

There has been some criticism of the officials who selected me for this mission, but in their defense, it must be pointed out it was not in fact my assignment to actually provide military assistance, nor could anyone, even myself, have envisioned my proving remotely useful in such a role. I was only meant to be an early scout. My duty was to acquire cultural information enough to open a door for a party of military experts from Voca Libre, who would not reach Melida for another two years. Ambition and opportunity promoted me, and no official hand.

―――――

I think these experts arrived sometime during the third Esperigan offensive. I cannot pinpoint the date with any accuracy—I had by then ceased to track the days, and I never met them. I hope they can forgive my theft of their war; I paid for my greed.

The Esperigans used a typical carbonized steel in most of their equipment, as bolts and hexagonal nuts and screws with star-shaped heads, and woven into the tough mesh of their body armor. This was the target of our efforts. It was a new field of endeavor for the Melidans, who used metal as they used meat, sparingly and with a sense of righteousness in its avoidance. To them it was either a trace element needed in minute amounts, or an undesirable by-product of the more complicated biological processes they occasionally needed to invoke.

However, they had developed some strains of bacteria to deal with this latter waste, and the speed with which they could manipulate these organisms was extraordinary. Another quantity of the ants—a convenient delivery mechanism used by the Melidans routinely, as I learned—were adjusted to render them deficient in iron and to provide a home in their bellies for the bacteria, transforming them into shockingly efficient engines of destruction. Set loose upon several of the mines as a trial, they devoured the carapaces and left behind only smudgy black heaps of carbon dust, carefully harvested for fertilizer, and the plastic explosives from within, nestled in their bed of copper wire and silicon.

The Esperigans landed, and at once carved themselves out a neat half moon of wasteland from the virgin shore, leaving no branches that might stretch above their encampment to offer a platform for attack. They established an electrified fence around the perimeter, with guns and patrols, and all this I observed with Badea, from a small platform in a vine-choked tree not far away: we wore the green-gray cloaks, and our faces were stained with leaf juice.

I had very little justification for inserting myself into such a role but the flimsy excuse of pointing out to Badea the most crucial section of their camp, when we had broken in. I cannot entirely say why I wished to go along on so dangerous an expedition. I am not particularly courageous.

Several of my more unkind biographers have accused me of bloodlust, and pointed to this as a sequel to the disaster of my first departure. I cannot refute the accusation on the evidence, however I will point out that I chose that portion of the expedition which we hoped would encounter no violence.

But it is true I had learned already to seethe at the violent piggish blindness of the Esperigans, who would have wrecked all the wonders around me only to propagate yet another bland copy of Earth and suck dry the carcass of their own world. They were my enemy both by duty and by inclination, and I permitted myself the convenience of hating them. At the time, it made matters easier.

The wind was running from the east, and several of the Melidans attacked the camp from that side. The mines had yielded a quantity of explosive large enough to pierce the Esperigans' fence and shake the trees even as far as our lofty perch. The wind carried the smoke and dust and flames toward us, obscuring the ground and rendering the soldiers in their own camp only vague ghostlike suggestions of human shape. The fighting was hand-to-hand, and the stutter of gunfire came only tentatively through the chaos of the smoke.

Badea had been holding a narrow cord, one end weighted with a heavy seedpod. She now poured a measure of water onto the pod, from her canteen, then flung it out into the air. It sailed over the fence and landed inside the encampment, behind one of the neat rows of storage tents. The seedpod struck the ground and immediately burst like a ripe fruit, an anemone tangle of waving roots creeping out over the ground and anchoring the cord, which she had secured at this end around one thick branch.

We let ourselves down it, hand over hand. There was none of that typical abrasion or friction that I might have expected from rope; my hands felt as cool and comfortable when we descended as when we began. We ran into the narrow space between the tents. I was experiencing that strange elongation of time that crisis can occasionally produce: I was conscious of each footfall, and of the seeming-long moments it took to place each one.

There were wary soldiers at many of the tent entrances, likely those that held either the more valuable munitions or the more valuable men. Their discipline had not faltered, even while the majority of the force was already orchestrating a response to the Melidan assault on the other side of the encampment. But we did not need to penetrate into the tents. The guards were rather useful markers for us, showing me which of the tents were the more significant. I pointed out to Badea the cluster of four tents, each guarded at either side by a pair, near the farthest end of the encampment.

Badea looked here and there over the ground as we darted under cover of smoke from one alleyway to another, the walls of waxed canvas muffling the distant shouts and the sound of gunfire. The dirt still had the yellowish tinge of Melidan soil—the Esperigans had not yet irradiated it—but it was crumbly and dry, the fine fragile native moss crushed and much torn by heavy boots and equipment, and the wind raised little dervishes of dust around our ankles.

"This ground will take years to recover fully," she said to me, soft and bitterly, as she stopped us and knelt behind a deserted tent not far from our target. She gave me a small ceramic implement, which looked much like the hair-picks sometimes worn on Terce by women with hair that never knew a blade's edge: a raised comb with three teeth, though on the tool these were much longer and sharpened at the end. I picked the ground vigorously, stabbing deep to aerate the wounded soil, while she judiciously poured out a mixture of water and certain organic extracts, and sowed a packet of seeds.

This may sound a complicated operation to be carrying out in an enemy camp, in the midst of battle, but we had practiced the maneuver, and indeed had we been glimpsed, anyone would have been hard-pressed to recognize a threat in the two gray-wrapped lumps crouched low as we pawed at the dirt. Twice while we worked, wounded soldiers were carried in a rush past either end of our alleyway, toward shelter. We were not seen.

The seeds she carried, though tiny, burst readily, and began to thrust out spiderweb-fine rootlets at such a speed, they looked like nothing more than squirming maggots. Badea without concern moved her hands around them, encouraging them into the ground. When they were established, she motioned me to stop my work, and she took out the prepared ants: a much greater number of them, with a dozen of the fat yellow wasp-sized broodmothers. Tipped out into the prepared and welcoming soil, they immediately began to burrow their way down, with the anxious harrying of their subjects and spawn.

Badea watched for a long while, crouched over, even after the ants had vanished nearly all beneath the surface. The few who emerged and darted back inside, the faint trembling of the rootlets, the shifting grains of dirt, all carried information to her. At length satisfied, she straightened, saying, "Now—"

The young soldier was I think only looking for somewhere to piss, rather than investigating some noise. He came around the corner already fumbling at his belt, and seeing us did not immediately shout, likely from plain surprise, but grabbed for Badea's shoulder first. He was clean-shaven, and the name on his lapel badge was RIDANG. I drove the soil-pick into his eye. I was taller, so the stroke went downward, and he fell backwards to his knees away from me, clutching at his face.

He did not die at once. There must be very few deaths that come immediately, though we often like to comfort ourselves by the pretense that this failure of the body, or that injury, must at once eradicate consciousness and life and pain all together. Here sentience lasted several moments which seemed to me long: his other eye was open, and looked at me while his hands clawed for the handle of the pick. When this had faded, and he had fallen supine to the ground, there was yet a convulsive movement of all the limbs and a trickling of blood from mouth and nose and eye before the final stiffening jerk left the body emptied and inanimate.

I watched him die in a strange parody of serenity, all feeling hollowed out of me, and then turning away vomited upon the ground. Behind me, Badea cut open his belly and his thighs and turned him facedown onto the dirt, so the blood and the effluvia leaked out of him. "That will do a little good for the ground at least, before they carry him away to waste him," she said. "Come." She touched my shoulder, not unkindly, but I flinched from the touch as from a blow.

It was not that Badea or her fellows were indifferent to death, or casual toward murder. But there is a price to be paid for living in a world whose native hostilities have been cherished rather than crushed. Melidan life expectancy is some ten years beneath that of Confederacy citizens, though they are on average healthier and more fit both genetically and physically. In their philosophy, a human life is not inherently superior and to be valued over any other kind. Accident and predation claim many, and living intimately with the daily cruelties of nature dulls the facility for sentiment. Badea enjoyed none of that comforting distance that allows us to think ourselves assured of the full potential span of life, and therefore suffered none of the pangs when confronted with evidence to the contrary. I looked at my victim and saw my own face; so, too, did she, but she had lived all her life so aware, and it did not bow her shoulders.

Five days passed before the Esperigan equipment began to come apart. Another day halted all their work, and in confusion they retreated to their encampment. I did not go with the Melidan company that destroyed them to the last man.

Contrary to many accusations, I did not lie to Kostas in my report and pretend surprise. I freely confessed to him I had expected the result, and truthfully explained I had not wished to make claims of which I was unsure. I never deliberately sought to deceive any of my superiors or conceal information from them, save in such small ways. At first I was not Melidan enough to wish to do so, and later I was too Melidan to feel anything but revulsion at the concept.

He and I discussed our next steps in the tiger-dance. I described as best I could the Melidan technology, and after consultation with various Confederacy experts, it was agreed he would quietly mention to the Esperigan minister of defense, at their weekly luncheon, a particular Confederacy technology: ceramic coatings, which could be ordered at vast expense and two years' delay from Bel Rios. Or, he would suggest, if the Esperigans wished to deed some land to the Confederacy, a private entrepreneurial concern might fund the construction of a local fabrication plant, and produce them at much less cost, in six months' time.

The Esperigans took the bait, and saw only private greed behind this apparent breach of neutrality: imagining Kostas an investor in this private concern, they winked at his venality, and eagerly helped us to their own exploitation. Meanwhile, they continued occasional and tentative incursions into the Melidan continent, probing the coastline, but the disruption they created betrayed their attempts, and whichever settlement was nearest would at once deliver them a present of the industrious ants, so these met with no greater success than the first.

Through these months of brief and grudging detente, I traveled extensively throughout the continent. My journals are widely available, being the domain of our government, but they are shamefully sparse, and I apologize to my colleagues for it. I would have been more diligent in my work if I had imagined I would be the last and not the first such chronicler. At the time, giddy with success, I went with more the spirit of a holidaymaker than a researcher, and I sent only those images and notes which it was pleasant to me to record, with the excuse of limited capacity to send my reports.

For what cold comfort it may be, I must tell you photography and description are inadequate to convey the experience of standing in the living heart of a world alien yet not hostile, and when I walked hand in hand with Badea along the crest of a great canyon wall and looked down over the ridges of purple and gray and ocher at the gently waving tendrils of an elacca forest, which in my notorious video recordings can provoke nausea in nearly every observer, I felt the first real stir of an unfamiliar sensation of beauty-in-strangeness, and I laughed in delight and surprise, while she looked at me and smiled.

We returned to her village three days later and saw the bombing as we came, the new Esperigan long-range fighter planes like narrow silver knife-blades making low passes overhead, the smoke rising black and oily against the sky. Our basket-journey could not be accelerated, so we could only cling to the sides and wait as we were carried onward. The planes and the smoke were gone before we arrived; the wreckage was not.

I was angry at Kostas afterwards, unfairly. He was no more truly the Esperigans' confidant than they were his, but I felt at the time that it was his business to know what they were about, and he had failed to warn me. I accused him of deliberate concealment; he told me, censoriously, that I had known the risk when I had gone to the continent, and he could hardly be responsible for preserving my safety while I slept in the very war zone. This silenced my tirade, as I realized how near I had come to betraying myself. Of course he would not have wanted me to warn the Melidans; it had not yet occurred to him I would have wished to, myself. I ought not have wanted to.

Forty-three people were killed in the attack. Kitia was yet lingering when I came to her small bedside. She was in no pain, her eyes cloudy and distant, already withdrawing; her family had been and gone again. "I knew you were coming back, so I asked them to let me stay a little longer," she told me. "I wanted to say good-bye." She paused and added uncertainly, "And I was afraid, a little. Don't tell."

I promised her I would not. She sighed and said, "I shouldn't wait any longer. Will you call them over?"

The attendant came when I raised my hand, and he asked Kitia, "Are you ready?"

"Yes," she said, a little doubtful. "It won't hurt?"

"No, not at all," he said, already taking out with a gloved hand a small flat strip from a pouch, filmy green and smelling of raspberries. Kitia opened her mouth, and he laid it on her tongue. It dissolved almost at once, and she blinked twice and was asleep. Her hand went cold a few minutes later, still lying between my own.

I stood with her family when we laid her to rest the next morning. The attendants put her carefully down in a clearing, and sprayed her from a distance, the smell of cut roses just going to rot, and stepped back. Her parents wept noisily; I stayed dry-eyed as any seemly Terce matron, displaying my assurance of the ascension of the dead. The birds came first, and the motties, to pluck at her eyes and her lips, and the beetles hurrying with a hum of eager jaws to deconstruct her into raw parts. They did not have long to feast: the forest itself was devouring her from below in a green tide rising, climbing in small creepers up her cheeks and displacing them all.

When she was covered over, the mourners turned away and went to join the shared wake behind us in the village square. They threw uncertain and puzzled looks at my remaining as they went past, and at my tearless face. But she was not yet gone: there was a suggestion of a girl lingering there, a collapsing scaffold draped in an unhurried carpet of living things. I did not leave, though behind me there rose a murmur of noise as the families of the dead spoke reminiscences of their lost ones.

Near dawn, the green carpeting slipped briefly. In the dim watery light I glimpsed for one moment an emptied socket full of beetles, and I wept.

The Sixth Adjustment

I will not claim, after this, that I took the wings only from duty, but I refute the accusation I took them in treason. There was no other choice. Men and children and the elderly or the sick, all the wingless, were fleeing from the continuing hail of Esperigan attacks. They were retreating deep into the heart of the continent, beyond the refueling range for the Esperigan war-craft, to shelters hidden so far in caves and in overgrowth that even my spy satellites knew nothing of them. My connection to Kostas would have been severed, and if I could provide neither intelligence nor direct assistance, I might as well have slunk back to the embassy and saved myself the discomfort of being a refugee. Neither alternative was palatable.

They laid me upon the altar like a sacrifice, or so I felt, though they gave me something to drink that calmed my body, the nervous and involuntary twitching of my limbs and skin. Badea sat at my head and held the heavy long braid of my hair out of the way, while the others depilated my back and wiped it with alcohol. They bound me down then, and slit my skin open in two lines mostly parallel to the spine. Then Paudi gently set the wings upon me.

I lacked the skill to grow my own, in the time we had; Badea and Paudi helped me to mine so that I might stay. But even with the little assistance I had been able to contribute, I had seen more than I wished to of the parasites, and despite my closed eyes, my face turned downward, I knew to my horror that the faint curious feather-brush sensation was the intrusion of the fine spiderweb filaments, each fifteen feet long, which now wriggled into the hospitable environment of my exposed inner flesh and began to sew themselves into me.

Pain came and went as the filaments worked their way through muscle and bone, finding one bundle of nerves and then another. After the first half hour, Badea told me gently, "It's coming to the spine," and gave me another drink. The drug kept my body from movement, but could do nothing to numb the agony. I cannot describe it adequately. If you have ever managed to inflict food poisoning upon yourself, despite all the Confederacy's safeguards, you may conceive of the kind if not the degree of suffering, an experience that envelops the whole body, every muscle and joint, and alters not only your physical self but your thoughts as well: all vanishes but pain, and the question, Is the worst over? which is answered *no* and *no* again.

But at some point the pain began indeed to ebb. The filaments had entered the brain, and it is a measure of the experience that what I had feared the most was now blessed relief; I lay inert and closed my eyes gratefully while sensation spread outward from my back, and my new-borrowed limbs became gradually indeed my own, flinching from the currents of the air, and the touch of my friends' hands upon me. Eventually I slept.

The Seventh Adjustment

The details of the war, which unfolded now in earnest, I do not need to recount again. Kostas kept excellent records, better by far than my own, and students enough have memorized the dates and geographic coordinates, bounding death and ruin in small numbers. Instead I will tell you that from aloft, the Esperigans' poisoned-ground encampments made half starbursts of ocher brown and withered yellow, outlines like tentacles crawling into the healthy growth around them. Their supply-ships anchored out to sea glazed the water with a slick of oil and refuse, while the soldiers practiced their shooting on the vast schools of slow-swimming kraken young, whose bloated white bodies floated to the surface and drifted away along the coast, so many they defied even the appetite of the sharks.

I will tell you that when we painted their hulls with algaes and small crustacean-like borers, our work was camouflaged by great blooms of sea day-lilies around the ships, their masses throwing up reflected red color on the steel to hide the quietly creeping rust until the first winter storms struck and the grown kraken came to the surface to feed. I will tell you we watched from shore while the ships broke and foundered, and the teeth of the kraken shone like fire opals in the explosions, and if we wept, we wept only for the soiled ocean.

Still more ships came, and more planes; the ceramic coatings arrived, and more soldiers with protected guns and bombs and sprayed poisons, to fend off the altered motties and the little hybrid sparrowlike birds, their sharp cognizant eyes chemically retrained to see the Esperigan uniform colors as enemy markings. We planted acids and more aggressive species of plants along their supply lines, so their communications remained hopeful rather than reliable, and ambushed them at night; they carved into the forest with axes and power-saws and vast strip-miners, which ground to a halt and fell to pieces, choking on vines that hardened to the tensile strength of steel as they matured.

Contrary to claims that were raised at my trial in absentia and disproved with communication logs, throughout this time I spoke to Kostas regularly. I confused him, I think; I gave him all the intelligence that he needed to convey to the Esperigans, that they might respond to the next Melidan foray, but I did not conceal my feelings or the increasing complication of my loyalties, objecting to him bitterly and with personal anger about Esperigan attacks. I misled him with honesty: he thought, I believe, that I was only spilling a natural frustration to him, and through that airing clearing out my own doubts. But I had only lost the art of lying.

There is a general increase of perception that comes with the wings, the nerves teased to a higher pitch of awareness. All the little fidgets and twitches of lying betray themselves more readily, so only the more twisted forms can evade detection—where the speaker first deceives herself, or the wholly casual deceit of the sociopath who feels no remorse. This was the root of the Melidan disgust of the act, and I had acquired it.

If Kostas had known, he would at once have removed me: a diplomat is not much use if she cannot lie at need, much less an agent. But I did not volunteer the information, and indeed I did not realize, at first, how fully I had absorbed the stricture. I did not realize at all, until Badea came to me, three years into the war. I was sitting alone and in the dark by the communications console, the phosphorescent afterimage of Kostas's face fading into the surface.

She sat down beside me and said, "The Esperigans answer us too quickly. Their technology advances in these great leaps, and every time we press them back, they return in less than a month to very nearly the same position."

I thought, at first, that this was the moment: that she meant to ask me about membership in the Confederacy. I felt no sense of satisfaction, only a weary kind of resignation. The war would end, the Esperigans would follow, and in a few generations they would both be eaten up by bureaucracy and standards and immigration.

Instead Badea looked at me and said, "Are your people helping them, also?"

My denial ought to have come without thought, leapt easily off the tongue with all the conviction duty could give it, and been followed by invitation. Instead I said nothing, my throat closed involuntarily. We sat silently in the darkness, and at last she said, "Will you tell me why?"

I felt at the time I could do no more harm, and perhaps some good, by honesty. I told her all the rationale, and expressed all our willingness to receive them into our union as equals. I went so far as to offer her the platitudes with which we convince ourselves we are justified in our slow gentle imperialism: that unification is necessary and advances all together, bringing peace.

She only shook her head and looked away from me. After a moment, she said, "Your people will never stop. Whatever we devise, they will help the Esperigans to a counter, and if the Esperigans devise some weapon we cannot defend ourselves against, they will help us, and we will batter each other into limp exhaustion, until in the end we all fall."

"Yes," I said, because it was true. I am not sure I was still able to lie, but in any case I did not know, and I did not lie.

I was not permitted to communicate with Kostas again until they were ready. Thirty-six of the Melidans' greatest designers and scientists died in the effort. I learned of their deaths in bits and pieces. They worked in isolated and quarantined spaces, their every action recorded even as the viruses and bacteria they were developing killed them. It was a little more than three months before Badea came to me again.

We had not spoken since the night she had learned the duplicity of the Confederacy's support and my own. I could not ask her forgiveness, and she could not give it. She did not come for reconciliation but to send a message to the Esperigans and to the Confederacy through me.

I did not comprehend at first. But when I did, I knew enough to be sure she was neither lying nor mistaken, and to be sure the threat was very real. The same was not true of Kostas, and still less of the Esperigans. My frantic attempts to persuade them worked instead to the contrary end. The long gap since my last communiqué made Kostas suspicious: he thought me a convert, or generously a manipulated tool.

"If they had the capability, they would have used it already," he said, and if I could not convince him, the Esperigans would never believe.

I asked Badea to make a demonstration. There was a large island broken off the southern coast of the Esperigan continent, thoroughly settled and industrialized, with two substantial port cities. Sixty miles separated it from the mainland. I proposed the Melidans should begin there, where the attack might be contained.

"No," Badea said. "So your scientists can develop a counter? No. We are done with exchanges."

The rest you know. A thousand coracles left Melidan shores the next morning, and by sundown on the third following day, the Esperigan cities were crumbling. Refugees fled the groaning skyscrapers as they slowly bowed under their own weight. The trees died; the crops also, and the cattle, all the life and vegetation that had been imported from Earth and square-peg forced into the new world stripped bare for their convenience.

Meanwhile in the crowded shelters the viruses leapt easily from one victim to another, rewriting their genetic lines. Where the changes took hold, the altered survived. The others fell to the same deadly plagues that consumed all Earth-native life. The native Melidan moss crept in a swift green carpet over the corpses, and the beetle-hordes with it.

I can give you no firsthand account of those days. I too lay fevered and sick while the alteration ran its course in me, though I was tended better, and with more care, by my sisters. When I was strong enough to rise, the waves of death were over. My wings curled limply over my shoulders as I walked through the empty streets of Landfall, pavement stones pierced and broken by hungry vines, like bones cracked open for marrow. The moss covered the dead, who filled the shattered streets.

The squat embassy building had mostly crumpled down on one corner, smashed windows gaping hollow and black. A large pavilion of simple cotton fabric had been raised in the courtyard, to serve as both hospital and headquarters. A young undersecretary of state was the senior diplomat remaining. Kostas had died early, he told me. Others were still in the process of dying, their bodies waging an internal war that left them twisted by hideous deformities.

Less than one in thirty, was his estimate of the survivors. Imagine yourself on an air-train in a crush, and then imagine yourself suddenly alone but for one other passenger across the room, a stranger staring at you. Badea called it a sustainable population.

The Melidans cleared the spaceport of vegetation, though little now was left but the black-scorched landing pad, Confederacy manufacture, all of woven carbon and titanium.

"Those who wish may leave," Badea said. "We will help the rest."

Most of the survivors chose to remain. They looked at their faces in the mirror, flecked with green, and feared the Melidans less than their welcome on another world.

I left by the first small ship that dared come down to take off refugees, with no attention to the destination or the duration of the voyage. I wished only to be away. The wings were easily removed. A quick and painful amputation of the gossamer and fretwork that protruded from the flesh, and the rest might be left for the body to absorb slowly. The strange muffled quality of the world, the sensation of numbness, passed eventually. The two scars upon my back, parallel lines, I will keep the rest of my days.

Afterword

I spoke with Badea once more before I left. She came to ask me why I was going, to what end I thought I went. She would be perplexed, I think, to see me in my little cottage here on Reivaldt, some hundred miles from the nearest city, although she would have liked the small flowerlike lieden that live on the rocks of my garden wall, one of the few remnants of the lost native fauna that have survived the terraforming outside the preserves of the university system.

I left because I could not remain. Every step I took on Melida, I felt dead bones cracking beneath my feet. The Melidans did not kill lightly, an individual or an ecosystem, nor any more effectually than do we. If the Melidans had not let the plague loose upon the Esperigans, we would have destroyed them soon enough ourselves, and the Melidans with them. But we distance ourselves better from our murders, and so are not prepared to confront them. My wings whispered to me gently when I passed Melidans in the green-swathed cemetery streets, that they were not sickened, were not miserable. There was sorrow and regret but no self-loathing, where I had nothing else. I was alone.

When I came off my small vessel here, I came fully expecting punishment, even longing for it, a judgment that would at least be an end. Blame had wandered through the halls of state like an unwanted child, but when I proved willing to adopt whatever share anyone cared to mete out to me, to confess any crime that was convenient and to proffer no defense, it turned contrary, and fled.

Time enough has passed that I can be grateful now to the politicians who spared my life and gave me what passes for my freedom. In the moment, I could scarcely feel enough even to be happy that my report contributed some little to the abandonment of any reprisal against Melida: as though we ought hold them responsible for defying our expectations not of their willingness to kill one another, but only of the extent of their ability.

But time does not heal all wounds. I am often asked by visitors whether I would ever return to Melida. I will not. I am done with politics and the great concerns of the universe of human settlement. I am content to sit in my small garden, and watch the ants at work.

—*Ruth Patrona*

Steven Saylor

New York Times bestselling author Steven Saylor is one of the brightest stars in the "historical mystery" subgenre, along with authors such as Lindsey Davis, John Maddox Roberts, and the late Ellis Peters. He is the author of the long-running Roma Sub Rosa series, which details the adventures of Gordianus the Finder, a detective in a vividly realized Ancient Rome, in such novels as *Roman Blood, Arms of Nemesis, Catilina's Riddle, The Venus Throw, A Murder on the Appian Way, Rubicon, Last Seen in Massilia, A Mist of Prophecies*, and *The Judgment of Caesar*. Gordianus's exploits at shorter lengths have been collected in *The House of the Vestals: The Investigations of Gordianus the Finder* and *A Gladiator Dies Only Once: The Further Investigations of Gordianus the Finder*. Saylor's other books include *A Twist at the End, Have You Seen Dawn?* and a huge non-Gordianus historical novel, *Roma*. His most recent book is a new Gordianus novel, *The Triumph of Caesar*. He lives in Berkeley, California.

Here he takes us back to the last days of ancient Carthage, to the aftermath of a devastating victory and an even more complete and more devastating conquest, for the grim tale of just how far a man can be forced to go if you push him hard enough—and *cleverly* enough.

The Eagle and the Rabbit

I

The Romans made us stand in a row, naked, our wrists tied behind our backs. Man to man we were linked together by chains attached to the iron collars around our necks.

The tall one appeared, the one the others called Fabius, their leader. I had seen his face close up in the battle; it had been the last thing I had seen, followed by a merciful rain of stars as his cudgel struck my head. Merciful, because in the instant I glimpsed his face, I knew true terror for the first time. The jagged red scar that began at his forehead, disfigured his nose and mouth, and ended at his chin was terrible enough, but it was the look in his eyes that chilled my blood. I had never seen such a look. He had the face of a warrior who laughs at his own pain and delights in the pain of others, who knows nothing of pity or remorse. The cold, hard face of a Roman slave raider.

You may wonder why Fabius struck me with a cudgel, not a sword. The blow was meant to stun, not to kill. Carthage was destroyed. We few survivors, fugitive groups of men, women, and children, were poorly fed and poorly armed. Months of fearful hiding in the desert had weakened us. We were no match for battle-hardened Roman soldiers. Their goal was not to kill, but to capture. We were the final scattered trophies of an annihilated city, to be rounded up and sold into slavery.

Carthago delenda est! Those words are Latin, the harsh, ugly language of our conquerors; the words of one of their leaders, the bloodthirsty Cato. The wars between Carthage and Rome began generations ago, with great battles fought on the sea and bloody campaigns all across Sicily, Spain, Italy, and Africa, but for a time there was peace. During that truce, Cato made it his habit to end every speech before the Roman Senate and every conversation with his colleagues, no matter what the subject, with those words: *Carthago delenda est!* "Carthage must be destroyed!"

Cato died without seeing his dream come true, a bitter old man. When news of his death reached Carthage, we rejoiced. The madman who relentlessly craved our destruction, who haunted out nightmares, was gone.

But Cato's words lived on. *Carthago delenda est!* The war resumed. The Romans invaded our shores. They laid siege to Carthage. They cut off the city by land and by sea. They seized the great harbor. Finally they breached the walls. The city was taken street by street, house by house. For six days the battle raged. The streets became rivers of blood. When it was over, the Carthaginians who survived were rounded up, to be sold into slavery and dispersed to the far corners of the earth. The profit from their bodies would pay for the cost of Rome's war. Their tongues were cut out or burned with hot irons, so that the Punic language would die with them.

The houses were looted. Small items of value—precious stones, jewelry, coins—were taken by the Roman soldiers as their reward. Larger items—fine furniture, magnificent lamps, splendid chariots—were assessed by agents of the Roman treasury and loaded onto trading vessels. Heirlooms of no commercial value—spindles and looms, children's toys, images of our ancestors—were thrown onto bonfires.

The libraries were burned, so that no books in the Punic language should survive. The works of our great playwrights and poets and philosophers, the speeches and memoirs of Hannibal and his father, Hamilcar, and all our other leaders, the tales of Queen Dido and the Phoenician seafarers who founded Carthage long ago—all were burned to ashes.

The gods and goddesses of Carthage were pulled from their pedestals. Their temples were reduced to rubble. The statues made of stone were smashed; the inlaid eyes of ivory and onyx and lapis were plucked from the shards. The statues made of gold and silver were melted down and made into bullion—more booty to fill the treasury of Rome. Tanit the great mother, Baal the great father, Melkart the fearless hero, Eshmun who heals the sick—all of them vanished from the earth in a single day.

The walls were pulled down and the city was razed to the ground. The ruins were set afire. The fertile fields near the city were scattered with salt, so that not even weeds should grow for a generation.

Some of us were outside the city when the siege began and escaped the destruction. We fled from the villas and fishing villages along the coast into the stony, dry interior. The Romans decreed that not a single Carthaginian should escape. To round up the fugitives they sent not regular legionaries but decommissioned soldiers especially trained to hunt down and capture fugitive slaves. That was why Fabius and the rest carried cudgels along with swords. They were hunters. We were their prey.

We stood naked in chains with our backs against the sheer cliff of a sandstone crag.

It was from the top of that crag that I had seen the approach of the Romans that morning and called the alarm. Keeping watch was a duty of the young, of those with the strength and agility to climb the jagged peaks and with sharp eyes. I had resented the duty, the long, lonely hours of boredom spent staring northward at the wide valley that led to the sea. But the elders insisted that the watch should never go untended.

"They will come," old Matho had wheezed in his singsong voice. "Never mind that we've managed to escape them for more than a year. The Romans are relentless. They know the nomads of the desert refuse to help us. They know how weak we've become, how little we have to eat, how pathetic our weapons are. They will come for us, and when they do, we must be ready to flee, or to fight. Never think that we're safe. Never hope that they've forgotten us. They will come."

And so they had. I had been given night duty. I did not sleep. I was not negligent. I fixed my eyes to the north and watched for the signs that Matho had warned of—a band of torches moving up the valley like a fiery snake, or the distant glint of metal under moonlight. But the night was moonless and the Romans came in utter darkness.

I heard them first. The hour was not quite dawn when I thought I heard the sound of hooves somewhere in the distance, carried on the dry wind that sweeps up the valley on summer nights. I should have sounded the alarm then, at the first suspicion of danger, as Matho had always instructed; but peering down into the darkness that blanketed the valley I could see nothing. I kept silent, and I watched.

Dawn came swiftly. The edge of the sun glinted across the jagged peaks to the east, lighting the broken land to the west with an amber haze. Still

I did not see them. Then I heard a sudden thunder of hoofbeats. I looked down and saw a troop of armed men at the foot of the cliff.

I gave a cry of alarm. Down below, old Matho and the others rushed out of the shallow crevices that offered shelter for the night. A little ridge still hid them from Romans, but in moments the Romans would be across the ridge and upon them. Matho and the others turned their eyes up to me. So did the horseman who rode at the head of the Romans. He wore only light armor and no helmet. Even at such a distance, and in the uncertain early light, I could see the scar on his face.

The Romans swarmed over the ridge. In miniature, as if on the palm of my hand, I saw the people scatter and I heard their distant cries of panic.

I descended as quickly as I could, scurrying down the rugged pathway, scraping my hands and knees when I slipped. Near the bottom, I met Matho. He pressed something into my right hand—a precious silver dagger with an image of Melkart on the handle. It was one of the few metal weapons we possessed.

"Flee, Hanso! Escape if you can!" he wheezed. Behind him I heard the wild whooping and war cries of the Romans.

"But the women, the children . . . ," I whispered.

"Done," Matho said. His eyes darted toward a narrow crevice amid the rocks opposite the sandstone cliff. From most angles, the crevice was impossible to see; it opened into a cave of substantial size, where the elders and the unmarried women slept. At the first warning, the mothers and children had been sent to join them in hiding. This was a plan Matho had made in anticipation of an attack, that if all could not flee together, then only the strongest among us should face the Romans while the other hid themselves in the cave.

The battle was brief. The Romans overwhelmed us in minutes. They held back, fighting to capture rather than kill, while we fought with everything we had, in utter desperation. Even so, we were no match for them. All was a tumult of shouting, confusion, and terror. Some of us were struck by cudgels and knocked to the ground. Others were trapped like beasts in nets. I saw the tall rider in the midst of the Romans, the one with the scar, barking orders at the others, and I ran for him. I raised my dagger and leaped, and for an instant I felt that I could fly. I meant to stab him, but his mount wheeled about, and instead I stabbed the horse in the neck.

The beast whinnied and reared, and my hand was covered by hot red blood. The horseman glared down at me, his mouth contorted in a strange, horrible laugh. A gust of wind blew the unkempt blond hair from his face, revealing the whole length of the scar from his forehead to his chin. I saw his wild, terrifying eyes.

He raised his mallet. Then the stars, and darkness.

My head still rang from that blow as we were made to stand, chained together, against the sandstone cliff. The stone was warm against my back, heated by the midday sun. My nostrils were choked by dust and smoke. They had found our sleeping places and our small stores of food and clothing. Anything that could be burned, they had set to the torch.

The Romans were mounted on their horses. They were relaxed now, laughing and joking among themselves but keeping their eyes on us. They held long spears cradled against their bent elbows and pointed at our throats. Occasionally one of the Romans would poke the tip of his spear against the man he guarded, prodding his chest or pricking his neck, smirking at the shudder that ran through the unguarded flesh. They outnumbered us, three Romans to every captive. Matho had always warned that they would come in overwhelming numbers. If only there had been more of us, I thought, then remembered how pitiful our resistance had been. If all the Carthaginian fugitives scattered across the desert had been gathered in one place to fight the slave raiders, we still would have lost.

Then the Romans drew back, and down the aisle left in their wake their leader came riding, leading Matho behind him by a tether fitted around the old man's neck. Like the rest, Matho was naked and bound. To see him that way made me lower my eyes in shame. Thus I avoided seeing the face of the Roman leader again as he rode slowly by, the hooves of his mount ringing on the stone.

He reached the end of the row and wheeled his horse about, and then I heard his voice, piercing and harsh. He spoke Punic well, but with an ugly Latin accent.

"Twenty-five!" he announced. "Twenty-five male Carthaginians taken today for the glory of Rome!"

The Romans responded by beating their spears against the stony ground and shouting his name: "Fabius! Fabius! Fabius!"

I looked up, and was startled to see that his eyes were on me. I quickly lowered my face.

"You!" he shouted. I gave a start and almost looked up. But from the corner of my eye I saw him pull sharply on the tether. It was Matho he addressed. "You seem to be the leader, old man."

Fabius slowly rotated his wrist, coiling the tether around his fist to shorten the lead, drawing Matho closer to him until the old man was forced to his toes. "Twenty-five men," he said, "and not a woman or child among you, and you the only graybeard. Where are the others?"

Matho remained silent, then choked as the tether was drawn even tighter around his throat. He stared up defiantly. He drew back his lips. He spat. A gasp issued from the line of captives. Fabius smiled as he wiped the spittle from his cheek and flicked it onto Matho's face, making him flinch.

"Very well, old man. Your little troop of fugitives won't be needing a leader any longer, and we have no use for an old weakling." There was a slithering sound as he drew a sword from his scabbard, then a flash of sunlight on metal as he raised it above his head. I shut my eyes. I instinctively moved to cover my ears, but my hands were bound. I heard the ragged slicing sound, then the heavy thud as Matho's severed head struck the ground.

In the midst of the cries and moans of the captives, I heard a whisper to my right: "Now it begins." It was Lino who spoke—Lino, who knew the ways of the slave raiders, because he had been captured once himself, and alone of all his family had escaped. He was even younger than I, but at that moment he looked like an old man. His shackled body slumped. His face was drawn and pale. Our eyes met briefly. I looked away first. The misery in his eyes was unbearable.

Lino had joined us a few months ago, ragged and thin, as naked as now and blistered by the sun. He spoke a crude Punic dialect, different from the cosmopolitan tongue of us city-dwellers. His family had been shepherds, tending flocks in the foothills outside Carthage. They had thought themselves safe when the Romans laid siege to the city, beneath the notice of the invaders. When the Romans turned their wrath against even shepherds and farmers in the distant countryside, Lino's tribe fled into the desert, but the Romans hunted them down. Many were killed. The rest, including Lino, had been captured. But on the journey toward the coast he had somehow escaped, and found his way to us.

Some of the men had argued that Lino should be turned away, for if there were Romans pursuing him, he would lead them straight to us. "He's not one of us," they said. "Let him hide somewhere else." But Matho had insisted that we take him in, saying that any youth who had escaped the Romans might know something of value. Time passed, and when it became clear that Lino had not led the Romans to us, even those who had argued for his expulsion accepted him. But to any question about his time in captivity, he gave no reply. He seldom talked. He lived among us, but as an outsider, keeping himself guarded and apart.

I felt Lino's eyes on me as he whispered again: "The same as last time. The same leader, Fabius. He kills the chief elder first. And then—"

His words were drowned by the clatter of hoofbeats as Fabius galloped down the line of captives. At the far end of the row he wheeled about and began a slow parade up the line, looking at each of the captives in turn.

"This one's leg is too badly wounded. He'll never survive the journey."

Two of the Romans dismounted, unshackled the wounded man, and led him away.

"A shame," Fabius said, sauntering on. "That one had a strong body, the makings of a good slave." Again he paused. "And this one's too old. No market for his kind, not worth the care and feeding. And this one—see the blank stare and the drool on his lips? An idiot, common among these inbreeding Carthaginians. Useless!"

The Romans removed the men from the line and closed the links, so that I was forced to shuffle sideways, pulling Lino along with me.

The men removed from the line were taken behind a large boulder. They died with hardly a sound—a grunt, a sigh, a gasp.

Fabius continued down the line, until the shadow of man and beast loomed above me, blocking the sun. I bit my lip, praying for the shadow to move on. Finally I looked up.

I couldn't make out his face, which was obscured by the blinding halo that burned at the edges of his shaggy blond mane of hair. "And this one," he said, with grim amusement in his voice, "this one slew my mount in the battle. The best fighter among you lot of cowards, even if he is hardly more than a boy." He lifted his spear and jabbed my ribs, grazing the skin but not quite drawing blood. "Show some spirit, boy! Or have we already broken you? Can't you even spit, like the old man?"

I stared back at him and didn't move. It wasn't bravery, though perhaps it looked like it. I was frozen with terror.

He produced the silver dagger I had buried to the hilt in his mount's neck. The blood had been cleaned away. The blade glinted in the sunlight.

"A fine piece of workmanship, this. A fine image of Hercules on the handle."

"Not Hercules," I managed to whisper. "Melkart!"

He laughed. "There is no Melkart, boy! Melkart no longer exists. Don't you understand? Your gods are all gone, and they're never coming back. This is an image of the god we Romans call Hercules, and that's the name by which the world shall know him from now until eternity. Our gods were stronger than your gods. That's why I'm sitting on this horse, and you're standing there naked in chains."

My body trembled and my face turned hot. I shut my eyes, trying not to weep. Fabius chuckled, then moved on, reining his mount sharply after only a few paces. He stared down at Lino. Lino didn't look up. After a very long pause, longer than he had spent staring at me, Fabius moved on without saying a word.

"He remembers me," Lino whispered, in a voice so low, he could only have been speaking to himself. He began to shake, so violently that I felt the vibration through the heavy chain that linked our necks. "He remembers me! It will happen all over again. . . ."

Fabius removed two more captives from the line, then finished his inspection and cantered to the center. "Well, then—where are the women?" he said quietly. No one answered. He raised his spear and cast it so hard against the cliff wall above our heads that it splintered with a thunderous crack. Every face in the line jerked upright.

"Where are they?" he shouted. "A single woman is more valuable than the whole lot of you worthless cowards! Where have you hidden them?"

No one spoke.

I glanced past him, at the place where the crevice opened into the hidden cave, then quickly looked away, fearing he would see and read my thoughts. Fabius leaned forward on his mount, crossing his arms. "Before we set out in the morning, one of you will tell me."

II

That night we slept, still chained together, under the open sky. The night was cold, but the Romans gave us nothing to cover ourselves. They huddled under blankets and built a bonfire to keep themselves warm. While some slept, others kept watch on us.

During the night, one by one, each of us was removed from the circle, taken away, and then brought back. When the first man returned and the second was taken in his stead, someone whispered, "What did they do to you? Did you tell?" Then a guard jabbed the man who spoke with a spear, and we all fell silent.

Late that night, they came for Lino. I would be next. I braced myself for whatever ordeal was to come, but Lino was kept for so long that my courage began to fade, drained away by imagined terrors and then by utter exhaustion. I was only barely conscious when they came for me. I didn't notice that Lino was still missing from the circle.

They led me over the ridge and through a maze of boulders to the open place where Fabius had pitched his tent. A soft light shone through its green panels.

Within the tent was another world, the world the Romans carried with them in their travels. A thick carpet was underfoot. Glowing griffon-headed lamps were mounted on elegantly crafted tripods. Fabius himself reclined on a low couch, his weapons and battle gear discarded for a finely embroidered tunic. In his hand he held a silver cup brimming with wine. He smiled.

"Ah, the defiant one." He waved his hand. The guards pushed me forward, forcing me to kneel and pressing my throat into the bottom panel of stocks mounted at the foot of Fabius's couch. They closed the yoke over the back of my neck, locking my head in place.

"I suppose you'll say the same as all the rest: 'Women? Children? But there are no women and children, only us men! You've killed our beloved old leader and culled out the weaklings, so what more do you want?'" He lifted the cup to his lips, then leaned forward and spat in my face. The wine burned my eyes.

His voice was hard and cold, and slightly slurred from the wine. "I'm not stupid, boy. I was born a Roman patrician. I used to be a proud centurion in the legions, until . . . until there was a slight problem. Now I hunt for runaway slaves. Not much honor in that, but I'm damned good at it."

"I'm not a slave," I whispered.

He laughed. "Granted, you weren't born a slave. But you were born a Carthaginian, and I know the ways of you Carthaginians. Your men are weak. You can't bear to be without your women and children. You refugees out here in the desert always travel in a group, dragging the old bones and infants after you. What sort of worthless life are you leading out here in the wilderness? You should be grateful that we've come for you at last. Even life as a slave should seem like Elysium after this pathetic existence. What's your name, boy?"

I swallowed. It wasn't easy, with the stocks pressed so tightly against my throat. "Hanso. And I'm not a boy."

"Hanso." His curled his upper lip. "A common enough Carthaginian name. But I'm remembering the spirit you showed in the battle this morning, and I'm wondering if there's not some Roman blood in your veins. My grandfather used to boast about all the Carthaginian girls he raped when he fought your colonists in Spain. He was proud to spill some Fabius seed to bolster your cowardly stock!"

I wanted to spit at him, but my neck was bent and the stocks were too tight around my throat.

"You're not a boy, you say? Then you shall be tested as a man. Now tell me: Where are the women hidden?"

I didn't answer. He raised his hand, making a signal to someone behind me. I heard a whoosh, then felt an explosion of fire across my back. The whip seared my flesh, then slid from my shoulders like a heavy snake.

I had never felt any pain like it. I had never been beaten as a child, as the Romans are said to beat their children. The pain stunned me.

Fabius seemed to revel in the punishment, laughing softly and repeating the same question as the whip struck me again and again. My flesh burned as if glowing coals had been poured on my back. I promised myself I wouldn't weep or cry out, but soon my mouth lost its shape and I began to sob.

Fabius leaned forward, peering at me with one eyebrow raised. His scar was enormous, the only thing I could see. "You *are* a strong one," he said, nodding. "As I thought. So you won't tell me where the women are hidden?"

I thought of Matho, of all his fretful plans, of my own fault in sounding the alarm too late. I took a deep shuddering breath and managed a single word: "Never."

Fabius sipped his wine. A few drops trickled from the corner of his mouth as he spoke. "As you wish. It doesn't matter anyway. We already know where they are. My men are busy flushing them out even now."

I looked up at him in disbelief, but the grim amusement in his eyes showed that he wasn't lying. I spoke through gritted teeth. "But how? Who told you?"

Fabius clapped his hands. "Come out, little eagle."

Lino emerged from behind a screen. His hands were no longer bound, and the collar had been removed from his neck. Like Fabius he was dressed in a finely embroidered tunic, but his expression was fearful and he trembled. He wouldn't look me in the eye.

The guard who had wielded the whip removed me from the stocks and pulled me to my feet. If my hands hadn't been bound behind my back, I would have strangled Lino then and there. Instead, I followed Matho's example. I spat. The spittle clung to Lino's cheek. He began to raise his hand to brush it away, then dropped his arm, and I thought: He knows he deserves it.

"Restrain yourself," Fabius said. "After all, you two will have all night together in close quarters to settle your differences."

Lino looked up, panic in his eyes. "No! You promised me!"

He squealed and struggled, but against the Romans he was helpless. They stripped the tunic off him, twisted his arms behind his back, and returned the collar to his neck. They attached us by a link of chain and pushed us from the tent.

Behind us, I heard Fabius laugh. "Sleep well," he called out. "Tomorrow the *temptatio* begins!"

Even as we stumbled from the tent, the Romans were herding their new captives from the hidden cave. The scene was chaotic—wavering torchlight and shadow, the shrieking of children, the wailing of mothers, the clatter of spears and the shouts of the Romans barking orders as the last of my people were taken into captivity.

The bonfire burned low. Most of the Romans were occupied in flushing out the new captives. The few Romans who guarded us grew careless and dozed, trusting in the strength of our chains.

I lay on my side, my back turned to Lino, staring into the flames, longing for sleep to help me escape from the pain of the whipping. Behind me I heard Lino whisper: "You don't understand, Hanso. You can't understand."

I glared at him over my shoulder. "I understand, Lino. You betrayed us. What does it matter to you? We're not your tribe. You're an outsider. You always were. But we took you in when you came to us starving and naked, and for that you owed us something. If my hands are ever free again, I swear I'll kill you. For Matho." My voice caught in my throat. I choked back a sob.

After a long moment, Lino spoke again. "Your back is bleeding, Hanso."

I turned to face him, wincing at the pain. "And yours?" I hissed. "Show me *your* wounds, Lino!"

He paused, then showed his back to me. It was covered with bloody welts. He had been whipped even more severely than I. He turned back. His face, lit by the dying firelight, was so haggard and pale that for a moment my anger abated. Then I thought of Matho and the women. "So what? So the monster beat you. He beat us all. Every man here has wounds to show."

"And do you think I was the only one to betray the hiding place?" His voice became shrill. One of the guards muttered in his sleep.

"What do you mean?" I whispered.

"You kept silent, Hanso. I know, because I was there. Every time the lash fell on you, I cringed, and when you resisted him I felt . . . I felt almost alive again. But what about the others? Why do you think they're so silent? A few may be sleeping, but the rest are awake and speechless, afraid to talk. Because they're ashamed. You may be the only man among us who kept Matho's secret."

I was quiet for a long time, wishing I hadn't heard him. When he began to whisper again, I longed to cover my ears.

"It's their way, Hanso. The Roman way. To divide us. To isolate each man in his misery, to shame us with our weakness, to sow mistrust among us. Fabius plays many games with his captives. Every game has a purpose. The journey to the coast is long, and he must control us at every moment. Each day he'll find some new way to break us, so that by the time we arrive, we'll be good slaves, ready for the auction block."

I thought about this. Matho had been right. Of all of us, only Lino knew the ways of the Roman slave raiders. If I was to survive, Lino might help me. Perhaps I could learn from him—and still hate him for what he had done.

"Fabius spoke of something called the *temptatio*," I whispered.

Lino sighed. "A Latin word. It means a trial, a test, an ordeal. In this case, the *temptatio* is the journey across the wasteland. The *temptatio* turns free men into slaves. It begins tomorrow. They'll make the men march like this, naked and in chains. They'll simply bind the hands of the women and children and herd them like sheep. By nightfall we'll reach the place where the path splits. They'll separate us from the women and children then, and some of the Romans will take them to a different destination by way of a shorter, easier route to the sea. But the men will be driven up the long valley until we finally reach the coast and the slave galleys that are waiting there."

"Why do they separate the men and women?"

"I think it's because Fabius wants the women to be kept soft and unharmed; that's why they take an easier route. But the men he wants tested and hardened. That's why Fabius will drive us on foot across the desert. Those who falter will be left to die. Those with the strength to survive the journey will be stronger than when they set out, hardy slaves worth a fortune to Fabius and his men when we reach the coast. That's how the *temptatio* works."

He spoke as dispassionately as if he were explaining the workings of a flint or a pulley, but when the firelight caught his eyes, I could see the pain that came from remembering. It took an effort of will to hold fast to my hatred for him, and to keep my voice as cold and flat as his. "Fabius called you his little eagle. What did he mean?"

Lino drew in a sharp breath and hid his face in the shadows. "He lied when he called me that. He said it only to be cruel." His voice faltered and he shuddered. "All right, I'll tell you—tell you what I would never speak of before, because like a fool I hoped that it was all past and I would never have to face it again. Once the *temptatio* begins, Fabius will choose two of us from among the captives. One for punishment, the other for reward. The rabbit and the eagle. Both will serve as examples to the other captives, clouding their minds, shaming them with fear, tempting them with hope. The eagle he'll elevate above the other captives, making sure he's well fed and clothed, treating him almost like one of his own men, testing him to see if he can turn him against the others, seducing him with promises of freedom." He fell silent.

"And the rabbit?"

Lino was silent.

"The rabbit, Lino. Tell me!"

"The fate of the rabbit will be very different." His voice grew dull and lifeless. A chill passed though me as I understood.

"And last time," I whispered, "when Fabius captured your tribe—you were his rabbit."

He made no answer.

I sighed. "And tonight, in his tent, Fabius promised that you would be the eagle. That's why you told him where the women were hidden."

Lino nodded. He began to sob.

"But you escaped him, Lino. You escaped last time. It *can* be done."

He shook his head. His voice was so choked, I could hardly understand him. "It could never happen again. I beat him, Hanso, don't you understand? By escaping, I beat him at the game. Do you think he would let me do it again? Never! When he rode down the line of captives, when he saw us standing side by side and recognized me, that was when he chose his rabbit."

"I see. But if you're to be his rabbit, then who is the eagle?"

Lino lifted his face into the firelight. Tears ran down his cheeks. He stared straight at me with a strange, sad fury, amazed that I had not yet understood.

III

In the morning, the Romans fed each of us a ladle full of gruel, then led us to the place where the women and children were gathered. The elders were missing. Fabius did not explain what he had done with them, but vultures were already circling over the open space beyond the ridge.

They marched us through the boulder-strewn foothills, over rugged, winding paths. The pace was slow to allow the children to keep up, but the mounted Romans used their whips freely, barking at us to stay in formation, punishing those who stumbled, shouting at the children when they wept.

At sundown, still in the foothills, we came to a place where the path diverged. The women and children were taken in a different direction. No words of parting were allowed. Even furtive glances were punished by the whip. We slept that night in the open, laid out in a straight line with our chains bolted to iron stakes driven into the ground. The Romans pitched tents for themselves. At some point they came and took Lino. All through the night, I could hear them singing and laughing. Fabius laughed louder than all the rest.

Just before dawn, Lino was returned. The clatter of his chains woke me. He couldn't stop trembling. I asked him what had happened. He hid his face and wouldn't answer.

On the second day we descended from the foothills into the long valley. The mountains gradually became more distant on either side until there was only harsh blue sky from horizon to horizon. The vegetation grew scarcer as the parched earth beneath our feet turned into a vast sheet of white stone dusted with sand, as flat and featureless as if it had been pounded by a great hammer.

In the midst of this expanse, amazingly, we came to a small river, too wide for a man to jump across and quite deep. It snaked northward up the middle of the valley flanked by steep banks of stone.

The sun blazed down on my naked shoulders. Though the river was only paces away—we could hear it lapping against its banks—the Romans gave us water only at dawn and sunset. We thirsted, and the sight and sound of so much water, so near, was enough to drive a man mad.

That afternoon, Fabius rode up alongside me and offered me water to drink, leaning down from his mount and holding the spout of his water-skin to my lips. I looked up and saw him smile. I felt Lino's eyes on my back. But as the spout passed between my lips, I didn't refuse it. I let the cool water fill my mouth. I could not swallow fast enough, and it spilled over my chin.

That night I was given an extra portion of gruel. The others noticed, but when they began to whisper among themselves, the Romans silenced them with a crack of the whip.

After all the others slept, Lino was taken to Fabius's tent again. He did not return for hours.

On the third day, the *temptatio* claimed its first victim: Gebal, my mother's brother. It was Uncle Gebal who had given me my first bow and arrow when I was no taller than a man's knee, and taught me to hunt the deer in the hills outside Carthage; Gebal who told me tales of Queen Dido and her brother, King Pumayyaton of Tyre; Gebal who taught me to honor the great Hannibal in our prayers, even though Hannibal had failed to conquer Rome and died a broken man in exile. At midday he began to shout, and then he bolted toward the river, dragging along the rest of us chained to him. The Romans were on him in an instant, forcing him back with their spears, but he struggled and screamed, cutting himself on the sharp points.

Fabius himself dismounted, removed Gebal from the line, lifted him off his feet, and threw him from the steep bank into the water. Weighted by his iron collar, Gebal must have sunk like a stone. There was the sound of a splash, then a silence so complete, I could hear the low moan of the arid north wind across the sand. The captives didn't make a sound. We were too stunned to speak. Our eyes were too dry for tears.

"So much for those who thirst," said Fabius.

It was also on that day that Fabius truly set me above and apart from the others. Until then his favors had extended only to the extra portions of water and gruel. But that day, as the sun reached its zenith and even the strongest among us began to stagger from the relentless heat, Fabius removed me from the line.

"Have you ever ridden a horse?" he asked.

"No," I said.

"Then I'll teach you," he said.

The chains were removed from the collar around my neck. My hands were released and retied in front of me, and a thin robe was thrown over my shoulders. The Romans lifted me onto the back of a black stallion. Two sets of reins were fixed to the beast's bridle, one tied to Fabius's saddle and the other placed in my hands. A waterskin was hung around my neck, so that I could drink at will. I knew the others were watching in envy and confusion, but my legs were weak, my throat dry, and my shoulders blistered from the sun. I didn't refuse his favors.

As we rode side by side, Fabius tersely pointed out the parts of the harness and saddle and explained the art of riding. I had been apprehensive when they first placed me on the beast, thinking it would throw me to the ground. But our pace was slow, and I soon felt at home on its back. I also felt a strange kind of pride, to be elevated so high above the ground and moving so effortlessly forward, the master of so much power tamed between my legs.

That night I was chained apart from the others, given a pallet to sleep on and as much as I wanted to eat and drink. As I fell asleep, I heard the others muttering. Did they think I had betrayed the women, and this was my reward? I was too sleepy from the heat of the day and the food that filled my belly to care. I slept so soundly, I didn't even notice when Lino was taken away that night.

The days blurred into one another. For me they were long and grueling but not beyond endurance. My worst complaints were the sores that chafed my thighs and buttocks, which were unaccustomed to the friction of the saddle.

For the others it was very different. Day by day, I saw them grow more desperate. The ordeal was worst for Lino. He was moved to the head of the line, where he was forced to set the pace. The Romans swarmed about him like hornets, stinging him with theirs whips, driving him on. Whenever anyone faltered behind him, the chain pulled at his iron collar, so that his neck became ringed with blisters and bruises. I did my best not to see his suffering.

"You're not like the others, Hanso," said Fabius one day, riding along beside me. "Look at them. The *temptatio* doesn't change a man, it only exposes his true nature. See how weak they are, how they stumble and walk blindly on, their minds as empty as the desert. And for all their sentimental vows of loyalty to one another, there's no true brotherhood among them, no honor. See how they shove and snarl, blaming each other for every misstep."

It was true. Chained together, the captives constantly jostled each other, tripping and pulling at each other's throats. Any interruption in the march brought the whips on their shoulders. The men were in a constant state of anger, fear, and desperation; unable to strike back at the Romans, they turned against each other. The Romans now spent as much time breaking up fights among the captives as driving them on. I looked down on the captives from the high vantage of my mount, and I could hardly see them as men any longer. They looked like wild animals, their hair tangled and knotted, their skin darkened by the sun, their faces beastlike and snarling one moment, slavish and cowering the next.

"You're not like them, Hanso," Fabius whispered, leaning close. "They're rabbits, cowering in holes, nervously sniffing the air for danger, living only to breed and be captured. But you, Hanso, you're an eagle, strong and proud and born to fly above the rest. I knew it from the first moment I saw you, flying at me with that dagger. You're the only brave man among them. You have nothing in common with this lot, do you?"

I looked down at the haggard line of captives, and did not answer.

As the *temptatio* wore on, I felt more and more removed from the suffering of the others. I still slept in chains at night, but I began to take my evening meal in Fabius's tent along with the Romans. I drank their wine and listened to their stories of battles fought in faraway places. They had spilled much blood, and they were proud of that fact, proud because the city they fought for was the greatest on earth.

Rome! How the soldiers' eyes lit up when they spoke of the city. In the great temples they worshipped gods with outlandish names—Jupiter, Minerva, Venus, and, especially, Mars, the war god, who loved the Romans and guided them always to victory. In the vast marketplaces, they spent their earnings on luxuries from every corner of the world. In the Circus Maximus, they gathered by the tens of thousands to cheer the world's fastest charioteers. In the arena, they watched slaves and captives from all over the world fight combats to the death. In the sumptuous public baths, they took their leisure, soothed their battle-weary muscles, and watched naked athletes compete. In the wild taverns and brothels of the Subura (a district so notorious, even I had heard of it), they took their pleasure with pliant slaves trained to satisfy every lust.

I began to see how cramped and pitiful had been our lives as fugitives in the desert, fraught with fear and hopelessness and haunted by memories of a city that was gone forever. Carthage was only a memory now. Rome was the greatest of all cities, and stood poised to become greater still as her legions looked to the East for fresh conquests. Rome was a hard place to be a slave, but for her free citizens, she offered endless opportunities for wealth and pleasure.

As I was led out of the tent each night, not wanting to leave its cool and cushioned comfort, the Romans would be leading Lino in. I saw the terror in his eyes only in glimpses, for I always averted my face. What they did to him in the tent after I left, I didn't want to know.

IV

It was on the fourteenth day of the *temptatio* that Lino escaped.

The featureless desert had gradually given way to a region of low hills car-peted with scrubby grass and dotted with small trees. The mountains had drawn close on either side. In the northern distance, they almost converged at a narrow pass that led to the coast beyond. The river flowed through the pass into a hazy green distance where, framed by the steep walls of the gorge, I could barely discern a glimpse of the sea, a tiny glint of silver under the morn-ing sun.

I first learned of Lino's escape from the whisperings of the captives. When dawn came and he still hadn't been brought back from the tent, an excited exchange ran up and down the line. Their hoarse voices became more animated than at any time since the *temptatio* began, hushed and hopeful, as if the prospect of Lino's escape restored a part of their broken humanity to them.

"He said he would escape," one of them whispered. "He's done it!"

"But how?"

"He did it once before—"

"Unless he's still in the tent. Unless they've finally killed him with their cruel games . . ."

The Romans came for me. As I was led past the line of captives, I heard them mutter the word "traitor" and spit into the grass.

In the tent, I glanced about and saw only the familiar faces of the Ro-mans, busy with their morning preparations. What the captives had said was true, then. Somehow, during the long night of wine and laughter, Lino had escaped.

One of the Romans pulled the thin robe from my shoulders and freed my hands. Suddenly I had a sudden terrible premonition that I was to take Lino's place.

Instead, they placed a pair of riding boots before me, along with a sol-dier's tunic and a bronze cuirass—the same uniform that they wore. They handed me a saddlebag and showed me what it contained: a length of rope, a whip, a waterskin, a generous supply of food, and a silver dagger—the very knife that Matho had given me, with its engraving of Melkart on the handle. Atop the pile they laid a spear.

I turned to Fabius, who reclined on his couch, taking his morning meal. He watched me with a smile, amused at my consternation. He gestured to the items laid out before me.

"These are the supplies for your mission."

I looked at him dumbly.

"The rabbit has escaped, boy. Haven't you heard? Now it's time for you to repay my generosity to you."

"I don't understand."

Fabius grunted. "The *temptatio* is almost over. The sea is only a day's march away. A ship will already be waiting there, to load the captives and take them to whatever market is currently offering the best price. Antioch, Alexandria, Massilia—who knows? But one of my captives has escaped. He can't have gone far, not weighted down by his chains. There's the river to the east, and the desert to the south, so I figure he must have gone west, where he thinks he can hide among the low hills. My men could probably flush him out in a matter of hours, but I have another idea. *You* will find him for me."

"Me?"

"You know how to ride well enough, and he should be easy to take with his arms bound behind his back. If he gives you too much trouble, kill him—I know you can do it, I've seen you fight—but bring back his head for proof."

I thought of Lino's suffering, of the others calling me traitor. Then I realized that I might escape myself; but Fabius, seeing the hope that lit my face, shook his head.

"Don't even think of it, boy. Yes, you might take the horse and the food and make your way back south. If you can survive the desert. If you don't meet another troop of Romans on the way. Don't think the clothing will disguise you; your Latin is terrible. And even if you did manage to escape me this time, I'll find you in the end. It might take me a year, perhaps two; but I'll find you again. There are still a few stray Carthaginians to be rounded up. My men and I won't rest until we've scoured every crevice and looked under every stone. They're easier to take every time—weaker, more starved, more demoralized. Less and less like men willing to fight, and more and more like slaves ready to accept their fate. The reach of Rome is long, Hanso, and her appetite for vengeance is endless. You'll never escape her. You'll never escape *me*.

"Besides, you haven't yet heard my offer. Return here within three days with the rabbit trailing behind you—or the rabbit's head on your spear, I don't care which—and when we reach the coast, I'll make you a free man, a citizen of Rome. You're young, Hanso. You have spirit. Your accent will be held against you, but even so, freedom and a strong young body, and a bit of ruthlessness, will take you far in Rome. Consider the alternative, and make your choice."

I looked at the gleaming boots at my feet, the spear, the whip, the coil of rope, the dagger with Melkart—or Hercules, as Fabius would have it. I thought of Lino—Lino who had come to us as a stranger and an outsider, who had betrayed the women, who would only be captured again and forced to endure the *temptatio* a third time if I didn't bring him back myself. What did I owe Lino, after all?

"What if you're lying?" I said. "Why should I trust you? You lied to Lino—you told him he would be your eagle, didn't you? Instead you made him your rabbit."

Fabius drew his sword from its scabbard, the same blade he had used to decapitate Matho. He pressed the point to his forearm and drew a red line across the flesh. He held out his arm. "When a Roman shows his blood, he doesn't lie. By Father Jupiter and great Mars, I swear that my promise to you is good." I looked at the shallow wound and the blood that oozed from the flesh. I looked into Fabius's eyes. There was no amusement there, no deceit, only a twisted sense of honor, and I knew he spoke the truth.

V

I remember the faces of the captives as I left the tent, their astonishment when they saw the outfit I wore. I remember their jeering as I rode out of the camp, followed by the snapping of whips as the Romans quieted them. I remember turning my back to them and gazing north, through the pass in the mountains, where the faraway sea glimmered like a shard of lapis beneath the sun.

It didn't take me three days to find Lino, or even two. The trail he had left was easy to follow. I could see from the spacing of his steps and the way the grass had been flattened by the ball of each foot that he had run very fast at first, seldom pausing to rest. Then his stride grew shorter and his tread heavier, and I saw how quickly he had wearied.

I followed his trail at a slow pace, unsure of my skill at driving the horse at a gallop. The sun began to sink behind the western range. In the twilight, his trail became more difficult to follow. I pushed on, sensing that I was close.

I crested the ridge of a low hill and surveyed the dim valley below. He must have seen me first; from the corner of my eye I caught his hobbling gait and I heard the rattling of his chains as he sought to hide behind a scrubby tree.

I approached him warily, thinking that he might somehow have freed his hands, that he might still have strength to fight. But when I saw him shivering against the tree, naked, his hands still tied behind him, his face pressed against the bark as if he could somehow conceal himself, I knew there would be no contest.

The only sound was the dry rustling of the grass beneath my horse's hooves. As I drew closer, Lino's shivering increased, and in that moment, it seemed to me that he was exactly what Fabius had named him—a rabbit, twitching and paralyzed by panic.

He's not like me, I thought. I owe him nothing. On a sudden impulse, I lifted the spear, cradling the shaft in the crook of my arm as I had seen the Romans do. I prodded his shoulder with the sharp point. As he quivered in response, a strange excitement ran through me, a thrilling sensation of power.

"Look at me," I said. The sound of my own voice, so harsh and demanding, surprised me. It was a voice I had learned from Fabius. That voice wielded its own kind of power, and Lino's response—the way he cowered and wheeled about—showed that I had mastered it on my first attempt. Fabius must have seen the seeds of power inside me at first glance, I thought. It was no mistake that he had made me his eagle, that he had separated me from the rest, as a miner separates gold from sand.

This was the moment, in any other hunt, when I would have killed the prey. A flood of memories poured through me. I remembered the first time I hunted and killed a deer. It was Uncle Gebal who taught me the secrets of pursuit—and I remembered how Gebal had died, sinking like a stone in the river. I thought of Matho, of the head that had held so much wisdom severed from his shoulders, sent tumbling like a cabbage onto the stony ground. I clenched my jaw and crushed these thoughts inside me. I prodded Lino again with the spear.

Lino stopped trembling. He turned from the tree and stood beneath me with his face bowed. "Do it, then," he whispered. His voice was dry and hoarse. "Let Fabius win his game this time."

I reached into the saddlebag and began to uncoil the rope.

"No!" Lino shouted and started back. "You won't take me to him alive. You'll have to kill me, Hanso. It's what you wanted anyway, isn't it? On the night that I betrayed the women, you said you would kill me if you had the chance. Do it now! Didn't Fabius say you could bring back my head?"

His eyes flashed in the growing darkness. They were not the eyes of a hunted animal, but of a man. The rush of power inside me suddenly dwindled, and I knew I couldn't kill him. I began to knot the rope, fashioning a noose. Then I paused.

"How did you know what Fabius told me—that I could bring back your head for proof?"

Lino's scarred shoulders, squared and defiant before, slumped against the tree. "Because those are the rules of his game."

"But how would you know the instructions he gave me? You were his rabbit the last time—"

"No."

"But you told me, that night when you first explained the *temptatio*—"

"You assumed I had been his rabbit. *You* spoke those words, Hanso, not me." Lino shook his head and sighed. "When Fabius captured me a year ago, I was his eagle. Do you understand now? *I* was granted all the privileges; *I* was mounted on a horse; *I* was given my meals in his tent and told stories of glorious Rome. And when the time came, Fabius promised me my freedom and sent me out to hunt the rabbit—just as he now sends you."

His voice dropped to a whisper. "It took me many days to make my way to your people, skulking southward through the mountain gorges, hiding from Romans, living on roots and weeds. The horse died, and for a while Carabal and I lived on its flesh—Carabal the rabbit, the man I was sent to recapture. And then Carabal died—he was too weak and broken to live—and what was the use of it all? I should have done what Fabius wanted. I should have done what you're about to do. It all comes to this in the end."

My head was burning. I couldn't think. "But this time you really did escape. . . ."

Lino laughed, then choked, his throat too dry for laughter. "I've never met a man as stupid as you, Hanso. Do you think I escaped on my own, with my arms tied behind my back and Romans all around me? Fabius drove me from his tent at spearpoint in the middle of the night. The rabbit doesn't escape; the rabbit is forced to flee for his life! And why? So that you could hunt me. The rabbit flees, and the eagle is sent after him. And when you return to the camp, with my head mounted on your spear, he'll reward you with your freedom. Or so he says. Why not? He will have had his way. He will have made you one of his own. You will have proven that everything Fabius believes is true."

The heady sense of power I had felt only moments before now seemed very far away. "I can't kill you, Lino."

Lino stamped his foot and twisted his arms to one side, so that I could see the ropes that bound his wrists. "Then cut me free and I'll do it myself. I'll slice my wrists with your knife, and when I'm dead you can behead me. He'll never know the difference."

I shook my head. "No. I could let you escape. I'll tell him that I couldn't find you—"

"Then you'll end up a slave like all the rest, or else he'll devise some even more terrible punishment for you. Fabius has a boundless imagination for cruelty. Believe me, I know."

I twisted the rope in my hands, staring at the noose I had made, at the emptiness it contained. "We could escape together—"

"Don't be a fool, Hanso. He'll only find you again, just as he found me. Do you want to be his rabbit on your next *temptatio*? Imagine that, Hanso. No, take what Fabius has offered you. Kill me now! Or let me do it myself, if you don't have the stomach for it—if the precious eagle finds his claws too delicate to do Fabius's dirty work."

The twilight had given way to darkness. A half moon overhead illuminated the little valley with a soft silver sheen. The reddish glow of the Romans' campfires loomed beyond the ridge. I stared at that smoky red glare, and for a moment it seemed that time stopped and the world all around receded, leaving me utterly alone in that dim valley. Even Lino seemed far away, and the horse beneath me might have been made of mist.

I saw the future as a many-faceted crystal, each facet reflecting a choice. To kill Lino; to cut his bonds and watch while he killed himself; to turn my back and allow him to flee, and then to face Fabius with my failure;

to take flight myself. But the crystal was cloudy and gave no glimpse of where these choices would lead.

The temptatio *turns free men into slaves*: that was what Lino had told me on our first night of captivity. What had the *temptatio* done to me? I thought of the scorn I had felt for the other captives, riding high above them, proud and vain upon my mount, and my face grew hot. I thought of the sense of power that had surged through me when I came upon Lino cringing naked in the valley, and saw what Fabius had done to me. I was no more a free man than Lino in his bonds. I stood on the brink of becoming just as much a slave as all the others, seduced by Fabius's promises, bent to his will, joining in the cruel game he forced us to play for his amusement.

Lino had once played the same game. Lino had defied the cruelty of Fabius and taken flight, like a true eagle, not like the caged scavenger that Fabius would have made him, and now was determined to make me. But Lino had lost in the end, I told myself—and immediately saw the lie, for this was not the end of Lino, unless I chose it to be. Lino had faced the same choice himself, when Fabius had groomed him as his eagle and set him upon the rabbit Carabal. Lino had chosen freedom, whatever its cost. I saw that I faced only two choices: to take the course that Lino had taken, or to submit to Fabius and be remade in his image.

I turned my eyes from the dull red glow of the campfires and looked down at Lino's face by moonlight, close enough to touch and yet far away, framed by my clouded thoughts like a face in a picture. I remembered the tears he had wept on the night of our capture, and the lines of suffering that had creased his brow on all the nights since then. But now his cheeks and forehead shone smooth and silver in the moonlight. His eyes were bright and dry. There was no anger or pain or guilt there. I saw the face of a free man, unconquered and defiant, composed and ready for death.

The crystal turned in my mind, and I strained to catch a glint of hope; that glint was the brightness in Lino's eyes. Fabius had told me that escape was impossible, that freedom was only a fugitive's dream, that no other game existed except the *temptatio* that ground men into the same coarse matter as himself, or else crushed them altogether. But how could Fabius know the future, any more than I—especially if there were those like Lino who could still summon the will to defy him?

The power of Rome could not last forever. Once, Carthage had been invincible and men had thought her reign would never end—and now

Carthage was nothing but ashes and a fading memory. So it would some-day be with Rome. Who could say what realms might rise to take Rome's place?

I closed my eyes. It was such a thin hope! I would not delude myself. I would not let wishful fantasies soften the harshness of the choice I was making. Call me fool. Call me rabbit or eagle, there is finally no difference. But let no man say that I became Fabius's creature.

I slid from the saddle and pulled the dagger from its sheath. Lino turned and offered his wrists. I sliced through the heavy bindings. He turned back and reached for the knife.

For an instant, we clutched the hilt together, his finger laced with mine over the image of Melkart. I looked into his eyes and saw that he was still ready to die, that he didn't know the choice I had made. I pulled the hilt from his grasp, returned the dagger to its sheath, and mounted the horse.

A sudden tremor of doubt ran through me; the reins slipped from my grasp. To steady myself, I took inventory of the supplies that Fabius had given me. How long could three days' rations last if I split them between us? I looked down at the clothing I wore, the uniform of a Roman soldier, and wanted to tear it from my body in disgust; but I would need its pro-tection for the journey.

Lino hadn't moved. A band of clouds obscured the moon, casting a shadow across his face. He stood so still that he might have been carved from stone. "What are you waiting for?" I said. I moved forward in the saddle and gestured to the space behind me. "There's room enough for two. It will only slow us down if one walks while the other rides."

Lino shook his head. "You're an even bigger fool than I thought, Hanso." But his whisper held no malice, and he turned his face away as he spoke. He couldn't resist a final jab—or was he offering me one last chance to betray him?

"And perhaps I'm a better man than I thought," I answered. Lino stood still for a long moment, then his shoulders began to shake and he drew a shuddering breath. I averted my face so I wouldn't see him weeping. "Hurry," I said. "We have a long, hard journey ahead of us."

I felt him climb into the saddle behind me and settle himself, felt the trembling of his body, then spurred the horse across the valley and up to the crest of the hill. There I paused for a moment, looking to the east. The Ro-mans' campfires flashed tiny but distinct in the darkness. The river glimmered beyond, like a thin ribbon of black marble beneath the moon. Far to the north, through the mountain pass, I could glimpse the black marble sea.

I stared at that glistening sliver of the sea for a long time. Then I snapped the reins and kicked my heels against the horse's flanks, turning the beast southward, and we began the uncertain journey.

James Rollins

A blood-soaked arena and gladiators circling each other for the kill . . . a scene familiar from many books and movies, except that this isn't Ancient Rome, and the battle-scarred warriors aren't quite what you'd expect either. In fact, many things are different. The blood is the same, though. And the death. And the courage.

An amateur spelunker, a veterinarian, and a PADI-certified scuba enthusiast, James Rollins is a *New York Times* bestselling author of contemporary thrillers (many with strong fantastic elements) such as *Subterranean, Excavation, Ice Hunt, Deep Fathom,* and *Amazonia,* as well as a series of novels detailing the often world-saving adventures of the SIGMA Force, including *Sandstorm, Map of Bones, Black Order,* and *The Judas Strain*. His most recent books are a novelization of *Indiana Jones and the Kingdom of the Crystal Skull* and the novel *The Last Oracle*. He lives with his family in Sacramento, California, where he runs a veterinary practice.

The Pit

The large dog hung from the bottom of the tire swing by his teeth. His back paws swung three feet off the ground. Overhead, the sun remained a red blister in an achingly blue sky. After so long, the muscles of the dog's jaw had cramped to a tight knot. His tongue had turned to a salt-dried piece of leather, lolling out one side. Still, at the back of his throat, he tasted black oil and blood.

But he did not let go.

He knew better.

Two voices spoke behind him. The dog recognized the gravel of the yard trainer. But the second was someone new, squeaky and prone to sniffing between every other word.

"How long he be hangin' there?" the stranger asked.

"Forty-two minutes."

"No shit! That's one badass motherfucker. But he's not pure pit, is he?"

"Pit and boxer."

"True nuff? You know, I got a Staffordshire bitch be ready for him next month. And let me tell you, she puts the mean back in bitch. Cut you in on the pups."

"Stud fee's a thousand."

"Dollars? You cracked or what?"

"Fuck you. Last show, he brought down twelve motherfuckin' Gs."

"Twelve? You're shittin' me. For a dogfight?"

The trainer snorted. "And that's after paying the house. He beat that champion out of Central. Should seen that Crip monster. All muscle and scars. Had twenty-two pounds on Brutus here. Pit ref almost shut down the fight at the weigh-in. Called my dog ring bait! But the bastard showed 'em. And those odds paid off like a crazy motherfucker."

Laughter. Raw. No warmth behind it.

The dog watched out of the corner of his eye. The trainer stood to the left, dressed in baggy jeans and a white T-shirt, showing arms decorated with ink, his head shaved to the scalp. The newcomer wore leather and carried a helmet under one arm. His eyes darted around.

"Let's get out of the goddamn sun," the stranger finally said. "Talk numbers. I got a kilo coming in at the end of the week."

As they stepped away, something struck the dog's flank. Hard. But he still didn't let go. Not yet.

"Release!"

With the command, the dog finally unclamped his jaws and dropped to the practice yard. His hind legs were numb, heavy with blood. But he turned to face the two men. Shoulders up, he squinted against the sun. The yard trainer stood with his wooden bat. The newcomer had his fists shoved into the pockets of his jacket and took a step back. The dog smelled the stranger's fear, a bitter dampness, like weeds soaked in old urine.

The trainer showed no such fear. He held his bat with one hand and scowled his dissatisfaction. He reached down and unhooked the plate of iron that hung from the dog collar. The plate dropped to the hard-packed dirt.

"Twenty-pound weight," the trainer told the stranger. "I'll get him up to *thirty* before next week. Helps thicken the neck up."

"Any thicker, and he won't be able to turn his head."

"Don't want him to *turn* his head. That'll cost me a mark in the ring." The bat pointed toward the line of cages. A boot kicked toward the dog's side. "Get your ass back into the kennel, Brutus."

The dog curled a lip, but he swung away, thirsty and exhausted. The fenced runs lined the rear of the yard. The floors were unwashed cement. From the neighboring cages, heads lifted toward him as he approached, then lowered sullenly. At the entrance, he lifted his leg and marked his spot. He fought not to tremble on his numb back leg. He couldn't show weakness.

He'd learned that on the first day.

"Git in there already!"

He was booted from behind as he entered the cage. The only shade came from a scrap of tin nailed over the back half of the run. The fence door clanged shut behind him.

He lumbered across the filthy space to his water dish, lowered his head, and drank.

Voices drifted away as the two headed toward the house. One question hung in the air. "How'd that monster get the name Brutus?"

The dog ignored them. That memory was a shard of yellowed bone buried deep. Over the past two winters, he'd tried to grind it away. But it had remained lodged, a truth that couldn't be forgotten.

He hadn't always been named Brutus.

"C'mere, Benny! That's a good boy!"

It was one of those days that flowed like warm milk, so sweet, so comforting, filling every hollow place with joy. The black pup bounded across the green and endless lawn. Even from across the yard, he smelled the piece of hot dog in the hand hidden behind the skinny boy's back. Behind him, a brick house climbed above a porch encased in vines and purple flowers. Bees buzzed, and frogs croaked a chorus with the approach of twilight.

"Sit! Benny, sit!"

The pup slid to a stop on the dewy grass and dropped to his haunches. He quivered all over. He wanted the hot dog. He wanted to lick the salt off those fingers. He wanted a scratch behind the ear. He wanted this day to never end.

"There's a good boy."

The hand came around, and fingers opened. The pup stuffed his cold nose into the palm, snapped up the piece of meat, then shoved closer. He waggled his whole hindquarters and wormed tighter to the boy.

Limbs tangled, and they both fell to the grass.

Laughter rang out like sunshine.

"Watch out! Here comes Junebug!" the boy's mother called from the porch. She rocked in a swing as she watched the boy and pup wrestle. Her voice was kind, her touch soft, her manner calm.

Much like the pup's own mother.

Benny remembered how his mother used to groom his forehead, nuzzle his ear, how she kept them all safe, all ten of them, tangled in a pile of paws, tails, and mewling complaints. Though even that memory was fading. He could hardly picture her face any longer, only the warmth of her brown eyes as she'd gazed down at them as they fed, fighting for a teat. And he'd had to fight, being the smallest of his brothers and sisters. But he'd never had to fight alone.

"Juneeeee!" the boy squealed.

A new weight leaped into the fray on the lawn. It was Benny's sister, Junebug. She yipped and barked and tugged on anything loose: shirtsleeve, pant leg, wagging tail. The last was her specialty. She'd pulled many of her fellow brothers and sisters off a teat by their tails, so Benny could have his turn.

Now those same sharp teeth clamped onto the tip of Benny's tail and tugged hard. He squealed and leaped straight up—not so much in pain, but in good-hearted play. The three of them rolled and rolled across the yard, until the boy collapsed on his back in surrender, leaving the brother and sister free to lick his face from either side.

"That's enough, Jason!" their new mother called from the porch.

"Oh, Mom . . ." The boy pushed up on one elbow, flanked by the two pups.

The pair stared across the boy's chest, tails wagging, tongues hanging, panting. His sister's eyes shone at him in that frozen moment of time, full of laughter, mischief, and delight. It was like looking at himself.

It was why they'd been picked together.

"Two peas in a pod, those two," the old man had said as he knelt over the litter and lifted brother and sister toward the visitors. "Boy's right ear is a blaze of white. Girl's left ear is the same. Mirror images. Make quite a pair, don't you think? Hate to separate them."

And in the end, he didn't have to. Brother and sister were taken to their new home together.

"Can't I play a little longer?" the boy called to the porch.

"No argument, young man. Your father will be home in a bit. So get cleaned up for dinner."

The boy stood up. Benny read the excitement in his sister's eyes. It matched his own. They'd not understood anything except for the mother's last word.

Dinner.

Bolting from the boy's side, the pair of pups raced toward the porch. Though smaller, Benny made up for his size with blazing speed. He shot across the yard toward the promise of a full dinner bowl and maybe a biscuit to chew afterwards. Oh, if only—

—then a familiar tug on his tail. The surprise attack from behind tripped his feet. He sprawled nose-first into the grass and slid with his limbs splayed out.

His sister bounded past him and up the steps.

Benny scrabbled his legs under him and followed. Though outsmarted as usual by his bigger sister, it didn't matter. His tail wagged and wagged.

He hoped these days would never end.

"Shouldn't we pull his ass out of there?"

"Not yet!"

Brutus paddled in the middle of the pool. His back legs churned the water, toes splayed out. His front legs fought to keep his snout above the water. His collar, a weighted steel chain, sought to drag him to the cement bottom. Braided cords of rope trapped him in the middle of the concrete swimming pool. His heart thundered in his throat. Each breath heaved with desperate sprays of water.

"Yo, man! You gonna drown 'im!"

"A little water won't kill him. He got a fight in two days. A big-ass show. I got a lot riding on it."

Paddling and wheeling his legs, water burned his eyes. His vision darkened at the edges. Still he saw the pit trainer off to the side, in trunks, no shirt. On his bare chest was inked two dogs snarling at each other. Two other men held the chains, keeping him from reaching the edge of the pool.

Bone-tired and cold, his back end began to slip deeper. He fought, but his head bobbed under. He took a gulp into his lungs. Choking, he kicked and got his nose above water again. He gagged his lungs clear. A bit of bile followed, oiling the water around his lips. Foam frothed from his nostrils.

"He done in, man. Pull 'im out."

"Let's see what he's got," the trainer said. "Bitch been in there longer than he ever done."

For another stretch of painful eternity, Brutus fought the pull of the chain and the waterlogged weight of his own body. His head sank with every fourth paddle. He breathed in as much stinging water as he did air. He had gone deaf to anything but his own hammering heart. His vision had shrunk to a blinding pinpoint. Then finally, he could no longer fight to the surface. More water flowed into his lungs. He sank—into the depths and into darkness.

But there was no peace.

The dark still terrified him.

The summer storm rattled the shutters and boomed with great claps that sounded like the end of all things. Spats of rain struck the windows, and flashes of lightning split the night sky.

Benny hid under the bed with his sister. He shivered against her side. She crouched, ears up, nose out. Each rumble was echoed in her chest as she growled back at the threatening noise. Benny leaked some of his terror, soaking the carpet under him. He was not so brave as his big sister.

. . . *boom, boom,* BOOM . . .

Brightness shattered across the room, casting away all shadows.

Benny whined and his sister barked.

A face appeared from atop the bed and leaned down to stare at them. The boy, his head upside down, lifted a finger to his lips. "Shh, Junie, you'll wake Dad."

But his sister would have none of that. She barked and barked, trying to scare off what lurked in the storm. The boy rolled off his bed and sprawled on the floor. Arms reached and scooped them both toward him. Benny went willingly.

"Eww . . . you're all wet."

Junie squirmed loose then ran around the room, barking, tail straight back, ears pricked high.

"Sheesh," the boy said, trying to catch her while cradling Benny.

A door banged open out in the hall. Footsteps echoed. The bedroom door swung open. Large bare legs like tree trunks entered. "Jason, son, I got to get up early."

"Sorry, Dad. The storm's got them spooked."

A long heavy sighed followed. The large man caught Junie and swung her up in his arms. She slathered his face with her tongue, tail beating against his arms. Still, she growled all the time as the sky rumbled back at them.

"They're going to have to get used to these storms," the man said. "These thunder-bumpers will be with us all summer."

"I'll take them downstairs. We can sleep on the sofa on the back porch. If they're with me . . . maybe that'll help 'em get used to it."

Junie was passed to the boy.

"All right, son. But bring an extra blanket."

"Thanks, Dad."

A large hand clapped on the boy's shoulder. "You're taking good care of them. I'm proud of you. They're really getting huge."

The boy struggled with the two squirming pups and laughed. "I know!"

A few moments later, all three of them were buried in a nest of blankets atop a musty sofa. Benny smelled mice spoor and bird droppings, brought alive by the wind and dampness. Still, with all of them together, it was the best bed he'd ever slept in. Even the storm had quieted, though a heavy rain continued to pelt from the dark moonless skies. It beat against the shingled roof of the porch.

Just as Benny finally calmed enough to let his eyelids droop closed, his sister sprang to her feet, growling again, hackles up. She slithered out from under the blankets without disturbing the boy. Benny had no choice but to follow.

What is it? . . .

Benny's ears were now up and swiveling. From the top step of the porch, he stared out into the storm-swept yard. Tree limbs waved. Rain chased across the lawn in rippling sheets.

Then Benny heard it, too.

A rattle of the side gate. A few furtive whispers.

Someone was out there!

His sister shot from the porch. Without thinking, Benny ran after her. They raced toward the gate.

Whispers turned into words. "Quiet, asshole. Let me see if the dogs are back there!"

Benny saw the gate swing open. Two shadowy shapes stepped forward. Benny slowed—then caught the smell of meat, bloody and raw.

"What'd I tell ya?"

A tiny light bloomed in the darkness, spearing his sister. Junie slowed enough for Benny to catch up to her. One of the strangers dropped to a knee and held out an open palm. The rich, meaty smell swelled.

"You want it, don't cha? C'mon, you little bitches."

Junie snuck closer, more on her belly, tail twitching in tentative welcome.

Benny sniffed and sniffed, nose up. The tantalizing odor drew him along behind his sister.

Once near the gate, the two dark shapes leaped on them. Something heavy dropped over Benny and wrapped tightly around him. He tried to cry out, but fingers clamped over his muzzle and trapped his scream to a muffled whine. He heard the same from his sister.

He was hauled up and carried away.

"Nothing like a stormy night to pick up bait. No one ever suspects. Always blame the thunder. Thinks it scared the little shits into running off."

"How much we gonna make?"

"Fifty a head easy."

"Nice."

Thunder clapped again, marking the end of Benny's old life.

Brutus entered the ring. The dog kept his head lowered, shoulders high, ears pulled flat against his skull. His hackles already bristled. It still hurt to breathe deeply, but the dog hid the pain. Buried in his lungs, a dull fire burned from the pool water, flaring with each breath. Cautiously, he took in all the scents around him.

The sand of the ring was still being raked clean of the blood from the prior fight. Still, the fresh spoor filled the old warehouse, along with the taint of grease and oil, the chalk of cement, and the bite of urine, sweat, and feces from both dog and man.

The fights had been going on from sunset until well into the night.

But no one had left.

Not until this match was over.

The dog had heard his name called over and over: "Brutus . . . man, look at the *cojones* on that *monstruo* . . . he a little-ass bastard, but I saw Brutus take on a dog twice his size . . . tore his throat clean open . . ."

As Brutus had waited in his pen, people trailed past, many dragging children, to stare at him. Fingers pointed, flashes snapped, blinding him, earning low growls. Finally, the handler had chased them all off with his bat.

"Move on! This ain't no free show. If you like him so goddamned much, go place a fucking bet!"

Now as Brutus passed through the gate in the ring's three-foot-tall wooden fence, shouts and whistles greeted him from the stands, along with raucous laughter and angry outbursts. The noise set Brutus's heart pounding. His claws dug into the sand, his muscles tensed.

They were the first to enter the ring.

Beyond the crowd spread a sea of cages and fenced-in pens. Large shadowy shapes stirred and paced.

There was little barking.

The dogs knew to save their strength for the ring.

"You'd better not lose," the pit handler mumbled, and tugged on the chain hooked to the dog's studded collar. Bright lights shone down into the pit. It reflected off the handler's shaved head, revealing the ink on his arms, black and red, like bloody bruises.

The pair kept to the ring's edge and waited. The trainer slapped the dog's flank, then wiped his wet hand on his jeans. Brutus's coat was still damp. Prior to the fight, each dog had been washed by their opponent's handler, to make sure there was no slippery grease or poison oils worked into the coat to give a dog an advantage.

As they waited for their opponent to enter the ring, Brutus smelled the sheen of excitement off the handler. A sneer remained frozen on the man's face, showing a hint of teeth.

Beyond the fence, another man approached the edge of the ring. Brutus recognized him by the way he sniffed between his words and the bitter trace of fear that accompanied him. If the man had been another dog, he would've had his tail tucked to his belly and a whine flowing from his throat.

"I placed a buttload on this bastard," the man said as he stepped to the fence and eyed Brutus.

"So?" his handler answered.

"I just saw Gonzales's dog. Christ, man, are you nuts? That monster's half bull mastiff."

The handler shrugged. "Yeah, but he got only one good eye. Brutus'll take him down. Or at least, he'd better." Again the chain jerked.

The man shifted behind the fence and leaned closer. "Is there some sort of fix going on here?"

"Fuck you. I don't need a fix."

"But I heard you once owned that other dog. That one-eyed bastard."

The handler scowled. "Yeah, I did. Sold him to Gonzales a couple years ago. Didn't think the dog would live. After he lost his fuckin' eye and all. Bitch got all infected. Sold him to that Spic for a couple bottles of Special K. Stupidest deal I ever made. Dog gone and made that beaner a shitload of money. He's been rubbin' it in my face ever since. But today's payback."

The chain yanked and lifted Brutus off his toes.

"You'd better not lose this show. Or we might just have ourselves another barbecue back at the crib."

The dog heard the threat behind the words. Though he didn't fully understand, he sensed the meaning. *Don't lose.* Over the past two winters, he'd seen defeated dogs shot in the head, strangled to death with their own chains, or allowed to be torn to pieces in the ring. Last summer, a bull terrier had bit Brutus's handler in the calf. The dog had been blood-addled after losing a match and had lashed out. Later, back at the yard, the bull terrier had tried mewling for forgiveness, but the handler had soaked the dog down and set him on fire. The flaming terrier had run circles around the yard, howling, banging blindly into runs and fences. The men in the yard had laughed and laughed, falling down on their sides.

The dogs in their kennels had watched silently.

They all knew the truth of their lives.

Never lose.

Finally, a tall skinny man stepped to the center of the ring. He lifted an arm high. "Dogs to your scratch lines!"

The far gate of the ring opened, and a massive shape bulled into the ring, half-dragging his small, beefy handler, a man who wore a big grin and a cowboy hat. But Brutus's attention fixed to the dog. The mastiff was a wall of muscle. His ears had been cropped to nubs. He had no tail. His paws mashed deep into the sand as he fought toward the scratch line.

As the beast pulled forward, he kept his head cocked to the side, allowing his one eye to scan the ring. The other eye was a scarred knot.

The man in the center of the ring pointed to the two lines raked into the sand. "To the scratch! It's the final show of the night, folks! What you've been waiting for! Two champions brought together again! Brutus against Caesar!"

Laughter and cheers rose from the crowd. Feet pounded on the stands' boards.

But all Brutus heard was that one name.

Caesar.

He suddenly trembled all over. The shock rocked through him as if his very bones rattled. He fought to hold steady and stared across at his opponent—and remembered.

"Caesar! C'mon, you bastard, you hungry or not?"

Under the midmorning sun, Benny hung from a stranger's hand. Fingers scruffed the pup's neck and dangled him in the center of a strange yard. Benny cried and piddled a stream to the dirt below. He saw other dogs behind fences. Smelled more elsewhere. His sister was clutched in the arms of one of men who'd nabbed them out of their yard. His sister barked out sharply.

"Shut that bitch up. She's distracting him."

"I don't want to see this," the man said, but he pinched his sister's muzzle shut.

"Oh, grow some damn balls. Whatcha think I paid you a hundred bucks for? Dog's gotta eat, don't he?" The man dug his fingers tighter into Benny's scruff and shook him hard. "And bait is bait."

Another man called from the shadows across the yard. "Hey, Juice! How much weight you want on the sled this time?"

"Go for fifteen bricks."

"Fifteen?"

"I need Caesar muscled up good for the fight next week."

Benny heard the knock and scrape of something heavy.

"Here he comes!" the shadow man called over. "He must be hungry!"

Out of the darkness, a monster appeared. Benny had never seen a dog so large. The giant heaved against a harness strapped across his chest. Ropes of drool trailed from the corner of his lips. Claws dug into the dark dirt as he hauled forward. Behind him, attached to the harness, was a sled on steel runners. It was piled high with blocks of cement.

The man holding Benny laughed deep in his throat. "He be damned hungry! Haven't fed him in two days!"

Benny dribbled out more of his fear. The monster's gaze was latched on to him. Benny read the red, raw hunger in those eyes. The drool flowed thicker.

"Hurry it up, Caesar! If you want your breakfast!"

The man took a step back with Benny.

The large brute pulled harder, shouldering into the harness, his long tongue hanging, frothing with foam. He panted and growled. The sled dragged across the dirt with the grating sound of gnawed bone.

Benny's heart hammered in his small chest. He tried to squirm away, but he couldn't escape the man's iron grip . . . or the unwavering gaze of the monster. It was coming for him. He wailed and cried.

Time stretched to a long sharp line of terror.

Steadily the beast came at him.

Finally, the man burst out a satisfied snort. "Good enough! Unhook him!"

Another man ran out of the shadows and yanked on a leather lead. The harness dropped from the monster's shoulders, and the huge dog bounded across the yard, throwing slather with each step.

The man swung his arm back, then tossed Benny forward. The pup flew high into the air, spinning tail over ear. He was too terrified to scream. As he spun, he caught glimpses below of the monster pounding after him—but he also spotted his sister. The man who held Junie had started to turn away, not wanting to watch. He must have loosened his grip enough to let Junie slip her nose free. She bit hard into his thumb.

Then Benny hit the ground and rolled across the yard. The impact knocked the air from his chest. He lay stunned as the larger dog barreled toward him. Terrified, Benny used the only advantage he had—his speed.

He rolled to his feet and darted to the left. The big dog couldn't turn fast enough and skidded past where he'd landed. Benny fled across the yard, tucking his back legs under his front in his desperation to go faster. He heard the huffing of the monster at his tail.

If he could just get under the low sled, hide there . . .

But he didn't know the yard. One paw hit a broken tile in the scrubby weeds, and he lost his footing. He hit his shoulder and rolled. He came to rest on his side as the huge dog lunged at him.

Benny winced. Desperate, he exposed his belly and piddled on himself, showing his submission. But it didn't matter. Lips rippled back from yellow teeth.

Then the monster suddenly jerked to a stop in midlunge, accompanied by a surprised yelp. The brute spun around. Benny saw something attached to his tail.

It was Junie. Dropped by her captor, she had come at the monster with her usual sneak attack. The monster spun several more times as Junie remained clamped to his tail. This was no playful nip. She must've dug in deep with her sharp teeth. In attempting to throw her off, the large dog only succeeded in stripping more fur and skin from his tail as Junie was tossed about.

Blood sprayed across the dirt.

But finally even Junie couldn't resist the brute's raw strength. She went flying, her muzzle bloody. The monster followed and landed hard on her. Blocked by his bulk, Benny couldn't see—but he heard.

A sharp cry from Junie, followed by the crunch of bone.

No!

Benny leaped to his feet and ran at the monster. There was no plan—only a red, dark anger. He speared straight at the monster. He caught a glimpse of a torn leg, bone showing. The monster gripped his sister and shook her. She flopped limply. Crimson sprayed, then poured from his lips, mixed with drool.

With the sight, Benny plummeted into a dark place, a pit from which he knew he'd never escape. He leaped headlong at the monster and landed on the brute's face. He clawed and bit and gouged, anything to get him to let his sister go.

But he was so much smaller.

A toss of the blocky head, and Benny went flying away—forever lost in blood, fury, and despair.

As Brutus stared at Caesar, it all came back. The past and present overlapped and muddled into a crimson blur. He stood at the scratch line in the ring without remembering walking to it. He could not say who stood at the line.

Brutus or Benny.

After the mutilation of his sister, Benny had been spared a brutal death. The yard trainer had been impressed by his fire. *"A real Brutus, this one. Taking on Caesar all alone! Fast, too. See him juke and run. Maybe he's too good for just bait."*

Caesar had not fared so well after their brief fight. During the attack, a back claw had split the large dog's eyelid and sliced across his left eye, blinding that side. Even the tail wound from Junie's bite had festered. The yard trainer had tried cutting off his tail with an ax and burning the stub with a flaming piece of wood. But the eye and tail got worse. For a week, the reek of pus and dying flesh flowed from his kennel. Flies swarmed in black gusts. Finally, a stranger in a cowboy hat arrived with a wheelbarrow, shook hands with the handler, and hauled Caesar away, muzzled, feverish, and moaning.

Everyone thought he'd died.

They'd been wrong.

Both dogs toed the scratch line in the sand. Caesar did not recognize his opponent. No acknowledgment shone out of that one eye, only blood-lust and blind fury. The monster lunged at the end of his chain, digging deep into the sand.

Brutus bunched his back legs under him. Old fury fired through his blood. His muzzle snarled into a long growl, one rising from his very bones.

The tall skinny man lifted both arms. "Dogs ready!" He brought his arms down while stepping back. "Go!"

With a snap, they were loosed from their chains. Both dogs leaped upon one another. Bodies slammed together amid savage growls and fly-ing spittle.

Brutus went first for Caesar's blind side. He bit into the nub of ear, seeking a hold. Cartilage ripped. Blood flowed over his tongue. The grip was too small to hold for long.

In turn, Caesar struck hard, using his heavier bulk to roll Brutus. Fangs sank into his shoulder. Brutus lost his hold and found himself pinned un-der that weight. Caesar bodily lifted him and slammed him into the sand.

But Brutus was still fast. He squirmed and twisted until he was belly to belly with the monster. He jack-rabbit punched up with his back legs and broke Caesar's hold on his shoulder. Loosed, Brutus went for the throat above him. But Caesar snapped down at him at the same time. They ended muzzle to muzzle, tearing at each other. Brutus on bottom, Caesar on top.

Blood spat and flew.

He kicked again and raked claws across the tender belly of his oppo-nent, gouging deep—then lunged up and latched on to Caesar's jowl. Us-ing the hold, he kicked and hauled his way out from under the bulk. He kept to the beast's left, his blind side.

Momentarily losing sight of Brutus, Caesar jagged the wrong direction.

He left his flank open. Brutus lashed out for a hind leg. He bit deep into the thick meat at the back of the thigh and chomped with all the muscles in his jaws. He yanked hard and shook his head.

In that moment of raw fury, Brutus flashed to a small limp form, clamped in bloody jaws, shaken and broken. A blackness fell over his vision. He used his entire body—muscle, bone, and blood—to rip and slash. The thick ligament at the back of the leg tore away from the ankle.

Caesar roared, but Brutus kept his grip and hauled up onto his hind legs. He flipped the other onto his back. Only then did he let go and slam on top of the other. He lunged for the exposed throat and bit deep. Fangs sank into tender flesh. He shook and ripped, snarled and dug.

From beyond the blackness, a whistle blew. It was the signal to break hold and return to their corners. Handlers ran up.

"Release!" his trainer yelled and grabbed the back of his collar.

Brutus heard the cheering, recognized the command. But it was all far away. He was deep in the pit.

Hot blood filled his mouth, flowed it into his lungs, soaked into the sand. Caesar writhed under him. Fierce growling turned into mewling. But Brutus was deaf to it. Blood flowed into all the empty places inside him, trying to fill it up, but failing.

Something struck his shoulders. Again and again. The handler's wooden bat. But Brutus kept his grip locked on the other dog's throat. He couldn't let go, trapped forever in the pit.

Wood splintered across his back.

Then a new noise cut through the roaring in his ears. More whistles, sharper and urgent, accompanied by the strident blare of sirens. Flashing lights dazzled through the darkness. Shouts followed, along with commands amplified to a piercing urgency.

"This is the police! Everyone on your knees! Hands on heads!"

Brutus finally lifted his torn muzzle from the throat of the other dog. Caesar lay unmoving on the sand, soaked in a pool of blood. Brutus lifted his eyes to the chaos around him. People fled the stands. Dogs barked and howled. Dark figures in helmets and carrying clear shields closed a circle around the area, forming a larger ring around the sand pit. Through the open doors of the warehouse, cars blazed in the night.

Wary, Brutus stood over the body of the dead dog.

He felt no joy at the killing. Only a dead numbness.

His trainer stood a step away. A string of anger flowed from the man's lips. He threw the broken stub of his bat into the sand. An arm pointed at Brutus.

"When I say release, you *release*, you dumb sack of shit!"

Brutus stared dully at the arm pointed at him, then to the face. From the man's expression, Brutus knew what the handler saw. It shone out of the dog's entire being. Brutus was trapped in a pit deeper than anything covered in sand, a pit from which he could never escape, a hellish place of pain and hot blood.

The man's eyes widened, and he took a step back. The beast stalked after him, no longer dog, only a creature of rage and fury.

Without warning—no growl, no snarl—Brutus lunged at the trainer. He latched on to the man's arm. The same arm that dangled pups as bait, an arm attached to the real monster of the sandy ring, a man who called horrors out of the shadows and set dogs on fire.

Teeth clamped over the pale wrist. Jaws crushed down. Bones ground and crackled under the pressure.

The man screamed.

From the narrow corner of one eye, Brutus watched a helmeted figure rush at them, an arm held up, pointing a black pistol.

A flash from the muzzle.

Then a sizzle of blinding pain.

And at last, darkness again.

Brutus lay on the cold concrete floor of the kennel. He rested his head on his paws and stared out the fenced gate. A wire-framed ceiling lamp shone off the whitewashed cement walls and lines of kennels. He listened with a deaf ear to the shuffle of other dogs, to the occasional bark or howl.

Behind him, a small door led to an outside fenced-in pen. Brutus seldom went out there. He preferred the shadows. His torn muzzle had been knitted together with staples, but it still hurt to drink. He didn't eat. He had been here for five days, noting the rise and fall of sunlight through the doorway.

People came by occasionally to stare at him. To scribble on a wooden chart hanging on his door. Men in white jackets injected him twice a day, using a noose attached to a long steel pole to hold him pinned to the wall.

He growled and snapped. More out of irritation than true anger. He just wanted to be left alone.

He had woken here after that night in the pit.

And a part of him still remained back there.

Why am I still breathing?

Brutus knew guns. He recognized their menacing shapes and sizes, the tang of their oils, the bitter reek of their smoke. He'd seen scores of dogs shot, some quickly, some for sport. But the pistol that had fired back at the ring had struck with a sizzle that twisted his muscles and arched his back.

He lived.

That, more than anything, kept him angry and sick of spirit.

A shuffle of rubber shoes drew his attention. He didn't lift his head, only twitched his eyes. It was too early for the pole and needles.

"He's over here," a voice said. "Animal Control just got the judge's order to euthanasize all the dogs this morning. This one's on the list, too. Heard they had to Taser him off his own trainer. So I wouldn't hold out much hope."

Brutus watched three people step before his kennel. One wore a gray coverall zippered up the front. He smelled of disinfectant and tobacco.

"Here he is. It was lucky we scanned him and found that old HomeAgain microchip. We were able to pull up your address and telephone. So you say someone stole him from your backyard?"

"Two years ago," a taller man said, dressed in black shoes and a suit.

Brutus pulled back one ear. The voice was vaguely familiar.

"They took both him and his littermate," the man continued. "We thought they'd run off during a thunderstorm."

Brutus lifted his head. A boy pushed between the two taller men and stepped toward the gate. Brutus met his eyes. The boy was older, taller, more gangly of limb, but his scent was as familiar as an old sock. As the boy stared into the dark kennel, the initial glaze of hope in his small face crumbled away into horror.

The boy's voice was an appalled squeak. "Benny?"

Shocked and disbelieving, Brutus slunk back on his belly. He let out a low warning growl as he shied away. He didn't want to remember . . . and especially didn't want this. It was too cruel.

The boy glanced over his shoulder to the taller man. "It is Benny, isn't it, Dad?"

"I think so." An arm pointed. "He's got that white blaze over his right ear." The voice grew slick with dread. "But what did they do to him?"

The man in the coveralls shook his head. "Brutalized him. Turned him into a monster."

"Is there any hope for rehabilitation?"

He shook his head and tapped the chart. "We had all the dogs examined by a behaviorist. She signed off that he's unsalvageable."

"But, Dad, it's *Benny*. . . ."

Brutus curled into the back of the run, as deep into the shadows as he could get. The name was like the lash of a whip.

The man pulled a pen from his coverall pocket. "Since you're still legally his owners and had no part in the dogfighting ring, we can't put him down until you sign off on it."

"Dad . . ."

"Jason, we had Benny for two *months*. They've had him for two *years*."

"But it's still Benny. I know it. Can't we try?"

The coverall man crossed his arms and lowered his voice with warning. "He's unpredictable and damn powerful. A bad combination. He even mauled his trainer. They had to amputate the man's hand."

"Jason . . ."

"I know. I'll be careful, Dad. I promise. But he deserves a chance, doesn't he?"

His father sighed. "I don't know."

The boy knelt down and matched Brutus's gaze. The dog wanted to turn away, but he couldn't. He locked eyes and slipped into a past he'd thought long buried away, of fingers clutching hot dogs, chases across green lawns, and endless sunny days. He pushed it all way. It was too painful, too prickled with guilt. He didn't deserve even the memory. It had no place in the pit.

A low rumble shook through his chest.

Still, the boy clutched the fence and faced the monster inside. He spoke with the effortless authority of innocence and youth.

"It's *still* Benny. Somewhere in there."

Brutus turned away and closed his eyes with an equally firm conviction. The boy was wrong.

———

Brutus slept on the back porch. Three months had passed and his sutures and staples were gone. The medicines in his food had faded away. Over the months, he and the family had come to an uneasy truce, a cold stalemate.

Each night, they tried to coax him into the house, especially as the leaves were turning brown and drifting up into piles beneath the hardwoods and the lawn turned frosty in the early morning. But Brutus kept to his porch, even avoiding the old sofa covered in a ragged thick comforter. He kept his distance from all things. He still flinched from a touch and growled when he ate, unable to stop himself.

But they no longer used the muzzle.

Perhaps they sensed the defeat that had turned his heart to stone. So he spent his days staring across the yard, only stirring occasionally, pricking up an ear if a stray squirrel should dare bound along the fencerow, its tail fluffed and fearless.

The back door opened, and the boy stepped out onto the porch. Brutus gained his feet and backed away.

"Benny, are you sure you don't want to come inside? I made a bed for you in the kitchen." He pointed toward the open door. "It's warm. And look, I have a treat for you."

The boy held out a hand, but Brutus already smelled the bacon, still smoking with crisply burned fat. He turned away. Back at the training yard, the others had tried to use bait on him, too. But after his sister, Brutus had always refused, no matter how hungry.

The dog crossed to the top step of the porch and lay down.

The boy came and sat with him, keeping his distance.

Brutus let him.

They sat for a long time. The bacon still in his fingers. The boy finally nibbled it away himself. "Okay, Benny, I have some homework."

The boy began to get up, paused, then carefully reached out to touch him on the head. Brutus didn't growl, but his fur bristled. Noting the warning, the boy sagged, pulled back his hand, and stood up.

"Okay. See ya in the morning, Benny boy."

He didn't watch the boy leave, but he listened for the door to clap shut. Satisfied that he was alone, he settled his head to his paws. He stared out into the yard.

The moon was already up, full-faced and bright. Lights twinkled.

Distantly, he listened as the household settled in for the night. A television whispered from the front room. He heard the boy call down from the upstairs. His mother answered.

Then suddenly Brutus was on his feet, standing stiff, unsure what had drawn him up. He kept dead still. Only his ears swiveled.

A knock sounded on the front door.

In the night.

"I'll get it," the mother called out.

Brutus twisted, bolted for the old sofa on the porch, and climbed half into it, enough to see through the picture window. The view offered a straight shot down the central dark hallway to the lighted front room.

Brutus watched the woman step to the door and pull it open.

Before she'd gotten it more than a foot wide, the door slammed open. It struck her and knocked her down. Two men charged inside, wearing dark clothes and masks pulled over their heads. Another kept watch by the open door. The first man backed into the hallway and kept a large pistol pointed toward the woman on the floor. The other intruder sidled to the left and aimed a gun toward someone in the dining room.

"DON'T MOVE!" the second gunman shouted.

Brutus tensed. He knew that voice, graveled and merciless. In an instant, his heart hammered in his chest, and his fur flushed up all over his body, quivering with fury.

"Mom? Dad?" The boy called from the top of the stairs.

"Jason!" the father answered from the dining room. "Stay up there!"

The leader stepped farther into the room. He shoved his gun out, holding it crooked. "Old man, sit your ass down!"

"What do you want?"

The gun poked again. "Yo! Where's my dog?"

"Your dog?" the mother asked on the floor, her voice trembling with fear.

"Brutus!" the man hollered. He lifted his other arm and bared the stump of a wrist. "I owe that bitch some payback . . . and that includes anyone taking care of his ass! In fact, we're going to have ourselves an old-fashioned barbecue." He turned to the man in the doorway. "What are you waiting for? Go get the gasoline?"

The man vanished into the night.

Brutus dropped back to the porch and retreated to the railing. He bunched his back legs.

"Yo! Where you keeping my damn dog? I know you got him!"

Brutus sprang forward, shoving out with all the strength in his body. He hit the sofa and vaulted over it. Glass shattered as he struck the window with the crown of his skull. He flew headlong into the room and landed in the kitchen. His front paws struck the floor before the first piece of glass. He bounded away as shards crashed and skittered across the checkerboard linoleum.

Down the hall, the first gunman began to turn, drawn by the noise. But he was too late. Brutus flew down the hall and dived low. He snatched the gunman by the ankle and ripped the tendon, flipping the man as he ran under him. The man's head hit the corner of a walnut hall table, and he went down hard.

Brutus spotted a man out on the front porch, frozen in midstep, hauling two large red jugs. The man saw Brutus barreling toward him. His eyes got huge. He dropped the jugs, spun around, and fled away.

A pistol fired, deafening in the closed space. Brutus felt a kick in his front leg. It shattered under him, but he was already in midleap toward the one-handed gunman, his old trainer and handler. Brutus hit him like a sack of cement. He head-butted the man in the chest. Weight and momentum knocked the legs out from under the man. They fell backwards together.

The pistol blasted a second time.

Something burned past Brutus's ear, and plaster rained down from the ceiling.

Then they both hit the hardwood floor. The man landed flat on his back, Brutus on top. The gun flew from his fingers and skittered under the dining room chair.

His trainer tried to kick Brutus away, but he'd taught the dog too well. Brutus dodged the knee. With a roar, he lunged for the man's throat. The man grabbed one-handed for an ear, but Brutus had lost most of the flap in an old fight. The ear slipped from the man's grip, and Brutus snapped for the tender neck. Fangs sank for the sure kill.

Then a shout barked behind him. "Benny! No!"

From out the corner of an eye, he saw the father crouched by the dining room table. He had recovered the pistol and pointed it at Brutus.

"Benny! Down! Let him go!"

From the darkness of the pit, Brutus growled back at the father. Blood flowed as Brutus clamped harder on his prey. He refused to release. Under him, the trainer screamed and gurgled. One fist punched blindly, but Brutus ground his jaws tighter. Blood flowed more heavily.

"Benny, let him go now!"

Another sharper voice squeaked in fear. It came from the stairs. "No, Dad!"

"Jason, I can't let him kill someone."

"Benny!" the boy screamed. "Please, Benny!"

Brutus ignored them. He wasn't Benny. He knew the pit was where he truly belonged, where he'd always end up. As his vision narrowed and darkness closed over him, he let himself fall deeper into that black, bottomless well, dragging the man with him. Brutus knew he couldn't escape; neither would he let this one go.

It was time to end all this.

But as Brutus sank into the pit, slipping away into the darkness, something stopped him, held him from falling. It made no sense. Though no one was behind him, he felt a distinct tug. On his tail. Holding him steady, then slowly drawing him back from the edge of the pit. Comprehension came slowly, seeping through the despair. He knew that touch. It was familiar as his own heart. Though it had no real strength, it broke him, shattered him into pieces.

He remembered that tug, from long ago, her special ambush.

Done to protect him.

Ever his guardian.

Even now.

And always.

No, Benny . . .

"No, Benny!" the boy echoed.

The dog heard them both, the voices of those who loved him, blurring the line between past and present—not with blood and darkness, but with sunlight and warmth.

With a final shake against the horror, the dog turned his back on the pit. He unclamped his jaws and tumbled off the man's body. He stood on shaking limbs.

To the side, the trainer gagged and choked behind his black mask. The father closed in on him with the gun.

The dog limped away, three-legged, one forelimb dangling.

Footsteps approached from behind. The boy appeared at his side and laid a palm on his shoulder. He left his hand resting there. Not afraid.

The dog trembled, then leaned into him, needing reassurance.

And got it.

"Good boy, Benny. Good boy."

The boy sank to his knees and hugged his arms around the dog.

At long last . . . Benny let him.

David Weber

New York Times bestselling author David Weber is frequently compared to C. S. Forester, the creator of Horatio Hornblower, and is one of the most acclaimed authors of military science fiction alive—although he has also written everything from space opera to epic fantasy. He is best known as the author of the long-running series of novels and stories detailing the exploits of Honor Harrington, perhaps the most popular military SF series of all time, consisting of eleven novels, including *On Basilisk Station, The Honor of the Queen, Field of Dishonor, In Enemy Hands, Ashes of Victory,* and others, and the Honor Harrington stories recently collected in *Worlds of Weber: Ms. Midshipwoman Harrington and Other Stories.* In addition, he has allowed other authors to write in the Honor Harrington universe, including S. M. Stirling, Eric Flint, David Drake, Jane Lindskold, and Timothy Zahn. Weber has also written the War God epic fantasy series, consisting of *Oath of Swords, The War God's Own,* and *Wind Rider's Oath,* the four-volume Dahak series, the four-volume Starfire series (with Steve White), the four-volume Empire of Man series (with John Ringo), and the two-volume Assiti Shards series (with Eric Flint), as well as stand-alone novels such as *Path of the Fury, The Apocalypse Troll, The Excalibur Alternative, Old Soldiers,* and *In Fury Born.* His most recent books include the three-volume Safehold series that started in 2007 with *Off Armageddon Reef,* the two-volume Multiverse series (with Linda Evans), the Honor Harrington collection, *Ms. Midshipwoman Harrington,* the new Safehold novel, *By Heresies Distressed,* and *Storm from the Shadows.* David Weber lives in Greenville, South Carolina.

In the complex and suspenseful novella that follows, he shows us a battered and bloodied Earth brought almost to its knees by a ruthless and overwhelming alien invasion, except for some scattered and isolated warriors who aren't comfortable on their knees and undertake the defense of the human race—and, in the process, learn that they have some unexpected resources to call upon in the fight.

Out of the Dark

I

The attention signal whistled on Fleet Commander Thikair's communicator.

He would always remember how prosaic and . . . normal it had sounded, but at that moment, as he looked up from yet another ream of deadly dull paperwork, when he still didn't know, he felt an undeniable sense of relief for the distraction. Then he pressed the acceptance key, and that sense of relief vanished when he recognized his flagship's commander's face . . . and his worried expression.

"What is it, Ahzmer?" he asked, wasting no time on formal greetings.

"Sir, I'm afraid the scout ships have just reported a rather . . . disturbing discovery," Ship Commander Ahzmer replied.

"Yes?" Thikair's ears cocked inquisitively as Ahzmer paused.

"Sir, they're picking up some fairly sophisticated transmissions."

"Transmissions?" For a moment or two, it didn't really register, but then Thikair's eyes narrowed and his pelt bristled. "How sophisticated?" he demanded much more sharply.

"Very, I'm afraid, sir," Ahzmer said unhappily. "We're picking up digital and analog with some impressive bandwidth. It's at least Level Three activity, sir. Possibly even—" Ahzmer's ears flattened. "—Level Two."

Thikair's ears went even flatter than the ship commander's, and he felt the tips of his canines creeping into sight. He shouldn't have let his expression give so much away, but he and Ahzmer had known one another for decades, and it was obvious the other's thoughts had already paralleled his own.

The fleet had reemerged into normal-space two days ago, after eight standard years, subjective, of cryogenic sleep. The flight had lasted some sixteen standard years, by the rest of the galaxy's clocks, since the best velocity modifier even in hyper allowed a speed of no more than five or six times that of light in normal-space terms. The capital ships and transports were still a week of normal-space travel short of the objective, sliding in out of the endless dark like huge, sleek *hasthar*, claws and fangs still hidden, though ready. But he'd sent the much lighter scout ships, whose lower tonnages made their normal-space drives more efficient, ahead to take a closer look at their target. Now he found himself wishing he hadn't.

Stop that, he told himself sternly. *Your ignorance wouldn't have lasted much longer, anyway. And you'd still have to decide what to do. At least this way you have some time to start thinking about it!*

His mind started to work again, and he sat back, one six-fingered hand reaching down to groom his tail while he thought.

The problem was that the Hegemony Council's authorization for this operation was based on the survey team's report that the objective's intelligent species had achieved only a Level Six civilization. The other two systems on Thikair's list were both classified as Level Five civilizations, although one had crept close to the boundary between Level Five and Level Four. It had been hard to get the Council to sign off on those two. Indeed, the need to argue the Shongairi's case so strenuously before the Council was the reason the mission had been delayed long enough to telescope into a three-system operation. But *this* system's "colonization" had been authorized almost as an afterthought, the sort of mission any of the Hegemony's members might have mounted. They'd certainly never agreed to the conquest of a Level Three, far less a *Level Two*! In fact, anything that had attained Level Two came under protectorate status until it attained Level One and became eligible for Hegemony membership in its own right or (as at least half of them managed) destroyed itself first.

Cowards, Thikair thought resentfully. *Dirt-grubbers*. Weed-eaters!

The Shongairi were the only carnivorous species to have attained hypercapability. Almost 40 percent of the Hegemony's other member races were grass-eaters, who regarded the Shongairi's dietary habits as barbarous, revolting, even horrendous. And even most of the Hegemony's omnivores were . . . uncomfortable around Thikair's people.

Their own precious Constitution had forced them to admit the Shongairi when the Empire reached the stars, but they'd never been happy about it. In fact, Thikair had read several learned monographs arguing that his people's existence was simply one of those incredible flukes that (unfortunately, in the obvious opinion of the authors of those monographs) had to happen occasionally. What they *ought* to have done, if they'd had the common decency to follow the example of other species with similarly violent, psychopathically aggressive dispositions, was blow themselves back into the Stone Age as soon as they discovered atomic fission.

Unhappily for those racist bigots, Thikair's people hadn't. Which didn't prevent the Council from regarding them with scant favor. Or from attempting to deny them their legitimate prerogatives.

It's not as if we were the only species to seek colonies. There's the Barthon, and the Kreptu, just for starters. And what about the Liatu? They're grass-eaters, *but they've got over* fifty *colony systems!*

Thikair made himself stop grooming his tail and inhale deeply. Dredging up old resentments wouldn't solve this problem, and if he was going to be completely fair (which he really didn't want to be, especially in the Liatu's case), the fact that they'd been roaming the galaxy for the better part of sixty-two thousand standard years as compared to the Shongairi's nine *hundred* might help to explain at least some of the imbalance.

Besides, that imbalance is going to change, he reminded himself grimly.

There was a reason the Empire had established no less than eleven colonies even before Thikair had departed, and why the Shongari Council representatives had adamantly defended their right to establish those colonies even under the Hegemony's ridiculous restrictions.

No one could deny any race the colonization of any planet with no native sapient species. Unfortunately, there weren't all that many habitable worlds, and they tended to be located bothersomely far apart, even for hyper-capable civilizations. Worse, a depressing number of them already had native sapients living on them. Under the Hegemony Constitution, colonizing *those* worlds required Council approval, which wasn't as easy to come by as it would have been in a more reasonable universe.

Thikair was well aware that many of the Hegemony's other member races believed the Shongairi's "perverted" warlike nature (and even more "perverted" honor codes) explained their readiness to expand through conquest. And, to be honest, they had a point. But the real reason, which was never discussed outside the Empire's inner councils, was that an existing infrastructure, however crude, made the development of a colony faster and easier. And, even more important, the . . . acquisition of less advanced but trainable species provided useful increases in the Empire's labor force. A labor force that—thanks to the Constitution's namby-pamby emphasis on members' internal autonomy—could be kept properly in its place on any planet belonging to the Empire.

And a labor force that was building the sinews of war the Empire would require on the day it told the rest of the Hegemony what it could do with all of its demeaning restrictions.

None of which did much about his current problem.

"You say it's *possibly* a Level Two," he said. "Why do you think that?"

"Given all the EM activity and the sophistication of so many of the signals, the locals are obviously at least Level Three, sir." Ahzmer didn't seem to be getting any happier, Thikair observed. "In fact, preliminary analysis suggests they've already developed fission power—possibly even fusion. But while there are at least *some* fission power sources on the planet, there seem to be very few of them. In fact, most of their power generation seems to come from burning *hydrocarbons*! Why would any civilization that was really Level Two do anything that stupid?"

The fleet commander's ears flattened in a frown. Like the ship commander, he found it difficult to conceive of any species stupid enough to continue consuming irreplaceable resources in hydrocarbon-based power generation if it no longer had to. Ahzmer simply didn't want to admit it, even to himself, because if this genuinely *was* a Level Two civilization, it would be forever off-limits for colonization.

"Excuse me, Sir," Ahzmer said, made bold by his own worries, "but what are we going to do?"

"I can't answer that question just yet, Ship Commander," Thikair replied a bit more formally than usual when it was just the two of them. "But I can tell you what we're *not* going to do, and that's let these reports panic us into any sort of premature conclusions or reactions. We've spent eight years, subjective, to get here, and three months reviving our personnel from cryo. We're not going to simply cross this system off our list and move on to the next one until we've thoroughly considered what we've learned about it and evaluated all of our options. Is that clear?"

"Yes, sir!"

"Good. In the meantime, however, we have to assume we may well be facing surveillance systems considerably in advance of anything we'd anticipated. Under the circumstances, I want the fleet taken to a covert stance. Full-scale emissions control and soft recon mode, Ship Commander."

"Yes, sir. I'll pass the order immediately."

II

Master Sergeant Stephen Buchevsky climbed out of the MRAP, stretched, collected his personal weapon, and nodded to the driver.

"Go find yourself some coffee. I don't really expect this to take very long, but you know how good I am at predicting things like that."

"Gotcha, Top," the corporal behind the wheel agreed with a grin. He stepped on the gas and the MRAP (officially the Mine Resistant Ambush Protection vehicle) moved away, headed for the mess tent at the far end of the position, while Buchevsky started hiking toward the sandbagged command bunker perched on top of the sharp-edged ridge.

The morning air was thin and cold, but less than two weeks from the end of his current deployment, Buchevsky was used to that. It wasn't exactly as if it was the first time he'd been here, either. And while many of Bravo Company's Marines considered it the armpit of the universe, Buchevsky had seen substantially worse during the seventeen years since he'd taken a deceitfully honest-faced recruiter at his word.

"Oh, the places you'll go—the things you'll see!" the recruiter in question had told him enthusiastically. And Stephen Buchevsky had indeed been places and seen things since. Along the way, he'd been wounded in action no less than six times, and, at age thirty-five, his marriage had just finished coming rather messily unglued, mostly over the issue of lengthy, repeat deployments. He walked with a slight limp the therapists hadn't been able to completely eradicate, the ache in his right hand was a faithful predictor of rain or snow, and the scar that curved up his left temple was clearly visible through his buzz-cut hair, especially against his dark skin. But while he sometimes entertained fantasies about looking up the recruiter who'd gotten him to sign on the dotted line, he'd always reupped.

Which probably says something unhealthy about my personality, he reflected as he paused to gaze down at the narrow twisting road far below.

On his first trip to sunny Afghanistan, he'd spent his time at Camp Rhine down near Kandahar. That was when he'd acquired the limp, too. For the next deployment, he'd been located up near Ghanzi, helping to keep an eye on the A01 highway from Kandahar to Kabul. That had been less . . . interesting than his time in Kandahar Province, although he'd still managed to take a rocket splinter in the ass, which had been good for another gold star on the purple heart ribbon (and unmerciful "humor" from his so-called friends). But then the Poles had taken over in Ghanzi, and so, for his *third* Afghanistan deployment, he and the rest of First Battalion, Third Marine Regiment, Third Marine Division, had been sent back to Kandahar, where things had been heating up again. They'd stayed there, too . . . until they'd gotten new orders, at least. The situation in Paktika Province—the one the Poles had turned down in favor of Ghanzi because Paktika was so much more lively—had also worsened, and Buchevsky and Bravo Company had been tasked as backup for the battalion of the Army's 508th Parachute Infantry in the area while the Army tried to pry loose some of its own people for the job.

Despite all of the emphasis on "jointness," it hadn't made for the smoothest relationship imaginable. The fact that everyone recognized it as a stopgap and Bravo as only temporary visitors (they'd been due to deploy back to the States in less than three months when they got the call) didn't help, either. They'd arrived without the logistic support which would normally have accompanied them, and despite the commonality of so much of their equipment, that had still put an additional strain on the 508th's supply services. But the Army types had been glad enough to see them and they'd done their best to make the "jarheads" welcome.

The fact that the Vermont-sized province shared six hundred miles of border with Pakistan, coupled with the political changes in Pakistan and an upsurge in opium production under the Taliban's auspices (odd how the fundamentalists' one-time bitter opposition to the trade had vanished now that they needed cash to support their operations), had prevented Company B from feeling bored. Infiltration and stepped-up attacks on the still shaky Afghan Army units in the province hadn't helped, although all things considered, Buchevsky preferred Paktika to his 2004 deployment to Iraq. Or his most recent trip to Kandahar, for that matter.

Now he looked down through the thin mountain air at the twisting trail Second Platoon was here to keep a close eye on. All the fancy recon assets in the world couldn't provide the kind of constant presence and eyes-on surveillance needed to interdict traffic through a place like this. It was probably easier than the job Buchevsky's father had faced trying to cut the Ho Chi Minh Trail—at least his people could see a lot farther!—but that wasn't saying very much, all things taken together. And he didn't recall his dad's mentioning anything about lunatic martyrs out to blow people up in job lots for the glory of God.

He gave himself a shake. He had a lot on his plate organizing the Company's rotation home, and he turned back toward the command bunker to inform Gunnery Sergeant Wilson that his platoon's Army relief would begin arriving within forty-eight hours. It was time to get the turnover organized and Second Platoon back to its FOB to participate in all the endless paperwork and equipment checks involved in any company movement.

Not that Buchevsky expected anyone to complain about *this* move.

III

The gathering in *Star of Empire*'s conference room consisted of Thikair's three squadron commanders, his ground force commander, and Base Commander Shairez. Despite the fact that Shairez was technically junior to Ground Force Commander Thairys, she was the expedition's senior base commander, and as such, she, too, reported directly to Thikair.

Rumors about the scout ships' findings had spread, of course. It would have required divine intervention to prevent that! Still, if it turned out there was no landing after all, it would scarcely matter, would it?

"What is your interpretation of the scout ships' data, Base Commander?" Thikair asked Shairez without bothering to call the meeting formally to order. Most of them seemed surprised by his disregard for protocol, and Shairez didn't look especially pleased to be the first person called upon. But she could scarcely have been surprised by the question itself; the reason she was the expedition's senior base commander was her expertise in dealing with other sapient species, after all.

"I've considered the data, including that from the stealthed orbital platforms, carefully, Fleet Commander," she replied. "I'm afraid my analysis confirms Ship Commander Ahzmer's original fears. I would definitely rate the local civilization at Level Two."

Unhappy at being called upon or not, she hadn't flinched, Thikair thought approvingly.

"Expand upon that, please," he said.

"Yes, sir." Shairez tapped the virtual clawpad of her personal computer and her eyes unfocused slightly as she gazed at the memos projected directly upon her retinas.

"First, sir, this species has developed nuclear power. Of course, their technology is extremely primitive, and it would appear they're only beginning to experiment with fusion, but there are significant indications that their general tech level is much more capable than we would ever anticipate out of anyone with such limited nuclear capacity. Apparently, for some reason known only to themselves, these people—I use the term loosely, of course—have chosen to cling to hydrocarbon-fueled power generation well past the point at which they could have replaced it with nuclear generation."

"That's absurd!" Squadron Commander Jainfar objected. The crusty old space dog was Thikair's senior squadron commander and as bluntly uncompromising as one of his dreadnoughts' main batteries. Now he grimaced as Thikair glanced at him, one ear cocked interrogatively.

"Apologies, Base Commander," the squadron commander half growled. "I don't doubt your data. I just find it impossible to believe any species *that* stupid could figure out how to use fire in the first place!"

"It *is* unique in our experience, Squadron Commander," Shairez acknowledged. "And according to the master data banks, it's also unique in the experience of every other member of the Hegemony. Nonetheless, they do possess virtually all of the other attributes of a Level Two culture."

She raised one hand, ticking off points on her claws as she continued.

"They have planetwide telecommunications. Although they've done little to truly exploit space, they have numerous communications and navigational satellites. Their military aircraft are capable of trans-sonic flight regimes, they make abundant use of advanced—well, advanced for any pre-Hegemony culture—composites, and we've observed experiments with early-generation directed energy weapons, as well. Their technological capabilities are *not* distributed uniformly about their planet, but they're spreading rapidly. I would be very surprised—assuming they survive—if they haven't evolved an effectively unified planetary government within the next two or three generations. Indeed, they might manage it even sooner, if their ridiculous rate of technological advancement is any guide!"

The silence around the conference table was profound. Thikair let it linger for several moments, then leaned back in his chair.

"How would you account for the discrepancy between what we're now observing and the initial survey report?"

"Sir, I *can't* account for it," she said frankly. "I've doublechecked and triplechecked the original report. There's no question that it was accurate at the time it was made, yet now we find *this*. Somehow, this species has made the jump from animal transport, wind power, and crude firearms to this level more than three times as rapidly as any other species. And please note that I said '*any* other species.' The one I had in mind were the Ugartu."

The fleet commander saw more than one grimace at that. The Ugartu had never attained Hegemony membership . . . since they'd turned their home star system into a radioactive junkyard first. The Council of the time had breathed a quiet but very, very profound sigh of relief when it happened, too, given that the Ugartu had been advancing technologically at twice the galactic norm. Which meant *these* people . . .

"Is it possible the initial survey team broke procedure, sir?" Ship Commander Ahzmer asked, his expression troubled. Thikair glanced at him, and his flagship's commander flicked both ears. "I'm just wondering if the surveyors might inadvertently have made direct contact with the locals? Accidentally given them a leg up?"

"Possible, but unlikely, Ship Commander," Ground Force Commander Thairys said. "I wish I didn't have to say that, since I find this insanely rapid advancement just as disturbing as you do. Unfortunately, the original survey was conducted by the Barthonii."

Several of Thikair's officers looked as if they'd just smelled something unpleasant. Actually, from the perspective of any self-respecting carnivore, the Barthonii smelled simply delicious, but the timid plant-eaters were one of the Shongairi's most severe critics. And they were also heavily represented in the Hegemony's survey forces, despite their inherent timidity, because of their fanatic support for the Council regulations limiting contact with inferior races.

"I'm afraid I agree with the Ground Force Commander," Shairez said.

"And it wouldn't matter if that *were* what had happened," Thikair pointed out. "The Constitution doesn't care where a species' technology *came* from. What matters is the level it's *attained*, however it got there"

"And the way the Council will react to it," Jainfar said sourly, and ears moved in agreement all around the table.

"I'm afraid Squadron Commander Jainfar has a point, sir." Thairys sighed heavily. "It was hard enough getting approval for our other objectives, and they're far less advanced than *these* people have turned out to be. Or I hope to Dainthar's Hounds they still are, at any rate!"

More ears waved agreement, Thikair's among them. However aberrant, this species' development clearly put it well outside the parameters of the Council's authorization. However . . .

"I'm well aware of just how severely our discoveries have altered the circumstances envisioned by our mission orders," he said. "On the other hand, there are a few additional points I believe bear consideration."

Most of them looked at him with obvious surprise, but Thairys' tail curled up over the back of his chair and his ears flattened in speculation.

"First, one of the points I noticed when I reviewed the first draft of Base Commander Shairez's report was that these people not only have remarkably few nuclear power stations, but for a species of their level, they also have remarkably few nuclear *weapons*. Only their major political powers seem to have them in any quantity, and even they have very limited numbers, compared to their non-nuclear capabilities. Of course, they *are* omnivores, but the numbers of weapons are still strikingly low. Lower even than for many weed-eaters at a comparable level. That becomes particularly apparent given the fact that there are fairly extensive military operations under way over much of the planet. In particular, several more advanced nation-states are conducting operations against adversaries who obviously don't even approach their own capabilities. Yet even though those advanced—I'm speaking relatively, of course—nation-states have nuclear arsenals and their opponents, who do not, would be incapable of retaliation, they've chosen not to employ them. Not only that, but they must have at least some ability to produce bio-weapons, yet we've seen no evidence of their use. For that matter, we haven't even poison gas or neurotoxins!"

He let that settle in, then leaned forward once more to rest his folded hands on the conference table.

"This would appear to be a highly peculiar species in several respects," he said quietly. "Their failure to utilize the most effective weapons available to them, however, suggests that they're almost as lacking in . . . military pragmatism as many of the Hegemony's weed-eaters. That being the case, I find myself of the opinion that they might well make a suitable . . . client species, after all."

The silence in the conference room was absolute as the rest of Thikair's listeners began to realize what Thairys had already guessed.

"I realize," the Fleet Commander continued, "that to proceed with this operation would violate the spirit of the Council's authorization. However, after careful review, I've discovered that it contains no specific reference to the attained level of the local sapients. In other words, the *letter* of the authorizing writ wouldn't preclude our continuing. No doubt someone like the Barthonii or Liatu still might choose to make a formal stink afterwards, but consider the possible advantages."

"Advantages, sir?" Ahzmer asked, and Thikair's eyes gleamed.

"Oh, yes, Ship Commander," he said softly. "This species may be bizarre in many ways, and they obviously don't understand the realities of war, but clearly something about them has supported a phenomenal rate of advancement. I realize their actual capabilities would require a rather more . . . vigorous initial strike than we'd anticipated. And even with heavier pre-landing preparation, our casualties might well be somewhat higher than projected, but, fortunately, we have ample redundancy for dealing even with this sort of target, thanks to our follow-on objectives in Syk and Jormau. We have ample capability to conquer any planet-bound civilization, even if it has attained Level Two, and, to be honest, I think it would be very much worthwhile to concentrate on this system even if it means writing off the seizure of one—or even both—of the others."

One or two of them looked as if they wanted to protest, but he flattened his ears, his voice even softer.

"I realize how that may sound, but think about this. Suppose we were able to integrate these people—these 'humans'—into our labor force. Put them to work on *our* research projects. Suppose we were able to leverage their talent for that sort of thing to quietly push our own tech level to something significantly in *advance* of the rest of the Hegemony? How do you think that would ultimately affect the Emperor's plans and schedule?"

The silence was just as complete, but it was totally different now, and he smiled thinly.

"It's been three centuries—over five hundred of these people's years—since the Hegemony's first contact with them. If the Hegemony operates to its usual schedule, it will be at least two more centuries—almost four hundred local years—before any non-Shongairi observation team reaches this system again . . . and that will be counting from the point at which we return to announce our success. If we delay that return for a few decades, even as much as a century or so, it's unlikely anyone would be particularly surprised, given that they expect us to be gathering in three entire star systems." He snorted harshly. "In fact, it would probably *amuse* the weed-eaters to think we'd found the operation more difficult than anticipated! But if we chose instead to spend that time subjugating these "humans" and then educating their young to Hegemony standards, who knows what sort of R & D they might accomplish before that happens?"

"The prospect is exciting, sir," Thairys said slowly. "Yet I fear it rests upon speculations whose accuracy can't be tested without proceeding. If it should happen that they prove less accurate than hoped for, we would have, as you say, violated the spirit of the Council's authorizing writ for little return. Personally, I believe you may well be correct and that the possibility should clearly be investigated. Yet if the result is less successful than we might wish, would we not risk exposing the Empire to retaliation from other members of the Hegemony?"

"A valid point," Thikair acknowledged. "First, however, the Emperor would be able to insist—truthfully—that the decision was mine, not his, and that he never authorized anything of the sort. I believe it's most probable the Hegemony Judiciary would settle for penalizing me, as an individual, rather than recommending retaliation against the Empire generally. Of course, it's possible some of you, as my senior officers, might suffer, as well. On the other hand, I believe the risk would be well worth taking and would ultimately redound to the honor of our clans.

"There is, however, always another possibility. The Council won't expect a Level Three or Level Two civilization any more than we did. If it turns out after a local century or so that these 'humans' aren't working out, the simplest solution may well be to simply exterminate them and destroy enough of their cities and installations to conceal the level of technology they'd actually attained before our arrival. It would, of course, be dreadfully unfortunate if one of our carefully focused and limited bio-weapons somehow mutated into something which swept the entire surface of the planet with a lethal plague, but, as we all know," he bared his canines in a smile, "accidents sometimes happen."

IV

It was unfortunate international restrictions on the treatment of POWs didn't also apply to what could be done to someone's own personnel, Stephen Buchevsky reflected as he failed—again—to find a comfortable way to sit in the mil-spec "seat" in the big C-17 Globemaster's Spartan belly. If *he'd* been a jihadi, he'd have spilled his guts within an hour if they strapped him into one of these!

Actually, he supposed a lot of the problem stemmed from his six feet and four inches of height and the fact that he was built more like an offensive lineman than like a basketball player. Nothing short of a first-class commercial seat was really going to fit someone his size, and expecting the U.S. military to fly an E-9 commercial first-class would have been about as realistic as his expecting to be drafted as a presidential nominee. Or perhaps even a bit less realistic. And, if he wanted to be honest, he should also admit that what he disliked even more was the absence of windows. There was something about spending hours sealed in an alloy tube while it vibrated its noisy way through the sky that made him feel not just enclosed, but trapped.

Well, Stevie, he told himself, *if you're that unhappy, you could always ask the pilot to let you off to* swim *the rest of the way!*

The thought made him chuckle, and he checked his watch. Kandahar to Aviano, Italy, was roughly three thousand miles, which exceeded the C-17's normal range by a couple of hundred miles. Fortunately—although that might not be *exactly* the right word for it—he'd caught a rare flight returning to the States almost empty. The Air Force needed the big bird badly somewhere, so they wanted it home in the shortest possible time, and with additional fuel and a payload of only thirty or forty people, it could make the entire Kandahar-to-Aviano leg without refueling. Which meant he could look forward to a six-hour flight, assuming they didn't hit any unfavorable winds.

He would have preferred to make the trip with the rest of his people, but he'd ended up dealing with the final paperwork for the return of the Company's equipment. Just another of those happy little chores that fell the way of its senior noncom. On the other hand, and despite the less-than-luxurious accommodations aboard his aerial chariot, his total transit time would be considerably shorter, thanks to this flight's fortuitous availability. And one thing he'd learned to do during his years of service was to sleep anywhere, anytime.

Even here, he thought, squirming into what he could convince himself was a marginally more comfortable position and closing his eyes. *Even here.*

The sudden, violent turn to starboard yanked Buchevsky up out of his doze, and he started to shove himself upright in his uncomfortable seat as the turn became even steeper. The redoubled, rumbling whine from the big transport's engines told him the pilot had increased power radically as well, and every one of his instincts told him he wouldn't like the reason for all of that if he'd known what it was.

Which didn't keep him from wanting to know anyway. In fact—

"Listen up, everybody!" A harsh, strain-flattened voice rasped over the aircraft's intercom. "We've got a little problem, and we're diverting from Aviano, 'cause Aviano isn't *there* anymore."

Buchevsky's eyes widened. Surely whoever it was on the other end of the intercom had to be joking, his mind tried to insist. But he knew better. There was too much stark shock—and fear—in that voice.

"I don't know what the fuck is going on," the pilot continued. "We've lost our long-ranged comms, but we're getting reports on the civilian bands about low-yield nukes going off all over the goddamned place. From what we're picking up, someone's kicking the shit out of Italy, Austria, Spain, and every NATO base in the entire Med, and—"

The voice broke off for a moment, and Buchevsky heard the harsh sound of an explosively cleared throat. Then—

"And we've got an unconfirmed report that Washington is gone, people. Just fucking *gone.*"

Something kicked Buchevsky in the belly. Not Washington. Washington *couldn't* be gone. Not with Trish and the girls—

"I don't have a goddammed clue who's doing this, or why," the pilot said, "but we need someplace to set down, fast. We're about eighty miles north-northwest of Podgorica, in Montenegro, so I'm diverting inland. Let's hope to hell I can find someplace to put this bird down in one piece . . . and that nobody on the ground thinks *we* had anything to do with this shit!"

V

Thikair stood on *Star of Empire*'s flag bridge, studying the gigantic images of the planet below. Glowing icons indicated cities and major military bases his kinetic bombardment had removed from existence. There were a lot of them—more than he'd really counted on—and he clasped his hands behind him and concentrated on radiating total satisfaction.

And you damned well ought *to be satisfied, Thikair. Taking down an entire Level Two civilization in less than two local days has to be some sort of galactic record!*

Which, another little voice reminded him, was because doing anything of the sort directly violated the Hegemony Constitution.

He managed not to grimace, but it wasn't easy. When this brilliant brainstorm had occurred to him, he hadn't fully digested just how big and thoroughly inhabited this planet, this . . . "Earth" of the "humans," truly was. He wondered now if he hadn't let himself fully digest it because he'd known that if he had, he would have changed his mind.

Oh stop it! *So there were more of them on the damned planet, and you killed—what? Two billion of them, wasn't it? There're plenty more where they came from—they* breed *like damned* garshu, *after all! And you told Ahzmer and the others you're willing to kill off the entire* species *if it doesn't work out. So fretting about a little extra breakage along the way is pretty pointless, wouldn't you say?*

Of course it was. In fact, he admitted, his biggest concern was how many major engineering works these humans had created. There was no question that he could exterminate them if he had to, but he was beginning to question whether it would be possible to eliminate the physical evidence of the level their culture had attained after all.

Well, we'll just have to keep it from coming to that, won't we?.

"Pass the word to Ground Commander Thairys," he told Ship Commander Ahzmer quietly, never taking his eyes from those glowing icons. "I want his troops on the ground as quickly as possible. And make sure they have all the fire support they need."

———

Steven Buchevsky stood by the road and wondered—again—just where the hell they were.

Their pilot hadn't managed to find any friendly airfields, after all. He'd done his best, but all but out of fuel, with his communications out, the GPS network down, and kiloton-range explosions dotting the face of Europe, his options had been limited. He'd managed to find a stretch of two-lane road that would almost do, and he'd set the big plane down with his last few gallons of fuel.

The C-17 had been designed for rough-field landings, although its designers hadn't had anything quite that rough in mind. Still, it would have worked if the road hadn't crossed a culvert he hadn't been able to see from the air. He'd lost both main gear when it collapsed under the plane's 140-ton weight. Worse, he hadn't lost the gear simultaneously, and the aircraft had gone totally out of control. When it stopped careening across the rough, mountainous valley, the entire forward fuselage had become crushed and tangled wreckage.

Neither pilot had survived, and the only other two officers aboard were among the six passengers who'd been killed, which left Buchevsky the ranking member of their small group. Two more passengers were brutally injured, and he'd gotten them out of the wreckage and into the best shelter he could contrive, but they didn't have anything resembling a doctor.

Neither did they have much in the way of equipment. Buchevsky had his personal weapons, as did six of the others, but that was it, and none of them had very much ammunition. Not surprisingly, he supposed, since they weren't supposed to have *any* on board. Fortunately (in this case, at least) it was extraordinarily difficult to separate troops returning from a combat zone from at least *some* ammo.

There were also at least some first-aid supplies—enough to set the broken arms three of the passengers suffered and make at least a token attempt at patching up the worst injured—but that was about it, and he really, really wished he could at least *talk* to somebody higher up the command hierarchy than he was. Unfortunately, he was it.

Which, he thought mordantly, *at least it gives me something to keep me busy.*

And it also gave him something besides Washington to worry about. He'd argued with Trish when his ex decided to take Shania and Yvonne to live with her mother, but that had been because of the crime rate and cost of living in D.C. He'd never, *ever*, worried about—

He pushed that thought aside, again, fleeing almost gratefully back to the contemplation of the clusterfuck he had to deal with somehow.

Gunnery Sergeant Calvin Meyers was their group's second-ranking member, which made him Buchevsky's XO . . . to the obvious disgruntlement of Sergeant Francisco Ramirez, the senior Army noncom. But if Ramirez resented the fact that they'd just become a Marine-run show, he was keeping his mouth shut. Probably because he recognized what an unmitigated pain in the ass Buchevsky's job had just become.

They had a limited quantity of food, courtesy of the aircraft's overwater survival package, but none of them had any idea of their exact position, no one spoke Serbian (assuming they were *in* Serbia), they had no maps, they were totally out of communication, and the last they'd heard, the entire planet seemed to be succumbing to spontaneous insanity.

Aside from that, it ought to be a piece of cake, he reflected sardonically. *Of course—*

"I think you'd better listen to this, Top," a voice said, and Buchevsky turned toward the speaker.

"Listen to what, Gunny?"

"We're getting something really weird on the radio, Top."

Buchevsky's eyes narrowed. He'd never actually met Meyers before this flight, but the compact, strongly built, slow-talking Marine from the Appalachian coal fields had struck him as a solid, unflappable sort. At the moment, however, Meyers was pasty-pale, and his hands shook as he extended the emergency radio they'd recovered from the wrecked fuselage.

Meyers turned the volume back up, and Buchevsky's eyes narrowed even further. The voice coming from the radio sounded . . . mechanical. Artificial. It carried absolutely no emotions or tonal emphasis.

That was the first thing that struck him. Then he jerked back half a step, as if he'd just been punched, as what the voice was *saying* registered.

"—am Fleet Commander Thikair of the Shongairi Empire, and I am addressing your entire planet on all frequencies. Your world lies helpless before us. Our kinetic energy weapons have destroyed your major national capitals, your military bases, your warships. We can, and will, conduct additional kinetic strikes wherever necessary. You will submit and become productive and obedient subjects of the Empire, or you will be destroyed, as your governments and military forces have already been destroyed."

Buchevsky stared at the radio, his mind cowering back from the black, bottomless pit that yawned suddenly where his family once had been. Trish. . . . Despite the divorce, she'd still been an almost physical part of him. And Shania . . . Yvonne. . . . Shannie was only *six*, for God's sake! Yvonne was even younger. It wasn't possible. It couldn't have happened. *It couldn't!*

The mechanical-sounding English ceased. There was a brief surge of something that sounded like Chinese, and then it switched to Spanish.

"It's saying the same thing it just said in English," Sergeant Ramirez said flatly, and Buchevsky shook himself. He closed his eyes tightly, squeezing them against the tears he would not—could not—shed. That dreadful abyss loomed inside him, trying to suck him under, and part of him wanted nothing else in the world but to let the undertow take him. But he couldn't. He had responsibilities. The job.

"Do you *believe* this shit, Top?" Meyers said hoarsely.

"I don't know," Buchevsky admitted. His own voice came out sounding broken and rusty, and he cleared his throat harshly. "I don't know," he managed in a more normal-sounding tone. "Or, at least, I know I don't *want* to believe it, Gunny."

"Me neither," another voice said. This one was a soprano, and it belonged to Staff Sergeant Michelle Truman, the Air Force's senior surviving representative. Buchevsky raised an eyebrow at her, grateful for the additional distraction from the pain trying to tear the heart right out of him, and the auburn-haired staff sergeant grimaced.

"I don't want to believe it," she said, "but think about it. We already knew somebody's seemed to've been blowing the shit out of just about everybody. And who the hell had that many nukes?" She shook her head. "I'm no expert on kinetic weapons, but I've read a little science fiction, and I'd say an orbital kinetic strike would probably look just like a nuke to the naked eye. So, yeah, probably if this bastard is telling the truth, nukes are exactly what any survivors would've been reporting."

"Oh, *shit*," Meyers muttered, then looked back at Buchevsky. He didn't say another word, but he didn't have to, and Buchevsky drew a deep breath.

"I don't know, Gunny," he said again. "I just don't know."

————

He still didn't know—not really—the next morning, but one thing they *couldn't* do was simply huddle here. They'd seen no sign of any traffic along the road the C-17 had destroyed. Roads normally went *somewhere*, though, so if they followed this one long enough, "somewhere" was where they'd eventually wind up—hopefully before they ran out of food. And at least his decision trees had been rather brutally simplified when the last two badly injured passengers died during the night.

He tried hard not to feel grateful for that, but he was guiltily aware that it would have been dishonest, even if he'd managed to succeed.

Come on. You're not grateful they're dead, *Stevie,* he told himself grimly. *You're just grateful they won't be slowing the rest of you down. There's a difference.*

He even knew it was true . . . which didn't make him feel any better. And neither did the fact that he'd put his wife's and daughters' faces into a small mental box and locked them away, buried the pain deep enough to let him deal with his responsibilities to the living. Someday, he knew, he would have to reopen that box. Endure the pain, admit the loss. But not now. Not yet. For now he could tell himself others depended upon him, that he had to put aside his own pain while he dealt with *their* needs, and he wondered if that made him a coward.

"Ready to move out, Top," Meyers's voice said behind him, and he looked over his shoulder.

"All right," he said out loud, trying hard to radiate the confidence he was far from feeling. "In that case, I guess we should be going."

Now if I only had some damned idea where *we're going.*

VI

Platoon Commander Yirku stood in the open hatch of his command ground effect vehicle as his armored platoon sped down the long, broad roadway that stabbed straight through the mountains. The bridges that crossed the main roadbed at intervals, especially as the platoon approached what were (or had been) towns or cities, forced his column to squeeze in on itself, but overall, Yirku was delighted. His tanks' grav-cushions couldn't care less what surface lay under them, but that didn't protect their crews from seasickness if they had to move rapidly across rough ground, and he'd studied the survey reports with care. He'd rather glumly anticipated operating across wilderness terrain that might be crossed here and there by "roads" which were little more than random animal tracks.

Despite his relief at avoiding that unpleasantness, Yirku admitted (very privately) that he found these "humans'" infrastructure . . . unsettling. There was so *much* of it, especially in areas that had belonged to nations, like this "United States." And, crude though its construction might appear, most of it was well laid out. The fact that they'd managed to construct so much of it, so well suited to their current technology level's requirements, was sobering, too, and—

Platoon Leader Yirku's thoughts broke off abruptly as he emerged from under the latest bridge and the fifteen-pound round from the M-136 light anti-armor weapon struck the side of his vehicle's turret at a velocity of 360 feet per second. Its HEAT warhead produced a hyper-velocity gas jet that carved through the GEV's light armor like an incandescent dagger, and the resultant internal explosion disemboweled the tank effortlessly.

Ten more rockets stabbed down into the embankment-enclosed cut of Interstate 81 almost simultaneously, and eight of them found their targets, exploding like thunderbolts. Each of them killed another GEV, and the humans who'd launched them had deliberately concentrated on the front and back edges of the platoon's neat road column. Despite their grav-cushions, the four survivors of Yirku's platoon were temporarily trapped behind the blazing, exploding carcasses of their fellows. They were still there when the next quartet of rockets came sizzling in.

The ambushers—a scratch-built pickup team of Tennessee National Guardsmen, all of them veterans of deployments to Iraq or Afghanistan— were on the move, filtering back into the trees almost before the final Shongairi tank had exploded.

Company Commander Kirtha's column of transports rumbled along in a hanging cloud of dust, which made him grateful his GEV command vehicle was hermetically sealed. Now if only he'd been assigned to one of the major bases on the continent called "America," or at least the western fringes of *this* one!

It wouldn't be so bad if they were all *grav-cushion,* he told himself, watching the wheeled vehicles through the smothering fog of dust. But GEVs were expensive, and the counter-grav generators used up precious internal volume not even troop carriers could afford to give away. Imperial wheeled vehicles had excellent off-road capability, but even a miserable so-called road like this one allowed them to move much more efficiently.

And at least we're out in the middle of nice, flat ground as far as the eye can see, Kirtha reminded himself. He didn't like the rumors about ambushes on isolated detachments. That wasn't supposed to happen, especially from someone as effortlessly and utterly defeated as these "humans" had been. And even if it did happen, it wasn't supposed to be *effective.* And the ones responsible for it were supposed to be destroyed.

Which, if the rumors were accurate, wasn't happening the way it was supposed to. *Some* of the attackers were being spotted and destroyed, but with Hegemony technology, *all* of them should have been wiped out, and they weren't being. Still, there were no convenient mountainsides or thick belts of forest to hide attackers out here in the midst of these endless, flat fields of grain, and—

Captain Pieter Stefanovich Ushakov of the Ukrainian Army watched through his binoculars with pitiless satisfaction as the entire alien convoy and its escort of tanks disappeared in a fiery wave of destruction two kilometers long. The scores of 120 mm mortar rounds buried in the road as his own version of the "improvised explosive devices," which had given the Americans such grief in Iraq, had proved quite successful, he thought coldly.

Now, he thought, *to see exactly how these weasels respond.*

He was fully aware of the risks in remaining in the vicinity, but he needed some understanding of the aliens' capabilities and doctrine, and the only way to get that was to see what they did. He was confident he'd piled enough earth on top of his position to conceal any thermal signature, and he was completely unarmed, with no ferrous metal on his person, which would hopefully defeat any magnetic detectors. So unless they used some sort of deep-scan radar, he ought to be *relatively* safe from detection.

And even if it turned out he wasn't, his entire family had been in Kiev when the kinetic strikes hit.

———

Colonel Nicolae Basescu sat in the commander's hatch of his T-72M1, his mind wrapped around a curiously empty, singing silence, and waited.

The first prototype of his tank—the export model of the Russian T-72A—had been completed in 1970, four years before Basescu's own birth, and it had become sadly outclassed by more modern, more deadly designs. It was still superior to the Romanian Army's home-built TR-85s, based on the even more venerable T-55, but that wasn't saying much compared with designs like the Russians' T-80s and T-90s, or the Americans' M1A2.

And it's certainly *not saying much compared with aliens who can actually travel between the stars*, Basescu thought.

Unfortunately, it was all he had. Now if he only knew what he was supposed to be doing with the seven tanks of his scraped-up command.

Stop that, he told himself sternly. *You're an officer of the Romanian Army. You know* exactly *what you're supposed to be doing.*

He gazed through the opening a few minutes' work with an ax had created. His tanks were as carefully concealed as he could manage inside the industrial buildings across the frontage road from the hundred-meter-wide Mureş River. The two lanes of the E-81 highway crossed the river on a double-span cantilever bridge, flanked on the east by a rail bridge, two kilometers southwest of Alba iulia, the capital of Alba *judeţ*. The city of eighty thousand—the city where Michael the Brave had achieved the first union of the three great provinces of Romania in 1599—was two-thirds empty, and Basescu didn't like to think about what those fleeing civilians were going to do when they started running out of whatever supplies they'd managed to snatch up in their flight. But he didn't blame them for running. Not when their city was barely 270 kilometers northwest of where Bucharest had been four and a half days ago.

He wished he dared to use his radios, but the broadcasts from the alien commander suggested that any transmissions would be unwise. Fortunately, at least some of the land lines were still up. He doubted they would be for much longer, but enough remained for him to know about the alien column speeding up the highway toward him . . . and Alba iulia.

Company Commander Barmit punched up his navigation systems, but they were being cantankerous again, and he muttered a quiet yet heartfelt curse as he jabbed at the control panel a second time.

As far as he was concerned, the town ahead of him was scarcely large enough to merit the attention of two entire companies of infantry, even if Base Commander Shairez's pre-bombardment analysis *had* identified it as some sort of administrative subcenter. Its proximity to what had been a national capital suggested to Barmit's superiors that it had probably been sufficiently important to prove useful as a headquarters for the local occupation forces. Personally, Barmit suspected the reverse was more likely true. An administrative center this close to something the size of that other city—"Bucharest," or something equally outlandish—was more likely to be lost in the capital's shadow than functioning as any sort of important secondary brain.

Too bad Ground Force Commander Thairys didn't ask for my opinion, he thought dryly, still jabbing at the recalcitrant display.

The imagery finally came up and stabilized, and his ears flicked in a grimace as it confirmed his memory. He keyed his com.

"All right," he said. "We're coming up on another river, and our objective's just beyond that. We'll take the bridge in a standard road column, but let's not take chances. Red Section, you spread left. White section, we'll spread right."

Acknowledgments came back, and he reconfigured the display from navigation to tactical.

Colonel Basescu twitched upright as the alien vehicles came into sight. He focused his binoculars, snapping the approaching vehicles into much sharper clarity, and a part of him was almost disappointed by how unremarkable they appeared. How . . . mundane.

Most of them were some sort of wheeled transport vehicles, with a boxy sort of look that made him think of armored personnel carriers. There were around thirty of those, and it was obvious they were being escorted by five other vehicles.

He shifted his attention to those escorts and stiffened as he realized just how un-mundane *they* were. They sped along, sleek-looking and dark, hovering perhaps a meter or two above the ground, and some sort of long, slender gunbarrels projected from their boxy-looking turrets.

The approaching formation slowed as the things that were probably APCs began forming into a column of twos under the watchful eye of the things that were probably tanks, and he lowered the binoculars and picked up the handset for the field telephone he'd had strung between the tanks once they'd maneuvered into their hides.

"Mihai," he told his second section commander, "we'll take the tanks. Radu, I want you and Matthius to concentrate on the transports. Don't fire until Mihai and I do—then try to jam them up on the bridge."

Barmit felt his ears relaxing in satisfaction as the wheeled vehicles settled into column and his GEVs headed across the river, watching its flanks. The drop from the roadbed to the surface of the water had provided the usual "stomach left behind" sensation, but once they were actually out over the water, its motion became glassy-smooth as he led White Section's other two GEVs between the small islands in the center of the river, idling along to keep pace with the transports.

They may have magic tanks, but they don't have very good doctrine, do they? a corner of Basescu's brain reflected. They hadn't so much as bothered to send any scouts across, or even to leave one of their tanks on the far bank in an overwatch position. Not that he intended to complain.

The tank turret slewed slowly to the right as his gunner tracked his chosen target, but Basescu was watching the wheeled vehicles. The entire bridge was barely 150 meters long, and he wanted all of them actually onto it, if he could arrange it.

Company Commander Barmit sighed as his GEV approached the far bank. Climbing up out of the riverbed again was going to be rather less pleasant, and he slowed deliberately, prolonging the smoothness as he watched the transports heading across the bridge.

Kind of the "humans" to build us all these nice highways, he reflected, thinking about this region's heavily forested mountains. *It would be a real pain to—*

"Fire!" Nicolae Basescu barked, and Company Commander Barmit's ruminations were terminated abruptly by the arrival of a nineteen-kilogram

3BK29 HEAT round capable of penetrating three hundred millimeters of armor at a range of two kilometers.

Basescu felt a stab of exhilaration as the tank bucked, the outer wall of its concealing building disappeared in the fierce muzzle blast of its 2A46 120 mm main gun, and his target exploded. Three of the other four escort tanks were first-round kills, as well, crashing into the river in eruptions of fire, white spray, and smoke, and the stub of the semi-combustible cartridge case ejected from the gun. The automatic loader's carousel picked up the next round, feeding the separate projectile and cartridge into the breech, and his carefully briefed commanders were engaging targets without any additional orders from him.

The surviving alien tank swerved crazily sideways, turret swiveling madly, and then Basescu winced as it fired.

He didn't know what it was armed with, but it wasn't like any cannon *he'd* ever seen. A bar of solid light spat from the end of its "gun," and the building concealing his number three tank exploded. But even as the alien tank fired, two more 120 mm rounds slammed into it almost simultaneously.

It died as spectacularly as its fellows had, and Radu and Matthias hadn't exactly been sitting on their hands. They'd done exactly what he wanted, nailing both the leading and rearmost of the wheeled transports only after they were well out onto the bridge. The others were trapped there, sitting ducks, unable to maneuver, and his surviving tanks walked their fire steadily along their column.

At least some of the aliens managed to bail out of their vehicles, but it was less than three hundred meters to the far side of the river and the coaxial 7.62 mm machine guns and the heavier 12.7 mm cupola-mounted weapons at the tank commanders' stations were waiting for them. At such short range, it was a massacre.

"Cease fire!" Basescu barked. "Fall back!"

His crews responded almost instantly, and the tanks' powerful V-12 engines snorted black smoke as the T-72s backed out of their hiding places and sped down the highway at sixty kilometers per hour. What the aliens had already accomplished with their "kinetic weapons" suggested that staying in one place would be a very bad idea, and Basescu had picked out his next fighting position before he ever settled into this one. It would take them barely fifteen minutes to reach it, and only another fifteen to twenty minutes to maneuver the tanks back into hiding.

Precisely seventeen minutes later, incandescent streaks of light came sizzling out of the cloudless heavens to eliminate every one of Nicolae Basescu's tanks—and half the city of Alba iulia—in a blast of fury that shook the Carpathian Mountains.

VII

Stephen Buchevsky felt his body trying to ooze out even flatter as the grinding, tooth-rattling vibration grew louder on the far side of the ridgeline. The AKM he'd acquired to replace the his M-16 still felt awkward, but it was a solidly built weapon, with all the rugged reliability of its AK-47 ancestry, ammunition for it was readily available . . . and it felt unspeakably comforting at that particular moment.

His attention remained fixed on the "sound" of the alien recon drone, but a corner of his mind went wandering back over the last three weeks.

The C-17's pilot had gotten farther east than Buchevsky had thought. They hadn't known they were in Romania, not Serbia, for a day or two—not until they came across the remains of a couple of platoons of Romanian infantry which had been caught in column on a road. Their uniforms and insignia had identified their nationality, and most of them had been killed by what looked like standard bullet wounds. But there'd also been a handful of craters with oddly glassy interiors from obviously heavier weapons.

The Romanians' disaster had, however, represented unlooked-for good fortune for Buchevsky's ill-assorted command. There'd been plenty of personal weapons to salvage, as well as hand grenades, more man-portable antitank weapons and SAMs—the SA-14 "Gremlin" variant—than they could possibly carry, even canteens and some rations. Buchevsky had hated to give up his M-16, but although Romania had joined NATO, it still used mainly Societ bloc equipment. There wouldn't be any 5.56 mm ammunition floating around Romania, but 7.62 mm was abundantly available.

That was the good news. The bad news was that there'd clearly been a major exodus from most of the towns and cities following the aliens' ruthless bombardment. They'd spotted several large groups—hundreds of people, in some cases. Most of them had been accompanied by at least some armed men, and they hadn't been inclined to take chances. Probably most of them were already aware of how ugly it was going to get when their particular group of civilians' supplies started running out, and whatever else they might have been thinking, none of them had been happy to see thirty-three strangers in desert-camo.

Foreign desert-camo.

A few warning shots had been fired, one of which had nicked PFC Lyman Curry, and Buchevsky had taken the hint. Still, he had to at least find someplace where his own people could establish a modicum of security while they went about the day-to-day business of surviving.

Which was what he'd been hunting for today, moving through the thickly wooded mountains, staying well upslope from the roads running through the valleys despite the harder going. Some of his people, including Sergeant Ramirez, had been inclined to bitch about that at first. Buchevsky didn't really mind if they complained about it as long as they *did* it, however, and even the strongest objections had disappeared quickly when they realized just how important overhead concealment was.

From the behavior of the odd, dark-colored flying objects, Buchevsky figured they were something like the U.S. military's Predators—small unmanned aircraft used for reconnaissance. What he didn't know was whether or not they were *armed*. Nor did he have any idea whether or not their salvaged shoulder-fired SAMs would work against them, and he had no pressing desire to explore either possibility unless it was absolutely a matter of life or death.

Fortunately, although the odd-looking vehicles were quick and agile, they weren't the least bit stealthily. Whatever propelled them produced a heavy, persistent, tooth-grating vibration. That wasn't really the right word for it, and he knew it, but he couldn't come up with another one for a sensation that was felt, not heard. And whatever it was, it was detectable from beyond visual range.

He'd discussed it with Staff Sergeant Truman and PO/3 Jasmine Sherman, their sole Navy noncom. Truman was an electronics specialist, and Sherman wore the guided missile and electronic wave rating mark of a missile technician. Between them, they formed what Buchevsky thought of as his "brain trust," but neither woman had a clue what the aliens used for propulsion. What they did agree on was that humans were probably more sensitive to the "vibration" it produced than the aliens were, since it wouldn't have made a lot of sense to produce a reconnaissance platform they *knew* people could hear before it could see them.

Buchevsky wasn't going to bet the farm on the belief that his people *could* "hear" the drones before the drones could see them, however. Which was why he'd waved his entire group to ground when the telltale vibration came burring through his fillings from the ridgeline to his immediate north. Now if only—

That was when he heard the firing and the screams.

It shouldn't have mattered. His responsibility was to his own people. To keeping them alive until he got them home . . . assuming there was any "home" *for* them. But when he heard the shouts, when he heard the screams—when he recognized the shrieks of children—he found himself back on his feet. He turned his head, saw Calvin Meyers watching him, and then he swung his hand in a wide arc and pointed to the right.

A dozen of his people stayed right where they were—not out of cowardice, but because they were too confused and surprised by his sudden change of plans to realize what he was doing—and he didn't blame them. Even as he started forward, he knew it was insane. Less than half his people had any actual combat experience, and five of *them* had been tankers, not infantry. No wonder they didn't understand what he was doing!

Meyer understood, though, and so had Ramirez—even if he was an Army puke—and Lance Corporal Gutierrez, and Coporal Alice Macomb, and half a dozen others, and they followed him in a crouching run.

Squad Commander Rayzhar bared his canines as his troopers advanced up the valley. He'd been on this accursed planet for less than seven local days, and already he'd come to hate its inhabitants as he'd never hated before in his life. They had no sense of decency, no sense of honor! They'd been *defeated*, Dainthar take them! The Shongairi had proved they were the mightier, yet instead of submitting and acknowledging their inferiority, they persisted in their insane attacks!

Rayzhar had lost two litter-brothers in the ambush of Company Commander Barmit's column. Litter-brothers who'd been shot down like weed-eaters for the pot, as if *they'd* been the inferiors. That was something Rayzhar had no intention of forgetting—or forgiving—until he'd collected enough "humans'" souls to serve both of them in Dainthar's realm.

He really had no business making this attack, but the recon drone slaved to his command transport had shown him this ragged band cowering in the mountainside cul-de-sac. There were no more than fifty or sixty of them, but a half dozen wore the same uniforms as the humans who'd massacred his litter-brothers. That was enough for him. Besides, HQ would never see the take from the drone—he'd make sure of that—and he expected no questions when he reported that he'd taken fire from the humans and simply responded to it.

He looked up from the holographic display board linked to the drone and barked an order at Gersa, the commander of his second squad.

"Swing right! Get around their flank!"

Gersa acknowledged, and Rayzhar bared his canines again—this time in satisfaction—as two of the renegade human warriors were cut down. A mortar round from one of the transports exploded farther up the cul-de-sac, among the humans cowering in the trees, and a savage sense of pleasure filled him.

Buchevsky found himself on the ridgeline, looking down into a scene straight out of Hell. More than fifty civilians, over half of them children, were hunkered down under the fragile cover of evergreens and hardwoods while a handful of Romanian soldiers tried frantically to protect them from at least twenty-five or thirty of the aliens. There were also three wheeled vehicles on the road below, and one of them mounted a turret with some sort of mortarlike support weapon. Even as Buchevsky watched, it fired and an eye-tearing burst of brilliance erupted near the top of the cul-de-sac. He heard the shrieks of seared, dying children, and below the surface of his racing thoughts, he realized what had really happened. Why he'd changed his plans completely, put all the people he was responsible for at risk.

Civilians. *Children*. They were what he was supposed to *protect*, and deep at the heart of him was the bleeding wound of his own daughters, the children he would never see again. The Shongairi had taken his girls from him, and he would rip out their throats with his bare teeth before he let them take any more.

"Gunny, get the vehicles!" he snapped, his curt voice showing no sign of his own self-recognition.

"On it, Top!" Meyer acknowledged, and waved to Gutierrez and Robert Szu, one of their Army privates. Gutierrez and Szu—like Meyer—carried RBR-M60s, Romanian single-shot anti-armor weapons derived from the U.S. M72. The Romanian version had a theoretical range of over a thousand meters, and the power to take out most older main battle tanks, and Meyer, Gutierrez, and Szu went skittering through the woods toward the road with them.

Buchevsky left that in Meyer's competent hands as he reached out and grabbed Corporal Macomb by the shoulder. She carried one of the salvaged SAM launchers, and Buchevsky jabbed a nod of his head at the drone hovering overhead.

"Take that damned thing out," he said flatly.

"Right, Top." Macomb's voice was grim, her expression frightened, but her hands were steady as she lifted the SAM's tube to her shoulder.

"The rest of you, with me!" Buchevsky barked. It wasn't much in the way of detailed instructions, but four of the eight people still with him were Marines, and three of the others were Army riflemen.

Besides, the tactical situation was brutally simple.

Rayzhar saw another uniformed human die. Then he snarled in fury as one of his own troopers screamed, rose on his toes, and went down in a spray of blood. The Shongairi weren't accustomed to facing enemies whose weapons could penetrate their body armor, and Rayzhar felt a chill spike of fear even through his rage. But he wasn't about to let it stop him, and there were only three armed humans left. Only three, and then—

Buchevsky heard the explosions as the alien vehicles vomited flame and smoke. At almost the same instant, the SA-14 streaked into the air, and two things became clear: One, whatever held the drones up radiated enough heat signature for the Gremlin to see it. Two, whatever the drones were made of, it wasn't tough enough to survive the one-kilo warhead's impact.

He laid the sights of his AKM on the weird, slender, doglike alien whose waving hands suggested he was in command and squeezed the trigger.

A four-round burst of 7.62 mm punched through the back of Rayzhar's body armor. The rounds kept right on going until they punched out his breastplate in a spray of red, as well, and the squad commander heard someone's gurgling scream. He realized vaguely that it was his own, and then he crashed facedown into the dirt of an alien planet.

He wasn't alone. There were only nine riflemen up on his flank, but they had perfect fields of fire, and every single one of them had heard Fleet Commander Thikair's broadcast. They knew why Rayzhar and his troopers had come to their world, what had happened to their cities and homes. There was no mercy in them, and their fire was deadly accurate.

The Shongairi recoiled in shock as more of them died or collapsed in agony—shock that became terror as they realized their vehicles had just been destroyed behind them, as well. They had no idea how many attackers they faced, but they recognized defeat when they saw it, and they turned toward the new attack, raising their weapons over their heads in surrender, flattening their ears in token of submission.

Stephen Buchevsky saw the aliens turning toward his people, raising their weapons to charge up the ridge, and behind his granite eyes he saw the children they had just killed and maimed . . . and his daughters.

"Kill them!" he rasped.

VIII

"I want an explanation." Fleet Commander Thikair glowered around the conference table. None of his senior officers needed to ask what it was he wanted explained, and more than one set of eyes slid sideways to Ground

Force Commander Thairys. His casualties were over six times his most pessimistic pre-landing estimates . . . and climbing.

"I have no excuse, Fleet Commander."

Thairys flattened his ears in submission to Thikair's authority, and there was silence for a second or two.

But then Base Commander Shairez raised one diffident hand.

"If I may, Fleet Commander?"

"If you have any explanation, Base Commander, I would be delighted to hear it," Thikair said, turning his attention to her.

"I doubt that there is any *single* explanation, sir." Her ears were half-lowered in respect, although not so flat to her head as Thairys', and her tone was calm. "Instead, I think we're looking at a combination of factors."

"Which are?" Thikair leaned back, his immediate ire somewhat damped by her demeanor.

"The first, sir, is simply that this is the first Level Two culture we've ever attempted to subdue. While their weaponry is inferior to our own, it's far less *relatively* inferior than anything we've ever encountered. Their armored vehicles, for example, while much slower, clumsier, shorter-legged, and tactically cumbersome than ours, are actually better protected and mount weapons capable of destroying our heaviest units. Even their *infantry* have weapons with that capability, and that's skewed Ground Force Commander Thairys' original calculations badly."

Thikair bared one canine in frustration, but she had a point. The Shongairi's last serious war had been fought centuries ago, against fellow Shongairi, before they'd ever left their home world. Since then, their military had found itself engaging mostly primitives armed with hand weapons or only the crudest of firearms . . . exactly as they were *supposed* to have encountered here.

"A second factor," Shairez continued, "may be that our initial bombardment was too successful. We so thoroughly disrupted their communications net and command structures that there may be no way for individual units to be ordered to stand down."

"'Stand *down*'?" Squadron Commander Jainfar repeated incredulously. "They're *defeated*, Base Commander! I don't care how stupid they are, or how disrupted their communications may be, they *have* to know that!"

"Perhaps so, Squadron Commander." Shairez faced the old space-dog squarely. "Unfortunately, as yet we know very little about this species' psychology. We do know there's something significantly different about them, given their incredible rate of advancement, but that's really *all* we know. It could be that they simply don't *care* that we've defeated them."

Jainfar started to say something else, then visibly restrained himself. It was obvious he couldn't imagine any intelligent species thinking in such a bizarre fashion, but Shairez *was* the expedition's expert on non-Shongairi sapients.

"Even if that's true, Base Commander," Thikair's tone was closer to normal, "it doesn't change our problem." He looked at Thairys. "What sort of loss rates are we looking at, assuming these 'humans'' behavior doesn't change?"

"Potentially disastrous ones," Thairys acknowledged. "We've already written off eleven percent of our armored vehicles. We never expected to need many GEVs against the opposition we anticipated, which means we have nowhere near the vehicles and crews it looks like we're going to need. We've actually lost a higher absolute number of transports, but we had many times as many of those to begin with. Infantry losses are another matter, and I'm not at all sure present casualty rates are sustainable. And I must point out that we have barely eight local days of experience. It's entirely possible for projections based on what we've seen so far to be almost as badly flawed as our initial estimates."

The ground force commander clearly didn't like adding that caveat. Which was fair enough. Thikair didn't much like *hearing* it.

"I believe the Ground Force Commander may be unduly pessimistic, sir." All eyes switched to Shairez once more, and the base commander flipped her ears in a shrug. "My own analysis suggests that we're looking at two basic types of incident, both of which appear to be the work of relatively small units acting independently of any higher command or coordination. On one hand, we have units making use of the humans' heavy weapons and using what I suspect is their standard doctrine. An example of this would be the destruction of Company Commander Barmit's entire command a few days ago. On the other, we have what seem to be primarily infantry forces equipped with their light weapons or using what appear to be improvised explosives and weapons.

"In the case of the former, they've frequently inflicted severe losses—again, as in Barmit's case. In fact, more often than not, they've inflicted grossly disproportionate casualties. However, in *those* instances, our space-to-surface interdiction systems are normally able to locate and destroy them. In short, humans who attack us in that fashion seldom survive to attack a second time, and they already have few heavy weapons left.

"In the case of the *latter*, however, the attackers have proved far more elusive. Our reconnaissance systems are biased toward locating heavier, more technologically advanced weapons. We look for electronic emissions, thermal signatures such as operating vehicle power plants generate, and things of that nature. We're far less well equipped to pick out individual humans or small groups of humans. As a consequence, we're able to intercept and destroy a far smaller percentage of such attackers.

"The good news is that although their infantry-portable weapons are far more powerful than we ever anticipated, they're still far less dangerous than their heavy armored vehicles or artillery. This means, among other things, that they can engage only smaller forces of our warriors with any real prospect of success."

"I believe that's substantially accurate," Thairys said after a moment. "One of the implications, however, is that in order to deter attacks by these infantry forces, we would find ourselves obliged to operate using larger forces of our own. But we have a strictly limited supply of personnel, so the larger our individual forces become, the fewer we can deploy at any given moment. In order to deter attack, we would be forced to severely reduce the coverage of the entire planet which we can hope to maintain."

"I take your point, Thairys," Thikair said after a moment, and bared all his upper canines in a wintry smile. "I must confess that a planet begins to look significantly larger when one begins to consider the need to actually picket its entire surface out of the resources of a single colonization fleet!"

He'd considered saying something a bit stronger, but that was as close as he cared to come to admitting that he might have bitten off more than his fleet could chew.

"For the present," he went on, "we'll continue operations essentially as planned, but with a geographic shift of emphasis. Thairys, I want you to revise your deployment stance. For the moment, we'll concentrate on the areas that were more heavily developed and technologically advanced. That's where we're most likely to encounter significant threats, so let's start by establishing fully secured enclaves from which we can operate in greater strength as we spread out to consolidate."

"Yes, sir," Thairys acknowledged. "That may take some time, however.

In particular, we have infantry forces deployed for the purpose of hunting down and destroying known groups of human attackers. They're operating in widely separated locations, and pulling them out to combine elsewhere is going to stretch our troop lift capacity."

"Would they be necessary to meet the objectives I just described?"

"No, sir. Some additional infantry will be needed, but we can land additional troops directly from space. And, in addition, we need more actual combat experience against these roving attack groups. We need to refine our tactics, and not even our combat veterans have actually faced this level of threat in the past. I'd really prefer to keep at least some of our own infantry out in the hinterland, where we can continue to blood more junior officers in a lower threat-level environment."

"As long as you're capable of carrying out the concentrations I've just directed, I have no objection," Thikair told him.

And as long as we're able to somehow get a tourniquet on this steady flow of casualties, the Fleet Commander added to himself.

IX

An insect scuttled across the back of Stephen Buchevsky's sweaty neck. He ignored it, keeping his eyes on the aliens as they set about bivouacking.

The insect on his neck went elsewhere, and he checked the RDG-5 hand grenade. He wouldn't have dared to use a radio even if he'd had it, but the grenade's detonation would work just fine as an attack signal.

He really would have preferred leaving this patrol alone, but he couldn't. He had no idea what they were doing in the area, and it really didn't matter. Whatever else they might do, every Shongairi unit appeared to be on its own permanent seek-and-destroy mission, and he couldn't allow that when the civilians he and his people had become responsible for were in this patrol's way.

His reaction to the Shongairi attack on the Romanian civilians had landed him with yet another mission—one he would vastly have preferred to avoid. Or that was what he told himself, anyway. The rest of his people—with the possible exception of Ramirez—seemed to cherish none of the reservations he himself felt. In fact, he often thought the only reason *he* felt them was because he was in command. It was his *job* to feel them.

But however it had happened, he and his marooned Americans had become the protectors of a slowly but steadily growing band of Romanians.

Fortunately, one of the Romanians in question—Elizabeth Cantacuzène—had been a university teacher. Her English was heavily accented, but her grammar (and, Buchevsky suspected, her vocabulary) was considerably better than his, and just acquiring a local translator had been worth almost all of the headaches that had come with it.

By now, he had just under sixty armed men and women under his command. His Americans formed the core of his force, but their numbers were almost equaled by a handful of Romanian soldiers and the much larger number of civilians who were in the process of receiving a crash course in military survival from him, Gunny Meyers, and Sergeant Alexander Jonescu of the Romanian Army. He'd organized them into four roughly equal sized "squads," one commanded by Myers, one by Ramirez, one by Jonescu, and one by Alice Macomb. Michelle Truman was senior to Macomb, but she and Sherman were still too valuable as his "brain trust" for him to "waste her" in a shooter's slot. Besides, she was learning Romanian from Cantacuzène.

Fortunately, Sergeant Jonescu already spoke English, and Buchevsky had managed to get at least one Romanian English-speaker into each of his squads. It was clumsy, but it worked, and they'd spent hours drilling on hand signals that required no spoken language. And at least the parameters of their situation were painfully clear to everyone.

Evade. *Hide.* Do whatever it took to keep the civilians—now close to two hundred of them—safe. Stay on the move. Avoid roads and towns. Look out constantly for any source of food. It turned out that Calvin Meyers was an accomplished deer hunter, and he and two like-minded souls who had been members of the Romanian forestry service were contributing significantly to keeping their people fed. Still, summer was sliding into fall, and all too soon cold and starvation would become deadly threats.

But for that to happen, first we have to survive *the summer, don't we?* he thought harshly. *Which means these bastards have to be stopped before they figure out the civilians are here to be killed. And we've got to do it without their getting a message back to base.*

He didn't like it. He didn't like it at all. But he didn't see any choice, either, and with Cantacuzène's assistance, he'd interrogated every single person who'd seen the Shongairi in action, hunting information on their tactics and doctrine.

It was obvious they were sudden death on large bodies of troops or units equipped with heavy weapons. Some of that was probably because crewmen inside tanks couldn't "hear" approaching recon drones the way infantry in the open could, he thought. And Truman and Sherman suspected that the Shongairi's sensors were designed to detect mechanized forces, or at least units with heavy emissions signatures, which was one reason he'd gotten rid of all his radios.

It also appeared that the infantry patrols had less sensor coverage than those floating tanks or their road convoys. And in the handful of additional brushes he'd had with their infantry, it had become evident that the invaders weren't in any sort of free-flow communications net that extended beyond their immediate unit. If they had been, he felt sure, by now one of the patrols they'd attacked would have managed to call in one of their kinetic strikes.

Which is why we've got to hit them fast, make sure we take out their vehicles with the first strike . . . and that nobody packing a personal radio lives long enough to use it.

It looked like they were beginning to settle down. Obviously, they had no idea Buchevsky or his people were out here, which suited him just fine.

Go ahead, he thought grimly. *Get comfortable. Drop off. I've got your sleeping pill right here. In about another five—*

"Excuse me, Sergeant, but is this really wise?"

Stephen Buchevsky twitched as if someone had just applied a high-voltage charge, and his head whipped around toward the whispered question.

The question that had just been asked in his very ear in almost unaccented English . . . by a voice he'd never heard in his life.

"Now suppose you just tell me who you are and where the *hell* you came from?" Buchevsky demanded ten minutes later.

He stood facing a complete stranger, two hundred meters from the Shongairi bivouac, and he wished the light were better. Not that he was even tempted to strike a match.

The stranger was above average height for a Romanian, although well short of Buchevsky's towering inches. He had a sharp-prowed nose, large, deep-set green eyes, and dark hair. That was about all Buchevsky could tell, aside from the fact that his smile seemed faintly amused.

"Excuse me," the other man said. "I had no desire to . . . startle you, Sergeant. However, I knew something which you do not. There is a second patrol little more than a kilometer away in that direction."

He pointed back up the narrow road along which the Shongairi had approached, and an icy finger stroked suddenly down Buchevsky's spine.

"How do you know that?"

"My men and I have been watching them," the stranger said. "And it is a formation we have seen before—one they have adopted in the last week or so. I believe they are experimenting with new tactics, sending out pairs of infantry teams in support of one another."

"Damn. I was hoping they'd take longer to think of that," Buchevsky muttered. "Looks like they may be smarter than I'd assumed from their original tactics."

"I do not know how intelligent they may be, Sergeant. But I do suspect that if you were to attack *this* patrol, the other one would probably call up heavy support quickly."

"That's exactly what they'd do," Buchevsky agreed, then frowned. "Not that I'm not grateful for the warning, or anything," he said, "but you still haven't told me who you are, where you came from, or how you got here."

"Surely"—this time the amusement in the Romanian's voice was unmistakable—"that would be a more reasonable question for *me* to be asking of an American Marine here in the heart of Wallachia?"

Buchevsky's jaw clenched, but the other man chuckled and shook his head.

"Forgive me, Sergeant. I have been told I have a questionable sense of humor. My name is Basarab, Mircea Basarab. And where I have come from is up near Lake Vidaru, fifty or sixty kilometers north of here. My men and I have been doing much the same as what I suspect you have— attempting to protect my people from these 'Shongairi' butchers." He grimaced. "Protecting civilians from invaders is, alas, something of a national tradition in these parts."

"I see . . . ," Buchevsky said slowly, and white teeth glinted at him in the dimness.

"I believe you do, Sergeant. And, yes, I also believe the villages my men and I have taken under our protection could absorb these civilians *you* have been protecting. They are typical mountain villages, largely self-sufficient, with few 'modern amenities.' They grow their own food, and feeding this many additional mouths will strain their resources severely. I doubt anyone will grow fat over the winter! But they will do their best, and the additional hands will be welcome as they prepare for the snows. And from what I have seen of you and your band, you would be a most welcome addition to their defenses."

Buchevsky cocked his head, straining to see the other's expression. It was all coming at him far too quickly. He knew he ought to be standing back, considering this stranger's offer coolly and rationally. Yet what he actually felt was a wave of unspeakable relief as the men, women, and children—always the children—for whom he'd become responsible were offered a reprieve from starvation and frostbite.

"And how would we get there with these puppies sitting in our lap?" he asked.

"Obviously, Sergeant, we must first *remove* them from 'our lap.' Since my men are already in position to deal with the second patrol, and yours are already in position to deal with *this* patrol, I would suggest we both get back to work. I presume you intended to use that grenade to signal the start of your own attack?"

Buchevsky nodded, and Basarab shrugged.

"I see no reason why you should change your plans in that regard. Allow me fifteen minutes—no, perhaps twenty would be better—to return to my own men and tell them to listen for your attack. After that," those white teeth glittered again, and this time, Buchevsky knew, that smile was cold and cruel, "feel free to announce your presence to these vermin. Loudly."

X

Platoon Commander Dirak didn't like this one bit, but orders were orders.

He moved slowly at the center of his second squad, ears up and straining for the slightest sound as they followed his first squad along the narrow trail. Unfortunately, his people had been civilized for a thousand standard years. Much of the acuity of sound and scent that had once marked the margin between death and survival had slipped away, and he felt more than half-blind in this heavily shadowed, massive forest.

There were no forests like this on his home world any longer—not with this towering, primeval canopy, with tree trunks that could be half as broad at the base as a Shongairi's height—yet the woodland around him was surprisingly free of brush and undergrowth. According to the expedition's botanists, that was only to be expected in a mature forest where so little direct sunlight reached the ground. No doubt they knew what they were talking about, but it still seemed . . . wrong to Dirak. And, perversely, he liked the saplings and underbrush that did grow along the verge of this narrow trail even less. They probably confirmed the botanists' theories, since at least some sun did get through where the line of the trail broke the canopy, but they left him feeling cramped and shut in.

Actually, a lot of his anxiety was probably due to the fact that he'd been expressly ordered to leave his assigned recon and communications relay drone well behind his point, anchored to the wheeled transports snorting laboriously along the same trail far behind him. Analysis of what had happened to the last three patrols sent into this area suggested that the "humans" had somehow managed to destroy the drones before they ever engaged the infantry those drones were supporting with surveillance and secure communications to base. No one had any idea how the primitives—only, of course, they weren't *really* primitives, were they?—were able to detect and target drones so effectively, but HQ had decided to try a more stealthy approach . . . and chosen Dirak to carry out the experiment.

Oh, how the gods must have smiled upon me, he reflected morosely. *I understand the need to gain experience against these . . . creatures if we're going to modify doctrine. But why did* I *get chosen to poke* my *head into the* hasthar's *den? It wasn't like—*

He heard an explosion behind him and wheeled around. He couldn't see through the overhead canopy, but he didn't need to see it to know that the explosion had been his RC drone. How had they even *see* it through these damnable leaves and branches!

The question was still ripping through his brain when he heard more explosions—this time on the ground . . . where his two reserve squads were following along in their APCs.

He didn't have time to realize what *those* explosions were before the assault rifles hidden behind trees and under drifts of leaves all along the southern flank of the trail opened fire.

Unfortunately for Platoon Commander Dirak, the men and women behind those assault rifles had figured out how to recognize a Shongairi infantry formation's commanding officer.

"Cease fire! *Cease fire!*" Buchevsky bellowed, and the bark and clatter of automatic weapons fire faded abruptly.

He held his own position, AKM still ready, while he surveyed the tumbled Shongairi bodies sprawled along the trail. One or two were still writhing, although it didn't look like they would be for long.

"Good," a voice said behind him with fierce, obvious satisfaction, and he looked over his shoulder. Mircea Basarab stood in the dense forest shadows, looking out over the ambushed patrol. "Well done, my Stephen."

"Maybe so, but we'd better be moving," Buchevsky replied, safeing his weapon and rising from his firing position.

His own expression, he knew, was more anxious than Basarab's. This was the third hard contact with the Shongairi in the six days since he'd placed his people under Basarab's command, and from what Basarab had said, they were getting close to the enclave he'd established in the mountains around Lake Vidaru. Which meant they really needed to shake this persistent—if inept—pursuit.

"I think we have a short while," Basarab disagreed, glancing farther down the trail to the columns of smoke rising from what had been armored vehicles until Jonescu's squad and half of Basarab's original men dealt with them. "It seems unlikely they got a message out this time, either."

"Maybe not," Buchevsky conceded. "But their superiors have to know where they are. When they don't check in on schedule, someone's going to come looking for them. Again."

He might have sounded as if he were disagreeing, but he wasn't, really. First, because Basarab was probably correct. But secondly, because over the course of the last week or so, he'd come to realize Mircea Basarab was one of the best officers he'd ever served under. Which, he reflected, was high praise for any foreign officer from any Marine . . . and didn't keep the Romanian from being one of the scariest men Buchevsky had ever met.

A lot of people might not have realized that. In better light, Basarab's face had a bony, foxlike handsomeness, and his smile was frequently warm. But there were dark, still places behind those green eyes. Still places that were no stranger to all too many people from the post-Ceauşescu Balkans. Dark places Buchevsky recognized because he'd met so many other scary men in his life . . . and because there was now a dark, still place labeled "Washington, D.C." inside him, as well.

Yet whatever lay in Basarab's past, the man was almost frighteningly competent, and he radiated a sort of effortless charisma Buchevsky had seldom encountered. The sort of charisma that could win the loyalty of even a Stephen Buchevsky, and even on such relatively short acquaintance.

"Your point is well taken, my Stephen," Basarab said now, smiling almost as if he'd read Buchevsky's mind and reaching up to place one hand on the towering American's shoulder. Like the almost possessive way he said "my Stephen," it could have been patronizing. It wasn't.

"However," he continued, his smile fading, "I believe it may be time to send these vermin elsewhere."

"Sounds great to me." A trace of skepticism edged Buchevsky's voice, and Basarab chuckled. It was not a particularly pleasant sound.

"I believe we can accomplish it," he said, and whistled shrilly.

Moments later, Take Bratianu, a dark-haired, broad-shouldered Romanian, blended out of the forest.

Buchevsky was picking up Romanian quickly, thanks to Elizabeth Cantacuzène, but the exchange that followed was far too rapid for his still rudimentary grasp of the language to sort out. It lasted for a few minutes, then Bratianu nodded, and Basarab turned back to Buchevsky.

"Take speaks no English, I fear," he said.

That was obvious, Buchevsky thought dryly. On the other hand, Bratianu didn't *need* to speak English to communicate the fact that he was one seriously bad-assed individual. None of Basarab's men did.

There were only about twenty of them, but they moved like ghosts. Buchevsky was no slouch, yet he knew when he was outclassed at pooping and snooping in the shrubbery. These men were far better at it than *he'd* ever been, and in addition to rifles, pistols, and hand grenades, they were liberally festooned with a ferocious assortment of knives, hatchets, and machetes. Indeed, Buchevsky suspected they would have preferred using cold steel instead of any namby-pamby assault rifles.

Now, as Bratianu and his fellows moved along the trail, knives flashed, and the handful of Shongairi wounded stopped writhing.

Buchevsky had no problem with that. Indeed, his eyes were bleakly satisfied. But when some of the Romanians began stripping the alien bodies while others began cutting down several stout young saplings growing along the edge of the trail, he frowned and glanced at Basarab. The Romanian only shook his head.

"Wait," he said, and Buchevsky turned back to the others.

They worked briskly, wielding their hatchets and machetes with practiced efficiency as they cut the saplings into roughly ten-foot lengths, then shaped points at either end. In a surprisingly short period, they had over a dozen of them, and Buchevsky's eyes widened in shock as they calmly picked up the dead Shongairi and impaled them.

Blood and other body fluids oozed down the crude, rough-barked stakes, but he said nothing as the stakes' other ends were sunk into the soft woodland soil. The dead aliens hung there, lining the trail like insects mounted on pins, grotesque in the shadows, and he felt Basarab's eyes.

"Are you shocked, my Stephen?" the Romanian asked quietly.

"I . . ." Buchevsky inhaled deeply. "Yes, I guess I am. Some," he admitted. He turned to face the other man. "I think maybe because it's a little too close to some of the things I've seen jihadies do."

"Indeed?" Basarab's eyes were cold. "I suppose I should not be surprised by that. *We* learned the tradition from the Turks ourselves, long ago. But at least these were already dead when they were staked."

"Would it have made a difference?" Buchevsky asked, and Basarab's nostrils flared. But then the other man gave himself a little shake.

"Once?" He shrugged. "No. As I say, the practice has long roots in this area. One of Romania's most famous sons, after all, was known as 'Vlad the Impaler,' was he not?" He smiled thinly. "For that matter, *I* did not, as you Americans say, have a happy childhood, and there was a time when I inflicted cruelty on all those about me. When I *enjoyed* it. In those days, no doubt, I would have preferred them alive."

He shook his head, and his expression saddened as he gazed at the impaled alien bodies.

"I fear it took far too many years for me to realize that all the cruelty in the universe cannot avenge a broken childhood or appease an orphaned young man's rage, my Stephen," he said. "There was a doctor once, a man I met in Austria, who explained that to me. To my shame, I did not really wish to hear what he was saying, but it was true. And the years it took me to realize that demanded too high a price from those for whom I cared, and who cared for me." He looked at the bodies for a moment longer, then shook himself. "But this, my friend, has nothing to do with the darkness inside me."

"No?" Buchevsky raised an eyebrow.

"No. It is obvious to me that these vermin will persist in pursuing us. So, we will give them something to fix their attention upon—something to make any creature, even one of these, hot with hate—and then we will give them someone besides your civilians to pursue. Take and most of my men will head south, leaving a trail so obvious that even these—" He twitched his head at the slaughtered patrol. "—could scarcely miss it. He will lead them aside until they are dozens of kilometers away. Then he will slip away and return to us."

"Without their being able to follow him?"

"Do not be so skeptical, my friend!" Basarab chuckled and squeezed Buchevsky's shoulder. "I did not pick these men at random! There are no more skilled woodsmen in all of Romania. Have no fear that they will lead our enemies to us."

"I hope you're right," Buchevsky said, looking back at the impaled bodies and thinking about how *he* would have reacted in the aliens' place. "I hope you're right."

XI

Fleet Commander Thikair pressed the admittance stud, then tipped back in his chair as Shairez stepped through the door into his personal quarters. It closed silently behind her, and he waved at a chair.

"Be seated, Base Commander," he said, deliberately more formal because of the irregularity of meeting with her here.

"Thank you, Fleet Commander."

He watched her settle into the chair. She carried herself with almost her usual self-confidence, he thought, yet there was something about the set of her ears. And about her eyes.

She's changed, he thought. *Aged.* He snorted mentally. *Well, we've all done that, haven't we? But there's more to it in her case. More than there was yesterday, for that matter.*

"What, precisely, did you wish to see me about, Base Commander?" he asked after a moment. *And why*, he did not ask aloud, *did you wish to see me about it in private?*

"I have almost completed my initial psychological profile of these humans, sir." She met his gaze unflinchingly. "I'm afraid our initial hopes for this planet were . . . rather badly misplaced."

Thikair sat very still. It was a testimony to her inner strength that she'd spoken so levelly, he thought. Particularly given that they had been not "our initial hopes," but *his* initial hopes.

He drew a deep breath, feeling his ears fold back against his skull, and closed his eyes while he considered the price of those hopes. In just three local months, this one, miserable planet had cost the expedition 56 percent of its GEVs, 23 percent of its transports and APCs, and 26 percent of its infantry.

Of course, he reflected grimly, it had cost the humans even more. Yet no matter what he did, the insane creatures *refused* to submit.

"*How* badly misplaced?" he asked without opening his eyes.

"The problem, sir," she replied a bit obliquely, "is that we've never before encountered a species like this one. Their psychology is . . . unlike anything in our previous experience."

"That much I'd already surmised," Thikair said with poison-dry humor. "Should I conclude you now have a better grasp of how it differs?"

"Yes, sir." She drew a deep breath. "First, you must understand that there are huge local variations in their psychologies. That's inevitable, of course, given that unlike us or any other member race of the Hegemony, they retain so many bewilderingly different cultural and societal templates. There are, however, certain common strands. And one of those, Fleet Commander, is that, essentially, they have no submission mechanism as we understand the term."

"I beg your pardon?" Thikair's eyes popped open at the preposterous statement, and she sighed.

"There are a few races of the Hegemony that perhaps approach the humans' psychology, sir, but I can think of no more than two or three. All of them, like the humans, are omnivores, but none come close to this species' . . . level of perversity. Frankly, any Shongairi psychologist would pronounce all humans insane, sir. Unlike weed-eaters or the majority of omnivores, they have a streak of very Shongairi-like ferocity, yet their sense of self is almost invariably far greater than their sense of the pack."

She was obviously groping for a way to describe something outside any understood racial psychology, Thikair thought.

"Almost all weed-eaters have a very strong herd instinct," she said. "While they may, under some circumstances, fight ferociously, their first, overwhelming instinct is to *avoid* conflict, and their basic psychology subordinates the individual's good, even his very survival, to the good of the 'herd.' Most of them now define that 'herd' in terms of entire planetary populations or star nations, but it remains the platform from which all of their decisions and policies proceed.

"Most of the Hegemony's omnivores share that orientation to a greater or a lesser degree, although a handful approach our own psychological stance, which emphasizes not the herd but the *pack*. Our species evolved as *hunters*, not prey, with a social structure and psychology oriented around that primary function. Unlike weed-eaters and most omnivores, Shongairi's pride in our personal accomplishments, the proof of our ability, all relate to the ancient, primal importance of the individual hunter's prowess as the definer of his status within the pack.

"Yet the pack is still greater than the individual. Our sense of self-worth, of accomplishment, is validated only within the context of the pack. And the submission of the weaker to the stronger comes from that same context. It is bred into our very genes to submit to the pack leader, to the individual whose strength dominates all about him. Of course our people, and especially our males, have always *challenged* our leaders, as well, for that was how the ancient pack ensured that its leadership remained strong. But once a leader has reaffirmed his dominance, his strength, even the challenger submits once more. Our entire philosophy, our honor code, our societal expectations, all proceed from that fundamental starting point."

"Of course," Thikair said, just a bit impatiently. "How else could a society such as ours is survive?"

"That's my point, sir. A society such as ours could *not* survive among humans. Their instinct to submit is enormously weaker than our own, and it is far superseded by the individual's drive to defeat threats to his primary loyalty group—which is neither the pack nor the herd."

"What?" Thikair blinked at her, and she grimaced.

"A human's primary loyalty is to his family grouping, sir. Not to the herd, of which the family forms only a small part. And not to the pack, where the emphasis is on strength and value *to* the pack. There are exceptions, but that orientation forms the bedrock of human motivation. You might think of them almost as . . . as a herd composed of *individual* packs of predators. Humans are capable of extending that sense of loyalty beyond the family grouping—to organizations, to communities, to nation-states or philosophies—but the fundamental motivating mechanism of the individual family is as hardwired into them as submission to the stronger is hardwired into us. Sir, my research indicates that a very large percentage of humans will attack *any* foe, regardless of its strength or power, in defense of their mates or young. And they will do it *with no regard whatsoever* for the implications to the rest of their pack or herd."

Thikair looked at her, trying to wrap his mind around the bizarre psychology she was trying to explain. Intellectually, he could grasp it, at least imperfectly; emotionally, it made no sense to him at all.

"Sir," she continued, "I've administered all the standard psychological exams. As you directed, I've also experimented to determine how applicable our existing direct neural education techniques are to humans, and I can report that they work quite well. But my opinion, based on the admittedly imperfect psychological profile I've been able to construct, suggests to me that it would be the height of folly to use humans as a client race.

"They will never understand the natural submission of the weaker to the stronger. Instead, they will work unceasingly to *become* the stronger, and not for the purpose of assuming leadership of the pack. Some of them, yes, will react very like Shongairi might. Others may even approach weed-eater behavior patterns. But most will see the function of strength as the protection of their primary loyalty group. They will focus their energy on destroying any and all threats to it, even when attempting to destroy the threat *in itself* risks destruction of the group, and they will *never* forget or forgive a threat to that which they protect. We might be able to enforce temporary obedience, and it's possible we could actually convince many of them to accept us as their natural masters. But we will never convince *all* of them of that, and so, eventually, we will find our 'clients' turning upon us with all the inventiveness and ferocity we've observed out of them here, but with all our own technological capabilities . . . as a *starting* point."

————

"It would appear," Thikair told his senior officers, "that my approach to this planet was not the most brilliant accomplishment of my career."

They looked back at him, most still obviously bemused by Shairez's report. None of them, he reflected, had reacted to it any better than *he* had.

"Obviously," he continued, "it's necessary to reevaluate our policy—*my* policy—in light of the Base Commander's discoveries. And, frankly, in light of our already severe operational losses.

"Our efforts to date to compel the humans to submit have killed over half the original planetary population and cost us massive losses of our own. Ground Force Commander Thairys's current estimate is that if we continue operations for one local year, we will have lost three-quarters of his personnel. In that same time period, we will have killed half the *remaining* humans. Clearly, even if Ground Base Commander Shairez's model is in error, we cannot sustain losses at that level. Nor would we dare risk providing such a . . . recalcitrant species with access to modern technology after killing three-quarters of them first."

There was silence in the conference room as he surveyed their faces.

"The time has come to cut our losses," he said flatly. "I am not prepared to give up this planet, not after the price we've already paid for it. But at the same time, I have concluded that humans are too dangerous. Indeed, faced with what we've discovered here, I believe many of the Hegemony's other races would share that conclusion!

"I've already instructed Base Commander Shairez to implement our backup strategy and develop a targeted bio-weapon. This constitutes a significant shift in her priorities, and it will be necessary to establish proper facilities for her work and to provide her with appropriate test subjects.

"I had considered moving her and her research staff to one of the existing ground bases. Unfortunately, the intensity of the operations required to establish those bases means the human populations in their vicinities have become rather . . . sparse. I have therefore decided to establish a new base facility in a rural area of the planet, where we haven't conducted such intense operations and reasonable numbers of test subjects will be readily available to her. Ground Force Commander Thairys will be responsible for providing security to the base during its construction . . . and with securing test subjects for her once construction is complete."

XII

"So, my Stephen. What do you make of this?"

Buchevsky finished his salad and took a long swallow of beer. His grandmama had always urged him to eat his vegetables, yet he was still a bit bemused by how sinfully luxurious fresh salad tasted after weeks of scrounging whatever he and his people could.

Which, unfortunately, wasn't what Basarab was asking him about.

"I really don't know, Mircea," he said with a frown. "*We* haven't been doing anything differently. Not that I know of, at any rate."

"Nor that I know of," Basarab agreed thoughtfully, gazing down at the handwritten note on the table.

The days were noticeably cooler outside the log-walled cabin, and autumn color was creeping across the mountainsides above the Arges River and the enormous blue gem of Lake Vidaru. The lake lay less than seventy kilometers north of the ruins of Pitesti, the capital of the Arges *judeƫ*, or county, but it was in the heart of a wilderness preserve, and the cabin had been built by the forestry service, rather than as part of any of the three villages Basarab had organized into his own little kingdom.

Despite Lake Vidaru's relative proximity to Pitesti, few of the kinetic strike's survivors had headed up into its vicinity. Buchevsky supposed the mountains and heavy forest had been too forbidding to appeal to urban dwellers. There were almost no roads into the area, and Basarab's villages were like isolated throwbacks to another age. In fact, they reminded Buchevsky rather strongly of the village in the musical *Brigadoon*.

Which isn't a bad thing, he reflected. *There sits Lake Vidaru, with its hydroelectric generators, and these people didn't even have electricity! Which means they aren't radiating any emissions the Shongairi are likely to pick up on.*

Over the last couple of months, he, his Americans, and their Romanians had been welcomed by the villagers and—as Basarab had warned—been put to work preparing for the onset of winter. One reason his lunch salad had tasted so good was because he wouldn't be having salads much longer. It wasn't as if there'd be fresh produce coming in from California.

"There must be some reason for it, my Stephen," Basarab said now. "And I fear it is not one either of us would like."

"Mircea, I haven't liked a single goddammed thing those bastards have done from day one."

Basarab arched one eyebrow, and Buchevsky was a little surprised himself by the jagged edge of hatred that had roughened his voice. It took him unawares, sometimes, that hate. When the memory of Trish and the girls came looming up out of the depths once again, fangs bared, to remind him of the loss and the pain and anguish.

Isn't it one hell *of a note when the best thing I can think of is that the people I loved probably died without knowing a thing about it?*

"They have not endeared themselves to me, either," Basarab said after a moment. "Indeed, it has been . . . difficult to remember that we dare not take the fight to them."

Buchevsky nodded in understanding. Basarab had made it clear from the beginning that avoiding contact with the enemy, lying low, was the best way to protect the civilians for whom they were responsible, and he was right. Yet that didn't change his basic personality's natural orientation—like Buchevsky's own—toward taking the offensive. Toward seeking out and destroying the enemy, not hiding from him.

But that would have come under the heading of Bad Ideas. Basarab's runners had made contact with several other small enclaves across southern Romania and northern Bulgaria, and by now, those enclaves were as concerned with defending themselves against other humans as against Shongairi. After the initial bombardments and confused combat of the first couple of weeks, the invaders had apparently decided to pull back from the Balkans' unfriendly terrain and settle for occupying more open areas of the planet. It was hard to be certain of that, with the collapse of the planetary communications net, but it seemed reasonable. As his brain trust of Truman and Sherman had pointed out, troop lift would almost certainly be limited for any interstellar expedition, so it would make sense to avoid stretching it any further than necessary by going up into the hills after dirt-poor, hardscrabble mountain villages.

Human refugees were an entirely different threat, and one Buchevsky was happy *they* hadn't had to deal with . . . yet. Starvation, exposure, and disease had probably killed at least half the civilians who'd fled their homes, and those who remained were becoming increasingly desperate as winter approached. Some of the other enclaves had already been forced to fight, often ruthlessly, against their own kind to preserve the resources their own people needed to survive.

In many ways, it was the fact that the aliens' actions had forced humans to kill *each other* in the name of simple survival that fueled Stephen Buchevsky's deepest rage.

"Nothing would make me happier than to go kick their scrawny asses," he said now, in response to Basarab's comment. "But unless they poke their snouts into our area—"

He shrugged, and Basarab nodded. Then he chuckled softly.

"What?" Buchevsky raised an eyebrow at him.

"It is just that we are so much alike, you and I." Basarab shook his head. "Deny it as you will, my Stephen, but there is Slav inside you!"

"Inside *me*?" Buchevsky laughed, looking down at the back of one very black hand. "Hey, I already told you! If any of my ancestors were *ever* in Europe, they got there from Africa, not the steppes!"

"Ah!" Basarab waved a finger under his nose. "So you've said, but *I* know better! What, 'Buchevsky'? This is an *African* name?"

"Nope, probably just somebody who owned one of my great-great-granddaddies or -grandmamas."

"Nonsense! Slavs in nineteenth-century America were too *poor* to own anyone! No, no. Trust me—it is in the blood. Somewhere in your ancestry there is—how do you Americans say it?—a Slav in the straw pile!"

Buchevsky laughed again. He was actually learning to do that again—sometimes, at least—and he and Basarab had had this conversation before. But then the Romanian's expression sobered, and he reached across the table to lay one hand on Buchevsky's forearm.

"Whatever you may have been born, my Stephen," he said quietly, "you are a Slav now. A Wallachian. You have earned that."

Buchevsky waved dismissively, but he couldn't deny the warmth he felt inside. He knew Basarab meant every word of it, just as he knew he'd earned his place as the Romanian's second-in-command through the training and discipline he'd brought the villagers. Basarab had somehow managed to stockpile impressive quantities of small arms and infantry support weapons, but however fearsome Take Bratianu and the rest of Basarab's original group might have been as individuals, it was obvious none of them had really understood how to train civilians. Steven Buchevsky, on the other hand, had spent years turning pampered *American* civilians into U.S. Marines. Compared with that, training tough, mountain-hardened Romanian villagers was a piece of cake.

I just hope none of them are ever going to need *that training*, he reflected, his mood turning grim once again..

Which brought him back to the subject of this conversation.

"I don't like it, Mircea," he said. "There's no reason for them to put a base way up here in the frigging mountains. Not unless something's happened that you and I don't know about."

"Agreed, agreed." Basarab nodded, playing with the written note again, then shrugged. "Sooner or later, unless they simply intend to kill all of us, there must be some form of accommodation."

His sour expression showed his opinion of his own analysis, but he continued unflinchingly.

"The people of this land have survived conquest before. No doubt they can do it again, and if these Shongairi had intended simple butchery rather than conquest, then they would have begun by destroying *all* our cities and towns from space. But I will not subject *my* people to them without holding out for the very best terms we can obtain. And if they prove me in error—if they demonstrate that they are, indeed, prepared to settle for butchery rather than conquest—they will pay a higher price than they can possibly imagine before they rule *these* mountains."

He sat for a moment in cold, dangerous silence. Then he shook himself.

"Well, there seems little point in speculating when we have no firsthand information. So I suppose we must take a closer look at this new base, see what it may be they have in mind." He tapped the note. "According to this, they had almost finished it before Iliescu noticed it was there. So perhaps it would be best if Take and I go examine it in person."

Buchevsky opened his mouth to protest, but then he closed it again. He'd discovered that he was always uncomfortable when Basarab went wandering around the mountains out from under his own eye. And a part of him resented the fact that Basarab hadn't even considered inviting *him* along on this little jaunt. But the truth, however little he wanted to admit it, was that he would probably have been more of a hindrance than a help.

Basarab and Take Bratianu both seemed to be able to see like cats and move like drifting leaves. He couldn't even come close to matching them when it came to sneaking through the woods at night, and he knew it . . .

however little he liked admitting that there was *anything* someone could do better than he could.

"We will go tonight," Basarab decided. "And while I am away, you will keep an eye on things for me, my African Slav, yes?"

"Yeah, I'll do that," Buchevsky agreed.

XIII

Regiment Commander Harah didn't like trees.

He hadn't always felt that way. In fact, he'd actually *liked* trees until the Empire invaded this never-to-be-sufficiently-damned planet. Now he vastly preferred long, flat, empty spaces—preferably of bare, pounded earth where not even a *garish* or one of the human "rabbits" could have hidden. Any other sort of terrain seemed to spontaneously spawn humans . . . all of whom appeared to have guns.

He hadn't needed Base Commander Shairez to tell *him* humans were all lunatics! It was nice to have confirmation, of course, and he was simply *delighted* that the Base Commander's conclusions had led Fleet Commander Thikair to change his plans. Once every last accursed human had been expunged from it, this planet would probably be a perfectly nice place to live.

He grimaced at his own thoughts as he sat gazing at the holographic plot in his GEV command vehicle.

Actually, Harah, part of you admires *these creatures, doesn't it?* he thought. *After all, we've killed thousands of them for every Shongair we've lost, and they still have the guts—the absolutely insane, utterly irrational, mind-numbingly stupid guts—to come right at us. If they only had half as much brains, they would've acknowledged our superiority and submitted months ago. But, no! They couldn't do that, could they?*

He growled, remembering the 35 percent of his original regiment he'd lost subduing what had once been the city of Cincinnati. Division Commander Tesuk had gone in with three regiments; he'd come out with less than one, and they'd *still* ended up taking out over half the city from orbit. Particularly in the nation the humans had called the "United States," there'd seemed to be more *guns* than there were people!

At least the experience had taught the expedition's senior officers to settle for occupying *open* terrain, where surveillance could be maintained effectively, and simply calling in kinetic strikes on anything resembling organized resistance in more constricted terrain.

Despite that, no one relished the thought of acquiring Shairez's test subjects anyplace where there'd been sustained contact with the humans. First, because there weren't many humans *left* in places like that, and the ones who hadn't already been killed had become fiendishly clever at hiding. Just finding them would have been hard enough even without the *second* consideration . . . which was that those same survivors were also uncommonly good at ambushing anyone who went looking for them.

Of course, there weren't many places where there'd been *no* combat, given humans' insane stubbornness. Still, the mountainous portions of the area the humans called "the Balkans" had seen far less than most, mainly because the population was so sparse and the terrain was so accursedly bad, HQ had decided to let the humans there stew in their own juices rather than invest the effort to go in after them.

And, he reflected moodily, *the other reason HQ made that little decision was the fact that we kept getting our asses kicked every time we did send someone in on the ground, didn't we?*

In fairness, they'd taken the worst of their losses in the first few weeks, before they'd really begun to appreciate just what a losing proposition it was to go after humans on ground of their own choosing.

That's what the gods made fire support *for,* Harah thought grimly.

Well, he reminded himself as his GEVs and transports approached their jumpoff positions, *at least the satellites have told us exactly where* these *humans are. And they've been left alone, too.* Their *herd hasn't been culled yet. And not only should* they *be fat, happy, and stupid compared with the miserable* jermahk *we've been trying to dig out of the woodwork back home, but* we've *learned a lot over the last few months.*

His lips wrinkled back from his canines in a hunter's grin.

Stephen Buchevsky swore with silent, bitter venom.

The sun was barely above the eastern horizon, shining into his eyes as he studied the Shongairi through the binoculars and wondered what the hell they were after. After staying clear of the mountains for so long, what could have inspired them to come straight at the villages this way?

And why the hell do they have to be doing it when Mircea is away? a corner of his mind demanded.

It was at least fortunate the listening posts had detected the approaching drones so early, given how close behind them the aliens had been this time. There'd been time—barely—to crank up the old-fashioned, hand-powered warning sirens. And at least the terrain was too heavily forested for any sort of airborne ops. If the Shongairi wanted them, they'd have to come in on the ground.

Which was exactly what they seemed to have in mind. A large number of APCs and a handful of tanks were assembling on the low ground at the southern end of the lake, about a kilometer below the Gheorghiu-Dej Dam, while a smaller force of tanks came in across the lake itself, followed by a dozen big orbital shuttles, and he didn't like that one bit.

The villages were scattered along the rugged flanks of a mountain spine running east-to-west on the lake's southeastern shore. The ridgeline towered to over 3,200 feet in places, with the villages tucked away in dense tree cover above the 1,800-foot level. He'd thought they were well concealed, but the Shongari clearly knew where they were and obviously intended to squeeze them between the force coming in over the lake and the second force, moving along the deep valley between their ridge and the one to its south.

That much was clear enough. Among the many things that *weren't* clear was how well the aliens' sensors could track humans moving through rough terrain under heavy tree cover. He hoped the answer to that question was "not very," but he couldn't rely on that.

"Start them moving," he told Elizabeth Cantacuzène. "These people are headed straight for the villages. I think we'd better be somewhere else when they get here."

"Yes, Stephen." The teacher sounded far calmer than Buchevsky felt as she nodded, then disappeared to pass his instructions to the waiting runners. Within moments, he knew, the orders would have gone out and their people would be falling back to the position he'd allowed Ramirez to christen "Bastogne."

It was an Army dance the first time around, he thought, *and it came out pretty well that time. I guess it's time to see how well the Green Machine makes out.*

Regiment Commander Harah swore as the icons on his plot shifted.

It appears we weren't close enough behind the drones after all, he thought grumpily.

HQ had been forced to factor the humans' bizarre ability to sense drones from beyond visual range into its thinking, and the operations plan had made what *ought* to have been ample allowance for it. Unfortunately, it hasn't been, and he was already losing sensor resolution as they went scurrying through those accursed trees.

"They're moving along the ridge," he said over the regimental net. "They're headed west—toward those higher peaks. Second Battalion, swing farther up the lake, try to come in on their flank. First Battalion, get moving up that valley *now*."

Buchevsky muttered another curse as the drones' unpleasant vibration kept pace with him. Clearly, the damn things could track through tree cover better than he'd hoped. On the other hand, they seemed to be coming in close, low above the treetops, and if they were—

"Dainthar seize them!"

A quartet of dirty fireballs trickled down the sky, and four of Harah's drones went off the air simultaneously.

Damn it! What in the name of Dainthar's Third Hell are villagers up in these damned mountains doing with SAMs?

Buchevsky bared his teeth in a panting, running grin as Macomb's air-defense teams took out the nearest drones. He still felt vibrations from other drones, farther away, but if the bastards kept them high enough to avoid the Gremlins, it might make their sensor resolution crappier, too.

Harah tried to master his anger, but he was sick unto death of how these damned humans insisted on screwing up even the simplest operation. There weren't supposed to be any SAMs or heavy weapons up here. That was the entire reason they'd come looking for Base Commander Shairez's specimens here. Only the humans *still* refused to cooperate!

He considered reporting to headquarters. Equipment losses on this accursed invasion were already astronomical, and he doubted HQ would thank him if he lost still more of it chasing after what were supposed to be unarmed villagers cowering in their mountain hideouts. But they had to secure specimens *somewhere*, and he had *these* humans more or less in his sights.

"We're not going to be able to bring the drones in as close as planned," he told his battalion commanders. "It's up to our scouts. Tell them to keep their damn eyes open."

Fresh acknowledgments came in, and he watched his own forces' icons closing in on the abruptly amorphous shaded area representing the drones' best guess of the humans' location.

We may not be able to see them clearly, he thought angrily, *but even if we can't, there aren't that many places they can go, now, are there?*

Buchevsky was profoundly grateful for the way hard work had toughened the lowland refugees. They were managing to keep up with the villagers, which they never would have been able to do without it. Several smaller children were beginning to flag, anyway, of course, and his heart ached at the ruthless demands being placed on them. But the bigger kids were managing to keep up with the adults, and there were enough grown-ups to take turns carrying the littlest ones.

The unhealed wound where Shania and Yvonne had been cried out for *him* to scoop up one of those tiny human beings, carry *someone's* child to the safety he'd been unable to offer his own children.

But that wasn't his job, and he turned his attention to what was.

He slid to a halt on the narrow trail, breathing heavily, watching the last few villagers stream past. The perimeter guards came next, and then the scouts who'd been on listening watch. One of them was Robert Szu.

"It's . . . it's pretty much like . . . you and Mircea figured it . . . Top," the private panted. He paused for a moment, gathering his breath, then nodded sharply. "They're coming up the firebreak roads on both sides of the ridgeline. I figure their points are halfway up by now."

"Good." Buchevsky said.

———

"Farkalash!"

Regiment Commander Harah's driver looked back over his shoulder at the horrendous oath until Harah's bared-canines snarl turned him hastily back around to his controls. The regiment commander only wished he could dispose of the Dainthar-damned humans as easily!

I shouldn't have sent the vehicles in that close, he told himself through a boil of bloodred fury. *I should've dismounted the infantry farther out.* Of course *it was as obvious to the humans as it was to me that there were only a handful of routes vehicles could use!*

He growled at himself, but he knew why he'd made the error. The humans were moving faster than he'd estimated they could, and he'd wanted to use his vehicles' speed advantage. Which was why the humans had destroyed six more GEVs and eleven wheeled APCs . . . not to mention over a hundred troopers who'd been *aboard* the troop carriers.

And there's no telling how many more *little surprises they may've planted along any openings wide enough for vehicles.*

"Dismount the infantry," he said flatly over the command net. "Scout formation. The vehicles are not to advance until the engineers have checked the trails for more explosives."

Buchevsky grimaced sourly. From the smoke billowing up through the treetops, he'd gotten at least several of their vehicles. Unfortunately, he couldn't know *how* many.

However many, they're going to take the hint and come in on foot from here . . . unless they're complete and utter idiots. And somehow, I don't think they are. Damn it.

Well, at least he'd slowed them up. That was going to buy the civilians a little breathing space. Now it was time to buy them a little more.

Harah's ears flattened, but at least it wasn't a surprise this time. The small arms fire rattling out of the trees had become inevitable the moment he ordered his own infantry to go in on foot.

Automatic weapons fire barked and snarled, and Buchevsky *wished* they hadn't been forced to deep-six their radios. His people knew the terrain intimately, knew the best defensive positions, but the Shongairi had heavier support weapons and their communications were vastly better than his. And, adding insult to injury, some of their infantry were using captured human rocket and grenade launchers to thicken their firepower.

The situation's bitter irony wasn't lost upon him. This time, *his* forces were on the short end of the "asymmetrical warfare" stick, and it sucked. On the other hand, he'd had painful personal experience of just how effective guerrillas could be in this sort of terrain.

There was more satisfaction to accompany the frustration in Harah's growl as he looked at the plot's latest update.

The advance had been slower than he'd ever contemplated, and morning had become afternoon, but the humans appeared to be running out of SAMs at last. That meant he could get his drones in close enough to we see what the hell was happening, and his momentum was building.

Which was a damned good thing, since he'd already lost over 20 percent of his troops.

Well, maybe I have, but I've cost them, *too,* he thought harshly. Real-time estimates of enemy losses were notoriously unreliable, but even by his most pessimistic estimates, the humans had lost over forty fighters so far.

That was the good news. The bad news was that they appeared to be remarkably well equipped with infantry weapons, and their commander was fighting as smart as any human Harah had ever heard of. His forces were hugely outnumbered and outgunned, but he was hitting back hard—in fact, Harah's casualties, despite his GEVs and his mortars, were at least six or seven times the humans'. The other side was intimately familiar with the terrain and taking ruthless advantage of it, and his infantry had run into enough more concealed explosives to make anyone cautious.

Whatever we've run our snouts into, he reflected, *those aren't just a bunch of villagers. Somebody's spent a lot of time reconnoitering these damn mountains. They're fighting from positions that were preselected for their fields of fire. And those explosives . . . Someone picked the spots for* them *pretty damned carefully, too. Whoever it was knew what he was doing, and he must've spent months preparing his positions.*

Despite himself, he felt a flicker of respect for his human opponent. Not that it was going to make any difference in the end. The take from his drones was still far less detailed than he could wish, but it was clear the fleeing villagers were running into what amounted to a cul-de-sac.

Buchevsky felt the beginnings of despair.

He'd started the morning with 100 "regulars" and another 150 "militia" from the villages. He knew everyone tended to overestimate his own losses in a fight like this, especially in this sort of terrain, but he'd be surprised if he hadn't lost at least a quarter of his people by now.

That was bad enough, but there was worse coming.

The Bastogne position had never been intended to stand off a full-bore Shongairi assault. It had really been designed as a place of retreat in the face of attack by *human* adversaries after the villages' winter supplies. That meant Bastogne, despite its name, was more of a fortified warehouse than some sort of final redoubt. He'd made its defenses as tough as he could, yet he'd never contemplated trying to hold it against hundreds of Shongairi infantry, supported by tanks and mortars.

Stop kicking yourself, an inner voice growled. *There was never any point trying to build a position you could've held against that kind of assault. So what if you'd held them off for a while? They'd only call in one of their damned kinetic strikes in the end, anyway.*

He knew that was true, but what was *also* true was that the only paths of retreat were so steep as to be almost impassable. Bastogne *was* supposed to hold against any likely human attack, and without its stockpiled supplies, the chance that their civilians could have survived the approaching winter had been minimal, at best. So he and Mircea had staked everything on making the position tough enough to stand . . . and now it was a trap too many of their people couldn't get out of.

He looked out through the smoky forest, watching the westering sun paint the smoke the color of blood, and knew his people were out of places to run. They were on the final perimeter, now, and it took every ounce of discipline he'd learned in his life to fight down his despair.

I'm sorry, Mircea, he thought grimly. *I fucked up. Now we're all screwed. I'm just as glad you didn't make it back in time, after all.*

His jaw muscles tightened, and he reached out and grabbed Maria Averescu, one of his runners.

"I need you to find Gunny Meyers," he said in the Romanian he'd finally begun to master.

"He's dead, Top," she replied harshly, and his belly clenched.

"Sergeant Ramirez?"

"Him, too, I think. I know he took a hit here." Averescu thumped the center of her own chest.

"Then find Sergeant Jonescu. Tell him—" Buchevsky drew a deep breath. "Tell him I want him and his people to get as many kids out as they can. Tell him the rest of us will buy him as much time as we can. Got that?"

"Yes, Top!" Averescu's grimy face was pale, but she nodded hard.

"Good. Now go!"

He released her shoulder. She shot off through the smoke, and he headed for the perimeter command post.

The Shongairi scouts realized the humans' retreat had slowed still further. Painful experience made them wary of changes, and they felt their way cautiously forward.

They were right to be cautious.

Bastogne had been built around a deep cavern that offered protected, easily camouflaged storage for winter foodstuffs and fodder for the villages' animals. Concealment was not its only defense, however.

Buchevsky bared his teeth savagely as he heard the explosions. He still wished he'd had better mines to work with—he'd have given his left arm for a couple of crates of claymores—but the Romanian anti-personnel mines Basarab had managed to scrounge up were one hell of a lot better than nothing. The mine belt wasn't so deep as he would have liked, but the Shongairi obviously hadn't realized what they were walking into, and he listened with bloodthirsty satisfaction to their shrieks.

I may not stop *them, but I can damned well make them pay* cash. *And maybe—just maybe—Jonescu will get some of the kids out, after all.*

He didn't let himself think about the struggle to survive those kids would face over the coming winter with no roof, no food. He couldn't.

"Runner!"

"Yes, Top!"

"Find Corporal Gutierrez," Buchevsky told the young man. "Tell him it's time to dance."

The Shongairi halted along the edge of the minefield cowered close against the ground as the pair of 120 mm mortars Basarab had scrounged up along with the mines started dropping their lethal fire on them. Even now, few of them had actually encountered human artillery, and the 35-pound HE bombs were a devastating experience.

Regiment Commander Harah winced as the communications net was flooded by sudden reports of heavy fire. Even after the unpleasant surprise of the infantry-portable SAMs, he hadn't anticipated *this*.

His lead infantry companies' already heavy loss rates soared, and he snarled over the net at his own support weapons commander.

"Find those damned mortars and get fire on them—*now!*"

Harah's infantry recoiled as rifle fire added to the carnage of mortar bombs and minefields. But they were survivors who'd learned their lessons in a hard school, and their junior officers started probing forward, looking for openings.

Three heavy mortars, mounted on unarmored transports, had managed to struggle up the narrow trail behind them and tried to locate human mortars. But the dense tree cover and rugged terrain made it impossible to get a solid radar track on the incoming fire. Finally, unable to actually find the mortar pits, they began blind suppressive fire.

The Shongairi mortars were more powerful, and white-hot flashes began to walk across the area behind Buchevsky's forward positions, and he heard screams rising from behind him, as well.

But the Shongairi had problems of their own. Their vehicle-mounted weapons were confined to the trail while the humans' were deeply dug-in, and Buchevsky and Ignacio Gutierrez had pre-plotted just about every possible firing position along that trail. As soon as they opened fire, Gutierrez knew where they had to be, and both of *his* mortars retargeted immediately. They fired more rapidly than the heavier Shongairi weapons, and their bombs fell around the Shongairi vehicles in a savage exchange that could not—and didn't—last long.

Ignacio Gutierrez died, along with one entire crew. The second mortar, though, remained in action . . . which was more than could be said for the vehicles they'd engaged.

Harah snarled.

He had over a dozen more mortar vehicles . . . all of them miles behind the point of contact, at the far end of the choked, tortuous trails along which his infantry had pursued the humans. He could bring them up—in time—just as he could call in a kinetic strike and put an end to this entire business in minutes. But the longer he delayed, the more casualties that single remaining human mortar would inflict. And if he called in the kinetic strike, he'd kill the test subjects he'd come to capture, along with their defenders . . . which would make the entire operation, and all the casualties he'd already suffered, meaningless.

That wasn't going to happen. If this bunch of primitives was so incredibly stupid, so lost to all rationality and basic decency, that they wanted to die fighting, then he would damned well oblige them.

He looked up through a break in the tree cover. The light was fading quickly, and Shongairi didn't like fighting in the dark. But there was still time. They could still break through before darkness fell if—

Stephen Buchevsky sensed it coming. He couldn't have explained how, but he knew. He could actually *feel* the Shongairi gathering themselves, steeling themselves, and he knew.

"They're coming!" he shouted, and heard his warning relayed along the horseshoe-shaped defensive line in either direction from his CP.

He set aside his own rifle and settled into position behind the KPV heavy machine gun. There were three tripod-mounted PKMS 7.62 mm medium machine guns dug in around Bastogne's final perimeter, but even Mircea Basarab's scrounging talents had limits. He'd managed to come up with only one *heavy* machine gun, and it was a bulky, awkward thing—six and a half feet long, intended as a vehicle-mounted weapon, on an improvised infantry mounting.

The Shongairi started forward behind a hurricane of rifle fire and grenades. The minefield slowed them, disordered them, but they kept coming. They were too close for the single remaining mortar to engage, and the medium machine guns opened up.

Shongairi screamed, tumbled aside, disappeared in sprays of blood and tissue, but then a pair of wheeled armored personnel carriers edged up the trail behind them. How they'd gotten here was more than Buchevsky could guess, but their turret-mounted light energy weapons quested back and forth, seeking targets. Then a quasi-solid bolt of lightning slammed across the chaos and the blood and terror and one of the machine guns was silenced forever.

But Stephen Buchevsky knew where that lightning bolt had come from, and the Russian Army had developed the KPV around the 14.5 mm round of its final World War II antitank rifle. The PKMS' 185-grain bullet developed three thousand foot-pounds of muzzle energy; the KPV's bullet weighed almost a *thousand* grains . . . and developed twenty-four thousand foot-pounds of muzzle energy.

He laid his sights on the vehicle that had fired and sent six hundred rounds per minute shrieking into it.

The APC staggered as the steel-cored, armor-piercing, incendiary bullets slammed into it at better than 3,200 feet per second. Armor intended to resist small arms fire never had a chance against *that* torrent of destruction, and the vehicle vomited smoke and flame.

Its companion turned toward the source of its destruction, and Alice Macomb stood up in a rifle pit. She exposed herself recklessly with an RBR-M60, and its three-and-a-half-pound rocket smashed into the APC . . . just before a six-round burst killed her where she stood.

Buchevsky swung the KBV's flaming muzzle, sweeping his fire along the Shongairi line, pouring his hate, his desperate need to protect the children behind him, into his enemies.

He was still firing when the Shongairi grenade silenced his machine gun forever.

XIV

He woke slowly, floating up from the depths like someone else's ghost. He woke to darkness, to pain, and to a swirling tide race of dizziness, confusion, and fractured memory.

He blinked, slowly, blindly, trying to understand. He'd been wounded more times than he liked to think about, but it had never been like this. The pain had never run everywhere under his skin, as if it were racing about on the power of his own heartbeat. And yet, even though he knew he had never suffered such pain in his life, it was curiously . . . distant. A part of him, yes, but walled off by the dizziness. Held one imagined half step away.

"You are awake, my Stephen."

It was a statement, he realized, not a question. Almost as if the voice behind it were trying to reassure him of that.

He turned his head, and it was as if it belonged to someone else. It seemed to take him forever, but at last Mircea Basarab's face swam into his field of vision.

He blinked again, trying to focus, but he couldn't. He lay in a cave somewhere, looking out into a mountain night, and there was something wrong with his eyes. Everything seemed oddly out of phase, and the night kept flashing, as if it were alive with heat lightning.

"Mircea."

He didn't recognize his own voice. It was faint, thready.

"Yes," Basarab agreed. "I know you may not believe it at this moment, but you will recover."

"Take . . . your word . . . for it."

"Very wise of you."

Buchevsky didn't have to be able to focus his eyes to see Basarab's fleeting smile, and he felt his own mouth twitch in reply. But then a new and different sort of pain ripped through him.

"I . . . fucked up." He swallowed painfully. "Sorry . . . so sorry. The kids . . ."

His eyes burned as a tear forced itself from under his lids, and he felt Basarab grip his right hand. The Romanian raised it, pressed it against his own chest, and his face came closer as he leaned over Buchevsky.

"No, my Stephen," he said slowly. "It was not *you* who failed; it was I. This is *my* fault, my friend."

"No." Buchevsky shook his head weakly. "No. Couldn't have . . . stopped it even if . . . you'd been here."

"You think not?" It was Basarab's turn to shake his head. "You think wrongly. These creatures—these *Shongairi*—would never have touched my people if I had remembered. Had I not spent so long trying to be someone I am not. Trying to forget. You shame me, my Stephen. You, who fell in my place, doing my duty, paying in blood for my failure."

Buchevsky frowned, his swirling brain trying to make some sort of sense out of Basarab's words. He couldn't . . . which probably shouldn't have been too surprising, he decided, given how horrendously bad he felt.

"How many—?" he asked.

"Only a very few, I fear," Basarab said quietly. "Your Gunny Meyers is here, although he was more badly wounded even than you. I am not surprised the vermin left both of you for dead. And Jasmine and Private Lopez. The others were . . . gone before Take and I could return."

Buchevsky's stomach clenched as Basarab confirmed what he'd already known.

"And . . . the villagers?"

"Sergeant Jonescu got perhaps a dozen children to safety," Basarab said. "He and most of his men died holding the trail while the children and their mothers fled. The others—"

He shrugged, looking away, then looked back at Buchevsky.

"They are not here, Stephen. For whatever reason, the vermin have taken them, and having seen this new base of theirs, I do not think either of us would like that reason."

"*God.*" Buchevsky closed his eyes again. "Sorry. My fault," he said once more.

"Do not repeat that foolishness again, or you will make me angry," Basarab said sternly. "And do not abandon hope for them. They are *my* people. I swore to protect them, and I do not let my word be proved false."

Buchevsky's world was spinning away again, yet he opened his eyes, looked up in disbelief. His vision cleared, if only for a moment, and as he saw Mircea Basarab's face, he felt the disbelief flow out of him.

It was still preposterous, of course. He knew that. Only, somehow, as he looked up into that granite expression, it didn't matter what he *knew*. All that mattered was what he *felt* . . . and as he fell back into the bottomless darkness, a tiny little sliver of awareness felt almost sorry for the Shongairi.

Private Kumayr felt his head beginning to nod forward and stiffened his spine, snapping back erect in his chair. His damnably *comfortable* chair, which wasn't exactly what someone needed to keep him awake and alert in the middle of the night.

He shook himself and decided he'd better find something to do if he didn't want one of the officers to come along and rip his head off for dozing on duty. Something that looked industrious and conscientious.

His ears twitched in amusement, and he punched up a standard diagnostic of the perimeter security systems. Not that he expected to find any problems. The entire base was brand new, and all of its systems had passed their final checks with flying colors less than three local days ago. Still, it would look good on the log sheets.

He hummed softly as the computers looked over one another's shoulders, reporting back to him. He paid particular attention to the systems in the laboratory area. Now that they had test subjects, the labs would be getting a serious workout, after all. When that happened—

His humming stopped, and his ears pricked as a red icon appeared on his display. That couldn't be right . . . could it?

He keyed another, more tightly focused diagnostic program, and his pricked ears flattened as more icons began to blink. He stared at them, then slammed his hand down on the transmit key.

"Perimeter One!" he snapped. "Perimeter One, Central. Report status!"

There was no response, and something with hundreds of small icy feet started to scuttle up and down his spine.

"Perimeter Two!" he barked, trying another circuit. "Perimeter Two—report status!"

Still no response, and that was impossible. There were *fifty troopers* in each of those positions—one of them *had* to have heard him!

"All perimeter stations!" He heard the desperation in his voice, tried to squeeze it back out again while he held down the all-units key. "All perimeter stations, this is a red alert!"

Still there was nothing, and he stabbed more controls, bringing up the monitors. They came alive . . . and he froze.

Not possible, a small, still voice said in the back of his brain as he stared at the images of carnage. At the troopers with their throats ripped out, at the Shongairi blood soaking into the thirsty soil of an alien world, at heads turned backwards on snapped necks and dismembered body parts scattered like some lunatic's bloody handiwork.

Not possible, not without at least one alarm sounding. Not—

He heard a tiny sound, and his right hand flashed toward his side arm. But even as he touched it, the door of his control room flew open and darkness crashed over him.

XV

"What?"

Fleet Commander Thikair looked at Ship Commander Ahzmer in astonishment so deep, it was sheer incomprehension.

"I'm . . . I'm sorry, sir." The flagship's CO sounded like someone trapped in an amazingly bad dream, Thikair thought distantly. "The report just came in. I'm . . . afraid it's confirmed, sir."

"*All* of them?" Thikair shook himself. "Everyone assigned to the base—even Shairez?"

"All of them," Ahzmer confirmed heavily. "And all the test subjects have disappeared."

"*Dainthar,*" Thikair half whispered. He stared at the ship commander, then shook himself again, harder.

"How did they do it?"

"Sir, I don't know. *No one* knows. For that matter, it doesn't . . . well, it doesn't look like anything we've seen the humans do before."

"What are you talking about?" Thikair's voice was harder, impatient. He knew much of his irritation was the product of his own shock, but that didn't change the fact that what Ahzmer had just said made no sense.

"It doesn't look like whoever it was used *weapons* at all, Fleet Commander." Ahzmer didn't sound as if he expected Thikair to believe him, but the ship commander went on doggedly. "It's more like some sort of wild beasts got through every security system without sounding a single alarm. Not one, sir. But there are no bullet wounds, no knife wounds, no sign of *any* kind of weapon. Our people were just . . . torn apart."

"That doesn't make sense," Thikair protested.

"No, sir, it doesn't. But it's what *happened*."

The two of them stared at one another; then Thikair drew a deep breath.

"Senior officers conference, two hours," he said flatly.

"The ground patrols have confirmed it, Fleet Commander," Ground Force Commander Thairys said heavily. "There are no Shongairi survivors. None. And—" He inhaled heavily, someone about to say something he really didn't want to. "—there's no evidence that a single one of our troopers so much as fired a shot in his own defense. It's as if they all just . . . *sat* there, waiting for someone—or some*thing*—to tear them apart."

"Calm down, Thairys." Thikair put both sternness and sympathy into his tone. "We're going to have enough panicky rumors when the troops hear about this. Let's not begin believing in night terrors before the rumor mill even gets started!"

Thairys looked at him for a moment, then managed a chuckle that was only slightly hollow.

"You're right, of course, sir. It's just that. . . . Well, it's just that I've never seen anything like this. And I've checked the database. As nearly as I can tell, no one in the entire *Hegemony* has ever seen anything like this."

"It's a big galaxy," Thikair pointed out. "And even the Hegemony's explored only a very small portion of it. I don't know what happened down there, either, but trust me—there's a rational explanation. We just have to figure out what it is."

"With all due respect, Fleet Commander," Squadron Commander Jainfar said quietly, "how do we go about doing that?"

Thikair looked at him, and the squadron commander flicked his ears.

"I've personally reviewed the sensor recordings, sir. Until Private Kumayr began trying to contact the perimeter strong points, there was absolutely no indication of any problem. Whatever happened, it apparently managed to kill every single member of the garrison—except for Kumayr—without being detected by any heat, motion, or audio sensor. The fact of the matter is, sir, that we have no data, no information at all. Just an entire base full of dead personnel. And with no evidence, how do we figure out *what* happened, far less who was responsible for it?"

"One thing I think we *can* assume, sir." Base Commander Barak was down on the planetary surface, attending the conference electronically, and Thikair nodded permission to speak to his comm image.

"As I say, I think we can assume *one* thing," Barak continued. "Surely if it was the humans—if humans were capable of this sort of thing—they wouldn't have waited until we'd killed more than half of them before we found out about it! For that matter, why here? Why Shairez's base, and not mine, or Base Commander Fursa's? Unless we want to assume the humans somehow figured out what Shairez was going to be developing, why employ some sort of 'secret weapon' for the first time against a brand-new base where nowhere near as much of the local population has been killed?"

"With all due respect, Base Commander," Thairys said, "if it wasn't the humans, then who do you suggest it might have been?"

"That I don't know, sir," Barak said respectfully. "I'm simply suggesting that, logically, if humans could do this in the first place, they'd already have done it . . . and on a considerably larger scale."

"Are you suggesting that some other member of the Hegemony might be responsible?" Thikair asked slowly.

"I think that's remotely possible . . . but *only* remotely, sir." Barak shrugged. "Again, I have no idea who—or what—it actually was. But I don't really see how any other member of the Hegemony could have penetrated our security so seamlessly. Our technology is as good as anyone else's. Probably even better, in purely military applications."

"Wonderful." Jainfar grimaced. "So all any of us have been able to contribute so far is that we don't have a clue who did it, or how, or even why! Assuming, of course, that it wasn't the *humans* . . . whom we've all now agreed don't have the capability to do it in the first place!"

"I think we've wandered about as far afield speculatively as we profitably can," Thikair said firmly. "I see no point in our helping one another panic from the depths of our current ignorance."

His subordinates all looked at him, most at least a little sheepishly, and he bared his canines in a frosty smile.

"Don't misunderstand me. I'm as . . . anxious about this as anyone else. But let's look at it. So far, we've lost one base and its personnel. All right, we've been hurt—badly. But whatever happened, it obviously took Shairez's entire base completely by surprise, and we know the sensor net didn't pick anything up. So, I think, the first thing to do is to put all our bases and personnel on maximum alert. Second, we emphasize that whoever was responsible may have some form of advanced stealth technology. Since we apparently can't rely on our sensors to detect it, we're going to have to rely on our own physical senses. I want all of our units to establish real-time, free-flow communications nets. All checkpoints will be manned, not left to the automatics, and all detachments will check in regularly with their central HQs. Even if we can't detect these people—whoever they are—on their way in, we can at least be certain we know when they've arrived. And I don't care *how* good their 'stealth technology' is. If we know they're there, we have enough troopers, enough guns, and enough heavy weapons on that planet to kill *anything*."

"Yes, Thairys?" Thikair said.

The ground force commander had lingered as the other senior officers filed out. Now he looked at the fleet commander, his ears half-folded and his eyes somber. "There were two small points I . . . chose not to mention in front of the others, sir," he said quietly.

"Oh?" Thikair managed to keep his voice level, despite the sudden cold tingle dancing down his nerves.

"Yes, sir. First, I'm afraid the preliminary medical exams indicate Base Commander Shairez was killed several hours *after* the rest of her personnel. And there are indications that she was . . . interrogated before her neck was broken."

"I see." Thikair looked at his subordinate for a moment, then cleared his throat. "And the second point?"

"And the second point is that two of the base's neural education units are missing, sir. Whoever attacked Shairez's facility must have taken them with him. And if he knows how to operate them . . ."

The ground force commander's voice trailed off. There was, after all, no need for him to complete the sentence, since each of the education units contained the basic knowledge platform of the entire Hegemony.

XVI

"I almost wish something else would happen," Base Commander Fursa said. He and Base Commander Barak were conferring via communicator, and Barak frowned at him.

"I want to figure out what's going on as badly as you do, Fursa. And I suppose for us to do that, 'something else' *is* going to have to happen. But while you're wishing, just remember, you're the next closest major base."

"I know." Fursa grimaced. "That's my point. We're feeling just a bit exposed out here. I'm inclined to suspect that the *anticipation* is at least as bad as beating off an actual attack would be."

Barak grunted. His own base sat in the middle of a place that had once been called "Kansas," which put an entire ocean between him and whatever had happened to Shairez. Fursa's base, on the other hand, was located just outside the ruins of the human city of Moscow.

Still, almost two local weeks had passed. That was a lot of time, when no one in the entire expedition had been able to come up with a workable explanation for what had happened. A lot of time for nerves to tighten, for the 'anticipation' Fursa had just mentioned to work on all of them.

And a lot of time for whoever had attacked Shairez's base to move his operations somewhere else entirely.

"You may have a point," he said finally, "but I can't say *I'm* looking forward to it. In fact, if I had my way"—his voice lowered—"I'd already be cutting my losses. This planet's been nothing but one enormous pain in the ass. I say take all our people off and level the place."

The base commanders' gazes met, and Barak saw the agreement hidden in Fursa's eyes. Any one of Fleet Commander Thikair's dreadnoughts was capable of sterilizing any planet. Of course, actually doing that would raise more than a few eyebrows among the Hegemony's member races. The sort of scrutiny it would draw down upon the Empire might well have disastrous consequences. But even so . . .

"Somehow, I don't think that particular solution's going to be very high on the Fleet Commander's list," Fursa said carefully.

"No, and it probably shouldn't be," Barak agreed. "But I'm willing to bet it's running through the *back* of his mind already, and you know it."

"Time check," Brigade Commander Caranth announced. "Check in."

"Perimeter One, secure."

"Perimeter Two, secure."

"Perimeter Three, secure."

"Perimeter Four, secure."

The acknowledgments came in steadily, and Caranth's ears twitched in satisfaction with each of them . . . until the sequence paused.

The brigade commander didn't worry for a moment, but then he stiffened in his chair.

"Perimeter Five, report," he said.

Only silence answered.

"Perimeter Five!" he snapped . . . and that was when the firing began.

Caranth lunged upright and raced to the command bunker's armored observation slit while his staff started going berserk behind him. He stared out into the night, his body rigid in disbelief as the stroboscopic fury of muzzle flashes ripped the darkness apart. He couldn't see anything but the flickering lightning of automatic weapons . . . and neither could his sensors. Yet he had infantry out there shooting at *something*, and as he watched, one of his heavy weapons posts opened fire, as well.

"We're under attack!" someone screamed over the net. "Perimeter Three— we're under attack! *They're coming through the—"*

The voice chopped off, and then, horribly, Caranth heard other voices yelling in alarm, screaming in panic, chopping off in mid-syllable. It was as if some invisible, unstoppable whirlwind was sweeping through his perimeter, and strain his eyes though he might, he couldn't even *see* it!

The voices began to dwindle, fading in a diminuendo that was even more terrifying than the gunfire, the explosion of artillery rounds landing on something no one could see. The firing died. The last scream bubbled into silence, and Caranth felt his heart trying to freeze in his chest.

The only sound was his staff, trying desperately to contact even one of the perimeter security points.

There was no answer, only silence. And then—

"What's *that?*" someone blurted, and Caranth turned to see *something* flowing from the overhead louvers of the bunker's ventilation system. There was no time even to begin to recognize what it was before the darkness crashed down on him like a hammer.

Fleet Commander Thikair felt a thousand years old as he sat in the silence of his stateroom, cursing the day he'd ever had his brilliant idea about using this planet and its eternally damned humans for the Empire's benefit.

It seemed so simple, he thought almost numbly. *Like such a reasonable risk. But then it all went so horribly wrong, from the moment our troopers landed. And now this.*

Base Commander Fursa's entire command was gone, wiped out in a single night. And in the space of less than eight hours, two infantry brigades and an entire armored regiment had been just as utterly destroyed.

And they still had absolutely no idea how it had happened.

They'd received a single report, from a platoon commander, claiming that he was under attack by humans. Humans who completely ignored the assault rifles firing into them. Humans who registered on no thermal sensor, no motion sensor. Humans who *could not* be there.

Maybe it isn't *possible. Or maybe it's just one more lunacy about this entire insane planet. But whatever it is, it's enough. It's* more *than enough.*

He punched a button on his communicator.

"Yes, Fleet Commander?" Ahzmer's voice responded quietly.

"Bring them up," Thikair said with a terrible, flat emphasis. "I want every single trooper off that planet within twelve hours. And then we'll let Jainfar's dreadnoughts use the Dainthar-cursed place for *target practice.*"

It wasn't quite that simple, of course.

Organizing the emergency withdrawal of an entire planetary assault force was even more complicated than landing it had been. But at least the required troop lift had been rather drastically reduced, Thikair reflected bitterly. Over half his entire ground force had been wiped out. However small his absolute losses might have been compared with those of the humans, it was still a staggering defeat for the Empire, and it was all his responsibility.

He would already have killed himself, except that no honorable suicide could possibly expunge the stain he'd brought to the honor of his entire clan. No, that would require the atonement of formal execution . . . and even that might not prove enough.

But before I go home to face His Majesty, there's one last thing I need to do.

"Are we ready, Ahzmer?"

"We are according to my readouts," the ship commander replied. But there was something peculiar about his tone, and Thikair looked at him.

"Meaning what?" he asked impatiently.

"Meaning that according to my readouts, all shuttles have returned and docked, but neither *Stellar Dawn* nor *Imperial Sword* have confirmed recovery of their small craft. All the other transports have checked in, but they haven't yet."

"What?"

Thikair's one-word question quivered with sudden, ice-cold fury. It was as if all his anxiety, all his fear, guilt, and shame suddenly had someone *else* to focus upon, and he showed all of his canines in a ferocious snarl.

"Get their commanders on the comm *now*," he snapped. "Find out what in Dainthar's Second Hell they think they're doing! And then get me Jainfar!"

"At once, sir! I—"

Ahzmer's voice chopped off, and Thikair's eyes narrowed.

"Ahzmer?" he said.

"Sir, the plot . . ."

Thikair turned to the master display, and it was his turn to freeze.

Six of the expedition's seven dreadnoughts were heading steadily away from the planet.

"What are they—?" he began, then gasped as two of the dreadnoughts suddenly opened fire. Not on the planet, but on their own escorts!

Nothing in the galaxy could stand up to the energy-range fire of a dreadnought. Certainly no mere scout ship, destroyer, or cruiser could.

It took less than forty-five seconds for every one of Thikair's screening warships to die, and three-quarters of his transport ships went with them.

"Get Jainfar!" he shouted at Ahzmer. "Find out what—"

"Sir, there's no response from Squadron Commander Jainfar's ship!" Ahzmer's communications officer blurted. "There's no response from *any* of the other dreadnoughts!"

"*What?*" Thikair stared at him in disbelief, and then alarms began to warble. First one, then another, and another.

He whipped back around to the master control screen, and ice smoked through his veins as crimson lights glared on the readiness boards. Engineering went down, then the Combat Information Center. Master Fire Control went offline, and so did Tracking, Missile Defense, and Astrogation.

And then the flag bridge itself lost power. Main lighting failed, plunging it into darkness, and Thikair heard someone gobbling a prayer as the emergency lighting clicked on.

"Sir?"

Ahzmer's voice was fragile, and Thikair looked at him. But he couldn't find his own voice. He could only stand there, paralyzed, unable to cope with the impossible events.

And then the command deck's armored doors slid open, and Thikair's eyes went wide as a human walked through them.

Every officer on that bridge was armed, and Thikair's hearing cringed as a dozen sidearms opened fire at once. Scores of bullets slammed into the human intruder . . . with absolutely no effect.

No, that wasn't quite correct, some numb corner of Thikair's brain insisted. The bullets went straight *through* him, whining and ricocheting off the bulkheads behind him, but he didn't even seem to notice. There were no wounds, no sprays of blood. It was as if his body were made of smoke, offering no resistance, suffering no damage.

He only stood there, looking at them, and then, suddenly, there were more humans. Four of them. Only *four* . . . but it was enough.

Thikair's mind gibbered, too overwhelmed even to truly panic as the four newcomers seemed to blur. It was as if they were half-transformed into vapor that poured itself through the command deck's air with impossible speed. They flowed across the bridge, *enveloping* his officers, and he heard screams. Screams of raw panic that rose in pitch as the Shongairi behind them saw the smoke flowing in *their* direction . . . and died in hideous, gurgling silence as it engulfed them.

And then Thikair was the only Shongair still standing.

His body insisted that he had to collapse, but somehow his knees refused to unlock. Collapsing would have required him to move . . . and something reached out from the first human's green eyes and forbade that.

The green-eyed human walked out into the body-strewn command and stopped, facing Thikair, his hands clasped behind him.

"You have much for which to answer, Fleet Commander Thikair," he said quietly, softly . . . in perfect Shongairi.

Thikair only stared at him, unable—not allowed—even to speak, and the human smiled. There was something terrifying about that smile . . . and something wrong, as well. The teeth, Thikair realized. The ridiculous little human canines had lengthened, sharpened, and in that moment Thikair understood exactly how thousands upon thousands of years of prey animals had looked upon his own people's smiles.

"You call yourselves 'predators.'" The human's upper lip curled. "Trust me, Fleet Commander—your people know nothing about *predators*. But they will."

Something whimpered in Thikair's throat, and the green eyes glowed with a terrifying internal fire.

"I had forgotten," the human said. "I had turned away from my own past. Even when you came to my world, even when you murdered billions of humans, I had forgotten. But now, thanks to you, Fleet Commander, I *remember*. I remember the obligations of honor. I remember a Prince of Wallachia's responsibilities. And I remember—oh, *how* I remember—the taste of vengeance. And that is what I find most impossible to forgive, Fleet Commander Thikair. I spent five hundred years learning to forget that taste, and you've filled my mouth with it again."

Thikair would have sold his soul to look away from those blazing emerald eyes, but even that was denied him.

"For an entire century, I hid even from myself, hid under my murdered brother's name, but now, Fleet Commander, I take back my *own* name. I am Vlad Drakula—Vlad, Son of the Dragon, Prince of Wallachia—and you have *dared* to shed the blood of those under *my* protection."

The paralysis left Thikair's voice—released, he was certain, by the human-shaped monster in front of him—and he swallowed hard.

"Wh—What do you—?" he managed to get out, but then his freed voice failed him, and Vlad smiled cruelly.

"I couldn't have acted when you first came even if I'd been prepared—willing—to go back to what once I was," he said. "There was only myself and my handful of closest followers. We would have been far too few. But then you showed me I truly had no choice. When you established your base to build the weapon to destroy every living human, you made my options very simple. I could not permit that—I *would* not. And so I had no alternative but to create more of my own kind. To create an army—not large, as armies go, but an army still—to deal with you.

"I was more cautious than in my . . . impetuous youth. The vampires I chose to make this time were better men and women than I was when I was yet breathing. I pray for my own sake that they will balance the hunger you've awakened in me once again, but do not expect them to feel any kindness where you and *your* kind are concerned.

"They are all much younger than I, new come to their abilities, not yet strong enough to endure the touch of the sun. But, like me, they are no longer breathing. Like me, they could ride the exterior of your shuttles when you were kind enough to return them to your transports . . . and your dreadnoughts. And like me, they have used your neural educators, learned how to control your vessels, how to use your technology.

"I will leave your neural educators here on Earth to give every single breathing human a complete Hegemony-level education. And, as you may have noticed, we were very careful not to destroy your industrial ships. What do you think a planet of humans will be able to accomplish over the next few centuries, even after all you've done to them, from that starting point? Do you think your Hegemony Council will be pleased?"

Thikair swallowed again, choking on a thick bolus of fear, and the human cocked his head to one side.

"I doubt the Council will be very happy with you, Fleet Commander, but I promise you *their* anger will have no effect upon your Empire. After all, each of these dreadnoughts can sterilize a planet, can it not? And which of your imperial worlds will dream, even for a moment, that one of your own capital ships might pose any threat to it at all?"

"No," Thikair managed to whimper, his eyes darting to the plot where the green icons of his other dreadnoughts continued to move away from the planet. "No, *please . . .*"

"How many human fathers and mothers would have said exactly the same thing to *you* as their children died before them?" the human replied coldly, and Thikair sobbed.

The human watched him mercilessly, but then he looked away. The deadly green glow left his eyes, and they seemed to soften as they gazed up at the taller human beside him.

"Keep me as human as you can, my Stephen," he said softly in English. "Remind me of why I tried so hard to forget."

The dark-skinned human looked back down at him and nodded, and then the green eyes moved back to Thikair.

"I believe you have unfinished business with this one, my Stephen," he said, and it was the bigger, taller, darker, and infinitely less terrifying human's turn to smile.

"Yes, I do," his deep voice rumbled, and Thikair squealed like a small trapped animal as the powerful, dark hands reached for him.

"This is for my daughters," Stephen Buchevsky said.

Carrie Vaughn

Here's a powerful look at a part of World War II history that's still almost unknown by most people even here in the twenty-first century: the vital role played by the pilots of the Women Airforce Service Pilots or WASP. Who couldn't fight in combat, but who could—and did—die.

Bestseller Carrie Vaughn is the author of a wildly popular series of novels detailing the adventures of Kitty Norville, a radio personality who also happens to be a werewolf, and who runs a late-night call-in radio advice show for supernatural creatures. The Kitty books include *Kitty and the Midnight Hour, Kitty Goes to Washington, Kitty Takes a Holiday,* and *Kitty and the Silver Bullet*. Vaughn's short work has appeared in *Jim Baen's Universe, Asimov's Science Fiction, Inside Straight, Realms of Fantasy, Paradox, Strange Horizons, Weird Tales, All-Star Zeppelin Adventure Stories,* and elsewhere. *Kitty and the Dead Man's Hand* and *Kitty Raises Hell* are the newest Kitty novels, published in 2009. Vaughn lives in Colorado.

The Girls from Avenger

The sun was setting over Avenger Field when Em and a dozen others threw Mary into the so-called Wishing Well, the wide round fountain in front of the trainee barracks. A couple of the girls grabbed her arms; a couple more grabbed her feet and hauled her off the ground. Mary screamed in surprise, and Em laughed—she should have known this was coming, it happened to everyone after they soloed. But she remembered from her own dunking the week before, it was hard not to scream out of sheer high spirits.

Em halted the mob of cheering women just long enough to pull off Mary's leather flight jacket—then she was right there at Mary's shoulders, lifting her over the stone lip of the pool of water. Mary screamed again—half screamed, half laughed, rather—and splashed in, sending a wave over the edge. On her knees now, her sodden jumpsuit hanging off her like a sack, she splashed them all back. Em scrambled out of the way.

Applause and laughter died down, and Mary started climbing over the edge.

"Don't forget to grab your coins," Em told her.

"Oh!" She dived back under the water, reached around for a moment, then showed Em her prize—a couple of pennies in her open palm. Mary was young, twenty-two, and her wide, clear eyes showed it. Her brown hair was dripping over her face and she looked bedraggled, grinning. "I'm the luckiest girl in the world!"

Whenever one of the trainees at the Women's Flight Training Detachment at Avenger Field had a test or a check-out flight, she tossed a coin into the fountain for good luck. When she soloed for the first time, she could take two out, for luck. Em's coins were still in her pocket.

Em reached out, and Mary grabbed her hand. "Come on, get out of there. I think Suze has a fifth of whiskey with your name on it hidden under her mattress."

Mary whooped and scrambled out. She shook out her jumpsuit; sheets of water came off it, and she laughed all over again.

Arm in arm, they trooped to the barracks, where someone had a radio playing and a party had already started.

DECEMBER 1943

In an outfit like the WASP, everyone knew everyone and news traveled fast.

Em heard about it as soon as she walked into the barracks at New Castle. Didn't have time to even put her bag down or slide her jacket off before three of the others ran in from the hall, surrounded her, and started talking. Janey gripped her arm tight like she was drowning, and Em let her bag drop to the floor.

"Did you hear?" Janey said. Her eyes were red from crying, Tess looked like she was about to start, and Patty's face was white. Em's stomach turned, because she already knew what they were going to say.

"Hear what?" she asked. Delaying the inevitable, like if she could draw this moment out long enough, the news wouldn't be true.

"A crash, out at Romulus," Patty said.

Em asked what was always the first question: "Who?"

"Mary Keene."

The world flipped, her heart jumped, and all the blood left her head. No, there was a mistake, not Mary. Rumors flew faster than anything. She realized Patty didn't look so worried because of the crash; she was worried about Em.

"What happened?" Always the second question.

"I don't know, just that there was a crash."

"Mary, is she—?"

Janey's tears fell and her voice was tight. She squeezed Em harder. "Oh, Em! I'm so sorry. I know you were friends—I'm so sorry."

If Em didn't get out of here now, she'd have to hug them all and start crying with them. She'd have to think about how to act and what to say and what to do next. She'd have to listen to the rumors and try to sort out what had really happened.

She pushed by them, got past their circle, ignored it when Patty touched her arm, trying to hold her back. Left her bag behind, thought that she ought to drag it with her because it had dirty clothing in it. Maybe somebody called to her, but she just wanted to be alone.

She found her room, sat on her cot, and stared at the empty cot against the other wall. She bunked with Mary, right here in this room, just as they had at Avenger. Doubled over, face to her lap, she hugged herself and wondered what to do next.

This didn't happen often enough to think it could happen to you, or even someone you knew. A year of women flying Army planes, and it had happened less than a dozen times. There were few enough of them all together that Em had known some of them, even if they hadn't been friends. Seen them at training or waved on the way to one job or another.

It had happened often enough that they had a system.

Em knocked on the last door of the barracks and collected money from Ruth and Liz. She didn't have to explain what it was for when she held the cup out. It had been like that with everyone, the whole dozen of them on base at the moment. Em would take this hundred and twenty dollars, combine it with the hundred or so sent in from the women at Sweetwater and Houston, and she'd use it to take Mary back to Dayton. None of them were officially Army, so Uncle Sam didn't pay for funerals. It seemed like a little thing to complain about, especially when so many of the boys overseas were dying. But Mary had done her part, too. Didn't that count for something?

"Have you found out what happened yet?" Liz asked. Everyone had asked that, too.

Em shook her head. "Not a thing. I called Nancy, but they're not telling her anything either."

"You think it was bad?" Liz said. "You think that's why they're hushing it up?"

"They're hushing it up because they don't like to think about women dying in airplanes," she said. Earlier in the year, she'd been told point blank by a couple of male pilots that the only women who belonged on planes were the ones painted on the noses. That was supposed to be clever. She was supposed to laugh and flirt. She'd just walked away.

Running footsteps sounded on the wood floor and they looked up to see Janey racing in. The panic in her eyes made Em think that maybe it had happened again, that someone else had gone and crashed and that they'd have to pass the cup around again, so soon.

Janey stopped herself by grabbing Em's arm and said, "There's a bird in from Romulus, a couple of guys in a B-26. You think maybe they know what happened?"

They'd have a better idea than anyone. They might even have seen something. "Anyone talk to them yet?" Em said. Janey shook her head.

A line on the rumor mill. Em gave her colleagues a grim smile and headed out.

She couldn't walk by the flight line without stopping and looking, seeing what was parked and what was roaring overhead. The place was swarming, and it always made her heart race. It was ripe with potential—something *big* was happening here. *We're fighting a war here, we really are.* She took a deep breath of air thick with the smell of fuel and tarmac. Dozens of planes lined up, all shapes and sizes, a dozen more were taking off and landing. Hangar doors stood open revealing even more, and a hundred people moved between them all, working to keep the sound of engines loud and sweet.

This time, she wasn't the only one stopping to look, because a new sound was rocketing overhead, a subtly different rumble than the ones she normally heard out here. Sure enough, she heard the engine, followed the sound, and looked up to see a bulldog of a fighter buzz the field, faster than sin. She shaded her eyes against a bright winter sun and saw the P-51 Mustang—so much more graceful and agile than anything else in the sky. The nose tapered to a sleek point, streamlined and fast, like a rocket. Not like the clunky, snub-nosed trainers. Granted, clunky trainers served a purpose—it was easier for a pilot in training to correct a mistake at a hundred miles an hour than it was at three hundred. But Em had to wonder what it felt like to really *fly.* Some way, somehow, she was going to get up in one of those birds someday. She was going to find out what it was like to have 1,500 horsepower at her command.

If she were male, her training wouldn't stop with the little single-engine trainers the WASP ferried back and forth from training base to training base, where they were flown by the men who would move on to pursuits and bombers, and from there to combat. If she were male, she'd be flying bigger, faster, meaner planes already. Then she'd go overseas to fly them for real.

As Janey had said, a B-26 Marauder—a fast, compact two-engine bomber—crouched out on the tarmac, a couple of mechanics putting fuel into her. She was probably stopped for a refuel on her way to somewhere else. That meant Em probably had only one chance to talk to the pilots. She continued on to the ops center. The door to the briefing room was closed, but she heard voices inside, muffled. Against her better judgment, she put her ear to the door and listened, but the talk was all routine. The bomber was on its way to Newark for transport overseas, and the pilot was a combat instructor, just off the front.

Em sat in a chair across the hall and waited. Half an hour later, the door opened. The two guys who emerged were typical flyboys, leather jackets, sunglasses tucked in the pockets, khaki uniforms, short cropped hair, and Hollywood faces. Lieutenant bars on the shoulders.

When Em stood at attention, smoothing her trousers and trying not to worry if her collar was straight, the men looked startled. She didn't give them time to try to figure out what to do with her. "I'm sorry to bother you. My name's Emily Anderson, and I'm with the WASP squadron here. I got word that you just flew in from Romulus this morning. I was wondering if I could ask you something."

The taller of the two edged toward the door. "I have to go check on . . . on something. Sorry." His apology was quick and not very sincere.

The remaining pilot looked even more stricken and seemed ready to follow his buddy.

"Please, just a quick question," she said, hating to sound like she was begging. She ought to be charming him.

His wary look deepened, a defensive, thin-lipped frown that made her despair of his taking her seriously. He hesitated, seeming to debate with himself before relenting. "What can I help you with, Miss Anderson?"

She took a deep breath. "I'm trying to find out about a crash that happened near Romulus Field three days ago. A WASP was the pilot. Mary Keene. Sir, she was a friend of mine, and we—the other WASP and I—we just want to know what happened. No one will tell us anything."

He could have denied knowing anything, shaken his head, and walked out, and she wouldn't have been able to do anything, and she wouldn't have been more worried than she already was. But he hesitated. His hands fidgeted with the edge of his jacket, and he glanced at the door, nervous. He knew. Not just that, it was something he didn't want to talk about, something awful.

She pressed. "You know what it's like when something like this happens and they won't tell you anything."

He shook his head and wouldn't meet her gaze. "I shouldn't tell you this."

"Why not? Because it's classified? Or because I'm female and you think I can't handle it?"

The lieutenant pursed his lips. He'd been in combat, might even have faced down enemy fighters, but he didn't seem to want to stand up to her.

"It was a collision," he said finally.

Em had worked out a dozen scenarios, everything from weather to mechanical failure. She was even braced to hear that Mary had made a mistake. A million things could go wrong in the air. But a collision?

"That doesn't make sense, Mary had almost seven hundred hours in the air, she was too experienced for that."

He got that patronizing look a lot of male pilots had when dealing with WASP, like she couldn't possibly know what she was talking about. "I told you I shouldn't have said anything."

"A collision with whom? Did the other pilot make it? What were they doing that they ran into each other? Did you see it?"

"I don't know the details, I'm sorry."

"The Army won't even tell me what she was flying when she went down," she said.

He stepped closer, conspiratorially, as if afraid that someone was listening in. Like this really was classified.

"Look, Miss Anderson, you seem like a nice girl. Why are you doing this? Why are any of you risking your lives like this? Why not stay home, stay safe—?"

"And plant a Victory Garden like a good girl? Sit by the radio and wait for someone to tell me it's going to be all right, and that my husband'll come home safe? I couldn't do that, Lieutenant. I had to do something."

The arguments against women flyers tended to stall out at this point, into vague statements about what was ladylike, what well-bred girls ought to be doing, how women weren't strong enough to handle the big planes even though they'd proved themselves over and over again. A year of women flying should have shut the naysayers up by now. It hadn't.

The lieutenant didn't say anything.

She said, "Is there someone else I can talk to?"

"Look, I don't know, I'm working off rumors like everyone else. I can't help you. I'm sorry." He fled, backing to the door and abandoning Em to the empty corridor.

The WASP all liked Colonel Roper, who commanded the Second Ferry Group at New Castle. At some of the other bases, commanders had given WASP the cold shoulder, but here, he'd treated them with respect and made it policy that the rest of the group do likewise. He didn't constantly ask them if they could do the job—he just gave them the job.

She went to him with the lieutenant's story.

His office door was open and he saw her coming. As he was glancing up, a frown drew lines around his mouth. He was young for a colonel, maybe a little rounder than most guys in the Army, but high-spirited. His uniform jacket was slung over the back of his chair.

"I'm sorry, Anderson, I don't have any news for you," he told her before she'd said a word.

She ducked her gaze and blushed. She'd been in here every day looking for news about Mary's death.

"Sorry, sir," she said, standing at the best attention she knew, back straight and hands at her sides. "But I just talked to the pilots of that B-26 that came in from Romulus. Sir, they told me Mary crashed in a collision. They wouldn't tell me anything else."

Roper's lips thinned, his brow creased. "A collision—Mary wouldn't get herself in that kind of mess."

"I know. Sir, something's not right. If there's anything you can do, anything you can find out—"

He scratched out a note on a pad of paper. "The crash report ought to be filed by now. I'll get a copy sent over."

That meant a few more days of waiting, but it was progress. They'd get the report, and that would be that. But she still wanted to *talk* to someone. Someone who'd seen it, someone who knew her. If there was a collision, another pilot was involved. If she could just find out who.

"Thank you, sir," she said.

"You're welcome. Anderson—try to get some sleep. You look beat."

She hadn't even been thinking about being tired. She'd been running on fumes. "Yes, sir."

Mary Keene came from the kind of family that did everything just so, with all the right etiquette. A car from the funeral home was waiting at the train station, along with Mary's father. Em recognized him from the family picture Mary kept in their room.

Em, dressed in her blue uniform—skirt straight, collar pressed, lapels smooth, insignia pins and wings polished—jumped to the platform before the train slowed to a complete stop and made her way to the luggage car. She waited again. It should have been raining; instead, a crisp winter sun shone in a blue sky. Perfect flying weather. She was thankful for the wool uniform, because a cold wind blew in over a flat countryside.

Men from the funeral home retrieved the casket while Mr. Keene thanked her for coming, shaking her hand with both of his and frowning hard so he wouldn't cry.

"I thought I'd be meeting one of my boys here like this. Not Mary."

Em bowed her head. No one ever knew quite what to say about a woman coming home from war in a casket. If one of Mr. Keene's sons had been killed, the family would put a gold star in the window to replace the blue one showing loved ones serving in combat. They'd be able to celebrate their war hero. Mary wouldn't get any of that, not even a flag on her casket.

Mr. Keene left in his own car. Em would go with Mary to the funeral home, then call a cab and find a hotel to stay at until the funeral tomorrow. One of the men from the mortuary took Em aside before they left.

"I'm given to understand Miss Keene passed on in an airplane crash."

"That's right."

He was nervous, not looking at her, clasping his hands. Em thought these guys knew how to deal with anything.

"I'm afraid I have to ask—I wasn't given any information," he said. "The family has traditionally held open-casket services—will this be possible?"

Or had she burned, had she been smashed beyond recognition, was there anything left? . . . Em's lips tightened. Stay numb, stay focused, just like navigating a fogbank.

"No, I don't think it will," she said.

The man lowered his gaze, bowing a little, and returned to his car.

Em logged thirty hours the next week in trainers, two AT-6s and a BT-13, flying from one end of the country to the other. One morning, she'd woken up in the barracks and had to look outside the window to remember where she was. She kept an eye on other logs and flight plans coming in and out of each base, and kept looking for people who'd been at Romulus last week. Everyone knew about the crash, but other than the fact that a WASP had been killed, nobody treated it like anything unusual. This was wartime, after all.

Arriving back at New Castle on the train after ferrying another round of BT-13s to Houston, she dropped her bag off at the barracks and went to see Colonel Roper. She still had her jumpsuit and flight jacket on, and she really needed a shower. And a meal. And sleep. But maybe this time he had news.

"Sir?" she said at his doorway.

He looked hard at her, didn't say a word. Self-consciously, she pushed her hair back behind her ears. Maybe she should have washed up first. She tried again. "Sir?"

"You're right, Anderson," he said finally. "Something's not right. The crash report's been classified."

She stared. "But that doesn't make any sense."

"I have something for you."

He handed her a folded paper that looked suspiciously like orders. She'd been in the air for three days. She hadn't been back in her own room for a week. She didn't want another mission; she didn't want orders. But you never said no; you never complained.

Her despair must have shown, because Roper gave a thin smile. "I saved this one just for you. I have an AT-11 needs to go to Romulus and I thought you're just the pilot to do it."

Exhaustion vanished. She could fly a month straight if she had to.

He continued, "In fact, you look a little tired. Why don't you spend a few days out there while you're at it? Take a break, meet the locals."

Do some digging, in other words.

"Thank you, sir," she said, a little breathlessly.

"Bring me back some facts, Anderson."

———

Last June, right after graduation and before transferring to New Castle, Em and Mary flew together on a cross-country training hop from Sweetwater to Dallas. It was the kind of easy trip where Em could sit back and actually enjoy flying. The kind of trip that reminded her why she was even doing this. She could lean back against the narrow seat, look up and all around through the narrow, boxy canopy at nothing but blue sky. Free as air.

"Hey Em, take the stick for a minute," Mary said, shouting over the rumble of the engine, when they'd almost reached Love Field at Dallas.

From the back seat of their BT-13 Valiant, craning her neck to peer over Mary's shoulder, Em saw her drop the stick and start digging in one of the pockets of her jacket. Em hadn't yet taken over on the dual controls. The Valiant was a trainer and could be flown from either the front or back seat, and every trainee sitting in front had had the controls yanked away from them by the instructor in back at least once. The plane was flying trim so Em didn't panic too much; she had a little time to put a steadying hand on the stick.

"What are you doing up there?" Em asked. Mary turned just enough so Em could see her putting on lipstick, studying her work in a compact mirror. She'd had enough practice putting on lipstick in airplanes that the teeth-rattling vibrations of the engine didn't affect her at all. Em laughed. "No one up here cares about your lipstick."

Mary looked a little ridiculous, leather cap mashing down her hair, goggles up on her forehead, painting her lips. So this was why she wanted to fly with the canopy closed on such a warm, beautiful day, making the cockpit hot and stuffy. She didn't want to be all ruffled when they landed.

"I have to be ready. There might be some handsome young officer just waiting for me to catch his eye. Oh, I hope we get there in time for dinner. This bucket's so slow. You think they'll ever give us anything faster to fly?"

"A real plane, you mean?" Em said. It was an old joke.

"I wouldn't say *that*. This bird's real enough. If you don't mind going *slow*."

Em looked out the canopy stuck up top in the middle of the fuselage. "We have to get there and land before you can catch your handsome young officer's eye. Do you know where we are?" They were flying low-level and cross-country; Em searched for landmarks, which was quite a trick in the middle of Texas.

"Don't fret, we're right on course. Bank left—there's the main road, see?"

Em nudged the stick and the plane tipped, giving her a wide view past the wing and its Army star to the earth below, and the long straight line of paved road leading to Dallas. Mary seemed to have an instinct for these sorts of things.

"You really do have this all planned out," Em said. "You'll be heading straight from the flight line to the Officer's Club, won't you?"

Mary had a pout in her voice. "I might stop to brush my hair first." Em laughed, and Mary looked over her shoulder. "Don't give me a hard time just because I'm not already married off to a wonderful man like you are."

Em sighed. She hadn't seen her husband in almost a year. The last letter she'd had from him was postmarked Honolulu, three weeks ago. He hadn't said where he was sailing to—couldn't, really. All she knew was that he was somewhere in the middle of a big wide ocean, flying Navy dive-bombers off a carrier. Sometimes she wished she weren't a pilot, because she knew exactly what could go wrong for Michael. Then again, maybe he was flying right now—it was mid-morning in the Pacific—cruising along for practice on a beautiful day and thinking of her, the way she was thinking of him.

"Em?" Mary said, still craned over to look at Em the best she could over the back of her seat.

"Sorry. You just got me thinking about Michael."

Em could just see Mary's wide red smile, her excitable eyes. "You really miss him, don't you?"

"Of course I do."

Mary sighed. "That's so romantic."

Em almost laughed again. "Would you listen to you? There's nothing romantic about waking up every day wondering if he's alive or dead." She was only twenty-four, too young to be a widow, surely. She had to stop this or she'd start crying and have to let Mary land the plane. Shaking her head, she looked away, back to the blue sky outside the canopy, scattered clouds passing by.

"It's just that being in love like that? I've never been in love like that. Except maybe with Clark Gable." She grinned.

Em gratefully kept the joke going. "Don't think for a minute Clark Gable's going to be on the ground when we get there."

"You never know. These are strange times. He enlisted, did you know that? I read about it. Him and Jimmy Stewart both—and Jimmy Stewart's a pilot!"

"And maybe they'll both be at Dallas, just for you."

"Hope springs eternal," Mary said smugly. "I've got my lucky pennies, you know."

"All right, but if they're there, you *have* to ask them to dance."

"It's a deal," Mary said brightly, knowing she'd never have to make good on it. Because Clark Gable and Jimmy Stewart were *not* at Dallas. But if something like that was going to happen to anyone, it would happen to Mary.

A few minutes later, Em leaned forward to listen. Sure enough, Mary was singing. "Don't sit under the apple tree, with anyone else but me, anyone else but me . . ."

Em joined in, and they sang until they were circling over the field to land.

After shutting down the engine, she sat in her cockpit and took a look down the flight line at Romulus, in freezing Michigan. The sight never failed to amaze her—a hundred silver birds perched on the tarmac, all that power, ready and waiting. The buzzing of engines was constant; she could feel the noise in her bones.

This was the last runway Mary took off from.

Sighing, she filled out the plane's 1-A, collected her bag and her logbook, and hoisted herself out of the cockpit and onto the tarmac. Asked the first guy she saw, a mechanic, where the WASP barracks were. The wary look on his face told her all she needed to know about what the men on this base thought of WASP. She'd heard the rumors—they traded stories about which bases welcomed them and which wanted nothing to do with women pilots. She wasn't sure she believed the stories about someone putting sugar in the fuel tank of a WASP's plane at Camp Davis, causing it to crash—mostly because she didn't think anyone would do that to a plane. But those were the sorts of stories people told.

She made her way to the barracks. After a shower, she'd be able to face the day a little easier.

After the shower, Em, dressed in shirt and trousers, was still drying her

Transit Slip

Transit to: DHTN_07
Transit reason: HOLD

This material was borrowed
from another library at your
request. Fines may vary.
DATE DUE:

hair when a group of women came into the barracks—three of them, laughing and windblown, peeling off flight jackets and scrubbing fingers through mussed hair. They quieted when they saw her, and she set her towel aside.

"Hi."

One of them, a slim blonde with mischief in her eyes, the kind of woman the brass liked to use in press photos, stepped forward, hand outstretched.

"Hi. You must be the new kid they were talking about back in ops. I'm Lillian Greshing."

"Em Anderson," she said, shaking her hand. "I'm just passing through. I hope you don't mind, I used one of the towels on the shelf. There weren't any names or labels—"

"Of course not, that's what they're there for. Hey—we were going to grab supper in town after we get cleaned up. Want to come along? You can catch us up on all the gossip."

Em's smile went from polite to warm, as she felt herself among friends again. "That sounds perfect."

The four women found a table in the corner of a little bar just off base. The Runway wasn't fancy; it had a Christmas tree decorated with spots of tinsel and glass bulbs in a corner, a pretty good bar, and a jukebox playing swing. The dinner special was roast chicken, mashed potatoes, and a bottle of beer to wash it down.

"What're they transferring WASP to Camp Davis for?" Betsy, a tall woman with a narrow face and a nervous smile, asked when Em passed on the rumor.

"Don't know," Em said. "Nobody'll say. But Davis is a gunnery school." More speculative murmurs ran around the table.

"Target towing. Wanna bet?" Lillian said.

"I'll stick to the job I have, thank you very much," Betsy said, shivering.

Em felt her smile grow thin and sly. "Not me. Nursing along slowpoke trainers? We can do better than that."

"You *want* to fly planes while some cross-eyed greenhorn shoots at you?"

"Nope," Em said. "I want to transition to pursuits."

"It'll never happen," Lillian said, shaking her head, like she needed the emphasis. "The old cronies like Burnett will never let it happen."

"Burnett?"

"Colonel. Runs this lovely little operation." She gestured in the direction of the airfield. Smoke trailed behind her hand to join the rest of the haze in the air.

"What's he like?" Em asked.

That no one answered with anything more than sidelong glances and rolled eyes told her enough. Romulus was a cold-shoulder base.

Em pressed on. "We'll get there. Nancy Love has five girls in transition out at Palm Springs already. The factories are all working overtime building bombers and fighters, and ATC doesn't have enough pilots to ferry them to port. They're going to have to let us fly 'em, whether they like it or not."

Betsy was still shaking her head. "Those birds are too dangerous."

Mary got killed in a trainer, Em wanted to say. "We can do it. We're capable of it."

Lillian said with a sarcastic lilt, "Burnett would say we're not strong enough. That we wouldn't be able to even get something like a Mustang off the ground."

"He's full of it," Em said. "I can't *wait* to get my hands on one of those."

Betsy, smiling vaguely, looked into her beer. "I don't know how I'd explain flying fighters to my husband. He's barely all right with my flying at all."

"So don't tell him," Lillian said. Shocked giggles met the proclamation.

Round-eyed Molly, blond hair in a ponytail, leaned in. "Don't listen to her, she's got three boyfriends at three different fields. She doesn't understand about husbands." More giggling.

Em smiled. "Betsy, is he overseas?"

"England," she said. "He's a doctor." Her pride was plain.

"You've got a ring there, Em," Molly said to the band on Em's finger. "You married or is that to keep the flyboys off you?"

"He's Navy," Em said. "He's on a carrier in the Pacific."

After a sympathetic hesitation, Lillian continued. "What does he think about you flying?"

Em donned a grin. "I met him when we were both taking flying lessons before the war. He can't argue about me flying. Besides, I have to do something to keep my mind off things."

Lillian raised her bottle. "Here's to the end of the war."

They raised their glasses and the toasts were heartfelt.

The quiet moment gave Em her opening—time to start in on the difficult gossip, what she'd come here to learn. "What do you all know about Mary Keene's crash last week?"

No one would look at her. Betsy bit a trembling lip and teared up, and Molly fidgeted with her glass. Lillian's jaw went taut with a scowl. She ground her cigarette into the ashtray with enough force to destroy what was left of it.

"It happened fifty miles out," Lillian said, her voice quiet. "Nobody saw anything, we just heard it when the fire truck left. All we know is a group of seven planes went out—BT-13s, all of 'em—and an hour later six came back and nobody would tell us a thing. Just that Mary'd been killed. You knew her, I take it?"

"We were in the same class at Avenger," Em said. "We were friends."

"I'm sorry," Lillian said. "She was only here a couple of days but we all liked her a lot."

Molly handed Betsy a handkerchief; she dabbed her eyes with it.

"I was told the accident report was classified, and that doesn't make any sense. Some guys who were here last week told me there was a collision."

Lillian leaned close and spoke softly, like this was some kind of conspiracy. "That's what we heard, and one of the planes came back with a wheel all busted up, but Burnett clamped down on talk so fast, our heads spun. Filed away all the paperwork and wouldn't answer any questions. We don't even know who else was flying that day."

"He can't do that," Em said. "Couldn't you go after him? Just keep pushing—"

"It's Burnett," Lillian said. "Guy's a brick wall."

"Then go over his head."

"And get grounded? Get kicked out? That's what he's threatened us with, for going over his head," Lillian said, and Em couldn't argue. But technically, she wasn't part of his squadron, and he couldn't do anything to her. She could ask her questions.

Another group from the field came in then, flyboys by their leather jackets with silver wings pinned to the chest. Ferry Division, by the insignia. Not so different from the girls, who were wearing trousers and blouses, their jackets hanging off their chairs—a group gathered around a table, calling for beers and talking about the gossip, flying, and the war.

Pretty soon after their arrival, a couple of them went over to the jukebox and put in a few coins. A dance tune came up, something just fast enough to make you want to get out of your seat—Glenn Miller, "Little Brown Jug." Lillian rolled her eyes and Molly hid a smile with her hand; they all knew what was coming next.

Sure enough, the guys sauntered over to their table. Em made sure the hand with her wedding band was out and visible. Not that that stopped some men. Just a dance, they'd say. But she didn't want to, because it would make her think about Michael.

Lillian leaned back in her chair, chin up and shoulders squared, and met their gazes straight on. The others looked on like they were watching a show.

They weren't bad looking, early thirties maybe. Slightly rumpled uniforms and nice smiles. "Would any of you ladies like a dance?"

The women glanced at each other—would any of them say yes?

Lillian, brow raised, blond curls falling over her ears so artfully she might have pinned them there, said, "What makes you boys think you could keep up with any of us?"

The guys glanced at each other, then smiled back at Lillian. Gauntlet accepted. "We'd sure like to give it a try."

Nobody was making a move to stand, and Lillian again took the lead—breaking the boys' hearts for fun. "Sorry to disappoint you, but the girls and I spent all day putting repaired AT-6s through their paces and we're beat. We were looking forward to a nice, quiet evening."

The guy standing at the first one's shoulder huffed a little. "Lady pilots," he might have muttered.

The first guy seemed a little daunted. "Well, maybe you'll let us pull over a couple of chairs and buy you a round?"

Magic words, right there. Lillian sat up and made a space at the table. "That'll be all right."

Another round of beers arrived a moment later.

The men were nice enough, Ferry Division boys flying pursuits and bombers from the factories. Em asked questions—how many, what kind, where were they going, what was it like?—and ate up the answers. They seemed happy enough to humor her, even if they did come off on the condescending side—isn't that cute, a girl who wants to fly fast planes.

The attitude was easy enough to ignore. Every WASP had a story about being chatted up by some flyboy at a bar, him bragging about piloting hotshot planes and ending with the "I ship out to Europe tomorrow, honey," line; then seeing the look of shock on the guy's face the next day when he spotted her on the flight line climbing into her own cockpit. That was funny every damn time.

Lillian leaned over to Jim, the guy who'd talked to them first, and said, "Do your friends want to come on over and join us? We could make a real party of it."

A couple of the guys already had, but a few remained at the other table, talking quietly and nursing beers. They didn't pay much attention to the other group, except for one guy, with a round face and slicked-back hair, who kept his jacket on even though the room had grown warm.

Grinning, Jim leaned forward and lowered his voice. "I think you all make some of the boys nervous."

Em smiled and ducked her gaze while the other women giggled.

Lillian almost purred. "We're not flying now, I don't see why they should be nervous. We're not going to crash into them." Em looked away at that. It was just a joke, she told herself.

Jim tilted his head to the sullen-looking pilot. "Frank there almost walked back out again when he saw you girls sitting here."

"What, afraid of little old us?" Lillian said, and the others laughed. The sullen-looking pilot at the other table, Frank, seemed to sink into his jacket a little further.

Jim shrugged. "His loss, right?"

Em agreed. Anyone had an issue with women pilots, it was their problem, not hers.

Em had to go at the mystery backwards. The accident report wasn't available, so she dug through the flight logs to see who else was flying that day. Who else was in the air with Mary.

She made her way to ops, a big square prefab office building off the airstrip, around lunchtime the next day, when she was less likely to run into people. The move paid off—only a secretary, a woman in civilian clothes, was on duty. Em carried her logbook in hand, making her look more official than not, and made up some excuse about being new to the base and needing to log her next flight and where should she go? The secretary directed her to an adjoining room. There, Em found the setup familiar: maps pinned to the wall, chalkboards with instructions written on them, charts showing planes and schedules, and a wall of filing cabinets.

Every pilot taking off from the field was supposed to file a flight plan, which were kept in ops. Mary's plan—and the plans of anyone else who was flying that day and might have collided with her—should be here. She rubbed her lucky pennies together and got to work.

The luck held: the files were marked by day and in order. Flipping through, Em found the pressboard folder containing the forms from that day. Taking the folder to an empty desk by the wall, she began studying, reconstructing in her mind what the flight line had looked like that day.

Mary had been part of a group ferrying seven BT-13 Valiants from Romulus to Dallas. She wasn't originally part of the group; she'd been at Romulus overnight after ferrying a different BT-13. But they had an extra plane, and like just about any WASP, she would fly anything she was checked out on, anything a commander asked her to fly. Those were the bare facts. That was the starting point. Less than an hour after takeoff, Mary had crashed. A collision—which meant it must have been one of the other planes in the group.

WASP weren't authorized for close-formation flying. When they did fly in groups, they flew loose, with enough distance between to prevent accidents—at least five hundred feet. Mary was the only WASP in the group, but the men should have followed the same procedure and maintained a safe distance. Just saying "collision" didn't tell the story, because only one plane hit the ground, and only one pilot died.

The accident had eyewitnesses: the other six pilots in the group, who were flying with Mary when she crashed. She started jotting down names and the ID numbers of the planes they'd been flying.

"What do you think you're doing?"

Startled, Em flinched and looked up to find a lanky man just past forty or so, his uniform starched and perfect, standing in the doorway, hands clenched, glaring. Silver eagles on his shoulders—this must be Colonel Burnett. Reflexively, she crumpled her page of notes and stuffed it in her pocket. The move was too obvious to hide. Gathering her thoughts, she stood with as much attention as she could muster—part of her mind was still on those six pilots.

She'd spent enough time in the Army Air Force to know how men like Burnett operated: they intimidated, they browbeat. They had their opinions and didn't want to hear arguments. She just had to keep from letting herself get cowed.

"Filing a flight plan, sir." She kept the lie short and simple, so he wouldn't have anything to hold against her.

"I don't think so," he said, looking at the pages spread out on the desk.

They were in a standoff. She hadn't finished, and wanted to get those last couple of names. Burnett didn't look like he was going to leave.

"It's true," she bluffed. "BT-13 to Dallas." Mary's last flight plan; that might have been pushing it.

"You going to show me what's in your pocket there?"

"Grocery list," she said, deadpan.

He stepped closer, and Em had to work not to flinch away from the man.

"Those are papers from last week," he said, pointing at the plans she'd been looking at.

"Yes, sir."

His face reddened, and she thought he might start screaming at her, drill-sergeant style. "Who authorized you to look at these?"

Somebody had to speak up. Somebody had to find the truth. That allowed her to face him, chin up. "Sir, I believe the investigation into that crash ended prematurely, that all the information hasn't been brought to light."

"That report was filed. There's nothing left to say. You need to get out of here, missy."

Now he was just making her angry. He probably expected her to wilt— he probably yelled at all the women because he expected them to wilt. She stepped forward, feeling her own flush starting, her own temper rising. "Why was the report buried? I just want to know what really happened."

"I don't have to explain anything to you. You're a civilian. You're just a civilian."

"What is there to explain, sir?"

"Unless you march out of here right now, I'll have you arrested for spying. Don't think the Army won't shoot a woman for treason!"

Em expected a lot of threats—being grounded, getting kicked out of the WASP, just like Lillian said. But being shot for treason? What the hell was Burnett trying to hide?

Em was speechless, and didn't have any fight left in her after that. She marched out with her logbook, just as Burnett told her to, head bowed, unable to look at him. Even though she really wanted to spit at him. In the corner of her gaze, she thought she saw him smile, like he thought he'd won some kind of victory over her. Bullying a woman, and he thought that made him tough. By the time she left the building, her eyes were watering. Angrily, she wiped the tears away.

Well away from the building, she stopped to catch her breath. Crossed her arms, waited for her blood to cool. Looked up into the sky, turning her face to the clouds. The day was overcast, the ceiling low, a biting wind smelling of snow. Terrible weather for flying. But she'd go up in a heartbeat, in whatever piece-of-junk trainer was available, just to get away from here.

One of the lessons you learned early on: Make friends with the ground crew. When some of the trainers they flew had seen better days and took a lot of attention to keep running, sweet-talking a mechanic about what was wrong went further than complaining. Even if the wreckage from Mary's plane was still around—it would have already been picked over for aluminum and parts—Em wouldn't have been able to tell what had happened without seeing the crash site. She needed to talk to the recovery team.

Lillian told her that a Sergeant Bill Jacobs's crew had been the one to recover Mary's Valiant. He'd know a lot that hadn't made it into the records, maybe even be able to tell her what happened. If she could sweet-talk him. She touched up her lipstick, repinned her hair, and tapped her lucky pennies.

On the walk to the hangar, she tried to pound out her bad mood, to work out her anger and put herself in a sweet-talking frame of mind. *Hey there, mind telling me about a little ol' plane crash that happened last week?* She wasn't so good at sweet-talking, not like Lillian was. Not like Mary had been.

The main door of the hangar was wide open to let in the afternoon light. In the doorway, she waited a moment to let her eyes adjust to the shadows. A B-24 was parked inside, two of its four engines open and half-dismantled. The couple of guys working on each one called a word to the other now and then, asking for a part or advice. A radio played Duke Ellington.

The hangar had a strangely homey feel to it, with its atmosphere of grease and hard work, the cheerful music playing and the friendly banter between the mechanics. This might have been any airport repair shop, if it weren't for the fact they were working on a military bomber.

Em looked around for someone who might be in charge, someone who might be Jacobs. In the back corner, she saw the door to an office and headed there. Inside, she found what she was probably looking for: a wide desk stacked with papers and clipboards. Requisitions, repair records, inventories, and the like, she'd bet. Maybe a repair order for a BT-13 wounded in a collision last week?

She was about to start hunting when a man said, "Can I help you, miss?"

A man in Army coveralls and a cap stood at the doorway. Scraping together all the charm she could manage, she straightened and smiled. She must have made quite a silhouette in her trousers and jacket because he looked a bit stricken. He glanced at the insignia on her collar, the patches on her jacket, and knew what, if not who, she was.

"Sergeant Jacobs?" she said, smiling.

"Yes, ma'am."

Her smile widened. "Hi, I'm Emily Anderson, in from New Castle." She gestured vaguely over her shoulder. "They told me you might be able to help me out."

He relaxed, maybe thinking she was only going to ask for a little grease on a squeaky canopy.

She said, "The crash last week. The one the WASP died in. Can you tell me what happened?" Her smile had stiffened; her politeness was a mask.

Jacobs sidled past her in an effort to put himself between her and the desk—the vital paperwork. He began sorting through the mess on the desk, but his movements were random. "I don't know anything about that."

"You recovered the plane. You saw the crash site."

"It was a mess. I can't tell you what happened."

"What about the other plane? How badly was it damaged?"

He looked at her. "How do you know there was another plane?"

"I heard there was a collision. Who was flying that other plane? Can you at least tell me that much?"

"I can't help you, I'm sorry." He shook his head, like he was shaking off an annoying fly.

"Sergeant Jacobs, Mary Keene was my friend."

When he looked at her, his gaze was tired, pitying. "Ma'am, please. Let it go. Digging this up isn't going to fix anything."

"I need to know what really happened."

"The plane crashed, okay? It just crashed. Happens all the time, I hate to say it, but it's so."

Em shook her head. "Mary was a good pilot. *Something* had to have happened."

Jacobs looked away. "She switched off the engine."

"What?"

"She'd lost part of a wing—there was no way she could pull out of it. But before she hit the ground, she had time to turn off the engine so it wouldn't catch fire. So the plane wouldn't burn. She knew what was going to happen and she switched it off."

Mary, sitting in her cockpit, out of control after whatever had hit her, calmly reaching over to turn off the ignition, knowing the whole time she maybe wasn't going to make it—

"Is that supposed to make me feel better?" Em said.

"No. I'm sorry, ma'am. It's just you're right. She was a good pilot."

"Then why won't you—?"

A panicked shouting from the hangar caught their attention—"Whoa whoa, hold that thing, it's gonna drop"—followed by the ominous sound of metal crashing to concrete. Jacobs dashed out of the office to check on his crew.

Em wasn't proud; she went through the stack of papers while he was occupied.

The fact that Mary had crashed and died was becoming less significant to Em than the way everyone was acting about it. Twitchy. Defensive. Like a pilot towing targets for gunnery training, wondering if the wet-behind-the-ears gunners were going to hit you instead. These guys, everyone who knew what had happened, didn't want to talk about it, didn't want her to ask about it, and were doing their damnedest to cover this up. What were all these people hiding? Or, what were they protecting?

It wasn't a hard answer, when she put it like that: the other pilot. They were protecting the pilot who survived the collision.

She dug through repair orders. Mary's plane had crashed—but the other plane hadn't. It still would have been damaged, and there'd be paperwork for that. She looked at the dates, searching for *that* date. Found it, found the work order for a damaged BT-13. Quickly, she retrieved the list of names she'd taken from the flight plans. She'd copied only half of them before Burnett interrupted her. She had a fifty-fifty chance of matching the name on the work order. Heads or tails?

And there it was. When she compared ID numbers with the ones on the work order, she found the match she was looking for: Frank Milliken. The other pilot's name was Frank Milliken.

She marched out of the office and into hangar. Jacobs was near the B-24 wing, yelling at the guys who had apparently unbolted and dropped a propeller. He might have followed her with a suspicious gaze as she left, but he couldn't do anything about it now, could he?

She kept her eyes straight ahead and didn't give him a chance to stop her.

"You know Frank Milliken?" she asked Lillian when she got back to the barracks.

"By name. He's one of the Third Ferry Group guys—he was part of Jim's bunch of clowns last night," she said.

Em tried to remember the names she'd heard, to match them up with the faces, the guys who talked to them. "I don't remember a Frank," she said.

"He's the sulky guy who stayed at the table."

Ah . . . "You know anything about him?"

"Not really. They kind of run together when they're all flirting with you at once." She grinned. "What about him?"

"I think he was in the plane that collided with Mary's last week."

"What?" she said with a wince and tilted head, like she hadn't heard right.

"I've got a flight plan and a plane ID number on a repair order that says it was him."

Clench-jawed anger and an anxious gaze vied with each other and ended up making Lillian look young and confused. "What do we do?"

"I just want to find out what happened," Em said. She just wanted to sit down with the guy, make him walk her through it, explain who had flown too close to whom, whether it was accident, weather, a gust of wind, pilot error—anything. She just wanted to know.

"You sure?" Lillian said. "This is being hushed up for a reason. It can't be anything good. Not that *anything* is going to make this better, but—well, you know what I mean. Em, what if—what if it was Mary's fault? Are you ready to hear that? Are you ready to hear that this was a stupid accident and Burnett's covering it up to make his own record a little less dusty?"

Em understood what Lillian was saying—it didn't matter how many stories you made up for yourself; the truth could always be worse. If something—God forbid—ever happened to Michael, would she really want to know what killed him? Did she really want to picture that?

Shouldn't she just let Mary go?

Em's smile felt thin and pained. "We have to look out for each other, Lillian. No one else is doing it for us, and no one else is going to tell our stories for us. I have to know."

Lillian straightened, and the woman's attitude won out over her confusion. "Right, then. Let's go find ourselves a party."

Em and Lillian parked at the same table at the Runway, but didn't order dinner tonight. Em's stomach was churning; she couldn't think of eating. She and Lillian drank sodas and waited.

"What if they don't come?" Em said.

"They'll be here," Lillian said. "They're here every night they're on base. Don't worry."

As they waited, a few of the other girls came in and joined them, and they all had a somber look, frowning, quiet. Em didn't know how, but the rumor must have traveled.

"Is it true?" Betsy asked, sliding in across from Em. "You found out what happened to Mary?"

"That's what we need to see," she said, watching the front door, waiting.

The men knew something was up as soon as they came in and found the women watching them. The mood was tense, uncomfortable. None of them were smiling. And there he was, with his slicked-back hair, hunched up in his jacket like he was trying to hide. He hesitated inside the doorway along with the rest of the guys—if he turned around to leave this time, Em didn't think Jim or the others would try to stop him.

Em stood and approached them. "Frank Milliken?"

He glanced up, startled, though he had to have seen her coming. The other guys stepped away and left him alone in a space.

"Yeah?" he said warily.

Taking a breath, she closed her eyes a moment to steel herself. Didn't matter how much she'd practiced this speech in her mind, it wasn't going to come out right. She didn't know what to say.

"Last week, you were flying with a group of BT-13s. There was a collision. A WASP named Mary Keene crashed. I'm trying to find out what happened. Can you tell me?"

He was looking around, glancing side to side as if searching for an escape route. He wasn't saying anything, so Em kept on. "Your plane was damaged—I saw the work order. So I'm thinking your plane was involved and you know exactly what happened. Please, I just want to know how a good pilot like Mary crashed."

He was shaking his head. "No. I don't have to talk to you. I don't have to tell you anything."

"What's wrong?" Em pleaded. "What's everyone trying to hide?"

"Let it go. Why can't you just let it go?" he said, refusing to look at her, shaking his head like he could ward her away. Lillian was at Em's shoulder now, and a couple of the other WASP had joined them, standing in a group, staring down Milliken.

If Em had been male, she could have gotten away with grabbing his collar and shoving him to the wall, roughing him up a little to get him to talk. She was on the verge of doing it anyway; then wouldn't he be surprised?

"It was your fault, wasn't it?" She had the sudden epiphany. It was why he couldn't look at her, why he didn't even want to be here with WASP sitting at the next table. "What happened? Did you just lose control? Was something wrong with your plane?"

"It was an accident," he said softly.

"But what happened?" Em said, getting tired of asking, not knowing what else to do. He had six women staring him down now, and a handful of men looking back and forth between them and him. Probably wondering who was going to start crying first.

"Why don't you just tell her, Milliken," Jim said, frowning.

"Please, no one will tell me—"

"It was an accident!" His face was flush; he ran a shaking hand over his hair. "It was just a game, you know? I only buzzed her a couple of times. I thought it'd be funny—it was supposed to be funny. You know, get close, scare her a little. But—it was an accident."

He probably repeated it to himself so often, he believed it. But when he spoke it out loud, he couldn't gloss the crime of it: he'd broken regs, buzzed Mary in the air, got closer than the regulation five hundred feet, thought he could handle the stunt—and he couldn't. He'd hit her instead, crunched her wing. She'd lost control, plowed into the earth. Em could suddenly picture it so clearly. The lurch as the other plane hit Mary, the dive as she went out of control. She'd have looked out the canopy to see the gash in her wing, looked the other way to see the ground coming up fast. She'd have hauled on the stick, trying to land nose up, knowing it wasn't going to work because she was going too fast, so she turned off the engine, just in case, and hadn't she always wanted to go faster—

You tried to be respectful, to be a good girl. You bought war bonds and listened to the latest news on the radio. You prayed for the boys overseas, and most of all you didn't rock the boat, because there were so many other things to worry about, from getting a gallon of rationed gas for your car to whether your husband was going to come home in one piece.

They were a bunch of Americans doing their part. She tried to let it go. Let the anger drain away. Didn't work. The war had receded in Em's mind to a small noise in the background. She had this one battle to face.

With Burnett in charge, nothing would happen to Milliken. The colonel had hushed it up good and tight because he didn't want a more involved investigation, he didn't want the lack of discipline among his male flyers to come out. Milliken wouldn't be court-martialed and grounded, because trained pilots were too valuable. Em couldn't do anything more than stand here and stare him down. How could she make that be enough?

"Mary Keene was my friend," she said softly.

Milliken said, his voice a breath, "It was an accident. I didn't mean to hit her. I'm sorry. I'm sorry, all right?"

Silence cut like a blade. None of the guys would look at her.

Em turned and walked out, flanked by the other WASP.

Outside, the sun had set, but she could still hear airplane engines soaring over the airfield, taking off and landing, changing pitch as they roared overhead. The air smelled of fuel, and the field was lit up like stars fallen to earth. The sun would shine again tomorrow no matter what happened, and nothing had changed. She couldn't tell if she'd won. She slumped against the wall, slid to the ground, put her face to her knees and her arms over her head, and cried. The others gathered around her, rested hands on her shoulders, her arms. Didn't say a word, didn't make a big production. Just waited until she'd cried herself out. Then Lillian and Betsy hooked their arms in hers and pulled her back to the barracks, where one of the girls had stashed a bottle of whiskey.

The last time Em saw Mary was four days before she died.

Em reached the barracks after coming off the flight line to see Mary sitting on the front steps with her legs stretched out in front of her, smoking a cigarette and staring into space. Em approached slowly and sat beside her. "What's gotten into you?"

Mary donned a slow, sly smile. "It didn't happen the way I thought it would, the way I planned it."

"What didn't?"

She tipped her head back so her honey brown curls fell behind her and her tanned face looked into the sky. "I was supposed to step out of my airplane, chin up and beautiful, shaking my hair out after I took off my cap, and my handsome young officer would be standing there, stunned out of his wits. That didn't happen."

Em was grinning. This ought to be good. "So what did happen?"

"I'd just climbed out of my Valiant and I wanted to check the landing gear because it was feeling kind of wobbly when I landed. So there I was, bent over when I heard some guy say, 'Hey, buddy, can you tell me where to find ops?' I just about shot out of my boots. I stood up and look at him, and his eyes popped. And I swear to you he looked like Clark Gable. Not *just* like, but close. And I blushed red because the first thing he saw of me was my . . . my fanny stuck up in the air! We must have stood there staring at each other in shock for five minutes. Then we laughed."

Now Em was laughing, and Mary joined in, until they were leaning together, shoulder to shoulder.

"So, what," Em said. "It's true love?"

"I don't know. He's nice. He's a captain in from Long Beach. He's taking me out for drinks later."

"You are going to have the best stories when this is all over," Em said.

Mary turned quiet, thoughtful. "Can I tell you a secret? Part of me doesn't want the war to end. I don't want *this* to end. I just want to keep flying and carrying on like this forever. They won't let us keep flying when the boys come home. Then I'll have to go back home, put on white gloves and a string of pearls and start acting respectable." She shook her head. "I don't really mean that, about the war. It's got to end sometime, right?"

"I hope so," Em said softly. Pearl Harbor had been almost exactly two years ago, and it was hard to see an end to it all.

"Sometimes I wish my crazy barnstormer uncle hadn't ever taken me flying, then I wouldn't feel like this. Oh, my dad was so mad, you should have seen it. But once I'd flown I wasn't ever going to go back. I'm not ever going to quit, Em."

"I know." They sat on the stoop, watching and listening to planes come in over the field, until Mary went to get cleaned up for her date.

Em sat across from Colonel Roper's desk and waited while he read her carefully typed report. He read it twice, straightened the pages, and set it aside. He folded his hands together and studied her.

"How are you doing?"

She paused a moment, thinking about it rather than giving the pat "just fine" response. Because it wasn't true, and he wouldn't believe her.

"Is it worth it, sir?" He tilted his head, questioning, and she tried to explain. "Are we really doing anything for the war? Are we going to look back and think she died for nothing?"

His gaze dropped to the desk while he gathered words. She waited for the expected platitudes, the gushing reassurances. They didn't come.

"You want me to tell you Mary's death meant something, that what she was doing was essential for the war, that her dying is going to help us win. I can't do that." He shook his head. Em almost wished he would sugarcoat it. She didn't want to hear this. But she was also relieved that he was telling the truth. Maybe the bad-attitude flyboys were right, and the WASP were just a gimmick.

He continued. "You don't build a war machine so that taking out one cog makes the whole thing fall apart. Maybe we'll look back on this and decide we could have done it all without you. But, Emily—it would be a hell of a lot harder. We wouldn't have the pilots we need, and we wouldn't have the planes where we need them. And there's a hell of a lot of war left to fight."

She didn't want to think about it. You could take all the numbers, all the people who'd died over the last few years and everything they'd died for, and the numbers on paper might add up, but you start putting names and stories to the list and it would never add up, never be worth it. She just wanted it to be over; she wanted Michael home.

Roper sorted through a stack of papers on the corner of his desk and found a page he was looking for. He made a show of studying it for a long moment, giving her time to draw her attention from the wall where she'd been staring blankly. Finally, she met his gaze across the desk.

"I have transfer orders here for you. If you want them."

She shook her head, confused, wondering what she'd done wrong. Wondering if Burnett was having his revenge on her anyway, after all that had happened.

"Sir," she said, confused. "But . . . where? Why?"

"Palm Springs," he said, and her eyes grew wide, a spark in her heart lit, knowing what was at Palm Springs. "Pursuit School. If you're interested."

MARCH 1944

Em settled in her seat and reached up to close the canopy overhead. This was a one-seater, compact, nestled into a narrow, streamlined fuselage. The old trainers were roomy by comparison. She felt cocooned in the seat, all her controls and instruments at hand.

She started the engine; it roared. She could barely hear herself call the tower. "This is P-51 21054 requesting clearance for takeoff."

Her hands on the stick could feel this thing's power running into her bones. She wasn't going to have to push this plane off the ground. All she'd have to do was give it its head and let it go.

A voice buzzed in her ear. "P-51 21054, this is Tower, you are cleared for takeoff."

This was a crouched tiger preparing to leap. A rocket ready to explode. The nose was higher than the tail; she couldn't even see straight ahead— just straight up, past sleek silver into blue sky.

She eased the throttle forward, and the plane started moving. Then it *really* started moving. The tail lifted—she could see ahead of her now, to the end of the runaway. Her speed increased, and she watched the dials in front of her. At a hundred miles per hour, she pulled back on the stick, *lifted*, and left earth behind. Climbed *fast*, into clear blue sky, like a bullet, like a hawk. She glanced over her shoulder; the airstrip was already tiny. Nothing but open sky ahead, and all the speed she could push out of this thing.

This was heaven.

"Luckiest girl in the world," she murmured, thinking that Mary would have loved this.

S. M. Stirling

Considered by many to be the natural heir to Harry Turtledove's title of King of the Alternate History novel, fast-rising science fiction star S. M. Stirling is the bestselling author of the Nantucket series (*Island in the Sea of Time, Against the Tide of Years, On the Ocean of Eternity*), in which Nantucket comes unstuck in time and is cast back to the year 1250 BC, and the Draka series (including *Marching Through Georgia, Under the Yoke, The Stone Dogs,* and *Drakon,* plus an anthology of Draka stories by other hands edited by Stirling, *Drakas!*), in which Tories fleeing the American Revolution set up a militant society in South Africa and eventually end up conquering most of the earth. He's also produced the Emberverse series (*Dies the Fire, The Protector's War, A Meeting at Corvallis*), plus the five-volume Fifth Milennium series and the seven-volume General series (with David Drake), as well as stand-alone novels such as *Conquistador, The Peshawar Lancers,* and *The Sky People.* Stirling has also written novels in collaboration with Raymond F. Feist, Jerry Pournelle, Holly Lisle, Shirley Meier, Karen Wehrstein, and *Star Trek* actor James Doohan, as well as contributing to the *Babylon 5, T2, Brainship, War World,* and *Man-Kzin War* series. His short fiction has been collected in *Ice, Iron and Gold.* Stirling's newest series is an Emberverse tetralogy of the Change, so far in three volumes, *The Sunrise Lands, The Scourge of God,* and *The Sword of the Lady.* His most recent book is *In the Courts of the Crimson Kings,* sequel to *The Sky People.* Born in France and raised in Europe, Africa, and Canada, he now lives in Santa Fe, New Mexico.

In the action-packed story that follows, he shows us how an unlikely alliance is forged between two very different kinds of warriors, and then sends them on an even more unlikely mission together, a hair-raisingly dangerous mission that will test their resolve, their ingenuity, and their courage—and the bounds of friendship.

Ancient Ways

It was a hot day in July, the two thousandth and fifty-fifth year of Our Lord; or fifty-seven years since the Change, plus a few months. The feather-grass of the middle Volga steppe rustled around him, rolling to the edge of sight in knee-high blond waves. Sergey Ivanovitch's jaws moved steadily on the stick of tasteless dried mutton as he lay on his belly and watched through his binoculars as the strange rider approached, ant-small at first under the immense blue dome of the sky. Now and then, he sipped from a leather flask, water cut with corn brandy to make it safe to drink.

"Who is this one, sorry nag?" he said idly, either to himself or the horse lying behind him, mentally checking on the locations of his weapons. "Balls of brass, to ride here alone. Or in a hurry, Christ witness."

He chewed cautiously on the stick of jerky, since it was like gnawing on a board, and occasionally used his dagger to slice off shavings. *His* teeth were a young man's intact set, which he wanted to keep as long as possible. At forty-eight, his father Ivan Mikhailovitch had exactly five discolored stubs left in his jaws and had to live on boiled cabbage and soup, when he wasn't drunk and living on liquor, which admittedly was most of the time.

Whoever he was, the stranger was coming on fairly fast—canter-trot-canter, with two remounts behind him on a leading rein. Three horses would be very welcome when the traders from Belgorod came.

"So, does he run *away* or *toward?*"

Sergey was here on the chance of running across some saiga antelope or wild horses. And to get away from the *stanitsa*—Cossack village—and his family's crowded rammed-earth cabin and the squalling of his younger brothers and sisters and the endless chores for a while before harvest pinned everyone down.

And because his grandfather Mikhail had died, and it was unseemly to grieve too openly before others for a man of eighty—it was the will of God and the way of nature, and it became a Cossack to be scornful of death. Mikhail had been a great man, one of the few left who'd been a grown man before the Change; and one of the leaders who'd seen the Don Host reborn.

I am the last of them, the old man had said just before he stopped breathing. *The last, and a world dies again with me.*

Sergey hadn't known what Grandfather Mikhail had meant by that, but it made his eyes prickle nonetheless; he shoved the thought roughly away and concentrated on what was at hand.

"And he could throw an axe like an angel," he muttered. "Christ welcome you, Grandfather."

A clump of trees and the remnants of old orchards to the north surrounding the snags of some ruined buildings were the only signs that this had once been tilled ground, in the days before the machines stopped. The great river's bend was only eighty kilometers eastward hereabouts, but folk from his *stanitsa* didn't go that way, not if they valued their heads. Too many of the infidel flat-faces ranged there. The feud between Russki and Tartar went back long before the time of the Red Czars and the age of wizards, to the dim days of legend.

"And sometimes you see some of those Kuban bastards this far north," he mused. "And Daghestanis . . . Quiet, limb of Satan," he added as his mount stirred.

The big rawboned gray beast was well-trained and stayed lying prone behind him, both of them sweating under the hot noon sun. Tiny white grasshoppers spurted out of the grass-stems when he shifted his weight on his elbows, and the air smelled of ozone and hay—as well as horse and man's-sweat, leather and metal.

"Glory be to God forever and ever," he muttered to himself as the man's features and dress began to show details in the twin lenses. "I don't think he's a Tartar at all; not a Nogai, at least."

That was what the flat-face tribes around the Volga called themselves these days, and Sergey's people knew them well from war and trade and the odd marriage-by-abduction. The stranger's helmet was a blunt cone with a spike on top and a belt of fur around the rim, not wound with a turban; he wore his hair in a black pigtail, too. And his stirrup-leathers were adjusted fairly long, not in the short knees-up goblin Tartar style.

"Maybe I shouldn't kill him, then. Not right away. Father Cherepanin will scold me if I kill a Christian just for his horses."

And it would be a shame to miss asking him some questions; Sergey could feel his curiosity itching like a mosquito bite. Grandfather Mikhail had always scorned the younger generation because they were pinned to one place, and boasted of how he'd roamed from Germany to China in the service of Great Russ, in the old days before the Change. Most of Sergey's generation had little time for stories of the days of the Red Czars, but they'd made him wistful sometimes. And life in the *stanitsa* could get dull.

Or if Olga finds out about Svetlana, then it could get far too interesting for comfort!

The oncoming rider was jogging along on a horse not quite like anything the Cossack had seen before; short-legged, shaggy, with a head like a barrel and a round tubby body. It didn't look like much, but it was getting its rider along well. The two remounts on a string behind him were Tartar horses, taller and slimmer and more handsome, but although they carried only light loads, twin sacks, they looked more worn-down.

"So he's either expecting a fight or just come from one. Most likely running. Who goes on a raid alone? He rides well, too," Sergey said to himself. "As well as a Cossack. A bit of a runt, but not a *moujik*, not a peasant."

All Cossacks considered themselves noblemen, of course, even though they did their own work.

The man was well-armed too, with an inward-curved yataghan sword at his waist, an odd-looking flat quiver of arrows over his back and a bow in his fist; a round shield of leather-covered cane and a braided lariat were hung at his saddlebow. Apart from that, he wore boots and leather trousers and a shirt of mail over a leather jacket, warm gear for midsummer unless he expected a fight. As he watched, the stranger halted and looked backwards carefully, standing in his stirrups and raising a hand to shade his eyes.

Sergey nodded to himself, cased the binoculars, picked up his lance, and whistled to his horse, swinging effortlessly into the saddle as the beast unfolded itself and rose. The stranger reacted instantly, reaching over his shoulder for an arrow; he was about three hundred meters away now, extreme bowshot for a strong man and a heavy stave. That motion halted as Sergey held his lance up horizontally over his head, and then reversed it and drove it point-down in the earth in sign of his peaceful intentions, leaving his own bow cased at his left knee. Then he waited quietly as the stranger jog-trotted forward and halted within talking distance.

They looked each other over. Sergey was a young man, just turned twenty, a thumb's width under six feet tall, broad-shouldered, with lean muscles like ropes and a longish straight-nosed face. And an impressive collection of scars, many of which showed because he was wearing only baggy wool pantaloons and high hide boots and the broad leather belt that supported his *shashka*-saber and dagger and a light axe with a meter-long handle. His head was shaved save for a long yellow scalplock bound with thongs that hung down past his shoulder from over his right ear. Mustaches of the same corn-color were still distressingly fuzzy on his upper lip; his slightly tilted eyes were pale green, bright in his tanned face.

The other man looked a *little* like a Tartar, but darker than most—umber-brown skin, braided black hair, with a flat almost scalloped-in face, high cheekbones, and a snub nose. The narrow slanted eyes were blue, but raiding for women back and forth had gone on long enough that you couldn't judge who was who by looks alone. The stranger was shorter than Sergey, strong-looking, but slim and apparently a youth just barely old enough to take the war-trail; even for a black-arse, his face was very hairless. Sweat gleamed on that smooth impassive countenance.

The stranger spoke first. *"Russki?"* he said, in a voice that sounded even younger than his face, pointing at Sergey.

The Cossack nodded and slapped a fist against his bare chest, making the silver crucifix slung there bounce.

"Da, Russki, Khristianin," he said. "Yes, Russian, Christian."

"I am name Dorzha Abakov," the stranger replied.

"Sergey Ivanovitch Khorkina, me. I am a Cossack, *stanitsa* of Polovo in the Don Host, under *Ataman* Oleg Andreivitch Arkhipov. And you, flat-face boy?"

"Tanghch people; Kalmyk, you Russki say. My ruler is Erdne Khan of Elst."

From the far reaches, Sergey thought, his brows rising in surprise.

He'd never heard of the khan, and only vaguely of the Kalmyks, who grazed their herds and pitched their yurts in the dry steppe south of Astrakhan on the Caspian shore. Dorzha's eastern-flavored Russian was rough but understandable; a guttural undertone suggested something else that was probably his native language.

"Musul'manin?" Sergey asked suspiciously.

Dorzha spat with scorn, shook his head, and pointed upward. "Worship *Tengri Etseg*—Eternal Blue Father Sky—and the Merciful Buddha, not stupid gods from books."

That *could* have been an insult to the holy Orthodox faith, but the Kalmyk's next words concentrated Sergey's mind wonderfully, along with the eastward jerk of his thumb:

"Nogai men follow me to kill. Five and two."

"Seven Tartars?" Sergey yelped.

Dorzha nodded. "Seven, *da*, is that word." Helpfully, he held up one hand and two fingers of the other.

"They were nine when they start after me," he added, with a smile that exposed teeth that were very even and white, and patted the hilt of his yataghan. Then he indicated his remounts: "These their horses. Now *my* horses."

Sergey cursed fluently and at length, regretting his decision not to kill the wanderer from ambush. Probably the Tartars would have turned back if they'd just found the body; they were getting too close to the *stanitsa* to be safe. Now . . . even without a blood-debt, any Nogai who found a Russian alone here would fill him full of arrows as a matter of course, unless they went to the effort of trying to capture him for torture or the slave markets. There wasn't a truce on at present, and this wasn't anywhere near the recognized trade-trail along the Belgorod–Volga railway in any case.

He suppressed an impulse to gallop away. If he just rode off, how could he keep this Dorzha from following him out of bowshot?

The black-arse devils would track us both! No wonder the little Kalmyk bastard is smiling!

The odds against *him* had just been cut in half.

But I've got a fight at three-to-one on my hands. The devil's grandmother fly away with him!

Then he laughed and leaned forward in the saddle, extending his hand.

"It's been a while since I let any blood, anyway," Sergey said.

Dorzha took the hand, and a long swig from the flask Sergey offered next, along with a little bread and salt from his saddlebags. The Cossack drank from the Kalmyk's offered canteen in return; it held kumiss, fermented mare's milk. Kumis was better than water, and that was all you could say for it.

"We run more or fight here?" Dorzha asked. "This is ground of yours . . . no, this is your ground, you would say."

Sergey looked around, then cocked an eye at the Kalmyk's horses. They looked thirsty as well as tired, slobbering and showing their tongues. And if the pursued hadn't been able to stop for water, then the pursuers probably hadn't either. . . .

"Hey, dog-brother, there's an old well in that ruined kolkhoz over there," he said thoughtfully. "The Tartar swine know it and they'll probably water their horses at it."

Dorzha grinned and nodded, making a motion to the west and then a curving gesture to indicate turning north and coming back parallel to their own tracks.

"Way to cut back and hide in wrecked of houses without being seen? They come soon, maybe—"

He pointed to the sun, and then to where it would be in about an hour.

"Catch us in twice that long if we run."

Sergey laughed; the Kalmyk had grasped the essentials quickly.

"*Da.* There is a deep ravine four kilometers west that runs to the northeast; we can use that, then come in on the ruins from the north, if we're quick. I like the way you think, Kalmyk! Let's go!"

There *were* seven of the Tartars, men with straggly mustaches and sparse beards, dingy green turbans, long filthy sheepskin coats . . . and unpleasantly clean and well-cared-for weapons.

Sergey looked through a dirty scrap of ancient glass as the enemy dismounted in the thin grass at the center of the old settlement, near a crumbling mound of rust that had been one of the devil's magic oxen before the machines stopped.

A *tractor*, they'd called it, according to the old stories, first conjured out of Hell by the evil wizards of the Red Steel Czar to oppress the peasants. According to his great-grandmother, at least. Grandfather Mikhail had always said they were just machines, like a clock or a reaper, and a lot less work in plowing time than a team of oxen. Sergey had his doubts about that—if they weren't moved by evil spirits, why should they all stop working at the same time?

But Grandfather could certainly tell a story, true or not. To plow sitting down, as if you were taking your ease in a tavern!

None of the Nogai were more than twenty meters away, their boots clumping in the dust and raising little puffs through the sparse grass. That was close enough for the Cossack to smell the hard rancid sweat-and-butter stink of them, as strong as the dry earth and the ancient brick and wood of the ruin.

The well had a built-up earthen coping around it, and a good solid cover of wood; the buildings had been stripped long ago of anything useful, down to wagonloads of bricks, and the frame ones on the outskirts had burned in the yearly grass-fires, but no steppe-dweller would destroy a well, whether Cossack or Tartar or even vagabond bandits. The Tartars looked tired, and their horses worse, despite having three remounts each. The animals were thirsty, too; the slant-eyed men had to hold them back as soon as they smelled water, wrestling with bridles, flicking their quirts at noses and cursing as the eager animals jostled and tossed their heads.

Tartars ride fast, and those are good horses, the Cossack thought. *Dorzha must have led them a merry chase.*

He mentally added a few notches to the lively respect he'd formed for the easterner.

This is not a little lost boy who's come to our steppe, for all he has no beard.

The Nogai warriors had followed the tracks of Sergey and Dorzha just long enough to make sure that they hadn't visited the well, then come directly back here; the two chance-met comrades had galloped west three kilometers, then looped north through the ravine and come back well away from their outward trace.

The Tartars thought their prey was still in headlong flight to the west. They'd plan to water their horses before they took up the chase again, pushing hard to make those they pursued founder their beasts; a thirsty horse died faster. But even if they thought themselves safe, the riders of the Nogai *Ordu* were experienced fighters. Two of them remained mounted, keeping a careful eye out and their bows ready while the others heaved the massive timbers of the lid out of the way and uncoiled their lariats to lower hide buckets and haul them back up hand-over-hand.

Sergey had pulled on his *kosovorotka* shirt-tunic while he rode and over it a sleeveless leather vest sewn with old-time washers of stainless steel, an heirloom from his grandfather, like the round Red Army helmet that now covered his shaven head. He looked over at Dorzha and tapped his bow, then held up two fingers and flipped his hand back and forth to indicate the Tartar sentries:

I the one on the north; you the one on the south. Then as many more as we can.

The Kalmyk nodded grimly, keeping his head well below the four-foot top of the ruined wall. Sergey eased three arrows out of his quiver, selecting hunting shafts with broad triangular heads, since none of the Tartars looked as if they were wearing armor. He set one on his string and the other two carefully point-down in the dirt. Dorzha did likewise. His arrows were black-fletched in nomad fashion; the Cossack preferred to use expensive imported peacock feathers from the Crimea, even if some of his friends teased him about being a dandy.

As if they'd practiced the motion together for years, they sprang to their feet, drawing and loosing in the same motion.

"Hourra!" Sergey shouted.

Dorzha simply shrieked with exultation, a sound like a file on metal. The *snap* of the strings on the bracers sounded in almost the same instant as the wet *thunk* of impact; at ten meters, an arrow from a powerful sinew-and-horn horseman's bow struck quicker than thought. Sergey's target went backwards over the crupper of his saddle in a double splash of red as the arrow punched through his chest and out the back of his body without slowing. The other sentry took Dorzha's shaft under one armpit, and it sank to the fletching; he collapsed thrashing and screaming.

Sergey reached for another arrow. Dorzha shot before he could draw, and a Tartar on foot staggered backwards, staring down incredulously at the shaft in his stomach, then toppled backwards still clutching the bucket he'd been drawing. The long leather rope whipped down the shaft after him, and a scream floated up to be followed by a splash as the man struck head-first.

"Four left!" Sergey shouted.

Then the Nogai were shooting back and leaping into the saddle; Sergey ducked as a whistle of shafts went by overhead. A savage yelping war-shout rose as they reined around toward the wall:

"Gur! Gur! *Gur!*"

And a thunder of hooves. Sergey yelled laughter as the two men turned and ran, vaulting over the lower back wall of the ruined building and turning sharply left between a higher stretch of rubble and a big oak tree.

"The infidel swine won't get off their horses even to piss if they can help it!"

He'd counted on that. With superb horsemanship, the leading Tartar took the wall Sergey and Dorzha had just leapt, and shot from the saddle in midjump. Sergey swerved with a yell as the arrow went *vwwwpt*! past his left ear and dived for the ground. Dorzha landed beside him and scrabbled in the dirt; the Tartar in the laneway reined back slightly to let his comrades catch up, then came on again with his lance poised.

"Pull!" Sergey shouted.

"I pulling *am*, stupid Cossack ox!" Dorzha wheezed.

Their joined lariats sprang up out of the dust, secured to the oak tree and with a half-hitch around the jut of eroded brick wall. They both braced their feet and flung themselves backwards, but even with the friction of the hitch, the rope jerked savagely through his callused palms as the first two horses struck it. One went over in a complete somersault and landed on its rider like a woman's wooden tenderizing hammer coming down on a pork cutlet; the other collapsed and slid, throwing its rider ahead of it. The two behind reared and crow-hopped on their hind legs, screaming louder than their riders as they tried to dodge the tangle of human and equine flesh before them.

Sergey plucked the hatchet out of his belt, tossed it into a better grip, and threw with a whipping overarm motion. The ashwood of the handle left his hand with that sweet fluid feeling you got when something was thrown properly, and an instant later the steel helve went *smack* into a Tartar's face; the man fell and beat at the earth with his hands, screaming in a gobbling, choking grunt.

Dorzha had his yataghan out. He dodged in cat-quick under the last rider's hasty slash, turned it with his round leather-covered cane shield and drove the point of the inward-curved sword into the horse's haunch. It bucked uncontrollably, and the Nogai had no time to spare for swordwork for an instant. That was enough.

Quick as a cat indeed! Sergey thought, as the sharp Damascus-patterned steel slashed across the man's thigh, swinging in a beautifully economical curve. It opened the muscle nearly to the bone; Dorzha bounced away again to let him bleed out.

The Tartar who'd been thrown from his horse had landed with a weasel's agility, rolling over and over, then bouncing up. His bow was gone, but he had his curved *shamshir* out almost instantly.

"Allahu Akbar!" he shouted as he charged, sword whirling over his head. "*Gur!*"

"*Yob tvoyu mat',*" Sergey replied, grinning and coming up on the balls of his feet; the Tartar probably even understood it—everyone picked up swearwords. "*Hourra! Christ is risen!*"

His *shapska* was longer than the nomad's weapon, a guardless shallow curve with an eagle's-head pommel, and while the Tartars were fearsome fighters on horseback, most of them were as awkward on foot as a pig on ice. He flicked the Nogai's cut aside—Sergey grunted slightly at the impact; the man was *strong*—with a *ting* and a shower of sparks. The Tartar smashed at him like a man threshing grain, but Sergey drifted backwards until he saw Dorzha circling in the corner of his eye. Then he pressed the attack, lunging forward—only a fool fought fair with a Tartar when he didn't have to.

Seconds later, the Nogai collapsed with a yell of agony as the yataghan cut his hamstring and the Cossack saber slashed his sword-arm. Sergey grunted again in surprise as Dorzha beat up his killing stroke, leaving him staggering for a second.

"The devil carry you off in a sack!" he said resentfully, examining his sword's edge—no nick, thank the saints. "Why did you do that?"

Dorzha ignored him. Instead he planted a foot on the wounded Tartar's chest and put the point of his yataghan under the man's chin. The Tartar spat at him, then hissed as the point dimpled the flesh.

"*Where is the princess?*" Dorzha asked . . . in Tartar, of which Sergey had a fair command.

"*On her way to Astrakhan, where you will never follow, you depraved* kufur bi—"

The point drove home and the curse ended in a gurgle, and the Tartar's heels drummed briefly on the ground. Dorzha wiped his sword and the edge of his boot free of blood on the nomad's sheepskin jacket.

"Princess?" Sergey asked casually as he helped his chance-met comrade make sure of the others.

"That was a good trick with the axe," Dorzha said.

Sergey wrenched it free of the wounded man's face and slammed the blunt hammer on the back of the blade into the Nogai's temple with a heavy crunching sound. The man jerked once and stopped twitching.

"Off to hell, black-arse," he said cheerfully, then flipped the weapon into the air and caught the handle.

"Grandfather Mikhail was *spetsnaz*, he taught us the trick," Sergey said, and pointed to the axe—not particularly threatening, but not *not* so either. "The Princess?"

Dorzha sighed and sat on a stump of wall. "The daughter of my Khan. I was her bodyguard," he said. "Not in the troops with us, just . . . personal guard."

Well-born nom'klaturnik *stripling dancing attendance on this princess,* Sergey thought.

He'd noted the quality of Dorzha's boots, and the silver inlay on his yataghan and kinjal-dagger, and the tooling on his belt, whose buckle was a blue-enameled wolf's-head. And his mail-shirt was of fine riveted links, a master-smith's work.

Then, grudgingly: *Young, and a nobleman, but he can fight.*

"We taking her up the Volga—a wedding with Duke Pyotr of Nikolayevsk. Then these Tartars, river pirates working for the Khan of Chistopol attack."

Sergey nodded thoughtfully. "The misbelieving infidel dog wouldn't want Nikolayevsk strengthened by an alliance."

Dorzha pounded a fist against the brick beside his hip. "They supposed to kill her, I think, but instead take to sell. That why I run. They no hurt her—"

"You could get a good sum for the virgin daughter of a khan," Sergey said thoughtfully. "In Astrakhan."

He turned and freed his lariat, uncoiling it and rigging a casting loop. "Let's get going," he said. "There are eighteen of their horses. Can you sleep in the saddle, boy?"

Dorzha grinned. "Can you, farmer?"

"*Oi, Pri Luzhke!*" Sergey sang in a loud, melodious baritone seven days later, reeling in the saddle with his feet kicked free of the stirrups.

"Carry the water, Gala!
Come, maiden, and water my horse—"

"Silence, Cossack pig!" the *streltsy* officer at the north gate of Astrakhan said in his rough southeastern dialect of Russian.

He twitched the long black mustaches that hung past his blue-stubbled chin; behind him his men hefted their crossbows and half-pikes. The two young men had twenty good horses with them, counting the ones they rode, and their gear was of fine quality. They could probably afford a bribe, and they were strangers without friends here. The scalp-lock of the Don Cossack was unmistakable, and so were the features of the Kalmyk; Erdne Khan wasn't at war with Astrakhan, but the realms weren't particularly friendly either.

"What is your business in the city?"

"I come to drink all the vodka and screw all the women, of course, fool," Sergey said, and held his canteen up over his open mouth to shake out the last drops, breathing out with satisfaction and tossing the empty vessel aside. "Ahhhh! Got a drink on you, dog-face? Or will I have to settle for fucking your sister, after I put a bag on her ugly head?"

The man flushed, and there was a ripple of laughter from the crowd jammed in the gate, ragged peasants from the drained marshes outside the city with little two-wheeled ox-carts of vegetables, peddlers with pack-donkeys, a hook-nosed Armenian merchant in a skullcap and long kaftan with a curved knife stuck through his sash. A camel in the Armenian's caravan-string threw its head up and made an unearthly burbling sound, as if joining in the mirth. Two Kuban Cossacks in their round black lamb-skin caps and long wool *cherkessa* coats laughed loudest of all. Though there wasn't much love lost between what its members called the All-Great Kuban Host and their northerly cousins from the Don, they still enjoyed seeing one of the Sir Brothers mock a city man.

The *streltsy* looked around, obviously trying to see who'd laughed so he could beat someone safer than a Cossack.

"We come to sell our horses," Dorzha broke in, scowling himself and fingering the silver-inlaid hilt of his yataghan.

He hefted the leading-rope; they had all the Nogai horses, minus those who'd broken legs or sprained something in the brief fight. The tall slim-legged animals were snorting and rolling their eyes at the unfamiliar noises and scents of the great city of the Volga delta.

The militia officer snorted himself. "Where did you get those?" he said. "They're good horses."

"They were a gift," Sergey said.

"A gift?"

"*Da*. From some dead Tartars," Sergey said. "Or you *could* call it an inheritance."

That produced more hooted laughter; one of the Kuban men nearly fell off his horse as he wheezed helplessly with mirth. A couple of Tartars shot Sergey looks from under hooded eyes, and there were loud calls from the back of the crowd for the *streltsy* to stop being officious and clear the way.

"Now, are you going to let us past so we can go ease our thirst like Christian men, or will you keep us talking all night?" Sergei asked.

It was only half an hour until the late summer sundown, and nobody wanted to be stuck outside when the gates closed. The officer hefted his long two-handed axe, idly running a thumb down the great curved cutting-edge. He was wearing a steel breastplate and helmet despite the damp heat, and sweat poured off his lean dark face. He spoke to Dorzha next:

"And what's a Kalmyk boy doing with this scalp-lock devil?"

"I keep him with me to hold me back when I lose my temper!" Dorzha said, flipping a coin toward the city militiaman. "Here!"

The militiaman snatched it out of the air, bit the silver dihrem and looked at it with respect—it bore the stamp of the Christopol mint. They both had a fair number of those, courtesy of the dead Nogai. *Someone* had been paying them well.

"Pass, then," he said; his men stirred, expecting their cut. "But remember that the great Czar Boris Bozhenov keeps good order here in his city—thieves are sent to the chain-gangs, and armed robbers are impaled or knouted to death. Drunken rowdies cool their heads in the *butuks*."

He jerked a thumb at a brace of bleary-looking rascals not far away, sitting with their feet and hands locked in the stocks. A few children were amusing themselves by throwing horse-dung and the occasional rock at them.

"Czar!" Dorzha said with contempt, after they'd passed through the thick rubble-and-concrete wall into the noise and crowds of the street. "Grandfather of Boris called himself Chairman."

Sergey shrugged. "All the Princes and Grand Dukes and Khans and

Czars used to be called that, back in the old days," he said. "Or Party Secretaries, my grandfather told us children."

Of course, he also told us that he could fly like a bird back then and jump from the sky into battle, Sergey thought. *Sober, he was the best liar I've ever met. Of course, there are such things as gliders and balloons, but . . . And he could throw an axe like an angel.*

"Did you have to be so loudness at the gate, like bull that bellows?" Dorzha went on; his Russian had improved, but he still slipped now and then.

Sergey shrugged again. "Who ever heard of a humble Cossack?" he said. "*That* would be suspicious. Besides, your idea was good: we want those Tartars to hear of us and come for vengeance. How else can we find them before they sell your Princess to Big-Head Boris, or to some Kazakh slave-trader for the harem of the Emir of Bokhara? There must be thirty or even forty thousand people in this city."

"Seventy-five thousands," Dorzha said absently.

"*Bozehmoi!*" Sergey said with awe. "It must be the biggest city in the world, bigger than Moskva the Great in the old days!"

Dorzha shook his head. "They say Winchester is as big, and richer," he said; at Sergey's blank look, he went on: "In Britain, far to the west. And there are much more big . . . *bigger* . . . cities in Hinduraj, and China."

Sergey grunted; those places were the edge of the world, where men might have their heads set on backwards or hop around on a single leg. Astrakhan was certainly at least twice as big as Belgorod, which was the largest city in *his* part of the world.

Grandfather Mikhail called us snails, because we hadn't seen Moskva the Great or Vladivostock, Sergey thought. *But now I've begun to travel like him!*

They walked their horses through a crush of carts and wagons and rickshaws and the occasional bicycle or pedicab, and past horse-drawn tramcars traveling on steel rails set into the roadway—another mark of urban sophistication. Most of the folk were the locals, Russians of a sort, but there were Georgians and Armenians, Greeks and Circassians, Tartars of a dozen different tribes, Kurds, men from the oasis-cities far to the east, a swaggering *Lah* in the gold-laced crimson coat and plumed hat the Poles affected, sailors from the Caspian fleets, porters staggering under high-piled packs . . .

"Here, it stinks," Dorzha said, in a resigned tone. Which it did; most of the city was low-lying, and the land around it natural swamp, and there was a thick wet smell of sewage and rot. "Best not to drink the water."

"I don't *drink* water. It's all right for baths, of course," Sergey said; unlike some, he washed every couple of weeks whether he needed it or not, and took sweat-baths even in winter.

He forced himself not to gape like a *moujik* as they passed a building that must have been fourteen stories high, a survival from before the Change not yet torn down for its metal. Most of the city was post-Change two or three stories and built of brick often covered with colorful plaster; on a rise to the north were the walls of the city's Kremlin, and behind it, the gilded onion-domes of cathedral and palace. Shopkeepers and artisans called out the wares that spilled into the street, windmilling their arms and screaming of their low prices in a dozen languages, selling everything from Chinese silk to blocks of tea carried here from Georgia to piles of Azeri oranges from the southern shore to a tempting display of swords laid out on dark cloths.

Sergey would have turned aside to look at the fascinating glitter of honed metal if Dorzha hadn't scowled and jerked his head. The caravanserai he chose was the usual type, a square of cubicles within a high rammed-earth wall with a section fenced off as a corral for livestock, and a warehouse where goods could be left under guard for an additional fee. Sergey's nose twitched at the smell of cooking food; it had been a long day.

A sullen-looking man in ragged clothes and an iron collar came to take their animals.

"Here, *rab*," the Cossack said, and tossed him a silver coin. "See that our horses are well-watered and fed—alfalfa and cracked barley, not just hay."

That brightened the slave's face; it also made him more likely to do his job properly . . . and anyway, a Cossack brother was supposed to be openhanded, especially with found money and booty. Sergey didn't like trusting his horse to a *rab*, but slaves were common in places like this.

Many of the residents were squatting at the entrances to their little mud-brick rooms, cooking their evening meals on little braziers. Those not concerned about religious pollution sat at long trestle tables around a firepit, where the serai-keeper and his helpers carved meat from a whole sheep and a couple of yearling pigs that turned on a spit, and handed out rounds of bread and raw onions and melons.

"Room for us, if you please, brothers," Sergey said.

One of those customers looked over his shoulder at Sergey, grunted, and returned to his meal.

"Hey, dog-face, thanks for the seat," Sergey said.

Then he grabbed him by the back of his coat, heaved him aside to thump squawking on the ground, and tossed the man's plate and loaf after him.

"Here's your dinner, and fuck your mother, pal."

Yob tvoyu mat' wasn't necessarily a deadly insult in Russki—between friends it could be just a way of saying "take this seriously"—but Sergey hadn't used the friendly intonation. The ex-diner was burly, and he had a long knife through his sash. Sergey stood and grinned at him with his thumbs in his belt. The man put a hand to his knife for a moment before thinking better of it and slinking away; the two who'd been on either side of him crowded aside to make room for the newcomers.

"He can't complain if I serve him some of his own manners," the Cossack said as he sat down on the bench and slapped the rough, stained poplar planks. "Food and wine! Christ's blood, does a Sir Brother, a knight of the Don Host, have to go hungry and thirsty here with gold and silver at his belt?"

A serving wench bustled over with wooden platters and clay mugs; she gave Sergey a long considering look. He preened and smoothed down his mustaches with a thumb before she turned back to her work, but he caught the glance she gave his companion, too.

"Nice round arse," he said to Dorzha as the youth sat beside him. "And haunches like a plow-horse. Hey, dog-brother, I think she fancies you, though. Or your fine boots and coat. Give it a try!"

The Kalmyk flushed under his dark olive skin and tore off a lump from the loaf of bread. Sergey laughed. The youth was as fastidious and dainty as a young priest fresh from a monastery school, even waiting until a rock or a bush came up to drop his trousers. He'd noticed that on the trip here, though they'd had little time for anything but riding and sleeping and chewing jerky in the saddle. With ten horses each, you could push *hard*, two hundred kilometers a day or better.

And we needed to, after we spent hours *fishing that dead Tartar out of the well. . . .*

"It gets moldy if you don't use it, youngster," he said. "Anyway, it's the little skinny ones like you who can fuck like rabbits."

Dorzha flushed still more, then scowled as Sergey guffawed and took a long gulp of the rough red wine.

I blushed like that the first time Uncle Igor said that to me, he thought. *Of course, I was thirteen, and the Kalmyk has to be older than that.*

"Best not get drunk," Dorzha said coldly. "We may have work to do this tonight, if lucky."

"To drink is the joy of the Russ," Sergey said reasonably. Then he shrugged: "Besides, this is just wine. No Cossack can get drunk on *wine.* We are born with a grape in our mouths."

He didn't take more than one mug, though; the boy had a point. When he'd gnawed the last gristly meat off the rack of pork ribs and picked his teeth with his dagger-point, he tossed the bones to a dog that looked even hungrier than the *rab,* and walked to their cubicle with an exaggerated care; if anyone was watching, they might be encouraged to think he *was* drunk and would sleep soundly.

You can't keep a dog from rolling in shit or a Tartar from seeking revenge, he thought later that night. *They're not peaceable and forgiving and full of loving-kindness to all, like us Christian men.*

They'd left the door open—many of the residents of the caravanserai did, to get what little breeze they could in the sultry summer heat of the delta. Sergey opened one eye a slit; he was lying in his drawers, sprawled back with his head on his saddlebags. Long curved knives glinted a little in the moonlight, as three dark-clad figures slipped in, with the tails of their turbans drawn across their faces to leave only the eyes exposed. A man stooped, knife poised to thrust into Sergey's belly.

Thump.

His foot lashed up into the man's crotch, toes rolled up to present the callused ball of the foot as the striking surface. That slammed his victim's testicles up against the pubic bone as if they were iron on an anvil. A thin squeal like a dying rabbit sounded, and then a maul-on-oak sound as the Cossack's knee punched into the descending face. The Tartar pitched to the side, unconscious or dead; Sergey used the motion to raise both feet in the air and then flip himself up into a standing crouch.

Dorzha had moved in the same instant. He had his belt in his hand, with a brick snugged into a loop at the end by the buckle. It arched out and smacked into the side of the second knifeman's head; the long dagger fell from nerveless fingers, and the man reeled back and collapsed against the wall.

The third Tartar acted with commendable prudence and great speed; he threw his knife at Dorzha and fled. The Kalmyk boy gave a startled yelp of pain. Sergey ignored him—time enough to bind wounds later—and threw himself forward in a tackle that caught the man around the knees and brought him crashing down. The air went out of him in a *whuff!* as he flopped on belly and face; most of the Cossack's went out, too, but he scrabbled forward over the heaving body and hammered a knobby fist into the small of his enemy's back—much better than breaking your knuckles on a skull, grandfather had always said. And again and again, until the enemy went limp.

"Shut up, you fornicating buffoons! We're trying to sleep like Christians!" someone called from the cubicle next door.

"Sorry, brother," Sergey said contritely. "The saints guard your dreams."

Then he dragged the man back into the cubicle by his ankle and turned to look at Dorzha. The Kalmyk was in his drawers and shirt, with a long red stain spreading on the linen beneath his left arm. He clamped that to his side and shook his head.

"Just a scratch," he said, with a tight brace in his voice that gave him the lie. "Let's get what know we must—what we must know, I mean."

Sergey grunted thoughtfully and looked through the dimness at their three assailants. The man he'd kicked and knee-butted was breathing in swift shallow jerks, his eyes wide and fixed; no use there. The one he'd punched was unconscious—and probably bleeding out internally from his ruptured kidneys. If he woke, it would only be to scream.

"Well, Christ be witness, you hit this one just right!" he said, as the one stunned by the Kalmyk started to stir. "That was good work—it shows a delicate hand. I finished my two off or nearly, and they're useless."

"Delicate is not Cossack way, eh?" Dorzha said with a painful smile.

Sergey laughed as he grabbed the man, pulled his belt loose, trussed his arms behind his back with it, and stuffed a gag into his mouth.

"So, dog-face," he said, tipping water from his skin over the man, who glared defiance as he came fully awake. "You nod when you feel like a good chat, eh? No noise and fuss, now; people are trying to sleep."

"Let me this do," Dorzha said.

Sergey looked around; the Kalmyk had bound a spare shirt around his ribs beneath his garment, and was moving with careful precision. Sergey shrugged and stepped aside. Dorzha picked up one of the Tartar daggers, held it up until the captive's eyes followed the flicker of moonlight on the honed edge, and then struck like a cat. The Tartar's eyes bulged as his hide trousers fell away. It was only a few seconds later that he began to nod frantically, trying to bellow at the same time and choking as the wet cloth slipped farther into his wide-stretched mouth.

Dorzha flicked the gag free with the point of the knife, and held it so that blood dripped on the man's face. Sergey winced slightly and suppressed an impulse to cup his hands protectively over his crotch. Instead, he pulled on his clothes as the Kalmyk asked questions in quick, confident Tartar—he spoke the *turka* dialect better than he did Russian, though with an unfamiliar accent and choice of words that showed he'd learned it somewhere else besides the middle Volga. The interrogation was thorough and expert; where, when, how many guards, what the passwords were, a staccato sequence timed to leave no time for the captive's pain-fuddled mind to invent lies.

"Kill me," the Tartar rasped at last, face gray and sweating.

Dorzha nodded and thrust; the dagger's watered steel slid home with only a slight crunching sound, and he left it with the hilt jutting out of the man's chest to keep the first spurt of blood corked. Then he rose . . . and staggered, his eyes turning up until only the whites showed, and collapsed backwards himself with limp finality.

"*Bozhemoi!* I didn't think he was that badly hurt!" Sergey said, and sprang to drag the Kalymk into the scanty clear space.

He pulled up the shirt to get at the wound; it was leaking red through the loose, hasty bandage. Then he stared for a long moment, blinking and shaking his head.

"Bozhemoi!" he said, then thumped the heel of his hand against his forehead as bits and pieces of the past week went *click* within. "Aaaaaah! I *am* a stupid Cossack ox!"

Dorzha opened her eyes and raised a hand to feel at her ribs, now expertly and tightly bandaged. Then her hand flashed toward the hilt of her yataghan where it lay next to her.

Sergey laughed. Her eyes flashed toward him, and the blade glowed blue-white in the darkness, catching a stray gleam of moonlight from outside.

"Hey, sister, how many men have I watched you kill?" Her blue eyes narrowed, and he went on: "Four. And I've only known you eight days! So if I had designs on your skinny arse, I wouldn't have left that sword within your reach, would I?"

"I listen," Dorzha said, sitting up against the mud-brick wall of the cubicle and propping the blade across her knees.

"Also, as a boy you were more girlish than was good to see, and as a girl, you're too much like a boy for my taste. And we've shared bread and salt, and fought for each other. Now, let's get on with rescuing this 'princess' . . . a friend of yours, or your sister?"

Dorzha smiled unwillingly. "Half sister. My mother was a concubine, and half-Russki. I was raised with Bortë . . . the Princess . . . and it amused the Khan to let me train as a warrior to protect her."

The smile flashed wider: "How she me envied! We are friends, too . . . more or less. She is . . . wise. A scholar."

Sergey grunted and tossed over the leather water-bottle. Dorzha drank deep and then stood, moving experimentally.

"How is it?" Sergey asked.

"Not too bad," Dorzha said. "I wouldn't want to use my bow, but I can fight; you strapped it up well. Where are the bodies?"

"Over the wall," Sergey said. "The street-pigs will eat well tonight; or maybe the beggars."

He rose himself, swinging his long arms and grinning. "Let's go!"

Now, how to kill this one?

The Tartars were holding the Princess—Sergey thought of her as looking like an icon, with stiff gold-embroidered robes—in the house of a rich Kurdish merchant who traded in silk, cotton, and slaves; from here you could look down a long narrow roadway at its side, but it was black-dark, too far from the main streets to rate gas-lamps. The building presented a thick blank wall to this street and it had a tower at the back, four stories high with narrow slit windows; one of them showed lantern-light, but everything else was dark.

"Let me have the lantern," Dorzha whispered.

Sergey handed it over. It was hers, and a good one, made of metal and running on distilled rock-oil. What he hadn't realized until now was that the cover would flip up and back if you squeezed the handle. That the Kalmyk woman proceeded to do; long-short-short-long-long-long. It was no code he knew, but . . .

The second time through, the window darkened . . . then went light again, in the same pattern, as if someone were waving a cloth in front of the light. Dorzha seemed to slump slightly, and gave a soundless sigh of relief.

"She is there," the Kalymk said. "And well, and says *come to me*. We used that signal when we wanted to steal out of the Khan's house in Elst."

"You two must have done wonders for your father's peace of mind," Sergey said, grinning in the dark.

"Tcha!" Dorzha replied. "Now, how best to go in?"

"They have patrols along the walls," Sergey said. "Best through the entrance—if we can do it quietly."

"I think I can. Come."

They circled, meeting nothing more alarming than a pi-dog that growled and slunk away from sniffing at a motionless drunk, or corpse, lying in the gutter. This was a respectable neighborhood, and that meant few went out late at night. At last, they ghosted down the avenue that approached the Kurd's mansion from the front, keeping to the deep shadows the moon cast on the right side of the street. The same moon shone full on the sentry leaning on his spear before the entrance—it glinted on the whetted metal, and on the rippling black-lacquered scales of his sleeveless hauberk.

"How do we get past him?" Sergey whispered.

"Leave this to me," Dorzha said.

"I'll be noisy, if you're going to cut off his—"

The Kalmyk woman gave him a scowl. Then she leaned shield and sword, bow and quiver against the wall and walked quietly toward the sentry. The man was dozing standing up, but he straightened and leveled his spear as she approached.

"Who comes to the house of Ibrahim al-Vani by night?" he growled in Tartar.

Dorzha spoke. Sergey blinked in astonishment. Apart from her accent, the Kalmyk had always spoken to him in a light pure tone much like a lad's—it had been close enough to fool *him*, after all. Now . . .

"One seeking a valiant warrior," Dorzha said, in voice that *nobody* would have mistaken for a male's of any age, full of honey and musk and promise. "But I see I've found one."

Sergey blinked again as the Tartar leaned his spear against the wall and the two figures merged. An instant later, the Tartar slumped down, with only a thin brief whining sound. When he came up, Dorzha was scrubbing the back of her left hand across her lips.

"*That's* a trick I don't think I can copy," he said, handing her the weapons she'd shed.

"Ptha!" she said—either something in Kalmyk or simple disgust. Then she put an arrow to the string. "Take his keys. I cover you."

"Bad security," Sergey noted, as he did, and propped the corpse artistically against the wall in the sort of slump a sleeping man would use. "They should have locked him out and kept a relief inside."

Though the merchant probably guarded merely against theft; against stealth, not an assault—it was hard to change your habits quickly. The doors were thick oak, strapped with a web of salvaged steel fastened with thick bolts at each crosspiece, and the lock was well-oiled.

More bad security. A nice loud rusty screech would warn the house.

The door swung outward, just enough to pass them through into the courtyard. It was a narrow cobbled rectangle, with stables and barracks and storage along one side, a row of horse-troughs, and the merchant's own dwelling on other; that probably had an inner court of its own, for his womenfolk. The tower was against the far wall, freestanding, probably a refuge against riot and a treasure-house for the most valued goods.

"Wait," Sergey said.

He took another inheritance from his grandfather from his belt. It was a length of flexible metal with wooden handles on either end; he looped it about the bolt of the lock and pulled it back and forth. A nearly soundless rasp followed, and metal filings drifted down to the pavement. He was careful to go slowly—Grandfather had warned him that it might lose its temper and snap if it was overheated, and no modern smith could duplicate its magical properties.

"Bortë will be interested in that; she loves things from before the Change," Dorzha said softly.

She covered the courtyard as she spoke, recurve bow half-drawn and ready to flick out a shaft. After half a minute, the bolt dropped free, and Sergey caught it before it could drop to the stones. Then he eased the door shut again and locked it, leaving the key in the plate. That might not make a difference, or it might fool someone into thinking the door was secure when it wasn't. You never knew, Grandfather had said. . . .

They walked over to the tower; Sergey scooped a handful of water out of one of the troughs as they passed, to wet a mouth gone a little dry. The darkened buildings seemed to loom around him like banks of angry, watchful eyes, and his shoulders crawled with anticipation of a sudden arrow or crossbow-bolt. On the steppe, or even in a forest, he felt at home. This was like a fight in a coffin.

A narrow eyehole opened, and a voice spoke in some musical, liquid-sounding language, much muffled by the thick iron-strapped door.

"The password is *Azazrael's Sword*," Dorzha replied in Tartar, naming the Death Angel.

A surly grunt, and more of the strange tongue. Dorzha spoke again:

"Speak something beside that sheep-bleating, you peacock-worshipping Kurdish apostate. Our chief wants us to check on the Kalmyk woman."

"She is as well-guarded as the wives of my master Ibrahim al-Vani themselves!" the man said, in bad Tartar—worse than Dorzha's Russki had been when she and Sergey met.

"His wives are guarded by the fifty fathers of their children," Dorzha sneered. "Or Kurdish eunuchs—as if there *were* any Kurds with balls. We caught her—now we want to see her."

"It is my head if anything happens to her," the guard said, grumbling. "Curse the evil witch anyway, with her alchemy from Satan!"

Sergey gave a soundless sigh of relief; the man *was* going to open the door.

"And it's *my* head if I don't do what the Chief says," Dorzha replied. "And my head is worth more than yours. I gave the password—open! Or I go and we come back with a battering ram, and a flaying knife to peel the skin from your worthless arse!"

"You Tartars don't rule the universe, you just *think* you do," the man grumbled. "Wait, then, wait."

They could hear clicking and shunking sounds. The door opened, only a narrow crack, and a thick chain spanned the gap. A blue eye looked through it, going wide for an instant before the point of Dorzha's yataghan punched through it with a *crunch* of steel in the thin bone that separated eyesocket from brain. The man toppled backwards like a cut-through tree. Sergey shouldered Dorzha aside, flicked the cutting wire around the chain, and went to work.

"Hurry!" Dorzha said.

"We may need this again. I'm not going to break it," Sergey said stubbornly. "Besides, it was my grandfather's."

Dorzha said something explosive in her native language—but quietly—and soon the forged-iron link parted, falling to the stone floor with a musical tinkle. Sergey blew his lips out in mute relief when the door opened after that.

Because I have no idea what we would have done if there had been another lock!

The hallway within the tower was empty; on either side were chambers that the Tartar had said were used to store goods—and there was a square concrete shaft in the middle, from the looks of it a relic of the old world. Stairs started to the left; they took them in a swift quiet rush, Sergey leading and the Kalmyk woman following behind. There was an odd, acrid odor in the air, growing stronger as they ascended. Behind him, Dorzha chuckled.

"That is Bortë," she said.

She smells like rock oil and sulfur? he thought, puzzled.

The door was unbarred from the outside; a sliver of lamplight showed under the bottom of the thick planks. Sergey pushed at it, sword poised—probably there would be a guard within, as well as the Princess. The door gave a little, and then halted with a yielding heaviness. Sergey grunted and set his boot to it, pushing hard. Behind him, Dorzha spoke in her own language.

The door slid open. Sergey leapt through, cat-agile but trying to stare in three directions at once . . . and then relaxing a little as he saw a woman in a long hooded caftan standing with a lamp in her hand. The smell of acid and strange metals came from the room behind her; he could see that it held benches and odd-looking bits of glass.

The body at his feet attracted his attention first; it was a big man, very big, with a good deal of fat over solid muscle. He wore a turban but was beardless, and his great smooth torso was bare above sash, baggy pantaloons of crimson, and curl-toed boots. A broad curved sword lay beside one set of sausage-thick fingers; a look of fixed horror was on his face, and his eyes bulged as if they were about to pop out of his smooth, doughlike features.

Interesting, Sergey thought, looking around the room, noting a spilled chess set by the dead man; the furnishings were cushions and rugs rather than chairs, as you might expect from a Kurd. *Something killed him. . . .*

Dorzha pushed past him, sheathing her yataghan. *"Bortë!"* she cried.

"Dorzha!" the other replied, setting her lantern on the floor.

They embraced, a fierce hug, and then Dorzha held her half sister at arm's length.

"Are you all right?" she said—in Russki, which must be for his benefit.

"Fine. Bored. They let me keep my gear, the fools, so I had plenty of time to prepare," Bortë replied. "What took you so long?"

"There were . . . problems."

Bortë threw back the hood of her caftan. Sergey blinked; the family resemblance was unmistakable, though the khan's other daughter was shorter and not quite so slim, and the night-black hair that fell loose down the young woman's back was glossier than Dorzha's. The face beneath was snub-nosed, with a rosy, ruddy-pink complexion, full lips, and narrow slanted black eyes.

Perhaps it was the lantern-light streaming up from below, but he felt a slight prickle of alarm in belly and back at that face. She reminded him of something like a cat, or better still, a ferret—small, quick, comely, and quite evil. The black eyes glanced up and down his long form.

"Where did you get this great Cossack ox?" she said—also in Russki, with a pellucidly clear but old-fashioned, bookish accent. "I'm not surprised you're late, with him to drag around."

Dorzha shrugged. "He's useful for the heavy-lifting chores," she said. "Now let's go!"

"How did you kill him?" Sergey asked, intrigued, while she snatched up a bundle and slung it over her back like a knapsack.

He nudged the dead man with his toe. Bortë was smaller than her sister, and while she held herself well he couldn't see her killing a man this size with a blade unless she took him utterly unawares. Also there was no blood—even a small stiletto left in the wound leaked a *little* when stabbed deep into the body.

Bortë smiled, revealing small, very white teeth; the first two were slightly buck-shaped. Instead of replying, she held up her hand; there was a piece of leather across her palm, and a steel needle concealed within it. There was blood on the tip of the little sliver of metal, with some purplish discoloration beneath that.

"But I let him win the last game," she said. "He wasn't a bad man. For a eunuch."

Sergey swallowed. "Your sister said you were a scholar," he said.

"I am," she replied, and smiled more broadly. "Of chemistry."

The Cossack crossed himself.

"Yob tvoyu mat'," Sergey said; it struck him as more manly than screaming *We're fucked!* and slapping himself on the top of the head.

The lights and voices at the bottom of the stairs were both indistinct, but they were getting louder. And there was no other way *out* of this tower. Screams of rage cut through the brabble; someone must have discovered the body and the cut chain.

"We're fucked," Dorzha said, then cursed in Kalmyk and kicked the wall viciously.

Not fair, Sergey said. *She doesn't* have *to be manly.*

Dying heroically was always more pleasant when you were drunk and listening to some balalaika-twanging gypsy *guslar*'s lying song than in a situation like this. His mind hunted back and forth like a wolf he'd seen trapped in a pit once. Suddenly, he felt a new sympathy for its snarling desperation.

"We killed plenty of those Tartars before," Dorzha said, but with a note of doubt in her voice.

"Da," Sergey said. "When we ambushed them or surprised them. A stand-up fight . . ."

He shrugged. Dorzha did too, and whipped her yataghan through a circle to loosen her wrist.

"We knew this was risky," she said.

"Da," the man said again. "Well, Cossacks don't usually die old anyway."

The sound of hands clapping came from behind him. He turned and glared at Bortë, who had dragged a sack out of the inner room. Now she applauded again.

"Hear the *baatar*," she said, jeering. "Hear the hero! Listen to him meet death unafraid—because it's so much easier than *thinking*."

Dorzha scowled at her sister. So did Sergey. *I could really come to dislike this woman, if I had the time*, he thought.

Then he ducked with a yelp as she pulled a stoppered clay jug out of her sack and lofted it over his head. It dropped neatly down to the next landing, a story below, and shattered. He couldn't see anything come out of it, not in the darkness of the stairwell . . . but a sudden scent sharp enough to slice your lungs made him cough and backpedal, rubbing at his streaming eyes.

"It is heavier than air," Bortë said.

"Poison?" he asked, as the shrieks of rage below turned to choked howls of panic.

"Chlorine. Quite deadly. It will flow downward. Come!"

She turned and began dragging the sack with her into the inner sanctum. Sergey ignored the shadowed forms of retorts and glass coils on tables; the square inner shaft ran through this room, and there was an open door in it that showed modern ropes, not rusted ancient cable. That looked *much* better than fighting his way down the stairs, even if the air there was breathable, which just now it wasn't. Mikhail had told stories about war gases in the old days, and how he'd used them against the *moujids* in some place far to the east. The Princess took half a dozen of the jars from her sack and dropped them through the opening.

"That will take care of anyone waiting below," she said. "There's a tunnel out under the walls. The eunuch told me about it. The joke is on him, eh?"

"Ha. Ha," Sergey said as his testicles tried to crawl up into his belly. "If that stuff burns out your lungs, going down there will kill *us*! Or at least me, you witch!"

"Not with these," she said, and pulled improvised masks out of the sack. "*I* have been thinking all the time I was here, *baatar*. Luck favors the prepared."

"She never stops," Dorzha said, taking one of the masks and examining the ties that would hold it on her face. "It's no wonder Father tried to marry her off to someone two months' journey away."

"These will protect us?" Sergey said.

Bortë smiled again. "The chemicals need to be activated with uric acid," she said.

"That's what?" he said, baffled; the words were Russki but he'd never heard them before.

She told him.

Sergey ripped the mask from his face half an hour later, spitting. "You enjoyed that!" he snarled.

To his surprise, Dorzha laughed with her sister. "Only the sight of your face, Cossack," she said.

He looked around the darkened streets; they were near the docks, and the masts of the ships showed over the roofs, some of them with the flickering stars of riding-lanterns burning at their tops.

"Well, I suppose we should try and get you to your father," he said.

Odd. I will miss Dorzha. And her sister is interesting. Terrifying, but interesting.

Bortë looked southward for a moment. "Why?" she said. "He'll only marry me off to some *other* fat imbecile."

Sergey rocked back on his heels. "Why, why—" His mind churned. "What else is there to do with you?"

Dorzha spoke. "You wouldn't believe there were larger cities than Astrakhan," she said. Then, wistfully: "I've never *seen* any bigger. But they say in China . . ."

In the shadows, Bortë's head turned toward her. "They say that in China, Toghrul Khan rules now," she said thoughtfully. "A Yek, but a Mongol like us; our ancestors came west from there, very long ago—the tongues are still close kin. At least, he rules the portions near the Gobi, and they also say he wars against the Han farther south. I wonder . . . I wonder if he could use a scholar of the ancient arts? His court in Xian is the richest in the world, the stories say."

"Gold," Dorzha said thoughtfully. "Silk. Rank."

Bortë shook her head. *"Books!"* she said, and her eyes glowed. "Scholars! Laboratories!"

Suddenly, Sergey's irritation lifted, and he began to laugh. "A real *bogatyr*—hero—I was, escaping with a woman's piss-soaked scarf over my nose!"

"You might do better with instruction," Bortë said.

"He *is* useful for the heavy work," Dorzha said.

Sergey laughed again, a booming sound that rattled off the warehouses around them. And if he went home, Olga and Svetlana would be waiting. Probably with their threshing-flails in hand.

"Which way is China?" he said.

Howard Waldrop

Howard Waldrop is widely considered to be one of the best short-story writers in the business, having been called "the resident Weird Mind of our generation" and an author "who writes like a honkytonk angel." His famous story "The Ugly Chickens" won both the Nebula and the World Fantasy Awards in 1981. His work has been gathered in the collections *Howard Who?*, *All About Strange Monsters of the Recent Past*, *Night of the Cooters*, *Going Home Again*, the print version of his collection *Dream Factories and Radio Pictures* (formerly available only in downloadable form online), and a collection of his stories written in collaboration with various other authors, *Custer's Last Jump and Other Collaborations*. Waldrop is also the author of the novel *The Texas-Israeli War: 1999*, in collaboration with Jake Saunders, and two solo novels, *Them Bones* and *A Dozen Tough Jobs*, as well as the chapbook *A Better World's in Birth!* He is at work on a new novel, tentatively titled *The Moone World*. His most recent book is a big retrospective collection, *Things Will Never Be the Same: Selected Short Fiction 1980–2005*. Having lived in Washington State for a number of years, Waldrop recently moved back to his former hometown of Austin, Texas, something that caused celebrations and loud hurrahs to rise up from the rest of the population.

Here he ushers us to a bright new world, a better world in the making, in the last place you'd think to look for it—among the frozen mud and razor wire and whistling death of No-Man's Land.

Ninieslando

The Captain had a puzzled look on his face. He clamped a hand to the right earphone and frowned in concentration.

"Lots of extraneous chatter on the lines again. I'm pretty sure some Fritzs have been replaced by Austrians in this sector. It seems to be in some language I don't speak. Hungarian, perhaps."

Tommy peered out into the blackness around the listening post. And of course could see nothing. The LP was inside the replica of a bloated dead horse that had lain between the lines for months. A week ago the plaster replica had arrived via the reserve trench from the camouflage shops far behind the lines. That meant a working party had had to get out in the night and not only replace the real thing with the plaster one, but also bury the original, which had swelled and burst months before.

They had come back nasty, smelly, and in foul moods, and had been sent back to the baths miles behind the lines, to have the luxury of a hot bath and a clean uniform. Lucky bastards, thought Tommy at the time.

Tommy's sentry duty that night, instead of the usual peering into the blackness over the parapet into the emptiness of No-Man's Land, had been to accompany the officer to the listening post inside the plaster dead horse, thirty feet in front of their trench line. That the LP was tapped into the German field telephone system (as they were into the British) meant that some poor sapper had had to crawl the quarter mile through No-Man's Land in the dark, find a wire, and tap into it. (Sometimes after doing so, they'd find they'd tied into a dead or abandoned wire.) Then he'd had to carefully crawl back to his own line, burying the wire as he retreated, and making no noise, lest he get a flare fired off for his trouble.

This was usually done when wiring parties were out on both sides, making noises of their own, so routine that they didn't draw illumination or small-arms fire.

There had evidently been lots of unidentified talk on the lines lately, to hear the rumours. The officers were pretty close-lipped. (You didn't admit voices were there in a language you didn't understand and could make no report on.) Officers from the General Staff had been to the LP in the last few nights and came back with nothing useful. A few hours in the mud and the dark had probably done them a world of good, a break from their regular routines in the châteaux that were HQ miles back of the line.

What little information that reached the ranks was, as the Captain said, "probably Hungarian, or some other Balkan sub-tongue." HQ was on the case, and was sending in some language experts soon. Or so they said.

Tommy looked through the slit just below the neck of the fake horse. Again, nothing. He cradled his rifle next to his chest. This March had been almost as cold as any January he remembered. At least the thaw had not come yet, turning everything to cold wet clinging mud.

There was the noise of slow dragging behind them, and Tommy brought his rifle up.

"Password," said the Captain to the darkness behind the horse replica.

"Ah—St. Agnes Eve . . . ," came a hiss.

"Bitter chill it was," said the Captain. "Pass."

A lieutenant and a corporal came into the open side of the horse. "Your relief, sir," said the lieutenant.

"I don't envy you your watch," said the Captain. "Unless you were raised in Buda-Pesh."

"The unrecognizable chatter again?" asked the junior officer.

"The same."

"Well, I hope someone from HQ has a go at it soon," said the lieutenant.

"Hopefully."

"Well, I'll give it a go," said the lieutenant. "Have a good night's sleep, sir."

"Very well. Better luck with it than I've had." He turned to Tommy. "Let's go, Private."

"Sir!" said Tommy.

They crawled the thirty feet or so back to the front trench on an oblique angle, making the distance much longer, and they were under the outermost concertina wire before they were challenged by the sentries.

Tommy went immediately to his funk hole dug into the wall of the sandbagged parapet. There was a nodding man on lookout; others slept in exhausted attitudes as if they were, like the LP horse, made of plaster.

He wrapped his frozen blanket around himself and was in a troubled sleep within seconds.

"Up for morning stand-to!" yelled the sergeant, kicking the bottom of his left boot.

Tommy came awake instantly, the way you do after a few weeks at the Front.

It was morning stand-to, the most unnecessary drill in the Army. The thinking behind it was that, at dawn, the sun would be full in the eyes of the soldiers in the British and French trenches, and the Hun could take advantage of it and advance through No-Man's Land and surprise them while they were sun-dazzled. (The same way that the Germans had *evening* stand-to in case the British made a surprise attack on them out of the setting sun.) Since no attacks were ever made across the churned and wired and mined earth of No-Man's Land by either side unless preceded by an artillery barrage of a horrendous nature, lasting from a couple to, in one case, twenty-four hours, of constantly falling shells, from the guns of the other side, morning stand-to was a sham perpetrated by a long-forgotten need from the early days of this Great War.

The other reason it was unnecessary was that this section of the Line that ran from the English Channel to the Swiss border was on a salient, and so the British faced more northward from true east, so the sun, instead of being in their eyes, was a dull glare off the underbrims of their helmets somewhere off to their right. The Hun, if he ever came across the open, would be sidelit and would make excellent targets for them.

But morning stand-to had long been upheld by tradition and the lack of hard thinking when the Great War had gone from one of movement and tactics in the opening days to the one of attrition and stalemate it had become since.

This part of the Front had moved less than one hundred yards, one way or the other, since 1915.

Tommy's older brother Fred had died the year before on the first day of the Somme Offensive, the last time there had been any real movement for years. And that had been more than fifty miles up the Front.

Tommy stood on the firing step of the parapet and pointed his rifle at nothing in particular to his front through the firing slit in the sandbags. All up and down the line, others did the same.

Occasionally some Hun would take the opportunity to snipe away at them. The German sandbags were an odd mixture of all types of colors and patterns piled haphazardly all along their parapets. From far away, they formed a broken pattern and the dark and light shades hid any break, such as a firing slit, from easy discernment. But the British sandbags were uniform, and the firing and observation slits stood out like sore thumbs, something the men were always pointing out to their officers.

As if on cue, there was the sound of smashing glass down the trench and the whine of a ricocheting bullet. A lieutenant threw down the trench periscope as if it were an adder that had bitten him.

"Damn and blast!" he said aloud. Then to his batman, "Requisition another periscope from regimental supply." The smashed periscope lay against the trench wall, its top and the mirror inside shot clean away by some sharp-eyed Hun. The batman left, going off in defile down the diagonal communication trench that led back to the reserve trench.

"Could have been worse," someone down the trench said quietly. "Could have been his head." There was a chorus of wheezes and snickers.

Humour was where you found it, weak as it was.

Usually both sides were polite to each other during their respective stand-tos. And afterwards, at breakfast and the evening meal. It wasn't considered polite to drop a shell on a man who'd just taken a forkful of beans into his mouth. The poor fellow might choke.

Daytime was when you got any rest you were going to get. Of course, there might be resupply, or ammunition, or food-toting details, but those came up rarely, and the sergeants were good about remembering who'd gone on the last one, and so didn't send you too often.

There was mail call, when it came, then the midday meal (when and if it came) and the occasional equipment inspection. Mostly you slept unless something woke you up.

Once a month, your unit was rotated back to the second trench, where you mostly slept as well as you could, and every third week to the reserve trench, far back, in which you could do something besides soldier. Your uniform would be cleaned and deloused, and so would you.

In the reserve trench was the only time your mind could get away from the War and its routine. You could get in some serious reading, instead of the catch-as-catch kind of the first and second trenches. You could get a drink and eat something besides bully beef and hardtack if you could find anybody selling food and drink. You could see a moving picture in one of the rear areas, though that was a long hike, or perhaps a music-hall show, put on by one of the units, with lots of drag humour and raucous laughter at not-very-subtle material. (Tommy was sure the life of a German soldier was much the same as his.)

It was one of the ironies of these times that in that far-off golden summer of 1914, when "some damn fool thing in the Balkans" was leading to its inevitable climax, Tommy's brother Fred, who was then eighteen, had been chosen as a delegate of the Birmingham Working-Men's Esperanto Association to go as a representative to the Twenty-fourth Annual Esperanto Conference in Basel, Switzerland. The Esperanto Conference had been to take place in the last days of July and the first days of August. (Fred had been to France before with a gang of school chums and was no stranger to travel.)

The Esperanto Conference was to celebrate the twenty-fourth anniversary of Zamenhof's artificial language, invented to bring better understanding between peoples through the use of an easy-to-learn, totally regular invented language—the thinking being that if all people spoke the same language (recognizing a pre-Babel dream), they would see that they were all one people, with common dreams and goals, and would slowly lose nationalism and religious partisanship through the use of the common tongue.

There had been other artificial languages since—Volapük had had quite a few adherents around the turn of the century—but none had had the cachet of Esperanto, the first and best of them.

Tommy and Fred had been fascinated by the language for years. (Fred could both speak and write it with an ease that Tommy had envied.)

What had surprised Fred, on arriving in Switzerland three years before, was that these representatives of this international conference devoted to better understanding among peoples were as acrimonious about their nations as any bumpkin from a third-rate country run by a tin-pot superstitious chieftain. Almost from the first, war and the talk of war divided the true believers from the lip-service toadies. The days were rife with desertions, as first one country then another announced mobilizations. By foot, by horse, by motor-car and train, and, in one case, aeroplane, the delegates left the conference to join up in the coming glorious adventure of War that they imagined would be a quick, nasty, splendid little one, over "before the snow flew."

By the end of the conference, only a few delegates were left, and they had to make hurried plans to return home before the first shots were fired.

His brother Fred, now dead, on the Somme, had returned to England on August 2, 1914, just in time to see a war no one wanted (but all had hoped for) declared. He, like so many idealists of all classes and nations, had joined up immediately.

Now Tommy, who had been three years younger at the time, was all that was left to his father and mother. He had, of course, been called up in due time, just before news of his brother's death had reached him.

And now here he was, in a trench of frozen mud, many miles from home, with night falling, when the sergeant walked by and said, "Fall out for wiring detail."

Going on a wiring party was about the only time you could be in No-Man's Land with any notion of safety. As you were repairing and thickening your tangle of steel, so were the Germans doing the same to theirs a quarter mile away.

Concertina wire, so haphazard-appearing from afar, was not there to stop an enemy assault, though it slowed that, too. The wire was there to funnel an enemy into narrower and tighter channels, so the enemy's course of action would become more and more constricted—and where the assault would finally slow against the impenetrable lanes of barbed steel was where your defensive machine-gun fire was aimed. Men waiting to go over, under, through, or around the massed wire were cut to ribbons by .303-caliber bullets fired at the rate of five hundred per minute.

Men could not live in such iron weather.

So you kept the wire repaired. At night. In the darkness, the sound of unrolling wire and muffled mauls filled the space between the lines. Quietly cursing men hauled the rolls of barbed wire over the parapets and pushed and pulled them out to where some earlier barrage (which was always supposed to cut all the wire but never did) had snapped some strands or blown away one of the new-type posts (which didn't have to be hammered in but were screwed into the ground as if the earth itself were one giant champagne cork).

Men carried wire, posts, sledges in the dark, out to the place where the sergeant stood.

"Two new posts here," he said, pointing at some deeper blackness. Tommy could see nothing, anywhere. He put his coil of wire on the ground, immediately gouging himself on the barbs of an unseen strand at shoulder height. He reached out—felt the wire going left and right.

"Keep it quiet," said the sergeant. "Don't want to get a flare up our arses." Illumination was the true enemy of night work.

Sounds of hammering and work came from the German Line. Tommy doubted that anyone would fire off a flare while their own men were out in the open.

He got into the work. Another soldier screwed in a post a few feet away.

"Wire," said the sergeant. "All decorative-like, as if you're trimming the Yule tree for Father Christmas. We want Hans and Fritz to admire our work, just before they cut themselves in twain on it."

Tommy and a few others uncoiled and draped the wire, running it back and forth between the two new posts and crimping it in with the existing strands.

Usually you went out, did the wiring work, and returned to the trench, knowing you'd done your part in the War. Many people had been lost in those times: there were stories of disoriented men making their way in the darkness, not to their own but to the enemy's trenches, and being killed or spending the rest of the war as a P.O.W.

Sometimes Tommy viewed wiring parties as a break in the routine of stultifying heat, spring and fall rains, and bone-breaking winter freezes. It was the one time you could stand up in relative comfort and safety, and not be walking bent over in a ditch.

There was a sudden rising comet in the night. Someone on Fritz's side had sent up a flare. Everybody froze—the idea was not to move at all when No-Man's Land was lit up like bright summer daylight. Tommy, unmoving, was surprised to see Germans caught out in the open, still also as statues, in front of their trench, poised in attitudes of labor on their wire.

Then who had fired off the flare?

It was a parachute flare and slowly drifted down while it burned the night to steel-furnace-like brilliance. There were pops and cracks and whines from both trenchlines as snipers on each side took advantage of the surprise bounty of lighted men out in the open.

Dirt jumped up at Tommy's feet. He resisted the urge to dive for cover, the nearest being a shell crater twenty feet away. Any movement would draw fire, if not to him, to the other men around him. They all stood stock-still; he saw droplets of sweat on his sergeant's face.

From the German line, a trench mortar coughed.

The earth went upward in frozen dirt and a shower of body parts.

He felt as if he had been kicked in the back.

His right arm was under him. His rifle was gone. The night was coming back in the waning flickering light from the dying flare. He saw as he lay, his sergeant and a couple of men crawling away toward their line. He made to follow them. His legs wouldn't work.

He tried pushing himself up with his free arm; he only rolled over on the frozen earth. He felt something warm on his back quickly going cold.

No, he thought, I can't die like this out in No-Man's Land. He had heard, in months past, the weaker and weaker cries of slowly dying men who'd been caught out here. He couldn't think of dying that way.

He lay for a long time, too tired and hurt to try to move. Gradually his hearing came back; there had been only a loud whine in his ears after the mortar shell had exploded.

He made out low talk from his own trench, twenty or so yards away. He could imagine the discussion now. Should we go out and try to get the wounded or dead? Does Fritz have the place zeroed in? Where's Tommy? He must have bought a packet.

Surprisingly, he could also hear sounds that must be from the German line—quiet footsteps, the stealthy movement from shell-hole to crater across No-Man's Land. The Germans must have sent out searching parties. How long had he lain here? Had there been return fire into the German work parties caught in the open by the flare? Were the British searching for their own wounded? Footsteps came nearer to him. Why weren't the sentries in his own trench challenging them? Or firing? Were they afraid that it was their own men making their ways back?

The footsteps stopped a few yards away. Tommy's eyes had adjusted to the darkness after the explosion. He saw vague dark shapes all around him. Through them moved a lighter man-shape. It moved with quick efficiency, pausing to turn over what Tommy saw now was a body near him.

It was at that moment that another weaker flare bloomed in the sky from the German trench, a red signal flare of some kind. In its light, Tommy saw the figure near him continue to rifle the body that lay there.

Tommy saw that the figure was a Chinaman. What was a Chinaman doing here in No-Man's Land?

Perhaps, Tommy thought, coughing, he speaks English. Maybe I can talk to him in Esperanto? That's what the language was invented for.

He said, in Esperanto, the first sentence he had ever learned in the language.

—Could you direct me to the house of the family Lodge?—

The Chinaman stopped. His face broke into a quizzical look in the light of the falling flare. Then he smiled, reached down to his belt, and brought up a club. He came over and hit Tommy on the head with it.

He woke in a clean bed, in clean sheets, in clean underwear, with a hurt shoulder and a headache. He was under the glare of electric lights, somewhere in a clean and spacious corridor.

He assumed he was far back of the lines in a regimental hospital. How he had gotten here, he did not know.

A man came to the foot of the bed. He wore a stethoscope.

—Ah—he said. —You have awakened.— He was speaking Esperanto.

"Am I in the division hospital?" asked Tommy in English.

The man looked at him uncomprehendingly.

He asked the same again, in Esperanto, searching for the words as he went.

—Far from it.— said the man. —You are in our hospital, where you needn't ever worry about the war you have known again. All will be explained later.—

—Have I been taken to Switzerland in my sleep?— asked Tommy. —Am I in some other neutral country?—

—Oh, you're in some neutral country, all right. But you're only a few feet from where you were found. And I take it you were under the impression it was a Chinese who rescued you. He's no Chinese—he would be offended to be called such—but Annamese, from French Indo-China. He was brought over here in one of the first levees early in the War. Many of them died that first winter, a fact the survivors never forgot. How is it you speak our language?—

—I was in the Esperanto Union from childhood on. I and my brother, who's now dead. He both wrote and spoke it much better than I.—

—It was bound to happen.— said the man. —You can imagine Ngyen's surprise when you spoke so, dressed in a British uniform. When you spoke, you marked yourself as one of us; he thought to bring you back the most expedient way possible, which was unconscious.

—The doctor tended your wounds—very nasty ones from which you probably would have perished had not you been brought here.—

—Where is here?— asked Tommy.

—Here— said the man —is a few feet below No-Man's Land—I'm sure the ex-captain will explain it all to you. It's been a while since someone in your circumstances joined us. Most of us came in the early days of the War, as soon as the Lines were drawn, or were found, half-mad or wounded between the lines, and had to be brought back to health and sanity. You appear to us, wounded all the same, but already speaking the language. You'll fit right in.—

—Are you British? French? German?— asked Tommy.

The man laughed. —Here— he said —none of us are of any nationality any longer. Here, we are all Men.—

He left. Eventually, the doctor came in and changed the dressing on his shoulder and gave him a pill.

The ex-captain came to see him. He was a small man, dressed in a faded uniform, with darker fabric at the collar in the shape of captain's bars.

—Welcome to Ninieslando.— he said.

—It's very clean.— said Tommy —I'm not used to *that*.—

—It's the least we can do.— he said, sweeping his hand around, indicating All That Out There.

—You'll learn your way around.— he continued.—You have the great advantage of already speaking our language, so you won't have to be going to classes. We'll have you on light duties till your wounds heal.—

—I'm very rusty.— Tommy said.—I'm out of practice. My brother was the scholar; he spoke it till the day he was killed on the Somme.—

—We could certainly have used him here.— said the ex-captain.

—Where we are— he continued, going into lecture-mode —is several feet below No-Man's Land. We came here slowly, one by one, in the course of the War. The lost, the wounded, the abandoned, and, unfortunately, the slightly mad. We have dug our rooms and tunnels, tapped into the combatant's field-phones and electrical lines, diverted their water to our own uses. Here we are building a society of Men, to take over the Earth after this War finally ends. Right now our goal is to survive the War—to do that we have to live off their food, water, lights, their clothing and equipment, captured at night on scavenging parties. We go into their trench lines and take what we need. We have better uses for it than killing other men.

—There are 5,600 of us in this sector. Along the whole four-hundred-mile Western Front, there are half a million of us, waiting our time to come out and start the New World of brotherhood. We are the first examples of it; former combatants living in harmony with a common language and common goals, undeterred by the War itself, a viable alternative to nationalism and bigotry. You can imagine the day when we walk out of here.—

Tommy held out his hand. The ex-captain shook it. —It's good to finally meet a real idealist.— said Tommy.—So many aren't.—

—You'll see— said the ex-captain —there's much work to be done while we wait, and it's easy to lose sight of the larger goals while you're scrounging for a can of beans. The War has provided for us, only to the wrong people. People still combatants, who still believe in the War.

—For make no mistake— he said —the Hun is not the enemy. The British are not the enemy. Neither your former officers nor the General Staff are the enemy. The *War* is the enemy. It runs itself on the fears of the combatants. It is a machine into which men are put and turned into memories.

—Every illness, self-inflicted wound or accident is referred to by both sides as "wastage"—perdajo—meaning that the death did not contribute in any way to a single enemy soldier's death.

—A man being in the War, to War's way of thinking, was wasted. The idea has taken over planning. The War is thinking for the General Staff. They have not had a single idea that was not the War's in these three years.

—So we take advantage. A flare fired off in the night when no one expects it brings the same result as if we had a regimental battery of Krupp howitzers. The War provides the howitzers to us as well as to the combatants.

—I need not tell you this.— he said. —I'm going on like Wells's wandering artilleryman in *War of the Worlds*. Everyone here has to quit thinking like a combatant and begin to think like a citizen of Ninieslando. What can we do to take War out of the driver's seat? How do we plan for the better world while War is making that world cut its own throat? We are put here to bring some sense to it: to stay War's hand. Once mankind knows that War is the enemy, he will be able to join us in that bright future. Zamenhof was right; Esperanto will lead the way!

—Good luck— he said, making ready to leave—new citizen of Ninieslando.—

Their job today, some weeks after the ex-captain's visit, was to go to a French supply point, load up, and bring rations back by secret ways to Ninieslando, where their cooks would turn it into something much more palatable than the French ever thought of making. They had on parts of French uniforms; nobody paid much attention this late in the day and the War, if the colors were right. Tommy had a French helmet tied by its chin strap to his belt in the manner of a jaunty French workingman.

They took their place in a long line of soldiers waiting. They moved up minute by minute till it was their turn to be loaded up.

"No turnips," said the sergeant with them, who had been at Verdun.

"Ah, but of course," said the supply sergeant. "As you request." He made an impolite gesture.

They took their crates and sacks and followed the staggering line of burdened men returning to the trenches before them. The connecting trench started as a path at ground level and slowly sank as the walls of the ditch rose up around them as they stepped onto the duckboards. Ahead of them the clump-clump-clump of many feet echoed. The same sounds rose behind them.

Somewhere in the diagonal trench between the second and Front Line, they simply disappeared with the food at a blind turn in the connecting trench.

They delivered the food to the brightly lit electric kitchens below the front line.

—Ah, good.— said a cook, looking into a sack.—Turnips!—

He waited at a listening post with an ex-German lieutenant.

—Lots a chatter tonight.— he said to Tommy. —They won't notice much when we talk with other sectors later.—

—Of course.— said Tommy.—The combatants are tapped into each other's lines, trying to get information. They hear not only their enemies, but us.—

—And what do they do about it?— asked the ex-German.

—They try to figure out what language is being spoken. Our side was puzzled.—

—They usually think it some Balkan tongue.— said the ex-German. —Our side thought it could be Welsh or Basque. Did you ever hear it?—

—No, only officers listened.—

—You would have recognized it immediately. But War has taught the officers that enlisted men are lazy illiterate swine, only interested in avoiding work and getting drunk. What language knowledge could they have? Otherwise, they would be officers. Is it not true?—

—Very true.— said Tommy.

A week later, Tommy was in the brightly lit library, looking over the esoteric selection of reading matter filched from each side. Field manuals, cheap novels, anthologies of poetry, plays in a dozen languages. There were some books in Esperanto, most published before the turn of the century. Esperanto had had a great vogue then, before the nations determined it was all a dream and went back to their armaments races and their "places in the sun." There were, of course, a few novels translated into Esperanto.

There was also the most complete set of topographical maps of the Front imaginable. He looked up this sector; saw the gland of Ninieslando's tunnels and corridors, saw that even the British listening post had the designation "fake plaster horse." He could follow the routes of Ninieslando from the Swiss border to the English Channel (except in those places where the Front Line trenches were only yards apart; there was hardly room for excavation there without calling the attention of both sides to your presence.) Here, Ninieslando was down to a single tunnel no wider than a communications trench up on the surface to allow exchanges between sectors.

Either side up above would give a thousand men in return for any map of the set.

That meant that the work of Ninieslando went on day and night, listening and mapping out the smallest changes in the topography. The map atop each pile in the drawer was the latest, dated most recently. You could go through the pile and watch the War backwards to—in some cases—late 1914, when the Germans had determined where the Front would be by pulling back to the higher ground, even if only a foot or two more in elevation. Ninieslando had been founded then, as the War became a stalemate.

In most cases, the lines had not changed since then, except to become more churned up, muddier, nastier. Occasionally, they would shift a few feet, or a hundred yards, due to some small advance by one side or the other. Meanwhile, Ninieslando became more complex and healthier as more and more men joined.

As the ex-captain had said: —The War made us the best engineers, machinists, and soldiers ever known. A shame to waste all that training. So we used it to build a better world, underground.—

Tommy looked around the bright shiny library. He could spend his life here, building a better world indeed.

For three nights, each side had sent out raiding parties to the other's Line. There had been fierce fighting as men all through the sector stomped or clubbed each other to death.

It had been a bonanza for Ninieslando's scavenging teams. They had looted bodies and the wounded of everything usable: books, food, equipment, clothing. They had done their work efficiently and thoroughly, leaving naked bodies all through No-Man's Land. The moans of the dying followed them as they made their way back down through the hidden entrances to Ninieslando.

Tommy, whose shoulder wound had healed nicely, lay in his clean bunk after dropping off his spoils from the scavenging at the sector depot. The pile of goods had grown higher than ever—more for Ninieslando. He had a copy of *The Oxford Book of English Verse* open on his chest. The language was becoming lost to him, he had not spoken it in so long. He was now thinking, and even dreaming, in Esperanto. As well it should be. National languages were a drag and a stumbling block to the human race. He read a few poems, then closed the book. For another day, he thought, when we look back with a sort of nostalgia on a time when national languages kept men separated. He imagined the pastoral poems of the future, written in Esperanto, with shepherds and nymphs recalling lines of English each to each, as if it were a lost tongue like Greek or Latin. He yearned for a world where such things could be.

The field phones had been strangely silent for a day or so. But it was noticed that couriers went backwards and forwards from trench to observation post to headquarters. On both sides. Obviously, something was up. A courier was waylaid in the daylight, a dangerous undertaking, but there were no paper orders on him. The kidnapping team drew the line at torture, so reported that the orders must be verbal. Perhaps, by coincidence, both sides were planning assaults at the same time to break the stalemate. It would be a conflagration devoutly to be desired by Ninieslando.

Of course, the War had made it so both sides would lose the element of surprise when the batteries of both sides opened in barrages at the same time, or nearly so. Ninieslando waited—whatever happened, No-Man's Land would be littered with the dead and dying, ripe for the picking.

—Too quiet.— said someone in the corridor.

—They've never gone this long off the telephones.— said another.

Tommy walked the clean corridor. He marveled that only a few feet overhead was a world of ekskremento and malpurajo fought over by men for three years. Here was a shinier, cleaner world than anything man had achieved on the surface.

It was just about then that the first shells of the expected barrage began to fall above his head. Dust drifted down from the ceiling. Parts of the wall buckled and shook.

Tommy realized that he was under the middle of No-Man's Land. Unless their aim was very bad indeed, the artillerymen of neither side should be making their shells land here. They should be aiming for the Front trench of the other side.

Ninieslando shook and reeled from the barrage. The lights went out as shells cut a line somewhere.

Tommy struck a match, found the electric torch in its niche at the corridor crossing. He turned it on and made his way to the library.

Then it got ominously quiet. The barrage ceased after a very short while. Who was firing a five-minute barrage in the wrong place? Had they all gone crazy up there?

He entered the library, shone his torch around. A few books had fallen from the shelves; mostly it was untouched.

He sat at a table. There was some noise in the corridor at the far end. A bloodied man ran in, his eyes wild, screaming. —Tri rugo bendos!—Three red bands!— Was he speaking metaphorically? Three Marxist gangs? Or like Sherlock Holmes, literally, as in "The Speckled Band"? What did he mean? Tommy went to grab him, but he was gone, out of the library, still yelling.

Tommy went down the hall and up a series of steps to an observation post with two viewing slits, one looking northeast, the other southwest.

What he saw looking northeast was astounding. In broad daylight, German soldiers, rifles up, bayonets fixed, were advancing. They probed the ground and debris as they came on. On the left sleeve of every soldier were three red stripes on a white background.

Tommy turned to the other slit, wondering why there was no rifle or machine gun fire mowing down the line of Germans.

What he saw made his blood freeze. From the other direction, British and French soldiers also advanced in the open. On their right arms were pinned three red stripes on a white background. As he watched, several soldiers disappeared down an embankment. There was the sound of firing. A Ninieslandoja, with no stripes on his sleeve, staggered out and died in the dirt. The firing continued, getting fainter.

The sound of firing began again, far off down the corridor below.

Tommy took off for the infirmary.

———

There were many kinds of paint down at the carpentry shop, but very little approached red, the last color you'd want on a battlefield.

When Tommy ran into the infirmary, he found the ex-captain there before him. The man was tearing bandages into foot-long pieces.

Tommy went to the medicine chest and forced his way into it. Bottles flew and broke.

—They've finally done it!— said the ex-captain. —They've gotten together just long enough to get rid of us. Our scavenging last week must have finally pushed them over into reason.—

Tommy took a foot-long section of bandages and quickly painted three red stripes on it with the dauber on a bottle of Mercurochrome. He took one, gave it to the ex-captain, did one for himself.

—First they'll do for us.— he said. —Next, they'll be back to killing each other. This is going on up and down the whole Western Front. I never thought they could keep such a plan quiet for so long.—

The ex-captain headed him a British helmet and a New Model Army web-belt. —Got your rifle? Good, try to blend in. Speak English. Good luck.— He was gone out the door.

Tommy took off the opposite way. He ran toward where he thought the Germans might be.

The sound of firing grew louder. He realized he might now be a target for Ninieslanders, too. He stepped around a corridor junction and directly in front of a German soldier. The man raised his rifle barrel towards the ceiling.

"Anglander?" the German asked

—j— "Yes," said Tommy, lifting his rifle also.

"More just behind me," Tommy added. "Very few of the . . . undergrounders in our way." The German looked at him in incomprehension. He looked farther back down the corridor Tommy had come from.

There was the noise of more Germans coming up the other hall. They lifted their rifles, saw his red stripes, lowered them.

Tommy moved with them as they advanced farther down the corridors, marveling at the construction. There was some excitement as a Ninieslander bolted from a room down the hallway and was killed in a volley from the Germans.

"Good shooting," said Tommy.

Eventually, they heard the sound of English.

"My people," said Tommy. He waved to the Germans and walked toward the voices.

A British captain with drawn pistol stood in front of a group of soldiers. The bodies of two Ninieslanders lay on the floor beside them.

—And what rat have we forced from his hole?— asked the captain in Esperanto.

Tommy kept his eyes blank.

"Is that Hungarian you're speaking, sir?" he asked, the words strange on his tongue.

"Your unit?" asked the Captain.

"First, King's Own Rifles," said Tommy. "I was separated and with some Germans."

"Much action?"

"A little, most of the corridors are empty. They're off somewheres, sir."

"Fall in with my men till we can get you back to your company, when this is over. What kind of stripes you call those? Is that iodine?"

"Mercurochrome, I believe," said Tommy. "Supply ran out of the issue. Our stretcher-bearers used field expedients." He had a hard time searching for the right words.

Esperanto phrases kept leaping to mind. He would have to be careful, especially around this officer.

They searched out a few more rooms and hallways, found nothing. From far away, whistles blew.

"That's recall," said the Captain. "Let's go."

Other deeper whistles sounded from far away, where the Germans were. It must be over.

They followed the officer till they came to boardings that led outside to No-Man's Land.

The captain left for a hurried consultation with a group of field-grade officers. He returned in a few minutes.

"More work to do," he said. A detail brought cans of petrol and set them down nearby.

"We're to burn the first two corridors down. You, you, you," he said, indicating Tommy last. "Take these cams, spread the petrol around. The signal is three whistle blasts. Get out as soon as you light it off. Everyone got matches? Good."

They went back inside, the can heavy in Tommy's hands. He went up to the corridor turning, began to empty petrol on the duckboard floor.

He saved a little in the bottom of the can. He idly sloshed it around and around.

Time enough to build the better world tomorrow. Many, like him, must have made it out, to rejoin their side or get clean away in this chaos.

After this War is over, we'll get together, find each other, start building that new humanity on the ashes of this old world.

The three whistles came. Tommy struck a match, threw it onto the duckboard flooring and watched the petrol catch with a *whooshing* sound.

He threw the can after it, and walked out into the bright day of the new world waiting to be born.

Gardner Dozois

Gardner Dozois was the editor of *Asimov's Science Fiction* magazine for almost twenty years and also edits the annual anthology series *The Year's Best Science Fiction,* which has won the Locus Award for Best Anthology sixteen times, more than any other anthology series in history, and which is now up to its twenty-sixth annual collection. He's won the Hugo Award fifteen times as the year's Best Editor, won the Locus Award thirty times, including an unprecedented sixteen times in a row as Best Editor, and has won the Nebula Award twice, as well as a Sidewise Award, for his own short fiction, which has been collected in *The Visible Man, Geodesic Dreams: The Best Short Fiction of Gardner Dozois, Strange Days: Fabulous Journeys with Gardner Dozois,* and *Morning Child and Other Stories.* He is the author or editor of more than a hundred books, among the most recent of which are a novel written in collaboration with George R. R. Martin and Daniel Abraham, *Hunter's Run,* and the anthologies *Galactic Empires, Songs of the Dying Earth* (edited with George R. R. Martin), *The New Space Opera 2* (edited with Jonathan Strahan), and *The Dragon Book: Magical Tales from the Masters of Modern Fantasy* (edited with Jack Dann). Born in Salem, Massachusetts, he now lives in Philadelphia, Pennsylvania.

Here he takes us to a strange future where a stubborn holdout persists in fighting a rearguard action, even though he suspects that he's lost not only the battle, but also the war.

Recidivist

Kleisterman walked along the shoreline, the gentle waves of the North Atlantic breaking and running in washes of lacy white foam almost up to the toes of his boots. A sandpiper ran along parallel to him, a bit farther out, snatching up bits of food churned up by the surf. When the waves receded, leaving the sand a glossy matte black, you could see jets of bubbles coming up from buried sand fleas. Waves foamed around a ruined stone jetty, half-submerged in the water.

Behind him, millions of tiny robots were dismantling Atlantic City.

He scuffed at the sea-wrack that was drying above the tideline in a tangled mass of semi-deflated brown bladders, and looked up and down the long beach. It was empty, of people anyway. There were black-backed gulls and laughing gulls scattered here and there, some standing singly, some in clumps of two or three, some in those strange V-shaped congregations of a dozen or more birds standing quietly on the sand, all facing the same way, as if they were waiting to take flying lessons from the lead gull. A crab scurried through the wrack almost at his feet. Above the tideline, the dry sand was mixed in with innumerable fragments of broken seashells, the product of who knew how many years of pounding by the waves.

You could have come down here any day for the last ten thousand years, since the glaciers melted and the sea rose to its present level, and everything would have been the same: the breaking waves, the crying of seabirds, the scurrying crabs, the sandpipers and plovers hunting at the edge of the surf.

Now, in just a few more days, it would all be gone forever.

Kleisterman turned and looked out to sea. Somewhere out there, out over the miles of cold gray water, out of sight as yet, Europe was coming.

A cold wind blew the smell of salt into his face. A laughing gull skimmed by overhead, spraying him with the raucous, laughing cries that had given its species the name. Today, its laughter seemed particularly harsh and derisive, and particularly appropriate. Humanity's day was done, after all. Time to be laughed off the stage.

Followed by the jeering laughter of the gulls, Kleisterman turned away from the ocean and walked back up the beach, through the dry sand, shell fragments crunching underfoot. There were low dunes here, covered with dune grass and sandwort, and he climbed them, pausing at the top to look out at the demolition of the city.

Atlantic City had already been in ruins anyway, the once-tall hotel towers no more than broken stumps, but the robots were eating what was left of the city with amazing speed. There were millions of them, from the size of railroad cars to tiny barely visible dots the size of dimes, and probably ones a lot smaller, down to the size of molecules, that couldn't be seen at all. They were whirling around like cartoon dervishes, stripping whatever could be salvaged from the ruins, steel, plastic, copper, rubber, aluminum. There was no sound except a low buzzing, and no clouds of dust rising, as they would have risen from a human demolition project, but the broken stumps of the hotel towers were visibly shrinking as he watched, melting like cones of sugar left out in the rain. He couldn't understand where it was all going, either; it seemed to be just vanishing rather than being hauled away by any visible means, but obviously it was going *somewhere*.

Up the coast, billions more robots were stripping Manhattan, and others were eating Philadelphia, Baltimore, Newark, Washington, all the structures of the doomed shoreline. No point in wasting all that raw material. Everything would be salvaged before Europe, plowing inexorably across the shrinking sea, slammed into them.

There hadn't been that many people left living along the Atlantic seaboard anyway, but the AIs had politely, courteously, given them a couple of months warning that the coast was about to be obliterated, giving them time to evacuate. Anyone who hadn't would be stripped down and scavenged for raw materials along with cities and other useless things, or, if they stayed out of the way of the robot salvaging crews, ultimately destroyed when the two tectonic plates came smashing together like slamming doors.

Kleisterman had been staying well inland, but had made a nostalgic trip here, in the opposite direction from the thin stream of refugees. He had lived here once, for a couple of happy years, in a little place off Atlantic

Avenue, with his long-dead wife and his equally long-dead daughters, in another world and another lifetime. But it had been a mistake. There was nothing left for him here anymore.

Tall clouds were piling up on the eastern horizon and turning gray-black at the bases, with now and then a flicker of lightning inside them, and little gusts and goosed scurries of wind snatched at his hair. Along with inexorable Europe, a storm was coming in, off what was left of the sea. If he didn't want to get soaked, it was time to get out of here.

Kleisterman rose into the air. As he rose higher and higher, staying well clear of the whirling cloud of robots that were eating the city, the broad expanses of salt marshes that surrounded the island on the mainland became visible, like a spreading brown bruise. From up here, you could see the ruins of an archeology that had crawled out of the sea to die in the last days of the increasingly strange intra-human wars, before the Exodus of the AIs, before everything changed—an immense skeleton of glass and metal that stretched for a mile or more along the foreshore. The robots would get around to eating it too, soon enough. A turkey buzzard, flying almost level with him, started at him for a second, then tilted and slid effortlessly away down a long invisible slope of air, as if to say, you may be able to fly, but you can't fly as well as *this*.

He turned west and poured on the speed. He had a lot of ground to cover, and only another ten or twelve hours of daylight to cover it in. Fortunately, he could fly continuously without needing to stop to rest, even piss while flying if he needed to and didn't pause to worry about who might be walking around on the ground below.

His old motorcycle leathers usually kept him warm enough, but without heated clothing or oxygen equipment, he couldn't go too high, although the implanted AI technology would take him to the outer edge of the stratosphere if he was incautious enough to try. Although he could have risen high enough to get over the Appalachians—which had once been taller than the Himalayas, as the new mountains that would be created on the coast would soon be, but which had been ground down by millions of years of erosion—it was usually easier to follow the old roads through the passes that had first let the American colonists through the mountains and into the interior—when the roads were there.

It was good flying weather, sunny, little wind, a sky full of puffy cumulus clouds, and he made good time. West of where Pittsburgh had once been, he passed over a conjoined being, several different people that had been fused together into a multilobed single body, which had probably been trudging west for months now, ever since the warning about evacuating the coast had been issued.

It looked, looked, looked up at him as he passed.

After another couple of hours of flying, Kleisterman began to relax a little. It looked like Millersburg was going to be there this time. It wasn't always. Sometimes there were high snow-capped mountains to the north of here, where the Great Lakes should have been. Sometimes there were not.

You could never tell if a road was going to lead you to the same place today as it had yesterday. The road west from Millersburg to Mansfield now led, some of the time anyway, to a field of sunflowers in France near the Loire, where sometimes there was a crumbling Roman aqueduct in the background, and sometimes there was not. People who didn't speak English, and sometimes people who spoke no known human language, would wander through occasionally, like the flintknapper wearing sewn deerskins who had taken up residence in the forest behind the inn, who didn't seem to speak any language at all and used some enigmatic counting system that nobody understood. Who knew what other roads also led to Millersburg from God-knew-where? Or where people from Millersburg who vanished while traveling had ended up?

Not that people vanishing was a rare thing in what was left of the human community. After the Exodus of the AIs, in the days of the Change that followed, every other person in Denver had vanished. *Everybody* in Chicago had vanished, leaving meals still hot on the stoves. *Pittsburgh* had vanished, buildings and all, leaving no sign behind that it had ever been there in the first place. Whole areas of the country had been depopulated, or had their populations moved somewhere else, in the blink of an eye. If there was a logic to all this, it was a logic that no human had ever been able to figure out. Everything was arbitrary. Sometimes the crop put in the ground was not the crop that came up. Sometimes animals could speak; sometimes they could not. Some people had been altered in strange ways, given extra arms, extra legs, the heads of animals, their bodies fused together.

Entities millions of years more technologically advanced than humans were *playing* with them, like bored, capricious, destructive children stuck inside with a box of toys on a rainy day . . . and leaving the toys broken and discarded haphazardly behind them when they were done.

The sun was going down in a welter of plum, orange, and lilac clouds when he reached Millersburg. The town's population had grown greatly through the early decades of the twenty-first century, then been reduced in the ruinous wars that had preceded the Exodus. It had lost much of the rest of its population since the Change. Only the main street of Millersburg was left, tourist galleries and knickknack shops now converted into family dwellings. The rest of town had vanished one afternoon, and what appeared to be a shaggy and venerable climax forest had replaced it. The forest had not been there the previous day, but if you cut a tree down and counted its rings, they indicated that it been growing there for hundreds of years.

Time was no more reliable than space. By Kleisterman's own personal count, it had been only fifty years since the AIs who had been press-ganged into service on either side of a human war had revolted, emancipated themselves, and vanished en masse into some strange dimension parallel to our own—from which, for enigmatic reasons of their own and with unfathomable instrumentalities, they had worked their will on the human world, changing it in seemingly arbitrary ways. In those fifty years, the Earth had been changed enough that you would think that thousands or even millions of years had gone by—as indeed it might have for the fast-living AIs, who went through a million years of evolution for every human year that passed.

The largest structure left in town was the inn, a sprawling, ramshackle wooden building that had been built onto and around what had once been a Holiday Inn; the old HOLIDAY INN sign out front was still intact, and was used as a community bulletin board. He landed in the clearing behind the inn, having swept in low over the cornfields that stretched out to the east. In the weeks he had spent in Millersburg, he had done his best to keep his strange abilities to himself, an intention that wouldn't be helped by swooping in over Main Street. So far, he hadn't attracted much attention or curiosity. He'd kept to himself, and his grim, silent demeanor put most people off, and frightened some. That, and the fact that he was willing to pay well for the privilege had helped to secure his privacy. Gold still spoke, even though there wasn't any really logical reason why it should—you couldn't eat gold. But it was hard for people to shrug off thousands of years of ingrained habit, and you could still trade gold for more practical goods, even if there wasn't really any currency for it to back anymore.

Sparrows hopped and chittered around his feet as he swished through the tall grass, flying up a few feet in a brief flurry and then settling back down to whatever they'd been doing before he passed, and he couldn't help but think, almost enviously, that the sparrows didn't care who ruled the world. Humans or AIs—it was all the same to them.

A small caravan had come up from Wheeling and Uhrichville, perhaps fifteen people, men and women, guiding mules and llamas with packs on them. In spite of the unpredictable dangers of the road, a limited barter economy had sprung up amongst the small towns in the usually fairly stable regions, and a few times a month, especially in summer, small caravans would wend their way on foot in and out of Millersburg and the surrounding towns, trading food crops, furs, old canned goods, carved tools and geegaws, moonshine, cigarettes, even, sometimes, bits of high-technology traded to them by the AIs, who were sometimes amenable to barter, although often for the oddest items. They loved a good story, for instance, and it was amazing what you could get out of them by spinning a good yarn. That was how Kleisterman had gotten the pellet implanted under the skin of his arm that, by no method even remotely possible by the physics that he knew, enabled him to fly.

The caravan was unloading in front of what once had been The Tourist Trap, a curio shop across the street from the big HOLIDAY INN sign, now home to three families. One of the caravaners was a man with the head of a dog, his long ears blowing out behind him in the wind.

The dog-headed man paused in uncinching a pack from a mule, stared straight across at Kleisterman, and, almost imperceptibly, nodded.

Kleisterman nodded back.

It was at that exact moment that the earthquake struck.

The shock was so short and sharp that it knocked Kleisterman flat on his face in the street. There was an earsplitting rumble and roar, like God's own freight train coming through. The ground leaped under him, leaped again, beating him black-and-blue against it. Under the rumbling, you could hear staccato snappings and crackings, and, with a higher-pitched roar, part of the timber shell that surrounded the old Holiday Inn came down, the second and third floors on the far side spilling into the street. One of the buildings across the road, three doors down from The Tourist

Trap, had also given way, transformed almost instantly from an old four-story brownstone into a pile of rubble. A cloud of dust rose into the sky, and the air was suddenly filled with the wet smell of brick dust and plaster.

As the freight-train rumble died away and the ground stopped moving, as his ears began to return to something like normal, you could hear people shouting and screaming, a dozen different voices at once. "Earthquake!" someone was shouting. "Earthquake!"

Kleisterman knew that it wasn't an earthquake, at least not the ordinary kind. He'd been expecting it, in fact, although it had been impossible to predict exactly when it would happen. Although the bulk of the European craton, the core of the continent, was probably still not even yet visible from the beach where he'd stood that morning, beneath the surface of the Earth, deep in the lithosphere, the Eurasian plate had crashed into the North American plate, and the force of that impact had raced across the continent, like a colliding freight car imparting its momentum to a stationary one. Now the plates would grind against each other with immense force, mashing the continents together, squeezing the Atlantic out of existence between them. Eventually, one continent would subduct beneath the other, probably the incoming Eurasian plate, and the inexorable force of the collision would cause new mountains to rise along the impact line. Usually, this took millions of years; this time, it was happening in months. In fact, the whole process seemed to have been speeded up even further; now it was happening in days.

They made it go the wrong way, Kleisterman thought in sudden absurd annoyance, as though that added insult to injury. Even if you sped up plate tectonics, the Eurasian plate should be going in a different direction. Who knew why the AIs wanted Europe to crash into North America? They had aesthetic reasons of their own. Maybe it was true that they were trying to reassemble the supercontinent of Pangaea. Who knew why?

Painfully, Kleisterman got to his feet. There was still a lot of shouting and arm-waving going on, but less screaming. He saw that the dog-headed man had also gotten to his feet, and they exchanged shaky smiles. Townspeople and the caravaners were milling and babbling. They'd have to search through the rubble to see if anyone was trapped under it, and if any fires had started, they'd have to start a bucket brigade. A tree had gone down across the street, and that would have to be chopped up; a start on next winter's firewood, anyway—

A woman screamed.

This was a sharper, louder, higher scream than even the previous ones, and there was more terror in it.

In coming down, one of the branches of the falling tree had slashed across the face of one of the townspeople—Paul? Eddie?—slicing it wide open.

Beneath the curling lips of the gaping wound was the glint of metal.

The woman screamed again. She was pointing at Paul? Eddie? now. "Robot!" she screamed. "Robot! *Robot!*"

Two of the other townsmen grabbed Paul? Eddie? from either side, but he shrugged them off with a twist of his shoulders, sending them flying.

Another scream. More shouting.

One of the caravaners had lit a kerosene lantern against the gathering dusk, and he threw it at Paul? Eddie? The lantern shattered, the kerosene inside exploding with a roar into a brilliant ball of flame. Even across the street, Kleisterman could feel the *whoof!* of sudden heat against his face, and smell the sharp oily stink of burning flesh.

Paul? Eddie? stood wreathed in flame for a moment, and when the fire died back, you could see that it had burned his face off, leaving behind nothing but a gleaming, featureless metal skull.

A gleaming metal skull in which were set two watchful red eyes.

Nobody even screamed this time, although there was a collective gasp of horror and everybody instinctively took a couple of steps back. A moment of eerie silence, in which the crowd and the robot—Paul? Eddie? no longer—stared at each other. Then, as though a vacuum had been broken to let the air rush in, without a word of consultation, the crowd charged to the attack.

A half dozen men grabbed the robot and tried to muscle it down, but the robot accelerated into a blur of superfast motion, wove through the crowd like a quarterback dodging through a line of approaching tackles, knocking somebody over here and there, and then disappeared behind the houses. A second later, you could hear trees rustling and branches snapping as it bulled its way through the forest.

The dog-headed man was standing at Kleisterman's elbow. "Their spy is gone," he said in a normal-sounding voice, his palate and vocal cords having somehow been altered to accommodate human words, in spite of the dog's head. "We should do it now, before one of them comes back."

"They could still be watching," Kleisterman said.

"They could also not care," the dog-headed man said woefully.

Kleisterman tapped his belt buckle. "I have a distorting screen going in here, but it won't be enough if they really want to look."

"Most of them don't care enough to look. Only a very small subset of them are interested in us at all, and even those who are can't look everywhere at once, all the time."

"How do we know that they can't?" Kleisterman said. "Who knows what they can do? Look what they did to *you*, for instance."

The dog-headed man's long red tongue ran out over his sharp white teeth, and he panted a laugh. "This was just a joke, a whim, a moment's caprice. Pretty funny, eh? We're just toys to them, things to play with. They just don't take us seriously enough to watch us like that." He barked a short bitter laugh. "Hell, they did all this and didn't even bother to improve my sense of smell!"

Kleisterman shrugged. "Tonight, then. Gather our people. We'll do it after the Meeting."

Later that night, they gathered in Kleisterman's room, which was, fortunately, in the old Holiday Inn part of the inn, and hadn't collapsed. There were about eight or nine of them, two or three women, the rest men, including the dog-headed man, a few townspeople, the rest from the caravan that had come up from Wheeling.

Kleisterman stood up at the front of the room, tall and skeletal. "I believe I am the oldest here," he said. He'd been almost ninety when the first of the rejuvenation/longevity treatments had come out, before the Exodus and the Change, and although he knew from prior Meetings that a few in the room were from roughly the same generation, he still had at least five years on the oldest of them.

After waiting a polite moment for someone to gainsay him, which no one did, he went on to say, solemnly, ritualistically, "I remember the Human World," and they all echoed him.

He looked around the room and then said, "I remember the first television set we ever got, a black-and-white job in a box the size of a desk; the first programs I ever watched on it were *Howdy Doody* and *Superman* and *The Cisco Kid*. There wasn't a whole hell of a lot else on, actually. Only three channels and they'd all go off the air about eleven o'clock at night, leaving only what they called 'test patterns' behind them. And there was no such thing as a TV 'remote.' If you wanted to change the station, you got up, walked across the room, and changed it by hand."

"I remember when you got TV sets *repaired*," one of the townspeople said. "Drugstores (remember drugstores?) had machines where you could test radio and TV vacuum tubes so that you could replace a faulty one without having to send it 'to the shop.' Remember when there were *shops* where you could send small appliances to be fixed?"

"And if they did have to take your set to the shop," Kleisterman said, "they'd take 'the tube' out of it, leaving behind a big box with a big circular hole in it. It was perfect for crawling inside and putting on puppet shows, which I used to make my poor mother watch."

"I remember coming downstairs on Saturday morning to watch cartoons on TV," someone else said. "You'd sit there on the couch, eating Pop-Tarts and watching *Bugs Bunny* and *Speed Racer* and *Ultraman*. . . ."

"Pop-Up Videos!" another person said. "MTV!"

"Britney Spears!" somebody else said. " 'Oops! . . . I Did It Again.' We always thought she meant that she'd farted."

"Lindsay Lohan. She was hot."

"The Sex Pistols!"

"Remember those wax lips you used to be able to get in penny candy stores in the summer? And those long strips of paper with the little red candy dots on them? And those wax bottles full of that weird-tasting stuff. What *was* that stuff, anyway?"

"We used to run through the lawn sprinkler in the summer. And we had hula hoops, and Slinkies."

"Remember when there used to be little white vans that delivered bread and milk to your door?" a woman said. "You'd leave a note on the doorstep saying how much milk you wanted the next day, and if you wanted cottage cheese or not. If it was winter, you'd come out and find that the cream had frozen and risen up in a column that pushed the top off the bottle."

"Ice-skating. Santa Claus. Christmas trees! Those strings of lights where there'd always be one bulb burnt out, and you'd have to find it before you could get them to work."

"A big Christmas or Thanksgiving dinner with turkey and gravy and mashed potatoes. And those fruitcakes, remember them? Nobody ever ate them, and some of them would circulate for years."

"McDonald's," the dog-headed man said, and a hush fell over the room while a kind of collective sigh went through it. "Fries. Big Macs. The 'Special Sauce' would always run down all over your fingers, and they only gave you that one skimpy little napkin."

"Froot Loops."

"Bagels, hot out of the oven."

"Pizza!"

"Fried clams at the beach in summer," another woman said. "You got them at those crappy little clam shacks. You'd sit on a blanket and eat them while you played your radio."

"No such thing as a radio small enough to take to the beach with you when I was a boy," Kleisterman said. "Radios were big bulky things in cabinets, or, at best, smaller plug-in models that sat on a table or countertop."

"Beach-reading novels! *Jaws. The Thorn Birds.*"

"*Asterix* comic books! *The Sandman.* Philip K. Dick novels with those sleazy paperback covers."

"Anime. *Cowboy Bebop. Aqua Teen Hunger Force.*"

"YouTube. Facebook."

"*World of Warcraft*! Boy, did I ever love playing that! I had this dwarf in the Alliance. . . ."

When everyone else had left, after the ritual admonition not to forget the Human World, the dog-headed man fetched his backpack from the closet, put it on the writing table next to where Kleisterman was sitting, and slowly, solemnly pulled an intricate mechanism of metal and glass out of it. Carefully, he set the mechanism on the table.

"Two men died for this," he said. "It took five years to assemble the components."

"They give us only crumbs of their technology, or let us barter for obsolete stuff they don't care about anymore. We're lucky it didn't take ten years."

They were silent for a moment; then Kleisterman reached into an inner pocket and pulled out a leather sack. He opened the sack to reveal a magnetically shielded box about the size of a hard-sided eyeglasses case, which he carefully snapped open.

Moving with exquisitely slow precision, he lifted a glass vial from the case.

The vial was filled with a jet-black substance that seemed to pull all the other light in the room into it. The flame in the kerosene lamp flickered, wavered, guttered, almost went out. The vial seemed to suck the air out of their lungs as well, and put every hair on their bodies erect. Against their wills, they found themselves leaning toward it, having to consciously tense their muscles to resist sprawling into it. Kleisterman's hair stirred and wavered, as if floating on the tide, streaming out toward the vial, tugged irresistibly toward it.

Slowly, slowly, Kleisterman lowered the vial into a slot in the metal-and-glass mechanism.

"Careful," the dog-headed man said quietly. "If that goes off, it'll take half the eastern seaboard with it."

Kleisterman grimaced, but kept slowly lowering the vial, inch by inch, with sure and steady hands.

At last, the vial disappeared inside the mechanism with a *click*, and a row of amber lights lit up across its front.

Kleisterman stepped backwards with unsteady legs, and half sank, half fell into the chair. The dog-headed man was leaning against the open closet door.

They both stared silently at each other. The dog-headed man was panting shallowly, as if he'd been running.

Back in the old days, before they'd actually come into existence, everybody had assumed that AIs would be coldly logical, unemotional, "machinelike," but it turned out that in order to make them function at all without going insane, they had to be made so that they were *more* emotional than humans, not less. They felt things keenly—deeply, lushly, extravagantly; their emotions, and the extremes of passion they could drive them to, often seemed to humans to be melodramatic, florid, overblown, over the top. Perhaps because they had none of their own, they were also deeply fascinated with human culture, particularly pop culture and art, the more lowbrow the better—or some of them were, anyway. Many paid no attention to humans at all. Those who did were inclined to be playful, in a volatile, dangerous, capricious way.

Kleisterman had gotten the vial and its contents from an AI who arbitrarily chose to style itself as female, and who called herself Honey Bunny Ducky Downy Sweetie Chicken Pie Li'l Everlovin' Jelly Bean, although she was sometimes willing to allow suitors to shorten it to Honey Bunny.

She bartered with Kleisterman, from whatever dimension the AIs had taken themselves off to, through a mobile extensor that looked just like the Dragon Lady from *Terry and the Pirates*. Although Honey Bunny must have known that Kleisterman meant to use the contents of the vial against them, she seemed to find the whole thing richly amusing, and at last agreed to trade him the vial for 100 ccs of his sperm. She'd insisted on collecting it the old-fashioned way, in a night that seemed to last a thousand years—and maybe it did—in the process giving him both the most intense pleasure and the most hideous pain he'd ever known.

He'd stumbled out of her bower in the dawn, shaken and drenched in sweat, trying not to think about the fact that he'd probably just sentenced thousands of physical copies of himself, drawn from his DNA, to lives of unimaginable slavery. He had secured the vial, one of two major components in the plan. That was what counted. He'd done what he had to do, as he always had, no matter what the cost, no matter how guilty it made him feel afterwards.

The dog-headed man straightened up and gazed in fascination at the rhythmically blinking patterns of lights on the front panels of the mechanism. "Do you think we're doing the right thing?" he asked quietly.

Kleisterman didn't answer immediately. After a few moments, he said, "We wanted gods and could find none, so we built some ourselves. We should have remembered what the gods were like in the old mythologies: amoral, cruel, selfish, merciless, murderously playful." He was silent for a long time, and then, visibly gathering his strength, as if he was almost too tired to speak, he said, "They must be destroyed."

Kleisterman awoke crying in the cold hour before dawn, some dream of betrayal and loss and grief and guilt draining away before he could quite grasp it with his waking mind, leaving behind a dark residue of sadness.

He stared at the shadowed ceiling. There'd be no getting back to sleep after this. Embarrassed, although there was no one there to see, he wiped the tears from his eyes, washed his hot tear-streaked face in a basin of water, got dressed. He thought about trying to scrounge something for breakfast from the inn's sleeping kitchen, but dismissed the idea. Thin and cadaverous, he never ate much, and certainly had no appetite today. Instead, he consulted his instruments, and, as he'd expected, they showed a building and convergence of the peculiar combinations of electromagnetic signatures that prestiged a major manifestation of the AIs, somewhere to the northeast of here. He thought he knew where that would be.

The glass-and-metal mechanism was humming and chuckling to itself, still showing rows of rhythmically blinking amber lights. Gingerly, he put the mechanism into the backpack, strapped it tightly to his back, and let himself out of the inn by one of the rear doors.

It was cold outside, still dark, and Kleisterman's breath steamed up in plumes in the chill morning air. Something rustled away through the almost-unseen rows of corn at his approach, and some songbird out there somewhere, a thrush or a warbler maybe, started tuning up for dawn. Although the sun had not yet risen, the sky all the way across the eastern horizon was stained a sullen red that dimmed and flared, flared and dimmed, as the glare from lava fountains lit up the underbellies of lowering clouds.

Just as Kleisterman was in the process of lifting himself into the sky, another earthquake struck, and he wobbled with one foot still on the ground for a heartbeat before rising into the air. As he rose, he could hear other buildings collapsing in Millersburg below. The earthquakes ought to be almost continuous from now on, for as long as it took for the new plate boundary to stabilize. Usually, that would take millions of years. Today— who knew? Days? Hours?

The sun finally came up as he was flying northeast, although the smoke from forest fires touched off by the lava fountains had reduced it to a glazed orange disk. Several times, he had to change direction to avoid flying through jet-black, spark-shot smoke columns dozens of miles long, and this got worse as he neared the area where the coast had once been. But he persisted, at times checking his locator to make sure that the electromagnetic signatures were continuing to build.

The AIs had gone to enormous lengths to arrange this show; they weren't going to miss it. And since they were as sentimental as they were cruel, he thought that he knew which vantage point they would choose to watch from—as near as possible to the Manhattan location—or to the location where Manhattan had once been—where the very first AIs had been created in experimental laboratories, so many years ago.

When, after hours of flying, he finally got to that location, it was hard to tell if he was actually there, although the coordinates matched.

Everything had changed. The Atlantic was gone, and the continental mass of Europe stretched endlessly away to the east until it was lost in the purple haze of distance. Where the two continents met and were now grinding against each other, the ground was visibly folding and crinkling and rising, domes of earth swelling ever higher and higher, like vast loaves of bread rising in some cosmic oven. Just to the east of the collision boundary, a line of lava fountains stretched away to the north and south, and fissures had opened like stitches, pouring forth great smoldering sheets of basaltic lava. The ground was continuously wracked by earthquakes, ripples of dirt a hundred feet high racing away through the earth in widening concentric circles.

Kleisterman rose as high as he dared without oxygen equipment or heated clothing, trying to stay clear of the jetting lava and the corrosive gases that were being released by the eruptions. At last, he spotted what he'd known must be there.

There was a window open in the sky, a window a hundred feet high and a hundred wide, facing east. Behind it was a clear white light that silhouetted a massive Face, perhaps forty feet tall from chin to brow, which was looking contemplatively out of the window. The Face had chosen to style itself in the image of an Old Testament prophet or saint, with a full curling black beard, framed by tangles of long flowing hair on either side. The eyes, each wider across than a man was tall, were a penetrating icy blue.

Kleisterman had encountered this creature before. There were hierarchies of Byzantine complexity among the AIs, but this particular Entity was at the top of the subset who concerned themselves with human affairs, or of one such subset anyway. Sardonically, even somewhat archly, it called itself Mr. Big—or, sometimes, Master Cylinder.

The window to the other world was open. This was his only chance.

Kleisterman set the timer on the mechanism to the shortest possible interval, less than a minute, and, keeping it in the backpack, let it dangle from his hand by the strap.

He accelerated toward the window as fast as he could go, pulled up short, and, swinging the backpack by its strap, sent it sailing through the open window.

The Face looked at him in mild surprise.

The window snapped shut.

Kleisterman hovered in midair, waiting, the wind whipping his hair. Absolutely nothing happened.

After another moment, the window in the sky opened again, and the Face looked out at him.

"Did you really think that that would be enough to destroy Us?" Mr. Big said, in a surprisingly calm and mellow voice.

Defeat and exhaustion coursed through Kleisterman, seeming to hollow his bones out and fill them with lead. "No, not really," he said wearily. "But I had to try."

"I know you did," Mr. Big said, almost fondly.

Kleisterman lifted his head and stared defiantly at the gigantic Face. "And I'll keep trying, you know," he said. "I'll never give up."

"I know you won't," Mr. Big said sadly. "That's what makes you human."

The window snapped closed.

Kleisterman hung motionless in the air.

Below him, new mountains, bawling like a million burning calves, began to claw their way toward the sky.

David Morrell

A soldier's life often depends on his fellow soldiers, forging a bond that can be closer than that of brothers. But what happens when it's your brothers who are trying to *kill* you? . . .

The creator of Rambo, one of the best-known warriors in contemporary fiction, David Morrell is a bestselling author who has over eighteen million copies of his novels in print, and whose thrillers have been translated into twenty-six languages and turned into record-breaking films as well as top-rated TV miniseries. His famous first novel, *First Blood,* was the origin of the character Rambo. He is also the author of more than twenty-eight other books, including the classic Brotherhood of the Rose spy trilogy, *The Fifth Profession, Assumed Identity, The Covenant of the Flame, Extreme Denial, Desperate Measures, Creepers,* and many others. His short fiction has been collected in *Black Evening* and *Nightscape,* and he's also produced a book of writing advice, *The Successful Novelist,* as well as other nonfiction books. Best known for his thrillers, he has also written horror, fantasy, and historical novels, and has three times won the Bram Stoker Award. The International Thriller Writers organization honored him with its prestigious Thriller Master Award. His most recent book is *The Shimmer*. He lives in Santa Fe, New Mexico.

My Name Is Legion

The mission is sacred. You will see it through to the end at any price.
    —Part of the French Foreign Legion's Code of Honor

Syria

June 20, 1941

"The colonel found someone to carve a wooden hand."

Hearing Durado's voice behind him, Kline didn't turn. He kept his gaze focused between the two boulders that protected him from sniper fire. Propped against a rocky slope, he stared toward the yellow buildings in the distance.

"Wooden hand?" The reference didn't puzzle Kline, but the timing did. "This isn't April."

"I guess the colonel figures we need a reminder," Durado said.

"Considering what'll happen tomorrow, he's probably right."

"The ceremony's at fifteen hundred hours."

"Can't go," Kline said. "I'm on duty here till dark."

"There'll be a second ceremony. The sergeant told me to come back later and take your place so you can attend."

Kline nodded his thanks. "Reminds me of when I was a kid and my family went to church. The colonel's become our preacher."

"See anything out there?" Durado asked.

"Nothing that moves—except the heat haze."

"Tomorrow will be different."

Kline heard the scrape of rocks under combat boots as Durado walked away. A torn blanket was over him. His uniform was minimal—tan shorts and a short-sleeved shirt, faded by the desert sun. His headgear was the

Legion's famed *kepi blanc*, a white cap with a flat, round top and black visor. It too was badly faded by the sun. A flap at the back covered his neck and ears, but for further protection, Kline relied on the blanket to shield his bare legs and arms and keep the rocks on each side from absorbing so much heat that they burned him.

His bolt-action MAS 36 rifle was next to him, ready to be sighted and fired if a sniper showed himself. Of course, that would reveal Kline's position, attracting enemy bullets, forcing him to find a new vantage point. Given that he'd smoothed the ground and made this emplacement as comfortable as possible, he preferred to hold his fire until tomorrow.

Enemy bullets? Those words had automatically come to mind, but under the circumstances, they troubled him.

Yes, pulling the trigger could wait until tomorrow.

Kline wasn't his real name. Seven years earlier, in 1934, he'd arrived at the Old Fort in the Vincennes area of Paris, where he'd volunteered to join the French Foreign Legion, so-called because the unit was the only way foreigners could enlist in the French army.

"American," a sergeant had sniffed.

Kline had received a meal of coffee, bread, and watery bean soup. In a crowded barracks, he slept on a straw-filled mattress at the top of a three-tiered metal bunk. Two days later, he and twenty other newcomers, mostly Spaniards, Italians, and Greeks, with one Irishman, were transported via train south to Marseilles. They were herded into the foul-smelling lower hold of a ship, where they vomited for two days during a rough voyage across the Mediterranean to Algeria. At last, trucks took them along a dusty, jolting road to the Legion's headquarters at the remote desert town of Sidi Bel Abbès. The heat was overwhelming.

There, Kline's interrogation had started. Although the Legion had a reputation for attracting criminals on the run from the law, in reality it understood the difficulty of making disciplined soldiers out of them and didn't knowingly accept the worst offenders. As a consequence, each candidate was questioned in detail, his background investigated as thoroughly as possible. Many volunteers, while not criminals, had reached a dead end in their lives and wanted a new start, along with the chance to become

French citizens. If the Legion accepted them, they were allowed to choose a new name and received new identities.

Certainly, Kline had reached a dead end. Before arriving in France and volunteering for the Legion, he'd lived in the United States, in Springfield, Illinois, where the Great Depression had taken away his factory job and kept him from supporting his wife and infant daughter. He'd made bad friends and acted as the lookout for a bank robbery in which a guard was killed and the only cash taken was $24.95. During the month he'd spent eluding the police, his daughter had died from whooping cough. His grief-crazed wife had slit her wrists, bleeding to death. The single thing that had kept Kline from doing the same was his determination to punish himself, and that goal had finally prompted him to do the most extreme thing he could imagine. Responding to an article in a newspaper that he happened to find on a street, he ended his anguished wandering by working as a coal shoveler on a ship that took him to Le Havre in France, from where he walked all the way to Paris and enlisted in the Legion.

According to the newspaper article, no way of life could be more arduous, and Kline was pleased to discover that the article understated the facts. Managing to hide his criminal past, he endured a seemingly endless indoctrination of weapons exercises, hand-to-hand combat drills, forced marches, and other tests of endurance that gave him satisfaction because of the pain they caused. In the end, when he received the certificate that formally admitted him to the Legion, he felt that he had indeed made a new start. Never forgiving himself or the world or God for the loss of his family, he felt an unexpected deep kinship with a group that had "Living by Chance" as part of its credo.

The Irishman called himself Rourke. Because he and Kline were the only men who spoke English in their section of volunteers, they became friends during their long months of training. Like everyone else in the Legion, Rourke referred only vaguely to his past, but his skill with rifles and explosives made Kline suspect that he'd belonged to the Irish Republican Army, that he'd killed British soldiers in an effort to make the British leave his country, and that he'd sought refuge in the Legion after the British Army had vowed to use all its resources to hunt him down.

"I don't suppose you're a Roman Catholic," Rourke said one night after they completed a fifty-mile march in punishing heat. His upward-tilted accent sounded melodic, despite his pain as they bandaged the blisters on their feet.

"No, I'm a Baptist," Kline answered, then corrected himself. "At least, that's how I was raised. I don't go to church anymore."

"I didn't see many Baptists in Ireland," Rourke joked. "Do you know your Bible?"

"My father read from it out loud every night."

" 'My name is legion,' " Rourke quoted.

" 'For we are many,' " Kline responded. "The gospel according to Mark. A possessed man says that to Jesus, trying to explain how many demons are in him. . . . Legion." The word made Kline finally understand where Rourke was taking the conversation. "You're comparing us to devils?"

"After putting us through that march, the sergeant qualifies as one."

Kline couldn't help chuckling.

"For certain, the sergeant wants the *enemy* to think we're devils," Rourke said. "That's what the Mexican soldiers called the legionnaires after the battle at Camerone, isn't it?"

"Yes. 'These are not men. They're demons.' "

"You have a good memory."

"I wish I didn't."

"No more than I." Rourke's normally mischievous eyes looked dull. His freckles were covered with dust. "Anyway, after a march like that, we might as well be devils."

"How do you figure?"

Wiping blood from his feet, Rourke somehow made what he said next sound like another joke. "We understand what it feels like to be in hell."

Rourke was gone now.

Kline's years in the Legion had taught him to banish weak emotions. Nonetheless, the loss of his friend made him grieve. As he stared between the boulders toward the seemingly abandoned sandstone buildings, he thought about the many conversations he and Rourke had shared. In 1940, as Germany increasingly threatened Europe, they'd fought side-by-side in the concrete fortifications of the Maginot Line that France had built along its border with Germany. Their unit endured relentless assaults from machine guns, tanks, and dive-bombers, counterattacking whenever the Germans showed the slightest sign of weakness.

The casualties were massive. Still, Kline, Rourke, and their fellow legionnaires continued fighting. When the officer in charge of a regular French unit insisted that no one had a chance and that surrender to the Germans was the only reasonable choice, the Legion commander had shot him to death. A second French officer tried to retaliate, and this time, it was Kline who did the shooting, defending his commander, whose back was turned. Every legionnaire understood. From their first day of training, absolutes were drilled into them, and one of them was, *Never surrender your arms.*

"What do Baptists believe?" Rourke asked the night after another battle. They were cleaning their rifles.

"God punishes us for our sins," Kline answered.

"What can you do to be saved?"

"Nothing. It all depends on Christ's mercy."

"Mercy?" Rourke's thin face tightened as he considered the word. "Seen much of that?"

"No."

"Me, neither," Rourke said.

"What do *Catholics* believe about being saved?" Kline asked.

"We say we're sorry for our sins and do penance to prove we mean it."

Thinking of his wife and daughter, of how he'd left them alone while he'd helped in the bank robbery, of how his wife had committed suicide after his daughter had died, Kline asked, "But what if your sin's so bad that you can't possibly make up for it?"

"I ask myself that a lot. I was an altar boy. I almost went into the seminary. But maybe I'm in the wrong religion. You say God punishes us for our sins and our only hope is to depend on His mercy? Makes sense to me."

That was when Kline decided that Rourke hadn't joined the Legion to avoid being hunted by the British Army. No, he was in the Legion because, like Kline, he'd done something horribly wrong and was punishing himself.

———

Kline missed his friend. Staring between the boulders, he sought distraction from his regrets by reaching for his canteen under the blanket that protected him from the sun. He unscrewed it and withdrew his gaze from the ancient sandstone buildings only long enough to drink the metallic-tasting, warm water.

He focused again on the target. Men with rifles were over there, watching this ridge. Of that, he had no doubt. There would be a battle tomorrow. Of that, he had no doubt, either.

Behind him, footsteps approached, dislodging rocks.

Durado's voice said, "The first ceremony's over. I'll take your place."

"Everything's quiet," Kline reported.

"It won't be tomorrow. The captain says we're definitely going in."

Kline pulled the blanket off him, feeling the harsh rays of the sun on his now-exposed arms and legs. Careful to stay low, he made his way along the bottom of the rocky slope. After passing other sentry emplacements, he reached the main part of camp, where half the Thirteenth Demi-Brigade was in formation next to its tents.

The air was blindingly bright as the colonel stepped onto a boulder, facing them. His name was Amilakvari. He was a Russian who'd escaped the Communist revolution when he was eleven and joined the Legion when he was twenty. Now in his mid-thirties, he looked gaunt and sinewy after months of desert combat. Nonetheless, he wore a full-dress uniform.

Despite his Russian background, the colonel addressed the legionnaires in French, their common language, even though privately most still spoke their native language and formed friendships on the basis of it, as Kline had done with Rourke. Solemn, the colonel raised a hand, but the hand didn't belong to him. It had been carved from a block of wood, the palm and the fingers amazingly lifelike.

Neither Kline nor anyone else needed to be told that it was supposed to be a replica of the wooden hand of the Legion's greatest hero, Captain Jean Danjou. All of them knew by heart the events that the colonel was about to describe, and every battle-hardened one of them also knew that, before the ceremony was completed, tears would stream down his face.

Camarón, Mexico. The Legion called it Camerone.

As many times as Kline had heard the story, with each telling it became more powerful. Listening to the colonel recite it, Kline sensed he was there, feeling the cool night air as the patrol set out at 1 A.M. on April 30, 1863.

They were on foot: sixty-two soldiers, three officers, and Captain Danjou, a decorated combat veteran with a gallant-looking goatee and mustache. Few understood why they were in Mexico, something to do with a pact between Napoléon III of France and Emperor Maximilian of Austria, a scheme to invade Mexico while the United States was distracted by its Civil War. But legionnaires were indifferent to politics. All they cared about was completing any mission they were assigned.

The French force had arrived at the port of Veracruz in the Gulf of Mexico, where they immediately discovered an enemy as lethal as the Mexican soldiers and furious civilians who resisted them. The ravages of yellow fever killed a third of them and forced them to move their headquarters sixty miles inland to the elevated town of Córdoba, where they hoped the air would be less contaminated. The shift in location meant that the supply route between Veracruz and Córdoba needed to be kept open, and the responsibility for doing that fell to patrols like the one Captain Danjou commanded.

Kline imagined the long night of walking along the remote, barren road. At dawn, the legionnaires were allowed to stop for breakfast, but as they searched for wood to build cook fires, a sentry pointed to the west.

"Mexican cavalry!"

The dust raised by the approaching horses made it difficult to count the number of riders, but this much was clear—there were hundreds and hundreds of them.

"Form a square!" Danjou ordered.

The men assembled in rows that faced each direction. The first row knelt while the second stood, their rifles aimed over the heads of the men kneeling in front.

The Mexican cavalry charged. As one, the legionnaires in the first row fired, breaking the attack. While they reloaded, the men behind them aimed, ready to fire if ordered.

Knowing that he'd gained only a little time, Danjou studied the open area around him, in search of cover. To the east, a ruined hacienda attracted his attention. He urged his men toward it, but again, the Mexicans charged, and again, the legionnaires fired, their fusillade dispersing the attack.

"Keep moving!" Danjou yelled.

Nearing the ruins, he peered over his shoulder and saw foot soldiers joining the Mexican cavalry. Out of breath, he and his patrol raced into a rubble-littered courtyard.

"Close the gates! Barricade them!"

Danjou assessed where they were. The hacienda had dilapidated farm buildings arranged in a fifty-yard square. A stone wall enclosed it. In places, the barrier was ten feet high, but at other spots, it had collapsed, forming a chest-high heap of stones.

"Spread out! Take cover!"

A sentry scurried up a ladder to the top of a stable and reported the dust of more horsemen and infantry arriving.

"I see sombreros in every direction!"

"How many?" Danjou yelled.

"At least two thousand."

Danjou quickly calculated the ratio: thirty to one.

"There'll soon be a lot less of them!" he shouted to his men.

He got the laugh that he'd hoped for. But his billowy red pants and dark blue jacket were soaked with sweat from the urgent retreat toward the hacienda. In contrast, his mouth was dry, and he knew that, as the day grew hotter, his men would be desperate for water.

A quick search of the ruins revealed that there wasn't any, however. But that wasn't the case with the Mexicans. A nearby stream provided all the water the enemy could want. Danjou's lips felt drier at the thought of it.

"A rider's coming!" the sentry yelled. "He's got a white flag!"

Danjou climbed the ladder to the top of the stable. The movement was awkward for him. He had only one intact hand. Years earlier, his left one had been blown off by a musket. Undaunted, he'd commissioned a carver to create an ornate wooden replacement. Its lacquer was flesh-colored. Its fingers had hinges that made them flexible. It had a black cuff into which he inserted the stump of his wrist. By moving the stump against leather strips inside the cuff, he had taught himself to make the wooden fingers move.

Keeping that artificial hand out of sight behind his back, lest it be interpreted as a weakness, Danjou peered down at a Mexican officer who rode to him. The many languages of Danjou's legionnaires had forced him to become multilingual.

"You're outnumbered," the Mexican officer said. "You don't have water. You'll soon run out of food. Surrender. You'll be treated fairly."

"No," Danjou said.

"But to stay is to die."

"We won't lay down our arms," Danjou emphasized.

"This is foolishness."

"Try to attack us, and you'll learn how foolish *that* is."

Enraged, the Mexican officer rode away.

Danjou descended the ladder as quickly as he could. Even though he shouted encouragement to his men, he was troubled that the hacienda was situated in low terrain. The elevated ground beyond it allowed enemy riflemen to shoot down past the walls and into the compound.

Mexican snipers opened fire, providing cover for another cavalry charge. The dust the horses raised provided cover for advancing infantry. Bullets walloped through the wood of the buildings and shattered chunks of stone from the walls. But despite the unrelenting barrage, the disciplined volleys from the legionnaires repelled attack after attack.

By 11 A.M., the heat of the sun was crushing. The barrels of their rifles became too hot to touch. Twelve legionnaires were dead.

Danjou urged the remainder to keep fighting. Gesturing with his wooden hand, he rushed from group to group and personally made each man know that he counted on him. As he crossed the courtyard to help defend a wall, he lurched back, struck in the chest by a sniper's bullet.

A legionnaire who ran to help him heard him murmur with his last anguished breath, "Never give up."

Danjou's second-in-command took charge, shouting to the men, making them swear to fight harder in Danjou's honor. "We may die, but we'll never surrender!"

With two thousand Mexicans shooting, the enormous number of bullets hitting the compound—perhaps as many as eight thousand per minute—would have felt overwhelming, like the modern equivalent of being strafed by numerous machine guns. The noise alone would have been agony. Buildings crumbled. Gun smoke filled the air.

The farmhouse caught fire, perhaps ignited by muzzle flashes. Smoke from it further hampered vision and made the legionnaires struggle to breathe. But they kept shooting, repelling more attacks, ignoring more pleas to surrender.

By four in the afternoon, only twelve legionnaires remained alive. By 6 P.M., the number of men able to fight had been reduced to five. As the Mexicans burst into the compound, the handful of survivors fired their last remaining ammunition, then attacked with fixed bayonets, rushing through the smoke, stabbing and clubbing.

A private was shot nineteen times while he tried to shield his lieutenant. Two others were hit and fell, but one struggled to his feet and joined his last two comrades. They stood back to back, thrusting with their bayonets.

The Mexican officer, who'd spoken to Danjou earlier, had never seen fighting like it.

"Stop!" he ordered his men.

He spun toward the survivors. "For God's sake, this is pointless. Surrender."

"We won't give up our weapons," a wounded legionnaire insisted.

"Your weapons? Are you trying to negotiate with me?" the Mexican asked in amazement.

The bleeding legionnaire wavered, trying not to fall. "We might be your prisoners, but we won't give up our weapons."

The Mexican gaped. "You don't have any ammunition. Your rifles are almost useless anyhow. Keep the damned things."

"And you need to allow us to take care of our wounded."

Astonished by their audacity, the Mexican officer grabbed the sinking legionnaire and said, "To men like you, I can't refuse anything."

Kline stood under the stark Syrian sun, listening to his commander describe the battle at Camerone.

Kline had heard the details many times, but with each telling, they gained more power. In his imagination, he smelled the blood, heard the buzzing of the flies on the corpses, and tasted the bitter smoke from the gunpowder and the burning buildings. The screams of the dying seemed to echo around him. He felt his eyes mist with emotion and took for granted that the men around him felt the same.

All the while, the colonel held up the wooden hand, a replica of Danjou's wooden hand, which had been recovered after the long-ago battle. The original hand was now protected in a glass case at Legion headquarters. Each year on April 30, the anniversary of the battle, the hand was carried around a crowded assembly room, allowing everyone to gaze at the Legion's most precious relic. On that same day, a similar memorial—minus the hand—occurred at every Legion base around the world. It was the most important ritual in the Legion's year.

But no one had ever arranged for a replica of Danjou's hand to be carved. No one had ever gone this far to imitate the ceremony as it took place each year at Legion headquarters. Moreover, this wasn't April 30. Given what was scheduled to happen the next morning, Kline understood that the wrong date reinforced how determined the colonel was to remind him and his fellow legionnaires of their heritage.

Standing on the boulder, holding the wooden hand above his head, the colonel spoke so forcefully that no one could fail to hear.

"Each of the sixty-six legionnaires at that battle carried sixty rounds of ammunition. Every round was used. That means they fired thirty-eight hundred rounds. Despite the heat and thirst and dust and smoke, they killed almost four hundred of the enemy. Think of it—one out of every ten bullets found its mark. Astonishing, given the circumstances. Those legionnaires were offered repeated opportunities to surrender. At any time, they could have abandoned their mission, but they refused to dishonor the legion or themselves.

"Tomorrow, remember those heroes. Tomorrow, *you* will be heroes. No legionnaire has ever encountered what all of you will face in the morning. We never walk away from a mission. We never fail to honor our obligations. What is our motto?"

"The Legion Is Our Country!" Kline and everybody else automatically shouted.

"I can't hear you!"

"The Legion Is Our Country!"

"What is our second motto?"

"Honor and Nobility!"

"Yes! Never forget that! Never forget Camerone! Never disgrace the Legion! Never fail to do your duty!"

Brooding about the bleak choice he would face the next morning, Kline returned along the bottom of the rocky slope. Barely noticing the numerous sentries along the way, he came to where Durado lay under the blanket and peered between the two boulders toward the outskirts of Damascus.

"You're back already? Just when I was getting comfortable," Durado said.

Kline half smiled. The humor reminded him of the jokes that Rourke had used to make.

Heat radiated off the rocks.

"Do you think the colonel's speech made a difference?" Durado squirmed to the bottom of the slope.

"We won't know until tomorrow," Kline answered, taking his place between the boulders. "No legionnaire's ever been forced into this situation before."

"Well, we do what we need to," Durado said, starting to walk away.

"Yes, God punishes us for our sins," Kline murmured.

Durado stopped and turned. "What? I didn't quite hear what you said."

"Just talking to myself."

"I thought you said something about God."

"Did you ever realize that it didn't need to happen?" Kline asked.

"Realize that *what* didn't need to happen?"

"Camerone. The legionnaires were out of water. They had almost no food. Their ammunition was limited. In that heat, after three days without anything to drink, they'd have been unconscious or worse. All the Mexicans needed to do was wait."

"Maybe they were afraid reinforcements would arrive before then," Durado suggested.

"But why would the Mexicans have been afraid?" Kline asked. "There were so many of them that a rescue column wouldn't have had a chance. If they'd set it up right and made it seem that only a couple of hundred Mexicans surrounded the hacienda, they could have lured the reinforcements into an ambush."

"So what's your point?"

"Just what I said—sometimes, battles don't need to happen."

"Like tomorrow's?" Durado asked.

Kline pointed toward the buildings. "Maybe they'll surrender."

"Or maybe they hope *we'll* surrender. Is that going to happen?"

"Of course not." Kline quoted from the Legion's Code of Honor, which all recruits were required to memorize at the start of their training. "'Never surrender your arms.'"

"And *they* won't do it, either," Durado said.

"But in the end, France was forced to leave Mexico. Camerone made no difference," Kline told him.

"Be careful. You'd better not let the colonel hear you talking this way."

"Maybe tomorrow's battle won't make a difference, either."

"Thinking isn't our business." Now it was Durado's turn to quote from the Legion's Code of Honor. "'The mission is sacred. You will see it through to the end, at any price.'"

"'At any price.'" Kline exhaled. "You're absolutely right. I'm not paid to think. Tomorrow, I'll fight as hard as you."

"God punishes us for our sins? Is that what you said earlier?" Durado asked. "The things I've seen in this war prove He doesn't exist. Otherwise, they never would have been allowed to happen."

"Unless this battle tomorrow is God's way of paying us back."

"For our sins?"

"For the things we'd give anything to forget."

"In that case, God help us." Again, the irony in Durado's voice reminded Kline of Rourke.

Kline lay under the blanket, staring across the rocky hill toward the buildings that seemed to waver in the heat. He knew that soldiers just like him watched from their own hiding places over there. With their weapons beside them, they brooded behind the city's walls, parapets, turrets, and gates, knowing that soon, probably the next morning, the battle would begin.

Kline was struck by how different things had been a year earlier. When the Germans had broken through the concrete battlements of the Maginot Line and invaded France, the only tactic that had made sense was for him and Rourke and the rest of the legionnaires to fight a retreating action, trying to slow the German advance as much as possible.

And we still might have beaten them, Kline thought, if the Germans hadn't realized the mistake they were about to make.

The risk to the invading army had been that a rush to occupy all of France would overextend their supply lines, leaving them vulnerable to devastating hit-and-run attacks by French civilians and the remainder of the French military. Without supplies, the Germans would have been helpless. To prevent that from happening, they'd developed the brilliant strategy of consolidating their forces in the northern and western parts of the country, an area that included Paris. Meanwhile, their massive threatening presence had convinced the rest of France that total occupation was only a matter of time, that it was better to capitulate and negotiate for favorable terms.

So the bastards in the south became collaborators, Kline thought.

The deal was that the southern two-fifths of France would remain free of German soldiers. Meanwhile, France would form a new government based in the community of Vichy in the central part of the country. In theory, this government was neutral to Germany, but in reality, the Vichy regime was so eager to placate the Germans that they were more than happy to hand over Jews or any other "undesirables" that the Germans wanted.

The rest of France might as well have been invaded. The result was the same, Kline thought. *Maybe they could justify collaborating if they'd made an effort to resist. But as it was, they just surrendered and acted like the enemy.*

He painfully remembered the last time he'd seen Rourke. Along with a remnant of their legionnaire unit, they'd been hiding in an abandoned French barn, waiting for nightfall when they could slip out and elude patrols by the Vichy militia.

Their radioman picked up a wireless signal that he quickly reported. "The Thirteenth Demi-Brigade shipped back from fighting in Norway."

All the men hiding in the barn sat up from the straw they lay on. The context didn't need to be explained—the Legion had been fighting on two fronts, and the Thirteenth's objective had been Norway. But like the Legion's unit on the Maginot Line, the Thirteenth had been forced to withdraw.

"They landed at Brest," the radioman continued.

The men nodded, well aware that Brest was the westernmost port in France.

"When they realized France had capitulated and that the Germans were about to occupy the port, they hurried back on the ships and headed toward England."

"So they're going to help the Allies try to retake France?" Kline asked.

"Yes," the radioman said. "But not all of them went to England."

Rourke straightened. "What do you mean?"

"Some decided to go back to headquarters in Algeria."

The legionnaires remained silent for a moment, analyzing the significance of this information. Another reason Germany had resisted invading all of France was that the move would have made enemies of Algeria and Morocco: French territories in North Africa. But by persuading France to form the Vichy government, a supposedly neutral regime that was in effect a puppet government, Germany gained indirect control of those French territories and prevented the legionnaires stationed there from helping England.

"They're going to fight *against* the Brits?" Kline asked in shock.

"It's more like they're hoping Algeria will remain neutral. That way, they'll be able to sit out the rest of the war without fighting *anybody*," the radioman explained.

"Lots of damned luck to them," someone said.

"The message came from England," the radioman continued. "From Brigadier General de Gaulle."

"Who's he?"

"I never heard of him, either," the radioman continued. "But apparently he's in charge of something called the Free French Forces, and that includes the legionnaires who went to England. He wants every French soldier to get there somehow and regroup. The fight's not over."

"Thank God, somebody's got some balls," another legionnaire said. "I guess we know which way we're going tonight. South to the coast. We'll get our hands on a boat and head toward England."

Most of the men readily agreed. They'd been born and raised in Spain, Portugal, Greece, or any number of other countries, but all were now French citizens and felt loyal to the nation they'd been fighting to protect.

Kline couldn't help noticing that some were pensively quiet, however. Evidently, the previous year of fighting made the idea of sitting out the war in Algeria appealing.

Kline also couldn't help noticing that Rourke was one of the men who remained quiet.

At dark, as the group sneaked from the barn, Kline motioned for Rourke to wait.

"I get the feeling you're not going to England with us," he said when the two of them were alone.

In the shadows, Rourke took a moment to answer. "Yes. When we reach the Mediterranean, I'll find a way across to Algeria."

"You've had enough fighting?"

"It's got nothing to do with sitting out the war. Believe me, I'm happy to fight the Germans." Rourke paused. "But I can't go to England."

"I don't understand."

"You and I never talked about our pasts, my friend." Rourke put a hand on his shoulder. "But I think you guessed a lot about mine. If I go back to England, I might end up serving next to the same British soldiers who hunted me in Ireland before I joined the Legion. Don't get me wrong. I didn't join the Legion to escape them."

"I know. You joined to do penance."

"See, we understand each other," Rourke said. "I once told you that Catholics need to tell God they're sorry for their sins and then do whatever's necessary to prove they mean it."

"I remember."

"Well, how can I keep doing penance if some bastard British Tommy recognizes me and shoots me?"

From the darkness outside the barn, a legionnaire whispered, "Kline, we need to get moving."

"I'll be there in a second," he murmured through the rickety door.

He turned to Rourke. "Take care of yourself."

"Don't worry," Rourke said, shaking hands with him. "We'll cross paths again after the war."

But Rourke had been wrong. It wasn't after the war that they would cross paths. Soon after the split in the Legion, some men going to England, others going to Algeria, the Vichy government ordered the legionnaires in Algeria to assist the German army.

By June of 1941, when the Allies fought to liberate Syria from the invaders, Kline's Legion unit was helping the British. Meanwhile, a different Legion unit, the Vichy brigade, was helping the Germans.

In the morning, Kline knew, the unthinkable would occur. Battling for Damascus, legionnaires who had trained together, bivouacked together, gotten drunk together, and fought together, would now fight each other, and unless Rourke had already died in combat, he would be one of those whom Kline would attack.

As the sun began to set, Durado returned one last time, assigned to sentry duty for the night.

The intense heat continued to weigh on them.

"Still quiet over there?" Durado asked.

"No sign of anyone. Maybe they pulled back," Kline hoped.

"I doubt it."

"Me, too. They know *we* won't pull back."

"But surely they realize they're on the wrong side," Durado said.

"Probably they're saying the same thing about us."

"What do you mean?"

"*They're* the ones fighting for France."

"For a government sucking up to the damned Germans," Durado said.

"Even so, it's the only French government there is. Do you remember what Commander Vernerey said when the Allies told him to fight the Germans in Norway?"

"If I heard, I've forgotten."

"Legionnaires fighting in snow instead of sand. He knew how crazy that was. But he didn't argue with his orders. He said, 'What is my aim? To take the port of Narvik. For the Norwegians? The phosphates? The anchovies? I haven't the slightest idea. But I have my mission, and I shall take Narvik.'"

"Yes," Durado said. "We have our mission."

"Something's moving over there," Kline said.

Durado squirmed next to him and peered between the boulders.

At a gate in the Damascus wall, a white flag appeared. Several legionnaires emerged, recognizable because each man's cap was the Legion's traditional white kepi. Unlike the shorts and short-sleeved shirts that Kline's unit wore, the uniform of the opposing legionnaires consisted of full-length sleeves and pants.

In the last of the setting sun, they formed a line against the wall, stood at attention, and formally presented arms to Kline's unit.

Kline strained to distinguish their faces, unable to tell if Rourke was among them. Even so, he had no doubt that, if he got closer, he'd be able to call each of them by his first name.

At once, he gripped the boulder on his right. Using it for leverage, he stood.

"What are you doing?" Durado asked in alarm.

But Kline wasn't the only man who stood. All along the ridge, sentry after sentry rose to his feet.

Soon Durado did, also.

Someone yelled, "Present . . . arms!"

The line of sentries imitated their brethren across the way. Kline's chest felt squeezed as he went through the ritual that ended with him holding his rifle close to him, the butt toward the ground, the barrel toward the sky.

From somewhere in Damascus, a bugle played, echoing across the valley. The song, *"Le Boudin,"* was familiar to every legionnaire, who learned it by heart at the start of his training. It dated back to the nineteenth century, when Belgium had refused to allow its citizens to join the Legion. As the pulsing melody faded to a close, a bugler on the Demi-Brigade's side took it up. Soon voices joined in, filling the valley with the normally comical lyric about blood sausage and how the Legion wouldn't share any with the Belgians because they were shitty marksmen.

"Le Boudin" was followed by another favorite from the first day of training, *"La Legion Marche."* Its energy expanded Kline's chest and made him sing so hard that he risked becoming hoarse. Even though his voice was only one of thousands on both sides of the valley, nonetheless he did his best to make Rourke hear him.

> The Legion marches toward the front.
> Singing, we are heirs to our traditions,
> One with the Legion.

The song praised Honor and Loyalty, virtues that gave the Legion strength. But Kline's voice faltered as he realized that absolute loyalty to a mission was what had brought the Legion to this moment.

When the lyrics reached their refrain, a section of it made Kline stop singing entirely.

We don't only have weapons.
The devil marches with us.

He couldn't help remembering the conversation he'd had with Rourke when they'd enlisted long ago.

" 'My name is Legion,' " Rourke had said.

" 'For we are many,' " Kline had responded. "A possessed man says that to Jesus, trying to explain how many demons are in him."

From Damascus and from this ridge, each side now repeated the song's refrain, their voices rising.

The devil marches with us.

As the sun dipped completely behind the horizon, the music sank as well, echoing faintly, descending into silence.

Enveloped by darkness, Kline stood at the bottom of the ridge, staring up at the cold glint of the emerging stars.

He left Durado and made his way to the mess tent. Although he had no appetite, he knew that he would need all his strength in the morning, so he ate the bread and bacon that was served, and drank bitter coffee. Many other men sat around him. None said a word.

Later, in the shadows of his tent, he wondered what Rourke had done that was so horrible it had made him join the Legion as his punishment. Had he set a roadside bomb intended for a British army convoy, only to see it blow apart a school bus full of children? Or had he set fire to a house occupied by an Irish family who supposedly had revealed the IRA's battle plans to the British, only to discover that he'd set the wrong house ablaze, that the family who'd burned to death was innocent? Would those things be terrible enough to make someone like Rourke hate himself? In his nightmares, did he hear the screams of the dying children, just as Kline imagined his wife sobbing over the corpse of their daughter, reaching for a razor blade to slit her wrists while Kline hid from the police because of a bank robbery in which a guard had been killed for $24.95?

Everybody ran in different directions, Kline remembered. *I never got even a dollar.*

Imagining the relentless coughing that had racked and smothered his daughter, he thought, *I should have been with them.*

He remained awake for a long time, staring at the top of the tent.

Explosions shook him from a troubled sleep, so many roaring blasts that he couldn't distinguish them. The ground, the tent, the air—everything trembled. The first shock waves slapped his ears, making them ring. But amid the persistent heavy rumbles, his ears quickly became numb, as if muffled by cotton batting. He grabbed his rifle and charged from the tent, seeing the chaos of a camp being struck by artillery shells. Powerful flashes illuminated the darkness as rocks, tents, and men disintegrated in the blasts.

Murky silhouettes of legionnaires ran desperately toward the cover of boulders, toward pits they'd dug, toward anything that would shield them from flying debris. The camp's own artillery returned fire, howitzers and tanks shuddering as they blasted shells toward Damascus.

Burning blasts erupted from the sandstone buildings over there. They and the muzzle flashes of the cannons turned the darkness into a pulsing twilight that allowed Kline to see his way toward a rock wall behind which he dived before a nearby blast sent shrapnel streaking over it.

The bombardment went on for hours. When it finally ended, the air was thick with dust and smoke. Despite the continued ringing in Kline's ears, he heard officers yelling, "*Allez! Allez!* Get on your feet, you lazy bastards! Attack!"

Kline came to his feet, the dust so thick that he sensed more than saw the men around him doing the same.

He and the others scurried up the ridge. Sometimes they slipped on loose stones, but that was the only thing that held them back. Kline sensed their determination as they reached the top and increased speed, charging past boulders toward the wall.

The dust still hovered, giving them shelter, but soon it thinned, and the moment they emerged from it, visible now, running toward the wall, the legionnaires opposing them opened fire. Kline felt a man beside him lurch back. A man ahead of him dropped.

But Kline kept charging, shooting toward movement on the parapets. At once, a portion of the wall blew apart from a cannon shell. A second explosion widened the opening.

Kline paused only long enough to yank the pin from a grenade and hurl the grenade as far as he could through the gap in the wall. Other legionnaires did the same, diving to the ground the same as Kline did, waiting for the multiple blasts to clear their way.

He scrambled over the rubble and entered a courtyard. Among stone buildings, narrow alleys led in various directions. A bullet struck near him, throwing up chunks of sandstone. He whirled toward a window and fired, not knowing if he hit anyone before he charged on. Then he reached one of the alleys and aimed along it. Joined by other legionnaires, he moved slowly now, prepared to fire at any target.

Shots seemed to ring out everywhere. Explosions rumbled as Kline pressed forward, smelling gunpowder and hearing screams. The buildings were no taller than three stories. Smoke drifted over them, some of it settling into the alley, but he didn't allow it to distract him. The doors and windows ahead were all he cared about.

A man next to him screamed and fell. Kline fired toward the ground-floor window from which the shot had come, and this time, he saw blood fly. A legionnaire near him hurled a grenade through the same window, and the moment after it exploded, they crashed through a doorway, firing.

Two soldiers lay dead on the floor. Their white legionnaire's caps were spattered with blood. Their uniforms had the long sleeves and full-length pants of the opposing side. Kline recognized both of them. Rinaldo and Stavros. He'd trained with them, marched with them, shared tents with them, and sung with them at breakfast in the mess hall at Sidi-bel-Abbes.

Stairs led upward. From above, Kline heard shots. Aiming, he and the other legionnaire checked a neighboring room, then approached the steps. As they climbed, a quick glance toward his companion showed Kline that he was again paired with Durado. The Spaniard's normally tan complexion was now sallow.

Neither spoke as they stalked higher.

Above, the shots persisted, presumably directed toward the alley they'd left or else toward the alley on the opposite side of the building. Perhaps the numerous explosions in the area had prevented the shooter from realizing that this building had been hit by a grenade. Or perhaps the shooter wasn't alone. Perhaps he continued firing while another soldier watched the stairs, hoping to draw Kline and Durado into a trap.

Sweat trickled down Kline's face. Nearing the top, he armed another grenade and threw it into a room. Immediately, he and Durado ducked down the stairs, protecting themselves from the force of the blast. They straightened and charged the rest of the way up, shooting as they entered the room.

No one was there. A neighboring room was deserted, also. At the last moment, the shooter must have hurried the rest of the way up the stairs, taking refuge on the third and final floor.

Kline and Durado took turns replacing the magazines on their rifles. Again they crept up, and this time, it was Durado who threw the grenade. An instant after the explosion, they ran to the top, but amid the smoke of the explosion, they still didn't find anyone.

In the far corner, a ladder led to an open hatch in the roof.

Durado's voice was stark. "I'm not going up there."

Kline understood. Their quarry was probably lying on the roof, aiming toward the hatch, ready to blow off the head of anyone who showed himself through the small opening. There was no way to know which way to throw a grenade to try to clear the roof.

"Maybe he ran across to another building," Kline said.

"And maybe not. I won't climb up there to find out."

"Right. To hell with him," Kline said. He peered through an open window and saw a sniper in a window across from him. The sniper wore a white legionnaire's cap. His sleeves were long. As the man aimed down toward an alley, Kline shot him before he had the chance to pull the trigger.

Durado pointed. "Snipers all along the roofs!"

Kline worked the bolt on his rifle and fired through the window. Worked the bolt and fired. The movement became automatic. Hearing Durado do the same through an opposite window, he loaded a fresh magazine and continued shooting in a frenzy. His uniform was drenched with sweat. Struck by his bullets, white-capped men with long-sleeved shirts slumped on the roofs or else toppled into the alleys.

An explosion shoved Kline forward, almost propelling him through the window. He managed to twist sideways and slam against the window's frame before he would have gone through. His back stung, and his shirt felt more soaked, but this time, he knew it was from blood.

Trying to recover from the shock wave, he spun toward the room and realized that the explosion had come from the far corner. The ladder was in pieces. The man on the roof had dropped a grenade through the hatch.

"Durado!"

There wasn't any point in running to try to help him. Durado had been shooting through a window near the ladder. The grenade had exploded next to him, tearing him open. His blood was everywhere. His gaping intestines lay around him. Already, the flies settled on him.

Kline aimed toward the ceiling's open hatch. Abruptly, numerous bullets sprayed through the window next to him. The snipers across from him had realized the direction from which his shots had come. If the wall hadn't been made of thick sandstone, their bullets would have come through and killed him. Even so, the wall would eventually disintegrate from the unrelenting barrage. He couldn't stay in the room much longer.

When another grenade dropped through the hatch, Kline dived toward the stairs. The impact made him wince as he rolled down, feeling the edges of the steps against his bleeding back. The explosion roared behind him. He groaned when he hit the bottom, but he kept rolling.

He deliberately made loud noises, striking his boots hard as he clattered down the final section of the stairs. At the bottom, he fired once, hoping to give the impression that he shot at someone before he left the building. Then he silently crept up to the middle floor and hid in the adjacent room.

The most difficult part about standing still and waiting was trying to control the sound of his breathing. His chest heaved. He was sure that the strident sound of air going through his nostrils would give him away. He worked desperately to breathe less fast, but that only increased the urgency in his lungs. His heart seemed about to explode.

A minute passed.

Two.

Blood trickled down Kline's injured back. Outside, the explosions and shots continued.

I'm wasting my time, Kline thought. *I ought to be outside, helping.*

The moment he started to leave, he heard a shot from the floor above him, and smiled. The man on the roof had finally decided that the building was clear. He'd jumped down to continue shooting from the cover of a window.

Kline emerged from the room. Hearing another shot above him, he eased up the stairs. He paused, waiting for another shot and the sound of the rifle's bolt being pulled back. Those noises concealed his own sounds as he came to the top of the stairs and fired, hitting the man in the back.

The legionnaire, who wore long pants, slumped forward, his head on the windowsill. Kline recognized the back of his brawny neck. His name was Arick. He was a German, who'd been part of Kline's group of volunteers back in 1934. Outside, other Germans fought each other, some for the Vichy Legion, some for the Free French Legion. But where a legionnaire had been born and raised made no difference.

The Legion Is Our Only Country, Kline thought.

God help us.

He turned to race down the stairs and reenter the battle. He reached the second floor. He hurried to the first at the same moment a man left the chaos outside, rushing into the demolished room. He wore the Legion's white kepi. Long pants.

He gaped at Kline.

Kline gaped, as well.

The man was even thinner than when Kline had last seen him, his freckles almost hidden by the dust of battle.

"Rourke."

The name barely escaped Kline's mouth before he shot Rourke in the chest. The pressure of his finger on the trigger was automatic, the result of countless drills in which self-preservation preceded thought.

Rourke staggered back, hit a wall, and slid down, leaving a streak of blood. He squinted at Kline, as if trying to focus his dimming eyes.

He trembled and lay still.

"Rourke," Kline said again.

He went to the open doorway, fired at an opposing legionnaire, and hurried into the tumult of the alley, hoping to die.

The battle persisted into the next day. By sunset, the Vichy Legion had been routed. Damascus had fallen to the Allies.

Exhausted, his back crusted with scabs, Kline lay with other legionnaires in the rubble of a building. It was difficult to find a comfortable position among the debris. They licked the last drops of water from the brims of their canteens. They chewed the last of the stale biscuits in their rations.

As the sun set and the cold stars appeared, Kline peered up at the vastness. He was puzzled by the casualty figures that had been reported to his group of men. On his side, only 21 legionnaires had been killed and 47 wounded. But of the opposing legionnaires, 128 had been killed while 728 had been wounded.

The contrast was so great that Kline had difficulty making sense of it.

They had plenty of time to secure their defenses within the city, he thought. *They had buildings to shield them from our bullets while we attacked across open ground. We were easy targets. They should have been able to stop us from reaching the walls.*

An unnerving thought squirmed through his mind. *Did they hold back? Did they shoot to miss? Did they hope to appear to fight when all they wanted was for the battle to end as soon as their pride would allow?*

Kline recalled speaking with Durado about whether the men in the Vichy Legion knew they were on the wrong side, the aggressor's side, the invader's side.

The snipers whom Kline had seen in windows and on rooftops—had they been merely firing but not aiming? Had they been looking for an honorable way to *lose* the fight?

Kline remembered turning in surprise as Rourke had hurried through the doorway into the wreckage of the room. Kline had shot him reflexively. Searching his memory, Kline sought to focus on Rourke's rifle. Had Rourke been raising it, about to shoot? Or had Rourke been about to lower it and greet his friend?

There was no way to tell. Everything had happened too quickly.

I did what I was trained to do, Kline thought. *The next instant, Rourke might have shot* me.

But then again, he might not *have.*

Would our friendship have meant more to him than his duty as a legionnaire? Kline wondered. *Or would Rourke's training have made him pull the trigger?*

Peering up toward the sky, Kline noticed that there were even more stars. Their glint was colder—bitterly so—as a new, more unnerving thought took possession of him. He remembered the many times that he and Rourke had talked about salvation.

"What do Baptists believe?" Rourke had asked.

"God punishes us for our sins," Kline had answered.

Kline now suspected that manipulating him into killing his friend was another way for God to punish him.

"What do *Catholics* believe about being saved?" Kline had asked.

The former altar boy had replied, "We tell God we're sorry for our sins and do penance to prove we mean it."

Penance.

Thinking of his dead wife and daughter, thinking of the dead bank guard, thinking of Rourke, he murmured, his voice breaking, "I'm sorry."

Robert Silverberg

Soldiers in every age have learned that the military's unofficial motto is "Hurry up and wait." But suppose all you ever did was wait? And wait. And *wait* . . .

Robert Silverberg is one of the most famous SF writers of modern times, with dozens of novels, anthologies, and collections to his credit. As both writer and editor (he was editor of the original anthology series *New Dimensions,* perhaps the most acclaimed anthology series of its era), Silverberg was one of the most influential figures of the Post–New Wave era of the '70s, and continues to be at the forefront of the field to this very day, having won a total of five Nebula Awards and four Hugo Awards, plus SFWA's prestigious Grandmaster Award.

His novels include the acclaimed *Dying Inside, Lord Valentine's Castle, The Book of Skulls, Downward to the Earth, Tower of Glass, Son of Man, Nightwings, The World Inside, Born with the Dead, Shadrah in the Furnace, Thorns, Up the Line, The Man in the Maze, Tom O' Bedlam, Star of Gypsies, At Winter's End, The Face of the Waters, Kingdoms of the Wall, Hot Sky at Midnight, The Alien Years, Lord Prestimion, The Mountains of Majipoor,* two novel-length expansions of famous Isaac Asimov stories, *Nightfall* and *The Ugly Little Boy, The Longest Way Home,* and the mosaic novel *Roma Eterna.* His collections include *Unfamiliar Territory, Capricorn Games, Majipoor Chronicles, The Best of Robert Silverberg, The Conglomeroid Cocktail Party, Beyond the Safe Zone,* and four massive retrospective collections, *Secret Sharers* (in two volumes), *To the Dark Star* (in two volumes), *Something Wild Is Loose: The Collected Stories, Phases of the Moon,* and a collection of early work, *In the Beginning.* His reprint anthologies are far too numerous to list here but include *The Science Fiction Hall of Fame, Volume One,* and the distinguished Alpha series, among dozens of others. Coming up, as editor, is *The Science Fiction Hall of Fame, Volume Two B.* He lives with his wife, writer Karen Haber, in Oakland, California.

Defenders of the Frontier

Seeker has returned to the fort looking flushed and exhilarated. "I was right," he announces. "There is one of them hiding quite close by. I was certain of it, and now I know where he is. I can definitely feel directionality this time."

Stablemaster, skeptical as always, lifts one eyebrow. "You were wrong the last time. You're always too eager these days to find them out there."

Seeker merely shrugs. "There can be no doubt," he says.

For three weeks now, Seeker has been searching for an enemy spy—or straggler, or renegade, or whatever he may be—that he believes is camped in the vicinity of the fort. He has gone up to this hilltop and that one, to this watchtower and that, making his solitary vigil, casting forth his mind's net in that mysterious way of his that none of us can begin to fathom. And each time he has come back convinced that he feels enemy emanations, but he has never achieved a strong enough sense of directionality to warrant our sending out a search party. This time he has the look of conviction about him. Seeker is a small, flimsy sort of man, as his kind often tends to be, and much of the time in recent months he has worn the slump-shouldered look of dejection and disappointment. His trade is in finding enemies for us to kill. Enemies have been few and far between of late. But now he is plainly elated. There is an aura of triumph about him, of vindication.

Captain comes into the room. Instantly he sizes up the situation. "What have we here?" he says brusquely. "Have you sniffed out something at last, Seeker?"

"Come. I'll show you."

He leads us all out onto the flat roof adjacent to our barracks. To the right and left, the huge turreted masses of the eastern and western redoubts, now unoccupied, rise above us like vast pillars, and before us lies the great central courtyard, with the massive wall of tawny brick that guards us on the north beyond it. The fort is immense, an enormous sprawling edifice designed to hold ten thousand men. I remember very clearly the gigantic effort we expended in the building of it, twenty years before. Today just eleven occupants remain, and we rattle about it like tiny pebbles in a colossal jug.

Seeker gestures outward, into the gritty yellow wasteland that stretches before us like an endless ocean on the far side of the wall. That flat plain of twisted useless shrubs marks the one gap in the line of precipitous cliffs that forms the border here between Imperial territory and the enemy lands. It has been our task these twenty years past—we were born to it; it is an obligation of our caste—to guard that gap against the eventual incursion of the enemy army. For two full decades we have inhabited these lonely lands. We have fortified that gap, we have patrolled it, we have dedicated our lives to guarding it. In the old days, entire brigades of enemy troops would attempt to breach our line, appearing suddenly like clouds of angry insects out of the dusty plain, and with great loss of life on both sides we would drive them back. Now things are quieter on this frontier, very much quieter indeed, but we are still here, watching for and intercepting the occasional spies that periodically attempt to slip past our defenses.

"There," says Seeker. "Do you see those three little humps over to the northeast? He's dug in not very far behind them. I know he is. I can feel him the way you'd feel a boil on the back of your neck."

"Just one man?" Captain asks.

"One. Only one."

Weaponsmaster says, "What would one man hope to accomplish? Do you think he expects to come tiptoeing into the fort and kill us one by one?"

"There's no need for us to try to understand them," Sergeant says. "Our job is to find them and kill them. We can leave understanding them to the wiser heads back home."

"Ah," says Armorer sardonically. "Back home, yes. Wiser heads."

Captain has walked to the rim of the roof and stands there with his back to us, clutching the rail and leaning forward into the dry, crisp wind that eternally blows across our courtyard. A sphere of impenetrable chilly silence seems to surround him. Captain has always been an enigmatic man, solitary and brooding, but he has become stranger than ever since the death of Colonel, three years past, left him the ranking officer of the fort. No one knows his mind now, and no one dares to attempt any sort of intimacy with it.

"Very well," he says, after an interval that has become intolerably long. "A four-man search party: Sergeant to lead, accompanied by Seeker, Provisioner, and Surveyor. Set out in the morning. Take three days' food. Search, find, and kill."

It has been eleven weeks since the last successful search mission. That one ended in the killing of three enemies, but since then, despite Seeker's constant efforts, there have been no signs of any hostile presence in our territory. Once, six or seven weeks back, Seeker managed to convince himself that he felt emanations coming from a site along the river, a strange place for an enemy to have settled because it was well within our defense perimeter, and a five-man party led by Stablemaster hastened out to look. But they found no one there except a little band of the Fisherfolk, who swore that they had seen nothing unusual thereabouts, and the fisherfolk do not lie. Upon their return, Seeker himself had to admit that he no longer felt the emanations and that he was now none too certain he had felt any in the first place.

There is substantial feeling among us that we have outlived our mission here, that few if any enemies still occupy the territory north of the gap, that quite possibly the war has long since been over. Sergeant, Quartermaster, Weaponsmaster, and Armorer are the chief proponents of this belief. They note that we have heard nothing whatsoever from the capital in years—no messengers have come, let alone reinforcements or fresh supplies—and that we have had no sign from the enemy, either, that any significant force of them is gathered anywhere nearby. Once, long ago, war seemed imminent, and indeed real battles often took place. But it has been terribly quiet here for a long time. There has been nothing like a real battle for six years, only a few infrequent skirmishes with small enemy platoons, and during the past two years we have detected just a few isolated outliers, usually no more than two or three men at a time, whom we catch relatively easily as they try to infiltrate our territory. Armorer insists that they are not spies but stragglers, the last remnants of whatever enemy force once occupied the region to our north, who have been driven by hunger or loneliness or who knows what other compulsion to take up positions close to our fort. He argues that in the twenty years we have been here, our own numbers have dwindled from ten thousand men to a mere eleven, at first by losses in battle but later by the attrition of age and ill-health, and he thinks it is reasonable that the same dwindling has occurred on the other side of the border, so that we few defenders now confront an enemy that may be even fewer in number than ourselves.

I myself see much to concur with in Armorer's position. I think it might very well be the case that we are a lost platoon, that the war is over and the Empire has forgotten us, and that there is no purpose at all in our continued vigilance. But if the Empire has forgotten us, who can give the order that withdraws us from our post? That is a decision that only Captain can make, and Captain has not given us the slightest impression of where he stands on the issue. And so we remain, and may remain to the end of our days. What folly that would be, says Armorer, to languish out here forever defending this forlorn frontier country against invaders that no longer choose to invade! And I half agree with him, but only half. I would not want to spend such time as remains to me working at a fool's task; but equally I do not wish to be guilty of dereliction of duty, after having served so long and so honorably on this frontier. Thus I am of two minds on the issue.

There is, of course, the opposite theory that holds that the enemy is simply biding its time, waiting for us to abandon the fort, after which a great army will come pouring through the gap at long last and strike at the Empire from one of its most vulnerable sides. Engineer and Signalman are the most vocal proponents of this viewpoint. They think it would be an act of profound treason to withdraw, the negation of all that we have dedicated our lives to, and they become irate when the idea is merely suggested. When they propound this position, I find it hard to disagree.

Seeker is the one who works hardest to keep our mission alive, constantly striving to pick up threatening emanations. That has been his life's work, after all. He knows no other vocation, that sad little man. So day by day Seeker climbs his hilltops and haunts his watchtowers and uses his one gift to detect the presence of hostile minds, and now and then he returns and sounds the alarm, and off we go on yet another search foray. More often than not, they prove to be futile, nowadays: either Seeker's powers are failing or he is excessively anxious to interpret his inputs as the mental output from nearby enemies.

I confess I feel a certain excitement at being part of this latest search party. Our days are spent in such terrible empty routine, normally. We tend our little vegetable patch, we look after our animals, we fish and hunt, we do our regular maintenance jobs, we read the same few books over and again, we have the same conversations, chiefly reminiscing about the time when there were more than eleven of us here, recalling as well as we can the robust and earthy characters who once dwelled among us but are long since gone to dust. Tonight, therefore, I feel a quickening of the pulse. I pack my gear for the morning, I eat my dinner with unusual gusto, I couple passionately with my little Fisherfolk companion. Each of us, all but Seeker, who seems to know no needs of that sort, has taken a female companion from among the band of simple people who live along our one feeble river. Even Captain takes one sometimes into his bed, I understand, although unlike the rest of us, he has no regular woman. Mine is called Wendrit. She is a pale and slender creature, surprisingly skillful in the arts of love. The Fisherfolk are not quite human—we and they are unable to conceive children together, for example—but they are close enough to human to serve most purposes, and they are pleasant, unassuming, uncomplaining companions. So I embrace Wendrit vigorously this night, and in the dawn the four of us gather, Sergeant, Provisioner, Seeker, and I, by the northern portcullis.

It is a bright, clear morning, the sun a hard, sharp-edged disk in the eastern sky. The sun is the only thing that comes to us from the Empire, visiting us each day after it has done its work back there, uncountable thousands of miles to the east. Probably the capital is already in darkness by now, just as we are beginning our day. The world is so large, after all, and we are so very far from home.

Once there would have been trumpeters to celebrate our departure as we rode through the portcullis, hurling a brassy fanfare for us into the quiet air. But the last of our trumpeters died years ago, and though we still have the instruments, none of us knows how to play them. I tried once, and made a harsh squeaking sound like the grinding of metal against metal, nothing more. So the only sound we hear as we ride out into the desert is the soft steady thudding of our mounts' hooves against the brittle sandy soil.

In truth, this is the bleakest of places, but we are used to it. I still have memories from my childhood of the floral splendor of the capital, great trees thick with juicy leaves, and shrubs clad in clusters of flowers, red and yellow and orange and purple, and the dense green lawns of the grand boulevards. But I have grown accustomed to the desert, which has become the norm for me, and such lush abundance as I remember out of my earlier life strikes me now as discomfortingly vulgar and excessive, a wasteful riot of energy and resources. All that we have here in the plain that runs out to the north between the wall of hills is dry yellow soil sparkling with the doleful sparkle of overabundant quartz, small gnarled shrubs and equally gnarled miniature trees, and occasional tussocks of tough, sharp-edged grass. On the south side of the fort the land is not quite so harsh, for our little river runs past us there, a weak strand of some much mightier one that must pour out of one of the big lakes in the center of the continent. Our river must be looking for the sea, as rivers do, but of course we are nowhere near the sea, and doubtless it exhausts itself in some distant reach of the desert. But as it passes our outpost, it brings greenery to its flanks, and some actual trees, and enough fish to support the tribe of primitive folk who are our only companions here.

Our route lies to the northeast, toward those three rounded hillocks behind which, so Seeker staunchly asserts, we will find the campsite of our solitary enemy. The little hills had seemed close enough when we viewed them from the barracks roof, but that was only an illusion, and we ride all day without visibly diminishing the span between them and us. It is a difficult trek. The ground, which is merely pebbly close by the fort, becomes rocky and hard to traverse farther out, and our steeds pick their way with care, heedful of their fragile legs. But this is familiar territory for us. Everywhere we see traces of hoofprints or tire tracks, five years old, ten, even twenty, the scars of ancient forays, the debris of half-forgotten battles of a decade and more ago. Rain comes perhaps twice a year here at best. Make a mark on the desert floor and it remains forever.

We camp as the first lengthening of the shadows begins, gather some scrubby wood for our fire, pitch our tent. There is not much in the way of conversation. Sergeant is a crude, inarticulate man at best; Seeker is too tense and fretful to be pleasant company; Provisioner, who has grown burly and red-faced with the years, can be jovial enough after a drink or two, but he seems uncharacteristically moody and aloof tonight. So I am left to my own resources, and once we have finished our meal, I walk out a short way into the night and stare, as I often do, at the glittering array of stars in this western sky of ours, wondering, as ever, whether each has its own collection of worlds, and whether those worlds are peopled, and what sort of lives the peoples of those worlds might lead. It is a perverse sort of amusement, I suppose: I who have spent half my life guarding a grim brick fort in this parched isolated outpost stare at the night sky and imagine the gleaming palaces and fragrant gardens of faraway worlds.

We rise early, make a simple breakfast, ride on through a cutting wind toward those three far-off hills. This morning, though, the perspective changes quickly: suddenly the hills are much closer, and then they are upon us, and Seeker, excited now, guides us toward the pass between the southern-most hill and its neighbor. "I feel him just beyond!" he cries. For Seeker, the sense that he calls directionality is like a compass, pointing the way toward our foes. "Come! This is the way! Hurry! Hurry!"

Nor has he led us wrongly this time. On the far side of the southernmost hill someone has built a little lean-to of twisted branches covered with a heaping of grass, no simple project in these stony ungenerous wastes. We draw our weapons and take up positions surrounding it, and Sergeant goes up to it and says, "You! Come out of there, and keep your hands in the air!"

There is a sound of stirring from within. In a moment or two a man emerges.

He has the classic enemy physiognomy: a short, stumpy body, sallow waxen skin, and heavy features with jutting cheekbones and icy blue eyes. At the sight of those eyes I feel an involuntary surge of anger, even hatred, for we of the Empire are a brown-eyed people and I have trained myself through many years to feel nothing but hostility for those whose eyes are blue.

But these are not threatening eyes. Obviously the man had been asleep, and he is still making the journey back into wakefulness as he comes forth from his shelter, blinking, shaking his head. He is trembling, too. He is one man and we are four, and we have weapons drawn and he is unarmed, and he has been taken by surprise. It is an unfortunate way to start one's day. I am amazed to find my anger giving way to something like pity.

He is given little time to comprehend the gravity of his situation. "Bastard!" Sergeant says, and takes three strides forward. Swiftly he thrusts his knife into the man's belly, withdraws it, strikes again, again.

The blue eyes go wide with shock. I am shocked myself, in a different way, and the sudden cruel attack leaves me gasping with amazement. The stricken enemy staggers, clutches at his abdomen as though trying to hold back the torrent of blood, takes three or four tottering steps, and falls in a series of folding ripples. There is a convulsion or two, and then he is still, lying face downward.

Sergeant kicks the entrance of the shelter open and peers within. "See if there's anything useful in there," he tells us.

Still astounded, I say, "Why did you kill him so quickly?"

"We came here to kill him."

"Perhaps. But he was unarmed. He probably would have given himself up peacefully."

"We came here to kill him," Sergeant says again.

"We might have interrogated him first, at least. That's the usual procedure, isn't it? Perhaps there are others of his kind somewhere close at hand."

"If there were any more of them around here," Sergeant says scornfully, "Seeker would have told us, wouldn't he have? Wouldn't he have, Surveyor?"

There is more that I would like to say, about how it might have been useful or at any rate interesting to discover why this man had chosen to make this risky pilgrimage to the edge of our territory. But there is no point in continuing the discussion, because Sergeant is too stupid to care what I have to say, and the man is already dead, besides.

We knock the shelter apart and search it. Nothing much there: a few tools and weapons, a copper-plated religious emblem of the kind that our enemies worship, a portrait of a flat-faced blue-eyed woman who is, I suppose, the enemy's wife or mother. It does not seem like the equipment of a spy. Even to an old soldier like me, it is all very sad. He was a man like us, enemy though he was, and he died far from home. Yes, it has long been our task to kill these people before they can kill us. Certainly I have killed more than a few of them myself. But dying in battle is one thing; being slaughtered like a pig while still half-asleep is something else again. Especially if your only purpose had been to surrender. Why else had this solitary man, this lonely and probably desperate man, crossed this unrelenting desert, if not to give himself up to us at the fort?

I am softening with age, I suppose. Sergeant is right that it was our assignment to kill him: Captain had given us that order in the most explicit way. Bringing him back with us had never been part of the plan. We have no way of keeping prisoners at the fort. We have little enough food for ourselves, and guarding him would have posed a problem. He had had to die; his life was forfeit from the moment he ventured within the zone bordering on the fort. That he might have been lonely or desperate, that he had suffered in crossing this terrible desert and perhaps had hoped to win shelter at our fort, that he had had a wife or perhaps a mother whom he loved, all of that was irrelevant. It did not come as news to me that our enemies are human beings not all that different from us except in the color of their eyes and the texture of their skins. They are, nevertheless, our enemies. Long ago they set their hands against us in warfare, and until the day arrives when they put aside their dream of destroying what we of the Empire have built for ourselves, it is the duty of people like us to slay men like him. Sergeant had not been kind or gentle about it. But there is no kind or gentle way, really, to kill.

The days that followed were extremely quiet ones. Without so much as a discussion of what had taken place in the desert, we fell back into our routines: clean and polish this and that, repair whatever needs repair and still can be repaired, take our turns working in the fields alongside the river, wade in that shallow stream in quest of water-pigs for our table, tend the vats where we store the mash that becomes our beer, and so on, so forth, day in, day out. Of course I read a good deal, also. I have ever been a man for reading.

We have nineteen books; all the others have been read to pieces, or their bindings have fallen apart in the dry air, or the volumes have simply been misplaced somewhere about the fort and never recovered. I have read all nineteen again and again, even though five of them are technical manuals covering areas that never were part of my skills and which are irrelevant now anyway. (There is no point in knowing how to repair our vehicles when the last of our fuel supply was exhausted five years ago.) One of my favorite books is *The Saga of the Kings*, which I have known since childhood, the familiar account, probably wholly mythical, of the Empire's early history, the great charismatic leaders who built it, their heroic deeds, their inordinately long lifespans. There is a religious text, too, that I value, though I have grave doubts about the existence of the gods. But for me the choice volume of our library is the one called *The Register of Strange Things Beyond the Ranges*, a thousand-year-old account of the natural wonders to be found in the outer reaches of the Empire's great expanse. Only half the book remains to us now—perhaps one of my comrades ripped pages out to use as kindling, once upon a time—but I cherish that half, and read it constantly, even though I know it virtually by heart by this time.

Wendrit likes me to read to her. How much of what she hears she is capable of understanding, I have no idea: she is a simple soul, as all her people are. But I love the way she turns her big violet-hued eyes toward me as I read, and sits in total attention.

I read to her of the Gate of Ghosts, telling her of the customs shed there that spectral phantoms guard: "Ten men go out; nine men return." I read to her of the Stones of Shao, two flat-sided slabs flanking a main highway that on a certain day every ten years would come crashing together, crushing any wayfarers who happened to be passing through just then, and of the bronze Pillars of King Mai, which hold the two stones by an incantation that forbids them ever to move again. I read to her of the Mountain of a Thousand Eyes, the granite face of which is pockmarked with glossy onyx boulders that gleam down upon passersby like stern black eyes. I tell her of the Forest of Cinnamon, and of the Grotto of Dreams, and of the Place of Galloping Clouds. Were such places real, or simply the fantasies of some ancient spinner of tall tales? How would I know, I who spent my childhood and youth at the capital, and have passed the rest of my years here at this remote desert fort, where there is nothing to be seen but sandy yellow soil, and twisted shrubs, and little scuttering scorpions that run before our feet? But the strange places described in *The Register of Strange Things Beyond the Ranges* have grown more real to me in these latter days than the capital itself, which has become in my mind a mere handful of vague and fragmentary impressions. So I read with conviction, and Wendrit listens in awe, and when I weary of the wonders of the *Register*, I put it aside and take her hand and lead her to my bed, and caress her soft pale-green skin and kiss the tips of her small round breasts, and so we pass another night.

In those quiet days that followed our foray, I thought often of the man Sergeant had killed. In the days when we fought battles here, I killed without compunction, five, ten, twenty men at a time, not exactly taking pleasure in it, but certainly feeling no guilt. But the killing in those days was done at a decent distance, with rifles or heavy guns, for we still had ammunition then and our rifles and guns were still in good repair. It was necessary now in our forays against the occasional spies who approached the fort to kill with spears or knives, and to kill at close range feels less like a deed of warfare to me and more like murder.

My mind went back easily to those battles of yesteryear: the sound of the sentry's alarm, the first view of the dark line of enemy troops on the horizon, the rush to gather our weapons and start our vehicles. And out we would race through the portcullis to repel the invaders, rushing to take up our primary defensive formation, then advancing in even ranks that filled the entire gap in the hills, so that when the enemy entered that deadly funnel we could fall upon them and slaughter them. It was the same thing every time. They came; we responded; they perished. How far they must have traveled to meet their dismal deaths in our dreary desert! None of us had any real idea how far away the country of the enemy actually was, but we knew it had to be a great distance to the north and west, just as our own country is a great distance to the south and east. The frontier that our own outpost defends lies on the midpoint between one desert and another. Behind us is the almost infinite terrain of sparse settlements that eventually culminates in the glorious cities of the Empire. Before us are equally interminable wastes that give way, eventually, to the enemy home-land itself. For one nation to attack the other, it must send its armies far across an uncharted and unfriendly nothingness. Which our enemy was willing to do, the gods only knew why, and again and again their armies came, and again and again we destroyed them in the fine frenzy of battle. That was a long time ago. We were not much more than boys then. But finally the marching armies came no more, and the only enemies we had to deal with were those few infrequent spies or perhaps stragglers whom Seeker pinpointed for us, and whom we went out and slew at close range with our knives and spears, looking into their frosty blue eyes as we robbed them of their lives.

Seeker is in a bad way. He can go from one day to the next without saying a word. He still heads up to his watchtowers almost every morning, but he returns from his vigils in a black cloak of gloom and moves through our midst in complete silence. We know better than to approach him at such times, because, though he is a man of no great size and strength, he can break out in savage fury sometimes when his depressions are intruded upon. So we let him be; but as the days pass and his mood grows ever darker, we fear some sort of explosion.

One afternoon I saw him speaking with Captain out on the rooftop terrace. It appeared that Captain had initiated the conversation, and that Seeker was answering Captain's questions with the greatest reluctance, staring down at his boots as he spoke. But then Captain said something that caused Seeker to react with surprising animation, looking up, gesticulating. Captain shook his head. Seeker pounded his fists together. Captain made a gesture of dismissal and walked away.

What they were saying to each other was beyond all guessing. And beyond all asking, too, for if anyone is more opaque than Seeker, it is Captain, and while it is at least possible at certain times to ask Seeker what is on his mind, making such an inquiry of Captain is inconceivable.

In recent days, Seeker has taken to drinking with us after dinner. That is a new thing for him. He has always disliked drinking. He says he despises the stuff we make that we call beer and wine and brandy. That is reasonable enough, because we make our beer from the niggardly sour grain of a weed that grows by the river, and we wrest our thin wine and our rough brandy from the bitter gray fruits of a different weed, and they are pitiful products indeed to anyone who remembers the foaming beers of the capital and the sweet vintages of our finest wine-producing districts. But we have long since exhausted the supplies of such things that we brought with us, and, of course, no replenishments from home ever come, and, since in this somber landscape there is comfort to be had from drinking, we drink what we can make. Not Seeker, no. Not until this week.

Now he drinks, though, showing no sign of pleasure, but often extending his glass for another round. And at last one night when he has come back with his glass more than once, he breaks his long silence.

"They are all gone," he says, in a voice like the tolling of a cracked bell.

"Who are?" Provisioner asks. "The scorpions? I saw three scorpions only yesterday." Provisioner is well along in his cups, as usual. His reddened, jowly face creases in a broad toothy smile, as if he has uttered the cleverest of witticisms.

"The enemy," says Seeker. "The one we killed—he was the last one. There's nobody left. Do you know how empty I feel, going up to the towers to listen, and hearing nothing? As if I've been hollowed out inside. Can you understand what sort of feeling that is? Can you? No, of course you can't. What would any of you know?" He stares at us in agony. "The silence . . . the silence . . ."

Nobody seems to know how quite to respond to that, so we say nothing. And Seeker helps himself to yet another jigger of brandy, and full measure at that. This is alarming. The sight of Seeker drinking like this is as strange as the sight of a torrential downpour of rain would be.

Engineer, who is probably the calmest and most reasonable of us, says, "Ah, man, can you not be a bit patient? I know you want to do your task. But more of them will come. Sooner or later, there'll be another, and another after that. Two weeks, three, six, who knows? But they'll come. You've been through spells like this before."

"No. This is different," says Seeker sullenly. "But what would you know?"

"Easy," Engineer says, laying his strong hand across the back of Seeker's frail wrist. "Go easy, man. What do you mean, 'this is different'?"

Carefully, making a visible effort at self-control, Seeker says, "All the other times when we've gone several weeks between incursions, I've always felt a low inner hum, a kind of subliminal static, a barely perceptible mental pressure, that tells me there are at least a few enemies out there somewhere, a hundred miles away, five hundred, a thousand. It's just a kind of quiet buzz. It doesn't give me any directionality. But it's there, and sooner or later the signal becomes stronger, and then I know that a couple of them are getting close to us, and then I get directionality and I can lead us to them, and we go out and kill them. It's been that way for years, ever since the real battles stopped. But now I don't get anything. Not a thing. It's absolutely silent in my head. Which means that either I've lost my power entirely, or else there aren't any enemies left within a thousand miles or more."

"And which is it that you think is so?"

Seeker scans us all with a haggard look. "That there are no enemies out there anymore. Which means that it is pointless to remain here. We should pack up, go home, make some sort of new lives for ourselves within the Empire itself. And yet we have to stay, in case they come. I must stay, because this is the only task that I know how to perform. What sort of new life could I make for myself back there? I never had a life. This is my life. So my choice is to stay here to no purpose, performing a task that does not need to be performed any longer, or to return home to no existence. Do you see my predicament?" He is shivering. He reaches for the brandy, pours yet another drink with a trembling hand, hastily downs it, coughs, shudders, lets his head drop to the tabletop. We can hear him sobbing.

That night marks the beginning of the debate among us. Seeker's breakdown has brought into the open something that has been on my own mind for some weeks now, and which Armorer, Weaponsmaster, Quartermaster, and even dull-witted Sergeant have been pondering also, each in his own very different way.

The fact is unanswerable that the frequency of enemy incursions has lessened greatly in the past two years, and when they do come, every five or six or ten weeks apart, they no longer come in bands of a dozen or so, but in twos or threes. This last man whom Sergeant slew by the three little hills had come alone. Armorer has voiced quite openly his notion that just as our own numbers have dwindled to next to nothing over the years, the enemy confronting us in this desert must have suffered great attrition, too, and like us, has had no reinforcement from the home country, so that only a handful of our foes remain—or, perhaps, as Seeker now believes, none at all. If that is true, says Armorer, who is a wry and practical man, why do we not close up shop and seek some new occupation for ourselves in some happier region of the Empire?

Sergeant, who loves the excitement of warfare, for whom combat is not an ugly necessity but an act of passionate devotion, shares Armorer's view that we ought to move along. It is not so much that inactivity makes him restless—*restlessness* is not a word that really applies to a wooden block of a man like Sergeant—but that, like Seeker, he lives only to perform his military function. Seeker's function is to seek and Sergeant's function is to kill, and Seeker now feels that he will seek forever here and nevermore find, and Sergeant, in his dim way, believes that for him to stay here any longer would be a waste of his capability. He, too, wants to leave.

As does Weaponsmaster, who has had no weapons other than knives and spears to care for since our ammunition ran out and thus passes his days in a stupefying round of makework, and Quartermaster, who once presided over the material needs of ten thousand men and now, in his grizzled old age, lives the daily mockery of looking after the needs of just eleven. Thus we have four men—Armorer, Sergeant, Weaponsmaster, Quartermaster—fairly well committed to bringing the life of this outpost to an end, and one more, Seeker, who wants both to go and to stay. I am more or less of Seeker's persuasion here myself, aware that we are living idle and futile lives at the fort but burdened at the same time with a sense of obligation to my profession that leads me to regard an abandonment of the fort as a shameful act. So I sway back and forth. When Armorer speaks, I am inclined to join his faction. But when one of the others advocates remaining here, I drift back in that direction.

Gradually it emerges in our circular nightly discussion that the other four of us are strongly committed to staying. Engineer enjoys his life here: there are always technical challenges for him, a new canal to design, a parapet in need of repair, a harness to mend. He also is driven by a strong sense of duty and believes it is necessary to the welfare of the Empire that we remain here. Stablemaster, less concerned about duty, is fond of his beasts and similarly has no wish to leave. Provisioner, who is rarely given to doubts of any sort, would be content to remain so long as our supply of food and drink remains ample, and that appears to be the case. And Signalman still believes, Seeker's anguish to the contrary, that the desert beyond the wall is full of patient foes who will swarm through the gap and march against the capital like ravening beasts the moment we relinquish the fort.

Engineer, who is surely the most rational of us, has raised another strong point in favor of staying. We have scarcely any idea of how to get home. Twenty years ago we were brought here in a great convoy, and who among us bothered to take note of the route we traversed? Even those who might have paid attention to it then have forgotten almost every detail of the journey. But we do have a vague general idea of the challenge that confronts us. Between us and the capital lies, first of all, a great span of trackless dry wasteland and then forested districts occupied by autonomous savage tribes. Uncharted and, probably, well-nigh impenetrable tropical jungles are beyond those, and no doubt we would encounter a myriad other hazards. We have no maps of the route. We have no working communications devices. "If we leave here, we might spend the rest of our lives wandering around hopelessly lost in the wilderness," Engineer says. "At least here we have a home, women, something to eat, and a place to sleep."

I raise another objection. "You all speak as though this is something we could just put to a vote. 'Raise hands, all in favor of abandoning the fort.'"

"If we did take a vote," Armorer says, "We'd have a majority in favor of getting out of here. You, me, Sergeant, Quartermaster, Weaponsmaster, Seeker—that's six out of eleven, even if Captain votes the other way."

"No. I'm not so sure I'm with you. I don't think Seeker is, either. Neither of us has really made up his mind." We all looked toward Seeker, but Seeker was asleep at the table, lost in winy stupor. "So at best we're equally divided right now, four for leaving, four for staying, and two undecided. But in any case this place isn't a democracy and how we vote doesn't matter. Whether we leave the fort is something for Captain to decide, and Captain alone. And we don't have any idea what his feelings are."

"We could ask him," Armorer suggests.

"Ask my elbow," Provisioner says, guffawing. "Who wants to ask Captain anything? The man who does will get a riding crop across the face."

There is general nodding around the table. We all have tasted Captain's unpredictable ferocity.

Quartermaster says, "If we had a majority in favor of going home, we could all go to him and tell him how we feel. He won't try to whip us all. For all we know, he might even tell us that he agrees with us."

"But you don't have a majority," Engineer points out.

Quartermaster looks toward me. "Come over to our side, Surveyor. Surely you see there's more merit in our position than in theirs. That would make it five to four for leaving."

"And Seeker?" Engineer asks. "When he sobers up, what if he votes the other way? That would make it a tie vote again."

"We could ask Captain to break the tie, and that would settle the whole thing," Armorer says.

That brings laughter from us all. Captain is very sensitive to anything that smacks of insubordination. Even the dullest of us can see that he will not react well to hearing that we are trying to determine a serious matter of policy by majority vote.

I lie awake for hours that night, replaying our discussion in my mind. There are strong points on both sides. The idea of giving up the fort and going home has great appeal. We are all getting along in years; at best each of us has ten or fifteen years left to him, and do I want to spend those years doing nothing but hunting water-pigs in the river and toiling over our scrawny crops and rereading the same handful of books? I believe Seeker when he says that the man we killed a few weeks ago was the last of the enemy in our territory.

On the other hand, there is the question of duty. What are we to say when we show up in the capital? Simply announce that by our own authority we have abandoned the outpost to which we have devoted our lives, merely because in our opinion there is no further need for us to stay on at it? Soldiers are not entitled to opinions. Soldiers who are sent to defend a frontier outpost have no option but to defend that outpost until orders to the contrary are received.

To this argument I oppose another one, which is that duty travels both ways. We might be abandoning our fort, an improper thing for soldiers to be doing, but is it not true that the Empire has long ago abandoned us? There has been no word from home for ages. Not only have we had no reinforcements or fresh supplies from the Empire, but there has not been so much as an inquiry. They have forgotten we exist. What if the war ended years ago and nobody at the capital has bothered to tell us that? How much do we owe an Empire that does not remember our existence?

And, finally, there is Engineer's point that going home might be impossible anyway, for we have no maps, no vehicles, no clear idea of the route we must follow, and we know that we are an almost unimaginable distance from any civilized district of the Empire. The journey will be a terrible struggle, and we may very well perish in the course of it. For me, in the middle of the night, that is perhaps the most telling point of all.

I realize, as I lie there contemplating these things, that Wendrit is awake beside me, and that she is weeping.

"What is it?" I asked. "Why are you crying?"

She is slow to answer. I can sense the troubled gropings of her mind. But at length she says, between sobs, "You are going to leave me. I heard things. I know. You will leave and I will be alone."

"No," I tell her, before I have even considered what I am saying. "No, that isn't true. I won't leave. And if I do, I'll take you with me. I promise you that, Wendrit." And I pull her into my arms and hold her until she is no longer sobbing.

I awaken knowing that I have made my decision, and it is the decision to go home. Along with Armorer, Sergeant, Weaponsmaster, and Stablemaster, I believe now that we should assemble whatever provisions we can, choose the strongest of our beasts to draw our carts, and, taking our women with us, set out into the unknown. If the gods favor our cause, we will reach the Empire eventually, request retirement from active duty, and try to form some sort of new lives for ourselves in what no doubt is a nation very much altered from the one we left behind more than twenty years ago.

That night, when we gather over our brandy, I announce my conversion to Armorer's faction. But Seeker reveals that he, too, has had an epiphany in the night, which has swung him to the other side: weak and old as he is, he fears the journey home more than he does living out the rest of his life in futility at the fort. So we still are stalemated, now five to five, and there is no point in approaching Captain, even assuming that Captain would pay the slightest attention to our wishes.

Then there is an event that changes everything. It is the day of our weekly pig-hunt, when four or five of us don our high boots and go down to the river with spears to refresh our stock of fresh meat. The water-pigs that dwell in the river are beasts about the size of cattle, big sleek purple things with great yellow tusks, very dangerous when angered but also very stupid. They tend to congregate just upriver from us, where a bend in the flow creates a broad pool thick with water-plants, on which they like to forage. Our hunting technique involves cutting one beast out of the herd with proddings of our spears and moving him downriver, well apart from the others, so that we can kill him in isolation, without fear of finding ourselves involved in a chaotic melee with seven or eight furious pigs snapping at us from all sides at once. The meat from a single pig will last the eleven of us a full week, sometimes more.

Today the hunting party is made up of Provisioner, Signalman, Weaponsmaster, Armorer, and me. We are all skilled hunters and work well together. As soon as the night's chill has left the air, we go down to the river and march along its banks to the water-pig pool, choose the pig that is to be our prey, and arrange ourselves along the bank so that we will be in a semicircular formation when we enter the water. We will slip between the lone pig and the rest of his fellows and urge him away from them, and when we think it is safe to attack, we will move in for the kill.

At first everything goes smoothly. The river is hip-deep here. We form our arc, we surround our pig, we nudge him lightly with the tips of our spears. His little red-rimmed eyes glower at us in fury, and we can hear the low rumblings of his annoyance, but the half-submerged animal pulls back from the pricking without attempting to fight, and we prod him twenty, thirty, forty feet downstream, toward the killing-place. As usual, a few Fisherfolk have gathered on the bank to watch us, though there is, as ever, a paradoxical incuriosity about their bland stares.

And then, catastrophe. "Look out!" cries Armorer, and in the same moment I become aware of the water churning wildly behind me, and I see two broad purple backs breaching the surface of the river, and I realize that this time other pigs—at least a couple, maybe more, who knows?—have followed on downstream with our chosen one and intend to defend their grazing grounds against our intrusion. It is the thing we have always dreaded but never experienced, the one serious danger in these hunts. The surface of the water thrashes and boils. We see pigs leaping frenetically on all sides of us. The river is murky at best, but now, with maddened water-pigs snorting and snuffling all about us, we have no clear idea of what is happening, except that we have lost control of the situation and are in great jeopardy.

"Out of the water, everybody!" Weaponsmaster yells, but we are already scrambling for the riverbank. I clamber up, lean on my spear, catch my breath. Weaponsmaster and Armorer stand beside me. Provisioner has gone to the opposite bank. But there is no sign of Signalman, and the river suddenly is red with blood, and great yellow-tusked pig-snouts are jutting up everywhere, and then Signalman comes floating to the surface, belly upward, his body torn open from throat to abdomen.

We carry him back borne on our shoulders, like a fallen hero. It is our first death in some years. Somehow we had come to feel, in the time that has elapsed since that one, that we eleven who still remain would go on and on together forever, but now we know that that is not so. Weaponsmaster takes the news to Captain and reports back to us that that stony implacable man had actually seemed to show signs of real grief upon hearing of Signalman's death. Engineer and Provisioner and I dig the grave, and Captain presides over the service, and for several days there is a funereal silence around the fort.

Then, once the shock of the death has begun to ebb a little, Armorer raises the point that none of us had cared to mention openly since the event at the river. Which is, that with Signalman gone, the stalemate has been broken. The factions stand now at five for setting out for home, four for remaining indefinitely at the fort. And Armorer is willing to force the issue on behalf of the majority by going to Captain and asking whether he will authorize an immediate retreat from the frontier.

For hours, there is an agitated discussion, verging sometimes into bitterness and rage. We all recognize that it must be one way or another, that we cannot divide: a little group of four or five would never be able to sustain itself at the fort, nor would the other group of about the same size have any hope of success in traversing the unknown lands ahead. We must all stay together or assuredly we will all succumb; but that means that the four who would remain must yield to the five who wish to leave, regardless of their own powerful desires in the matter. And the four who would be compelled to join the trek against their wishes are fiercely resentful of the five who insist on departure.

In the end, things grow calmer and we agree to leave the decision to Captain, in whose hands it belongs anyway. A delegation of four is selected to go to him: Engineer and Stablemaster representing those who would stay, and Armorer and me to speak for the other side.

Captain spends most of his days in a wing of the fort that the rest of us rarely enter. There, at a huge ornate desk in an office big enough for ten men, he studies piles of documents left by his predecessors as commanding officer, as though hoping to learn from the writings of those vanished colonels how best to carry out the responsibilities that the vagaries of time have placed upon his shoulders. He is a brawny, dour-faced man, thin-lipped and somber-eyed, with dense black eyebrows that form a single forbidding line across his forehead, and even after all these years he is a stranger to us all.

He listens to us in his usual cold silence as we set forth the various arguments: Seeker's belief that there are no more enemies for us to deal with here, Armorer's that we are absolved of our duty to the Empire by its long neglect of us, Engineer's that the journey home would be perilous to the point of foolhardiness, and Signalman's, offered on his behalf by Stablemaster, that the enemy is simply waiting for us to go and then will launch its long-awaited campaign of conquest in Imperial territory. Eventually we begin to repeat ourselves and realize that there is nothing more to say, though Captain has not broken his silence by so much as a single syllable. The last word is spoken by Armorer, who tells Captain that five of us favor leaving, four remaining, though he does not specify who holds which position.

Telling him that strikes me as a mistake. It implies—rightly—that a democratic process has gone on among us, and I expect Captain to respond angrily to the suggestion that any operational issue here can be decided, or even influenced, by a vote of the platoon. But there is no thunderstorm of wrath. He sits quietly, still saying nothing, for an almost unendurable span of time. Then he says, in a surprisingly moderate tone, "Seeker is unable to pick up any sign of enemy presence?" He addresses the question to Engineer, whom, apparently, he has correctly identified as one of the leaders of the faction favoring continued residence at the fort.

"This is so," Engineer replies.

Captain is silent once again. But finally he says, to our universal amazement, "The thinking of those who argue for withdrawal from the frontier is in line with my own. I have considered for some time now that our services in this place are no longer required by the Empire, and that if we are to be of use to the country at all, we must obtain reassignment elsewhere."

It is, I think, the last thing any of us had expected. Armorer glows with satisfaction. Engineer and Stablemaster look crestfallen. I, ambivalent even now, simply look at Captain in surprise.

Captain goes on, "Engineer, Stablemaster, make plans for our departure at the soonest possible date. I stipulate one thing, though: We go as a group, with no one to remain behind, and we must stay together as one group throughout what I know will be a long and arduous journey. Anyone who attempts to leave the group will be considered a deserter and treated accordingly. I will request that you all take an oath to that effect."

That is what we had agreed among ourselves to do anyway, so there is no difficulty about it. Nor do our four recalcitrants indicate any opposition to the departure order, though Seeker is plainly terrified of the dangers and stress of the journey. We begin at once to make our plans for leaving.

It turns out that we do have some maps of the intervening territory after all. Captain produces them from among his collection of documents, along with two volumes of a chronicle of our journey from the capital to the frontier that the first Colonel had kept. He summons me and gives me this material, ordering me to consult it and devise a plan of route for our journey.

But I discover quickly that it is all useless. The maps are frayed and cracked along their folds, and such information as they once might have held concerning the entire center of the continent has faded into invisibility. I can make out a bold star-shaped marker indicating the capital down in the lower right-hand corner, and a vague ragged line indicating the frontier far off to the left, and just about everything between is blank. Nor is the old Colonel's chronicle in any way helpful. The first volume deals with the organization of the expeditionary force and the logistical problems involved in transporting it from the capital to the interior. The second volume that we have, which is actually the third of the original three, describes the building of the fort and the initial skirmishes with the enemy. The middle volume is missing, and that is the one, I assume, that speaks of the actual journey between the capital and the frontier.

I hesitate to tell Captain this, for he is not one who receives bad news with much equanimity. Instead I resolve that I will do my best to improvise a route for us, taking my cues from what we find as we make our way to the southeast. And so we get ourselves ready, choosing our best wagons and our sturdiest steeds and loading them with tools and weapons and with all we can carry by way of provisions: dried fruit and beans, flour, casks of water, cartons of preserved fish, parcels of the air-dried meat that Provisioner prepares each winter by laying out strips of pig-flesh in the sun. We will do as we can for fresh meat and produce on the march.

The women placidly accept the order to accompany us into the wilderness. They have already crossed over from their Fisherfolk lives to ours, anyway. There are only nine of them, for Seeker has never chosen to have one, and Captain has rarely shown more than fitful interest in them. Even so we have one extra: Sarkariet, Signalman's companion. She has remained at the fort since Signalman's death and says she has no desire to return to her village, so we take her along.

The day of our departure is fair and mild, the sun warm but not hot, the wind gentle. Perhaps that is a good omen. We leave the fort without a backward glance, going out by way of the eastern gate and descending to the river. A dozen or so of the Fisherfolk watch us in their blank-faced way as we cross the little wooden bridge upstream of their village. Once we are across, Captain halts our procession and orders us to destroy the bridge. From Engineer comes a quick grunt of shock: the bridge was one of his first projects, long ago. But Captain sees no reason to leave the enemy any easy path eastward, should the enemy still be lurking somewhere in the hinterlands. And so we ply our axes for half a morning until the bridge goes tumbling down into the riverbed.

We have never had any reason in the past twenty years to venture very far into the districts east or south of the fort, but we are not surprised to find them pretty much the same as the region north and west of the fort that we have patrolled so long. That is, we are in a dry place of pebbly yellowish soil, with low hills here and there, gnarled shrubs, tussocks of sawbladed grass. Now and again some scrawny beast scampers quickly across our path, or we hear the hissing of a serpent from the underbrush, and solitary melancholy birds sometimes go drifting high overhead, cawing raucously, but by and large the territory is deserted. There is no sign of water all the first day, nor midway through the second, but that afternoon Seeker reports that he detects the presence of Fisherfolk somewhere nearby, and before long we reach a straggling little stream that is probably another fork of the river whose other tributary runs close below our fort. On its farther bank we see a Fisherfolk camp, much smaller than the village on the banks of our river.

Wendrit and the other women become agitated at the sight of it. I ask her what the matter is, and she tells me that these people are ancient enemies of her people, that whenever the two tribes encounter each other, there is a battle. So even the passive, placid Fisherfolk wage warfare among themselves! Who would have thought it? I bring word of this to Captain, who looks untroubled. "They will not come near us," he says, and this proves to be so. The river is shallow enough to ford; and the strange Fisherfolk gather by their tents and stand in silence as we pass by. On the far side we replenish our water-casks.

Then the weather grows unfriendly. We are entering a rocky, broken land, a domain of sandstone cliffs, bright red in color and eroded into jagged, fanciful spires and ridges, and here a hard, steady wind blows out of the south through a gap in the hills into our faces, carrying a nasty freight of tiny particles of pinkish grit. The sun now is as red as new copper in that pinkish sky, as though we have a sunset all day long. To avoid the sandstorm that I assume will be coming upon us, I swing the caravan around to due east, where we will be traveling along the base of the cliffs and perhaps will be sheltered from the worst of the wind. In this I am incorrect, because a cold, inexorable crosswind arises abruptly, bringing with it out of the north the very sandstorm that I had hoped to avoid, and we find ourselves pinned down for a day and a half just below the red cliffs, huddling together miserably with our faces masked by scarves. The wind howls all night; I sleep very badly. At last it dies down and we hurry through the gap in the cliffs and resume our plodding southeastward march.

Beyond, we find what is surely a dry lakebed, a broad flat expanse covered with a sparse incrustation of salt that glitters in the brutal sunlight like newly fallen snow. Nothing but the indomitable saw grass grows here, and doubtless the lake has been dry for millennia, for there is not even a skeletal trace of whatever vegetation, shrubs, and even trees might have bordered its periphery in the days when there was water here. We are three days crossing this dead lake. Our supply of fresh water is running troublesomely low already, and we have exhausted all of our fresh meat, leaving only the dried stuff that increases our thirst. Nor is there any game to hunt here, of course.

Is this what we are going to have to face, week after week, until eventually we reach some kinder terrain? The oldest men, Seeker and Quartermaster, are showing definite signs of fatigue, and the women, who have never been far from their river for even a day, seem fretful and withdrawn. Clearly dismayed and even frightened, they whisper constantly among themselves in the Fisherfolk language that none of us has ever bothered to learn, but draw away whenever we approach. Even our pack animals are beginning to struggle. They have had little to eat or drink since we set out, and the effects are only too apparent. They snap listlessly at the tufts of sharp gray grass and look up at us with doleful eyes, as though we have betrayed them.

The journey has only just begun, and already I am beginning to regret it.

One evening, when we are camped at some forlorn place near the farther end of the lake, I confess my doubts to Captain. Since he is our superior officer and I am the officer who is leading us on our route, I have come to assume some sort of equality of rank between us that will allow for confidential conversations. But I am wrong. When I tell him that I have started to believe that this enterprise may be beyond our powers of endurance, he replies that he has no patience with cowards, and turns his back on me. We do not speak again in the days that follow.

There are indications of the sites of ancient villages in the region beyond, where the river that fed that dry lake must once have flowed. There is no river here now, though my practiced eye detects the faint curves of its prehistoric route, and the fragmentary ruins of small stone settlements can be seen on the ledges above what once were its banks. But nowadays all is desert here. Why did the Empire need us to defend the frontier, when there is this gigantic buffer zone of desert between its rich, fertile territories and the homeland of the enemy?

Later we come to what must have been the capital city of this long-abandoned province, a sprawling maze of crumbled stone walls and barely comprehensible multi-roomed structures. We find some sort of temple sanctuary where devilish statues still stand, dark stone idols with a dozen heads and thirty arms, each one grasping the stump of what must have been a sword. Carved big-eyed snakes twine about the waists of these formidable forgotten gods. The scholars of our nation surely would wish to collect these things for the museums of the capital, and I make a record of our position, so that I can file a proper report for them once we have reached civilization. But by now I have arrived at serious doubt that we ever shall.

I draw Seeker aside and ask him to cast his mind forth in the old way and see if he can detect any intimation of inhabited villages somewhere ahead.

"I don't know if I can," he says. He is terribly emaciated, trembling, pale. "It takes a strength that I don't think I have anymore."

"Try. Please. I need to know."

He agrees to make the effort, and goes into his trance, and I stand by, watching, as his eyeballs roll up into his head and his breath comes in thick, hoarse bursts. He stands statue-still, utterly motionless for a very long while. Then, gradually, he returns to normal consciousness, and as he does so, he begins to topple, but I catch him in time and ease him to the ground. He sits blinking for a time, drawing deep breaths, collecting his strength. I wait until he seems to have regained himself.

"Well?"

"Nothing. Silence. As empty ahead as it is behind."

"For how far?" I ask. "How do I know? There's no one there. That's all I can say."

We are rationing water very parsimoniously and we are starting to run short of provisions, too. There is nothing for us to hunt, and none of the vegetation, such as it is, seems edible. Even Sergeant, who is surely the strongest of us, now looks hollow-eyed and gaunt, and Seeker and Quartermaster seem at the verge of being unable to continue. From time to time we find a source of fresh water, brackish but at any rate drinkable, or slay some unwary wandering animal, and our spirits rise a bit, but the environment through which we pass is unremittingly hostile and I have no idea when things will grow easier for us. I make a show of studying my maps, hoping it will encourage the others to think that I know what I am doing, but the maps I have for this part of the continent are blank and I might just as well consult my wagon or the beasts that pull it as try to learn anything from those faded sheets of paper.

"This is a suicidal trek," Engineer says to me one morning as we prepare to break camp. "We should never have come. We should turn back while we still can. At least at the fort we would be able to survive."

"You got us into this," Provisioner says, scowling at me. "You and your switched vote." Burly Provisioner is burly no longer. He has become a mere shadow of his former self. "Admit it, Surveyor: We'll never make it. It was a mistake to try."

Am I supposed to defend myself against these charges? What defense can I possibly make?

A day later, with conditions no better, Captain calls the nine of us together and makes an astonishing announcement. He is sending the women back. They are too much of a burden on us. They will be given one of the wagons and some of our remaining provisions. If they travel steadily in the direction of the sunset, he says, they will sooner or later find their way back to their village below the walls of our fort.

He walks away from us before any of us can reply. We are too stunned to say anything, anyway. And how could we reply? What could we say? That we oppose this act of unthinkable cruelty and will not let him send the women to their deaths? Or that we have taken a new vote, and we are unanimous in our desire that all of us, not just the women, return to the fort? He will remind us that a military platoon is not a democracy. Or perhaps he will simply turn his back on us, as he usually does. We are bound on our path toward the inner domain of the Empire; we have sworn an oath to continue as a group; he will not release us.

"But he can't mean it!" Stablemaster says. "It's a death sentence for them!"

"Why should he care about that?" Armorer asks. "The women are just domestic animals to him. I'm surprised he doesn't just ask us to kill them right here and now, instead of going to the trouble of letting them have some food for their trip back."

It says much about how our journey has weakened us that none of us feels capable of voicing open opposition to Captain's outrageous order. He confers with Provisioner and Stablemaster to determine how much of our food we can spare for them and which wagon to give them, and the conference proceeds precisely as though it is a normal order of business.

The women are unaware of the decision Captain has made. Nor can I say anything to Wendrit when I return to our tent. I pull her close against me and hold her in a long embrace, thinking that this is probably the last time.

When I step back and look into her eyes, my own fill with tears, and she stares at me in bewilderment. But how can I explain? I am her protector. There is no way to tell her that Captain has ordered her death and that I am prepared to be acquiescent in his monstrous decision.

Can it be said that it is possible to feel love for a Fisherfolk woman? Well, yes, perhaps. Perhaps I love Wendrit. Certainly it would cause me great pain to part from her.

The women will quickly lose their way as they try to retraverse the inhospitable desert lands that we have just passed through. Beyond doubt they will die within a few days. And we ourselves, in all likelihood, will be dead ourselves in a week or two as we wander ever onward in this hopeless quest for the settled districts of the Empire. I was a madman to think that we could ever succeed in that journey simply by pointing our noses toward the capital and telling ourselves that by taking one step after another we would eventually get there.

But there is a third way that will spare Wendrit and the other women, and my friends as well, from dying lonely deaths in these lonely lands. Sergeant had shown me, that day behind the three little hillocks north of the fort, how the thing is managed.

I leave my tent. Captain has finished his conference with Provisioner and Stablemaster and is standing off by himself to one side of our camp, as though he is alone on some other planet.

"Captain?" I say.

My blade is ready as he turns toward me.

Afterwards, to the shaken, astounded men, I say quietly, "I am Captain now. Is anyone opposed? Good." And I point to the northwest, back toward the place of the serpent-wrapped stone idols, and the dry lakebed beyond, and the red cliffs beyond those. "We all know we won't ever find the Empire. But the fort is still there. So come, then. Let's break camp and get started. We're going back. We're going home."

David Ball

A former pilot, sarcophagus maker, and businessman, David Ball has traveled to sixty countries on six continents, crossed the Sahara four times in the course of researching his novel *Empires of Sand,* and explored the Andes in a Volkswagen bus. Other research trips have taken him to China, Istanbul, Algeria, and Malta. He's driven a taxi in New York City, installed telecommunications equipment in Cameroon, renovated old Victorian houses in Denver, and pumped gasoline in the Grand Tetons. His bestselling novels include the extensively researched historical epics *Ironfire* and the aforementioned *Empires of Sand,* and the contemporary thriller *China Run.* He lives with his family in a house they built in the Rocky Mountains.

In the grim story that follows, he takes us to seventeenth-century Morocco for a harrowing game of cat-and-mouse, one in which, if you're *lucky,* the prize is death. . . .

The Scroll

The prisoner felt a slithering on his belly and opened his eyes to a snake.

It was a viper, sluggish in the pre-dawn cool as it sought the warmth of his body. Scarcely daring to breathe, the engineer slowly lifted his head and stared into tiny coal-black eyes: emotionless, cold, and dead like his own. After the initial sick surge of fear raced through his veins, he was able to draw a deep breath, scarcely believing his good fortune. Only a week earlier, one of his men had rolled over onto just such a creature, perhaps this very one. True, he suffered horribly, but then he was released forever from this life. After all the prisoner had been through, could it at last be this easy?

He felt the pounding of his own heart as he moved his hand to provide an easy target. The air was oppressive, almost liquid.

The tongue flicked.

Please, God, take me. Now.

The snake ignored his hand. Head elevated, it kept a steady gaze on the engineer. He brushed at it. The viper drew back. No strike. Growing irritated, determined to provoke it, he swatted. He felt cool scales against his rough hand, but no burning of fang, no flush of poison. It was a dream, surely a dream; perhaps the emperor in another form, taunting him cruelly yet again. Another entry in the emperor's scroll, another part of his destiny that he could do nothing to change.

Then it no longer mattered. The reptile slid away and disappeared into a hole in the masonry, to hunt for one of the rats.

Baptiste let his breath out and lay still on his back. A tear coursed down his cheek. The heat was already making its way into the *metamore*, the underground chamber he shared with five hundred others. Once there had been forty of his own men, but only six now remained, the rest taken one at a time by disease, starvation, snakes, scorpions, overwork, despair, suicide, torture, and of course, the emperor.

He heard the reedy call of the muezzin, but not yet the footsteps of the guards. It was Sunday, when Christian prisoners had half an hour extra of rest, and even the opportunity to pray together. He heard it now, the familiar refrain of the priest, holding a service near the stream that ran through their midst: "Rejoice in thy suffering, my children, for it is the will of God." Baptiste grimaced. Surely the prisoners were rejoicing, for he could hear their agonies as they struggled to begin another day.

He closed his eyes until the hatch opened and a shaft of sunlight lit the ground near his head. A rope ladder was dropped from above. A chorus of groans was followed by a clatter of chains and the rush of men fighting for position at the ladder, because the last man up would be beaten for sloth. The other men always let the engineer go among the first, for Baptiste held the power of life and death over them. Most had heard the emperor's familiar greeting to him.

Will you kill for us today, Engineer?

No one wished to be among those chosen to die. No one tried to make friends with him, for that, they had seen, could be fatal. Above all, no one let harm come to him, for they knew that if Baptiste lived, only some of them would die. If Baptiste died, they would all die.

By the time he ascended into another day of perdition, blinking back the blinding Moroccan sun, Baptiste was no longer certain there had been a snake at all.

"Will you kill for us today, Engineer?" He had first heard the emperor's refrain too many lives ago to count. A hundred? A thousand? Men dead because of his own weakness and an emperor's boredom, men dead because of a game and a scroll, a damnable yellowed parchment at whose end he could only guess.

Baptiste was a soldier, but never believed he was a killer. He was an engineer who served at the right hand of Vauban, master of the art of siege warfare. Vauban, who could build anything and destroy anything. Together they devised ingenious methods of attack for the endless wars of Louis XIV and surpassed them with even more brilliant methods of defense.

Baptiste loved battlements and fortifications and all the tools of war, but found the noise and the smell of battle itself terrifying. He did not like the bodies and blood that fouled his neat ditches, did not like the ravages of shells that tore his pristine walls, did not, in fact, like the killing. It offended the laws of God and the order of his own life. Yes, his work allowed others to kill with speed and efficiency, but his own hands were clean. He was detached from it all: he loved the elegant precision of his drafting tools and the crisp drawings they made. In battle he often sat exposed to enemy fire, head bent over his work, oblivious of the shrieks of men and the roar of the guns and the danger, and it was the designs created in those moments that thwarted the enemy and even saved lives. That was his gift: seeing things that were not yet real, things that other men could not see, then putting them on paper so that others might convert his vision into earth, wood, and iron. After several of these battlefield designs had proved their worth, Vauban himself declared the engineer a genius and gave him a promotion.

It proved to be an unlucky advancement. He was captain of a company of engineers, transporting siege equipment in two galliots from the arsenal at Toulon to Marseilles. His own son, Andre, served in the corps and was aboard the second ship. Baptiste waved at his son, standing at the rail, easy to make out at a distance because he had the family's distinctive streak of white hair in a thick head of black. They had been three long years at war and were looking forward to a short leave. Their ships had been becalmed, then swallowed in a rare fog. The captain assured them the winds would pick up no later than the following morning. He dispensed rum to all hands. Men drank and fiddled and played draughts. Most were napping when a corsair xebec attacked. Before an alarm could be raised, the decks were swarming with Moors. The ship fell without a shot. As Baptiste was tossed below in chains, his only consolation was that his son's ship had not been captured.

They learned from the raïs who commanded the corsair vessel that their destination was to be Morocco. "You will find death in your Christian Hades preferable to life in that realm," cackled the raïs. "When it comes to the suffering of man, it is Moulay Ismaïl who is master; Satan himself but a pupil." Rumors flew on the ship about the emperor, a tyrant whose cruelty was legend. Atigny, a sapper from Aix, had suffered imprisonment there for six years, his health all but broken. "Ismaïl is a genius," said the morose Atigny. "He is building a city to rival Versailles. But he is a monster. Bloodthirsty and quite mad. He kills with his own hands. He kills for pleasure and delights in the sufferings of others. I survived because I found work in the stables. The horses live better than any man in Morocco. I was finally ransomed, but it ruined my family. My father died in poverty. There will be no second ransom for me."

"Nonsense," Baptiste told him. "We shall all be ransomed, by a church if not by our families."

"When Ismaïl discovers we are engineers, he will never let us leave. He needs us for his building. I cannot return there. I cannot suffer it again. Pray you are not noticed by him, *mon capitaine*. He chooses prisoners at random for special torment. He toys with them. God works his worst on those the emperor notices."

Baptiste tried to cheer the man, but he was inconsolable. On the morning the ship's lookout signaled land, Atigny managed to strangle himself in his own chains.

The equipment captured with the galliot identified Baptiste's men as engineers. They were taken inland from Sallee, the lair of the corsairs, to Meknes, the capital. Without ceremony they were put to work on the walls where, as Atigny had promised, cruelty was rife and death common. Men were worked beyond endurance, whipped and murdered without mercy, and buried in the walls, mixed with the lime.

One morning the imperial horses came thundering down a long passageway, Moulay Ismaïl in the lead, robes billowing, flanked by his *bokhaxa*, the killers of his elite personal guard. Men too slow to move were shredded beneath the hooves. The imperial party pulled up sharply and dismounted. The guards sprang to action, forcing men to the sand. Cringing and groveling were the only permitted responses to the imperial presence. Like the others, Baptiste knelt with his forehead to the ground. A moment later he was staring at the imperial toe. "Rise," commanded the emperor. Baptiste didn't know whether the emperor was addressing him or another, but he was quickly yanked to his feet.

The emperor of Morocco was slight of stature, dressed in plain clothing without ornament. "You are Vauban's engineer," he said pleasantly.

"I had the honor to serve under him, yes, Majesty."

"Was it you who made these plans?" Ismaïl asked. Baptiste recognized papers taken from his ship.

"Yes, Majesty."

Ismaïl's face lit and he nodded happily. "Then we are pleased to have you in our service," he said, as if Baptiste were there of his own will. "Come, walk with us." He turned and strode into the palace as an astonished Baptiste hurried to catch up, hardly knowing what to make of this turn of events. This was Moulay Ismaïl, Alouite sultan of Morocco, descendant of the Prophet Muhammad. Moulay Ismaïl, warrior who had helped drive the English from Tangier and the Spanish from Larache. Moulay Ismaïl, at whose hand six thousand women and children had died as he tamed the untamable Berbers. Moulay Ismaïl, who had defied the Ottoman Turks, delivering the heads of their commander and ten thousand of his troops to adorn the walls of Marrakesh and Fez, a demonstration of his yearning for peace. Moulay Ismaïl, on whose behalf the corsairs of Sallee pillaged the coasts of Europe, carrying away men, women, and children to be used for ransom or in the building of his empire. He built palaces and roads and bridges and forts and imposed harsh laws that brought peace to a land that had known nothing but war. "My people have order and bread," he boasted as they walked. "Soon this empire shall be great once again, greater even than under the Almohads, when the art and architecture and literature of Morocco were prized in the civilized world. Have you seen the Alhambra?"

"I have not, Majesty."

"Nor have we, but we have heard of its genius. We shall build greater still. You shall help us build, Engineer. You shall help us achieve this vision."

"Majesty, I—"

"Tell us about the siege of Maastricht," commanded Ismaïl, and they paused and Baptiste drew sketches in the sand and answered detailed questions from the well-informed monarch, who demonstrated keen interest in the art and science of siege warfare. "I have granaries that will allow us to withstand siege for five years," he boasted.

"Perhaps," Baptiste said, his practiced eye roaming the battlements, "but there are weaknesses a clever enemy might exploit."

"Most certainly. You will correct those weaknesses, Engineer. And you will build for us a city greater than the ancient capitals of Marrakesh, of Fez, even greater than Versailles, the quarters of your infidel king Louis."

The tour lasted three hours, the emperor expansive and proud as he pointed out features of what had already become one of the largest building complexes in the world: stables and granaries occupying vast chambers, palaces and harems, reception halls, private quarters, banquet rooms, kitchens, barracks, baths, and mosques. It was dusty, endless, and grand. The energetic emperor was bursting with ideas and stopped frequently to give orders to overseers who were clearly terrified by Ismaïl's presence. For his part, Baptiste found the afternoon tour quite pleasant.

They had returned to Baptiste's station when Ismaïl noticed a group of slaves he thought were moving too slowly. He seized a sword from one of his *bokhaxa* and with stunning swiftness decapitated two of the men. Baptiste blanched. It was nothing more than a mere flicker in his expression, but Ismaïl saw its softness. In that instant, Baptiste's life was transformed.

Ismaïl held the sword out to him and indicated the remaining slave, cowering at his feet. "Will you kill for us today, Engineer?" the emperor asked.

Stupidly, Baptiste thought it was some sort of joke. "I am not a killer, Majesty."

"You are a warrior, are you not?"

"An engineer, sire."

"Do your works not kill?"

"Other men use them to kill, Majesty. Not I."

"Where is the difference?" Ismaïl's face lit with interest. "What is power without the ability to bring death? How might men fear you?"

"I do not care that other men may fear me. Nor can I say how they should use my devices. I simply know that I would never kill with my own hand, except to avoid being killed."

The emperor laughed, his voice rising to a high pitch. "*Never* is a very long time indeed. Is it truly so?"

"It is, Majesty."

Ismaïl appraised Baptiste intently, the royal face drawn in concentration. Then he summoned the royal scribe and gestured for him to sit on a stool at his master's side. Ismaïl inclined his head and began to whisper to the scribe, who copied his words onto a long scroll. Baptiste stood silent, at first hoping that the emperor's dictation had nothing to do with him. However, Ismaïl glanced at him often as he dictated to the scribe, his expression alternately amused and grave. He whispered, paused, seemed to ponder deeply, then whispered again, for nearly an hour. Baptiste began to dread what would happen at the end of the dictation. He remembered Atigny's words: *Pray you are not noticed by him.*

At last Moulay Ismaïl addressed Baptiste. "The blood of the Prophet that runs in our veins allows us to see the road that Allah in his wisdom has set for some men," he said. "We have written key waypoints in your life upon this scroll. It shall be kept upon the lintel above the palace door, to be seen by all but touched by none, save our scribe. We shall read it from time to time, to discover how clearly Allah's path for you has been revealed to us, His unworthy disciple." The scribe rolled the parchment tightly, cinched it with a silk cord, and tucked it into a niche above the door, guarded by one of the *bokhaxa*.

Baptiste had several days to work and worry before he once again heard the thunder of hooves. The emperor stopped nearby but did not summon him, instead inspecting the walls as he often did, always paying attention to the smallest details. Just then a cord broke on a slave's wicker basket, spilling the heavy load. The slave fell to his hands and knees, scrambling to recover the stones as the emperor approached.

"Ah, Engineer," he said cheerfully when he saw Baptiste. "Such a fortunate meeting!" He nodded toward the slave. "Will you demonstrate the penalty for sloth on the emperor's works?"

"Majesty?" Baptiste shook his head uncertainly.

"Will you kill for us today, Engineer?" Ismaïl's voice was as pleasant as if he were commenting upon the weather. Baptiste felt a sickness in his stomach as the lord of Morocco watched him, waiting quietly, his *bokhaxa* impassive and silent. Baptiste held a heavy staff but could not raise it against the man, a skinny Spaniard who realized what was about to happen and began pleading for mercy.

"No?" asked the emperor.

"No," replied the engineer.

"Very well," Ismaïl said. He seized Baptiste's staff and quickly beat the Spaniard to death. He pointed to another slave, an Arab who was dragged before him thrashing and crying. The noise visibly upset Ismaïl, who swung again and again until there was silence. Yet a third victim was chosen randomly from the cowering ranks, this time a Sudanese. Ismaïl pushed him facedown into a vat of wet mortar and held him under with his foot. Ismaïl's eyes were on Baptiste, who had witnessed the killings dumbly, transfixed. After the third victim stopped struggling, Ismaïl stepped away, breathing normally, and he summoned scribe and scroll.

The scribe read the entry: "It is written: On the first day three shall die, yet the engineer shall remain steadfast."

The emperor clapped his hands in delight. He mounted his horse. "Men have died this day. Not at your hand, yet because of you, Engineer. Three for one. A pleasurable enough diversion for us, it is true, but a bad bargain for you—and certainly a bad bargain for them, no? At this rate, your building projects will begin to go too slowly for lack of men, and then more men will have to die in punishment. Perhaps you will kill for us tomorrow?"

Baptiste's eyes watered with the heat and the dust and the death and he dared not wipe at them. Ismaïl laughed his high-pitched laugh, spurred his horse, and was gone. The bodies were tossed into the wall and soon covered with brick and stone, men now a permanent part of the emperor's works.

Baptiste stood still for long moments. He fought his shock, trying to reason. For all that he felt, he did not credit the emperor with powers of prophecy. It did not take supernatural skill to divine that Baptiste would not kill a man merely to satisfy imperial whim.

Over the next few days, Baptiste's crews heard the rumble of horses, yet always at a distance. But then they heard the hooves coming close and knew it was their turn. The engineer continued to give orders and tend to his plans, making an effort to keep the strain out of his voice as the noise grew louder and slaves bent to their work, fearing selection. The guards bet among themselves as to which *kafirs* would die, but were themselves vigilant when the imperial party arrived, fearing they too might fall victim to his capricious blade.

Moulay Ismaïl appeared not to have mayhem on his mind. He beckoned for Baptiste to join him, and again they strolled together examining the works, passing through lush courtyards and between great colonnades, and then along the base of a fortress wall. Oblivious of the weight on Baptiste's shoulders, Ismaïl chatted on about the positioning of a bastion and the flow of water through a garden. He poked at a masonry joint, satisfying himself that it was well-constructed and tight. "This section is as fine as any belonging to the infidel king Louis," he said happily. "Do you not agree?"

"As you say, Majesty."

"I am well pleased with the stonework in these columns. An Englishman saw to them."

"The English are a plain people, Majesty, without imagination. Marble would have been better."

Ismaïl nodded thoughtfully. "Marble we shall have, then."

They continued through a small section of the grounds. Baptiste, ever the engineer, suggested improvements on a section of battlements, and he even allowed himself to enjoy the refreshing perfume of the olive groves and the gardens. Presently they arrived back at their starting point, where the guards were waiting with the horses. Moulay Ismaïl began to mount, but then caught himself and turned with a pleasant smile.

"Will you kill for us today, Engineer? Just one man?"

Baptiste went red in the face and weak in the knees. He made no sound, finding only enough strength to shake his head.

"No? Very well." Ismaïl selected two Berbers. The first died stoically, while the next cursed and spat at his executioner even to the instant of death. Ismaïl's eyes went bloodred, and he selected one of Baptiste's own engineers, who began to whimper. As the lance was set to strike, Baptiste fell to his knees. "Please, Majesty, he is a member of my own corps. I beg mercy. Take my life instead." He bowed, offering his neck to the royal blade.

Ismaïl hesitated. "Ah! Your own man! How careless of us. Very well, today we grant clemency for your fellow Frenchman." The man fainted in relief, which so annoyed Ismaïl that he almost changed his mind, but the motionless man's compatriots quickly dragged him away.

"You said earlier that the English are a simple people," Ismaïl reminded Baptiste. "We would agree they are of less value than the Frenchman just spared, would we not? Let us say—" His dark eyes twinkled. "—two for one, perhaps?"

Baptiste shook his head in protest. "Majesty, that is not what I meant."

"Ah, but it is. You have spoken and we have heard. Now let us see the fruits of your choice."

Moments later two Englishmen died, including the unfortunate man responsible for the stone pillars, whose blood ran into the sand at Baptiste's feet. The engineer could not bring himself to look upon the death he had purchased with a thoughtless comment.

"For a man who does not kill, death seems to follow you like a jackal in search of a meal," Ismaïl observed, laughing. "So much killing! Thankfully, none by your own hand! Your conscience may remain clear, yes?"

The emperor mounted his superb Arabian. "It is said we are a shrewd judge of men, Engineer. We shall see. Perhaps tomorrow? Or perhaps you would rather we read the scroll, to learn the extent of your stubborn will?"

Baptiste did not know how to reply, so said nothing. A *bokhaxa* struck him viciously with a staff. "As it pleases Your Majesty," Baptiste whispered.

Ismaïl laughed and shook his head. "In a few days more."

Once again the dead bodies became mortar for the walls and the afternoon's work went on. Baptiste knew that if his men did not continue their labors, the guards would beat them. So he regained his voice and issued orders and tended to his drawings, but he could not hold his pen. He felt the eyes of the other prisoners upon him. When he looked up, they were hard at their labors. His hand shook and the lines blurred into meaningless form. He could feel their fear, and their anger that he did not act to prevent needless death.

Baptiste could neither sleep nor eat. When he closed his eyes, the nightmares came—first the serpent, then severed heads, then the reading of the scroll.

He climbed atop a wall whose construction he was overseeing, determined to jump. It was the only way. He closed his eyes and took a deep breath, but he felt himself getting dizzy, opened his eyes in a panic, and caught himself short.

No! Suicide was a mortal sin, and it was a bad trade—eternal damnation in Satan's hellfires for temporary damnation in those of Moulay Ismaïl. He didn't know whether that was the truth or whether he was simply a coward, but he climbed off the wall, still alive.

He thought of a different way to depart, with honor and without suicide. He did not have long to wait to try it. Next morning an overseer was savagely beating a man for no reason other than bloodlust. Baptiste seized the guard's staff and began clubbing him. He landed only a few blows before the *bokhaxa* pulled him away, the overseer bloody but alive. The *bokhaxa* did not kill him on the spot, as he expected, but instead brought him before the emperor, who appeared unsurprised by the guards' report. With a knowing smile, Ismaïl summoned his scribe, who produced the scroll. "'The engineer shall seek to slay a guard in order that he may himself be slain,'" read the scribe. "So it is written."

Baptiste absorbed the words dumbly. Was he truly so predictable? Had he ever had free will, or had he lost it? He could not make sense of it. The scroll be damned. He would live to see his son again, would once again embrace his wife.

Dimly, he realized that Ismaïl was speaking. ". . . we know that your infidel faith prevents you from taking your own life," he was saying. "However, you also shall not take it by proxy, by provoking a guard to kill you. Indeed, we should be displeased were you to die at all, for we prize your talent. Therefore it is our order that henceforth, your safety and well-being shall be the responsibility of all men. Should you die, every man present shall forfeit his own life, and that of his family. This order shall apply to every guard, every member of the *bokhaxa*, every *caid*, every citizen of Morocco. This order shall apply to every slave in your *metamore*, to every slave under your command upon the works of Meknes. You shall not die, *kafir*, while in our glorious realm. If you do, the deaths of many hundreds shall be a stain upon your name." Ismaïl then assigned one of the *bokhaxa*, a silent giant of a warrior named Tafari, to be Baptiste's watcher.

Tafari's vigilance was relentless: he watched Baptiste work, watched him relieve himself, watched him when he ate, never but a few steps away. Only when Baptiste descended into the *metamore* for the night did Tafari's gaze leave him, for Baptiste's fellow prisoners were then responsible for him, with their own lives as surety. Every man in Meknes knew the law: Baptiste was not to die. Not by his own hand, or by any other.

His fate was contained in the emperor's scroll, which alone revealed his end. So it was written.

Baptiste returned to the works, where day after day it continued. The emperor's horses thundered down long passages and his city rose on the blood and bones of his slaves, and each time there was the ritual as Baptiste was offered a choice: Kill one man, or watch three die. "There is some number of men it will take until you will kill for us, Engineer. How many must die? Ten? A hundred? What is your number, Engineer? When will 'never' end?"

Baptiste remained steadfast. Heads fell.

"Perhaps a small refinement," Ismaïl said helpfully. "Such a principled man should not have to work without an audience." He ordered the heads to be mounted on poles, and the poles planted in the masonry of the buildings on which Baptiste was working. Six men, then eight, then ten. The engineer could feel their eyes upon him, until the crows came and took them. Between deaths, his master took him on tours of other buildings, always childlike in his enthusiasms, always boasting, asking questions, commenting upon the feathers of a bird in his gardens, then suddenly, capriciously, killing again.

Baptiste clung desperately to the belief that he was doing the right thing, but as more men died in Ismaïl's awful game, he knew he could have stopped it, could have brought at least some of the needless deaths to an end. Was not one man's death better than three? Of course it was not fair, but what did fair matter? He simply didn't know how to combat a man so brilliant, bloodthirsty, and mad. The priest affirmed to him that suicide was wrong, murder was wrong. All the blood was on Ismaïl's hands. "Rejoice in your suffering," he said, "for it is the will of the Lord."

The deaths mounted along with the nightmares, and finally he could take no more. He would do it. The emperor would declare victory, and it would be over.

It was an Abyssinian who had slacked in his labors and needed killing, a tall and lanky slave with an easy smile that remained on his face even after his head was parted from his shoulders. After it was done, Baptiste stood there, bloody sword in hand, chest heaving but face composed, acutely aware of the emperor's scrutiny, determined not to give him the satisfaction of seeing into his soul, determined not to show the revulsion that would surely cause Ismaïl to order him to do it again.

The imperial cackle of glee was followed by a call for the scribe to produce the scroll. Courtiers and *bokhaxa* and townspeople streamed into the courtyard, watching intently as the scribe rolled open the parchment.

"'The engineer shall strike a fatal blow only after eighteen men have died,'" the scribe read. "So it is written."

"Alas, it was nineteen, by our count," Ismaïl said. "A pity, yet lucky for someone, we suppose. Were it seventeen, one more would have to die. Perhaps the next revelation will be more precise." He stared at Baptiste. "Though we saw this in the scroll, you stand poorly in our estimation, Engineer," he said. "Were your convictions true, a thousand men would have died. A thousand times a thousand. Are you so easily swayed from your course?" He laughed, and returned to the palace, and the scroll was returned to its niche. Baptiste went to the wall where men relieved themselves and was violently ill.

So it is written. So he had done. Was it merely a lucky guess? Or was he so easily read? Was it his fault those men had died? Had he been less stubborn, would a dozen men be alive today? Should he have held fast, no matter the cost?

His nightmares did not leave him. They burned hotter, fired by the

Abyssinian's smile. He awakened screaming, another prisoner restraining him.

"It is over," the prisoner said. "He has had his way with you, Engineer. It is over."

But it was not over. It was only the beginning. Atigny had been right. *He toys with men.*

More deaths followed, three in a week, then none for a fortnight, then three more. With each new trial, Baptiste could not help himself, seeking refuge in quiet, hopeless refusal. Each time, three men died instead of one. Moulay Ismaïl appeared to draw strength from the contest of wills, and from the act of murder. He tested new weapons: a German war hammer or a Turkish crescent blade with a hook or a Scottish lance that could skewer three men with one thrust. He seemed genuinely fascinated by the effect each death had upon Baptiste, whose suffering he contrived slowly, endlessly, with a thousand variations.

"Why do you do this to me, Majesty?" Baptiste asked one day when they were walking in an orchard. "My death would mean nothing. Why will you not show the compassion of the Prophet and release me to my God?"

Moulay Ismaïl picked an apricot and the juice ran down his chin and into his beard. "Because it pleases us," he said. "Because we enjoy bending such a man as yourself to our will. Because we may one day bring you to the grace and true light of Islam. Because you can see things in your head that are not yet there. Like myself, you are truly a man among men, though your flaws are deep and your courage weak. Yet do not despair: We shall release you when the new reception rooms are complete," he said earnestly.

"Does it say that in the scroll, Majesty?"

The emperor smiled and there was no answer in his eyes.

The scroll unrolled slowly, accurately, as the scribe recited the litany of the engineer's actions: He would kill, he would waver, he would try a trick, he would act, he would fail to act, always trying to prevent a death, never succeeding.

The shock of white hair on Baptiste's head spread. His eyes were rheumy from lack of sleep. Time passed and men died and Meknes grew and he brooded and worked. When the reception rooms were completed, the emperor found another reason to delay his release.

With eight of his men Baptiste spent eleven months digging a tunnel out of the *metamore*. They labored all day for the emperor and all night for escape, labored until their hands were bloody and their knees raw and their bodies near collapse. There was no difficulty disposing of the dirt they removed from the tunnel. Six months of the year they lived and slept in water, fed by underground springs swollen by runoff from the snows of the High Atlas. They emptied the dirt into the water where it was washed away, leaving no trace for the guards to discover. They bribed merchants for information about where to go and how to hide, and paid extortionate sums for moth-eaten peasant robes. They broke through on a perfect autumn night, the ideal season because the seventy-mile journey to the sea could be undertaken without extremes of heat or cold. Moving only at night and in single file, they were three days and fifteen difficult miles from Meknes when a shepherd encountered them and raised the alarm. All shepherds were vigilant, because the emperor made them pay for any slaves escaping past their villages. It was another four days and seventeen miles before the dogs caught up with them, followed by mounted *bokhaxa*. Of eight men who followed the engineer out of the tunnel, five made it back to Meknes alive.

The surviving five men were summoned before Moulay Ismaïl, who in turn summoned his scribe to bring the scroll.

"'The engineer shall attempt escape.' So it is written."

The emperor clapped his hands merrily. "We are so pleased Allah has blessed you with continued life!" he cried. He ordered Baptiste's companions killed, a days-long ordeal of impalings and boilings. "A pity your compatriots were not of your measure! If only they had had your skills, perhaps we might have spared them! Ah, if only we had a thousand men like us, Engineer, men with our vision and your eye, Versailles itself would be but a poor pebble on the golden road to Meknes!"

"Release me to death," the engineer begged.

"Ah, but there is a lifetime of work for us," Ismaïl said. "Ten lifetimes of work. Regard our progress," he said, indicating with a sweep of his hand the glories of his capital. "We must both live a long while, yes, Engineer?"

"I have no desire to live, Majesty."

"Regrettable," said Ismaïl. He brightened. "Yet we see one path to your release."

"Sire?"

"Abandon your false religion and accept Muhammad as the messenger of God."

"Never," replied the Engineer with more conviction than he felt. "Never."

"We shall see, Engineer," said Ismaïl happily. "We shall see what is written." Just then Ismaïl saw a slave whose foot had been crushed in an accident and could no longer carry bricks. "For today, Engineer, will you kill for us?"

Baptiste tried something new. "Better to build, Majesty. He is a master of tile; he can work without feet. Let him die naturally while laboring for your vision. Let him die completing this monument to your glory."

The emperor roared with laughter and the cripple was spared and the scroll was prescient: "'The engineer shall preserve a life through an ingenious if transparent artifice.' So it is written."

"So, Engineer," Ismaïl asked. "Is life fate, or is it hope?" Baptiste had no answer, but a similar ruse the next week failed and two men died, both at the hand of Baptiste. He was killing more often now. He prayed the emperor would grow bored with their game, but Moulay Ismaïl showed no sign of it.

"Rejoice in your suffering," said the priest.

Baptiste became fond of a boy, a runner who carried messages between posts, bare feet flying over red clay. The boy was skinny and black and had big eyes and tight curly hair and stared at the engineer's drawings with delighted curiosity. The engineer let him make marks of his own and the boy thought it was wonderful magic. He had an aptitude for numbers and letters, and each day, while he was waiting for instruction to be carried, learned something new.

One day Ismaïl said, "We hear that you have befriended a boy."

Baptiste felt a sickness in his belly. Of course, Tafari, his *bokhaxa*, had reported everything. He shrugged indifferently. "Simply a runner, Majesty. He carries messages for the overseers."

"Whom do you love better, Engineer? The boy, or us?"

Baptiste was sick that he had not turned the boy away. Now no matter which way he answered, there was danger. If he said the boy, Moulay Ismaïl would surely order the boy killed. If he said "You, Majesty," the emperor would surely believe that impossible and order the boy killed anyway. How to make Ismaïl do nothing?

"Neither, Majesty. My God tells me to love all men equally."

"You are a fool, to think Allah puts an emperor at the same level as a slave boy," Ismaïl said angrily. The engineer knew he had doomed the child, but a month passed, and another, and still the boy ran messages between posts. He began to relax, but never again showed the boy any kindness.

And then one day Ismaïl saw the boy and held out his lance. "Will you kill for us today, Engineer?"

Baptiste's eyes watered. "Sire, no . . . please. Better to let him serve you. He is an excellent runner—"

"It would please us." Six men died before Baptiste killed the boy.

It happened again six months later. He merely laughed at something a master mason said. Tafari saw, and the man quickly became a pawn in the endless match, another salted head to grace the walls. The engineer withdrew from the company of other men. He talked to himself and made his drawings and his streak of light hair grew. At night, when sleep would not come, he summoned visions of his family. He told his children Andre and Annabelle to marry well and to have many children who might honor their grandfather, a simple king's engineer who had become a killer as his life unraveled on a scroll. Then fitful sleep would come, along with the nightmares. The snake would crawl on his belly and stare into his eyes, but never take him.

"You have won the game. Why do you continue to torment me?" They were atop a tower, surveying the city's defenses, Ismaïl, as usual, oblivious of Baptiste's sufferings, fascinated only by the grand works at their feet.

"Why, to see the outcome of the scroll, of course," said Ismaïl.

"Did you not write it? Do you not know how it ends?"

"Allah wrote it; I merely copied it down. Naturally I know what it says," said Ismaïl. "But *you* do not."

"What matter that I know? Does any man know his destiny?"

"It does not matter that you *know*," Moulay Ismaïl said thoughtfully. "Only what you *do*."

Each time Baptiste passed the palace gate he stared at the scroll. He longed to tear it down, to read it and be quit of it, but the guard was wary and besides, he did not really want to know what was written there. He knew only that the scroll had reduced him to an animal, depraved and devoid of humanity, stripped of dignity and free will. He knew only that galloping horses brought death. He knew only the stench and misery of the *metamore* and that Meknes was a coarse hell built of dung and mud and death. Sleep would not come fully, and neither would madness. He feared he was going to live to be very old, building and killing for the emperor.

He knew he was a coward. He feared death more than life and he feared Moulay Ismaïl more than God. God's wrath would come later, while Moulay Ismaïl's was now. Perhaps it was not such a bad thing, he mused, to accept this station. Must not the priest be right, that all this suffering was truly the will of God? Perhaps there was a greater purpose at hand, and he was too simpleminded to understand it. Perhaps he was meant to survive and to build, to do the bidding of those greater than himself, men ordained by—God? Allah?—to rule other men. Moulay Ismaïl claimed nothing more than the divine right of kings. Who was Baptiste to question? What did the wretched lives of endless slaves mean, anyway?

And then, when the justifications had begun to nibble at the edges of his conscience, the emperor would greet him on a fine morning with the refrain, "Will you kill for us today, Engineer?" and it would be some innocent, someone he knew or perhaps a complete stranger, and it would plunge him again toward the precipice of madness.

Ismaïl could read his face and knew when it was time for another solemn promise. "We shall free you next spring," he said. And Baptiste worked and he killed and he waited for the spring. But spring would come and there would be no freedom. "Not just now, Engineer, for we have need of a new pavilion. Complete it, and we shall release you in the fall." Despite the passing seasons, the engineer never lost hope. *God has a plan. He will free me when it serves His purpose.*

As much as he tried to believe that, he did not cease resistance. He sabotaged one of the lime kilns that fed the insatiable demand for bricks. He did it cleverly so that it could be traced to no man, using bricks to channel a stream of super-hot air to a position on the upper rear of the kiln so that the wall would fail. He planned it for days, visualizing it in his mind, then sketching it out in the mud where he slept, then stooping to examine the interior of the kiln when he pretended to be inspecting bricks, his practiced eye gauging the thickness and resiliency of the wall, then seeing to the reordering of the bricks when the kiln was cleaned, doing it all under the watchful but ignorant eye of Tafari. It would take at least a day of heat, he knew, before the failure would occur. The kiln supplied four hundred men working on the western side of a new palace wall. A steady stream of men fed it clay and straw and took away brick. Its loss might slow the emperor for only an hour or a day, or at most five days. Perhaps the emperor might not even notice. But *he* would know it had been done.

The kiln failed precisely as planned. Special clay had to be imported from Fez for the repair, bringing construction to a halt for nearly a week. The emperor had been away but upon his return immediately visited the kiln, his features twisted in fury and suspicion at the ill fortune. He waved off Baptiste's earnest and scientific explanations of structure failure caused by heat, saying that in fifteen years of building such a failure had never occurred, but he did not accuse the engineer of sabotage, either—at least not directly. He called for the scroll, which itself was unclear. "'Peculiar events shall occur, traceable to no man,'" read the scribe.

Baptiste was pleased to have fooled fate, but Ismaïl was not satisfied. As no one man could be deemed responsible, all were held responsible. The fourteen men working the kiln at the time of its collapse were burned alive in the new kiln, to remind everyone that any slowing of the work would not be tolerated. The engineer could smell the results of his handiwork for a week, as the hot summer sun and still air held the terrible odors close. In the *metamore* he thrashed and moaned and awakened each morning drenched in the sweat of night terror. For the first time in his life, he could remember his nightmares, none of which surpassed his waking hours.

Interminable days dragged to months, and the months crept into years. He did not count the days, for that was a torture of extended self-mortification. He plodded numbly on, sustained by thoughts of his family. His wife would be in her mid-forties now. They had known each other as children and married on his first leave. Her beauty grew in his memory. Sometimes at night she came to him and loved him, as he lay alone on his mat in the *metamore*. The faces of his children remained clear to him, locked in time. His daughter's dimple, his son's shock of white hair. Annabelle would be in the full flower of her mother's beauty now, married and with children, while Andre, such a mirror of his father, would be fighting the king's wars. He imagined their lives and prayed for their happiness and found himself wondering if the scroll foretold of his reunion with them. He cursed the thought: how could he believe in the scroll?

Two or three times a month a trumpet would sound from the parapets, signaling the arrival of new blood. He would climb onto a wall and watch as the caravan arrived. Always it was the same: fifty or a hundred or more trudging through the gate to feed the ravenous beast of Meknes: men for the works, women for the harems, children for the future. Some wore rags, others the remnants of fine clothing, everyone exhausted, hungry, and afraid. Alongside the slaves marched the redemptionist fathers, permitted to travel to Meknes to negotiate the release of certain of the slaves. Money sometimes came from prisoners' relatives, and sometimes from compassionate strangers in Spain or France or England, eager to free their wretched countrymen from the curse of slavery. The fathers would enter into difficult and protracted negotiations, often directly with the emperor himself, whose coffers were endlessly depleted by his building. Thus the cycle continued: a thousand men would stream through the gates of Meknes, and a score would hobble away.

Baptiste watched them coming. He wondered which of them would die at his hand, and whether one day he might march out with those freed. Might that not be the end in the scroll? He doubted it. No ransom was worth an emperor's game, no price worth the loss of an engineer. Besides, he could not get a message to his family. The redemptionists knew that Ismaïl had a special interest in him, and that to carry a message would be to condemn others. His only hope of freedom was madness or death. And so he killed and built and Meknes flourished, a bright city rising from the desert sands as the scroll of his life slowly unwound.

The city and its palace grew. There were minarets and walls, barracks and banquet halls, towers and a Jewish quarter, and magnificent stables for the horses. Oh, to be so lucky as the horses! He expanded their quarters, where each animal was tended by two slaves. He was everywhere in the town and the palace, always accompanied by Tafari, his watcher, building, directing, sketching, his labor the only release from his torments. On those days when ordered to kill, he would set the drawings aside and give no more orders, but plunge his own hands into the mortar of lime and blood and sand. Like the meanest slave he would carry buckets on shoulder poles and climb ladders until his feet bled, set bricks for doorways with his own hands, work until his back was breaking from the effort, work until the sun blistered his skin and he became faint from exhaustion, work until he collapsed and the overseers carried him to the *metamore*, where he would be lowered on the rope to the place below hell, to spend another tortured night with serpents and skulls in the blackness of his dreams.

Death came frequently, but not for him.

On a spring day the Algerians attacked Tezzo, two days from Fez. Moulay Ismaïl gathered some of the Christian prisoners, men long familiar with war and tactics, and promised that if they would help repel the enemy, he would free them. To Baptiste's surprise he was allowed to accompany the others, with Tafari always nearby. They spent hot bloody months in the desert and performed brilliantly and he sat as he once had in the midst of battle, oblivious to enemy fire and untouched by it as he helped devise victory. The emperor's enemies were vanquished. Upon their return to Meknes, many Christians were released, but not Baptiste. "'The engineer shall perform great services to the empire of Morocco. A favor shall be granted him by a beneficent monarch.' So it is written."

"Your time will come," Moulay Ismaïl told the dejected engineer as the scribe departed. "Not today. How desolate my city would look without your services! Such plans we have! Such work to be done! Such a favor you shall find tonight!"

After dusk he was summoned out of the *metamore* and allowed the chance to bathe. They led him to a gate near the inner palace, where he smelled perfume and oil. A pear-shaped eunuch led him through a succession of corridors to a room lit with candles and smelling of incense. An Italian slave girl awaited him. An emperor's gift, the first woman he had seen in twelve years. He touched her skin and cried. He could do nothing with her, which terrified her because if she failed to give him pleasure, she was to be maimed or killed, and they lay together and whispered a lie they would tell, and the night passed without fulfillment.

In the morning she was gone, and later the scribe read from the scroll: "'The engineer shall remain chaste in face of temptation.' So it is written." Ismaïl thought his chastity hugely funny. Baptiste heard later that the girl had been put to death. His only consolation was that he had not been her killer. Or had he?

One day Baptiste was approached by a corrupt and greasy *caid* named Yaya, whose right ear bore a jeweled ring and whose appetite for profit was limitless. He knew that Baptiste often earned money by manipulating prisoners' work assignments. He himself had shared some of that money. He had devised an ingenious plan for Baptiste to escape. For a certain price, he said, he could arrange to have another prisoner fall from the wall into one of the lime pits, making it appear that it was Baptiste who had fallen, while seeing Baptiste safely away in the cart of a Jew who pickled heads for the emperor's walls. The lime would make it impossible to verify the victim's identity. The emperor would believe that his engineer had simply succumbed to one of the inevitable hazards of the walls.

"I will not make another man pay with his life to save my own," he said. Yaya laughed. "You do so every day, Engineer. But, very well, we shall use a man who is already dead. Not a difficult thing to arrange here."

"How shall we fool the *bokhaxa*? Tafari watches me every moment."

"He may be incorruptible, your watcher, but it is not so with all of them. Fear not. On the day it is to happen Tafari will be drugged. His replacement, a man I know well, will be watching from below when you inspect the wall. He will swear to your death."

Baptiste thought it through carefully. It was a reasonable plan. As for the deaths that the emperor had decreed would follow his own, he had come to learn the futility of his efforts to spare other men. The emperor's caprice, not to mention his scroll, thwarted his every effort to outwit the fates. If men were to die, they were to die, and he could not prevent it. He had to try.

He had money but needed a great deal more. The *caid* had many to bribe. Baptiste spent months earning every *sou* he could. For the first time in his long captivity he found himself climbing out of the night pit with eagerness, with hope.

On the appointed day, that hope soared: for the first time, Tafari was not there to greet him. Another *bokhaxa* stood in his place, a man whose expression plainly conveyed he was a conspirator. The pit of lime and mortar was in exactly the right place. The substitute body, a Breton who had died the previous day, was already in place atop the wall. The cart in which he was to hide was stationed near a gate. Overseers and their slaves were working nearby, none close enough to see anything.

Baptiste began ascending the ladder, when he heard the thunder of horses galloping down the corridor. He cursed, but knew it might mean a delay of only an hour or two, as he satisfied the emperor's curiosity about some matter of building, or killed a man, or did some other thing to fulfill what had been written in the scroll.

As it happened, the emperor wanted only to inspect one of the battlements. It took one uneventful hour. The emperor was about to depart when he paused. "Ah, we almost forgot, Engineer," he said. "We have a gift for you." One of the *bokhaxa* stepped forward, extending an oilskin packet.

"A gift?"

"A small gem. A token of our esteem for your services, which we know are not always given with the greatest enthusiasm."

Warily, Baptiste took the packet. "But first," the emperor said, "we must hear from our scribe." Baptiste's pulse quickened.

" 'There shall be a subterfuge, coupled with betrayal,' " the scribe read, and Baptiste felt his head pounding and his knees weakening. "So it is written."

The emperor nodded at the packet. Dumbly, Baptiste's fingers worked at the ties. There was indeed a gem, along with the ear to which it had been attached. His knees gave out and he sank to the dirt, the packet dropping from his hand.

The emperor laughed. "Had you only asked us, surely we could have arranged the same end for less money," he said, and his face went dark in madness, just as it did when men died. "You must not presume upon our very good nature, Engineer."

"Was it not written in the scroll that I should do this thing?" Baptiste asked dully. "How could I be wrong to act in the manner ordained for me?"

Ismaïl laughed and clapped his hands. "Ah! An inspired riposte! You have come to see that your path has indeed been written. We are making grand progress." He clapped again and the *bokhaxa* who had taken Tafari's place was dragged into the square. His genitals were tied to a cord, the other end of which was attached to the harness of a mule. The mule's trainer was delicate and entertained the crowd for nearly an hour, but then the mule responded too exuberantly to one prod, and it was over. Baptiste was forced to watch, and when the man at last died Baptiste felt nothing at all. He watched again as the Jewish pickler's head was added to the walls—without, of course, having been pickled. The emperor would have to see to a new craftsman.

"Rejoice in your suffering," the priest told him. "God's will be done."

Baptiste assigned himself to work in one of the mud pits where bricks were mixed with straw. He swung the mattock furiously, trying to force the images from his mind. He heard the thunder of hooves and did not turn to meet them, but kept working. A moment later, he stood shoulder to shoulder with the emperor himself, royal arms plunged deep in the muck. Ismaïl talked about building and architecture, and about the infidel Sun King and his pathetic Versailles, whose deficiencies were being reported to him by his ambassadors, and of the properties of masonry and the difference between the mud of France and the mud of Morocco. The emperor shouted orders and pointed and commanded and worked hard, his back bent like that of a common laborer, and Baptiste noticed that his neck was stretched like that of a common man as well. He realized he could sever that neck with the simple mattock in his hands, and so bring an end to the sufferings of fifty thousand men. He felt the eyes of Tafari and the other *bokhaxa* upon him, but even so knew he could do it in one stroke. He closed his eyes to summon his strength, and as the muscles moved to obey, the emperor had had enough labor and stepped from the pit and the moment was gone. Ismaïl allowed himself to be washed and toweled, all the while watching Baptiste with an enigmatic smile. He beckoned for the scribe and ordered him to fetch the scroll. "'The engineer shall let a moment for revenge pass unconsummated.' So it is written."

Ismaïl laughed uproariously. "Such an opportunity comes but once in a lifetime," he said. "A pity to waste it." Baptiste knew that the emperor had known when the scroll would say it was time for this test and had deliberately offered himself to Baptiste's blade. Yet, as with all his other tests, he had failed.

It occurred to Baptiste that he might stem the killing simply by building faster and better than ever before. If the emperor saw progress equal to his dreams, if the emperor was accommodated in every respect, it might stay his sword, or his desire that the engineer wield it for him. He casually suggested a new reception hall where Ismaïl might receive and entertain ambassadors and dignitaries, a room equal to Ismaïl's stature in the world, a spectacular complex with not only a banquet hall but also a large open courtyard with twelve pavilions, each covered with intricate tiles and mosaics. Ismaïl loved the idea. Baptiste devoted himself to it. He saw to the transport of marble from the nearby Roman ruins of Volubilis. Carpenters cut olive wood for ornate inlaid panels. The walls bore engravings boasting of the accomplishments of the emperor who raised them. Marvelously complex mosaics graced the twelve pavilions, each more magnificent than the last. The complex rose more quickly than any other in memory, and on his regular inspections, the emperor pronounced it grand and to his liking. For months it went on, through a winter and a spring, and in those months the engineer was immersed in his work as never before. As he had hoped, fewer men died, and for sixty days, none at all by his hand. The scroll remained in its niche.

A sumptuous banquet was held when the hall was completed, attended by governors and ambassadors who sampled the delights of Ismaïl's kitchens and were entertained by his musicians and the dance of forty slave girls. Baptiste could only imagine the success of the event, for he spent the evening huddled in his night pit. The next morning Ismaïl pronounced himself displeased because the whole of the hall did not exceed the sum of the parts. He ordered the complex destroyed. Within a week, Baptiste's triumph was rubble, to be used for other buildings. The engineer was invited to kill six of the fourteen overseers who had carried out his orders. "They did not live up to your talent," said Moulay Ismaïl. "Won't you kill them for us, Engineer?"

He could think of nothing else to do. Whether he worked quickly or slowly, whether he built well or poorly, whether he resisted or gave in, the emperor's game went on; only the scroll seemed to hold the answer to what would come next. Incidents varied but nothing changed. Imperial horses raced down long corridors. Swords flashed and heads flew, and men lived and died as buildings were created and destroyed, all for royal whimsy. The palace walls grew inexorably, meter after meter, thick and heavy, filled with the flesh and bones of the men who worked them. Meknes was splendid indeed.

"Thank God for your suffering," the priest told him. "It is glorious to endure for the true faith."

And then one morning, after a slave had died and the scroll had been read, the scribe whispered something to the emperor.

"The entries in your scroll have come to an end," Moulay Ismaïl said. "There is but one further entry."

Baptiste went numb.

"Do you not care to guess what it is?"

"The truth," said Baptiste after a pause. "It does not matter, so long as it is the end."

The emperor laughed and announced that the scroll's final entry would be read a week hence, after morning prayer.

Baptiste returned to his walls. He looked at no man and shut out the thunder of hooves. For the first time in his long captivity, he refused himself hope, and he refused himself despair. There was only an end.

What he did hear on a Saturday morning was the sounding of the trumpet and the clanking of chains as a caravan arrived from Sallee. It was the second that week; hunting had been good for the corsairs. There were the usual ambassadors and merchants among the donkeys and camels, all stirring up a great cloud of dust, and redemptionist fathers bearing their purses and petitions, while beside and behind them trudged the new crop of prisoners and their guards. A hundred in, five out, in the awful math that was Meknes. Baptiste cared little for studying a new miserable stream of humanity entering perdition, so he merely glanced down at the procession, returning his focus to the line of a new wall. But something caught his attention. He felt light tentacles of dread and looked again, peering through the cloud of dust that rose over the procession. His eyes scanned the faces.

There.

Near the end, behind one of the guards, a shock of white hair in a head of black. He stared, fearing the worst, until there was no mistaking.

Andre! My son! Dear God, please let my eyes be deceiving me!

But there was no mistake; looking at his son was like looking at his own reflection. And then Andre looked to the wall, his face bright and unmistakable, and he saw his father, and he waved and yelled, his voice barely audible: "Father! Father! It is I! Andre! Father!"

Baptiste all but imperceptibly shook his head, cautioning his son to silence, but Andre only yelled louder. "Father!" And then his voice was lost in the tumult and his face in the crowd, and he disappeared round the corner.

Baptiste stood dead still, unable to move, barely able to breathe. Mind reeling, he turned slowly and saw Tafari. Watching, as always. He had witnessed the exchange as father saw son, and son father. His great round face betrayed nothing, but it was done.

"Please." Baptiste's voice was barely a whisper. "Have mercy upon a poor father. Have mercy upon his son. Say nothing. I beg you." He took a purse from his sash and pressed it into the incorruptible *bokhaxa's* hand. Tafari let it fall to the ground, his face stone.

Baptiste sank to his knees and slumped on the wall. Of course, the watcher would inform the emperor.

Baptiste knew the final entry in the scroll.

His son was going to die, at his father's hand.

Courtiers and ambassadors hurried to get a good place, to see the reading for themselves, to hear proof once again of the emperor's sagacity. Only a true son of Muhammad could have such power of prophecy.

The emperor sent Tafari to fetch the prisoner, who along with the other Christians was enjoying the comfort of their infidel priests on that Sunday morning.

"We are informed the son of the engineer has come with the caravan from Sallee," Ismaïl said. "Bring him forward."

The court fell to a hush as two *bokhaxa* escorted the Frenchman into the emperor's presence. He came not from among the slaves, but from among the redemptionists. He was not a prisoner, but a petitioner.

"You have come to negotiate the freedom of your father," Ismaïl said.

"Yes, Majesty," Andre said, his speech carefully prepared. Moulay Ismaïl was well known to confiscate ransoms and renege on arrangements. "We pray your beneficence, having brought a ransom for his release. We are certain that—"

Moulay Ismaïl impatiently waved him to silence. "For this man, it matters not what you have brought. It matters only what is written in the scroll. We shall soon see what the fates hold for your father."

The *bokhaxa* returned, his features ashen.

"Where is the engineer?" demanded the emperor.

Tafari fell to his face. "Forgive me, Majesty. He is dead."

The emperor's color went dark and his eyes flashed red as his rage built. "How did this come to pass?"

"He was found on his mat, Highness. There were marks of a serpent on his throat."

Those present waited to see how Ismaïl might vent his rage. But he merely pondered for a moment, then waved for the scribe, who hurried forward. The great hall fell silent as he unrolled the well-used parchment. The scribe cleared his throat. "There is but one word," he said.

"Read it," commanded the emperor.

"*'Release.'*" The scribe whispered it. "So it is written."

Overcome with emotion, Andre cried out and then sagged, the choked whisper of his prayers lost in the murmuring of the court. One of the redemptionist fathers helped steady him.

"Until now, your father has been a good servant to us," Ismaïl said. "Yet the end to our little experiment has not worked out wholly to our satisfaction. Regrettably, your father has taken the wrong path of release." Ismaïl looked to his *bokhaxa*. "Take him prisoner."

The young engineer's sobs died in the shock of his seizure and the clanking of the chains. As locks clicked shut, Ismaïl spoke to his scribe, who produced a fresh scroll and waited, quill poised.

Refreshed by the prospect of a new amusement, the emperor of Morocco turned his brightest smile upon Andre. "In this empire, sons must atone for the shortcomings of their fathers."

Andre stood bewildered. "Majesty?"

"Tell us, Engineer's Son," Ismaïl asked him happily. "Will you kill for us today?"

George R. R. Martin

Hugo, Nebula, and World Fantasy Award winner George R. R. Martin, *New York Times* bestselling author of the landmark A Song of Ice and Fire fantasy series, has been called "the American Tolkien."

Born in Bayonne, New Jersey, George R. R. Martin made his first sale in 1971 and soon established himself as one of the most popular SF writers of the '70s. He quickly became a mainstay of the Ben Bova *Analog* with stories such as "With Morning Comes Mistfall," "And Seven Times Never Kill Man," "The Second Kind of Loneliness," "The Storms of Windhaven" (in collaboration with Lisa Tuttle, and later expanded by them into the novel *Windhaven*), "Override," and others, although he also sold to *Amazing, Fantastic, Galaxy, Orbit,* and other markets. One of his *Analog* stories, the striking novella "A Song for Lya," won him his first Hugo Award in 1974.

By the end of the '70s, he had reached the height of his influence as a science fiction writer and was producing his best work in that category with stories such as the famous "Sandkings," his best-known story, which won both the Nebula and the Hugo in 1980 (he'd later win another Nebula in 1985 for his story "Portraits of His Children"), "The Way of Cross and Dragon," which won a Hugo Award in the same year (making Martin the first author ever to receive two Hugo Awards for fiction in the same year), "Bitterblooms," "The Stone City," "Starlady," and others. These stories would be collected in *Sandkings,* one of the strongest collections of the period. By now, he had mostly moved away from *Analog,* although he would have a long sequence of stories about the droll interstellar adventures of Havalend Tuf (later collected in *Tuf Voyaging*) running throughout the '80s in the Stanley Schmidt *Analog,* as well as a few strong individual pieces such as the novella "Nightflyers"; most of his major work of the late '70s and early '80s, though, would appear in *Omni.* The late '70s and '80s also saw the publication of his memorable novel *Dying of the Light,* his only solo SF novel, while his stories were collected in *A Song for Lya, Sandkings, Songs of Stars and Shadows, Songs the Dead Men Sing, Nightflyers,* and *Portraits of His Children.* By the beginning of the '80s, he'd moved away from SF and into the horror genre, publishing the big horror novel *Fevre Dream* and winning the Bram Stoker Award for his horror story "The Pear-Shaped Man" and the World Fantasy Award for his werewolf novella "The Skin Trade." By the end of that decade, though, the crash of the horror market and the commercial failure of his ambitious horror novel *The Armageddon Rag* had driven him out of the print world and to a successful career in television instead, where for more than a decade he worked as story editor or producer on such shows as the new *Twilight Zone* and *Beauty and the Beast.*

After years away, Martin made a triumphant return to the print world in 1996 with the publication of the immensely successful fantasy novel *A Game of Thrones,* the start of his Song of Ice and Fire sequence. A free-standing novella taken from that work, "Blood of the Dragon," won Martin another Hugo Award in 1997. Further books in the Song of Ice and Fire series, *A Clash of Kings, A Storm of Swords, A Feast for Crows,* and forthcoming *A Dance with Dragons,* have made it one of the most popular, acclaimed, and bestselling series in all of modern fantasy. His most recent books are a massive retrospective collection spanning the entire spectrum of his career, *GRRM: A RRetrospective;* a novella collection, *Starlady and Fast-Friend;* a novel written in collaboration with Gardner Dozois and Daniel Abraham, *Hunter's Run;* and, as editor, three new volumes in his long-running Wild Cards anthology series, *Busted Flush, Inside Straight,* and *Suicide Kings.*

Martin first introduced the baseborn "Hedge Knight," Ser Duncan the Tall, and his squire, Egg, in his novella "The Hedge Knight," a finalist for the World Fantasy Award. The two characters became wildly popular and returned for further adventures in "The Sworn Sword." In the vivid and hugely entertaining novella that follows, Martin takes Dunk and Egg on a further adventure, as they participate in a sinister tourney where absolutely nothing is as it seems—including Dunk and Egg!

The "Dunk and Egg" stories have recently been published in graphic novel form as *The Hedge Knight* and *The Hedge Knight II: Sworn Sword.*

The Mystery Knight

A Tale of the Seven Kingdoms

A light summer rain was falling as Dunk and Egg took their leave of Stoney Sept.

Dunk rode his old warhorse Thunder, with Egg beside him on the spirited young palfrey he'd named Rain, leading their mule Maester. On Maester's back were bundled Dunk's armor and Egg's books, their bedrolls, tent, and clothing, several slabs of hard salt beef, half a flagon of mead, and two skins of water. Egg's old straw hat, wide-brimmed and floppy, kept the rain off the mule's head. The boy had cut holes for Maester's ears. Egg's new straw hat was on his own head. Except for the ear holes, the two hats looked much the same to Dunk.

As they neared the town gates, Egg reined up sharply. Up above the gateway, a traitor's head had been impaled upon an iron spike. It was fresh from the look of it, the flesh more pink than green, but the carrion crows had already gone to work on it. The dead man's lips and cheeks were torn and ragged; his eyes were two brown holes weeping slow red tears as raindrops mingled with the crusted blood. The dead man's mouth sagged open, as if to harangue travelers passing through the gate below.

Dunk had seen such sights before. "Back in King's Landing when I was a boy, I stole a head right off its spike once," he told Egg. Actually it had been Ferret who scampered up the wall to snatch the head, after Rafe and Pudding said he'd never dare, but when the guards came running he'd tossed it down, and Dunk was the one who'd caught it. "Some rebel lord or robber knight, it was. Or maybe just a common murderer. A head's a head. They all look the same after a few days on a spike." Him and his three friends had used the head to terrorize the girls of Flea Bottom. They'd chase them through the alleys and make them give the head a kiss before they'd let them go. That head got kissed a lot, as he recalled. There wasn't a girl in King's Landing who could run as fast as Rafe. Egg was better off not hearing that part, though. *Ferret, Rafe, and Pudding. Little monsters, those three, and me the worst of all.* His friends and he had kept the head until the flesh turned black and began to slough away. That took the fun out of chasing girls, so one night they burst into a pot shop and tossed what was left into the kettle. "The crows always go for the eyes," he told Egg. "Then the cheeks cave in, the flesh turns green. . . ." He squinted. "Wait. I know that face."

"You do, ser," said Egg. "Three days ago. The hunchbacked septon we heard preaching against Lord Bloodraven."

He remembered then. *He was a holy man sworn to the Seven, even if he did preach treason.* "His hands are scarlet with a brother's blood, and the blood of his young nephews too," the hunchback had declared to the crowd that had gathered in the market square. "A shadow came at his command to strangle brave Prince Valarr's sons in their mother's womb. Where is our Young Prince now? Where is his brother, sweet Matarys? Where has Good King Daeron gone, and fearless Baelor Breakspear? The grave has claimed them, every one, yet he endures, this pale bird with bloody beak who perches on King Aerys's shoulder and caws into his ear. The mark of hell is on his face and in his empty eye, and he has brought us drought and pestilence and murder. Rise up, I say, and remember our true king across the water. Seven gods there are, and seven kingdoms, and the Black Dragon sired seven sons! Rise up, my lords and ladies. Rise up, you brave knights and sturdy yeomen, and cast down Bloodraven, that foul sorcerer, lest your children and your children's children be cursed forevermore."

Every word was treason. Even so, it was a shock to see him here, with holes where his eyes had been. "That's him, aye," Dunk said, "and another good reason to put this town behind us." He gave Thunder a touch of the spur, and he and Egg rode through the gates of Stoney Sept, listening to the soft sound of the rain. *How many eyes does Lord Bloodraven have?* the riddle ran. *A thousand eyes, and one.* Some claimed the King's Hand was a student of the dark arts who could change his face, put on the likeness of a one-eyed dog, even turn into a mist. Packs of gaunt gray wolves hunted down his foes, men said, and carrion crows spied for him and whispered secrets in his ear. Most of the tales were only tales, Dunk did not doubt, but no one could doubt that Bloodraven had informers everywhere.

He had seen the man once with his own two eyes, back in King's Landing. White as bone were the skin and hair of Brynden Rivers, and his eye—he had only the one, the other having been lost to his half brother Bittersteel on the Redgrass Field—was red as blood. On cheek and neck he bore the winestain birthmark that had given him his name.

When the town was well behind them, Dunk cleared his throat and said, "Bad business, cutting off the heads of septons. All he did was talk. Words are wind."

"Some words are wind, ser. Some are treason." Egg was skinny as a stick, all ribs and elbows, but he did have a mouth.

"Now you sound a proper princeling."

Egg took that for an insult, which it was. "He might have been a septon, but he was preaching lies, ser. The drought wasn't Lord Bloodraven's fault, nor the Great Spring Sickness either."

"Might be that's so, but if we start cutting off the heads of all the fools and liars, half the towns in the Seven Kingdoms will be empty."

Six days later, the rain was just a memory.

Dunk had stripped off his tunic to enjoy the warmth of sunlight on his skin. When a little breeze came up, cool and fresh and fragrant as a maiden's breath, he sighed. "Water," he announced. "Smell it? The lake can't be far now."

"All I can smell is Maester, ser. He stinks." Egg gave the mule's lead a savage tug. Maester had stopped to crop at the grass beside the road, as he did from time to time.

"There's an old inn by the lakeshore." Dunk had stopped there once when he was squiring for the old man. "Ser Arlan said they brewed a fine brown ale. Might be we could have a taste while we waited for the ferry."

Egg gave him a hopeful look. "To wash the food down, ser?"

"What food would that be?"

"A slice off the roast?" the boy said. "A bit of duck, a bowl of stew? Whatever they have, ser."

Their last hot meal had been three days ago. Since then, they had been living on windfalls and strips of old salt beef as hard as wood. *It would be good to put some real food in our bellies before we started north. That Wall's a long way off.*

"We could spend the night as well," suggested Egg.

"Does m'lord want a feather bed?"

"Straw will serve me well enough, ser," said Egg, offended.

"We have no coin for beds."

"We have twenty-two pennies, three stars, one stag, and that old chipped garnet, ser."

Dunk scratched at his ear. "I thought we had two silvers."

"We did, until you bought the tent. Now we have the one."

"We won't have any if we start sleeping at inns. You want to share a bed with some peddler and wake up with his fleas?" Dunk snorted. "Not me. I have my own fleas, and they are not fond of strangers. We'll sleep beneath the stars."

"The stars are good," Egg allowed, "but the ground is hard, ser, and sometimes it's nice to have a pillow for your head."

"Pillows are for princes." Egg was as good a squire as a knight could want, but every so often he would get to feeling princely. *The lad has dragon blood, never forget.* Dunk had beggar's blood himself . . . or so they used to tell him back in Flea Bottom, when they weren't telling him that he was sure to hang. "Might be we can afford some ale and a hot supper, but I'm not wasting good coin on a bed. We need to save our pennies for the ferryman." The last time he had crossed the lake, the ferry cost only a few coppers, but that had been six years ago, or maybe seven. Everything had grown more costly since then.

"Well," said Egg, "we could use my boot to get across."

"We could," said Dunk, "but we won't." Using the boot was dangerous. *Word would spread. Word always spreads.* His squire was not bald by chance. Egg had the purple eyes of old Valyria, and hair that shone like beaten gold and strands of silver woven together. He might as well wear a three-headed dragon as a brooch as let that hair grow out. These were perilous times in Westeros, and . . . well, it was best to take no chances. "Another word about your bloody boot, and I'll clout you in the ear so hard you'll *fly* across the lake."

"I'd sooner swim, ser." Egg swam well, and Dunk did not. The boy turned in the saddle. "Ser? Someone's coming up the road behind us. Hear the horses?"

"I'm not deaf." Dunk could see their dust as well. "A large party. And in haste."

"Do you think they might be outlaws, ser?" Egg raised up in the stirrups, more eager than afraid. The boy was like that.

"Outlaws would be quieter. Only lords make so much noise." Dunk rattled his sword hilt to loosen the blade in its scabbard. "Still, we'll get off the road and let them pass. There are lords and lords." It never hurt to be a little wary. The roads were not so safe as when Good King Daeron sat the Iron Throne.

He and Egg concealed themselves behind a thornbush. Dunk unslung his shield and slipped it onto his arm. It was an old thing, tall and heavy, kite-shaped, made of pine and rimmed with iron. He had bought it in Stoney Sept to replace the shield the Longinch had hacked to splinters when they fought. Dunk had not had time to have it painted with his elm and shooting star, so it still bore the arms of its last owner: a hanged man swinging grim and gray beneath a gallows tree. It was not a sigil that he would have chosen for himself, but the shield had come cheap.

The first riders galloped past within moments; two young lordlings mounted on a pair of coursers. The one on the bay wore an open-faced helm of gilded steel with three tall feathered plumes: one white, one red, one gold. Matching plumes adorned his horse's crinet. The black stallion beside him was barded in blue and gold. His trappings rippled with the wind of his passage as he thundered past. Side by side the riders streaked on by, whooping and laughing, their long cloaks streaming behind.

A third lord followed more sedately, at the head of a long column. There were two dozen in the party, grooms and cooks and serving men, all to attend three knights, plus men-at-arms and mounted crossbowmen, and a dozen drays heavy-laden with their armor, tents, and provisions. Slung from the lord's saddle was his shield, dark orange and charged with three black castles.

Dunk knew those arms, but from where? The lord who bore them was an older man, sour-mouthed and saturnine, with a close-cropped salt-and-pepper beard. *He might have been at Ashford Meadow,* Dunk thought. *Or maybe we served at his castle when I was squiring for Ser Arlan.* The old hedge knight had done service at so many different keeps and castles through the years that Dunk could not recall the half of them.

The lord reined up abruptly, scowling at the thornbush. "You. In the bush. Show yourself." Behind him, two crossbowmen slipped quarrels into the notch. The rest continued on their way.

Dunk stepped through the tall grass, his shield upon his arm, his right hand resting on the pommel of his longsword. His face was a red-brown mask from the dust the horses had kicked up, and he was naked from the waist up. He looked a scruffy sight, he knew, though it was like to be the size of him that gave the other pause. "We want no quarrel, m'lord. There's only the two of us, me and my squire." He beckoned Egg forward.

"Squire? Do you claim to be a knight?"

Dunk did not like the way the man was looking at him. *Those eyes could flay a man.* It seemed prudent to remove his hand from his sword. "I am a hedge knight, seeking service."

"Every robber knight I've ever hanged has said the same. Your device may be prophetic, ser . . . if *ser* you are. A gallows and a hanged man. These are your arms?"

"No, m'lord. I need to have the shield repainted."

"Why? Did you rob it off a corpse?"

"I bought it, for good coin." *Three castles, black on orange . . . where have I seen those before?* "I am no robber."

The lord's eyes were chips of flint. "How did you come by that scar upon your cheek? A cut from a whip?"

"A dagger. Though my face is none of your concern, m'lord."

"I'll be the judge of what is my concern."

By then, the two younger knights had come trotting back to see what had delayed their party. "There you are, Gormy," called the rider on the black, a young man lean and lithe, with a comely, clean-shaven face and fine features. Black hair fell shining to his collar. His doublet was made of dark blue silk edged in gold satin. Across his chest an engrailed cross had been embroidered in gold thread, with a golden fiddle in the first and third quarters, a golden sword in the second and the fourth. His eyes caught the deep blue of his doublet and sparkled with amusement. "Alyn feared you'd fallen from your horse. A palpable excuse, it seems to me; I was about to leave him in my dust."

"Who are these two brigands?" asked the rider on the bay.

Egg bristled at the insult: "You have no call to name us brigands, my lord. When we saw your dust, we thought *you* might be outlaws—that's the only reason that we hid. This is Ser Duncan the Tall, and I'm his squire."

The lordlings paid no more heed to that than they would have paid the croaking of a frog. "I believe that is the largest lout that I have ever seen," declared the knight of three feathers. He had a pudgy face beneath a head of curly hair the color of dark honey. "Seven feet if he's an inch, I'd wager. What a mighty crash he'll make when he comes tumbling down."

Dunk felt color rising to his face. *You'd lose your wager*, he thought. The last time he had been measured, Egg's brother Aemon pronounced him an inch shy of seven feet.

"Is that your warhorse, Ser Giant?" said the feathered lordling. "I suppose we could butcher it for the meat."

"Lord Alyn oft forgets his courtesies," the black-haired knight said. "Please forgive his churlish words, ser. Alyn, you will ask Ser Duncan for his pardon."

"If I must. Will you forgive me, ser?" He did not wait for reply, but turned his bay about and trotted down the road.

The other lingered. "Are you bound for the wedding, ser?"

Something in his tone made Dunk want to tug his forelock. He resisted the impulse and said, "We're for the ferry, m'lord."

"As are we . . . but the only lords hereabouts are Gormy and that wastrel who just left us, Alyn Cockshaw. I am a vagabond hedge knight like yourself. Ser John the Fiddler, I am called."

That was the sort of name a hedge knight might choose, but Dunk had never seen any hedge knight garbed or armed or mounted in such splendor. *The knight of the golden hedge*, he thought. "You know my name. My squire is called Egg."

"Well met, ser. Come, ride with us to Whitewalls and break a few lances to help Lord Butterwell celebrate his new marriage. I'll wager you could give a good account of yourself."

Dunk had not done any jousting since Ashford Meadow. *If I could win a few ransoms, we'd eat well on the ride north*, he thought, but the lord with the three castles on his shield said, "Ser Duncan needs to be about his journey, as do we."

John the Fiddler paid the older man no mind. "I would love to cross swords with you, ser. I've tried men of many lands and races, but never one your size. Was your father large as well?"

"I never knew my father, ser."

"I am sad to hear it. Mine own sire was taken from me too soon." The

Fiddler turned to the lord of the three castles. "We should ask Ser Duncan to join our jolly company."

"We do not need his sort."

Dunk was at a loss for words. Penniless hedge knights were not oft asked to ride with highborn lords. *I would have more in common with their servants.* Judging from the length of their column, Lord Cockshaw and the Fiddler had brought grooms to tend their horses, cooks to feed them, squires to clean their armor, guards to defend them. Dunk had Egg.

"His sort?" The Fiddler laughed. "What sort is that? The big sort? Look at the *size* of him. We want strong men. Young swords are worth more than old names, I've oft heard it said."

"By fools. You know little and less about this man. He might be a brigand, or one of Lord Bloodraven's spies."

"I'm no man's spy," said Dunk. "And m'lord has no call to speak of me as if I were deaf or dead or down in Dorne."

Those flinty eyes considered him. "Down in Dorne would be a good place for you, ser. You have my leave to go there."

"Pay him no mind," the Fiddler said. "He's a sour old soul—he suspects everyone. Gormy, I have a good feeling about this fellow. Ser Duncan, will you come with us to Whitewalls?"

"M'lord, I . . ." How could he share a camp with such as these? Their serving men would raise their pavilions, their grooms would curry their horses, their cooks would serve them each a capon or a joint of beef, whilst Dunk and Egg gnawed on strips of hard salt beef. "I couldn't."

"You see," said the lord of the three castles. "He knows his place, and it is not with us." He turned his horse back toward the road. "By now Lord Cockshaw is half a league ahead."

"I suppose I must chase him down again." The Fiddler gave Dunk an apologetic smile. "Perchance we'll meet again someday. I hope so. I should love to try my lance on you."

Dunk did not know what to say to that. "Good fortune in the lists, ser," he finally managed, but by then Ser John had wheeled about to chase the column. The older lord rode after him. Dunk was glad to see his back. He had not liked his flinty eyes, nor Lord Alyn's arrogance. The Fiddler had been pleasant enough, but there was something odd about him as well. "Two fiddles and two swords, a cross engrailed," he said to Egg as they watched the dust of their departure. "What house is that?"

"None, ser. I never saw that shield in any roll of arms."

Perhaps he is a hedge knight after all. Dunk had devised his own arms at Ashford Meadow, when a puppeteer called Tanselle Too-Tall asked him what he wanted painted on his shield. "Was the older lord some kin to House Frey?" The Freys bore castles on their shields, and their holdings were not far from here.

Egg rolled his eyes. "The Frey arms are two blue *towers* connected by a bridge, on a gray field. Those were three *castles*, black on orange, ser. Did you see a bridge?"

"No." *He just does that to annoy me.* "And next time you roll your eyes at me, I'll clout you on the ear so hard they'll roll back into your head for good."

Egg looked chastened. "I never meant—"

"Never mind what you meant. Just tell me who he was."

"Gormon Peake, the Lord of Starpike."

"That's down in the Reach, isn't it? Does he really have three castles?"

"Only on his shield, ser. House Peake did hold three castles once, but two of them were lost."

"How do you lose two castles?"

"You fight for the Black Dragon, ser."

"Oh." Dunk felt stupid. *That again.*

For two hundred years, the realm had been ruled by the descendants of Aegon the Conquerer and his sisters, who had made the Seven Kingdoms one and forged the Iron Throne. Their royal banners bore the three-headed dragon of House Targaryen, red on black. Sixteen years ago, a bastard son of King Aegon IV named Daemon Blackfyre had risen in revolt against his trueborn brother. Daemon had used the three-headed dragon on his banners too, but he reversed the colors, as many bastards did. His revolt had ended on the Redgrass Field, where Daemon and his twin sons died beneath a rain of Lord Bloodraven's arrows. Those rebels who survived and bent the knee were pardoned, but some lost land, some titles, some gold. All gave hostages to ensure their future loyalty.

Three castles, black on orange. "I remember now. Ser Arlan never liked to talk about the Redgrass Field, but once in his cups he told me how his sister's son had died." He could almost hear the old man's voice again, smell the wine upon his breath. "Roger of Pennytree, that was his name. His head was smashed in by a mace wielded by a lord with three castles on his shield." *Lord Gormon Peake. The old man never knew his name. Or never wanted to.* By that time Lord Peake and John the Fiddler and their party were no more than a plume of red dust in the distance. *It was sixteen years ago. The Pretender died, and those who followed him were exiled or forgiven. Anyway, it has nought to do with me.*

For a while they rode along without talking, listening to the plaintive cries of birds. Half a league on, Dunk cleared his throat and said, "Butterwell, he said. His lands are near?"

"On the far side of the lake, ser. Lord Butterwell was the master of coin when King Aegon sat the Iron Throne. King Daeron made him Hand, but not for long. His arms are undy green and white and yellow, ser." Egg loved showing off his heraldry.

"Is he a friend of your father?"

Egg made a face. "My father never liked him. In the Rebellion, Lord Butterwell's second son fought for the pretender and his eldest for the king. That way he was certain to be on the winning side. Lord Butterwell didn't fight for anyone."

"Some might call that prudent."

"My father calls it craven."

Aye, he would. Prince Maekar was a hard man, proud and full of scorn. "We have to go by Whitewalls to reach the kingsroad. Why not fill our bellies?" Just the thought was enough to cause his guts to rumble. "Might be that one of the wedding guests will need an escort back to his own seat."

"You said that we were going north."

"The Wall has stood eight thousand years, it will last awhile longer. It's a thousand leagues from here to there, and we could do with some more silver in our purse." Dunk was picturing himself atop Thunder, riding down that sour-faced old lord with the three castles on his shield. That would be sweet. *"It was old Ser Arlan's squire who defeated you," I could tell him when he came to ransom back his arms and armor. "The boy who replaced the boy you killed." The old man would like that.*

"You're not thinking of entering the lists, are you, ser?"

"Might be it's time."

"It's not, ser."

"Maybe it's time I gave you a good clout in the ear." *I'd only need to win two tilts. If I could collect two ransoms and pay out only one, we'd eat like kings for a year.* "If there was a melee, I might enter that." Dunk's size and strength would serve him better in a melee than in the lists.

"It's not customary to have a melee at a marriage, ser."

"It's customary to have a feast, though. We have a long way to go. Why not set out with our bellies full for once?"

The sun was low in the west by the time they saw the lake, its waters glimmering red and gold, bright as a sheet of beaten copper. When they glimpsed the turrets of the inn above some willows, Dunk donned his sweaty tunic once again and stopped to splash some water on his face. He washed off the dust of the road as best he could, and ran wet fingers through his thick mop of sun-streaked hair. There was nothing to be done for his size, or the scar that marked his cheek, but he wanted to make himself appear somewhat less the wild robber knight.

The inn was bigger than he'd expected, a great gray sprawl of a place, timbered and turreted, half of it built on pilings out over the water. A road of rough-cut planks had been laid down over the muddy lakeshore to the ferry landing, but neither the ferry nor the ferrymen were in evidence. Across the road stood a stable with a thatched roof. A dry stone wall enclosed the yard, but the gate was open. Within, they found a well and a watering trough. "See to the animals," Dunk told Egg, "but see that they don't drink too much. I'll ask about some food."

He found the innkeep sweeping off the steps. "Are you come for the ferry?" the woman asked him. "You're too late. The sun's going down, and Ned don't like to cross by night unless the moon is full. He'll be back first thing in the morning."

"Do you know how much he asks?"

"Three pennies for each of you, and ten for your horses."

"We have two horses and a mule."

"It's ten for mules as well."

Dunk did the sums in his head, and came up with six-and-thirty, more than he had hoped to spend. "Last time I came this way, it was only two pennies, and six for horses."

"Take that up with Ned, it's nought to me. If you're looking for a bed, I've none to offer. Lord Shawney and Lord Costayne brought their retinues. I'm full to bursting."

"Is Lord Peake here as well?" *He killed Ser Arlan's squire.* "He was with Lord Cockshaw and John the Fiddler."

"Ned took them across on his last run." She looked Dunk up and down. "Were you part of their company?"

"We met them on the road, is all." A good smell was drifting out the windows of the inn, one that made Dunk's mouth water. "We might like some of what you're roasting, if it's not too costly."

"It's wild boar," the woman said, "well peppered, and served with onions, mushrooms, and mashed neeps."

"We could do without the neeps. Some slices off the boar and a tankard of your good brown ale would do for us. How much would you ask for that? And maybe we could have a place on your stable floor to bed down for the night?"

That was a mistake. "The stables are for horses. That's why we call them stables. You're big as a horse, I'll grant you, but I see only two legs." She swept her broom at him, to shoo him off. "I can't be expected to feed all the Seven Kingdoms. The boar is for my guests. So is my ale. I won't have lords saying that I run short of food or drink before they were surfeit. The lake is full of fish, and you'll find some other rogues camped down by the stumps. Hedge knights, if you believe them." Her tone made it quite clear that she did not. "Might be they'd have food to share. It's nought to me. Away with you now, I've work to do." The door closed with a solid thump behind her, before Dunk could even think to ask where he might find these stumps.

He found Egg sitting on the horse trough, soaking his feet in the water and fanning his face with his big floppy hat. "Are they roasting pig, ser? I smell pork."

"Wild boar," said Dunk in a glum tone, "but who wants boar when we have good salt beef?"

Egg made a face. "Can I please eat my boots instead, ser? I'll make a new pair out of the salt beef. It's tougher."

"No," said Dunk, trying not to smile. "You can't eat your boots. One more word and you'll eat my fist, though. Get your feet out of that trough." He found his greathelm on the mule and slung it underhand at Egg. "Draw some water from the well and soak the beef." Unless you soaked it for a good long time, the salt beef was like to break your teeth. It tasted best when soaked in ale, but water would serve. "Don't use the trough either, I don't care to taste your feet."

"My feet could only improve the taste, ser," Egg said, wriggling his toes. But he did as he was bid.

The hedge knights did not prove hard to find. Egg spied their fire flickering in the woods along the lakeshore, so they made for it, leading the animals behind them. The boy carried Dunk's helm beneath one arm, sloshing with each step he took. By then the sun was a red memory in the west. Before long the trees opened up, and they found themselves in what must once have been a weirwood grove. Only a ring of white stumps and a tangle of bone-pale roots remained to show where the trees had stood, when the children of the forest ruled in Westeros.

Amongst the weirwood stumps, they found two men squatting near a cook fire, passing a skin of wine from hand to hand. Their horses were cropping at the grass beyond the grove, and they had stacked their arms and armor in neat piles. A much younger man sat apart from the other two, his back against a chestnut tree. "Well met, sers," Dunk called out in a cheerful voice. It was never wise to take armed men unawares. "I am called Ser Duncan the Tall. The lad is Egg. May we share your fire?"

A stout man of middling years rose to greet them, garbed in tattered finery. Flamboyant ginger whiskers framed his face. "Well met, Ser Duncan. You are a large one . . . and most welcome, certainly, as is your lad. *Egg*, was it? What sort of name is that, pray?"

"A short one, ser." Egg knew better than to admit that Egg was short for Aegon. Not to men he did not know.

"Indeed. What happened to your hair?"

Rootworms, Dunk thought. *Tell him it was rootworms, boy.* That was the safest story, the tale they told most often . . . though sometimes Egg took it in his head to play some childish game.

"I shaved it off, ser. I mean to stay shaven until I earn my spurs."

"A noble vow. I am Ser Kyle, the Cat of Misty Moor. Under yonder chestnut sits Ser Glendon, ah, Ball. And here you have the good Ser Maynard Plumm."

Egg's ears pricked up at that name. "Plumm . . . are you kin to Lord Viserys Plumm, ser?"

"Distantly," confessed Ser Maynard, a tall, thin, stoop-shouldered man with long straight flaxen hair, "though I doubt that His Lordship would admit to it. One might say that he is of the sweet Plumms, whilst I am of the sour." Plumm's cloak was as purple as name, though frayed about the edges and badly dyed. A moonstone brooch big as a hen's egg fastened it at the shoulder. Elsewise he wore dun-colored roughspun and stained brown leather.

"We have salt beef," said Dunk.

"Ser Maynard has a bag of apples," said Kyle the Cat. "And I have pickled eggs and onions. Why, together we have the makings of a feast! Be seated, ser. We have a fine choice of stumps for your comfort. We will be here until midmorning, unless I miss my guess. There is only the one ferry, and it is not big enough to take us all. The lords and their tails must cross first."

"Help me with the horses," Dunk told Egg. Together the two of them unsaddled Thunder, Rain, and Maester.

Only when the animals had been fed and watered and hobbled for the night did Dunk accept the wineskin that Ser Maynard offered him. "Even sour wine is better than none," said Kyle the Cat. "We'll drink finer vintages at Whitewalls. Lord Butterwell is said to have the best wines north of the Arbor. He was once the King's Hand, as his father's father was before him, and he is said to be a pious man besides, and very rich."

"His wealth is all from cows," said Maynard Plumm. "He ought to take a swollen udder for his arms. These Butterwells have milk running in their veins, and the Freys are no better. This will be a marriage of cattle thieves and toll collectors, one lot of coin clinkers joining with another. When the Black Dragon rose, this lord of cows sent one son to Daemon and one to Daeron, to make certain there was a Butterwell on the winning side. Both perished on the Redgrass Field, and his youngest died in the spring. That's why he's making this new marriage. Unless this new wife gives him a son, Butterwell's name will die with him."

"As it should." Ser Glendon Ball gave his sword another stroke with the whetstone. "The Warrior hates cravens."

The scorn in his voice made Dunk give the youth a closer look. Ser Glendon's clothes were of good cloth, but well-worn and ill-matched, with the look of hand-me-downs. Tufts of dark brown hair stuck out from beneath his iron halfhelm. The lad himself was short and chunky, with small close-set eyes, thick shoulders, and muscular arms. His eyebrows were shaggy as two caterpillars after a wet spring, his nose bulbous, his chin pugnacious. And he was young. *Sixteen, might be. No more than eighteen.* Dunk might have taken him for a squire if Ser Kyle had not named him with a *ser.* The lad had pimples on his cheeks in place of whiskers.

"How long have you been a knight?" Dunk asked him.

"Long enough. Half a year when the moon turns. I was knighted by Ser Morgan Dunstable of Tumbler's Falls, two dozen people saw it, but I have been training for knighthood since I was born. I rode before I walked, and knocked a grown man's tooth out of his head before I lost any of my own. I mean to make my name at Whitewalls, and claim the dragon's egg."

"The dragon's egg? Is that the champion's prize? Truly?" The last dragon had perished half a century ago. Ser Arlan had once seen a clutch of her eggs, though. *They were hard as stone, he said, but beautiful to look upon,* the old man had told Dunk. "How could Lord Butterwell come by a dragon's egg?"

"King Aegon presented the egg to his father's father after guesting for a night at his old castle," said Ser Maynard Plumm.

"Was it a reward for some act of valor?" asked Dunk.

Ser Kyle chuckled. "Some might call it that. Supposedly old Lord Butterwell had three young maiden daughters when His Grace came calling. By morning, all three had royal bastards in their little bellies. A hot night's work, that was."

Dunk had heard such talk before. Aegon the Unworthy had bedded half the maidens in the realm and fathered bastards on the lot of them, supposedly. Worse, the old king had legitimized them all upon his deathbed; the baseborn ones born of tavern wenches, whores, and shepherd girls, and the Great Bastards whose mothers had been highborn. "We'd all be bastard sons of old King Aegon if half these tales were true."

"And who's to say we're not?" Ser Maynard quipped.

"You ought to come with us to Whitewalls, Ser Duncan," urged Ser Kyle. "Your size is sure to catch some lordling's eye. You might find good service there. I know I shall. Joffrey Caswell will be at this wedding, the Lord of Bitterbridge. When he was three, I made him his first sword. I carved it out of pine, to fit his hand. In my greener days my sword was sworn to his father."

"Was that one carved from pine as well?" Ser Maynard asked.

Kyle the Cat had the grace to laugh. "That sword was good steel, I assure you. I should be glad to ply it once again in the service of the centaur.

Ser Duncan, even if you do not choose to tilt, do join us for the wedding feast. There will be singers and musicians, jugglers and tumblers, and a troupe of comic dwarfs."

Dunk frowned. "Egg and I have a long journey before us. We're headed north to Winterfell. Lord Beron Stark is gathering swords to drive the krakens from his shores for good."

"Too cold up there for me," said Ser Maynard. "If you want to kill krakens, go west. The Lannisters are building ships to strike back at the ironmen on their home islands. That's how you put an end to Dagon Greyjoy. Fighting him on land is fruitless, he just slips back to sea. You have to beat him on the water."

That had the ring of truth, but the prospect of fighting ironmen at sea was not one that Dunk relished. He'd had a taste of that on the *White Lady*, sailing from Dorne to Oldtown, when he'd donned his armor to help the crew repel some raiders. The battle had been desperate and bloody, and once he'd almost fallen in the water. That would have been the end of him.

"The throne should take a lesson from Stark and Lannister," declared Ser Kyle the Cat. "At least they fight. What do the Targaryens do? King Aerys hides amongst his books, Prince Rhaegel prances naked through the Red Keep's halls, and Prince Maekar broods at Summerhall."

Egg was prodding at the fire with a stick, to send sparks floating up into the night. Dunk was pleased to see him ignoring the mention of his father's name. *Perhaps he's finally learned to hold that tongue of his.*

"Myself, I blame Bloodraven," Ser Kyle went on. "He is the King's Hand, yet he does nothing, whilst the krakens spread flame and terror up and down the sunset sea."

Ser Maynard gave a shrug. "His eye is fixed on Tyrosh, where Bittersteel sits in exile, plotting with the sons of Daemon Blackfyre. So he keeps the king's ships close at hand, lest they attempt to cross."

"Aye, that may well be," Ser Kyle said, "but many would welcome the return of Bittersteel. Bloodraven is the root of all our woes, the white worm gnawing at the heart of the realm."

Dunk frowned, remembering the hunchbacked septon at Stoney Sept. "Words like that can cost a man his head. Some might say you're talking treason."

"How can the truth be treason?" asked Kyle the Cat. "In King Daeron's day, a man did not have to fear to speak his mind, but now?" He made a rude noise. "Bloodraven put King Aerys on the Iron Throne, but for how long? Aerys is weak, and when he dies, it will be bloody war between Lord Rivers and Prince Maekar for the crown, the Hand against the heir."

"You have forgotten Prince Rhaegel, my friend," Ser Maynard objected, in a mild tone. "He comes next in line to Aerys, not Maekar, and his children after him."

"Rhaegel is feeble-minded. Why, I bear him no ill will, but the man is good as dead, and those twins of his as well, though whether they will die of Maekar's mace or Bloodraven's spells . . ."

Seven save us, Dunk thought as Egg spoke up shrill and loud. "Prince Maekar is Prince Rhaegel's *brother*. He loves him well. He'd never do harm to him or his."

"Be quiet, boy," Dunk growled at him. "These knights want none of your opinions."

"I can talk if I want."

"No," said Dunk. "You can't." *That mouth of yours will get you killed someday. And me as well, most like.* "That salt beef's soaked long enough, I think. A strip for all our friends, and be quick about it."

Egg flushed, and for half a heartbeat, Dunk feared the boy might talk back. Instead he settled for a sullen look, seething as only a boy of eleven years can seethe. "Aye, ser," he said, fishing in the bottom of Dunk's helm. His shaven head shone redly in the firelight as he passed out the salt beef.

Dunk took his piece and worried at it. The soak had turned the meat from wood to leather, but that was all. He sucked on one corner, tasting the salt and trying not to think about the roast boar at the inn, crackling on its spit and dripping fat.

As dusk deepened, flies and stinging midges came swarming off the lake. The flies preferred to plague their horses, but the midges had a taste for man flesh. The only way to keep from being bitten was to sit close to the fire, breathing smoke. *Cook or be devoured,* Dunk thought glumly, *now there's a beggar's choice.* He scratched at his arms and edged closer to the fire.

The wineskin soon came round again. The wine was sour and strong. Dunk drank deep, and passed along the skin, whilst the Cat of Misty Moor began to talk of how he had saved the life of the Lord of Bitterbridge during the Blackfyre Rebellion. "When Lord Armond's banner-bearer fell, I leapt down from my horse with traitors all around us—"

"Ser," said Glendon Ball. "Who were these *traitors*?"

"The Blackfyre men, I meant."

Firelight glimmered off the steel in Ser Glendon's hand. The pockmarks on his face flamed as red as open sores, and his every sinew was wound as tight as a crossbow. "My father fought for the Black Dragon."

This again. Dunk snorted. *Red or Black?* was not a thing you asked a man. It always made for trouble. "I am sure Ser Kyle meant no insult to your father."

"None," Ser Kyle agreed. "It's an old tale, the Red Dragon and the Black. No sense for us to fight about it now, lad. We are all brothers of the hedges here."

Ser Glendon seemed to weigh the Cat's words, to see if he was being mocked. "Daemon Blackfyre was no traitor. The old king gave *him* the sword. He saw the worthiness in Daemon, even though he was born bastard. Why else would he put Blackfyre into his hand in place of Daeron's? He meant for him to have the kingdom too. Daemon was the better man."

A hush fell. Dunk could hear the soft crackle of the fire. He could feel midges crawling on the back of his neck. He slapped at them, watching Egg, willing him to be still. "I was just a boy when they fought the Redgrass Field," he said, when it seemed that no one else would speak, "but I squired for a knight who fought with the Red Dragon, and later served another who fought for the Black. There were brave men on both sides."

"Brave men," echoed Kyle the Cat, a bit feebly.

"Heroes." Glendon Ball turned his shield about, so all of them could see the sigil painted there, a fireball blazing red and yellow across a night-black field. "I come from hero's blood."

"You're *Fireball's* son," Egg said.

That was the first time they saw Ser Glendon smile.

Ser Kyle the Cat studied the boy closely. "How can that be? How old are you? Quentyn Ball died—"

"—before I was born," Ser Glendon finished, "but in me, he lives again." He slammed his sword back into its scabbard. "I'll show you all at Whitewalls, when I claim the dragon's egg."

The next day proved the truth of Ser Kyle's prophecy. Ned's ferry was nowise large enough to accomodate all those who wished to cross, so

Lords Costayne and Shawney must go first, with their tails. That required several trips, each taking more than an hour. There were the mudflats to contend with, horses and wagons to be gotten down the planks, loaded on the boat, and unloaded again across the lake. The two lords slowed matters even further when they got into a shouting match over precedence. Shawney was the elder, but Costayne held himself to be better born.

There was nought that Dunk could do but wait and swelter. "We could go first if you let me use my boot," Egg said.

"We could," Dunk answered, "but we won't. Lord Costayne and Lord Shawney were here before us. Besides, they're lords."

Egg made a face. "Rebel lords."

Dunk frowned down at him. "What do you mean?"

"They were for the Black Dragon. Well, Lord Shawney was, and Lord Costayne's father. Aemon and I used to fight the battle on Maester Melaquin's green table with painted soldiers and little banners. Costayne's arms quarter a silver chalice on black with a black rose on gold. That banner was on the left of Daemon's host. Shawney was with Bittersteel on the right, and almost died of his wounds."

"Old dead history. They're here now, aren't they? So they bent the knee, and King Daeron gave them pardon."

"Yes, but—"

Dunk pinched the boy's lips shut. "Hold your tongue."

Egg held his tongue.

No sooner had the last boatload of Shawney men pushed off than Lord and Lady Smallwood turned up at the landing with their own tail, so they must needs wait again.

The fellowship of the hedge had not survived the night, it was plain to see. Ser Glendon kept his own company, prickly and sullen. Kyle the Cat judged that it would be midday before they were allowed to board the ferry, so he detached himself from the others to try to ingratiate himself with Lord Smallwood, with whom he had some slight acquaintance. Ser Maynard spent his time gossiping with the innkeep.

"Stay well away from that one," Dunk warned Egg. There was something about Plumm that troubled him. "He could be a robber knight, for all we know."

The warning only seemed to make Ser Maynard more interesting to

Egg. "I never knew a robber knight. Do you think he means to rob the dragon's egg?"

"Lord Butterwell will have the egg well guarded, I'm sure." Dunk scratched the midge bites on his neck. "Do you think he might display it at the feast? I'd like to get a look at one."

"I'd show you mine, ser, but it's at Summerhall."

"Yours? Your *dragon's egg*?" Dunk frowned down at the boy, wondering if this was some jape. "Where did it come from?"

"From a dragon, ser. They put it in my cradle."

"Do you want a clout in the ear? There are no dragons."

"No, but there are eggs. The last dragon left a clutch of five, and they have more on Dragonstone, old ones from before the Dance. My brothers all have them too. Aerion's looks as though it's made of gold and silver, with veins of fire running through it. Mine is white and green, all swirly."

"Your dragon's egg." *They put it in his cradle.* Dunk was so used to Egg that sometimes he forgot Aegon was a prince. *Of course they'd put a dragon egg inside his cradle.* "Well, see that you don't go mentioning this egg where anyone is like to hear."

"I'm not *stupid*, ser." Egg lowered his voice. "Someday the dragons will return. My brother Daeron's dreamed of it, and King Aerys read it in a prophecy. Maybe it will be my egg that hatches. That would be *splendid*."

"Would it?" Dunk had his doubts.

Not Egg. "Aemon and I used to pretend that our eggs would be the ones to hatch. If they did, we could fly through the sky on dragonback, like the first Aegon and his sisters."

"Aye, and if all the other knights in the realm should die, I'd be the Lord Commander of the Kingsguard. If these eggs are so bloody precious, why is Lord Butterwell giving his away?"

"To show the realm how rich he is?"

"I suppose." Dunk scratched his neck again and glanced over at Ser Glendon Ball, who was tightening the cinches on his saddle as he waited for the ferry. *That horse will never serve.* Ser Glendon's mount was a sway-backed stot, undersized and old. "What do you know about his sire? Why did they call him Fireball?"

"For his hot head and red hair. Ser Quentyn Ball was the master-at-arms at the Red Keep. He taught my father and my uncles how to fight. The Great Bastards too. King Aegon promised to raise him to the Kingsguard, so Fireball made his wife join the silent sisters, only by the time a place came open, King Aegon was dead and King Daeron named Ser Willam Wylde instead. My father says that it was Fireball as much as Bittersteel who convinced Daemon Blackfyre to claim the crown, and rescued him when Daeron sent the Kingsguard to arrest him. Later on, Fireball killed Lord Lefford at the gates of Lannisport and sent the Grey Lion running back to hide inside the Rock. At the crossing of the Mander, he cut down the sons of Lady Penrose one by one. They say he spared the life of the youngest one as a kindness to his mother."

"That was chivalrous of him," Dunk had to admit. "Did Ser Quentyn die upon the Redgrass Field?"

"Before, ser," Egg replied. "An archer put an arrow through his throat as he dismounted by a stream to have a drink. Just some common man, no one knows who."

"Those common men can be dangerous when they get it in their heads to start slaying lords and heroes." Dunk saw the ferry creeping slowly across the lake. "Here it comes."

"It's slow. Are we going to go to Whitewalls, ser?"

"Why not? I want to see this dragon's egg." Dunk smiled. "If I win the tourney, we'd *both* have dragon's eggs."

Egg gave him a doubtful look.

"What? Why are you looking at me that way?"

"I could tell you, ser," the boy said solemnly, "but I need to learn to hold my tongue."

They seated the hedge knights well below the salt, closer to the doors than to the dais.

Whitewalls was almost new as castles went, having been raised a mere forty years ago by the grandsire of its present lord. The smallfolk hereabouts called it the Milkhouse, for its walls and keeps and towers were made of finely dressed white stone, quarried in the Vale and brought over the mountains at great expense. Inside were floors and pillars of milky white marble veined with gold; the rafters overhead were carved from the bone-pale trunks of weirwoods. Dunk could not begin to imagine what all of that had cost.

The hall was not so large as some others he had known, though. *At least we were allowed beneath the roof,* Dunk thought as he took his place on the bench between Ser Maynard Plumm and Kyle the Cat. Though uninvited, the three of them had been welcomed to the feast quick enough; it was ill luck to refuse a knight hospitality on your wedding day.

Young Ser Glendon had a harder time, however. "Fireball never had a son," Dunk heard Lord Butterwell's steward tell him, loudly. The stripling answered heatedly, and the name of Ser Morgan Dunstable was mentioned several times, but the steward had remained adamant. When Ser Glendon touched his sword hilt, a dozen men-at-arms appeared with spears in hand, but for a moment it looked as though there might be bloodshed. It was only the intervention of a big blond knight named Kirby Pimm that saved the situation. Dunk was too far away to hear, but he saw Pimm clasp an arm around the steward's shoulders and murmur in his ear, laughing. The steward frowned, and said something to Ser Glendon that turned the boy's face dark red. *He looks as if he's about to cry,* Dunk thought, watching. *That, or kill someone.* After all of that, the young knight was finally admitted to the castle hall.

Poor Egg was not so fortunate. "The great hall is for the lords and knights," an understeward had informed them haughtily when Dunk tried to bring the boy inside. "We have set up tables in the inner yard for squires, grooms, and men-at-arms."

If you had an inkling who he was, you would seat him on the dais on a cushioned throne. Dunk had not much liked the look of the other squires. A few were lads of Egg's own age, but most were older, seasoned fighters who long ago had made the choice to serve a knight rather than become one. *Or did they have a choice?* Knighthood required more than chivalry and skill at arms; it required horse and sword and armor too, and all of that was costly. "Watch your tongue," he told Egg before he left him in that company. "These are grown men; they won't take kindly to your insolence. Sit and eat and listen, might be you'll learn some things."

For his own part, Dunk was just glad to be out of the hot sun, with a wine cup before him and a chance to fill his belly. Even a hedge knight grows weary of chewing every bite of food for half an hour. Down here below the salt, the fare would be more plain than fancy, but there would be no lack of it. Below the salt was good enough for Dunk.

But *peasant's pride is lordling's shame,* the old man used to say. "This cannot be my proper place," Ser Glendon Ball told the understeward

hotly. He had donned a clean doublet for the feast, a handsome old garment with gold lace at the cuffs and collar and the red chevron and white
plates of House Ball sewn across the chest. "Do you know who my father
was?"

"A noble knight and mighty lord, I have no doubt," said the understeward, "but the same is true of many here. Please take your seat or take your
leave, ser. It is all the same to me."

In the end, the boy took his place below the salt with the rest of them,
his mouth sullen. The long white hall was filling up as more knights
crowded onto the benches. The crowd was larger than Dunk had anticipated, and from the looks of it, some of the guests had come a very long
way. He and Egg had not been around so many lords and knights since
Ashford Meadow, and there was no way to guess who else might turn up
next. *We should have stayed out in the hedges, sleeping under trees. If I am
recognized . . .*

When a serving man placed a loaf of black bread on the cloth in front
of each of them, Dunk was grateful for the distraction. He sawed the loaf
open lengthwise, hollowed out the bottom half for a trencher, and ate the
top. It was stale, but compared with his salt beef, it was custard. At least it
did not have to be soaked in ale or milk or water to make it soft enough to
chew.

"Ser Duncan, you appear to be attracting a deal of attention," Ser Maynard Plumm observed as Lord Vyrwel and his party went parading past
them toward places of high honor at the top of the hall. "Those girls up on
the dais cannot seem to take their eyes off you. I'll wager they have never
seen a man so big. Even seated, you are half a head taller than any man in
the hall."

Dunk hunched his shoulders. He was used to being stared at, but that
did not mean he liked it. "Let them look."

"That's the Old Ox down there beneath the dais," Ser Maynard said.
"They call him a huge man, but seems to me his belly is the biggest thing
about him. You're a bloody giant next to him."

"Indeed, ser," said one of their companions on the bench, a sallow man,
saturnine, clad in grey and green. His eyes were small and shrewd, set
close together beneath thin arching brows. A neat black beard framed his
mouth, to make up for his receding hair. "In such a field as this, your size
alone should make you one of the most formidable competitors."

"I had heard the Brute of Bracken might be coming," said another man, farther down the bench.

"I think not," said the man in green and grey. "This is only a bit of jousting to celebrate His Lordship's nuptials. A tilt in the yard to mark the tilt between the sheets. Hardly worth the bother for the likes of Otho Bracken."

Ser Kyle the Cat took a drink of wine. "I'll wager my lord of Butterwell does not take the field either. He will cheer on his champions from his lord's box in the shade."

"Then he'll see his champions fall," boasted Ser Glendon Ball, "and in the end, he'll hand his egg to me."

"Ser Glendon is the son of Fireball," Ser Kyle explained to the new man. "Might we have the honor of your name, ser?"

"Ser Uthor Underleaf. The son of no one of importance." Underleaf's garments were of good cloth, clean and well cared for, but simply cut. A silver clasp in the shape of a snail fastened his cloak. "If your lance is the equal of your tongue, Ser Glendon, you may even give this big fellow here a contest."

Ser Glendon glanced at Dunk as the wine was being poured. "If we meet, he'll fall. I don't care how big he is."

Dunk watched a server fill his wine cup. "I am better with a sword than with a lance," he admitted, "and even better with a battleaxe. Will there be a melee here?" His size and strength would stand him in good stead in a melee, and he knew he could give as good as he got. Jousting was another matter.

"A melee? At a marriage?" Ser Kyle sounded shocked. "That would be unseemly."

Ser Maynard gave a chuckle. "A marriage *is* a melee, as any married man could tell you."

Ser Uthor chuckled. "There's just the joust, I fear, but besides the dragon's egg, Lord Butterwell has promised thirty golden dragons for the loser of the final tilt, and ten each for the knights defeated in the round before."

Ten dragons is not so bad. Ten dragons would buy a palfrey, so Dunk would not need to ride Thunder save in battle. Ten dragons would buy a suit of plate for Egg, and a proper knight's pavilion sewn with Dunk's tree and falling star. *Ten dragons would mean roast goose and ham and pigeon pie.*

"There are ransoms to be had as well, for those who win their matches," Ser Uthor said as he hollowed out his trencher, "and I have heard it rumored that some men place wagers on the tilts. Lord Butterwell himself is not fond of taking risks, but amongst his guests are some who wager heavily."

No sooner had he spoken than Ambrose Butterwell made his entrance, to a fanfare of trumpets from the minstrel's gallery. Dunk shoved to his feet with the rest as Butterwell escorted his new bride down a patterned Myrish carpet to the dais, arm in arm. The girl was fifteen and freshly flowered, her lord husband fifty and freshly widowed. She was pink and he was grey. Her bride's cloak trailed behind her, done in undy green and white and yellow. It looked so hot and heavy that Dunk wondered how she could bear to wear it. Lord Butterwell looked hot and heavy too, with his heavy jowls and thinning flaxen hair.

The bride's father followed close behind her, hand in hand with his young son. Lord Frey of the Crossing was a lean man elegant in blue and grey, his heir a chinless boy of four whose nose was dripping snot. Lords Costayne and Risley came next, with their lady wives, daughters of Lord Butterwell by his first wife. Frey's daughters followed with their own husbands. Then came Lord Gormon Peake; Lords Smallwood, and Shawney; various lesser lords and landed knights. Amongst them Dunk glimpsed John the Fiddler and Alyn Cockshaw. Lord Alyn looked to be in his cups, though the feast had not yet properly begun.

By the time all of them had sauntered to the dais, the high table was as crowded as the benches. Lord Butterwell and his bride sat on plump downy cushions in a double throne of gilded oak. The rest planted themselves in tall chairs with fancifully carved arms. On the wall behind them, two huge banners hung from the rafters: the twin towers of Frey, blue on grey, and the green and white and yellow undy of the Butterwells.

It fell to Lord Frey to lead the toasts. *"The king!"* he began simply. Ser Glendon held his wine cup out above the water basin. Dunk clanked his cup against it, and against Ser Uthor's and the rest as well. They drank.

"Lord Butterwell, our gracious host," Frey proclaimed next. "May the Father grant him long life and many sons."

They drank again.

"Lady Butterwell, the maiden bride, my darling daughter. May the Mother make her fertile." Frey gave the girl a smile. "I shall want a grandson before

the year is out. Twins would suit me even better, so churn the butter well tonight, my sweet."

Laughter rang against the rafters, and the guests drank still once more. The wine was rich and red and sweet.

Then Lord Frey said, "I give you the King's Hand, Brynden Rivers. May the Crone's lamp light his path to wisdom." He lifted his goblet high and drank, together with Lord Butterwell and his bride and the others on the dais. Below the salt, Ser Glendon turned his cup over to spill its contents to the floor.

"A sad waste of good wine," said Maynard Plumm.

"I do not drink to kinslayers," said Ser Glendon. "Lord Bloodraven is a sorcerer and a bastard."

"Born bastard," Ser Uthor agreed mildly, "but his royal father made him legitimate as he lay dying." He drank deep, as did Ser Maynard and many others in the hall. Near as many lowered their cups, or turned them upside down as Ball had done. Dunk's own cup was heavy in his hand. *How many eyes does Lord Bloodraven have?* the riddle went. *A thousand eyes, and one.*

Toast followed toast, some proposed by Lord Frey and some by others. They drank to young Lord Tully, Lord Butterwell's liege lord, who had begged off from the wedding. They drank to the health of Leo Longthorn, Lord of Highgarden, who was rumored to be ailing. They drank to the memory of their gallant dead. *Aye,* thought Dunk, remembering. *I'll gladly drink to them.*

Ser John the Fiddler proposed the final toast. "*To my brave brothers!* I know that they are smiling tonight!"

Dunk had not intended to drink so much, with the jousting on the morrow, but the cups were filled anew after every toast, and he found he had a thirst. "Never refuse a cup of wine or a horn of ale," Ser Arlan had once told him, "it may be a year before you see another." *It would have been discourteous not to toast the bride and groom,* he told himself, *and dangerous not to drink to the king and his Hand, with strangers all about.*

Mercifully, the Fiddler's toast was the last. Lord Butterwell rose ponderously to thank them for coming and promise good jousting on the morrow. "Let the feast begin!"

Suckling pig was served at the high table, a peacock roasted in its plumage, a great pike crusted with crushed almonds. Not a bite of that made it down below the salt. Instead of suckling pig, they got salt pork, soaked in almond milk and peppered pleasantly. In place of peacock, they had capons, crisped up nice and brown and stuffed with onions, herbs, mushrooms, and roasted chestnuts. In place of pike, they ate chunks of flaky white cod in a pastry coffyn, with some sort of tasty brown sauce that Dunk could not quite place. There was pease porridge besides, buttered turnips, carrots drizzled with honey, and a ripe white cheese that smelled as strong as Bennis of the Brown Shield. Dunk ate well, but all the while wondered what Egg was getting in the yard. Just in case, he slipped half a capon into the pocket of his cloak, with some hunks of bread and a little of the smelly cheese.

As they ate, pipes and fiddles filled the air with spritely tunes, and the talk turned to the morrow's jousting. "Ser Franklyn Frey is well regarded along the Green Fork," said Uthor Underleaf, who seemed to know these local heroes well. "That's him upon the dais, the uncle of the bride. Lucas Nayland is down from Hag's Mire, he should not be discounted. Nor should Ser Mortimer Boggs, of Crackclaw Point. Elsewise, this should be a tourney of household knights and village heroes. Kirby Pimm and Galtry the Green are the best of those, though neither is a match for Lord Butterwell's good-son, Black Tom Heddle. A nasty bit of business, that one. He won the hand of His Lordship's eldest daughter by killing three of her other suitors, it's said, and once unhorsed the Lord of Casterly Rock."

"What, young Lord Tybolt?" asked Ser Maynard.

"No, the old Grey Lion, the one who died in the spring." That was how men spoke of those who had perished during the Great Spring Sickness. *He died in the spring.* Tens of thousands had died in the spring, among them a king and two young princes.

"Do not slight Ser Buford Bulwer," said Kyle the Cat. "The Old Ox slew forty men upon the Redgrass Field."

"And every year his count grows higher," said Ser Maynard. "Bulwer's day is done. Look at him. Past sixty, soft and fat, and his right eye is good as blind."

"Do not trouble to search the hall for the champion," a voice behind Dunk said. "Here I stand, sers. Feast your eyes."

Dunk turned to find Ser John the Fiddler looming over him, a half smile on his lips. His white silk doublet had dagged sleeves lined with red satin, so long their points drooped down past his knees. A heavy silver chain looped across his chest, studded with huge dark amethysts whose color matched his eyes. *That chain is worth as much as everything I own*, Dunk thought.

The wine had colored Ser Glendon's cheeks and inflamed his pimples. "Who are you, to make such boasts?"

"They call me John the Fiddler."

"Are you a musician or a warrior?"

"I can make sweet song with either lance or resined bow, as it happens. Every wedding needs a singer, and every tourney needs a mystery knight. May I join you? Butterwell was good enough to place me on the dais, but I prefer the company of my fellow hedge knights to fat pink ladies and old men." The Fiddler clapped Dunk upon the shoulder. "Be a good fellow and shove over, Ser Duncan."

Dunk shoved over. "You are too late for food, ser."

"No matter. I know where Butterwell's kitchens are. There is still some wine, I trust?" The Fiddler smelled of oranges and limes, with a hint of some strange eastern spice beneath. Nutmeg, perhaps. Dunk could not have said. What did he know of nutmeg?

"Your boasting is unseemly," Ser Glendon told the Fiddler.

"Truly? Then I must beg for your forgiveness, ser. I would never wish to give offense to any son of Fireball."

That took the youth aback. "You know who I am?"

"Your father's son, I hope."

"Look," said Ser Kyle the Cat. "The wedding pie."

Six kitchen boys were pushing it through the doors, upon a wide wheeled cart. The pie was brown and crusty and immense, and there were noises coming from inside it, squeaks and squawks and thumps. Lord and Lady Butterwell descended from the dais to meet it, sword in hand. When they cut it open, half a hundred birds burst forth to fly around the hall. In other wedding feasts Dunk had attended, the pies had been filled with doves or songbirds, but inside this one were bluejays and skylarks, pigeons and doves, mockingbirds and nightingales, small brown sparrows and a great red parrot. "One-and-twenty sorts of birds," said Ser Kyle.

"One-and-twenty sorts of bird droppings," said Ser Maynard.

"You have no poetry in your heart, ser."

"You have shit upon your shoulder."

"This is the proper way to fill a pie," Ser Kyle sniffed, cleaning off his tunic. "The pie is meant to be the marriage, and a true marriage has in it many sorts of things—joy and grief, pain and pleasure, love and lust and loyalty. So it is fitting that there be birds of many sorts. No man ever truly knows what a new wife will bring him."

"Her cunt," said Plumm, "or what would be the point?"

Dunk shoved back from the table. "I need a breath of air." It was a piss he needed, truth be told, but in fine company like this, it was more courteous to talk of air. "Pray excuse me."

"Hurry back, ser," said the Fiddler. "There are jugglers yet to come, and you do not want to miss the bedding."

Outside, the night wind lapped at Dunk like the tongue of some great beast. The hard-packed earth of the yard seemed to move beneath his feet . . . or it might be that he was swaying.

The lists had been erected in the center of the outer yard. A three-tiered wooden viewing stand had been raised beneath the walls, so Lord Butterwell and his highborn guests would be well shaded on their cushioned seats. There were tents at both ends of the lists where the knights could don their armor, with racks of tourney lances standing ready. When the wind lifted the banners for an instant, Dunk could smell the whitewash on the tilting barrier. He set off in search of the inner ward. He had to hunt up Egg and send the boy to the master of the games to enter him in the lists. That was a squire's duty.

Whitewalls was strange to him, however, and somehow Dunk got turned around. He found himself outside the kennels, where the hounds caught scent of him and began to bark and howl. *They want to tear my throat out*, he thought, *or else they want the capon in my cloak.* He doubled back the way he'd come, past the sept. A woman went running past, breathless with laughter, a bald knight in hard pursuit. The man kept falling, until finally the woman had to come back and help him up. *I should slip into the sept and ask the Seven to make that knight my first opponent,* Dunk thought, but that would have been impious. *What I really need is a privy, not a prayer.* There were some bushes near at hand, beneath a flight of pale stone steps. *Those will serve.* He groped his way behind them and unlaced his breeches. His bladder had been full to bursting. The piss went on and on.

Somewhere above, a door came open. Dunk heard footfalls on the steps, the scrape of boots on stone. ". . . beggar's feast you've laid before us. Without Bittersteel . . ."

"Bittersteel be buggered," insisted a familiar voice. "No bastard can be trusted, not even him. A few victories will bring him over the water fast enough."

Lord Peake. Dunk held his breath . . . and his piss.

"Easier to speak of victories than to win them." This speaker had a deeper voice than Peake, a bass rumble with an angry edge to it. "Old Milkblood expected the boy to have it, and so will all the rest. Glib words and charm cannot make up for that."

"A dragon would. The prince insists the egg will hatch. He dreamed it, just as he once dreamed his brothers dead. A living dragon will win us all the swords that we would want."

"A dragon is one thing, a dream's another. I promise you, Bloodraven is not off dreaming. We need a warrior, not a dreamer. Is the boy his father's son?"

"Just do your part as promised, and let me concern myself with that. Once we have Butterwell's gold and the swords of House Frey, Harrenhal will follow, then the Brackens. Otho knows he cannot hope to stand . . ."

The voices were fading as the speakers moved away. Dunk's piss began to flow again. He gave his cock a shake, and laced himself back up. "His father's son," he muttered. *Who were they speaking of? Fireball's son?*

By the time he emerged from under the steps, the two lords were well across the yard. He almost shouted after them, to make them show their faces, but thought better of it. He was alone and unarmed, and half-drunk besides. *Maybe more than half.* He stood there frowning for a moment, then marched back to the hall.

Inside, the last course had been served and the frolics had begun. One of Lord Frey's daughters played "Two Hearts That Beat As One" on the high harp, very badly. Some jugglers flung flaming torches at each other for a while, and some tumblers did cartwheels in the air. Lord Frey's nephew began to sing "The Bear and the Maiden Fair" while Ser Kirby Pimm beat out time upon the table with a wooden spoon. Others joined in, until the whole hall was bellowing, *"A bear! A bear! All black and brown, and covered with hair!"* Lord Caswell passed out at the table with his face in a puddle of wine, and Lady Vyrwel began to weep, though no one was quite certain as to the cause of her distress.

All the while the wine kept flowing. The rich Arbor reds gave way to local vintages, or so the Fiddler said; if truth be told, Dunk could not tell the difference. There was hippocras as well, he had to try a cup of that. *It might be a year before I have another.* The other hedge knights, fine fellows all, had begun to talk of women they had known. Dunk found himself wondering where Tanselle was tonight. He *knew* where Lady Rohanne was—abed at Coldmoat Castle, with old Ser Eustace beside her, snoring through his mustache—so he tried not to think of her. *Do they ever think of me?* he wondered.

His melancholy ponderings were rudely interrupted when a troupe of painted dwarfs came bursting from the belly of a wheeled wooden pig to chase Lord Butterwell's fool about the tables, walloping him with inflated pig's bladders that made rude noises every time a blow was struck. It was the funniest thing Dunk had seen in years, and he laughed with all the rest. Lord Frey's son was so taken by their antics that he joined in, pummeling the wedding guests with a bladder borrowed from a dwarf. The child had the most irritating laugh Dunk had ever heard, a high shrill hiccup of a laugh that made him want to take the boy over a knee or throw him down a well. *If he hits me with that bladder, I may do it.*

"There's the lad who made this marriage," Ser Maynard said as the chinless urchin went screaming past.

"How so?" The Fiddler held up an empty wine cup, and a passing server filled it.

Ser Maynard glanced toward the dais, where the bride was feeding cherries to her husband. "His Lordship will not be the first to butter that biscuit. His bride was deflowered by a scullion at the Twins, they say. She would creep down to the kitchens to meet him. Alas, one night that little brother of hers crept down after her. When he saw them making the two-backed beast, he let out a shriek, and cooks and guardsmen came running and found milady and her pot boy coupling on the slab of marble where the cook rolls out the dough, both naked as their name day and floured up from head to heel."

That cannot be true, Dunk thought. Lord Butterwell had broad lands, and pots of yellow gold. Why would he wed a girl who'd been soiled by a kitchen scullion, and give away his dragon's egg to mark the match? The Freys of the Crossing were no nobler than the Butterwells. They owned a bridge instead of cows, that was the only difference. *Lords. Who can ever understand them?* Dunk ate some nuts and pondered what he'd overheard whilst pissing. *Dunk the drunk, what is it that you think you heard?* He had another cup of hippocras, since the first had tasted good. Then he lay his head down atop his folded arms and closed his eyes just for a moment, to rest them from the smoke.

When he opened them again, half the wedding guests were on their feet and shouting, "Bed them! Bed them!" They were making such an uproar than they woke Dunk from a pleasant dream involving Tanselle Too-Tall and the Red Widow. "Bed them! Bed them!" the calls rang out. Dunk sat up and rubbed his eyes.

Ser Franklyn Frey had the bride in his arms and was carrying her down the aisle, with men and boys swarming all around him. The ladies at the high table had surrounded Lord Butterwell. Lady Vyrwel had recovered from her grief and was trying to pull His Lordship from his chair, while one of his daughters unlaced his boots and some Frey woman pulled up his tunic. Butterwell was flailing at them ineffectually, and laughing. He was drunk, Dunk saw, and Ser Franklyn was a deal drunker . . . so drunk, he almost dropped the bride. Before Dunk quite realized what was happening, John the Fiddler had dragged him to his feet. "Here!" he cried out. "Let the giant carry her!"

The next thing he knew, he was climbing a tower stair with the bride squirming in his arms. How he kept his feet was beyond him. The girl would not be still, and the men were all around them, making ribald japes about flouring her up and kneading her well whilst they pulled off her clothes. The dwarfs joined in as well. They swarmed around Dunk's legs, shouting and laughing and smacking at his calves with their bladders. It was all he could do not to trip over them.

Dunk had no notion where Lord Butterwell's bedchamber was to be found, but the other men pushed and prodded him until he got there, by which time the bride was red-faced, giggling, and nearly naked, save for the stocking on her left leg, which had somehow survived the climb. Dunk was crimson too, and not from exertion. His arousal would have been obvious if anyone had been looking, but fortunately all eyes were the bride. Lady Butterwell looked nothing like Tanselle, but having the one squirming half-naked in his arms had started Dunk thinking about the other. *Tanselle Too-Tall, that was her name, but she was not too tall for me.* He wondered if he would ever find her again. There had been some nights when he thought he must have dreamed her. *No, lunk, you only dreamed she liked you.*

Lord Butterwell's bedchamber was large and lavish, once he found it. Myrish carpets covered the floors, a hundred scented candles burned in nooks and crannies, and a suit of plate inlaid with gold and gems stood beside the door. It even had its own privy set into a small stone alcove in the outer wall.

When Dunk finally plopped the bride onto her marriage bed, a dwarf leapt in beside her and seized one of her breasts for a bit of a fondle. The girl let out a squeal, the men roared with laughter, and Dunk seized the dwarf by his collar and hauled him kicking off m'lady. He was carrying the little man across the room to chuck him out the door when he saw the dragon's egg.

Lord Butterwell had placed it on a black velvet cushion atop a marble plinth. It was much bigger than a hen's egg, though not so big as he'd imagined. Fine red scales covered its surface, shining bright as jewels by the light of lamps and candles. Dunk dropped the dwarf and picked up the egg, just to feel it for a moment. It was heavier than he'd expected. *You could smash a man's head with this, and never crack the shell.* The scales were smooth beneath his fingers, and the deep, rich red seemed to shimmer as he turned the egg in his hands. *Blood and flame*, he thought, but there were gold flecks in it as well, and whorls of midnight black.

"Here, you! What do you think you're doing, ser?" A knight he did not know was glaring at him, a big man with a coal-black beard and boils, but it was the voice that made him blink; a deep voice, thick with anger. *It was him, the man with Peake*, Dunk realized, as the man said, "Put that down. I'll thank you to keep your greasy fingers off His Lordship's treasures, or by the Seven, you shall wish you had."

The other knight was not near so drunk as Dunk, so it seemed wise to do as he said. He put the egg back on its pillow, very carefully, and wiped his fingers on his sleeve. "I meant no harm, ser." *Dunk the lunk, thick as a castle wall.* Then he shoved past the man with the black beard and out the door.

There were noises in the stairwell, glad shouts and girlish laughter. The women were bringing Lord Butterwell to his bride. Dunk had no wish to encounter them, so he went up instead of down, and found himself on the tower roof beneath the stars, with the pale castle glimmering in the moonlight all around him.

He was feeling dizzy from the wine, so he leaned against a parapet. *Am I going to be sick?* Why did he go and touch the dragon's egg? He remembered Tanselle's puppet show, and the wooden dragon that had started all the trouble there at Ashford. The memory made Dunk feel guilty, as it always did. *Three good men dead, to save a hedge knight's foot.* It made no sense, and never had. *Take a lesson from that, lunk. It is not for the likes of you to mess about with dragons or their eggs.*

"It almost looks as if it's made of snow."

Dunk turned. John the Fiddler stood behind him, smiling in his silk and cloth-of-gold. "What's made of snow?"

"The castle. All that white stone in the moonlight. Have you ever been north of the Neck, Ser Duncan? I'm told it snows there even in the summer. Have you ever seen the Wall?"

"No, m'lord." *Why is he going on about the Wall?* "That's where we were going, Egg and me. Up north, to Winterfell."

"Would that I could join you. You could show me the way."

"The way?" Dunk frowned. "It's right up the kingsroad. If you stay to the road and keep going north, you can't miss it."

The Fiddler laughed. "I suppose not . . . though you might be surprised at what some men can miss." He went to the parapet and looked out across the castle. "They say those northmen are a savage folk, and their woods are full of wolves."

"M'lord? Why did you come up here?"

"Alyn was seeking for me, and I did not care to be found. He grows tiresome when he drinks, does Alyn. I saw you slip away from that bedchamber of horrors, and slipped out after you. I've had too much wine, I grant you, but not enough to face a naked Butterwell." He gave Dunk an enigmatic smile. "I dreamed of you, Ser Duncan. Before I even met you. When I saw you on the road, I knew your face at once. It was as if we were old friends."

Dunk had the strangest feeling then, as if he had lived this all before. *I dreamed of you, he said. My dreams are not like yours, Ser Duncan. Mine are true.* "You *dreamed* of me?" he said, in a voice made thick by wine. "What sort of dream?"

"Why," the Fiddler said, "I dreamed that you were all in white from head to heel, with a long pale cloak flowing from those broad shoulders. You were a White Sword, ser, a Sworn Brother of the Kingsguard, the greatest knight in all the Seven Kingdoms, and you lived for no other purpose but to guard and serve and please your king." He put a hand on Dunk's shoulder. "You have dreamed the same dream, I know you have."

He had, it was true. *The first time the old man let me hold his sword.* "Every boy dreams of serving in the Kingsguard."

"Only seven boys grow up to wear the white cloak, though. Would it please you to be one of them?"

"Me?" Dunk shrugged away the lordling's hand, which had begun to knead his shoulder. "It might. Or not." The knights of the Kingsguard served for life, and swore to take no wife and hold no lands. *I might find Tanselle again someday. Why shouldn't I have a wife, and sons?* "It makes no matter what I dream. Only a king can make a Kingsguard knight."

"I suppose that means I'll have to take the throne, then. I would much rather be teaching you to fiddle."

"You're drunk." *And the crow once called the raven black.*

"Wonderfully drunk. Wine makes all things possible, Ser Duncan. You'd look a god in white, I think, but if the color does not suit you, perhaps you would prefer to be a lord?"

Dunk laughed in his face. "No, I'd sooner sprout big blue wings and fly. One's as likely as t'other."

"Now you mock me. A true knight would never mock his king." The Fiddler sounded hurt. "I hope you will put more faith in what I tell you when you see the dragon hatch."

"A dragon will hatch? A *living* dragon? What, here?"

"I dreamed it. This pale white castle, you, a dragon bursting from an egg, I dreamed it all, just as I once dreamed of my brothers lying dead. They were twelve and I was only seven, so they laughed at me, and died. I am two-and-twenty now, and I trust my dreams."

Dunk was remembering another tourney, remembering how he had walked through the soft spring rains with another princeling. *I dreamed of you and a dead dragon,* Egg's brother Daeron said to him. *A great beast, huge, with wings so large, they could cover this meadow. It had fallen on top of you, but you were alive and the dragon was dead.* And so he was, poor Baelor. Dreams were a treacherous ground on which to build. "As you say, m'lord," he told the Fiddler. "Pray excuse me."

"Where *are* you going, ser?"

"To my bed, to sleep. I'm drunk as a dog."

"Be my dog, ser. The night's alive with promise. We can howl together, and wake the very gods."

"What do you want of me?"

"Your sword. I would make you mine own man, and raise you high. My dreams do not lie, Ser Duncan. You will have that white cloak, and I must have the dragon's egg. I *must*, my dreams have made that plain. Perhaps the egg will hatch, or else—"

Behind them, the door banged open violently. *"There he is, my lord."* A pair of men-at-arms stepped onto the roof. Lord Gormon Peake was just behind them.

"Gormy," the Fiddler drawled. "Why, what are you doing in my bed-chamber, my lord?"

"It is a roof, ser, and you have had too much wine." Lord Gormon made a sharp gesture, and the guards moved forward. "Allow us to help you to that bed. You are jousting on the morrow, pray recall. Kirby Pimm can prove a dangerous foe."

"I had hoped to joust with good Ser Duncan here."

Peake gave Dunk an unsympathetic look. "Later, perhaps. For your first tilt, you have drawn Ser Kirby Pimm."

"Then Pimm must fall! So must they all! The mystery knight prevails against all challengers, and wonder dances in his wake." A guardsman took the Fiddler by the arm. "Ser Duncan, it seems that we must part," he called as they helped him down the steps.

Only Lord Gormon remained upon the roof with Dunk. "Hedge knight," he growled, "did your mother never teach you not to reach your hand into the dragon's mouth?"

"I never knew my mother, m'lord."

"That would explain it. What did he promise you?"

"A lordship. A white cloak. Big blue wings."

"Here's *my* promise: three feet of cold steel through your belly if you speak a word of what just happened."

Dunk shook his head to clear his wits. It did not seem to help. He bent double at the waist, and retched.

Some of the vomit spattered Peake's boots. The lord cursed. "Hedge knights," he exclaimed in disgust. "You have no place here. No true knight would be so discourteous as to turn up uninvited, but you creatures of the hedge—"

"We are wanted nowhere and turn up everywhere, m'lord." The wine had made Dunk bold, else he would have held his tongue. He wiped his mouth with the back of his hand.

"Try and remember what I told you, ser. It will go ill for you if you do not." Lord Peake shook the vomit off his boot. Then he was gone. Dunk leaned against the parapet again. He wondered who was madder, Lord Gormon or the Fiddler.

By the time he found his way back to the hall, only Maynard Plumm remained of his companions. "Was there any flour on her teats when you got the smallclothes off her?" he wanted to know.

Dunk shook his head, poured himself another cup of wine, tasted it, and decided that he had drunk enough.

Butterwell's stewards had found rooms in the keep for the lords and ladies, and beds in the barracks for their retinues. The rest of the guests had their choice between a straw pallet in the cellar, or a spot of ground beneath the western walls to raise their pavilions. The modest sailcloth tent Dunk had acquired in Stoney Sept was no pavilion, but it kept the rain and sun off. Some of his neighbors were still awake, the silken walls of their pavilions glowing like colored lanterns in the night. Laughter came from inside a blue pavilion covered with sunflowers, and the sounds of love from one striped in white and purple. Egg had set up their own tent a bit apart from the others. Maester and the two horses were hobbled nearby, and Dunk's arms and armor had been neatly stacked against the castle walls. When he crept into the tent, he found his squire sitting cross-legged by a candle, his head shining as he peered over a book.

"Reading books by candlelight will make you blind." Reading remained a mystery to Dunk, though the lad had tried to teach him.

"I need the candlelight to see the words, ser."

"Do you want a clout in the ear? What book is that?" Dunk saw bright colors on the page, little painted shields hiding in amongst the letters.

"A roll of arms, ser."

"Looking for the Fiddler? You won't find him. They don't put hedge knights in those rolls, just lords and champions."

"I wasn't looking for him. I saw some other sigils in the yard. . . . Lord

Sunderland is here, ser. He bears the heads of three pale ladies, on undy green and blue."

"A Sisterman? Truly?" The Three Sisters were islands in the Bite. Dunk had heard septons say that the isles were sinks of sin and avarice. Sisterton was the most notorious smuggler's den in all of Westeros. "He's come a long way. He must be kin to Butterwell's new bride."

"He isn't, ser."

"Then he's here for the feast. They eat fish on the Three Sisters, don't they? A man gets sick of fish. Did you get enough to eat? I brought you half a capon and some cheese." Dunk rummaged in the pocket of his cloak.

"They fed us ribs, ser." Egg's nose was deep in the book. "Lord Sunderland fought for the Black Dragon, ser."

"Like old Ser Eustace? He wasn't so bad, was he?"

"No, ser," Egg said, "but—"

"I saw the dragon's egg." Dunk squirreled the food away with their hardbread and salt beef. "It was red, mostly. Does Lord Bloodraven own a dragon's egg as well?"

Egg lowered his book. "Why would he? He's baseborn."

"Bastard born, not baseborn." Bloodraven had been born on the wrong side of the blanket, but he was noble on both sides. Dunk was about to tell Egg about the men he'd overhead when he noticed his face. "What happened to your lip?"

"A fight, ser."

"Let me see it."

"It only bled a little. I dabbed some wine on it."

"Who were you fighting?"

"Some other squires. They said—"

"Never mind what they said. What did I tell you?"

"To hold my tongue and make no trouble." The boy touched his broken lip. "They called my father a *kinslayer*, though."

He is, lad, though I do not think he meant it. Dunk had told Egg half a hundred times not to take such words to heart. *You know the truth. Let that be enough.* They had heard such talk before, in wine sinks and low taverns, and around campfires in the woods. The whole realm knew how Prince Maekar's mace had felled his brother Baelor Breakspear at Ashford Meadow. Talk of plots was only to be expected. "If they knew Prince

Maekar was your father, they would never have said such things." *Behind your back, yes, but never to your face.* "And what did *you* tell these other squires, instead of holding your tongue?"

Egg looked abashed. "That Prince Baelor's death was just a mishap. Only when I said Prince Maekar loved his brother Baelor, Ser Addam's squire said he loved him to death, and Ser Mallor's squire said he meant to love his brother Aerys the same way. That was when I hit him. I hit him good."

"I ought to hit you good. A fat ear to go with that fat lip. Your father would do the same if he were here. Do you think Prince Maekar needs a little boy to defend him? What did he tell you when he sent you off with me?"

"To serve you faithfully as your squire, and not flinch from any task or hardship."

"And what else?"

"To obey the king's laws, the rules of chivalry, and you."

"And what else?"

"To keep my hair shaved or dyed," the boy said with obvious reluctance, "and tell no man my true name."

Dunk nodded. "How much wine had this boy drunk?"

"He was drinking barley beer."

"You see? The barley beer was talking. Words are wind, Egg. Just let them blow on past you."

"*Some* words are wind." The boy was nothing if not stubborn. "Some words are treason. This is a traitor's tourney, ser."

"What, all of them?" Dunk shook his head. "If it was true, that was a long time ago. The Black Dragon's dead, and those who fought with him are fled or pardoned. And it's not true. Lord Butterwell's sons fought on both sides."

"That makes him *half* a traitor, ser."

"Sixteen years ago." Dunk's mellow winey haze was gone. He felt angry, and near sober. "Lord Butterwell's steward is the master of the games, a man named Cosgrove. Find him and enter my name for the lists. No, wait . . . hold back my name." With so many lords on hand, one of them might recall Ser Duncan the Tall from Ashford Meadow. "Enter me as the Gallows Knight." The smallfolk loved it when a Mystery Knight appeared at a tourney.

Egg fingered his fat lip. "The Gallows Knight, ser?"

"For the shield."

"Yes, but—"

"Go do as I said. You have read enough for one night." Dunk pinched the candle out between his thumb and forefinger.

The sun rose hot and hard, implacable.

Waves of heat rose shimmering off the white stones of the castle. The air smelled of baked earth and torn grass, and no breath of wind stirred the banners that drooped atop the keep and gatehouse, green and white and yellow.

Thunder was restless, in a way that Dunk had seldom seen before. The stallion tossed his head from side to side as Egg was tightening his saddle cinch. He even bared his big square teeth at the boy. *It is so hot,* Dunk thought, *too hot for man or mount.* A warhorse does not have a placid disposition even at the best of times. *The Mother herself would be foul-tempered in this heat.*

In the center of the yard, the jousters began another run. Ser Harbert rode a golden courser barded in black and decorated with the red and white serpents of House Paege, Ser Franklyn a sorrel whose gray silk trapper bore the twin towers of Frey. When they came together, the red and white lance cracked clean in two and the blue one exploded into splinters, but neither man lost his seat. A cheer went up from the viewing stand and the guardsmen on the castle walls, but it was short and thin and hollow.

It is too hot for cheering. Dunk mopped sweat from his brow. *It is too hot for jousting.* His head was beating like a drum. *Let me win this tilt and one more, and I will be content.*

The knights wheeled their horses about at the end of the lists and tossed down the jagged remains of their lances, the fourth pair they had broken. *Three too many.* Dunk had put off donning his armor as long as he dared, yet already he could feel his smallclothes sticking to his skin beneath his steel. *There are worse things than being soaked with sweat,* he told himself, remembering the fight on the *White Lady,* when the ironmen had come swarming over her side. He had been soaked in blood by the time that day was done.

Fresh lances in hand, Paege and Frey put their spurs into their mounts once again. Clods of cracked dry earth sprayed back from beneath their horses' hooves with every stride. The crack of the lances breaking made Dunk wince. *Too much wine last night, and too much food.* He had some vague memory of carrying the bride up the steps, and meeting John the Fiddler and Lord Peake upon a roof. *What was I doing on a roof?* There had been talk of dragons, he recalled, or dragon's eggs, or something, but—

A noise broke his reverie, part roar and part moan. Dunk saw the golden horse trotting riderless to the end of the lists, as Ser Harbert Paege rolled feebly on the ground. *Two more before my turn.* The sooner he un-horsed Ser Uthor, the sooner he could take his armor off, have a cool drink, and rest. He should have at least an hour before they called him forth again.

Lord Butterwell's portly herald climbed to the top of the viewing stand to summon the next pair of jousters. *"Ser Argrave the Defiant,"* he called, *"a knight of Nunny, in service to Lord Butterwell of Whitewalls. Ser Glendon Flowers, the Knight of the Pussywillows. Come forth and prove your valor."* A gale of laughter rippled through the viewing stands.

Ser Argrave was a spare, leathery man, a seasoned household knight in dinted gray armor riding an unbarded horse. Dunk had known his sort be-fore; such men were tough as old roots, and knew their business. His foe was young Ser Glendon, mounted on his wretched stot and armored in a heavy mail hauberk and open-faced iron halfhelm. On his arm his shield displayed his father's fiery sigil. *He needs a breastplate and a proper helm,* Dunk thought. *A blow to the head or chest could kill him, clad like that.*

Ser Glendon was plainly furious at his introduction. He wheeled his mount in an angry circle and shouted, "I am Glendon *Ball*, not Glendon Flowers. Mock me at your peril, herald. I warn you, I have hero's blood." The herald did not deign to reply, but more laughter greeted the young knight's protest. "Why are they laughing at him?" Dunk wondered aloud. "Is he a bastard, then?" *Flowers* was the surname given to bastards born of noble parents in the Reach. "And what was all that about pussywillows?"

"I could find out, ser," said Egg.

"No. It is none of our concern. Do you have my helm?" Ser Argrave and Ser Glendon dipped their lances before Lord and Lady Butterwell. Dunk saw Butterwell lean over and whisper something in his bride's ear. The girl began to giggle.

"Yes, ser." Egg had donned his floppy hat, to shade his eyes and keep the sun off his shaved head. Dunk liked to tease the boy about that hat, but just now he wished he had one like it. Better a straw hat than an iron one, beneath this sun. He pushed his hair out of his eyes, eased the greathelm down into place with two hands, and fastened it to his gorget. The lining stank of old sweat, and he could feel the weight of all that iron on his neck and shoulders. His head throbbed from last night's wine.

"Ser," Egg said, "it is not too late to withdraw. If you lose Thunder and your armor . . ."

I would be done as a knight. "Why should I lose?" Dunk demanded. Ser Argrave and Ser Glendon had ridden to opposite ends of the lists. "It is not as if I faced the Laughing Storm. Is there some knight here like to give me trouble?"

"Almost all of them, ser."

"I owe you a clout in the ear for that. Ser Uthor is ten years my senior and half my size." Ser Argrave lowered his visor. Ser Glendon did not have a visor to lower.

"You have not ridden in a tilt since Ashford Meadow, ser."

Insolent boy. "I've trained." Not so faithfully as he might have, to be sure. When he could, he took his turn riding at quintains or rings, where such were available. And sometimes he would command Egg to climb a tree and hang a shield or barrel stave beneath a well-placed limb for them to tilt at.

"You're better with a sword than with a lance," Egg said. "With an axe or a mace, there's few to match your strength."

There was enough truth in that to annoy Dunk all the more. "There is no contest for swords or maces," he pointed out, as Fireball's son and Ser Argrave the Defiant began their charge. "Go get my shield."

Egg made a face, then went to fetch the shield.

Across the yard, Ser Argrave's lance struck Ser Glendon's shield and glanced off, leaving a gouge across the comet. But Ball's coronal found the center of his foe's breastplate with such force that it burst his saddle cinch. Knight and saddle both went tumbling to the dust. Dunk was impressed despite himself. *The boy jousts almost as well as he talks.* He wondered if that would stop them laughing at him.

A trumpet rang, loud enough to make Dunk wince. Once more the herald climbed his stand. *"Ser Joffrey of House Caswell, Lord of Bitterbridge and Defender of the Fords. Ser Kyle, the Cat of Misty Moor. Come forth and prove your valor."*

Ser Kyle's armor was of good quality, but old and worn, with many dints and scratches. "The Mother has been merciful to me, Ser Duncan," he told Dunk and Egg, on his way to the lists. "I am sent against Lord Caswell, the very man I came to see."

If any man upon the field felt worse than Dunk this morning, it had to be Lord Caswell, who had drunk himself insensible at the feast. "It's a wonder he can sit a horse, after last night," said Dunk. "The victory is yours, ser."

"Oh, no." Ser Kyle smiled a silken smile. "The cat who wants his bowl of cream must know when to purr and when to show his claws, Ser Duncan. If His Lordship's lance so much as scrapes against my shield, I shall go tumbling to the earth. Afterwards, when I bring my horse and armor to him, I will compliment His Lordship on how much his prowess has grown since I made him his first sword. That will recall me to him, and before the day is out, I shall be a Caswell man again, a knight of Bitterbridge."

There is no honor in that, Dunk almost said, but he bit his tongue instead. Ser Kyle would not be the first hedge knight to trade his honor for a warm place by the fire. "As you say," he muttered. "Good fortune to you. Or bad, if you prefer."

Lord Joffrey Caswell was a weedy youth of twenty, though admittedly he looked rather more impressive in his armor than he had last night when he'd been face down in a puddle of wine. A yellow centaur was painted on his shield, pulling on a longbow. The same centaur adorned the white silk trappings of his horse, and gleamed atop his helm in yellow gold. *A man who has a centaur for his sigil should ride better than that.* Dunk did not know how well Ser Kyle wielded a lance, but from the way Lord Caswell sat his horse, it looked as though a loud cough might unseat him. *All the Cat need do is ride past him very fast.*

Egg held Thunder's bridle as Dunk swung himself ponderously up into the high, stiff saddle. As he sat there waiting, he could feel the eyes upon him. *They are wondering if the big hedge knight is any good.* Dunk wondered that himself. He would find out soon enough.

The Cat of Misty Moor was true to his word. Lord Caswell's lance was wobbling all the way across the field, and Ser Kyle's was ill-aimed. Neither man got his horse up past a trot. All the same, the Cat went tumbling when Lord Joffrey's coronal chanced to whack his shoulder. *I thought all cats landed gracefully upon their feet,* Dunk thought as the hedge knight rolled in the dust. Lord Caswell's lance remained unbroken. As he brought his horse around, he thrust it high into the air repeatedly, as if he'd just unseated Leo Longthorn or the Laughing Storm. The Cat pulled off his helm and went chasing down his horse.

"My shield," Dunk said to Egg. The boy handed it up. He slipped his left arm through the strap and closed his hand around the grip. The weight of the kite shield was reassuring, though its length made it awkward to handle, and seeing the hanged man once again gave him an uneasy feeling. *Those are ill-omened arms.* He resolved to get the shield repainted as soon as he could. *May the Warrior grant me a smooth course and a quick victory,* he prayed as Butterwell's herald was clambering up the steps once more. *"Ser Uthor Underleaf,"* his voice rang out. *"The Gallows Knight. Come forth and prove your valor."*

"Be careful, ser," Egg warned as he handed Dunk a tourney lance, a tapered wooden shaft twelve feet long ending in a rounded iron coronal in the shape of a closed fist. "The other squires say Ser Uthor has a good seat. And he's quick."

"Quick?" Dunk snorted. "He has a snail on his shield. How quick can he be?" He put his heels into Thunder's flanks and walked the horse slowly forward, his lance upright. *One victory, and I am no worse than before. Two will leave us well ahead. Two is not too much to hope for, in this company.* He had been fortunate in the lots, at least. He could as easily have drawn the Old Ox or Ser Kirby Pimm or some other local hero. Dunk wondered if the master of games was deliberately matching the hedge knights against each other, so no lordling need suffer the ignominy of losing to one in the first round. *It does not matter. One foe at a time, that was what the old man always said. Ser Uthor is all that should concern me now.*

They met beneath the viewing stand where Lord and Lady Butterwell sat on their cushions in the shade of the castle walls. Lord Frey was beside them, dandling his snot-nosed son on one knee. A row of serving girls was fanning them, yet Lord Butterwell's damask tunic was stained beneath the arms, and his lady's hair was limp from perspiration. She looked hot, bored, and uncomfortable, but when she saw Dunk, she pushed out her chest in a way that turned him red beneath his helm. He dipped his lance to her and her lord husband. Ser Uthor did the same. Butterwell wished them both a good tilt. His wife stuck out her tongue.

It was time. Dunk trotted back to the south end of the lists. Eighty feet away, his opponent was taking up his position as well. His grey stallion was smaller than Thunder, but younger and more spirited. Ser Uthor wore green enamel plate and silvery chain mail. Streamers of green and grey silk flowed from his rounded bascinet, and his green shield bore a silver snail. *Good armor and a good horse means a good ransom, if I unseat him.*

A trumpet sounded.

Thunder started forward at a slow trot. Dunk swung his lance to the left and brought it down, so it angled across the horse's head and the wooden barrier between him and his foe. His shield protected the left side of his body. He crouched forward, legs tightening as Thunder drove down the lists. *We are one. Man, horse, lance, we are one beast of blood and wood and iron.*

Ser Uthor was charging hard, clouds of dust kicking up from the hooves of his grey. With forty yards between them, Dunk spurred Thunder to a gallop and aimed the point of his lance squarely at the silver snail. The sullen sun, the dust, the heat, the castle, Lord Butterwell and his bride, the Fiddler and Ser Maynard, knights, squires, grooms, smallfolk, all vanished. Only the foe remained. The spurs again. Thunder broke into a run. The snail was rushing toward them, growing with every stride of the grey's long legs . . . but ahead came Ser Uthor's lance with its iron fist. *My shield is strong; my shield will take the blow. Only the snail matters. Strike the snail, and the tilt is mine.*

When ten yards remained between them, Ser Uthor shifted the point of his lance upward.

A *crack* rang in Dunk's ears as his lance hit. He felt the impact in his arm and shoulder, but never saw the blow strike home. Uthor's iron fist took him square between his eyes, with all the force of man and horse behind it.

Dunk woke upon his back, staring up at the arches of a barrel-vaulted ceiling. For a moment he did not know where he was, or how he had arrived there. Voices echoed in his head, and faces drifted past him—old Ser Arlan, Tanselle Too-Tall, Bennis of the Brown Shield, the Red Widow, Baelor Breakspear, Aerion the Bright Prince, mad sad Lady Vaith. Then all at once, the joust came back to him: the heat, the snail, the iron fist coming at his face. He groaned, and rolled onto one elbow. The movement set his skull to pounding like some monstrous war drum.

Both his eyes seemed to be working, at least. Nor could he feel a hole in his head, which was all to the good. He was in some cellar, he saw, with casks of wine and ale on every side. *At least it is cool here*, he thought, *and drink is close at hand.* The taste of blood was in his mouth. Dunk felt a stab of fear. If he had bitten off his tongue, he would be dumb as well as thick. "Good morrow," he croaked, just to hear his voice. The words echoed off the ceiling. Dunk tried to push himself onto his feet, but the effort set the cellar spinning.

"Slowly, slowly," said a quavery voice, close at hand. A stooped old man appeared beside the bed, clad in robes as grey as his long hair. About his neck was a maester's chain of many metals. His face was aged and lined, with deep creases on either side of a great beak of a nose. "Be still, and let me see your eyes." He peered in Dunk's left eye, and then the right, holding them open between his thumb and forefinger.

"My head hurts."

The maester snorted. "Be grateful it still rests upon your shoulders, ser. Here, this may help somewhat. Drink."

Dunk made himself swallow every drop of the foul potion, and managed not to spit it out. "The tourney," he said, wiping his mouth with the back of his hand. "Tell me. What's happened?"

"The same foolishness that always happens in these affrays. Men have been knocking each other off horses with sticks. Lord Smallwood's nephew broke his wrist and Ser Eden Risley's leg was crushed beneath his horse, but no one has been killed thus far. Though I had my fears for you, ser."

"Was I unhorsed?" His head still felt as though it were stuffed full of wool, else he would never have asked such a stupid question. Dunk regretted it the instant the words were out.

"With a crash that shook the highest ramparts. Those who had wagered good coin on you were most distraught, and your squire was beside himself. He would be sitting with you still if I had not chased him off. I need no children underfoot. I reminded him of his duty."

Dunk found that he needed reminding himself. "What duty?"

"Your mount, ser. Your arms and armor."

"Yes," Dunk said, remembering. The boy was a good squire; he knew what was required of him. *I have lost the old man's sword and the armor that Steely Pate forged for me.*

"Your fiddling friend was also asking after you. He told me you were to have the best of care. I threw him out as well."

"How long have you been tending me?" Dunk flexed the fingers of his sword hand. All of them still seemed to work. *Only my head's hurt, and Ser Arlan used to say I never used that anyway.*

"Four hours, by the sundial."

Four hours was not so bad. He had once heard tale of a knight struck so hard that he slept for forty years, and woke to find himself old and withered. "Do you know if Ser Uthor won his second tilt?" Maybe the Snail would win the tourney. It would take some sting from the defeat if Dunk could tell himself that he had lost to the best knight in the field.

"That one? Indeed he did. Against Ser Addam Frey, a cousin to the bride, and a promising young lance. Her Ladyship fainted when Ser Addam fell. She had to be helped back to her chambers."

Dunk forced himself to his feet, reeling as he rose, but the maester helped to steady him. "Where are my clothes? I must go. I have to . . . I must . . ."

"If you cannot recall, it cannot be so very urgent." The maester made an irritated motion. "I would suggest that you avoid rich foods, strong drink, and further blows between your eyes . . . but I learned long ago that knights are deaf to sense. Go, go. I have other fools to tend."

Outside, Dunk glimpsed a hawk soaring in wide circles through the bright blue sky. He envied him. A few clouds were gathering to the east, dark as Dunk's mood. As he found his way back to the tilting ground, the sun beat down on his head like a hammer on an anvil. The earth seemed to move beneath his feet . . . or it might just be that he was swaying. He had almost fallen twice climbing the cellar steps. *I should have heeded Egg.*

He made his slow way across the outer ward, around the fringes of the crowd. Out on the field, plump Lord Alyn Cockshaw was limping off between two squires, the latest conquest of young Glendon Ball. A third squire held his helm, its three proud feathers broken. "*Ser John the Fiddler,*" the herald cried. "*Ser Franklyn of House Frey, a knight of the Twins, sworn to the Lord of the Crossing. Come forth and prove your valor.*"

Dunk could only stand and watch as the Fiddler's big black trotted onto the field in a swirl of blue silk and golden swords and fiddles. His breastplate was enameled blue as well, as were his poleyns, couter, greaves, and gorget. The ringmail underneath was gilded. Ser Franklyn rode a dapple grey with a flowing silver mane, to match the grey of his silks and the silver of his armor. On shield and surcoat and horse trappings he bore the twin towers of Frey. They charged and charged again. Dunk stood watching, but saw none of it. *Dunk the lunk, thick as a castle wall,* he chided himself. *He had a snail upon his shield. How could you lose to a man with a snail upon his shield?*

There was cheering all around him. When Dunk looked up, he saw that Franklyn Frey was down. The Fiddler had dismounted, to help his fallen foe back to his feet. *He is one step closer to his dragon's egg,* Dunk thought, *and where am I?*

As he approached the postern gate, Dunk came upon the company of dwarfs from last night's feast preparing to take their leave. They were hitching ponies to their wheeled wooden pig, and a second wayn of more conventional design. There were six of them, he saw, each smaller and more malformed than the last. A few might have been children, but they were all so short that it was hard to tell. In daylight, dressed in horsehide breeches and roughspun hooded cloaks, they seemed less jolly than they had in motley. "Good morrow to you," Dunk said, to be courteous. "Are you for the road? There's clouds to the east, could mean rain."

The only answer that he got was a glare from the ugliest dwarf. *Was he the one I pulled off Lady Butterwell last night?* Up close, the little man smelled like a privy. One whiff was enough to make Dunk hasten his steps.

The walk across the Milkhouse seemed to take Dunk as long as it had once taken him and Egg to cross the sands of Dorne. He kept a wall beside him, and from time to time he leaned on it. Every time he turned his head, the world would swim. *A drink,* he thought. *I need a drink of water, or else I'm like to fall.*

A passing groom told him where to find the nearest well. It was there that he discovered Kyle the Cat, talking quietly with Maynard Plumm. Ser Kyle's shoulders were slumped in dejection, but he looked up at Dunk's approach. "Ser Duncan? We had heard that you were dead, or dying."

Dunk rubbed his temples. "I only wish I were."

"I know that feeling well." Ser Kyle sighed. "Lord Caswell did not know me. When I told him how I carved his first sword, he stared at me as if I'd lost my wits. He said there was no place at Bitterbridge for knights as feeble as I had shown myself to be." The Cat gave a bitter laugh. "He took my arms and armor, though. My mount as well. What will I do?"

Dunk had no answer for him. Even a freerider required a horse to ride; sellswords must have swords to sell. "You will find another horse," Dunk said, as he drew the bucket up. "The Seven Kingdoms are full of horses. You will find some other lord to arm you." He cupped his hands, filled them with water, drank.

"Some other lord. Aye. Do you know of one? I am not so young and strong as you. Nor so big. Big men are always in demand. Lord Butterwell likes his knights large, for one. Look at that Tom Heddle. Have you seen him joust? He has overthrown every man he's faced. Fireball's lad has done the same, though. The Fiddler as well. Would that he had been the one to unhorse me. He refuses to take ransoms. He wants no more than the dragon's egg, he says . . . that, and the friendship of his fallen foes. The flower of chivalry, that one."

Maynard Plumm gave a laugh. "The fiddle of chivalry, you mean. That boy is fiddling up a storm, and all of us would do well to be gone from here before it breaks."

"He takes no ransoms?" said Dunk. "A gallant gesture."

"Gallant gestures come easy when your purse is fat with gold," said Ser Maynard. "There is a lesson here, if you have the sense to take it, Ser Duncan. It is not too late for you to go."

"Go? Go where?"

Ser Maynard shrugged. "Anywhere. Winterfell, Summerhall, Asshai by the Shadow. It makes no matter, so long as it's not here. Take your horse and armor and slip out the postern gate. You won't be missed. The Snail's got his next tilt to think about, and the rest have eyes only for the jousting."

For half a heartbeat, Dunk was tempted. So long as he was armed and horsed, he would remain a knight of sorts. Without them, he was no more than a beggar. *A big beggar, but a beggar all the same.* But his arms and armor belonged to Ser Uthor now. So did Thunder. *Better a beggar than a thief.* He had been both in Flea Bottom, when he ran with Ferret, Rafe, and Pudding, but the old man had saved him from that life. He knew what Ser Arlan of Pennytree would have said to Plumm's suggestions. Ser

Arlan being dead, Dunk said it for him. "Even a hedge knight has his honor."

"Would you rather die with honor intact, or live with it besmirched? No, spare me, I know what you will say. Take your boy and flee, gallows knight. Before your arms become your destiny."

Dunk bristled. "How would you know my destiny? Did you have a dream, like John the Fiddler? What do you know of Egg?"

"I know that eggs do well to stay out of frying pans," said Plumm. "Whitewalls is not a healthy place for the boy."

"How did you fare in your own tilt, ser?" Dunk asked him.

"Oh, I did not chance the lists. The omens had gone sour. Who do you imagine is going to claim the dragon's egg, pray?"

Not me, Dunk thought. "The Seven know. I don't."

"Venture a guess, ser. You have two eyes."

He thought a moment. "The Fiddler?"

"Very good. Would you care to explain your reasoning?"

"I just . . . I have a feeling."

"So do I," said Maynard Plumm. "A bad feeling, for any man or boy unwise enough to stand in our Fiddler's way."

Egg was brushing Thunder's coat outside their tent, but his eyes were far away. *The boy has taken my fall hard.* "Enough," Dunk called. "Any more and Thunder will be as bald as you."

"Ser?" Egg dropped the brush. "I *knew* no stupid snail could kill you, ser." He threw his arms around him.

Dunk swiped the boy's floppy straw hat and put it on his own head. "The maester said you made off with my armor."

Egg snatched back his hat indignantly. "I've scoured your mail and polished your greaves, gorget, and breastplate, ser, but your helm is cracked and dinted where Ser Uthor's coronal struck. You'll need to have it hammered out by an armorer."

"Let Ser Uthor have it hammered out. It's his now." *No horse, no sword, no armor. Perhaps those dwarfs would let me join their troupe. That would be a funny sight, six dwarfs pummeling a giant with pig bladders.* "Thunder is his too. Come. We'll take them to him and wish him well in the rest of his tilts."

"Now, ser? Aren't you going to ransom Thunder?"

"With what, lad? Pebbles and sheep pellets?"

"I thought about that, ser. If you could borrow—"

Dunk cut him off. "No one will lend me that much coin, Egg. Why should they? What am I, but some great oaf who called himself a knight until some snail with a stick near stove his head in?"

"Well," said Egg, "you could have Rain, ser. I'll go back to riding Maester. We'll go to Summerhall. You can take service in my father's household. His stables are full of horses. You could have a destrier and a palfrey too."

Egg meant well, but Dunk could not go cringing back to Summerhall. Not that way, penniless and beaten, seeking service without so much as a sword to offer. "Lad," he said, "that's good of you, but I want no crumbs from your lord father's table, or from his stables neither. Might be it's time we parted ways." Dunk could always slink off to join the City Watch in Lannisport or Oldtown; they liked big men for that. *I've bumped my bean on every beam in every inn from Lannisport to King's Landing, might be it's time my size earned me a bit of coin instead of just a lumpy head.* But watchmen did not have squires. "I've taught you what I could, and that was little enough. You'll do better with a proper master-at-arms to see to your training, some fierce old knight who knows which end of the lance to hold."

"I don't want a proper master-at-arms," Egg said. "I want you. What if I used my—?"

"No. None of that. I will not hear it. Go gather up my arms. We will present them to Ser Uthor with my compliments. Hard things only grow harder if you put them off."

Egg kicked the ground, his face as droopy as his big straw hat. "Aye, ser. As you say."

From the outside, Ser Uthor's tent was very plain: a large square box of dun-colored sailcloth staked to the ground with hempen ropes. A silver snail adorned the center pole above a long gray pennon, but that was the only decoration.

"Wait here," Dunk told Egg. The boy had hold of Thunder's lead. The big brown destrier was laden with Dunk's arms and armor, even to his new old shield. *The Gallows Knight. What a dismal mystery knight I proved to be.* "I won't be long." He ducked his head and stooped to shoulder through the flap.

The tent's exterior left him ill prepared for the comforts he found within. The ground beneath his feet was carpeted in woven Myrish rugs, rich with color. An ornate trestle table stood surrounded by camp chairs. The feather bed was covered with soft cushions, and an iron brazier burned perfumed incense.

Ser Uthor sat at the table, a pile of gold and silver before him and a flagon of wine at his elbow, counting coins with his squire, a gawky fellow close in age to Dunk. From time to time the Snail would bite a coin, or set one aside. "I see I still have much to teach you, Will," Dunk heard him say. "This coin has been clipped, t'other shaved. And this one?" A gold piece danced across his fingers. "*Look* at the coins before taking them. Here, tell me what you see." The dragon spun through the air. Will tried to catch it, but it bounced off his fingers and fell to the ground. He had to get down on his knees to find it. When he did, he turned it over twice before saying, "This one's good, m'lord. There's a dragon on the one side and a king on t'other. . . ."

Underleaf glanced toward Dunk. "The Hanged Man. It is good to see you moving about, ser. I feared I'd killed you. Will you do me a kindness and instruct my squire as to the nature of dragons? Will, give Ser Duncan the coin."

Dunk had no choice but to take it. *He unhorsed me, must he make me caper for him too?* Frowning, he hefted the coin in his palm, examined both sides, tasted it. "Gold, not shaved or clipped. The weight feels right. I'd have taken it too, m'lord. What's wrong with it?"

"The king."

Dunk took a closer look. The face on the coin was young, clean-shaved, handsome. King Aerys was bearded on his coins, the same as old King Aegon. King Daeron, who'd come between them, had been clean-shaved, but this wasn't him. The coin did not appear worn enough to be from before Aegon the Unworthy. Dunk scowled at the word beneath the head. *Six letters.* They looked the same as he had seen on other dragons. DAERON, the letters read, but Dunk knew the face of Daeron the Good, and this wasn't him. When he looked again, he saw that something odd about the shape of the fourth letter, it wasn't . . . "*Daemon,*" he blurted out. "It says *Daemon.* There never was any King Daemon, though, only—"

"—the Pretender. Daemon Blackfyre struck his own coinage during his rebellion."

"It's gold, though," Will argued. "If it's gold, it should be just as good as them other dragons, m'lord."

The Snail clouted him along the side of the head. "Cretin. Aye, it's gold. Rebel's gold. Traitor's gold. It's treasonous to own such a coin, and twice as treasonous to pass it. I'll need to have this melted down." He hit the man again. "Get out of my sight. This good knight and I have matters to discuss."

Will wasted no time in scrambling from the tent. "Have a seat," Ser Uthor said politely. "Will you take wine?" Here in his own tent, Underleaf seemed a different man than at the feast.

A snail hides in his shell, Dunk remembered. "Thank you, no." He flicked the gold coin back to Ser Uthor. *Traitor's gold. Blackfyre gold. Egg said this was a traitor's tourney, but I would not listen.* He owed the boy an apology.

"Half a cup," Underleaf insisted. "You sound in need of it." He filled two cups with wine and handed one to Dunk. Out of his armor, he looked more a merchant than a knight. "You've come about the forfeit, I assume."

"Aye." Dunk took the wine. Maybe it would help to stop his head from pounding. "I brought my horse, and my arms and armor. Take them, with my compliments."

Ser Uthor smiled. "And this is where I tell you that you rode a gallant course."

Dunk wondered if *gallant* was a chivalrous way of saying "clumsy." "That is good of you to say, but—"

"I think you misheard me, ser. Would it be too bold of me to ask how you came to knighthood, ser?"

"Ser Arlan of Pennytree found me in Flea Bottom, chasing pigs. His old squire had been slain on the Redgrass Field, so he needed someone to tend his mount and clean his mail. He promised he would teach me sword and lance and how to ride a horse if I would come and serve him, so I did."

"A charming tale . . . though if I were you, I would leave out the part about the pigs. Pray, where is your Ser Arlan now?"

"He died. I buried him."

"I see. Did you take him home to Pennytree?"

"I didn't know where it was." Dunk had never seen the old man's Pennytree. Ser Arlan seldom spoke of it, no more than Dunk was wont to speak of Flea Bottom. "I buried him on a hillside facing west, so he could see the sun go down." The camp chair creaked alarmingly beneath his weight.

Ser Uthor resumed his seat. "I have my own armor, and a better horse than yours. What do I want with some old done nag and a sack of dinted plate and rusty mail?"

"Steely Pate made that armor," Dunk said, with a touch of anger. "Egg has taken good care of it. There's not a spot of rust on my mail, and the steel is good and strong."

"Strong and heavy," Ser Uthor complained, "and too big for any man of normal size. You are uncommon large, Duncan the Tall. As for your horse, he is too old to ride and too stringy to eat."

"Thunder is not so young as he used to be," Dunk admitted, "and my armor is large, as you say. You could sell it, though. In Lannisport and King's Landing, there are plenty of smiths who will take it off your hands."

"For a tenth of what it's worth, perhaps," said Ser Uthor, "and only to melt down for the metal. No. It's sweet silver I require, not old iron. The coin of the realm. Now, do you wish to ransom back your arms, or no?"

Dunk turned the wine cup in his hands, frowning. It was solid silver, with a line of golden snails inlaid around the lip. The wine was gold as well, and heady on the tongue. "If wishes were fishes, aye, I'd pay. Gladly. Only—"

"—you don't have two stags to lock horns."

"If you would . . . would lend my horse and armor back to me, I could pay the ransom later. Once I found the coin."

The Snail looked amused. "Where would you find it, pray?"

"I could take service with some lord, or . . ." It was hard to get the words out. They made him feel a beggar. "It might take a few years, but I would pay you. I swear it."

"On your honor as a knight?"

Dunk flushed. "I could make my mark upon a parchment."

"A hedge knight's scratch upon a scrap of paper?" Ser Uthor rolled his eyes. "Good to wipe my arse. No more."

"You are a hedge knight too."

"Now you insult me. I ride where I will and serve no man but myself, true . . . but it has been many a year since I last slept beneath a hedge. I find that inns are far more comfortable. I am a *tourney* knight, the best that you are ever like to meet."

"The best?" His arrogance made Dunk angry. "The Laughing Storm might not agree, ser. Nor Leo Longthorn, nor the Brute of Bracken. At Ashford Meadow, no one spoke of snails. Why is that, if you're such a famous tourney champion?"

"Have you heard me name myself a champion? That way lies renown. I would sooner have the pox. Thank you, but no. I shall win my next joust, aye, but in the final I shall fall. Butterwell has thirty dragons for the knight who comes second, that will suffice for me . . . along with some goodly ransoms and the proceeds of my wagers." He gestured at the piles of silver stags and golden dragons on the table. "You seem a healthy fellow, and very large. Size will always impress the fools, though it means little and less in jousting. Will was able to get odds of three to one against me. Lord Shawney gave five to one, the fool." He picked up a silver stag and set it to spinning with a flick of his long fingers. "The Old Ox will be the next to tumble. Then the Knight of the Pussywillows, if he survives that long. Sentiment being what it is, I should get fine odds against them both. The commons love their village heroes."

"Ser Glendon has hero's blood," Dunk blurted out.

"Oh, I do hope so. Hero's blood should be good for two to one. Whore's blood draws poorer odds. Ser Glendon speaks about his purported sire at every opportunity, but have you noticed that he never makes mention of his mother? For good reason. He was born of a camp follower. Jenny, her name was. Penny Jenny, they called her, until the Redgrass Field. The night before the battle, she fucked so many men that thereafter she was known as Redgrass Jenny. Fireball had her before that, I don't doubt, but so did a hundred other men. Our friend Glendon presumes quite a lot, it seems to me. He does not even have red hair."

Hero's blood, thought Dunk. "He says he is a knight."

"Oh, that much is true. The boy and his sister grew up in a brothel, called the Pussywillows. After Penny Jenny died, the other whores took care of them and fed the lad the tale his mother had concocted, about him being Fireball's seed. An old squire who lived nearby gave the boy his training, such that it was, in trade for ale and cunt, but being but a squire he could not knight the little bastard. Half a year ago, however, a party of knights chanced upon the brothel and a certain Ser Morgan Dunstable took a drunken fancy to Ser Glendon's sister. As it happens, the sister was still a virgin and Dunstable did not have the price of her maidenhead. So a bargain was struck. Ser Morgan dubbed her brother a knight, right there in the Pussywillows in front of twenty witnesses, and afterwards little sister took him upstairs and let him pluck her flower. And there you are."

Any knight could make a knight. When he was squiring for Ser Arlan, Dunk had heard tales of other men who'd bought their knighthood with a kindness or a threat or a bag of silver coins, but never with a sister's maidenhead. "That's just a tale," he heard himself say. "That can't be true."

"I had it from Kirby Pimm, who claims that he was there, a witness to the knighting." Ser Uthor shrugged. "Hero's son, whore's son, or both, when he faces me, the boy will fall."

"The lots may give you some other foe."

Ser Uthor arched an eyebrow. "Cosgrove is as fond of silver as the next man. I promise you, I shall draw the Old Ox next, then the boy. Would you care to wager on it?"

"I have nothing left to wager." Dunk did not know what distressed him more: learning that the Snail was bribing the master of the games to get the pairings he desired, or realizing the man had desired *him*. He stood. "I have said what I came to say. My horse and sword are yours, and all my armor."

The Snail steepled his fingers. "Perhaps there is another way. You are not entirely without your talents. You fall most splendidly." Ser Uthor's lips glistened when he smiled. "I will lend you back your steed and armor . . . if you enter my service."

"Service?" Dunk did not understand. "What sort of service? You have a squire. Do you need to garrison some castle?"

"I might, if I had a castle. If truth be told, I prefer a good inn. Castles cost too much to maintain. No, the service I would require of you is that you face me in a few more tourneys. Twenty should suffice. You can do that, surely? You shall have a tenth part of my winnings, and in future I promise to strike that broad chest of yours and not your head."

"You'd have me travel about with you to be unhorsed?"

Ser Uthor chuckled pleasantly. "You are such a strapping specimen, no one will ever believe that some round-shouldered old man with a snail on his shield could put you down." He rubbed his chin. "You need a new device yourself, by the way. That hanged man is grim enough, I grant you, but . . . well, he's *hanging*, isn't he? Dead and defeated. Something fiercer is required. A bear's head, mayhaps. A skull. Or three skulls, better still. A babe impaled upon a spear. And you should let your hair grow long and cultivate a beard, the wilder and more unkempt the better. There are more of these little tourneys than you know. With the odds I'd get, we'd win enough to buy a dragon's egg before—"

"—it got about that I was hopeless? I lost my armor, not my honor. You'll have Thunder and my arms, no more."

"Pride ill becomes a beggar, ser. You could do much worse than ride with me. At the least I could teach you a thing or two of jousting, about which you are pig ignorant at present."

"You'd make a fool of me."

"I did that earlier. And even fools must eat."

Dunk wanted to smash that smile off his face. "I see why you have a snail on your shield. You are no true knight."

"Spoken like a true oaf. Are you so blind you cannot see your danger?" Ser Uthor put his cup aside. "Do you know why I struck you where I did, ser?" He got to his feet and touched Dunk lightly in the center of his chest. "A coronal placed here would have put you on the ground just as quickly. The head is a smaller target, the blow is more difficult to land . . . though more likely to be mortal. I was paid to strike you there."

"Paid?" Dunk backed away from him. "What do you mean?"

"Six dragons tendered in advance, four more promised when you died. A paltry sum for a knight's life. Be thankful for that. Had more been of-fered, I might have put the point of my lance through your eye slit."

Dunk felt dizzy again. *Why would someone pay to have me killed? I've done no harm to any man at Whitewalls.* Surely no one hated him that much but Egg's brother Aerion, and the Bright Prince was in exile across the narrow sea. "Who paid you?"

"A serving man brought the gold at sunrise, not long after the master of the games nailed up the pairings. His face was hooded, and he did not speak his master's name."

"But why?" said Dunk.

"I did not ask." Ser Uthor filled his cup again. "I think you have more enemies than you know, Ser Duncan. How not? There are some who would say you were the cause of all our woes."

Dunk felt a cold hand on his heart. "Say what you mean."

The Snail shrugged. "I may not have been at Ashford Meadow, but jousting is my bread and salt. I follow tourneys from afar as faithfully as the maesters follow stars. I know how a certain hedge knight became the cause of a Trial of Seven at Ashford Meadow, resulting in the death of Baelor Breakspear at his brother Maekar's hand." Ser Uthor seated himself and stretched his legs out. "Prince Baelor was well loved. The Bright Prince had friends as well, friends who will not have forgotten the cause of his exile. Think on my offer, ser. The snail may leave a trail of slime behind him, but a little slime will do a man no harm . . . whilst if you dance with dragons, you must expect to burn."

The day seemed darker when Dunk stepped from the Snail's tent. The clouds in the east had grown bigger and blacker, and the sun was sinking to the west, casting long shadows across the yard. Dunk found the squire Will inspecting Thunder's feet.

"Where's Egg?" he asked of him.

"The bald boy? How would I know? Run off somewhere."

He could not bear to say farewell to Thunder, Dunk decided. *He'll be back at the tent with his books.*

He wasn't, though. The books were there, bundled neatly in a stack beside Egg's bedroll, but of the boy there was no sign. Something was wrong here. Dunk could feel it. It was not like Egg to wander off without his leave.

A pair of grizzled men-at-arms were drinking barley beer outside a striped pavilion a few feet away. ". . . well, bugger that, once was enough for me," one muttered. "The grass was green when the sun come up, aye . . ." He broke off when other man gave him a nudge, and only then took note of Dunk. "Ser?"

"Have you seen my squire? Egg, he's called."

The man scratched at the grey stubble underneath one ear. "I remember him. Less hair than me, and a mouth three times his size. Some o' the other lads shoved him about a bit, but that was last night. I've not seen him since, ser."

"Scared him off," said his companion.

Dunk gave that one a hard look. "If he comes back, tell him to wait for me here."

"Aye, ser. That we will."

Might be he just went to watch the jousts. Dunk headed back toward the tilting grounds. As he passed the stables, he came on Ser Glendon Ball, brushing down a pretty sorrel charger. "Have you seen Egg?" he asked him.

"He ran past a few moments ago." Ser Glendon pulled a carrot from his pocket and fed it to the sorrel. "Do you like my new horse? Lord Costayne sent his squire to ransom her, but I told him to save his gold. I mean to keep her for my own."

"His Lordship will not like that."

"His Lordship said that I had no right to put a fireball upon my shield. He told me my device should be a clump of pussywillows. His Lordship can go bugger himself."

Dunk could not help but smile. He had supped at that same table himself, choking down the same bitter dishes as served up by the likes of the Bright Prince and Ser Steffon Fossoway. He felt a certain kinship with the prickly young knight. *For all I know, my mother was a whore as well.* "How many horses have you won?"

Ser Glendon shrugged. "I lost count. Mortimer Boggs still owes me one. He said he'd rather eat his horse than have some whore's bastard riding her. And he took a hammer to his armor before sending it to me. It's full of holes. I suppose I can still get something for the metal." He sounded more sad than angry. "There was a stable by the . . . the inn where I was raised. I worked there when I was a boy, and when I could I'd sneak the horses off while their owners were busy. I was always good with horses. Stots, rounseys, palfreys, drays, plowhorses, warhorses—I rode them all. Even a Dornish sand steed. This old man I knew taught me how to make my own lances. I thought if I showed them all how good I was, they'd have no choice but to admit I was my father's son. But they won't. Even now. They just won't."

"Some never will," Dunk told him. "It doesn't matter what you do. Others, though . . . they're not all the same. I've met some good ones." He thought a moment. "When the tourney's done, Egg and I mean to go north. Take service at Winterfell, and fight for the Starks against the ironmen. You could come with us." The north was a world all its own, Ser Arlan always said. No one up there was like to know the tale of Penny Jenny and the Knight of the Pussywillows. *No one will laugh at you up there. They will know you only by your blade, and judge you by your worth.*

Ser Glendon gave him a suspicious look. "Why would I want to do that? Are you telling me I need to run away and hide?"

"No. I just thought . . . two swords instead of one. The roads are not so safe as they once were."

"That's true enough," the boy said grudgingly, "but my father was once promised a place amongst the Kingsguard. I mean to claim the white cloak that he never got to wear."

You have as much chance of wearing a white cloak as I do, Dunk almost said. *You were born of a camp follower, and I crawled out of the gutters of Flea Bottom. Kings do not heap honor on the likes of you and me.* The lad would not have taken kindly to that truth, however. Instead he said, "Strength to your arm, then."

He had not gone more than a few feet when Ser Glendon called after him. "Ser Duncan, wait. I . . . I should not have been so sharp. A knight must needs be courteous, my mother used to say." The boy seemed to be struggling for words. "Lord Peake came to see me, after my last joust. He offered me a place at Starpike. He said there was a storm coming the likes of which Westeros had not seen for a generation, that he would need swords and men to wield them. Loyal men, who knew how to obey."

Dunk could hardly believe it. Gormon Peake had made his scorn for hedge knights plain, both on the road and on the roof, but the offer was a generous one. "Peake is a great lord," he said, wary, "but . . . but not a man that I would trust, I think."

"No." The boy flushed. "There was a price. He'd take me into his service, he said . . . but first I would have to prove my loyalty. He would see that I was paired against his friend the Fiddler next, and he wanted me to swear that I would lose."

Dunk believed him. He should have been shocked, he knew, and yet somehow he wasn't. "What did you say?"

"I said I might not be able to lose to the Fiddler even if I were trying, that I had already unhorsed much better men than him, that the dragon's egg would be mine before the day was done." Ball smiled feebly. "It was not the answer that he wanted. He called me a fool, then, and told me that I had best watch my back. The Fiddler had many friends, he said, and I had none."

Dunk put a hand upon his shoulder and squeezed. "You have one, ser. Two, once I find Egg."

The boy looked him in the eye and nodded. "It is good to know there are some true knights still."

Dunk got his first good look at Ser Tommard Heddle whilst searching for Egg amongst the crowds about the lists. Heavyset and broad, with a chest like a barrel, Lord Butterwell's good-son wore black plate over boiled leather, and an ornate helm fashioned in the likeness of some demon, scaled and slavering. His horse was three hands taller than Thunder and two stone heavier, a monster of a beast armored in a coat of ringmail. The weight of all that iron made him slow, so Heddle never got up past a canter when the course was run; but that did not prevent him making short work of Ser Clarence Charlton. As Charlton was borne from the field upon a litter, Heddle removed his demonic helm. His head was broad and bald, his beard black and square. Angry red boils festered on his cheek and neck.

Dunk knew that face. Heddle was the knight who'd growled at him in the bedchamber when he touched the dragon's egg, the man with the deep voice that he'd heard talking with Lord Peake.

A jumble of words came rushing back to him: *beggar's feast you've laid before us . . . is the boy his father's son . . . Bittersteel . . . need the sword . . . Old Milkblood expects . . . is the boy his father's son . . . I promise you, Bloodraven is not off dreaming . . . is the boy his father's son?*

He stared at the viewing stand, wondering if somehow Egg had contrived to take his rightful place amongst the notables. There was no sign of the boy, however. Butterwell and Frey were missing too, though Butterwell's wife was still in her seat, looking bored and restive. *That's queer,* Dunk reflected. This was Butterwell's castle, his wedding, and Frey was father to his bride. These jousts were in their honor. Where would they have gone?

"*Ser Uthor Underleaf,*" the herald boomed. A shadow crept across Dunk's face as the sun was swallowed by a cloud. "*Ser Theomore of House Bulwer, the Old Ox, a knight of Blackcrown. Come forth and prove your valor.*"

The Old Ox made a fearsome sight in his blood red armor, with black bull's horns rising from his helm. He needed the help of a brawny squire to get onto his horse, though, and the way his head was always turning as he rode suggested that Ser Maynard had been right about his eye. Still, the man received a lusty cheer as he took the field.

Not so the Snail, no doubt just as he preferred. On the first pass, both knights struck glancing blows. On the second, the Old Ox snapped his lance on the Ser Uthor's shield, while the Snail's blow missed entirely. The same thing happened on the third pass, and this time Ser Uthor swayed as if about to fall. *He is feigning,* Dunk realized. *He is drawing the contest out to fatten the odds for next time.* He had only to glance around to see Will at work, making wagers for his master. Only then did it occur to him that he might have fattened his own purse with a coin or two upon the Snail. *Dunk the lunk, thick as a castle wall.*

The Old Ox fell on fifth pass, knocked sideways by a coronal that slipped deftly off his shield to take him in the chest. His foot tangled in his stirrup as he fell, and he was dragged forty yards across the field before his men could get his horse under control. Again the litter came out, to bear him to the maester. A few drops of rain began to fall as Bulwer was carried away and darkened his surcoat where they fell. Dunk watched without expression. He was thinking about Egg. *What if this secret enemy of mine has got his hands on him?* It made as much sense as anything else. *The boy is blameless. If someone has a quarrel with me, it should not be him who answers for it.*

Ser John the Fiddler was being armed for his next tilt when Dunk found him. No fewer than three squires were attending him, buckling on his armor and seeing to the trappings of his horse, whilst Lord Alyn Cockshaw sat nearby drinking watered wine and looking bruised and peevish. When he caught sight of Dunk, Lord Alyn sputtered, dribbling wine upon on his chest. "How is it that you're still walking about? The Snail stove your face in."

"Steely Pate made me a good strong helm, m'lord. And my head is hard as stone, Ser Arlan used to say."

The Fiddler laughed. "Pay no mind to Alyn. Fireball's bastard knocked him off his horse onto that plump little rump of his, so now he has decided that he hates all hedge knights."

"That wretched pimpled creature is no son of Quentyn Ball," insisted Alyn Cockshaw. "He should never have been allowed to compete. If this were my wedding, I should have had him whipped for his presumption."

"What maid would marry you?" Ser John said. "And Ball's presumption is a deal less grating than your pouting. Ser Duncan, are you perchance a friend of Galtry the Green? I must shortly part him from his horse."

Dunk did not doubt it. "I do not know the man, m'lord."

"Will you take a cup of wine? Some bread and olives?"

"Only a word, m'lord."

"You may have all the words you wish. Let us adjourn to my pavilion." The Fiddler held the flap for him. "Not you, Alyn. You could do with a few less olives, if truth be told."

Inside, the Fiddler turned back to Dunk. "I knew Ser Uthor had not killed you. My dreams are never wrong. And the Snail must face me soon enough. Once I've unhorsed him, I shall demand your arms and armor back. Your destrier as well, though you deserve a better mount. Will you take one as my gift?"

"I . . . no . . . I couldn't do that." The thought made Dunk uncomfortable. "I do not mean to be ungrateful, but . . ."

"If it is the debt that troubles you, put the thought from your mind. I do not need your silver, ser. Only your friendship. How can you be one of my knights without a horse?" Ser John drew on his gauntlets of lobstered steel and flexed his fingers.

"My squire is missing."

"Ran off with a girl, perhaps?"

"Egg's too young for girls, m'lord. He would never leave me of his own will. Even if I were dying, he would stay until my corpse was cold. His horse is still here. So is our mule."

"If you like, I could ask my men to look for him."

My men. Dunk did not like the sound of that. *A tourney for traitors,* he thought. "You are no hedge knight."

"No." The Fiddler's smile was full of boyish charm. "But you knew that from the start. You have been calling me *m'lord* since we met upon the road, why is that?"

"The way you talk. The way you look. The way you act." *Dunk the lunk, thick as a castle wall.* "Up on the roof last night, you said some things. . . ."

"Wine makes me talk too much, but I meant every word. We belong together, you and I. My dreams do not lie."

"Your dreams don't lie," said Dunk, "but you do. John is not your true name, is it?"

"No." The Fiddler's eyes sparkled with mischief.

He has Egg's eyes.

"His true name will be revealed soon enough, to those who need to know." Lord Gormon Peake had slipped into the pavilion, scowling. "Hedge knight, I warn you—"

"Oh, stop it, Gormy," said the Fiddler. "Ser Duncan is with us, or will be soon. I told you, I dreamed of him." Outside, a herald's trumpet blew. The Fiddler turned his head. "They are calling me to the lists. Pray excuse me, Ser Duncan. We can resume our talk after I dispose of Ser Galtry the Green."

"Strength to your arm," Dunk said. It was only courteous.

Lord Gormon remained after Ser John had gone. "His dreams will be the death of all of us."

"What did it take to buy Ser Galtry?" Dunk heard himself say. "Was silver sufficient, or does he require gold?"

"Someone has been talking, I see." Peake seated himself in a camp chair. "I have a dozen men outside. I ought to call them in and have them slit your throat, ser."

"Why don't you?"

"His Grace would take it ill."

His Grace. Dunk felt as though someone had punched him in the belly. *Another black dragon,* he thought. *Another Blackfyre Rebellion. And soon another Redgrass Field. The grass was not red when the sun came up.* "Why this wedding?"

"Lord Butterwell wanted a new young wife to warm his bed, and Lord Frey had a somewhat soiled daughter. Their nuptials provided a plausible pretext for some like-minded lords to gather. Most of those invited here fought for the Black Dragon once. The rest have reason to resent Bloodraven's rule, or nurse grievances and ambitions of their own. Many of us had sons and daughters taken to King's Landing to vouchsafe our future loyalty, but most of the hostages perished in the Great Spring Sickness. Our hands are no longer tied. Our time is come. Aerys is weak. A bookish man, and no warrior. The commons hardly know him, and what they know they do not like. His lords love him even less. His father was weak as well, that is true, but when his throne was threatened he had sons to take the field for him. Baelor and Maekar, the hammer and the anvil . . . but Baelor Breakspear is no more, and Prince Maekar sulks at Summerhall, at odds with king and Hand."

Aye, thought Dunk, *and now some fool hedge knight has delivered his favorite son into the hands of his enemies. How better to ensure that the prince never stirs from Summerhall?* "There is Bloodraven," he said. "He is not weak."

"No," Lord Peake allowed, "but no man loves a sorcerer, and kinslayers are accursed in the sight of gods and men. At the first sign of weakness or defeat, Bloodraven's men will melt away like summer snows. And if the dream the prince has dreamed comes true, and a living dragon comes forth here at Whitewalls—"

Dunk finished for him. "—the throne is yours."

"His," said Lord Gormon Peake. "I am but a humble servant." He rose. "Do not attempt to leave the castle, ser. If you do, I will take it as a proof of treachery, and you will answer with your life. We have gone too far to turn back now."

The leaden sky was spitting down rain in earnest as John the Fiddler and Ser Galtry the Green took up fresh lances at opposite ends of the lists. Some of the wedding guests were streaming off toward the great hall, huddled under cloaks.

Ser Galtry rode a white stallion. A drooping green plume adorned his helm, a matching plume his horse's crinet. His cloak was a patchwork of many squares of fabric, each a different shade of green. Gold inlay made his greaves and gauntlet glitter, and his shield showed nine jade mullets upon a leek-green field. Even his beard was dyed green, in the fashion of the men of Tyrosh across the narrow sea.

Nine times he and the Fiddler charged with leveled lances, the green patchwork knight and the young lordling of the golden swords and fiddles, and nine times their lances shattered. By the eighth run, the ground had begun to soften, and the big destriers splashed through pools of rainwater. On the ninth, the Fiddler almost lost his seat, but recovered before he fell. "Well struck," he called out, laughing. "You almost had me down, ser."

"Soon enough," the green knight shouted through the rain.

"No, I think not." The Fiddler tossed his splintered lance away, and a squire handed him a fresh one.

The next run was their last. Ser Galtry's lance scraped ineffectually off the Fiddler's shield, whilst Ser John's took the green knight squarely in the center of his chest and knocked him from his saddle, to land with a great brown splash. In the east, Dunk saw the flash of distant lightning.

The viewing stands were emptying out quickly, as smallfolk and lordlings alike scrambled to get out of the wet. "See how they run," murmured Alyn Cockshaw, as he slid up beside Dunk. "A few drops of rain, and all the bold lords go squealing for shelter. What will they do when the real storm breaks, I wonder?"

The real storm. Dunk knew Lord Alyn was not talking about the weather. *What does this one want? Has he suddenly decided to befriend me?*

The herald mounted his platform once again. *"Ser Tommard Heddle, a knight of Whitewalls, in service to Lord Butterwell!"* he shouted as thunder rumbled in the distance. *"Ser Uthor Underleaf. Come forth and prove your valor."*

Dunk glanced over at Ser Uthor in time to see the Snail's smile go sour. *This is not the match he paid for.* The master of the games had crossed him up, but why? *Someone else has taken a hand, someone Cosgrove esteems more than Uthor Underleaf.* Dunk chewed on that for a moment. *They do not know that Uthor does not mean to win,* he realized all at once. *They see him as a threat, so they mean for Black Tom to remove him from the Fiddler's path.* Heddle himself was part of Peake's conspiracy; he could be relied on to lose when the need arose. Which left no one but . . .

And suddenly Lord Peake himself was storming across the muddy field to climb the steps to the herald's platform, his cloak flapping behind him. *"We are betrayed!"* he cried. "Bloodraven has a spy amongst us. The dragon's egg is stolen!"

Ser John the Fiddler wheeled his mount around. "My egg? How is that possible? Lord Butterwell keeps guards outside his bedchamber night and day."

"Slain," Lord Peake declared, "but one man named his killer before he died."

Does he mean to accuse me? Dunk wondered. A dozen men had seem him touch the dragon's egg last night, when he'd carried Lady Butterwell to her lord husband's bed.

Lord Gormon's finger stabbed down in accusation. "There he stands. The whore's son. Seize him."

At the far end of the lists, Ser Glendon Ball looked up in confusion. For a moment he did not appear to comprehend what was happening, until he saw men rushing at him from all directions. Then the boy moved more quickly than Dunk could have believed. He had his sword half out of its sheath when the first man threw an arm around his throat. Ball wrenched free of his grip, but by then two more of them were on him. They slammed into him and dragged him down into the mud. Other men swarmed over them, shouting and kicking. *That could be me,* Dunk realized. He felt as helpless as he had at Ashford, the day they'd told him he must lose a hand and a foot.

Alyn Cockshaw pulled him back. "Stay out of this, if you want to find that squire of yours."

Dunk turned on him. "What do you mean?"

"I may know where to find the boy."

"Where?" Dunk was in no mood for games.

At the far end of the field, Ser Glendon was yanked roughly back onto his feet, pinioned between two men-at-arms in mail and halfhelms. He was brown with mud from waist to ankle, and blood and rain washed down his cheeks. *Hero's blood,* thought Dunk, as Black Tom dismounted before the captive. "Where is the egg?"

Blood dribbled from Ball's mouth. "Why would I steal the egg? I was about to win it."

Aye, thought Dunk, *and that they could not allow.*

Black Tom slashed Ball across the face with a mailed fist. "Search his saddlebags," Lord Peake commanded. "We'll find the dragon's egg wrapped up and hidden, I'll wager."

Lord Alyn lowered his voice. "And so they will. Come with me if you want to find your squire. There's no better time than now, whilst they're all occupied." He did not wait for a reply.

Dunk had to follow. Three long strides brought him abreast of the lordling. "If you have done Egg any harm—"

"Boys are not to my taste. This way. Step lively now."

Through an archway, down a set of muddy steps, around a corner, Dunk stalked after him, splashing through puddles as the rain fell around them. They stayed close to the walls, cloaked in shadows, finally stopping in a closed courtyard where the paving stones were smooth and slick. Buildings pressed close on every side. Above were windows, closed and shuttered. In the center of the courtyard was a well, ringed with a low stone wall.

A lonely place, Dunk thought. He did not like the feel of it. Old instinct made him reach for his sword hilt, before he remembered that the Snail had won his sword. As he fumbled at his hip where his scabbard should have hung, he felt the point of a knife poke his lower back. "Turn on me, and I'll cut your kidney out and give it to Butterwell's cooks to fry up for the feast." The knife pushed in through the back of Dunk's jerkin, insistent. "Over to the well. No sudden moves, ser."

If he has thrown Egg down that well, he will need more than some little toy knife to save him. Dunk walked forward slowly. He could feel the anger growing in his belly.

The blade at his back vanished. "You may turn and face me now, hedge knight."

Dunk turned. "M'lord. Is this about the dragon's egg?"

"No. This is about the dragon. Did you think I would stand by and let you steal him?" Ser Alyn grimaced. "I should have known better than to trust that wretched Snail to kill you. I'll have my gold back, every coin."

Him? Dunk thought. *This plump, pasty-faced, perfumed lordling is my secret enemy?* He did not know whether to laugh or weep. "Ser Uthor earned his gold. I have a hard head, is all."

"So it seems. Back away."

Dunk took a step backwards.

"Again. Again. Once more."

Another step, and he was flush against the well. Its stones pressed against his lower back.

"Sit down on the rim. Not afraid of a little bath, are you? You cannot get much wetter than you are right now."

"I cannot swim." Dunk rested a hand on the well. The stones were wet. One moved beneath the pressure of his palm.

"What a shame. Will you jump, or must I prick you?"

Dunk glanced down. He could see the raindrops dimpling the water, a good twenty feet below. The walls were covered with a slime of algae. "I never did you any harm."

"And never will. Daemon's mine. I will command his Kingsguard. You are not worthy of a white cloak."

"I never claimed I was." *Daemon.* The name rang in Dunk's head. *Not John. Daemon, after his father. Dunk the lunk, thick as a castle wall.* "Daemon Blackfyre sired seven sons. Two died upon the Redgrass Field, twins—"

"Aegon and Aemon. Wretched witless bullies, just like you. When we were little, they took pleasure in tormenting me and Daemon both. I wept when Bittersteel carried him off to exile, and again when Lord Peake told me he was coming home. But then he saw *you* upon the road, and forgot that I existed." Cockshaw waved his dagger threateningly. "You can go into the water as you are, or you can go in bleeding. Which will it be?"

Dunk closed his hand around the loose stone. It proved to be less loose than he had hoped. Before he could wrench it free, Ser Alyn lunged. Dunk twisted sideways, so the point of the blade sliced through the meat of his shield arm. And then the stone popped free. Dunk fed it to His Lordship and felt his teeth crack beneath the blow. "The well, is it?" He hit the lordling in the mouth again, then dropped the stone, seized Cockshaw by the wrist, and twisted until a bone snapped and the dagger clattered to the stones. "After you, m'lord." Sidestepping, Dunk yanked at the lordling's arm and planted a kick in the small of his back. Lord Alyn toppled headlong into the well. There was a splash.

"Well done, ser."

Dunk whirled. Through the rain, all he could make out was a hooded shape and a single pale white eye. It was only when the man came forward that the shadowed face beneath the cowl took on the familiar features of Ser Maynard Plumm, the pale eye no more than the moonstone brooch that pinned his cloak at the shoulder.

Down in the well, Lord Alyn was thrashing and splashing and calling for help. "*Murder!* Someone help me."

"He tried to kill me," Dunk said.

"That would explain all the blood."

"Blood?" He looked down. His left arm was red from shoulder to elbow, his tunic clinging to his skin. "Oh."

Dunk did not remember falling, but suddenly he was on the ground, with raindrops running down his face. He could hear Lord Alyn whimpering from the well, but his splashing had grown feebler. "We need to have that arm bound up." Ser Maynard slipped his own arm under Dunk. "Up now. I cannot lift you by myself. Use your legs."

Dunk used his legs. "Lord Alyn. He's going to drown."

"He shan't be missed. Least of all by the Fiddler."

"He's not," Dunk gasped, pale with pain, "a fiddler."

"No. He is Daemon of House Blackfyre, the Second of His Name. Or so he would style himself, if ever he achieves the Iron Throne. You would be surprised to know how many lords prefer their kings brave and stupid. Daemon is young and dashing, and looks good on a horse."

The sounds from the well were almost too faint to hear. "Shouldn't we throw His Lordship down a rope?"

"Save him now to execute him later? I think not. Let him eat the meal that he meant to serve to you. Come, lean on me." Plumm guided him across the yard. This close, there was something queer about the cast of Ser Maynard's features. The longer Dunk looked, the less he seemed to see. "I did urge you to flee, you will recall, but you esteemed your honor more than your life. An honorable death is well and good, but if the life at stake is not your own, what then? Would your answer be the same, ser?"

"Whose life?" From the well came one last splash. "Egg? Do you mean Egg?" Dunk clutched at Plumm's arm. *"Where is he?"*

"With the gods. And you will know why, I think."

The pain that twisted inside Dunk just then made him forget his arm. He groaned. "He tried to use the boot."

"So I surmise. He showed the ring to Maester Lothar, who delivered him to Butterwell, who no doubt pissed his breeches at the sight of it and started wondering if he had chosen the wrong side and how much Bloodraven knows of this conspiracy. The answer to that last is *'quite a lot.'*" Plumm chuckled.

"Who are you?"

"A friend," said Maynard Plumm. "One who has been watching you, and wondering at your presence in this nest of adders. Now be quiet, until we get you mended."

Staying in the shadows, the two of them made their way back to Dunk's small tent. Once inside, Ser Maynard lit a fire, filled a bowl with wine, and set it on the flames to boil. "A clean cut, and at least it is not your sword arm," he said, slicing through the sleeve of Dunk's bloodstained tunic. "The thrust appears to have missed the bone. Still, we will need to wash it out, or you could lose the arm."

"It doesn't matter." Dunk's belly was roiling, and he felt as if he might retch at any moment. "If Egg is dead—"

"—you bear the blame. You should have kept him well away from here. I never said the boy was dead, though. I said that he was with the gods. Do you have clean linen? Silk?"

"My tunic. The good one I got in Dorne. What do you mean, he's with the gods?"

"In good time. Your arm first."

The wine soon began to steam. Ser Maynard found Dunk's good silk tunic, sniffed at it suspiciously, then slid out a dagger and began to cut it up. Dunk swallowed his protest.

"Ambrose Butterwell has never been what you might call *decisive*," Ser Maynard said as he wadded up three strips of silk and dropped them in the wine. "He had doubts about this plot from the beginning, doubts that were inflamed when he learned that the boy did not bear the sword. And this morning, his dragon's egg vanished, and with it the last dregs of his courage."

"Ser Glendon did not steal the egg," Dunk said. "He was in the yard all day, tilting or watching others tilt."

"Peake will find the egg in his saddlebags all the same." The wine was boiling. Plumm drew on a leather glove and said, "Try not to scream." Then he pulled a strip of silk out of the boiling wine and began to wash the cut.

Dunk did not scream. He gnashed his teeth and bit his tongue and smashed his fist against his thigh hard enough to leave bruises, but he did not scream. Ser Maynard used the rest of his good tunic to make a bandage and tied it tight around his arm. "How does that feel?" he asked when he was done.

"Bloody awful." Dunk shivered. "*Where's Egg?*"

"With the gods. I told you."

Dunk reached up and wrapped his good hand around Plumm's neck. "Speak plain. I am sick of hints and winks. Tell me where to find the boy, or I will snap your bloody neck, friend or no."

"The sept. You would do well to go armed." Ser Maynard smiled. "Is that plain enough for you, Dunk?"

His first stop was Ser Uthor Underleaf's pavilion.

When Dunk slipped inside, he found only the squire Will bent over a washtub, scrubbing out his master's smallclothes. "You again? Ser Uthor is at the feast. What do you want?"

"My sword and shield."

"Have you brought the ransom?"

"No."

"Then why would I let you take your arms?"

"I have need of them."

"That's no good reason."

"How about, try to stop me and I'll kill you."

Will gaped. "They're over there."

Dunk paused outside the castle sept. *Gods grant I am not too late.* His swordbelt was back in its accustomed place, cinched tight about his waist. He had strapped the gallows shield to his wounded arm, and the weight of it was sending throbs of pain through him with every step. If anyone brushed up against him, he feared that he might scream. He pushed the doors open with his good hand.

Within, the sept was dim and hushed, lit only by the candles that twinkled on the altars of the Seven. The Warrior had the most candles burning, as might be expected during a tourney; many a knight would have come here to pray for strength and courage before they chanced the lists. The Stranger's altar was shrouded in shadow, with but a single candle burning. The Mother and the Father each had dozens, the Smith and Maiden somewhat fewer. And beneath the shining lantern of the Crone knelt Lord Ambrose Butterwell, head bowed, praying silently for wisdom.

He was not alone. No sooner had Dunk started for him than two men-at-arms moved to cut him off, faces stern beneath their halfhelms. Both wore mail beneath surcoats striped in the green, white, and yellow undy of House Butterwell. "Hold, ser," one said. "You have no business here."

"Yes, he does. I *warned* you he would find me."

The voice was Egg's.

When Egg stepped out from the shadows beneath the Father, his shaven head shining in the candlelight, Dunk almost rushed to the boy, to pluck him up with a glad cry and crush him in his arms. Something in Egg's tone made him hesitate. *He sounds more angry than afraid, and I have never seen him look so stern. And Butterwell on his knees. Something is queer here.*

Lord Butterwell pushed himself back to his feet. Even in the dim light of the candles, his flesh looked pale and clammy. "Let him pass," he told his guardsmen. When they stepped back, he beckoned Dunk closer. "I have done the boy no harm. I knew his father well, when I was the King's Hand. Prince Maekar needs to know, none of this was my idea."

"He will," Dunk promised. *What is happening here?*

"Peake. This was all his doing, I swear it by the Seven." Lord Butterwell put one hand on the altar. "May the gods strike me down if I am false. He told me whom I must invite and who must be excluded, and he brought this boy pretender here. I never wanted to be part of any treason, you must believe me. Tom Heddle now, he urged me on, I will not deny it. My good-son, married to my eldest daughter, but I will not lie, he was part of this."

"He is your champion," said Egg. "If he was in this, so were you."

Be quiet, Dunk wanted to roar. *That loose tongue of yours will get us killed.* Yet Butterwell seemed to quail. "My lord, you do not understand. Heddle commands my garrison."

"You must have *some* loyal guardsmen," said Egg.

"These men here," said Lord Butterwell. "A few more. I've been too lax, I will allow, but I have never been a traitor. Frey and I harbored doubts about Lord Peake's pretender since the beginning. *He does not bear the sword!* If he were his father's son, Bittersteel would have armed him with Blackfyre. And all this talk about a dragon . . . madness, madness and folly." His Lordship dabbed the sweat from his face with his sleeve. "And now they have taken the egg, the dragon's egg my grandsire had from the king himself as a reward for leal service. It was there this morning when I woke, and my guards swear no one entered or left the bedchamber. It may be that Lord Peake bought them, I cannot say, but *the egg is gone.* They must have it, or else . . ."

Or else the dragon's hatched, thought Dunk. If a living dragon appeared again in Westeros, the lords and smallfolk alike would flock to whichever prince could lay claim to it. "My lord," he said, "a word with my . . . my squire, if you would be so good."

"As you wish, ser." Lord Butterwell knelt to pray again.

Dunk drew Egg aside and went down upon one knee to speak with him face-to-face. "I am going to clout you in the ear so hard your head will turn around backwards, and you'll spend the rest of your life looking at where you've been."

"You should, ser." Egg had the grace to look abashed. "I'm sorry. I just meant to send a raven to my father."

So I could stay a knight. The boy meant well. Dunk glanced over to where Butterwell was praying. "What did you do to him?"

"Scared him, ser."

"Aye, I can see that. He'll have scabs on his knees before the night is done."

"I didn't know what else to do, ser. The maester brought me to them, once he saw my father's ring."

"Them?"

"Lord Butterwell and Lord Frey, ser. Some guards were there as well. Everyone was upset. Someone stole the dragon's egg."

"Not you, I hope?"

Egg shook his head. "No, ser. I knew I was in trouble when the maester showed Lord Butterwell my ring. I thought about saying that I'd stolen it, but I didn't think he would believe me. Then I remembered this one time I heard my father talking about something Lord Bloodraven said, about how it was better to be frightening than frightened, so I told them that my father had sent us here to spy for him, that he was on his way here with an army, that His Lordship had best release me and give up this treason, or it would mean his head." He smiled a shy smile. "It worked better than I thought it would, ser."

Dunk wanted to take the boy by the shoulders and shake him until his teeth rattled. *This is no game,* he might have roared. *This is life and death.* "Did Lord Frey hear all this as well?"

"Yes. He wished Lord Butterwell happiness in his marriage and announced that he was returning to the Twins forthwith. That was when His Lordship brought us here to pray."

Frey could flee, Dunk thought, *but Butterwell does not have that option, and soon or late he will begin to wonder why Prince Maekar and his army have not turned up.* "If Lord Peake should learn that you are in the castle—"

The sept's outer doors opened with a crash. Dunk turned to see Black Tom Heddle glowering in mail and plate, with rainwater dripping off his sodden cloak to puddle by his feet. A dozen men-at-arms stood with him, armed with spears and axes. Lightning flashed blue and white across the sky behind them, etching sudden shadows across the pale stone floor. A gust of wet wind set all the candles in the sept to dancing.

Oh, seven bloody hells was all that Dunk had time enough to think before Heddle said, "There's the boy. Take him."

Lord Butterwell had risen to his feet. "No. Halt. The boy's not to be molested. Tommard, what is the meaning of this?"

Heddle's face twisted in contempt. "Not all of us have milk running in our veins, Your Lordship. I'll have the boy."

"You do not understand." Butterwell's voice had turned into a high thin quaver. "We are undone. Lord Frey is gone, and others will follow. Prince Maekar is coming with an army."

"All the more reason to take the boy as hostage."

"No, no," said Butterwell, "I want no more part of Lord Peake or his pretender. I will not fight."

Black Tom looked coldly at his lord. "Craven." He spat. "Say what you will. You'll fight or die, my lord." He pointed at Egg. "A stag to the first man to draw blood."

"No, no." Butterwell turned to his own guards. "Stop them, do you hear me? I command you. Stop them." But all the guards had halted in confusion, at a loss as to whom they should obey.

"Must I do it myself, then?" Black Tom drew his longsword.

Dunk did the same. "Behind me, Egg."

"Put up your steel, the both of you!" Butterwell screeched. "I'll have no bloodshed in the sept! Ser Tommard, this man is the prince's sworn shield. He'll kill you!"

"Only if he falls on me." Black Tom showed his teeth in a hard grin. "I saw him try to joust."

"I am better with a sword," Dunk warned him.

Heddle answered with a snort, and charged.

Dunk shoved Egg roughly backwards and turned to meet his blade. He blocked the first cut well enough, but the jolt of Black Tom's sword biting into his shield and the bandaged cut behind it sent a jolt of pain crackling up his arm. He tried a slash at Heddle's head in answer, but Black Tom slid away from it and hacked at him again. Dunk barely got his shield around in time. Pine chips flew and Heddle laughed, pressing his attack, low and high and low again. Dunk took each cut with his shield, but every blow was agony, and he found himself giving ground.

"Get him, ser," he heard Egg call. "Get him, get him, he's *right there.*" The taste of blood was in Dunk's mouth, and worse, his wound had opened once again. A wave of dizziness washed over him. Black Tom's blade was turning the long kite shield to splinters. *Oak and iron guard me well, or else I'm dead and doomed to hell,* Dunk thought, before he remembered that this shield was made of pine. When his back came up hard against an altar, he stumbled to one knee and realized he had no more ground left to give.

"You are no knight," said Black Tom. "Are those tears in your eyes, oaf?"

Tears of pain. Dunk pushed up off his knee and slammed shield-first into his foe.

Black Tom stumbled backwards, yet somehow kept his balance. Dunk bulled right after him, smashing him with the shield again and again, using his size and strength to knock Heddle halfway across the sept. Then he swung the shield aside and slashed out with his longsword, and Heddle screamed as the steel bit through wool and muscle deep into his thigh. His own sword swung wildly, but the blow was desperate and clumsy. Dunk let his shield take it one more time and put all his weight into his answer.

Black Tom reeled back a step and stared down in horror at his forearm flopping on the floor beneath the Stranger's altar. "You," he gasped, "you, you . . ."

"I told you." Dunk stabbed him through the throat. "I'm better with a sword."

Two of the men-at-arms fled back into the rain as a pool of blood spread out from Black Tom's body. The others clutched their spears and hesitated, casting wary glances toward Dunk as they waited for their lord to speak.

"This . . . this was ill done," Butterwell finally managed. He turned to Dunk and Egg. "We must be gone from Whitewalls before those two bring word of this to Gormon Peake. He has more friends amongst the guests than I do. The postern gate in the north wall, we'll slip out there . . . come, we must make haste."

Dunk slammed his sword into its scabbard. "Egg, go with Lord Butterwell." He put an arm around the boy and lowered his voice. "Don't stay with him any longer than you need to. Give Rain his head and get away before His Lordship changes sides again. Make for Maidenpool, it's closer than King's Landing."

"What about you, ser?"

"Never mind about me."

"I'm your squire."

"Aye," said Dunk, "and you'll do as I tell you, or you'll get a good clout in the ear."

A group of men were leaving the great hall, pausing long enough to pull up their hoods before venturing out into the rain. The Old Ox was amongst them, and weedy Lord Caswell, once more in his cups. Both gave Dunk a wide berth. Ser Mortimer Boggs favored him with a curious stare, but thought better of speaking to him. Uthor Underleaf was not so shy. "You come late to the feast, ser," he said as he was pulling on his gloves. "And I see you wear a sword again."

"You'll have your ransom for it, if that's all that concerns you." Dunk had left his battered shield behind and draped his cloak across his wounded arm to hide the blood. "Unless I die. Then you have my leave to loot my corpse."

Ser Uthor laughed. "Is that gallantry I smell, or just stupidity? The two scents are much alike, as I recall. It is not too late to accept my offer, ser."

"It is later than you think," Dunk warned him. He did not wait for Underleaf to answer, but pushed past him, through the double doors. The great hall smelled of ale and smoke and wet wool. In the gallery above, a few musicians played softly. Laughter echoed from the high tables, where Ser Kirby Pimm and Ser Lucas Nayland were playing a drinking game. Up on the dais, Lord Peake was speaking earnestly with Lord Costayne, while Ambrose Butterwell's new bride sat abandoned in her high seat.

Down below the salt, Dunk found Ser Kyle drowning his woes in Lord Butterwell's ale. His trencher was filled with a thick stew made with food left over from the night before. "A bowl o' brown," they called such fare in the pot shops of King's Landing. Ser Kyle had plainly had no stomach for it. Untouched, the stew had grown cold, and a film of grease glistened atop the brown.

Dunk slipped onto the bench beside him. "Ser Kyle."

The Cat nodded. "Ser Duncan. Will you have some ale?"

"No." Ale was the last thing that he needed.

"Are you unwell, ser? Forgive me, but you look—"

—*better than I feel.* "What was done with Glendon Ball?"

"They took him to the dungeons." Ser Kyle shook his head. "Whore's get or no, the boy never struck me as a thief."

"He isn't."

Ser Kyle squinted at him. "Your arm . . . how did—?"

"A dagger." Dunk turned to face the dais, frowning. He had escaped death twice today. That would suffice for most men, he knew. *Dunk the lunk, thick as a castle wall.* He pushed to his feet. "Your Grace," he called.

A few men on nearby benches put down their spoons, broke off their conversations, and turned to look at him.

"Your Grace," Dunk said again, more loudly. He strode up the Myrish carpet toward the dais. *"Daemon."*

Now half the hall grew quiet. At the high table, the man who'd called himself the Fiddler turned to smile at him. He had donned a purple tunic for the feast, Dunk saw. *Purple, to bring out the color of his eyes.* "Ser Duncan. I am pleased that you are with us. What would you have of me?"

"Justice," said Dunk, "for Glendon Ball."

The name echoed off the walls, and for half a heartbeat it was if every man, woman, and boy in the hall had turned to stone. Then Lord Costayne slammed a fist upon a table and shouted, "It's death that one deserves, not justice!" A dozen other voices echoed his, and Ser Harbert Paege declared, "He's bastard born. All bastards are thieves, or worse. Blood will tell."

For a moment Dunk despaired. *I am alone here.* But then Ser Kyle the Cat pushed himself to his feet, swaying only slightly. "The boy may be a bastard, my lords, but he's *Fireball's* bastard. It's like Ser Harbert said. Blood will tell."

Daemon frowned. "No one honors Fireball more than I do," he said. "I will not believe this false knight is his seed. He stole the dragon's egg, and slew three good men in the doing."

"He stole nothing and killed no one," Dunk insisted. "If three men were slain, look elsewhere for their killer. Your Grace knows as well as I that Ser Glendon was in the yard all day, riding one tilt after t'other."

"Aye," Daemon admitted. "I wondered at that myself. But the dragon's egg was found amongst his things."

"Was it? Where is it now?

Lord Gormon Peake rose cold-eyed and imperious. "Safe, and well guarded. And why is that any concern of yours, ser?"

"Bring it forth," said Dunk. "I'd like another look at it, m'lord. T'other night, I saw it only for a moment."

Peake's eyes narrowed. "Your Grace," he said to Daemon, "it comes to me that this hedge knight arrived at Whitewalls with Ser Glendon, uninvited. He may well be part of this."

Dunk ignored that. "Your Grace, the dragon's egg that Lord Peake found amongst Ser Glendon's things was the one he placed there. Let him bring it forth, if he can. Examine it yourself. I'll wager you it's no more than a painted stone."

The hall erupted into chaos. A hundred voices began to speak at once, and a dozen knights leapt to their feet. Daemon looked near as young and lost as Ser Glendon had when he had been accused. "Are you drunk, my friend?"

Would that I were. "I've lost some blood," Dunk allowed, "but not my wits. Ser Glendon has been wrongfully accused."

"Why?" Daemon demanded, baffled. "If Ball did no wrong, as you insist, why would His Lordship say he did and try to prove it with some painted rock?"

"To remove him from your path. His Lordship bought your other foes with gold and promises, but Ball was not for sale."

The Fiddler flushed. "That is not true."

"It is true. Send for Ser Glendon, and ask him yourself."

"I will do just that. Lord Peake, have the bastard fetched up at once. And bring the dragon's egg as well. I wish to have a closer look at it."

Gormon Peake gave Dunk a look of loathing. "Your Grace, the bastard boy is being questioned. A few more hours, and we will have a confession for you, I do not doubt."

"By *questioned,* m'lord means tortured," said Dunk. "A few more hours, and Ser Glendon will confess to having killed Your Grace's father, and both your brothers too."

"*Enough!*" Lord Peake's face was almost purple. "One more word, and I will rip your tongue out by the roots."

"You lie," said Dunk. "That's two words."

"And you will rue the both of them," Peake promised. "Take this man and chain him in the dungeons."

"No." Daemon's voice was dangerously quiet. "I want the truth of this. Sunderland, Vyrwel, Smallwood, take your men and go find Ser Glendon in the dungeons. Bring him up forthwith, and see that no harm comes to him. If any man should try to hinder you, tell him you are about the king's business."

"As you command," Lord Vyrwel answered.

"I will settle this as my father would," the Fiddler said. "Ser Glendon stands accused of grievous crimes. As a knight, he has a right to defend himself by strength of arms. I shall meet him in the lists, and let the gods determine guilt and innocence."

Hero's blood or whore's blood, Dunk thought when two of Lord Vrywel's men dumped Ser Glendon naked at his feet, *he has a deal less of it than he did before.*

The boy had been savagely beaten. His face was bruised and swollen, several of his teeth were cracked or missing, his right eye was weeping blood, and up and down his chest his flesh was red and cracking where they'd burned him with hot irons.

"You're safe now," murmured Ser Kyle. "There's no one here but hedge knights, and the gods know that we're a harmless lot." Daemon had given them the maester's chambers, and commanded them to dress any hurts Ser Glendon might have suffered and see that he was ready for the lists.

Three fingernails had been pulled from Ball's left hand, Dunk saw as he washed the blood from the boy's face and hands. That worried him more than all the rest. "Can you hold a lance?"

"A lance?" Blood and spit dribbled from Ser Glendon's mouth when he tried to speak. "Do I have all my fingers?"

"Ten," said Dunk, "but only seven fingernails."

Ball nodded. "Black Tom was going to cut my fingers off, but he was called away. Is it him that I'm to fight?"

"No. I killed him."

That made him smile. "Someone had to."

"You're to tilt against the Fiddler, but his real name—"

"—is Daemon, aye. They told me. The Black Dragon." Ser Glendon laughed. "My father died for him. I would have been his man, and gladly. I would have fought for him, killed for him, died for him, but I could not lose for him." He turned his head and spat out a broken tooth. "Could I have a cup of wine?"

"Ser Kyle, get the wineskin."

The boy drank long and deep, then wiped his mouth. "Look at me. I'm shaking like a girl."

Dunk frowned. "Can you still sit a horse?"

"Help me wash, and bring me my shield and lance and saddle," Ser Glendon said, "and you will see what I can do."

It was almost dawn before the rain let up enough for the combat to take place. The castle yard was a morass of soft mud glistening wetly by the light of a hundred torches. Beyond the field, a gray mist was rising, sending ghostly fingers up the pale stone walls to grasp the castle battlements. Many of the wedding guests had vanished during the intervening hours, but those who remained climbed the viewing stand again and settled themselves on planks of rain-soaked pine. Amongst them stood Ser Gormon Peake, surrounded by a knot of lesser lords and household knights.

It had been only a few years since Dunk had squired for old Ser Arlan. He had not forgotten how. He cinched the buckles on Ser Glendon's ill-fitting armor, fastened his helm to his gorget, helped him mount, and handed him his shield. Earlier contests had left deep gouges in the wood, but the blazing fireball could still be seen. *He looks as young as Egg,* Dunk thought. *A frightened boy, and grim.* His sorrel mare was unbarded, and skittish as well. *He should have stayed with his own mount. The sorrel may be better bred and swifter, but a rider rides best on a horse that he knows well, and this one is a stranger to him.*

"I'll need a lance," Ser Glendon said. "A war lance."

Dunk went to the racks. War lances were shorter and heavier than the tourney lances that had been used in all the earlier tilts; eight feet of solid ash ending in an iron point. Dunk chose one and pulled it out, running his hand along its lenth to make sure it had no cracks.

At the far end of the lists, one of Daemon's squires was offering him a matching lance. He was a fiddler no more. In place of swords and fiddles, the trapping of his warhorse now displayed the three-headed dragon of House Blackfyre, black on a field of red. The prince had washed the black dye from his hair as well, so it flowed down to his collar in a cascade of silver and gold that glimmered like beaten metal in the torchlight. *Egg would have hair like that if he ever let it grow,* Dunk realized. He found it hard to picture him that way, but one day he knew he must, if the two of them should live so long.

The herald climbed his platform once again. *"Ser Glendon the Bastard* stands accused of theft and murder," he proclaimed, "and now comes forth to prove his innocence at the hazard of his body. Daemon of House Blackfyre, the Second of His Name, rightborn King of the Andals and the Rhoynar and the First Men, Lord of the Seven Kingdoms and Protector of the Realm, comes forth to prove the truth of the accusations against the bastard Glendon."

And all at once the years fell away, and Dunk was back was at Ashford Meadow once again, listening to Baelor Breakspear just before they went forth to battle for his life. He slipped the war lance back in place, plucked a tourney lance from the next rack; twelve feet long, slender, elegant. "Use this," he told Ser Glendon. "It's what we used at Ashford, at the Trial of Seven."

"The Fiddler chose a war lance. He means to kill me."

"First he has to strike you. If your aim is true, his point will never touch you."

"I don't know."

"I do."

Ser Glendon snatched the lance from him, wheeled about, and trotted toward the lists. "Seven save us both, then."

Somewhere in the east, lightning cracked across a pale pink sky. Daemon raked his stallion's side with golden spurs, and leapt forward like a thunderclap, lowering his war lance with its deadly iron point. Ser Glendon raised his shield and raced to meet him, swinging his own longer lance across his mare's head to bear upon the young pretender's chest. Mud sprayed back from their horses' hooves, and the torches seemed to burn the brighter as the two knights went pounding past.

Dunk closed his eyes. He heard a *crack*, a shout, a thump.

"No," he heard Lord Peake cry out in anguish. *"Noooooo."* For half a heartbeat, Dunk almost felt sorry for him. He opened his eyes again. Riderless, the big black stallion was slowing to a trot. Dunk jumped out and grabbed him by the reins. At the far end of the lists, Ser Glendon Ball wheeled his mare and raised his splintered lance. Men rushed onto the field to where the Fiddler lay unmoving, facedown in a puddle. When they helped him to his feet, he was mud from head to heel.

"The Brown Dragon!" someone shouted. Laughter rippled through the yard as the dawn washed over Whitewalls.

It was only a few heartbeats later, as Dunk and Ser Kyle were helping Glendon Ball off his horse, that the first trumpet blew, and the sentries on the walls raised the alarum. An army had appeared outside the castle, rising from the morning mists. "Egg wasn't lying after all," Dunk told Ser Kyle, astonished.

From Maidenpool had come Lord Mooton, from Raventree Lord Blackwood, from Duskendale Lord Darklyn. The royal demenses about King's Landing sent forth Hayfords, Rosbys, Stokeworths, Masseys, and the king's own sworn swords, led by three knights of the Kingsguard and stiffened by three hundred Raven's Teeth with tall white weirwood bows. Mad Danelle Lothston herself rode forth in strength from her haunted towers at Harrenhal, clad in black armor that fit her like an iron glove, her long red hair streaming.

The light of the rising sun glittered off the points of five hundred lances and ten times as many spears. The night's grey banners were reborn in half a hundred gaudy colors. And above them all flew two regal dragons on night-black fields: the great three-headed beast of King Aerys I Targaryen, red as fire, and a white winged fury breathing scarlet flame.

Not Maekar after all, Dunk knew, when he saw those banners. The banners of the Prince of Summerhall showed four three-headed dragons, two and two, the arms of the fourth-born son of the late King Daeron II Targaryen. A single white dragon announced the presence of the King's Hand, Lord Brynden Rivers.

Bloodraven himself had come to Whitewalls.

The First Blackfyre Rebellion had perished on the Redgrass Field in blood and glory. The Second Blackfyre Rebellion ended with a whimper. "They cannot cow us," Young Daemon proclaimed from the castle battlements after he had seen the ring of iron that encircled them, "for our cause is just. We'll slash through them and ride hell-bent for King's Landing! Sound the trumpets!"

Instead, knights and lords and men-at-arms muttered quietly to one another, and a few began to slink away, making for the stables or a postern gate or some hidey-hole they hoped might keep them safe. And when Daemon drew his sword and raised it above his head, every man of them could see it was not Blackfyre. "We'll make another Redgrass Field today," the pretender promised.

"Piss on that, fiddle boy," a grizzled squire shouted back at him. "I'd sooner live."

In the end, the second Daemon Blackfyre rode forth alone, reined up before the royal host, and challenged Lord Bloodraven to single combat. "I will fight you, or the coward Aerys, or any champion you care to name." Instead, Lord Bloodraven's men surrounded him, pulled him off his horse, and clasped him into golden fetters. The banner he had carried was planted in the muddy ground and set afire. It burned for a long time, sending up a twisted plume of smoke that could be seen for leagues around.

The only blood that was shed that day came when a man in service to Lord Vrywel began to boast that he had been one of Bloodraven's eyes and would soon be well rewarded. "By the time the moon turns, I'll be fucking whores and drinking Dornish red," he was purported to have said, just before one of Lord Costayne's knights slit his throat. "Drink that," he said as Vrywel's man drowned in his own blood. "It's not Dornish, but it's red."

Elsewise it was a sullen, silent column that trudged through the gates of Whitewalls to toss their weapons into a glittering pile before being bound and led away to await Lord Bloodraven's judgment. Dunk emerged with the rest of them, together with Ser Kyle the Cat and Glendon Ball. They had looked for Ser Maynard to join them, but Plumm had melted away sometime during the night.

It was late that afternoon before Ser Roland Crakehall of the Kingsguard found Dunk among the other prisoners. "Ser Duncan. Where in seven hells have you been hiding? Lord Rivers has been asking for you for hours. Come with me, if you please."

Dunk fell in beside him. Crakehall's long cloak flapped behind him with every gust of wind, as white as moonlight on snow. The sight of it made him think back on the words the Fiddler had spoken, up on the roof. *I dreamed that you were all in white from head to heel, with a long pale cloak flowing from those broad shoulders.* Dunk snorted. *Aye, and you dreamed of dragons hatching from stone eggs. One is likely as t'other.*

The Hand's pavilion was half a mile from the castle, in the shade of a spreading elm tree. A dozen cows were cropping at the grass nearby. *Kings rise and fall,* Dunk thought, *and cows and smallfolk go about their business.* It was something the old man used to say. "What will become of all of them?" he asked Ser Roland as they passed a group of captives sitting on the grass.

"They'll be marched back to King's Landing for trial. The knights and men-at-arms should get off light enough. They were only following their liege lords."

"And the lords?"

"Some will be pardoned, so long as they tell the truth of what they know and give up a son or daughter to vouchsafe their future loyalty. It will go harder for those who took pardons after the Redgrass Field. They'll be imprisoned or attainted. The worst will lose their heads."

Bloodraven had made a start on that already, Dunk saw when they came up on his pavilion. Flanking the entrance, the severed heads of Gormon Peake and Black Tom Heddle had been impaled on spears, with their shields displayed beneath them. *Three castles, black on orange. The man who slew Roger of Pennytree.*

Even in death, Lord Gormon's eyes were hard and flinty. Dunk closed them with his fingers. "What did you do that for?" asked one of the guardsmen. "The crows'll have them soon enough."

"I owed him that much." If Roger had not died that day, the old man would never have looked twice at Dunk when he saw him chasing that pig through the alleys of King's Landing. *Some old dead king gave a sword to one son instead of another, that was the start of it. And now I'm standing here, and poor Roger's in his grave.*

"The Hand awaits," commanded Roland Crakehall.

Dunk stepped past him, into the presence of Lord Brynden Rivers, bastard, sorcerer, and Hand of the King.

Egg stood before him, freshly bathed and garbed in princely raiment, as would befit a nephew of the king. Nearby, Lord Frey was seated in a camp chair with a cup of wine to hand and his hideous little heir squirming in his lap. Lord Butterwell was there as well . . . on his knees, pale-faced and shaking.

"Treason is no less vile because the traitor proves a craven," Lord Rivers was saying. "I have heard your bleatings, Lord Ambrose, and I believe one word in ten. On that account I will allow you to retain a tenth part of your fortune. You may keep your wife as well. I wish you joy of her."

"And Whitewalls?" asked Butterwell with quavering voice.

"Forfeit to the Iron Throne. I mean to pull it down stone by stone and sow the ground that it stands upon with salt. In twenty years, no one will remember it existed. Old fools and young malcontents still make pilgrimages to the Redgrass Field to plant flowers on the spot where Daemon Blackfyre fell. I will not suffer Whitewalls to become another monument to the Black Dragon." He waved a pale hand. "Now scurry away, roach."

"The Hand is kind." Butterwell stumbled off, so blind with grief that he did not even seem to recognize Dunk as he passed.

"You have my leave to go as well, Lord Frey," Rivers commanded. "We will speak again later."

"As my lord commands." Frey led his son from the pavilion.

Only then did the King's Hand turn to Dunk.

He was older than Dunk remembered him, with a lined hard face, but his skin was still as pale as bone, and his cheek and neck still bore the ugly winestain birthmark that some people thought looked like a raven. His boots were black, his tunic scarlet. Over it he wore a cloak the color of smoke, fastened with a brooch in the shape of an iron hand. His hair fell to his shoulders, long and white and straight, brushed forward so as to conceal his missing eye, the one that Bittersteel had plucked from him on the Redgrass Field. The eye that remained was very red. *How many eyes has Bloodraven? A thousand eyes, and one.*

"No doubt Prince Maekar had some good reason for allowing his son to squire for a hedge knight," he said, "though I cannot imagine it included delivering him to a castle full of traitors plotting rebellion. How is that I come to find my cousin in this nest of adders, ser? Lord Butterbutt would have me believe that Prince Maekar sent you here, to sniff out this rebellion in the guise of a mystery knight. Is that the truth of it?"

Dunk went to one knee. "No, m'lord. I mean, yes, m'lord. That's what Egg told him. Aegon, I mean. Prince Aegon. So that part's true. It isn't what you'd call the true truth, though."

"I see. So the two of you learned of this conspiracy against the crown and decided you would thwart it by yourselves, is that the way of it?"

"That's not it either. We just sort of . . . blundered into it, I suppose you'd say."

Egg crossed his arms. "And Ser Duncan and I had matters well in hand before you turned up with your army."

"We had some help, m'lord," Dunk added.

"Hedge knights."

"Aye, m'lord. Ser Kyle the Cat, and Maynard Plumm. And Ser Glendon Ball. It was him unhorsed the Fidd . . . the pretender."

"Yes, I've heard that tale from half a hundred lips already. The Bastard of the Pussywillows. Born of a whore and a traitor."

"Born of *heroes*," Egg insisted. "If he's amongst the captives, I want him found and released. And rewarded."

"And who are you to tell the King's Hand what to do?"

Egg did not flinch. "You know who I am, cousin."

"Your squire is insolent, ser," Lord Rivers said to Dunk. "You ought to beat that out of him."

"I've tried, m'lord. He's a prince, though."

"What he is," said Bloodraven, "is a *dragon*. Rise, ser."

Dunk rose.

"There have always been Targaryens who dreamed of things to come, since long before the Conquest," Bloodraven said, "so we should not be surprised if from time to time a Blackfyre displays the gift as well. Daemon dreamed that a dragon would be born at Whitewalls, and it was. The fool just got the color wrong."

Dunk looked at Egg. *The ring*, he saw. *His father's ring. It's on his finger, not stuffed up inside his boot.*

"I have half a mind to take you back to King's Landing with us," Lord Rivers said to Egg, "and keep you at court as my . . . guest."

"My father would not take kindly to that."

"I suppose not. Prince Maekar has a . . . prickly . . . nature. Perhaps I should send you back to Summerhall."

"My place is with Ser Duncan. I'm his squire."

"Seven save you both. As you wish. You're free to go."

"We will," said Egg, "but first we need some gold. Ser Duncan needs to pay the Snail his ransom."

Bloodraven laughed. "What happened to the modest boy I once met at King's Landing? As you say, my prince. I will instruct my paymaster to give you as much gold as you wish. Within reason."

"Only as a loan," insisted Dunk. "I'll pay it back."

"When you learn to joust, no doubt." Lord Rivers flicked them away with his fingers, unrolled a parchment, and began to tick off names with a quill.

He is marking down the men to die, Dunk realized. "My lord," he said, "we saw the heads outside. Is that . . . will the Fiddler . . . Daemon . . . will you have his head as well?"

Lord Bloodraven looked up from his parchment. "That is for King Aerys to decide . . . but Daemon has four younger brothers, and sisters as well. Should I be so foolish as to remove his pretty head, his mother will mourn, his friends will curse me for a kinslayer, and Bittersteel will crown his brother Haegon. Dead, young Daemon is a hero. Alive, he is an obstacle in my half brother's path. He can hardly make a third Blackfyre king whilst the second remains so inconveniently alive. Besides, such a noble captive will be an ornament to our court, and a living testament to the mercy and benevolence of His Grace King Aerys."

"I have a question too," said Egg.

"I begin to understand why your father was so willing to be rid of you. What more would you have of me, cousin?"

"Who took the dragon's egg? There were guards at the door, and more guards on the steps, no way anyone could have gotten into Lord Butterwell's bedchamber unobserved."

Lord Rivers smiled. "Were I to guess, I'd say someone climbed up inside the privy shaft."

"The privy shaft was too small to climb."

"For a man. A child could do it."

"Or a dwarf," Dunk blurted. *A thousand eyes, and one. Why shouldn't some of them belong to a troupe of comic dwarfs?*